P9-CBB-915

It was a testimony meeting, the Saints rising to their feet to give impromptu speeches about their love for God.

Here is where I am at home, Dinah thought, touched by real faith, surrounded by women who depended on her. Here is my family. How could I have thought otherwise. As that surety grew within her she felt the light also grow, with a fire that burned behind her eyes. Suddenly the woman who was speaking stopped and Dinah realized that the woman was looking at *her*, and Dinah was sure she could see the light coming out of her eyes. The woman began to speak again; but now the words did not come in the accents of Lancashire. It was the gift of tongues and Dinah realized that she understood her. Without thinking, Dinah leapt to her feet and began to translate. She hardly understood herself; all that mattered was to speak.

Finally the woman stopped speaking and Dinah felt the words fade within her. What had she said? It frightened her, it thrilled her, it gave her peace. Father, she said silently, I will follow you forever, across the sea, away from my husband if need be, over the mountains of death, through whatever storms of suffering. The light was in her again, dim now but unquenchable, and all would be justified in the end, whenever the end might be.

Look for these Tor Books by Orson Scott Card

ORSON SCOTT CARD

SAINTS

TOR

A TOM DOHERTY ASSOCIATES BOOK

This is a work of fiction. All the characters and events portrayed in this book are fictional, and any resemblance to real people or incidents is purely coincidental.

SAINTS

Copyright © 1984 by Orson Scott Card

All rights reserved, including the right to reproduce this book or portions thereof in any form.
Previously published under the title A WOMAN OF DESTINY.

First Tor Edition: June 1988

A TOR Book

Published by Tom Doherty Associates, Inc.
49 West 24th Street
New York, NY 10010

Cover art by Hiram Richardson

ISBN: 0-812-58140-7
Can. No.: 0-812-58141-5

Printed in the United States of America

0   9   8   7   6   5   4   3   2   1

For Kristine,
who showed me the mind and
heart of a perfect woman.

⊷⊷⊷ BOOK ONE ⊶⊶⊶

*In which kindly Providence
takes notice of a deserving family
and makes their lives interesting.*

🌿 First Word 🌿

This is all we have of Dinah Kirkham now: a lock of hair in an envelope, color nondescript; five photographs taken in her fifties or later, including the famous picture of her looking with disdain at Brigham Young; a will, in which she left her small fortune to the Mormon Church; and a brutally frank journal, which is now kept under lock and key in the Church archives, where no historian may read it. Too late. I read it, and now you hold this book in your hands.

The pictures are not kind to her. A recent historian, somewhat given to cleverness at the expense of the dead, wrote, "Dinah Kirkham was an ugly old woman, and age had only improved her." Indeed, she looks more lively in her funeral picture than in any other: the mortician twisted her lips into an unpleasant smile, as if she had just been told an enemy had died in agony and could not help but gloat. But let us be fair: No photographs from that time are flattering; everyone looks severe, the clothing styles were ugly, and makeup was forbidden to virtuous women. Other evidence is kinder to her: She was loved by three husbands, all of whom had ample opportunity to compare her with other women. Those

3

who knew her wrote that she was beautiful in her youth and handsome in her matronhood. Photographs are deceitful—they can give us patterns of black and white, but not the eyes to see what her contemporaries saw.

Besides, it doesn't matter much how Dinah looked. She was called the Prophetess by many thousands, the champion of the weak and heartbroken, advocate of plural marriage and female suffrage, speaker in tongues and healer of the sick. When she died, the Salt Lake *Tribune* needed only the small headline, "Aunt Dinah Passes Away." The line at her viewing was a half-mile long for eleven hours; they turned the rest away, or they could not have buried her.

And oh, how they wanted to bury her. She was a relic of the wrong century by then. She knew too well what the businessmen were up to. If they had known of her journal then, they would have burned it.

She was also my great aunt. I didn't mean to write about her. I set out to write about her brother Charlie, who wrote mediocre hymns that have somehow become the favorite anthems of four million Latter-Day Saints. She was only background for me.

Background, until I found her journal, sitting in a file where it shoudn't have been, overlooked for years, mentioned in no catalogue. I read a dozen pages at random and knew what a treasure I had found; I told no one, but simply Xeroxed and Xeroxed and Xeroxed until I had it all.

And now I know her far too well to be content with writing her biography. Instead I have decided to write her life as if it were the life of a great hero. Why not? It was. Yet this is too large for me: the task I have set myself is not Boswell's but Homer's, and my failure is determined before I start. I am a worm of a scholar, best at burrowing, but now at last come up for air. Bear me. I will intrude on you, I will annoy you, but I will also do my best to carry you into the life of the only person I've ever known who was loved by all who really knew her, and yet was worthy of more love than she received.

—O. Kirkham, Salt Lake City, 1981

1

John Kirkham
Manchester 1829

THE DAY JOHN KIRKHAM abandoned his family, he came home early from work. It was midafternoon, and Manchester bustled with business. He dodged carts and wagons and carriages all the way home. He remembered that when he was a young man he walked for pleasure, sending the carriage home early from the store. And then, when they had lost the house and moved into the rooms over the store, he had walked not at all, if he could help it. He was irritated by business, ashamed of the sweat of his brow. Sweat was for less sensitive men, the near-animals who made their nails and wove their endless cloth and tended their machinery in the factories that pumped the air out of the sky and replaced it with foul coal smoke.

This was not the first day John had left early. Many times, pushing another man's broom in another man's store, he had become impatient and taken his box of paints and pens and coals, and a sheaf of papers, and headed out of the city, beyond

Broughton to the north or Ardwick to the east, to where the
scenes were rustic and unspoiled, to where the carriages did
not come.

There was no grace in carriages, or in any of the works of
men, John was sure. To him all buildings were blocky pro-
tuberances from the surface of the earth; Manchester was a
vast blemish. He could not paint with a carriage in the scene;
the thought of drawing a shop or factory would never have
occurred to him. Instead he had always painted the gentle, wild
scenes by the River Medlock, upstream of Manchester where
the water was drinkable and fish had strength to leap.

But now he had painted everything within a day's going
and coming of Manchester. Even if he had not, he had no will
to paint anything near this city, even if he saw something new.
Tied to the shop by his need for money, where the work dulled
him and slowed his mind and heart, he could not paint his best.
True, the painters in London were forced to paint portraits,
dull visions of dull people, in order to finance themselves in
style. But at least they painted for their bread and were received
as artists in society, not forced to bear the crude manners of
factory men, not forced to smile and deferently give them what
they wanted for their coins, their precious and grudgingly given
pennies and shillings. A real painter never had fingers so stiff
from gripping a broom that he could not hold a brush.

So today John left work early, but did not go to the countryside. Instead he headed home.

Home was surely not where he had intended to go. He had
meant to go east, keep walking until he reached London, where
a discriminating audience would soon recognize his talent. But,
as always, his feet would not let him leave Anna, not without
seeing her one last time. He tried to remember—hadn't he felt
this way before? Hadn't he meant to leave, and then changed
his mind because of Anna's comfortable ways?

Busy people passed him, hurrying, shoving sometimes, jos-
tling and scrambling for place in the dirty streets. John refused
to let his heart beat as quickly as theirs. His footsteps were
slower. More relaxed. He could hear the silent criticisms as
the busy men went by. Idler. Slacker. If you have no hurry,
don't take place on the road. But I am not on the road, John
answered. I am walking in the meadow God meant this place
to be. You have hidden it in stone, but still my feet can feel

the grass, my ears can hear the bees dozing on the dandelions.

Home was one apartment in a long building that stretched the length of a block of Bedford Street. It was a nice enough place, their cottage, but definitely middle class. Definitely middle-bordering-on-lower class. Not the home of a gentleman. I was meant to be a gentleman, John Kirkham thought bitterly. If the universe were properly run I would manage a great estate and paint in the garden in the afternoon. God is perfect when it comes to nature, but he's far too whimsical with the lives of men. Bees don't dig badger holes, yet I take small money and wait on barbarians. I have been mislaid in a world of brick. If my father had had the good sense to be as impotent as he was stupid, I might have had my soul placed in a different family, with the right advantages. The stone walls of the great houses in the countryside. Some men should not have had children.

"Father."

"Dinah. Your cheek is dirty. Your mother ought to wash you more."

His ten-year-old daughter looked up at him with her inscrutable face. She neither smiled nor frowned nor anything at all. Like a cat, her eyes just stared into his face, as if she knew what lay behind his eyes. He felt a rush of guilt, knowing that he had decided to leave. Damn this girl for her silence, for her seeing eyes.

"Enough of that," he said to her. "What's for supper?"

"Isn't ready yet."

"Of course it isn't, girl; I'm home early, do you think I don't know that?" He was ashamed to be annoyed, yet could not curb either the annoyance or the shame. "Why aren't you in school?"

She said nothing, only looked at him. Of course he remembered why. The girls were sent home earlier than the boys. But she could make a civil answer, couldn't she? He wanted to shake her. Answer me, damn you. What are you thinking? Speak, child, or I'll know the devil's in you. But he knew from experience that nothing would get words from this child unless she felt the need to speak. Her school uniform was frayed, faded, and too small. Not my fault. It was my father who gambled it all away. It's not my fault for my father's sins.

He brushed past his lithe daughter and entered the cottage. Onions were strong in the air. That meant no meat tonight, so there were onions to give some flavor to the potatoes. The endless potatoes, poor man's food. Filthy Papist Irishman's food. John resented the potatoes without letting himself draw a connection between the low wages he brought home and the hours he spent away from the shop to play with a paintbrush that earned no money.

"Anna," he said. Anna was surprised to see him home. Well, be surprised if you like, Anna. Life is rude shocks, Anna, and the rudest of all is the shock of learning where you must live your life, and that you may never leave that place. But I will leave.

"Are you ill, to be home early?"

He shook his head. "Only tired."

He ignored the frown on Anna's forehead. Only tired. His own words were an accusation: she was also tired, but where could *she* go to escape from her work?

Charlie came down the stairs, a book under his arm. He was small for seven years old, but bright and eager. Was I bright and eager at seven? John did not think so. He had been a moody child, had grown to be a melancholy man. Brightness was Anna's manner, and Charlie was Anna's boy. "Papa, are you ill?"

Again no. "I just couldn't bear the shop any longer, and old Martin couldn't bear me, and so we agreed to part company." He saw Anna's eyes go wide with fear. "Only for the afternoon, Anna. I haven't lost my place." He spoke snidely, angrily; how dare she care about his *place* when she didn't give a damn about his soul. Fine with *you* if your husband never achieves what he was born to do, just so he brings home money. Never mind how the earning of it ruins him.

She clattered the spoons on the table; she was angry that he had spoken so sharply to her. It was unfair, and he was sorry. "You should have been the man, Anna," he said mildly. "You'd be rich by now."

"And you'd look fine in a fancy gown, John," she said, smiling at him. Again he felt contempt for her, for being so changeable of mood. When *he* was sad, he stayed quite glum all day; another sign of the weakness of women, that they could not hold a humour.

Charlie came to his mother and began reciting. The sound of it throbbed in John's head; he would have left, but his languor sank him deep into the chair and he could not move.

Know then thyself, presume not God to scan;
The proper study of mankind is man.

Wretched boy. Miserable boy. Your mother's son to the core. Read read read. Recite it once, recite it twice until all the family can say the words along with you. And the boy's worst habit was to get well into a piece he had done a hundred times and then stop, leaving the last few lines to hammer endlessly through his father's head.

"Born but to die, and reasoning but to err."

What sort of miserable stuff is Anna teaching to the boy? Born but to die. Sounds downright Papist. Anna *will* have the children read, *will* have them go to school, whatever it costs, however it means that he must do his endless, meaningless toil and be content eating potatoes and onions, so the children can have their books. It's not as if the boy *understood* any of what he spouted. Ta-DUM ta-DUM ta-DUM ta-DUM ta-DUM.

Created half to rise and half to fall;
Great lord of all things, yet a prey to all;
Sole judge of truth, in endless error hurled:
The glory, jest, and riddle of the world.

Just as John was about to cry aloud, about to run from the house begging for silence, for respite from the boy's rote wisdom, just then came Dinah's gentle hand on his forehead, stroking, calming. He did not open his eyes and look at her; did not speak to her, because she would not answer. He just slumped in his chair and let her gentle hands minister to his inward pain. His younger son might be unbearable, but his daughter had a good heart and a knack for kindness. Of course I won't go. How could anyone imagine I would leave here? They love me, they depend on me, I know my duty and I will not go.

Then Charlie began on Gray's Elegy, and John got up and left the room. Damn the inglorious Miltons. Would God they all were mute.

From the window of his upstairs room John Kirkham watched the street. No flower sellers here, no one crying "strawberries, raspberries, fresh and sweet!" The venders were wise enough to know there was no money here. But once John had known their cries. Hadn't his father had a house in the country and a house in town? Hadn't all sorts of people come to visit them? The man who did the family portrait when John was only five— the man with the paints, who made a mirror image of the family that did not disappear when you walked away from it—ah, the miracle of it, and so I learned to paint. My father encouraged me: the rich should have some pleasant way to pass their time, he said. How are the mighty fallen. The old man died with three mortgages on the house and enough gambling debts to obliterate a much larger fortune. First the house had gone, then the country estate, then even the store they had bought, leaving only what he could earn in menial labor, all because his father loved the excitement of the gaming tables.

My father left me ruin. What will I leave my son?

My son. Only one son, of course, and there he was on the street below, walking home. Robert, thirteen years old now, and showing signs of growing tall; lanky, with hands already large and manly; only the effeminate books his mother forced him to carry to and from the school, only the books marred him. Oh, Robert, you are beautiful, you are my only hope, I will leave you more than debts and bitter memories.

Robert looked up at his father, raised his hand, and waved. I will not go. How could I leave my son?

He looked away from the window to the paintings on the walls. Wretched trash, all of them; only hours after he finished each one he had begun to notice the flaws, how the sheep were in the wrong place, how the shepherd was too much in the foreground, how the hills were not distant enough, how the trees looked like a drawing and not like the real thing. He had modeled them from nature, but his image wasn't true. I have no control, he said silently. I have no restraint. And he thought of the lovely woman by the brook. Her smile made him kiss her, her lips made him caress her, her breasts made him bear her to the meadow grass and take her, and all for the sake of his lack of self-restraint he now was trapped in this cottage with this woman and her reciting children and her achingly sweet body that was always eager for him, that never could be satisfied. You drain all my genius from me in your body at night, you thief, he accused her. And yet when she reached and touched him, he could not say no. Could never, never tell her no. She was much too strong for him. She went at loving as if she enjoyed it, which was certainly not proper and, he sometimes feared, not Christian.

It was deep in the night, and he lay awake in bed. He listened to her heavy breathing, slow in the dark beside him. He had tried, but nothing could satisfy her. He could hear the voice of God whispering, "John Kirkham, I put you on the earth to paint, and you did not paint. If you could have pulled away from that temptress the devil put in your path, you could have painted. It was your choice." And God cried out to a terrible angel standing in fire beside him, "Take the iron and put out his eyes!" The angel dipped the iron into the flames and came closer, closer.

John woke, the last sound of his scream ringing in the air. Anna was awake beside him, patting him. "A dream, John, that's all."

A dream. He had fallen asleep, on this of all nights. That's what Anna's body did to him. He twisted his head around to see the window—no light drifted in past the shutters, so he at least hadn't slept through all the hours of darkness. Anna kissed him, and the lips were like needles, so sharply did his cheek tingle. Then she rolled over, went back to sleep. He reached for her, touched the hair that spilled across the sheets, and he almost said, "Anna, I cannot leave you, not ever." But then the lump in his throat subsided, and his resolution returned, and he waited, sleepless, until her breaths were the breaths of sleep again.

He carefully arose and dressed. When he was ready, he pulled two boxes from under the bed, the one partly filled with money, the other filled to the brim with paints and brushes and papers.

He toyed with the idea of taking the whole moneybox— after all, hadn't he earned this money? Hadn't he as much need to eat as anyone, and far less idea of what he would live on once he got to London?

And then, ashamed, he thought of taking nothing, for surely they would need it all.

In the end, he carefully counted out three pounds and left the rest, sure that he was taking only a tiny portion of a rather large cache of money. He did not know that with the price of food rising, Anna had long since stopped saving money, and for months had been dipping into the savings under their bed. It would have made no difference. If he had known, it would have made him all the more certain he must leave.

He tiptoed to the door, carrying the paintbrush and his shoes.

He closed the door to his and Anna's room and stepped carefully down the stairs. He did not open the door of Robert's and Charlie's room, for fear they would waken, for fear that seeing Robert he wouldn't have the heart to leave. And he did not walk to Dinah's cot in the kitchen. He did not need to. She was wide awake to meet him at the foot of the stairs.

"Father," she said.

"Sh," he answered. "Go back to bed."

But she did not go back to bed, only stood there in her nightgown, watching him. Look at someone else with your sharp eyes, girl. I won't be held back now. She said nothing, and the silence tore him.

"I'm not going far, Dinah," he insisted. "And I'll come back soon."

A lie, of course it was a lie, he knew it as he spoke and saw that she knew it also. Oh, no, of course she *believed* him. Of course she *believed* that he'd come home. But already behind her inscrutable face she was making plans, figuring ways to get along without him. I need you, said her expressionless face; I don't need you at all. Well, to hell with you women and your miserable dependency, your infuriating independence. I am free of you forever, free of you all.

He closed the door behind him and set out for London. Within minutes it seemed he was out of Manchester, walking on a country road. The morning dawned in his face, with all nature spread between the light and his eyes. Cows mooed, and whimsically and joyously he answered them, earning the curious stares of the farmers—the poor farmers, who understood nothing, to whom cows were nothing more than machines for consuming grass and turning it to shit. No one understands. Only God and I, and there are things that I can teach him, too.

2

Anna Banks Kirkham
Manchester, 1829

ANNA REACHED OUT in her sleep; her hand stretched out and touched the body that lay breathing warmly beside her. But it was not her husband's body; the habitual movement was interrupted. She awoke.

"Dinah," she whispered in surprise. "What are you doing here? Where's your father?"

Dinah awoke slowly, as if the sleep were her fortress, and she was slow to surrender it.

"Where's father? Where's your father?"

"He went out," Dinah answered.

"Went out! It's still nighttime!"

"He had his paints."

Innocent enough, it was surely innocent enough. Then why did he say nothing to her, if he meant to arise early and go paint? No, no, she knew it was more than a painting trip this time; knew at once, in fact, that John Kirkham had left her for good. Dinah must have seen the grief and fear in her face, for the girl began to tremble.

13

"Hush, be still; why are you shaking, child?" Anna asked.

"I'm cold," Dinah answered.

"So am I," Anna whispered. "But we'll be strong women together, won't we, Dinah, and help each other. Won't we? Won't we?" And after holding her daughter for a while, Anna felt the clenched arms grow limp, felt the girl's hot breath get slow. Sleep, child. Sleep, child. Over and over Anna said the words to herself. Sleep, child. He said he loved me. And the children, said he loved the children. Sleep, child. He'll be back before breakfast. Sleep, sleep, child.

But he did not come for breakfast. Charlie took it all calmly enough, but Robert's questions showed that he could not be fooled. Dinah was quiet, of course: Who could tell what this strange child thought behind her silence?

She sent Robert and Dinah off to school, and once the breakfast dishes were cleared away, she told Charlie to bring the Bible and come with her as she did the laundry. She lugged the large basket down the stairs. Of course he'll come back. I have all his shirts here, he must come back and get them.

"Tell me the piece you learned yesterday, from the Bible, Charlie."

"The Song of Songs, which is Solomon's," he said. "'Let him kiss me with the kisses of his mouth, for thy love is better than wine.'"

She turned on him in fury. "Who told you to learn that piece!"

"No one," he said.

She saw that he was terrified. How could he have known? She softened toward him. "Charlie, another book. Not that one. That's all. Just not that one."

So he began to recite a passage out of *Wealth of Nations*. John had always sneered at her for having the boy learn Adam Smith as if he were Homer. "He doesn't understand a word of it," John had said. "And the Psalms! No one understands *those* but God and King David, and I'm not altogether sure about God."

Charlie droned on about diminishing supply and increasing demand. The Song of Songs. The first time the Song of Songs meant something to her was at a picnic with John Kirkham by the River Medlock, far upriver of Manchester, up where the water was perfect and clear. They were only ten days from their wedding, and he had read passages of Song of Songs as they leaned in the grass of the riverbank. It was too much for her, his voice, his beauty, and her own desire. She let him take her—or did she force herself upon him?—she was never sure. Enough that they had sinned; immediately afterward they burned so with shame that they knelt and prayed for forgiveness of the sin. She thought that surely God would strike them down for their impudence, to pray after fornication. Yet even as she prayed, Anna had wondered how God could have been so cruel as to create man and woman in such a way that they could not resist each other's beauty, and then command them upon threat of eternal torment not to have each other till the black-frocked pastor gave consent.

Oddly, she remembered, John was more ashamed of his loss of self-control than she had been, and on their wedding night he had trembled and fumbled so that she could hardly believe he was not a virgin. "Just like before, John," she had whispered. "It should work a second time, don't you think?" And he laughed and mumbled something about being out of his element when he couldn't hear the rush of clear water and the singing of a bird. "It'll be a lonely winter, then," she had answered, "till the birds come back and the rivers thaw." John adapted quickly. Six pregnancies, and three children who lived into their second year. We may not be good at money, but children we can make.

"Why are you crying, Mother?"

"I'm not."

Charlie helped her wring the shirts, and they carried the heavy basket into the house together. There was Robert, books in hand, standing at the foot of the stairs.

"Why aren't you in school?" she asked sharply.

"He's never coming back."

Since she couldn't argue, she reached out and held him. He clung to her, and cried a little, hiding the shame of his tears in his mother's shoulder.

Charlie looked on in puzzlement, and finally, to Anna's annoyance and Robert's rage, began to cry. "Hold me, Mother! I'm sad!" So she held him, and shook her head at Robert to stop him from saying anything cutting to his little brother.

All afternoon she kept the boys busy at household tasks. She half-expected Dinah to show up at noon, or at least before the close of school. Was she that much stronger than Robert, that she could bear to be among the other children at a time like this? But there was another reason why Dinah was so strong. She had believed her father's final words to her.

She looked around the moment she got home. "Is he back yet?"

"No," Anna said.

"Then soon," she said confidently.

"He won't be back," Robert said.

"He said he would," Dinah answered. That settled it. There could be no more argument. I have failed you somewhere in your education, Anna said silently to her daughter. I didn't teach you to recognize a lie. I didn't teach you that fathers abandon families and lie to their children as they leave.

For once, Dinah was not quiet at night. Instead she talked and talked, and the longer she went on, the clearer it became that she, too, knew that John had left them all for good. "He'll come back and give us carriage rides tomorrow," Dinah said. "He'll come back with marzipan. He'll have a beautiful painting of the king on his horse. And he won't be tired, so he'll be glad to play with us."

Charlie was drinking it in, but Robert could not bear it. "Why do you lie about carriage rides?"

"It's not a lie!" Dinah shouted back at him.

Anna was not used to hearing Dinah shout. "Children, enough of that now. We don't know where your father went, or when he'll bother to come home or tell us something of what he means to do. And in the meantime, it's better not to think of him returning. That way when he comes it'll be a surprise."

Robert frowned. "I don't need to have you trick me to be happy. I'm almost a man now, and I can bear the truth."

Can you? Then try this truth, Anna thought. My time of month is five days late. Only six times in my life has such a thing happened, and each time it meant there was a child in me. See what you make of such a parting gift from my loving husband. I wonder if you'd want the truth, if you guessed even a tenth of what lies ahead of us. Less than twenty pounds in the box under the bed, after what he so kindly took. Bear that for a while, and see how straight you stand.

Those were her thoughts; her voice, when she spoke, was kinder. "You aren't *almost* a man, Robert, you *are* a man, and must act like one for our sake. You must be strong, like a father to Charlie and Dinah and a good right arm to me."

It was only then that Dinah openly admitted what had happened. And at the age of ten, she was already something like the woman she was going to be. "If father's gone, then we'll have no money," she said. "We'll have to stop going to school."

"Not right away," Anna said. "The week's tuition is already paid."

"And his paintings," Dinah said. "We can sell them."

It was a horrifying thought—the paintings, I can't sell my husband's paintings! How could this child think of such a thing!

But by week's end, Anna knew her daughter was right. She sold the frames for ten and sixpence. The man took the canvases as well, but only gave her three shillings for them. Anna didn't think twice. They couldn't eat canvas; and if three shillings was all the paint was worth, so be it. It was the only patrimony John Kirkham's children would ever get. Anna thought of giving a shilling to each child. Here, Robert, here, Charlie, your inheritance. Here, Dinah, your dowry. Thank your loving father.

When she came home to the bare-walled cottage, bearing the payment, Robert brought in a stack of books from the other room. "These, too," he said.

"No," Anna answered.

"His paintings, and not the books?" It was a quiet rebellion, but no less dangerous for all that.

"Aye," she said. "We keep the books, we sell the paintings. Because we're not tradesmen, we're better than that. My father was a learned man, and even wrote a book. We will read and we will write, and we will think great thoughts because those that don't might as well be sheep."

Then she counted out their money on the table. "Enough for three months," she said. "If we scrimp."

"I'll take work," Robert said.

"And so will I, and so no doubt will Dinah, and Charlie's only seven but in a few years he'll earn his pennies, too. But you're all children, and they scarce pay grown men enough to stay alive in the sort of work you'd have to do. And what can *I* do, blessed as I am with John's last gift to me?" She tried to laugh, to make her worry seem like exasperation, but the children were not fooled. Humble as their cottage was, it was too rich for them now. And before the money ran out, Anna found them another place.

The man wasn't there yet to cart their goods, but the furniture was stacked in the street, ready to be loaded. Dinah went alone upstairs. She found Robert there, sitting with his back

to the wardrobe in what had been his father's and mother's
room. The wardrobe belonged to the landlord, and would stay.
He did not look up when Dinah entered. Only stared at the
wall where the paper had faded above the headboard of his
parents' bed.

"Sir Redcrosse," Dinah said.

At that he stirred and looked at her. He remembered the
ancient game they had played, and smiled at her. "Fair Lady
Una, I fear this is no fit habitation for thee."

"Enough for me or any Christian, if the love of God is
here."

Robert resisted the game for a moment; he was too old, he
was a man, he couldn't play with his sister as they had in the
attic of the store, when they had lived above it. He laughed;
he shook his head; he refused.

But Dinah's dream was too strong for him—it always was.
She showed no sign of being Dinah Kirkham at all. She was
Una, and she pled with him to help her on her way. "But
beware of the dread monster Error," she warned him, and her
voice was so afraid and yet so stern with authority that he could
only whisper to her, "I fear you misjudge me, Lady. A knight
I am called, but my armor is borrowed, and my arm is yet
untried in battle."

She reached out and touched his cheek. "Sir Redcrosse,
every knight must fight his first battle, and if it is against a
great enemy, so much more the worship that will come to him
in victory."

"You're too good at this," Robert said, making his last try
at ending the game.

"If you won't fight for my good, Sir Redcrosse," Dinah
whispered, "then I am surely alone."

She was so mournful that it touched his heart despite his
unwillingness to play. He got to his feet, he looked down at
his sister, who looked upward to him with so much hope, and
he believed her. She saw him as Sir Redcrosse, and so it must
be true. In the hour before the carter came to load the furniture
and bear them all away, Sir Redcrosse slew Error, killed the
dragon, and discerned the false Duessa, restoring Una to her
rightful place.

"Thank you, my lord," Dinah said to him at the end.

"I don't know which you do better, Dinah. Una or Duessa."

Dinah at last returned to herself, and laughed sadly, laughed in a way that made Robert think she must surely be older than her mere ten years. "I do best with the one that's really me." Robert did not ask her which that was. He thought he knew.

They walked before the cart up Portland Street to Piccadilly and from there through the heart of mercantile Manchester. They had not been poor long enough for their clothing to be wretched, but Robert keenly felt the fact that the men who got in and out of carriages were dressed in a way that would have made his father look and feel rather fine, and not as tired and emptied-out as he had looked since Robert had been old enough to notice such things. The men in fine clothing greeted each other jovially on the street, but said nothing, gave no sign they even saw the many common tradesmen who passed by on errands through the streets.

"Why are they rich?" Robert asked his mother.

"Hush," she said, not wishing to be conspicuous, though in fact no one paid them the slightest notice.

"Why are they so fine? Why not us?"

"Because they have the money," Anna said impatiently.

"And how did they get it?" asked Robert.

"By being wise and educated and deserving and by praying to God always."

Robert was silent for a few moments, and Anna thought she had done with the foolish conversation.

"I," he announced loudly, shattering her delusion, "shall also be wise and educated and deserving and pray to God always."

"You still won't be rich," Dinah said. Anna looked sharply at her daughter, wondering, as she always did, how much her daughter really understood.

"Why not!" Robert demanded.

"Because," Dinah answered, "they won't give any of their money to such a poor boy as you."

Robert digested this idea in silence for awhile. A carriage came briskly through the street, horses atrot, and the driver cursed at their carter, who only shrugged. The man inside the carriage seemed not to notice the argument, did not seem to notice the street at all. Robert watched after him, and finally said, "If they won't give me any money, then I'll take it from them."

Anna grabbed his jacket from behind, whirled him around,

and held him by the ears as she spoke directly into his face. "Take? You never take what belongs to another man, Robert, not as long as you're my son! And if I hear you talk like that again you'll not *be* my son, for I won't have a coveter and a thief in my family!"

"I didn't mean it." Robert was ashamed, and frightened, too. Anna did not often get so angry.

"We're educated people, God-fearing people, and I swear to God before you, my children, that we shall be honest in the sight of God, even if it means we starve!"

"All well and good, mum," said the carter behind her, "but if we must keep stopping in the road we'll never get wherever it is we're getting."

As they went up Long Mill Gate Road the buildings changed. The money had stayed behind in the heart of the city, or had been deftly carried to the nicest neighborhoods. Here the offices gave way to cheap shops, and the shops began to look filthy, with shabby buildings opening to courts knee-deep in rubbish. The people changed, too, and now the family was rather unusually well-dressed, and instead of ignoring them as the businessmen had done, the passersby stared. Such people as lived in this borough recognized bad fortune when they saw it; they had sampled enough to be connoisseurs. They watched the Kirkhams pass, and were careful to step back, to be ready to run or ward away the evil chance if they should come too near. The smell of cheap alcohol was pungent in the streets, along with other odors that it would not do to identify.

"What's it like where we're going?" Charlie asked.

"I don't know," answered his mother. "I only know the price, which is cheap, and the place, which isn't far now."

"Any farther," Robert mumbled, "and we'll be living with the hogs."

They turned off the road just before the bridge over the River Irk, and the carter could only go a little way on the rough turning. "Close as I can go, mum."

Anna looked at the row houses that fronted on the river. They looked abandoned, the doors swinging open, neither glass nor boards in the windows. "How much farther is it?" she asked.

"Oh, you're here. Number four must be the fourth cottage in."

The fourth cottage looked no better than the rest—abandoned, dead, unlivable.

"I must go see."

Anna took Robert's hand, commanded the other children to stay with the cart, and walked along the uneven path leading to the fourth cottage. As they approached, the smell got more and more pungent, and there was no denying what it was—human excrement in varying stages of decay.

"We've been cheated," Robert said softly.

"Not for the first time," Anna answered.

A shutter opened above them, and a woman's head poked out. "You new?" asked the woman.

"I think so," Anna said. "You mean someone lives here?"

"Lovely place, an't it?" The woman giggled. "But you don't live on the ground floor. You live above." The woman was incredibly thin, and though she giggled, there wasn't a trace of a smile on her face. "Are you in number four?"

Yes.

"Looks like we're neighbors. Folks died of cholera in number four. Or something. My name's Barton. Nomi Barton."

"Kirkham, Anna. Which one is number four?"

"Three down from here. They starts the numbers from the other end, Lord knows why. You get upstairs through the ground floor, but tread careful, hi-ho!" The shutter closed.

Anna led the way into the house that would be their home. The stench was overpowering. The floor had been used as a privy for a long time, and was still used that way, judging from the pools of urine shining in the light from the courtyard windows. Their feet skidded on the floor. Anna held her skirts high, found the stairway in the dim light, and gingerly made her way to it, climbed the creaking treads, and opened the door at the top of the stairs.

Better, the upstairs room, but only by contrast. The plaster walls were chipped, in some places right down to the brick. And daylight came through on such a spot, proof that the walls were only one brick thick. The floor was grimy, the ceiling webbed, and the ash from the fireplace had been strewn across the floor.

"Mother, we can't," said Robert.

"What we must we can, and what we can we will," she

said. Her mother had always said it, and she hoped that it was true.

"Surely God loves us better than to make us live here."

Anna had no answer for that. She walked around the room, as if she were hoping to find a door leading somewhere else, somewhere livable. Someone screamed, not far away, screamed and then began jabbering and shouting, the voice finally trailing away into nothing. A dog barked. Anna remembered her father's dogs, and knew they would never have been permitted to sleep in such a place as this. Her mother's wooden floors, always gleaming; fine places on a proud kitchen table; four rooms with only three of them in the family, so that her father had a library. But he had died, the college had taken back the rooms, and even the library had gone to help John Kirkham pay his impossible burden of debt.

There would be no lace curtains at these windows, she knew. And she wondered what her children would remember, when they got to be her age. *She* could remember romping down the stairs with the dogs, sliding down the banister, splashing in mud and getting a delicious and half-hearted whipping for it from a father who had not forgotten about unsanctioned fun. But *her* children—they'd remember only that they must walk carefully downstairs, and instead of cut flowers in a bowl, they would know only the smell of—

She leaned her head against the doorjamb and breathed deeply to keep herself from weeping. Robert looked at her in awe. He did not know what went on in adult minds, but he knew that his mother was in pain.

"It's all right, Mother. We'll clean it up in no time."

"Aye," his mother said bitterly.

"And I'll work hard, and soon we'll have enough money to move away."

"I'm not the kind of woman," Anna said softly, "who lives in such a place."

"Then we'll make it the sort of place where a woman such as you can live."

Anna turned to him, gravely touched his cheek. "If only your father..." she said, then repented of the thought, and said instead, "I can depend on you, can't I?"

Robert nodded, troubled at his mother's intensity.

"We must move the furniture inside," she said, suddenly

businesslike. "The beds will go by the window, the dresser under it, the table here. Will that be good?"

No, of course not, nothing would be good, but neither of them would say it now, and when they returned to the children—for Robert was not one of the children now—they were cheerful. "Just needs a bit of fixing up," Robert told them.

"Will you help us with the furniture?" Anna asked the carter.

"Aye, for two shillings."

"Two shillings! Two shillings was your price to bring everything here!"

"The horse brung it here, mum, but the horse won't carry it upstairs. I charges for me the same as for the horse. S'only fair."

"Fair. Do as you like, then, we'll carry it ourselves. But kindly wait here until we're through, so we don't have to set it all out in the mud. There'll be an extra tuppence for you if you wait."

"My money, mum."

"I'll pay you when we've unloaded everything. Charlie, you wait here with the man. Robert and Dinah, you hold one end of the bed and I'll hold the other, while this strong man watches us do a man's work." The carter was oblivious to her abuse—it would take much harsher language for him to notice he was being insulted. It took a half hour to get the two beds upstairs, and the clothing and the table took nearly as long again. The two children couldn't carry too far without resting, and Anna was weakened more than a little by the pregnancy.

They returned last of all for the bureau, but the cart was gone. Charlie was standing where it had been, trying to whistle. Anna knew at once what had happened. The dresser was easily worth half a pound, much better payment than the two shillings Anna would have given the carter. "Charlie! Why didn't you tell us he was leaving!"

"Oh, he'll be back, Mother," Charlie said. "He only had to help a friend in Broughton."

"If he has friends in Broughton I'm a duke!" Robert shouted. "The man's stole our bureau!"

"He hasn't! He told me to stand here so I could whistle when he's looking for this place again!"

"You haven't the brains of a louse, Charlie!" Robert shouted, until his mother's hand on his shoulder silenced him. "He's only seven," she said. "How should he know when a man like that has lied?"

"We told him to stay with the cart!"

"You better stop crabbing me!" Charlie retorted.

"Enough," Anna said, and she led them back to the cottage. As they came in the front door on the ground floor, a man was climbing into the room from the courtyard.

"What are you doing here?" Anna challenged him.

"Come to piss, mum," said the man.

"You can do that elsewhere."

"As good a place as any."

"This is my cottage, and this is my floor."

"I'm urgent, mum," he said, unbuttoning his trousers.

Robert stepped forward, his foot splashing slightly on the floor. "You heard my mother."

"It's not like I'm the first," the man said. It was plain he was amused that someone as small as Robert meant to challenge him.

"The man before you was the last." Robert *was* afraid, but angry, too, and the anger won. But the man didn't bother getting angry, just turned his back and began urinating into the corner. Anna put her hand on Robert's shoulder. "You can't teach a pig to use a chamberpot," she said, and she led the children up the stairs.

Their bundles of clothing sat on the beds they had so laboriously carried up the stairs. There was nowhere else to set them, with no bureau; the floor was far too dirty for them to put anything there, not yet, anyway. Anna took a candle from a bag, set it in a holder, lit it. As if the candle had been a cue, rain started falling outside. Almost immediately water started dripping through the roof and ceiling, and puddling where it oozed out from behind a wall.

"It's a blessing," said Anna. "Now we needn't fetch water for the cleaning." And for the next two hours, until dark came in earnest, they washed the walls and floor of their upstairs room, and brushed the webs from the ceiling. The place was reasonably clean.

"We'll hunt up the wood tomorrow for some more shelves," Anna said. "We must spare the money to keep our goods off the floor." She was tired from the labor, bent from the discouragement, and she sat against the table, looking at the children who watched her from the beds where they sat.

"We can live here," she insisted to them.

"Aye, Mother," Robert said.

"It stinks," Charlie said, and the smell grew worse because he said so.

"Tomorrow," Anna said, "we'll clean downstairs."

"Tomorrow I'll find work," Robert said.

Anna nodded. Then she used the candle to start a coal fire in the hearth. Supper would be potatoes burnt by the fire— they did not yet know where they could get water nearby, except the River Irk, which was filthy. Anna thought of asking the neighbor where they might find water, but she had seemed a repulsive woman, and in Anna's middle-class soul there was no room yet for the admission that she was now, however much against her will, at that woman's social level. Surely money did not make that much difference. Surely breeding and the thoughts of the heart were what made the difference between human beings and scum.

The children were asleep, Robert and Charlie in one bed, Dinah in the bed she would share with her mother, when Anna heard a sound downstairs, a snuffling sound, like an animal. Impossible for it to be anything good. Anna took the candle, opened the door, and went partway down the stairs. The sound came from the nearest corner of the room, and as her eyes got used to the dimness Anna saw that it was a man, drunken and filthy, on his hands and knees in the slime on the floor, vomiting out the night's drink and dinner. The man saw the light and looked up.

"Oh, mum, I'm sick," he said.

"Clearly," Anna answered.

"God a bed? Got a bed for me? Man needs a bed."

"Then go home to your wife," Anna told him curtly, "but get out of here."

The man started crying and shakily stood, walking a few steps toward the stairs. "Mum, I haven't got a wife, her died, and haven't got a home, landlord outed me on my arse, take pity on me, mum." He put a foot up on the stairs.

"Get out," Anna said, beginning to be afraid.

"Not a civil way to talk to a man what's out of work through no fault of his own—"

He took another step up the stairs, and then Anna heard a noise behind her. One of the children. "Get back inside," she whispered, "nothing's wrong." She heard the door close behind her, and almost wished the child had not obeyed. A foolish wish, of course. The children were not ready to cope with a drunken man who had completely forgotten himself.

"Where's your man, mum?" asked the drunk.

"Asleep. I trust you won't require me to wake him."

"Just want a bed, mum," said the man, lurching up the stairs toward her. He reached toward her; she recoiled, retreated a step. "Got no husband, have you?"

"Yes I have. Get off my stairs."

"Don't I smell sweet to you, mum? Got shit on my boots, mum? How are such a lady, living here? How did you get across this floor with your feet all pretty, did you fly?" His soiled hand touched her sleeve, caught at her fingers as she pulled away. The slime on his hand was cold and wet. She cried out faintly.

"Please go away."

"Want a bed. Raining out," the man said. "Man's got a right to sleep dry."

"I'd help you if I could, but there's no room, none at all—"

"None of that, mum. Don't mean you no harm, but—"

The vomit on his breath was strong, and weary as she was, pregnant and sensitive to smells, Anna thought she would faint. She almost stumbled as her foot sought the next step, found nothing. She was at the top of the stairs, and had no hope against such a lout, drunk as he was. She was not so much afraid of what he might do as she was afraid of the children seeing him and discovering how helpless she was now to protect them. It would terrify them. God knows it terrified *her*.

The door behind her opened. The man looked from her to the door as Anna half-turned to try to get the children to go back, to stay out of the way. She had no time to say anything, however. Robert rushed by her and swung the heavy iron stewpot, striking the man in the shoulder. The drunk roared, reached at Robert, who was staggering back, recovering his balance after the exertion. He didn't touch the boy, however, for at that moment Dinah shoved forward and kicked the man squarely in the crotch. He bellowed, lost his balance, tumbled backward down the stairs.

"No!" cried Anna, terrified that they had killed him. But the man immediately scrambled to his feet and fled out the door. As soon as he was gone, Anna ushered the children back into their room. "I'm relieved to see that Charlie's still asleep." Anna said. "I half expected to see him turn up next with a musket."

"Won't have nobody talk to you like that," Robert said, his voice trembling.

"Won't have *anybody*," Anna corrected him. "You should have let me handle it."

"I'll kill him if he comes back," Dinah said.

"No talk of killing," Anna said, violently scrubbing her hand and sleeve with a rag, trying to get rid of the slime.

"Don't be angry, Mother," Robert said. "We only meant to help."

Suddenly Anna found herself crying, not stern at all, not rebuking, but reaching out to Robert and Dinah, hugging them and saying, "Thank you, thank you."

At last they were calmed down enough to sleep. Only a few quiet words. "How did Dinah know to kick a man like that?" Robert asked.

"I don't know," Anna answered. "But I'm glad she knew."

Charlie woke a little as she covered Robert in the same bed. "I dreamed bad," he said.

"I'm sorry," Anna said. "Did you say your prayers?"

"I prayed three times and the dream went away."

"It's all better then, isn't it?"

Charlie nodded gravely, believing it. So easily, thought Anna, so easily such a little one can be given peace.

The children slept, and now Anna trembled, now she quietly crept out the door and stepped a short way down the stairs and leaned over the wobbly banister and vomited into the foul room. And when she was empty, she still retched and retched until, exhausted, she returned weakly to her bed. She was ashamed of her weakness, and tried to excuse it. It was the smell, the fear, the helplessness, the loss of her husband, most of all the shame of having fallen to such a depth as this.

"Mother."

"Hush, Dinah. Go to sleep."

"How will Father know to find us here, when he comes back?"

How could she tell the girl that her father would never come back, that he was also proud, that his shame would always keep him away? Still less could she explain that if he came, she'd shut the door in his face, treat him like the man they had driven from their stairs. I hate him, Dinah, I'll never forgive him; even if he *is* your father, he's the cause of all this, and I pray every night that there's a miserable room in hell for men who abandon their families. She couldn't say any of that. So she told the comforting lie: "I left word with the neighbors. He'll know the way."

Dinah nodded inscrutably; for a moment Anna had the queer feeling that her daughter knew the true answer, and had only asked the question to test her mother, to see whether Anna would trust her with the truth. But of course not, Dinah was only ten, only a child, and she missed her father after these weeks. Of course she did. God help her—she's had to strike a man to save us, and if he had died, she would have been the one who tumbled him down the stairs. Ten years old, and she had reached willingly to cause a death, if Providence had turned it that way. What will happen to you, Dinah, you and my sons, what will happen to you when the need gets greater, and our strength grows less?

Can't be helped. All in the hands of God, can't be helped. We will pray as we have always prayed, and God will care for us, as he sees best.

Next day before breakfast she went downstairs and began sweeping the filth off the floor, including her own vomit, which was no less foul than any other. One by one the children came down to help, and it was done before their first meal at noon. "Tastes better," Robert said, holding up his cold potato, "without the smell of downstairs sauce."

❧ 3 ❧

Robert Kirkham
Manchester, 1829

DESPITE THE BRAVE FRONT he tried to put on it, Robert did not face new things easily. He never had. Dinah's birth had been catastrophic to him, and he had reacted almost as badly to Charlie's, even though he was six when his younger brother was born. The other three children had not lived more than a few days—their deaths had been a relief to him. Was it sinful of him? As he grew older, he wondered about himself, but he was really no more monstrous than most children are.

Robert knew beyond doubt how things ought to be. The family ought to live in rooms above a store. There ought to be customers. His mother ought to say, "My strong boy. What would I do without you?" Just as the sunlight ought to slant so in summer, hot and shimmery, and then at a steeper, colder angle in the winter afternoons. In his earliest years he had studied the customers and knew who would buy, who would haggle, and who would cheat; he had also studied the dust trembling in the sunlight streaming through the window, yet for all his study never knew which drifting wisp of it would pass too near the edge, would slip outside the walls of the sunbeam and be lost.

I am lost, he said to himself. He feared the strange silence of this place; the walls were all wrong; and worst of all, the wrongest thing of all was that his father's step never came here, that he could no longer conjure a memory of his father's face, even in the darkest night. Am lost.

And yet there were things even here that he could count on. He would awake in the morning when he heard the door close from his mother going off to fetch water. He would rise, set out the plates, stoke the fire, and then, if she was not back yet, lean against the bare wall and look at the arrangement of the plates. God bless me, thought he, but I do a neat job of it.

A morning like any other. Cold potato again, and less of it than ever. Mother looking afraid but smiling cheerfully despite the way that Charlie, damn him, whined for more. And when at last Charlie was buried in his book, Robert said, "Will you take me to find work, or must I go alone?"

As if by habit Anna shook her head. Robert rolled up his sleeves and stretched out his arms. "If you won't let me use them, you might as well cut them off." Ah, it was a melodramatic moment. But it was no actor's ploy; Anna saw that the boy would not be denied. In truth, she had no further will to deny him. Starvation was only weeks away, and *she* had had no luck in finding work.

So Robert and Anna stood at the door of Ambrose and Brewster, an impressive hulk of smudged brick that loomed over Chapel Street. Anna held Robert's hand, and she spoke for him, but he had no illusions. Her hand would go, and he would stay, and it would all be new and terrible. Only this made it bearable: that he had chosen it.

"Mum?" asked the thick and confident man who opened the door.

"I wondered," Anna said, "if you have need of a fine young man."

"A child?"

"You see that Robert is tall for his age, and strong."

"Eleven?"

"Thirteen."

"Looks like eleven, and soft. We pay him for what he does, not what his mother thinks of him." The man wrote *doffer* in his book, and the name *Robert*. "He gets dinner at noon, tea at four if you live close. Work stops at ten, and then wash up. Master's particular about washing up."

"So am I," Anna said. She was relieved that they cared about cleanliness. Robert was not. He did not hear cleanliness. He heard that Master was particular.

"Will you treat him well?" Anna asked.

"They don't do much work if we beat them too much, mum. But they also don't do much if we don't maintain normal and necessary discipline."

A few beatings were to be expected; no adults thought twice about it, unless it was excessive. Robert had been beaten at school as a matter of course. Anna suspected that the stories she had heard of cruelty in the factories were much overdone. "You'll find Robert's a good boy."

"Three a week."

"I had rather hoped for more, him being so large for his age."

"Well, then," said the overseer, drawing a line through Robert's name in the book. "We don't want him, if he's already being trained to be greedy." He closed the book and made as if to turn away.

Anna was flustered, but Robert knew that this was just another form of haggling: he knew it well from his earliest memories of his father's store. "Sir," Robert said, "start me at three, and I'll work so hard that in six weeks you'll not be able to say your prayers for paying me so little."

The man turned around and squinted at Robert. "Cocky little devil, aren't you? Begging your pardon, mum. Well, I can't give you more than two and six, at first, seeing how you're so smart-spoken and have greedy blood. But if you do as well as you brag, boy, you'll have your rise, we don't pay but what's fairly owed."

He could tell his mother wanted to refuse, wanted to take him away and find another place, or better still send him back to school somehow. But the money was low and the food near gone, and so he pulled his hand from hers and reluctantly she agreed to it. So it was done, and Anna went off and left him there. Oddly, when she let go his hand the noise of the factory

suddenly became louder, reached out to him and touched him
and enveloped him; he could feel the throbbing of the machinery
for the first time, as if the quiet pulse of her hand had been
enough to drown it out before.

The overseer's fingers came around behind his neck, large
and strong, stronger than his father's hand; by it he was pro-
pelled into the factory, where the smell of coal and the whine
and screech and hum and clatter of machinery took hold of
him and drew him in despite his terror. It came to him like the
thunder and lightning from Mount Sinai, like hearing the voice
of a God whose face could not be seen. Lord, the world is
burning, but it is not consumed! The rites of the factory had
more strength than the stately Anglican service, for the silence
of the Church could be no match for this. Trembling into his
bones, hammering at his ears, this was omnipotence, Almighty
Coalfire and His Son the Steam Engine, and everywhere the
power brought by endless whistling belts to each spinning jenny,
like the Holy Ghost touching the heart of every man: Praise
God, from whom all blessings flow; fear God and live, yes,
fear him and live, become careless of him and you will die.

"You hear me, boy? Never touch one of those belts for an
instant or you're dead on the spot, the belts'll snatch you and
crush you into the machinery in a second, and nothing for you
but the grave, boy, if we can find enough pieces of you to fill
a box."

It was a religion Robert could understand. "Aye, sir," he
said reverently. He saw the hundreds of women, each bent over
her work, the bins of unspun wool being sucked dry by the
power of the machines, the digested thread spewing from them,
hurtling around huge bobbins, all by the force of the belts that
seemed alive, they sang so. "I'll be careful."

The hand at his back tightened, held his neck and his hair
in a crushing, tearing grip.

"Did I ask you to speak?"

"No, sir!"

The hand tightened more. "I say, did I ask you to speak?"
This time Robert only shook his head.

"Then keep still. In this place, that rule is law. Not a word
except what's required for the work, and that's damned little
except what's said by me. In other factories they talk and get
careless, but here you keep still and think about your work and

there's no accidents that way, or fewer, anyway. Do you understand?"

Robert caught himself in time and nodded his answer instead of saying yes.

The overseer left him and stepped farther into the cavernous room. Boys Robert's age and younger were rushing back and forth carrying bobbins. The overseer collared one and pulled him to where Robert waited. "New doffer. Teach him in fifteen minutes or I'll have your hide."

The boy glared at Robert, but led him to the spinning jenny he had been heading for with his empty bobbin. The woman there did not stop her work, not even to look up at them. Instead she said softly, so that it was almost impossible to hear her, "A new one?"

The boy nodded. The woman's face went ugly for a moment, but she just nodded and went on working. The boy whispered something to Robert. "What?" Robert asked.

The boy slapped his face. Robert was stunned, and might have made reply except for the woman hissing softly and shaking her head. The boy grabbed Robert's shirt front, pulled him close, and whispered in his ear. "Not a sound out loud, not that the bastard overseer can hear, or we'll all three be strapped!" The whisper was vehement. Robert nodded quickly. "All right then, strip off those shoes and stockings and take off that jacket so you can get to work." Robert looked where the boy was pointing—a room full of coats and shoes and stockings. Robert quickly went to it, took off his shoes and socks. As he hung up his coat on a peg, he noticed that many of the coats were women's, as were many of the shoes, mingled right among the men's. He was startled—surely the factory would not do anything so indecent as to require the women to remove their stockings in the same room as the men. He puzzled on this for a moment.

"Dawdling?"

He turned to see the overseer gazing at him with deep, bright eyes, and he was so afraid that he spoke to defend himself. "No sir, I was just—"

He was silenced by the sting of the overseer's strap against his arm. It was a piece of an old belt that once had carried power; now it carried only authority, and yet the force of it, like all other force within the factory, came ultimately from the unseen coalfire, which sent the black dust everywhere, coming from nowhere, to burn in the nose and lungs and spread to fill all Manchester with its soot. This was what the overseer carried in his hand, and Robert's awe only deepened.

"Not a word," said the overseer. "Now were you dawdling?"

Robert shook his head. The strap fell again, stinging twice as badly as before.

"Not a word, and still less a lie. Dawdling? I asked you."

Robert nodded.

"I thought so." The overseer grabbed him by the arm, spun him around, and landed three vicious blows across the high part of his back, between his shoulders. They were agonizing, caught as Robert was with just his shirt. Robert cried out, and the overseer heaved him into the coats hanging on the wall. It was all the boy could do to keep from crying from the pain.

"Learn your trade quickly," said the overseer, "and make no mistakes, and you won't feel this strap again." And again Robert was alone in the cloak room.

When he got back to the spinning jenny, the boy assigned to him said nothing, just began showing Robert how to dismantle the frame of thread, remove the full bobbin, rush it to the rollers, and return with an empty bobbin and replace it in the frame. One doffer served six jennies, and it was only a few moments before Robert was required to change a frame entirely on his own.

It was not just fear of the strap that kept Robert from doing well at first; the very novelty of everything he was doing and the speed at which it had to be done had him so terrified that he was lucky to remember where the bobbin was on the machines. The operator of one of the first jennies he changed alone became impatient and whispered, "Quick, damn you, boy, or I fall behind!" It only made Robert more tense, less able to move quickly, and when he finally had the frame off and the bobbin out, he lost his balance and stumbled toward the belts and straps that whirred madly only a few inches away from him.

The operator cried out, grabbing him by the arm. His free hand brushed against a belt. The belt caught his hand and threw it brutally against the jenny. It could have been worse, could have caught his hand between strap and metal and shorn it off at the wrist. As it was, it tore a gouge out of his flesh, bruised his hand, twisted his wrist, and so frightened him that he felt nauseated and faint.

"What's going on!" roared the overseer. "Why the shouting and screaming! Why isn't the boy working!"

No one said anything. The operator just lifted Robert's bleeding hand.

"Stanch that blood! Do you want to stain the thread?"

The operator made as if to help Robert to a place where his hand could be bound, but the overseer jabbed at her with the strap. "Not you! Where's the turnboy!"

A nine-year-old appeared from farther up the line. The overseer tersely told him to take care of the problem. The nine-year-old had no sense of urgency—what was another boy's blood to him?—and sauntered easily to the washroom, where he directed Robert to put his hand under a spigot, which poured out ice-cold water. It numbed the pain.

"Can I talk here?" Robert asked.

"Ye're talkin', an't ye?"

"Will my hand be all right?"

The boy shrugged. "If it is, ye go back to work in a minute, and do double to make up for the time lost. If it isn't, ye go home and no more come here to work." In other words, the hand was all right whether it was injured or not, because it *had* to be.

"What's a turnboy?"

"Me," said the boy. Then he grinned. "Turnboy's what tells everybody their turn."

"Turn for what?"

"To pluck daisies. And they only have a few seconds, so when yer turn comes, fellow, ye'd best have the need." The hand was bound now, and skillfully, so that Robert still had full use of it. "Ye're na cripple on this one. Be more careful, there's nothin' I can do if yer head be crushed."

Kind words and a note of concern: They were people here, not just pieces of the machine or fingers of the overseer. And hadn't the operator grabbed him and probably saved his life? As ancient Israel had discovered, God could be lived with, and so could even his prophets, it was possible to survive even in the shadow of the power of God, even after God had touched his hand and struck his back and taught him that the first virtue of power was its pain.

By dinner Robert had the knack of it, and though he wasn't near as quick as the other boys, he got it done and kept up. He noticed how the others had such a keen eye for the overseer that they could stop now and then and chat with each other, with the rollers, with even the operators. The women had learned to trust the doffers' eyes—if the boy spoke, it was because, for the moment, it was safe to speak. Robert hadn't their trust yet, and didn't deserve it—he wasn't sure enough of his work to take his eyes off it to see where the man with the strap was lurking. Yet there was hope, for the other boys could do it, and someday he'd manage it as well.

Dinner came with a whistle at noon, and there was a mad scramble for shoes; Robert got his near last, trying to be courteous, and so lost five minutes of the precious forty-five alotted. He ran home—ten more minutes gone—and found Dinah and Charlie there with no food prepared, no dinner even begun.

"What have you been doing all morning?" Robert shouted.

"Reading," said Charlie. Dinah held up her mending.

"Don't you know I have but fifteen minutes at home, or they take my wages for being late? The food must be ready when I get here!"

Dinah looked at him coldly; she said nothing, but he could hear her words all the same: Who are you to give orders?

"I'm who earns what Father ought to earn, that's who I am, and it means my meals are ready when I need them!" He groaned and threw himself on the bed where Charlie was lying with his book.

"Get off me," Charlie shouted.

"Get off the bed. I need to rest." He was not trying to offend; he had simply never been so exhausted in his life, and the longest part of the day was yet ahead. His muscles ached from the unusual labor, his back and hand ached, he had no thought to be deferent. Either Charlie understood that, or Robert's tone frightened him—he silently went over to Anna's and Dinah's bed. Dinah set water to boil in the fireplace, then walked to the foot of the bed and looked at Robert's back.

"Why are you bleeding?"

"Hurt my hand in the machinery."

"Not your hand. Your back."

Robert raised his head from the sheet. "Is it bleeding?"

"You didn't know?"

"Knew it hurt, didn't know the strap drew blood."

"Strap?"

"Overseer."

Dinah looked horrified. At that Robert knew he had said too much. "You won't tell Mother, will you? She might take me out of there, and we need the money. I'm getting better at it—I won't get beaten too often." Dinah's eyes stayed wide, and Robert knew he could not take her silence for assent. "Promise, both of you, that you won't tell Mother."

They promised. He drank tea and took a cold potato with him, so he could eat while walking back. Yet he was oddly cheerful. For the first time in years all was as it should be. He thought of Dinah's awe at the blood he had shed for them and was content.

🐾 4 🐾

Anna Banks Kirkham
Manchester, 1829

ANNA WAS ALREADY BONE WEARY. The child in her was not heavy enough to weigh her down yet, but it sucked strength from her constantly, and the long walk in the hot sun was costing her dearly. She had gone through the great row houses of the rich, and had been told the same everywhere. "It's girls we want, woman, not old ones who've never been trained. Just girls."

Once, weary enough to forget herself, Anna had mentioned Dinah. "Ten years old and strong and willing and smart as a whip."

The butler, who had charge of screening candidates for employment, looked interested. "Bring her by. We might be able to pay her two shillings a week, if she works out."

But the maid who showed her to the back door stepped outside with her. "Mum, don't bring your daughter, not to this house."

"Why not?"

"Because the master likes to plant in fields that aren't his own."

Anna was not too surprised—rumors of this kind of thing were rampant in the middle class, where the best gossip was of the failings of the rich. "She's only ten," Anna said, as if that made all the difference.

"Aye," said the maid. "I know. He also likes to plow new soil." And the woman had ducked back inside, leaving Anna to wander through the narrow gap that led to the street.

This afternoon she had begun looking in at the larger estates outside of Manchester, where the houses were surrounded by land, with long drives. Usually the gatekeeper would tell her, "We an't lookin', mum. No hiring today." Occasionally there was no gatekeeper, or he would merely shrug and let her by.

One such place had a drive lined with roses. Anna leaned over and smelled one. She remembered that John had often compared her to a rose. Often before they were married. And after, too, but where before he had said much about the blossom and the scent and the softness of the petals, in after years he made more mention of the thorns. It was a rueful memory, yet not entirely unkind. She did not stand long, bent over the rose; the flower might speak of her youth, but the pain in her back and thighs and ankles spoke of age and the infant in her, ravenously draining her of strength.

Apparently the butler was observant. He was already speaking angrily when he opened the servants' door. "I saw you stop at the roses! You didn't pluck one, did you?"

"No!"

"I doubt it! I know your kind. What do you want?"

"Work."

"Work," he answered, mockingly. "And when you hear we don't have work, you'll be asking for a hot meal all the same, won't you?"

"You've accused me now of being a thief and a beggar, sir, but I assure you that I'm neither."

"I'm glad to hear it. We don't have work, so you can go."

It was too much for her. She might be forced to look for servants' work, but she had grown up in another class. She had treated her father's servants with dignity, and could not bear this butler treating her so rudely. "Indeed I *can* go, and indeed I *shall* go, but if you had come honestly asking for work at *my* door I'd have given you a glass of water before you left. But then, I can't expect *you* to be a gentleman. You're only a servant, and no doubt born to be worse."

She turned away, thinking to leave, but the butler barred her passage. "Oh, I'm *just* a servant, am I? And what if I was to accuse you of stealing, my fine lady? There'd be a search then, wouldn't there, and quite a row, and I'd see to it we didn't stop at the petticoats."

"Let me go."

"When you humbly beg my pardon for your sluttish manners."

Just a moment before, the butler's face had seemed impervious to emotion, but now it was twisted with rage, and Anna began to wonder if he might be mad. Certainly his eyes were unstable, darting back and forth in his fury, and she thought he might be capable of violence. So, hating herself for a coward, she bowed her head and apologized. "I'm sorry, sir. I spoke out of turn."

The butler was not satisfied, however, and kept her there another five minutes, calling her names so foul she sometimes did not even understand. She bore it as her penance; she had sinned when she spoke haughtily to him, and now God was kind enough to chastise her immediately, instead of saving the punishment for later. God's punishments were always easier to bear when they came immediately: then there was not the agonizing process of discovering what sin the punishment was for, so she could finally repent of it and be reprieved.

When at last he let her go, she was livid with shame and unvented rage. The hot sun reflecting painfully from the gravel drive helped little, and near the gate she finally succumbed to her feelings and reached out, plucked a white rose, and stepped on it, twisting her foot to grind it into the fine stones of the drive. The smell of it came up hot and sweet. I am learning, God. I haven't your finesse, but the result's the same, isn't it?

And then she caught herself in the blasphemy and was afraid. Was there no end to her sinfulness and pride? O God, she prayed, O God, O God—but she could not think of anything to say afterward. What was it that she wanted from God? Forgiveness? Punishment? Relief?

Work. That was all she wanted. Work, so that from her

pores she could squeeze pennies and shillings like sweat and keep her little ones alive.

And as if God had heard her, a carriage turned into the lane, a fine carriage enclosed against the dust of the dry day. Anna felt a rush of fear, for there was the crushed rose, and God seemed to be upbraiding her promptly today. Then she stepped back to let the carriage pass, and thought of nothing but how nice it would be to ride the miles back home instead of walking. The horses pranced beautifully. As they passed, she noticed that their eyes looked frightened and dangerous. And then a voice from the carriage cried, "Peter, ho up!"

The driver drew in the reins, and the carriage stopped only a few paces beyond her. Her fear returned. The owner of the estate had seen the flower—or worse, seen her crush it.

The carriage door opened. Anna was unsure what she was expected to do. Finally the voice from the carriage called out, "Must I send a postman with a letter inviting you to come?" Anna carefully approached the carriage, stood on the ground outside the open door. Inside a wizened-looking old man was peering out at her intently.

"Sir?" she asked.

"Not him," said the voice. "Me." Anna stepped to her right, saw that a much younger and fatter man sat across from the old one.

"That's my father," said the younger man. "He's old and mad and knows nothing, so you needn't address yourself to him."

The old man giggled. The sound rattled in his throat.

The younger man leaned forward. "Did you come to beg, or for work?"

"Work."

"What do you do?"

"Anything, sir. Cleaning, and I'm a fair cook and a better laundress." She had said the words a dozen times since noon, but they still tasted foul in her mouth. I'm a professional man's wife, she said in her mind. But outside her manner was obsequious, for she had always known servants, and had the knack of imitating them.

"Anything. Well, then you'll do. We've an old servant who died a few days ago, and I don't want to fuss with training children to the work. Ten shillings a week, Sunday off, report at six and you may leave at seven in the evening, unless we need you."

Anna bowed her head. "I doubt your butler will be happy to have me working for you."

"I doubt I give a damn. My name is Hulme."

"Anna Kirkham."

"I will meet you in the library, Anna, in half an hour."

He tapped with his cane, and the carriage started forward. The old man giggled as the younger Hulme reached out and closed the carriage door.

The dust rose behind the carriage, and Anna turned her face away to breathe clearer air. Ten shillings a week. With Robert's two and sixpence it was not enough—eighteen shillings a week were needed just to live.

But she had had no other offers, and if worse came to worst she could quit and find other work, she told herself. Yet she knew as she started back up the drive that she would not quit. That this was where she would start work and have to keep working until the baby came.

"Master's got no judgment when it comes to hiring," said the butler to the cook. Anna overheard as she came from the library. "He'll hire a hog if it was easier than looking for quality."

Anna said nothing. She could quote Adam Smith and Samuel Johnson; she understood Locke and *Leviathan*. What mattered it if the butler taught the other servants to snub her? She was here, not for friendship, but for survival. She docilely followed the head housekeeper upstairs to learn her duties. Silently she thanked God she was rarely sick when pregnant; she would have to be utterly reliable here, hardworking and regular, so that no offense could be charged against her. Yet she could not stop herself from thinking that if God really meant to be kind to her, he might more conveniently have blessed her not to be pregnant at all, or even to have money enough not to have to work, or best of all to have a husband at home, earning well so that she could spend her life educating her children, which was all she cared about, all that she was really good at.

And then, of course, she had to beg forgiveness for having criticized God's treatment of her, for didn't God understand her heart and know what she deserved? I am circled about by my own sins, my thorny wickedness; if I am ever freed at all it will be by thy grace; oh, give me grace, my Lord, though I'm unworthy.

Seventeen beds to turn daily. Seventeen rooms to sweep, dust, and air. Windows to wash, floors to scrub, rugs to carry out and beat. She followed the housekeeper and let her feet learn the steps, let her hands learn the work, while her mind endlessly recited poetry in meaningless repetitions. Most of all these words kept coming back to her: But follow me, and I will bring thee where no shadow stays thy coming.

❧ 5 ❧

Robert Kirkham
Manchester, 1829

IT WAS AFTER DARK, long after supper, and they were working by gaslight when the doffer across from Robert fell into
the straps and was killed. The boy had been tired all day, and
Robert had watched him lurch to and fro under the weight of
full bobbins—and only slightly less under the weight of the
empty ones. They had talked at supper. Or, rather, Robert had,
trying to strike up some sort of conversation. The boy hadn't
answered—just ate the bread he had brought in his pocket and
turned away to sleep the rest of the time.

"His mother's sick," Liza told Robert quietly. "He tends
her all night while she's dying, and comes here to try to earn
enough by day to keep them both alive."

"His father?"

"Crippled. And the other children all in the workhouse."
Her voice broke at that. "They all depend on him, poor boy,
and he only earns his three a week. It'd be a mercy if she'd

die soon, so he could sleep at night. It isn't right for a child to kill himself this way."

On their way back into the factory from supper—they only had twenty minutes for it—Robert noticed that two of the operators were harshly shaking the sleeping boy to wake him.

"Can't they be gentler?" Robert asked.

"And not wake him? If he's late he loses his place."

Now no fear will wake him, Robert thought. They had closed down the power to the jennies while they extricated the twisted and broken body from the belts. Everyone was grateful for the rest, even though they grieved for the boy's death. The overseer walked back and forth, nervously rubbing his hands together, saying, "Terrible, terrible, a dreadful thing to happen," though Robert was not altogether sure which bothered the overseer more, the boy's death or the stoppage of work.

Robert was ashamed of it, but the death in the machinery brought him a strange kind of peace. It was because the death was so inevitable; he had sensed it almost from the start, that the power of this place was the power to give life, to give death. Work for money, money for food, food for life; and now the other side of the power, the thirst of the belts, they must drink also, must drink a fluid richer than the sweat that constantly specked its surface. He had known the death was coming from the start. Now it had come, the waiting was over, and to his relief the machinery had taken someone else. Now how long until the engines demanded their next propitiation?

Robert finished putting his bobbin back into its place in the frame; already his work had formed such habits in him that he could do it without thinking. It would take time to get the belts moving again. He took the opportunity to wander off into the roller room. He did not know what he had been looking for until he found it. One of the large machines there had broken down, and three men were laboring to repair it. They were the ones who had been carrying pieces of metal back and forth all day, and Robert stood and watched him silently as they continued their work. It was plain they understood the unintelligible metal lacework, knew what each part was for and how it ought to move. Robert, uninitiated, looked at their inscrutable labors in awe.

Yet not so much awe that he could not try to figure it out. From the belt to the rollers, that was what he could understand.

The belt turns the shafts, the shafts turn other belts, gears and pistons and all fit together, engaging and disengaging to wind spool after spool of thread. All of it felt good and true and powerful and he worshiped, for it was beautiful. Except in one place, where he saw that it could not work.

"You've got it wrong," he said.

One of the men, a cheerful-looking fellow of about twenty with grease liberally covering his face, looked over at him.

"Oh. We have?"

"You've got two belts connected to this shaft here, and they go opposite ways."

The man looked where Robert pointed. Another one said, "We haven't got time for this, Aaron!" But Aaron led Robert closer. "You see this lever? It chooses which of these will engage or disengage over here. You see that? So the machine can go two ways, if the operator wants, forward or backward. You see that? It isn't a mistake. It's just damn good engineering."

Robert was embarrassed and stammered an apology.

"Don't be sorry. It takes a keen eye to know which way these belts will go. You're a doffer, right?"

Robert nodded.

"Too bad. An eye like that should be an engineer."

The man who had interrupted before climbed out from under one of the machines. "Say, little doffer, do you like the way they beat you in there?"

Robert said nothing. It was a question too fraught with danger to answer it straight out.

"Well, if you like it, boy, you'll be glad to know that the machines have started up in there, and if you dally here a moment longer you'll be blue from your arse to your ankles."

Now Robert heard a sound he had only been vaguely conscious of before—the spinning jennies going at full power. He turned, ran back into the room, and made it to the fullest frame before the operator had time to get impatient and call the overseer. Then he saw that the operator was Liza, and remembered that this was the jenny where the boy had been caught up in the straps. No wonder this place had been empty for him. She made no sign of wanting to scold him, though her face was hard and set. As he fiddled with the frame to loose the bobbin, he saw that her eyes were full of tears.

"Careful," he whispered, leaning near her. "If you can't see clearly, it could happen bad with you."

She nodded. It was friendship here, as much as was possible, and words like that might save a hand. A life. But her tears, they stayed with him more than the boy's death. Her face, ruddy, funny-looking and cheerful, twisted up from crying. Wasn't right, that's all, and yet was necessary, in this place it was needful that tears also fall upon the singing metal.

And when he left at ten o'clock, his body all over in pain, his legs so weary that his feet slapped the pavement like a cripple's feet, then he left his body and dwelt, for a time, only in his mind. He saw Liza crying for the boy, only it was his mother crying for him, only it was St. Mary crying for the slain Lord.

There was singing in the ugly streets beyond Hanging Ditch. The men were drunk, cheerfully singing bawdy songs whose meaning always just eluded Robert; or they mournfully lamented some long-dead hero as a substitute for mentioning the miseries of their present, unromantic life. A slight breeze rattled the rubbish in the streets. It was the mournful songs that most accorded with Robert's temper, and when he reached Ducie Bridge and the turning to his family's cottage, he could not stop himself from weeping. It was not for the boy in the factory whose corpse had been stowed in the corner in a bloody cloth for his family to come for him; the tears were for the pain in his body, for the knowledge he would spend another day at the factory tomorrow and the next day and the next day forever. It was for the squalor he now lived in and the memory of better days in childhood. It was for his father, who would not return, for the two and sixpence that were all he had to lay upon the table to ease his mother's heavy burden. It was for the child Robert, who was dead, replaced by a melancholy old man whose feet spastically slapped against the road as he walked.

He leaned against the corner of the row and wept into his sleeve, wept until he could not weep anymore; then he waited until he judged his eyes would show no sign of his tears before he walked the short way along the riverbank to the cottage.

Anna greeted him with a smile. "Oh, you look weary, Robert. But I bought a fish today, and that should do you good, to have something besides gruel and potatoes and tea, though heaven knows God has blessed us more than we deserve to give us even that much." She kissed him, but he saw behind the smile and knew that she, too, had lost something in her heart today.

"How did it go?"

She affected delight. "I have a position. Upstairs domestic in a fine rich house in Broughton." She laughed and cheerfully described the house, the stern housekeeper, the rough-spoken butler. Dinah and Charlie were awestruck at the number of rooms with no one to sleep in them, at the library full of books to the second-story ceiling, at the kitchen with three ovens and three stoves, at the drive lined with roses. Robert noticed something else: all the other servants were described as humorous characters, not as potential friends. And he asked the other question, which ruined it all.

"How much?"

"Ten a week," Anna said, still smiling.

"With mine that's twelve and six, and we'd be starving even if we had a pound."

"We have our savings."

"Aye, until that money's gone, and buying fish will finish it much sooner than we like."

Anna's smile became wistful. "Robert, Robert, can't we at least be cheerful tonight? I'm so tired."

"So am I." His body shuddered involuntarily. "A boy died at the factory today. Fell asleep and got caught in the machinery."

Anna gave a little cry. Charlie, of course, was immediately full of questions, but Dinah hushed him. And Anna put a close to the dismal conversation by saying, "At least we can thank God it wasn't you."

"Yes, and while we're thanking God, let's thank Him He hasn't burned down the house around our ears, or had us beaten and robbed and left for dead—"

"Robert!" Anna said.

"Oh, pardon me, Mother, I spoke prematurely. God probably has all that planned for us in the next few weeks, and my thanks would be out of turn."

Her hand swung toward him; something stopped her, though, before she slapped him. It would have made no difference. He did not flinch, and yet felt the pain as surely as if the hand had struck.

"Don't tell me, Mother," he whispered, "that you haven't wondered whether God really loves us."

"And what if He doesn't? Are we so perfect that we deserve favors from Him?"

In that moment Robert discovered that he didn't believe in God. Not the God his mother taught, anyway. What does He ever do? He lets a boy die of weariness, which will also mean the death of his ailing mother, and probably the beginning of his father's career as a beggar. He lets terrible things happen in the world, and never acts to make sure they happen only to the wicked. What sort of weakling God is that, who can't reward His friends? If there is a God He has a shaft somewhere powered by belts that run in opposite directions, making Him forever powerful, and forever impotent. As good as dead. Not worth getting angry at. Not worth arguing about.

"I'm sorry, Mother."

She decided to accept his surrender. "A bad day?"

"I do well now. They never have to strap me. I'm treated kindly." And then, to ease the tension in the room, he said, "I shan't be a doffer long, I think. I've decided to be an engineer. Man said I had an eye for it."

He sounded cheerful enough to convince his mother, who was eager to believe. "I'm glad," she said.

And then: "Are there any girl doffers?"

Robert was too tired to catch her drift before he answered. "Aye, a few. Women do everything men do, except overseering, and the engineers are all men."

"Any girls as young as Dinah?"

"No." Now he understood. "They never hire them so young."

"Are you sure? I think they do. Perhaps if Dinah worked too, them being so kind and all—"

"No," Robert said vehemently. "They won't take her."

Anna looked at him in surprise. "Robert, it's good for a girl to stay home and all, but you know we need the money. It might make all the difference."

"I won't have it."

"You won't? Why not?"

Robert did not answer.

Anna was not a fool. "You lied, of course. They aren't kind at all there. They still beat you, even when you do well."

"It's good enough for me, because I can bear it."

From the dimly lit edge of the room Dinah spoke. "They also punished the girls in school, and I bore that."

"In school the girls were punished lighter than the boys. They make no difference between them at the factory."

Anna was standing now, had walked behind Robert, was touching his shirt. "What are these stains, Robert? Are they blood?"

"Yes," Dinah answered, before Robert could deny it.

"The strap?"

"I tell you I can bear it, but Dinah can't."

"What did you do, that they'd punish you so hard as to draw blood? I'll have words with that overseer, I will!"

"It was only once he drew blood, and I deserved it." How could he tell her that if she complained it would be the ruin of him, whether they sacked him or not? "I swore at him."

"You what?" Already the lie was working, for her anger had become surprise.

"Never mind. But I'd rather he forgot that time he beat me, the sooner the better."

"You swore?"

"I told him to go to hell."

Anna was shocked, outraged. It made Robert want to laugh or scream at her, he could not decide which. In a world like this, his mother could actually be irate at the thought that her son spoke some of the world's language. Yet she *was* angry, and he had deliberately provoked her, and so he bore it. "You're a Kirkham, your father's son and mine, and in all our tribulations have you ever heard either him or me speak one ugly word?"

"Never."

"I don't know where you learned to say such a thing. Not from me. Surely not from me."

"No, not from you."

"If he hadn't already punished you, you can be assured I would," Anna said. "I won't have my children acting like common boys and girls. You are not common. You must never be common." Her voice trembled with emotion. All the day's humiliations were in her voice now. "We may have to live and work among the lowest scum of mankind, but we don't have to think or talk or act as they do. We can't ever forget who we are!"

Yet after all had quieted down, as they were quietly undressing for sleep, Dinah said, in a voice that denied any thought of compromise, "I'll go to work as a doffer tomorrow."

Robert turned on her. "You *shall* not."

"You needn't worry about me," Dinah said. "I shan't tell the overseer to go to hell, and so I'll be all right."

He would have argued more, but for the look in Dinah's eyes. She stared him down; he looked at her and remembered that only a few nights ago she had kicked a man and sent him tumbling down the stairs. I will do what I will, she said to Robert with her silent gaze, and he hadn't the power to argue with her anymore. "Do as you like," he said.

You might have thought that what Robert went through would have taught him compassion. And he learned it, I suppose, after his fashion. But it was a fastidious sort of charity, a selective pity. He could grieve for strangers, but never quite forgave his family for their inconvenient insistence on not behaving as he thought they should. Nothing was ever as it ought to be. It would be his life's work, he realized, just beginning to set the world to rights. But he would not fight it through tonight. Let Dinah do as she likes and be damned. Soon enough—how well Robert could foresee it—she'd run into trouble there, and want his help or his comfort. And he knew with satisfaction that then he would have his revenge for her disregard of him—he *would* comfort and help her, you see, and then they would know that he was *right*, they should have listened to *him*.

In his dreams again and again the overseer raised his whip, but the strap did not fall on Robert's back. It fell on Dinah, and the blows seemed heavy enough to cut her in two.

☙ 6 ❧

Charlie Banks Kirkham
Manchester, 1830

IT WAS THE BIRTH of the baby that took the last of the savings. The midwife had to be paid in advance. They had to buy a blanket to line the crate they would use as a cradle. And when the midwife, after a seven-hour labor, insisted that they call a doctor, the doctor took all the money that was left, and muttered even so that no man knew poverty but the man who made his living from the poor.

Charlie was sure, as he watched the events through his childish eyes, that they were being persecuted by fate. Actually, however, they were lucky. The doctor was so disgusted by the squalor of the neighborhood and his low fee that he didn't actually touch Anna, which doubtless saved her life—if he had examined her he would have given her an infection that her body had no strength to resist.

In fact, Providence, after so long a quarrel with the family, was downright kind to them now, for the baby died. That meant no one to nurse. No one to weary them with nightlong wakings. Mother could go back to work as soon as she healed. Charlie admitted no doubt that she would heal. We will let her rest, Charlie assured himself, and she will get better.

Charlie watched her all day, for of course Robert and Dinah couldn't afford to stay away from work. He watched as she tossed back and forth on the bed, usually unconscious, sometimes delirious. He could hardly tell when she was in her right mind and when she was not. She might call him over and talk to him clearly about what she would do as soon as she was well, and then end the conversation by calling him John and saying strange things that Charlie didn't understand. She would talk sometimes about the baby, how beautiful she was, her pretty black curls, her turned-up nose, though the infant had died within hours of birth, and Anna had never seen her.

It made him afraid. For the first day he tried to read and memorize passages to please her, as if performing that daily ritual in exactly the right way would restore her. Surely if he memorized and recited she would remember her proper role and catechize him on what he had just read. But no passage from *Wealth of Nations* would rouse her, and when he quoted the Queen Mab speech from *Romeo and Juliet,* she wept and wept and would not be comforted, calling out again and again for her little girl. Charlie did not know that one of the children born and died before his own life began had been called Mab. He only knew that he had recited and caused his mother to grieve; he blamed himself, and it made him try all the harder to bring her to herself. He went back and forth to the well to bring cool water and bathe her fevered face and arms. He kept silent for hours once, and another time kept up a constant stream of talk. When he was silent she grew afraid and began to cry out; when he talked she seemed to become confused, and tossed and turned until he thought she would throw herself from the bed in her writhing.

By the time Robert brought Mr. Whitesides, Charlie was so filled with guilt for his mother's suffering that he was ready to do anything that might help. He did not notice that Robert approached the subject cautiously; it did not occur to him that Robert was afraid he would say no. For, inadvertently, Robert began the conversation in such a way that Charlie could not refuse.

"Charlie, since Mother's been so sick she's had no wages, and with her wages stopped we'll soon be out on the streets to starve unless we can do something to take up the slack."

Charlie, obsessed as he was with his mother's condition, immediately imagined her, delirious and raving and burning up with fever, forced to sit in the road and beg.

"There's a man, Charlie, who's willing to take you for an apprentice. He'll feed and shelter you, and train you for a trade."

"Will I have wages, then?" Charlie asked.

Robert shook his head. "You're too young for wages, Charlie, only eight years old; you wouldn't earn enough to pay for what you eat. But if you go with Mr. Whitesides, you'll at least stop eating up part of our little money here. That'll be a help."

And, miserably, Charlie agreed. The best thing he could do would be to leave, to stop harming his mother, to stop costing them money. Robert only confirmed what he had already feared: that he caused more harm than good in the family. "I'll go," Charlie said.

Then Robert went downstairs and brought Whitesides up with him. The man was tall and thin and wore a coal-black suit that didn't fit him and a top hat that looked to be the perfect home for lice. His hair was also black, and his skin was dark and stained.

Whitesides was all business. He smiled and shook Charlie's hand briskly, then said to Robert, "All right, I need the mother's permission, the boy can't do it."

"She's asleep," Charlie said.

Whitesides smiled broadly. "And I'd never think of interrupting her slumber, lad, except that it's a Sunday, and it costs me money to be standing about on a Sunday."

Robert nodded and went to the bed where Anna lay. He touched her gently, then shook her until her eyes opened. Charlie knew immediately that she did not know what she was about—she had one of the looks of madness on her. But only he would know that. Dinah and Robert hadn't been around her enough since the birth to know.

"Mother?"

"Hmmm?"

"This is Mr. Whitesides, Mother."

She giggled. "Such a bright name for so dark a man."

"Mother, Mr. Whitesides is in the chimney-cleaning business."

"A sweep?"

Whitesides raised his hands in genial protest. "Oh, no, ma'am, a director of sweeps, a superintendent of sweeps, but never a sweep myself. I'm much too big for the chimneys anymore." So it was that Charlie first learned what trade Robert had chosen for him for the rest of his life.

Anna smiled bashfully and touched her hair. "Robert, how can you bring me company to see me in bed? I must look like a monster from the deep."

"Not at all, ma'am," said Whitesides. "Charming to the core. Boy here says you have a sweep to give me."

Robert interrupted. "Charlie, Mother. He's still small. Mr. Whitesides is willing to take him on as an apprentice."

"My Charlie, a sweep?"

"It's not a bad life," Whitesides said, and as he talked his hands came alive and inscribed spiderwebs in the air. "The boys earns an honest living during the working days, and in the schoolish time of year I sends 'em to the finest of teachers that moderate money can afford so they grows up to be what any mother could be proud of. And it's a jolly time for the boys, they gets to see Manchester like no other boys ever does." Whitesides reached over and pulled on Charlie's cheek. "You like a jolly time with the boys, don't you?" The hand was a claw, and Charlie's cheek hurt.

Anna tried to make sense of what was going on. "My Charlie's a reader."

"I love a good book myself," said Whitesides.

"And the best of it is," Robert said, "Mr. Whitesides doesn't ask an apprentice fee."

"Oh, I never needs it. The boys is useful to me from the start. I have a special training method that has them up the chimney the first day. They always catches on quick, especially boys what comes from fine homes like yours."

Anna's face looked troubled. She didn't understand what was expected of her. Of course, Robert and Mr. Whitesides didn't know how to interpret her face as Charlie did. "Never mind, boy," said Whitesides. "She doesn't want to."

Charlie came closer to his mother. "Let me tell her." He reached out and touched her face, and she instantly turned to his hand. "Mother, we're down to our last nothing, and Robert's found a way for me to earn my keep. Is it all right?"

"Not in the factory, son. I'll have no son of mine working in a factory."

Charlie felt Robert stiffen—now he knew she was in her madness. But it made no difference, really. Charlie was sure that even if she were quite herself she would consent to it. Why should she not? Charlie was useless, worse than useless around home; better if he at last earned his own way. "It's no factory, Mother. He says I can read with him."

"Oh, do, yes, do!" she said. "And he'll teach you geometry and Latin, too, and raise you up to be as wise as you ought to be!" Clearly she now took Whitesides to be a teacher. Well, I'm not lying, Charlie told himself. He'll teach me a trade, and that makes him a teacher, even if it isn't in a school. "You'll take care of my little boy, won't you?"

"Of course, Ma'am."

It was then that Dinah came in. She had gone to the cathedral to pray for their mother—somehow it was always assumed that religious duties properly belonged to the women of the family. She saw Whitesides and seemed immediately to know what was going on. Charlie thought it was part of Dinah's seemingly infinite cleverness; in fact, she and Robert had discussed the idea of putting Charlie out as apprentice before.

"We're family," Dinah said. "We stay together."

Robert whirled on her, his face bright with anger, yet his voice a whisper. "Stay together, is it? Do they put us all out on the street together with no roof at all over our heads? Do we all together watch Mother die? What's together? Do you think we'll care about together in the cemetery?"

"I'll do it," Charlie said. "I'm glad to."

Robert's outburst had done nothing to bend Dinah's determination, but Charlie's willingness changed everything for her. "Charlie," she said, "do you *want* to be a sweep?"

Charlie hardly knew what it was that sweeps did. He was only eight, and like any child of the time he admired the small boys dressed in cut-up men's clothes who seemed completely free on the streets, romping and cursing and crying out for business. He thought it wonderfully romantic to be such a boy, unwanted by his family but still happy with his lot. "Better than anything else," he answered her.

It was then that Whitesides produced the papers and held

them out for Anna to sign. Anna took the pen willingly enough. Of course, Dinah had to block things one more time—it was her way. "What do the papers *say?*" she asked.

Whitesides looked annoyed. Robert sighed in impatience. "Dinah, they're apprenticeship papers. They say what all papers say."

"There's words," Dinah said, "and the words will bind us and we ought to know what they say."

Whitesides laughed at that. "Truth to tell, little girl, I had a lawyer do it all up in fine language, and I don't know a bit of what it means myself." And he held out the papers for her to read them.

Dinah didn't understand the legal language and might have caused more fuss about it, except that she noticed that Anna did not sign herself as Anna Kirkham. She signed herself Anna Banks. To Dinah, that was proof that the papers didn't mean anything after all, and so it didn't matter what they said. Robert also noticed it, but took it only as a sign that his father was gone for good, as if his mother had divorced him. Charlie did not see it; he was too occupied with wondering what it would be like to stand on the top of a chimney or get as dirty as he pleased, without having to wash. And as for Whitesides, he saw her sign but knew as little as if he hadn't—for he couldn't read a word to save his life. That was one reason why he already hated Charlie more than any other boy he'd ever had, and loved him more, too, in his dark way: the boy knew how to read, and that made him powerful and strange and wise. So clever, aren't you, Whitesides said silently, you children reading, you woman signing. But these papers give me the boy, he's mine and never yours again, and he'll soon find out how much of good his books'll do him when he's up to his arse in ashes.

As Charlie left the house, he heard his mother call to him. "In all your education, son," she said, "don't forget the Lord of heaven."

"This is Raymond," said Whitesides. "He's my best boy."

Raymond, a cocky twelve-year-old, took a deep bow. His hair was long and shaggy, his face stained, but his smile was completely winning. Charlie smiled back.

"*Was* my best boy," Whitesides amended. "For *you* shall be my best boy now, Charlie."

Charlie was confused but pleased at the thought of it. "I'll try to be, Mr. Whitesides," he said.

"You may call me *master*," Whitesides said. "Raymond here, he's too fat." He took a pinch at Raymond's waistline. There wasn't anything loose enough to grab, but Whitesides grabbed it anyway. Raymond bent slightly with the pain of the claw pulling at his skin, but the smile never left his face. "Raymond can't get up the chimney so good anymore. So he's my teacher. He teaches boys. And Charlie, here, he's a smart lad, Raymond. He can *read*."

"Oh, he'll learn fast, he will, Master," Raymond said. Smiling.

"All my boys learns fast, Charlie. Or the boys suffers."

It was the first open statement of Whitesides's teaching method. The second came a moment later. Whitesides bent and smiled in Charlie's face. "You aren't smiling, boy. My boys is happy. My boys smiles." And he cheerfully struck Charlie across the head, knocking him to the floor.

"Smile," Whitesides said, grinning. It was impossible. Charlie had rarely been hit in his life—even at his most depressed and angry, John Kirkham had been gentle with his children, and Anna scarcely less so. "Charlie, you *must* smile or I'll think you aren't happy with me." And Whitesides kicked him in the hip. Charlie screamed with the pain.

Raymond, still smiling, tugged at Whitesides' coat. "If you break his bones, Master, he can't climb."

"He must smile," Whitesides said. "I won't have any sadness near me. It's a sad world, Charlie, and it's our duty given us by God to smile and bring gladness to every heart."

Charlie, tears running down his cheeks, holding his painful hip, smiled.

"Ah, Charlie, that's no smile. That's no smile." Whitesides lifted his foot and used it to shove Charlie flat on the floor. Then he pressed down, putting more and more weight on Charlie's stomach. Charlie felt the air go out of his lungs as his stomach caved easily to the pressure. The pain became intense. He whimpered high in his throat.

"Careful, Master," said Raymond, smiling.

"A real smile, Charlie," said Whitesides.

And Charlie put a ghastly grimace of pain on his face, desperately trying to make it a smile so he could breathe again, so the terrible pain in his stomach would go away. He wished, desperately, to be home. He would sit beside his mother and repeat the words of Mercutio about Queen Mab. "She it is who presses girls and teaches them to bear, making them women of good carriage." Was that how it went? And what next? "There is in every society or neighborhood an ordinary or average rate both of wages and profit." No, that was Adam Smith, not Shakespeare. Sorry, Mother. I'll get it right next time.

"Smile from the heart, Charlie," said Whitesides.

"The fool hath said in his heart, there is no such thing as justice." Did he say it? No—it was Leviathan, speaking back to him in his mind. He had no notion what the words meant—he rarely did—but they seemed very important to him right now.

"Or I'll find your heart and feed it to you," said Whitesides even more cheerfully.

Charlie thought he saw his mother's sleeping face as she lay in bed, the baby beside her in the minutes before they realized the infant was dead. He would have screamed, but he had no air at all in him, and then the world went white and then red and then black.

He awoke a moment later, choking and gagging. The weight was gone from his stomach, but his gut ached as if it had been torn inside, and he gasped for breath against the pain and rolled over, curling up to let his organs find their natural place again. When the pain subsided a little, Charlie began to cry.

"Can't cry," Raymond said. Charlie looked up to find that the boy's face, mercifully, was not smiling. Already Charlie knew that that meant Whitesides was not near at hand. "Can't cry, it makes it worse. Just smile all the time. Pretty soon you learn to smile in your sleep. Stomach all right?"

Charlie shook his head.

"Well, get used to it. There's a sort of sense in what he does. Chimney sweeps has to be tough, and if you live through the first few weeks, you get tough." Raymond laughed mirthlessly. "I don't suppose you're hungry?"

"Where is he?"

"Out making appointments. He does it every Sunday. Wasted a lot of time getting *you*, has to make it up. But don't think of running home. He locks the door from the outside."

Painfully Charlie got up, careful not to put any more strain than necessary on his stomach. As soon as he stood up his head went dizzy; he fell to his knees and vomited on the floor.

"They all does it," Raymond said. "Now you'll want to eat for sure."

Charlie cleaned up the mess, and Raymond was right. He felt much better now, and was able to eat the cheap soup that Raymond poured into a platter. Not a trace of meat in it, and some of the vegetables were unidentifiable. "Don't ask," Raymond said, anticipating the question. "Whitesides makes the soup."

"Are there any books?" Charlie asked.

"Books?"

"To read. If we go to school, I thought there might be books here."

"School?"

Now Charlie realized how he had been cheated. All lies about school, lies just to get Mother to sign. And Robert was in on it. Charlie was sure of that. After all, Robert was the one who brought Whitesides. Robert was the one who hated him and wanted him to go. Dinah and Mother still wanted Charlie to be home, and only Robert had made him go, only Robert had lied to him and brought this man to take him away and lock him in a room and hurt him. I hate you, Charlie said silently to his brother. I'll get free and come back and tell Mother what you did.

Even better than the soup, the hatred eased the pain; it worked so well that he was even able to smile at Whitesides when he finally returned. You and Robert may have conspired to torture me, but I will not let you see how much you hurt me.

❥ 7 ❧

Anna Banks Kirkham
Manchester, 1830

ANNA AWOKE THINKING CLEARLY for the first time since labor. She had no memory beyond the midwife saying, "It's a girl, Annie." And then, as so many times before, she remembered the other words, the later words. "She's dead. Ah, it'll break Anna's heart." All the pity in the world in the voice that said it, but no pity at all in the God that did it. No, no, not God! God didn't do it! Forgive me for the thought, don't punish me for my sin by killing this one, let me have this one alive—

This time, however, she fought back against the grief, held it at bay and kept her thoughts clear. She remembered now how often this same moment had come, and how each time she had retreated into dreams of the infant in her arms. Was it true that John had come back to her? No, that was part of the dreaming. So much dreaming—what was true and what wasn't? No matter. She wasn't dreaming now, and soon enough she'd find out the truth of all.

She felt weak, and her belly ached deep when she tried to sit. But she knew this pain—she had met it before, and defeated it. She rolled to the edge of the bed and let her legs slide to the floor. She knelt and prayed, thanking God for his mercy in letting her survive and begging his forgiveness for anything sinful she might have said in her illness. Then she slowly got to her feet and walked to the table, where a small remnant of cheese lay, uncovered. Not like Charlie, to leave the cheese on the table. He must just be out getting water. He only left the cheese this way for a moment, knowing he'd be back soon. She got back in bed, waiting for him to come back so he could tell her what day it was, and how the child was buried, and what name they had given to her, and whether she had been baptized in time.

But the hours passed, and Charlie did not come home, and she began to worry. Again she got up, and this time combed her filthy, tangled hair and dressed herself and slowly, painfully went down the stairs, calling Charlie's name. He did not answer. He was not at any near neighbor's cottage. She could see across the river that he was not at the plug beyond Scotland Bridge where they drew clean water. Perhaps he was at the market. Don't worry, she told herself. No need to imagine the worst. He's off on some errand for Robert, that's all.

She came back when the noon bells began. Nomi Barton was outside, loading her scant furniture into a cart.

"Moving?" Anna asked, to be polite.

"No, just bringin' my sticks out to air," Nomi answered with good-natured sarcasm. "Don't you know? Didn't the landlord notice you?"

"Notice me what?"

"The lease reverts, is what the man read to me last evenin'. The lease reverts and everyone must come out because the buildings is comin' down."

"Coming down?"

"You don't think they'll go *up*, do you?" Nomi cackled grimly. "No, when they knocks down these old walls, the place comes down for sure."

"When?"

"Three or four days, I think. End of the month. I was lucky and found me a cottage I can have a bit early. Others is bound to spend a night or two in the cold."

Anna hurried upstairs, hoping to find Charlie there. All she found was the notice nailed to the door. She read it quickly. The owner of the building had lost his lease on the land; a consortium of wealthy men was going to build a factory on the spot with a new fifty-year lease.

Robert and Dinah came home for dinner a few minutes later. They arrived together, and came slowly up the stairs—too slowly, Anna thought as they came, for she remembered how they used to thunder up and down stairs back when they were children. Now they were weary adults, they plodded, and it broke her heart to hear the funereal cadence. She knew Charlie was not with them. Charlie was too quick of step; he had not yet been touched enough by life.

When they came in, they didn't see her at first; silently they went about the business of getting dinner quickly. For a moment Anna was hurt that their first thought wouldn't have been to see how their ailing mother was doing. But of course not, she told herself. They think that Charlie has been caring for me all day. Poor children. They have the walk, they have the expressions of age, they have been given the duties of adults and done better than many who are supposedly of the proper age. And yet Robert is still so slight, though he is taller, and his face is still so smooth, his hair so free. Dinah's eyes are still large and deep, hinting at naivete and unfathomable things, and her hair is thick, her body lithe as a child's; she still stands tiptoe to reach across the table. God have mercy on them. All my children now are gone.

Robert gravely set out the platters; Dinah cut up the potatoes and sprinkled precious pepper over the top. She did it with such ceremony that Robert burst out laughing. Suddenly all was changed. Robert's whole body came alive, Dinah smiled and leaned on the table, shaking with silent laughter, and Anna realized that they were children still, able to be joyful in a moment.

It came as such a relief to her that she laughed, too; they heard her, and turned, and after the moment it took them to realize that she was alert now, in her right mind now, they plunged into embraces and rejoicing and tears. Anna set aside the worry about Charlie not being home, forgot for a moment that they were going to lose the house, even overlooked the ache for the child that she had borne and never knew, and celebrated with them: They were glad that she was better, and she rejoiced that they were glad.

And not only glad for that. "I talked to the maintenance man today," Robert said. "I'm in, starting next week. To repair machinery. It's a step to becoming an engineer. And I'll be paid like a man. A pound a week. More than we all used to make together. And the maintenance man, Joe Purny, he tells me there's places to the other side of Oldham Road, beyond Great Ancoats. Better built than these, newer, and not much more a month rent."

Dinah walked to the door where the eviction notice was posted, tore it down, brought it into the room and, with a flourish tore it into little pieces. "What do we care about that?" she said.

And then, suddenly, Dinah's expression went grim.

"What is it?" Anna asked.

"Charlie," Dinah answered.

"What about him?" Anna asked. "He's been away all morning."

"Oh my God," said Robert. "She doesn't remember."

Anna did not think to rebuke him for his blasphemous language. His words had more import than mere offensiveness.

"What's happened to Charlie?"

"He'll never find us if we move," Dinah said.

"What have we done?" Robert whispered. "I had no hope then. How could I have known?"

"What have you done!" Anna shouted.

Robert buried his face in his hands. Dinah looked at him contemptuously. "You wouldn't hear my voice then, but now it's my voice must tell the news." Dinah faced her mother, and paused a moment, searching for words. They did not come easily to her, not because she could not think of any words, but because they were all so imprecise. "You signed the paper two days ago. Charlie's gone, apprenticed to a chimney sweep."

Anna looked at them in horror. "Charlie! To a chimney sweep!"

Robert looked up, his eyes already inflamed from tears—not of grief for Charlie, but of shame for having made a wrong decision for the family. "We were only weeks from starvation, Mother. It was a way to save his life."

Charlie, who reads poetry and philosophy, Charlie who has

a mind like a god and the disposition of an angel—climbing up and down chimneys and walking the streets covered with soot. It was impossible. It could not be. Anna came to herself enough to realize that Robert was watching her with terrible apprehension for her verdict on him. She hated what he had done, but he was only a child, and it was her duty to comfort him. "You thought it was for the best, Robert," she said. "As God is my witness I will get him back."

"How?" Robert asked. "You signed a paper."

"I wasn't in my right mind!" Anna said.

"It was written by a solicitor," Robert said, sure that it meant the contract was irrevocable.

"The problem isn't the paper," Dinah said. "The problem is—where *is* he?"

"I don't know," Robert said. "I met the man on the street. I saw him with a small boy, and I thought, there's a place for Charlie, and I talked to him and he came to our house on Sunday. I don't know where he lives."

"His name," Anna said.

"Whitesides. But it's not so bad, Mother. He'll send Charlie to school."

Anna shook her head and laughed bitterly. "Did he say so? And since when was there a chimney sweep who could even read? He wouldn't know how to find a school. You knew no better, Robert—you and Charlie both, so trusting you're easy victims to anyone with a lie that says what you want to hear. So trusting. But I will get him back."

Dinah didn't ask again, but the question still hung in the air: How? Her son, the jewel of her life, was gone; she would do anything; she would swallow pride and beg if she had to. "I will ask Mr. Hulme to help me."

"But, Mother," Dinah said, "you surely lost your place when you—"

"I won't ask for my place. I'll ask him how I can find my son."

For a moment they sat in silence. Then Robert leapt to his feet. "How long have we been here? How long has it been?" And with scarcely another word, he and Dinah left the cottage running, for if they were late to the factory they would be docked, and even the smallest loss of pay was one night colder or one dinner with no food, and that might mean the difference between marginal health and plunging over the edge into sickness, exhaustion, unemployment, beggary, starvation, and death.

After they ran off to work, Anna sat in the cottage for a half hour, trying to find in the Bible what was in God's mind when He blessed them with one hand while cursing them a thousandfold with the other. Finally she closed the Bible, unsatisfied, and left to see Hulme to ask his help. She would get her son back whether it was God's will or not. God's will had done them little good so far. Now she would see how well she did with her own.

8

Charlie Kirkham
Manchester, 1830

CHARLIE ALMOST FORGOT his fear of Whitesides as the housekeeper led them to the fireplace, for the house was magnificent beyond his dreams. He had no way of knowing that it was rather an ordinary middle-class home; his only point of comparison was the places he remembered living, and he couldn't even remember the comfortable rooms above the store, back when his father still owned his own shop. So the varnished wooden floor, the thick rugs, the paintings on the wall, the carefully placed furniture all spoke to him of heaven: this is what comes to good people after they die. Frankly, Charlie gawked.

Raymond, of course, had been in many homes richer than this one and knew it wasn't much. He nudged Charlie and said so—in a whisper, of course. But when Raymond spoke Charlie realized something that gave him confidence. Raymond's thick, lower-class speech, uneducated and full of cant, would forever bar him from belonging in a house like this, let alone one better. Charlie, however, spoke with his mother's clear, educated speech, which still echoed *her* father's Cambridge pronunciation; if he were not dressed in old and threadbare clothing, he could easily belong here, and indeed probably had a clearer speech and more elegant language than the owner of the house. Charlie didn't put it to himself so clearly, however. All that passed through his mind was the thought, I ought to be in a place like this. And with the thought came the unrecognized resolution, I *will* have a house like this. He felt it as a right— or rather he felt his poverty as a wrong. If God ever set the world to rights, Charlie Kirkham would live like this.

The housekeeper tapped the brick of the fireplace. "This is the one. And please be quick—we have company tonight, and we must be able to have a roaring fire without smoke. And try not to spray ash everywhere, it's near impossible to clean." She spoke with the conscious snobbery of servants trying to cloak themselves in their masters' elevated status.

Whitesides, smiling, reached up inside the fireplace and felt the brick.

"I thought I said, ma'am, that there be no fire in here last night."

"The master got cold. When he is cold, there's a fire."

"This is hot enough to scorch, ma'am. It must have been put out only a few hours ago at most."

The housekeeper narrowed her eyes. "Oh, a regular scientist, he is. Next you'll be telling me how many pounds of coal we burned. Will you do the job or not? You're not the only sweeps in town, I hear."

"But we're the only ones in this house, ma'am. You're welcome to go find another, if you think you can get one quick enough. But there you are. We'll do it, but the charge is more, in case of damage to my boys."

The housekeeper chuckled. "If there be damage, sweep, then we'll talk about paying extra. These don't look like they're worth much anyway." And with that she swept out of the room, her bouncing stride belying the airs she affected.

"What a proud day," Whitesides said when she was gone. "Your first day up a chimney, Charlie. Does it please you?"

Charlie, whose cheeks already hurt from smiling, smiled more broadly and said, "It does, Master."

"Then up you go."

Charlie hesitated. He was not an athletic child, and had never climbed a chimney in his life—had never, in fact, climbed a tree. He had no notion how to begin.

"Charlie looks reluctant, wouldn't you say, Raymond?"

Raymond laughed. "More stupid than slow, I'd say, right Charlie?"

Whitesides came close to Charlie and squatted down so his eyes were on a level with the boy's. "You take off your shoes and socks, Charlie."

Once his feet were bare, Charlie started to take off his coat. Raymond stopped him. "Unless you want to scrape your elbows raw, boy, and have ash in your arse and armpits, you leave the coat on."

Now Whitesides took a long, sharp pin out of his lapel and, with a flourish, handed it to Raymond. "You help the boy up the chimney, Raymond," he said. "You give him a bit of a desire to climb high and fast."

"What's that for?" Charlie asked.

"You look worried, Charlie."

Charlie smiled more broadly.

"Much better, Charlie. And now faces, Charlie, there mustn't be faces in the chimney, mustn't there?" Whitesides reached into the voluminous pocket of his coat and pulled out a blackened wad of knit. Charlie took it gingerly, opened it. It was a mask, with holes for eyes and nothing else. It had once been red, or partly red. "It's been up ten thousand chimneys twice ten thousand times, Charlie, and up one more with you today."

Charlie started to put it on, filthy as it was, but Raymond stopped him. "Dip it." Charlie didn't understand. Raymond pointed to a bucket of water the housekeeper had set out for them. "Dip it. Wet it so you can breathe."

Charlie dipped it in the water and picked it out. The water had not penetrated much.

"Soak it. Wet clear through."

Charlie dipped it again, squished it several times in the water, then pulled it out, heavy and dripping. Was he to put it on like that? He looked at Raymond, then smiled at Whitesides. They were watching him intently. No advice from them, and he dared not ask, so he slipped the filthy mask over his head. Cold water dribbled down his neck into his shirt. He shuddered. Whitesides giggled.

"Most boys wrings it out," said Whitesides. He giggled again.

Raymond sauntered to the hearth and Charlie followed. The bricks were rough under the white paint; inside, unpainted, there would be nothing to mitigate the sharp points and harsh edges against his feet and hands, nothing but the soot itself. Inwardly Charlie recoiled from the touch of the brick. It would hurt him. And now that hurting was a fresh memory, it terrified him more than it had when he had never known real pain.

He leaned his head back and looked up. Far above was a dim light. It looked miles away. And there was no ladder, no step cut into the brick, nothing at all to help him up the shaft. Yet he had to climb it, for Raymond held a needle whose use would not be tailorwork, Charlie was certain.

"How?" Charlie whispered to the boy beside him.

"It's elbows and knees does it, Charlie, and your back. You push against the walls and it holds you up."

Now Charlie felt the heat of the bricks seeping into his feet. He began to lift one foot, then the other. He heard Whitesides giggle and say something about a clever dance.

"Will you give me a boost?" Charlie asked.

"Of course," said Raymond. "But you need the chipper and the brush, you know. Get right to the top and chip your way down—keeps the ash out of your eyes."

Suddenly Whitesides' head was in the hearth, inches from them. "Aye, Raymond, you ought to write a book, my boy. You're taking time, my lads, and time is money, and money is bread, and bread is dear, and if you want full stomachs tonight you'll hasten hasten hasten."

Raymond cupped his hands to give Charlie a lift. As Charlie placed his foot in the stirrup and braced one hand on Raymond's shoulder, he said softly, "Please don't stick me, Raymond."

Loudly Raymond answered, "Stick you? It's worth my life if I don't stick you, jack!"

"Aye, that's the answer," said Whitesides. Raymond gave Charlie a rueful grin that at least hinted that he'd regret doing it.

The air was close in the chimney as Charlie climbed into it. The bricks were warm, and the ash stung his lungs despite the wet mask. Charlie scrabbled for a handhold, but there was nothing; the bricks scraped his hands and hurt him when he banged his elbows on them. Soot slipped from the sides of the chimney, avalanched into Charlie's shirt and down his back. He slid downward, his foot slamming into Raymond's upturned face, the brick scraping his knees.

"Damn you!" Raymond cried. "Keep your foot out of my face, you little bastard!"

"Watch your language, my young friend," said Whitesides cheerfully. "We can't let the good folk here get theirselves offended."

Raymond pushed Charlie upward again, and this time he rose high enough to find a small ridge in the brick where he could hook his fingers, giving him enough purchase so that he didn't slide downward. He pressed his back firmly against one side, his toes against the other, and tried not to tremble in fear, for he dared not loosen his hold to climb higher, and yet he knew that if he stayed—

"Doesn't he like to climb?" he heard Whitesides say.

"You're turned wrong!" Raymond called up to him. "It's the other way, pressing outward with your knees and elbows!"

"Doesn't he like chimneys?"

"I love the chimneys," Charlie called down, trying to turn himself in the chimney so that he faced one of the narrow walls instead of one of the wide ones. His muscles were not toned for pressing outward; it took all his strength just to stay up, facing that way. But now his back was not pressed against a wall, and he could climb a little. It was slow, and he was terrified.

There was no warning. Just a sudden, agonizing pain in his foot. He cried out; his leg by reflex shot upward, and he lost his hold. He started to slide downward, which drove the needle deeper. Then he felt the shaft slide out of the wound, and he hung in the chimney, gasping, until the needle came into the sole of the other foot. He shouted and desperately elbowed his way upward into the chimney, banging and bruising his knees and elbows, scraping and burning his hands and feet, but climbing. And now that he was getting higher, he had no choice but to climb, for the soot was so thick and slick that if he stopped moving for an instant he began to fall, and a fall from this height would surely break a leg, if it didn't kill him.

The higher he rose, however, the cooler the bricks became. He began to slow down. He hadn't realized Raymond was climbing after him, until the needle came again. This time was the deepest, the most painful of all, and the hurt took his breath away for a moment; then he climbed again, faster than before, and now Raymond didn't follow him. The chimney was so caked with soot and ash that it narrowed, making the climbing easier, though breathing was harder all the time. Dust rose in the chimney, stinging his eyes, and despite the wet mask it burned in his throat.

He looked down. Raymond's face was so far below him that he looked like a bug, and Charlie felt a terrible vertigo, a feeling, not that he would fall, but that he already was falling.

"Keep climbing!" Raymond shouted. His voice rang in the chimney.

"I'll never get down again!"

As if the voice came from hell he heard Whitesides call out gleefully, "Down's easy, boy! Nothing's so easy as down!"

"All the way to the top!" Raymond called.

His elbows and knees throbbed with pain, his hands were raw, his arms and legs were exhausted, but he climbed upward because he had no choice. And at last, not daring to look down again, he reached the top, flung his arms out over the lip of the chimney, and hung there, up to his armpits in ash, but his face at last free to breath.

He had never realized Manchester was so large. From this house on Manor Street in Ardwick he could see a battery of chimneys, like cannons firing into the sky. The pall that always hung low over the city on a still day seemed to be pouring down a thousand spouts, or shooting up from them—the illusion kept changing as he watched.

Sound also rose to the rooftops, but oddly there was none of the bustle of a city. Instead he heard the birds by the River Medlock not far distant, and the genteel carriages passing brusquely in the streets. The cry of beggars was not heard here, nor the whine and stomp of machinery. They could be different worlds, the one his ears heard and the one his eyes saw.

The shouting from below, inside the chimney, reminded him of what he had come for. Turning, he braced his back against the chimney and began chipping away the soot. It was easy enough work—the soot was not hard to chip away—but it was miserable. For every pound of soot that dropped past his legs, down to the bottom, it seemed sixteen ounces turned to dust and drifted upward into his eyes and hair and mouth. He shut his eyes often as he worked. Yet, struggling with the soot, he was able to keep his mind off misery, except the stinging of his feet, the aching of his legs, his elbows; it became almost a game to him, getting the soot off and brushing the dust away until brick showed through a bit.

It took him nearly an hour to work his way down, and, as Raymond had promised, it was easy. Staring at the brick ahead of him, he forgot how far away the ground was and began to take some pride in accomplishing the cleaning as well as he did.

But his legs, under constant tension, grew weaker and weaker. He began coughing, and the phlegm tasted of ash; tears streamed out of his eyes, and he could not wipe them because of the mask. Gradually even the pinpricks in his feet were numb compared to the vast ache of his entire body.

And at last when he let himself slide downward a few inches there was suddenly nothing for his toes to brace against. He had reached the bottom of the chimney. He fell.

Not far, of course, but there was a deep pile of loose ash in the hearth, and when he landed in it the dust flew in a great cloud through the room, settling on the walls, the ceiling, the bare floor. What had once been plastered white was now a dingy gray. And Whitesides was smiling.

"Careless boy," he said. "Careless, careless." And he dragged Charlie from the hearth and began beating him, raising a cloud of dust on the first blow and bringing no cry of pain from Charlie at all. Charlie was too tired to care. His brain had shut off the pain, and since the pain was all he felt of the world, he might as well have been asleep.

Except that he kept smiling and smiling until Whitesides stopped.

The housekeeper cursed and threatened, but she finally paid and let them go, since she couldn't clean the room while the filthy sweeps were still in it.

Back in their rooms, the fresh air and limbering walk made Charlie more alert, despite the aches. At first he was glad for a bath and cheerfully carried water up to fill the tub. Charlie stripped and was surprised to find that the ash had spread right through his clothes so that he was grey everywhere that he wasn't black. The ash itched; the bath would be welcome. But

Whitesides insisted on bathing the boy himself, and filled a bucket with lye and salt and water. He dipped a harsh brush into the bucket again and again. It got the ash and dust off, but cut the skin and put the salt into the new wounds on every stroke.

"Not so hard, please," Charlie begged.

"Isn't my boy Charlie happy? Doesn't he like to be clean?"

And Charlie smiled, standing naked in the tub as the water began to turn black, and then even blacker with his blood as it dripped an ever darker crimson down his legs. He smiled, and silently decided that they could put him in jail or hang him or poison him but he would not work for this man for seven years, or one year, or one week, or one more day if he could help it. He smiled until Whitesides deftly pulled the brush across his young and tender loins, and then again, and then again; Charlie screamed and fainted, and knew nothing more until morning.

❧ 9 ❧

Charlie and Dinah
Manchester, 1830

DINAH CARRIED AN ARMLOAD of pots and pans and loaded them on the cart. When she turned around, she paused a moment to glare at the bored workmen waiting for the Kirkhams to vacate their cottage. They took no notice of her wrath.

Robert and Mother emerged from the building, carrying a trunk. One of the men muttered, "Lot of work for nothing. Might as well tear it down with the rubbish inside as out." It won some laughs from the other workmen, but got no response from the Kirkhams. Robert held his peace because of his mother's hand on his arm. Dinah held her peace because she knew that if she spoke what was in her heart she would surely burn in hell. She turned her back on the men and went inside.

Back inside the now-empty room, she was surprised to find herself sad at leaving the hideous place. They had come there in their first grief at Father's going—surely it should have no hold on her heart. It had always been cold more than a few feet from the fire, and the smell had never entirely left down-stairs. The place was cramped and ugly and a shameful sort of home for them. But she could not bear the thought of leaving it, for when they left, the workmen would kill the place, and with it something would die. Not something of Dinah, but something of the family. All they had now of Charlie would surely die. For there he was reading in the corner; there he was at the fire, preparing food for her and Robert when they came home for dinner; there he was in his bed quarreling with his brother and yet crying quietly when Robert refused to play with him.

Dinah felt something bitter that she did not want to name. *Charlie did not need to leave us. In all our poverty, it was only our loss of faith, only our fear that split us up.*

But not my *fear.*

No, she did not blame Robert. Rather she recognized inside herself something that she only now began to understand. When she had seen Father on the night he left, she had believed the lie that he would soon be back. Yet underneath her naivete she had been wise; she had felt a terrible loss and an anger that was so cold that she had to crawl into her mother's bed to stay warm enough to sleep.

And when Robert had explained that there was no choice but to send Charlie off with the sweep, she had found no words for argument. Yet again, she felt that cold anger, that sense of loss and grief. She had *known* that it did not need to be this way, had known that once again a man who thought he was wise was being wrong and cruel.

She had always been stubborn, had always thought her own thoughts. But now she knew that when she felt that sureness in herself, it would be true. She would never trust anyone again, she was sure. Only herself. Only the wise grief inside her.

And now, once again, she felt that inward agony of loss. Mother had tried to find Charlie. Robert had searched. Even Hulme had been so generous that he let Mother look for him for three days before she had to return to work. They had not found him. Manchester was too large, and no one noticed sweeps except when their chimneys were dirty. At last someone had told Robert that he had seen a sweep with a few boys heading out of Manchester toward Liverpool. The description was vague, but seemed to fit, and Anna and Robert had decided they had no choice but to be content with that. Perhaps later, when Charlie came back, they'd find him. In a few weeks they'd look for him again.

Dinah knew better. They were wrong. Charlie was in Manchester, and Charlie would come back. But when he came, because of those workmen with their crows, their hammers, their gunpowder and fuses—because of them Charlie would find nothing, the building gone and no one to tell him the way to where his family lived.

Well, it isn't so. He will find *me*. I will be waiting for him, and I will bring him home.

"Dinah, what are you still doing here?" Robert stood in the door.

"Nothing." Annoyed at his peremptory tone, she turned and faced her older brother. "Wishing for Charlie," she said.

Robert wordlessly turned and walked down the stairs. Dinah knew she had been cruel; it was an unfair weapon to use on Robert, and it was low of her to wield it so readily.

She followed him downstairs. The carter was actually helping load the last sacks of clothing and pans as Dinah came out the front door. The workmen, seeing the end of their wait was near, were a bit freer of tongue as they began to pry at the doorjamb. "And where do such folks go from here?" one asked.

"Couldn't find a place worse than this—got to be better for them."

The note of kindness died with the next man's laugh. "Wherever they goes soon gets like this. Scum always forms on the top of the porridge."

The cart lurched forward. Silently Dinah walked ahead, letting her mother and brother watch to see that nothing fell from the cart. Her shoes slapped and sucked in the mud. She did nothing to soften her steps. Let the mud have its way with her; it would wash.

She stopped on the hard surface of the road and turned to wait for the others. The horse strained to pull the cart up the slope, and Dinah joined the others in helping to push. Her arms were strong now, though she was only eleven; carrying bobbins in the factory had firmed her body so that she felt she could have pushed the cart alone.

Behind them came the first of the explosions. They did not turn. Only when the cart was well up on the road did they glance back. One end of the building was in ruins, only a small section of wall standing. As they turned to leave, another explosion shuddered the ground. This time they saw the walls belly out or convulse inward, the lines of bricks undulating and finally sinking emphatically into a sea of dust. As the noise of the explosion faded, they could hear the gay laughter of the workmen, as if it were a holiday.

"It's nice to see someone who enjoys his work," Anna said drily.

The carter hooted. "The devil does *that*, mum! The devil does *that!*"

At first Dinah walked near Mother and Robert. She hated the way Robert was giving directions to the carter. She hated the way he made decisions and Mother blithely went along. For she recognized in Robert's manner an almost perfect imitation of Father, the way he spoke, expecting to be obeyed. *Almost* perfect, because in Father there had always been a weakness, an inadvertent humility that turned his commands into requests, his petitions into pleas. Robert lacked that. Robert was as strong as his father had not been, and Mother, still weak from her delivery, still broken in spirit from the loss of her new infant and her youngest son and her home, all in the last few weeks—Mother seemed to accept Robert's leadership gratefully.

Well, *I* do not accept it.

She strode forward, ahead of the cart. Why should she follow along behind, forced to endure her mother's obedience to a mere boy?

"Dinah," Mother said.

She pretended not to hear.

"Dinah," said Robert. "It's better if you walk with us."

I am not your daughter, boy.

"Dinah, we'll stay together!" Robert said.

Dinah turned and faced him, but did not move. The cart came up to her, and she did not move. There they stood in the middle of the street, people swirling around them, and Dinah would not move.

"*Will* you not make a scene here!" Robert's request, far from being a plea, was a command.

Dinah would not bear it. "The man who sleeps with Mother is my father. The man who sleeps with me will be my husband. Tell me, Robert, where do *you* sleep?"

"Children," Mother pled helplessly.

Dinah watched Robert's face go red. She knew that because she held her tongue so much, people thought she was dull or inarticulate. On the contrary, she knew that her tongue could sting, that she had a knack for finding the weakest place in other people and probing it directly with her daggered words. And now that she had let herself go this far, she would not soften it. "How will Charlie find us, Robert?" She asked because she was certain he had not so much as thought of the question.

"He'll look up the factory, and they'll tell him where we live."

Dinah did not bother reminding Robert that they had never taken Charlie with them to the factory, so he did not know the way. She did not remind him that because they had rarely talked about the factory at home, there was a good chance that Charlie would not even remember the company's name. She only looked at him coldly until he was forced to glance away. Then she turned her back on him and strode off toward their new house. She heard the cart start moving after them. She heard the carter chuckle and say, "Pity the man who weds *her*." She shrugged off the insult. The man she married would be such a man that she would never need to speak to him that way. The man she married would have had the faith not to force Charlie to leave. The man she married would have real authority, not usurped power that belonged to someone who had gone. The man she married would by God be stronger than her. It did not occur to her that there might not be any such man in the world.

Dinah led all the way home, and that night whenever Robert and Anna spoke to her, it was with deference. Once Mother screwed up her courage enough to say, "I think you ought to speak more kindly to Robert. He's got so much responsibility, and he's so young."

"If I'm too much of a burden for him, I'll leave. I have money enough to keep myself now, plenty of other girls do."

Anna was angry. "I've lost enough of my children!"

"Then you'd best keep Robert in check. If he has his way he'll soon be the only child you have." It was cruel and, worse, untrue. But she did not unsay it. In silence she continued to unpack and set out their pitiful belongings. As the sun was setting she walked to the door and opened it.

"Where are you going?" Anna asked.

"To the old house."

"Why?"

"Someone should be there, in case Charlie comes."

"He won't come," Robert said. "He's not even in Manchester." Dinah looked at him coldly. This time he did not look away. "Remember that tomorrow's Monday, and you have to work."

Dinah walked out the door, pulling it closed behind her. Let him tell her to come home early—she would come home because she needed her strength, not because of his command. She would not argue with him, nor did she care so much for him that she would deliberately damage her own health to flout him. That much she would grant him—the authority to stand at the edge of the sea and command the waves to roll, the tide to ebb.

The opportunity for escape did not come until Charlie had been with Whitesides for a day over two weeks. In the daylight hours he was never out of Whitesides' sight. By night Whitesides slept with the key to the room on a chain around his neck. When Whitesides went out alone, he shot a bolt that had been installed on the outside of the room; he came home reeking of alcohol, but showing no sign of drunkenness except a great deal of affection for Charlie and Raymond, which he showed by beery kisses on their lips, which they had to pretend they enjoyed.

Despite knowing he would soon return, they managed to enjoy his absences. They had little in common—Raymond was only a farmer's son, the ninth child in a family that could not decently support two, and Charlie's love of reading meant nothing to him. Nor did Raymond miss his family. "They were as wonderful as slugs, if you get my meaning," Raymond said. "Old Whitesides's tough and a bastard if there ever was one, but I'm eatin', an't I? And I'm gettin' into the best rich houses and trompin' dust on the floor, and every now and then I get to piss in their gardens, which does my heart good, I can tell you."

But friendly and cheerful as Raymond managed to be when Whitesides was gone, when the master came back Raymond was one of the enemy. Not that he didn't mean well, and he obviously mitigated Charlie's suffering as much as he could

without Whitesides noticing. But he was thoroughly Whitesides' tool, and could no more disobey him than fly. Charlie
confided nothing to him about his plan to escape at the first
opportunity.

The second day of work had been worse, if possible, than
the first, because all the sores of the day before were reopened
and stung worse than before, and Raymond had used the needle
again until Charlie could hardly walk; his muscles rebelled and
would not take him up the chimney until pain drove him up.
By the third day, however, he was toughening, and it finally
occurred to him that the life was physically endurable after all,
though it left him exhausted and the scrubbing at the end of
the day never stopped hurting.

His decision to run away, however, did not waver. It was
not his body that suffered most. Even though his family had
sent him away, he knew they had not dreamed his life would
be like this. They loved him, and the thought of them put him
where he no longer let Whitesides' tortures put him—near
tears. He was eight, and had lost his father only half a year
before. The loss of all the rest of his family was more than he
was willing to bear.

His opportunity came when their work moved out of Ardwick and into the older houses in middle-class Chorlton. The
architecture was different—the houses stood close together,
but they rambled a bit more, and instead of rising two stories
sheer from ground to roof, there were gables and roofs on
wings extending from the ground floor, too.

Charlie watched to see if Whitesides would notice the difference and guard him closer, but the man seemed oblivious.
Perhaps he thought that because Charlie was being cooperative
and climbing well—and smiling uninterruptedly—there was
nothing more to worry about. In fact, in the last few days
Whitesides had been growing almost maudlin in his affection.
Later, remembering the man—something he would generally
avoid doing—Charlie would wonder if Whitesides even knew
what he was doing to his boys. Perhaps the sweep thought that
all was well with them, and his cruelty was nothing but good
discipline, necessary to keep the wicked little creatures in the
strait and narrow way.

It was not a theological strait and narrow way that Charlie
confronted now: the chimney was stone, which made it at once

harder and easier to climb. There were handholds and toeholds all the way up, making the passage quick and easy; the stones, however, jutted into his back painfully whenever he leaned back. It didn't matter to Charlie, however. It was only on the down climb that the stones would matter, when he had to lean against the back wall to work. And he was determined that he would never climb down the inside of this chimney.

"Can't get up!" he shouted down the chimney.

"Why not!" Raymond cried from below.

"There's a stone crumbled out, blocks the way."

A few moments of silence below, and then Whitesides himself stuck his head in the chimney more than two stories below. "Can you lift it?"

"Maybe!" Charlie grunted as if he were working. Actually, he was sitting quite comfortably on the lip of the chimney, scraping the sides of the chimney with his feet so soot would fall down inside. He hoped Whitesides got an eyeful. There would be no way for the sweep to get a clear view of the top of the chimney. Charlie kept up the scraping as he pulled the damp mask from his head. His face was instantly cold from the slight breeze on his wet skin; in a moment, his hair also went cold. He took off his jacket. Black as it was, it would brand him as a sweep's boy wherever he went. The breeze immediately cut through his shirt. He reconsidered. What good would it do to escape Whitesides if the weather got him? He fingered the wet mask. Soot came off it onto his hands. He couldn't bear the thought of wearing it again. So the decision stayed. He dropped the mask on the high side of the roof, above the chimney, then draped his coat over half the opening so anyone looking up the shaft would think there was someone in it.

Charlie swung his legs out of the chimney and looked over the city. From where he was only a small patch of street was visible; all the rest of the world was chimneys and roofs, gables, slopes, steep pitches, cupolas, dormers, and the hundred shapes and heights of the erupting stacks. Smoke rose from all the pillars like the leaves rising above the trunks of the forest, only grey and not green, dead and not living; and the wind did not rustle the smoke like leaves, it carried it, settled it out, dropped the soot onto the city like an eternal, deadly autumn. Whenever Charlie remembered Manchester in later life—indeed, whenever he thought of any city—the image that flickered in his mind was not the buildings seen from the street, not the river, not even the various cottages, good or bad, his family lived in over the years. All those things were themselves, very particular. The city itself, the whole of Manchester, was the dangerous forest of coal smoke, conjured by cruel necromancers and abetted by the blood of little boys with needles in their feet.

Charlie shook himself and shivered in the breeze, which was not strong, but strong enough to freeze him, wet and thinclad as he was. If he was to go, it must be now. In his fear he wished that he were home with his mother already, holding her hand, going to sleep with her fingers patting his back, reading to her and winning her love. This was no place for him, he did not belong here, certainly he should never have been allowed to come here. There was something bitterly wrong with the world. He deserved better than this from God.

No help for him now but his own wit, luck, and strength. He carefully lowered himself down the outside of the chimney, turning as he did so that he hung by the armpits, his head leaning over the shaft. "I've nearly got it free now!" he called. "Stand back, it's going to fall!" That'd keep them from the chimney for a minute or so. He dropped the rest of the way to the roof. It was steep, but he caught the upper corner of the chimney and so did not slide. He carefully laid the brush and bar on top of the mask on the high side of the chimney, so they would not fall and would not be visible from the street. Let *them* climb up if they want it back.

He remembered that below this stretch of roof was a first-floor gable that would catch him if he fell. He was careful anyway, and just as well: when he got to the rain gutter, he could see that his memory of the house was skewed. He had come out the wrong chimney, and below him was nothing but a two-story drop onto flagstones.

He made his way carefully but quickly along the rain gutter until he reached the corner; instead of a gable, the roof sloped all the way around, and now he was only four feet away from the roof of the neighboring house. He made the decision instantly, and only climbed up enough to get a running start that let him land like a frog sprawled against the other roof.

There was still no uproar from the house he had left, and

he began to believe he might really get away. The house he was climbing over met the corner of the block, and he was able to let himself down onto the roof over the entrance, and from the drop down to the ground, not on Rosamond, where they had gone into the house, but on Rumford Street.

He could not go straight home—the chance of running into Whitesides immediately was too great. So he dodged up and down the elegant streets until he came to the high wall of the burying ground, climbed over, and dropped inside among the tombstones and the graves.

Now he felt he could rest a moment—but not long. Coatless and barefoot in the middle of February, he hadn't a chance in the world of living through the night unless he got indoors before dark. Yet now it occurred to him for the first time that he might have nowhere to go. He had no way of knowing what had happened to his family since he left. His mother had been sick. What if she had died? And if he got there, what surety did he have that Robert wouldn't send for Whitesides to take him back again. It was a ghastly thought, what would happen to him if Whitesides got hands on him after this. Robert would surely never do it; yet in Charlie's memory, Robert had emerged more and more as the villain. Robert only wanted to be rid of him. Robert was jealous because Mother loved him, jealous because Charlie read so much better and because Mother had kept the books for him even after the paintings were sold. Robert wouldn't want him back.

It was the wind that sent him on his way. Perhaps he could stay downstairs for the night, hide until Robert left for work, and see Mother then, if she had lived through the illness. Perhaps he could listen at the door and hear how things were. One thing was certain—he had to go somewhere, and there was nowhere else to go.

He followed a circuitous route to avoid Whitesides, who in Charlie's mind was just around every corner, or dogging his heels to catch him if he stopped. He ran as much as he had breath to run, as much to keep warm as to evade pursuit. And when he got near home, he crossed Irk downstream, to approach the cottage from across the river, in case Whitesides was already lurking there, waiting for him to arrive.

He walked up the west bank of Irk, glancing east across the river now and then to look for his row. When he recognized a factory bridge off Horrocks Avenue he realized that somehow he had passed his house. For a moment he was disoriented, wondering if he had been walking the wrong way; then he decided he must have got tired and inattentive, and missed the cottage and not even noticed Scotland Bridge.

On the way back downstream he recognized Scotland Bridge immediately. But, unbelievably, the row of cottages was gone and the land was smooth, except where new foundation piles were sunk into the earth.

He sat on the bank of the river and stared, looking back and forth, trying to figure out what had happened. It was impossible that his home could simply disappear. Yet there was no mistake—this *was* Scotland Bridge, and all the other buildings were unchanged. Where was his family? How could he possibly find them?

He almost crossed the river to look for some clue as to where his family had gone, but in time he noticed the tall mangy black hat bobbing among the piles. Whitesides was there, and obviously he expected Charlie to come from cityside instead of riverside. Charlie shivered, as much from dread as from the cold, and carefully made his way back from the river to a point where he would not be visible to Whitesides.

Pacing back and forth could keep him somewhat warm, but he had no layer of fat to insulate him. The ground was cold. He was hungry and thirsty and knew better than to drink the water of Irk, which had more manure in it than a pasture. Still Whitesides lingered, for hours it seemed, until at last a cold thin rain came up and Whitesides stalked away. Charlie, his teeth chattering, waited a little longer in the rain, then crossed Scotland Bridge and walked to where he figured the cottage had been. There were plenty of loose bricks around. He had to pick his way carefully in the gathering darkness. A wind came up, driving the rain in gusts that struck him like ice, and finally he took shelter in the lee of one of the piles. There was no high ground—by avoiding the wind he accepted the water that flowed toward him, seeking the river. The rain tasted slightly of the coal dust it had gathered from the air, yet it was all the water Charlie was likely to get, and he even dipped some out of the streams flowing along the ground, though he knew it could be poisoned. He did not think he could live without a drink. Hunger he was used to, but not utter fasting, not such burning thirst.

A thousand times as he sat there he hoped it would be Robert

who found his corpse there among the ruins. Let him find me
lying here starving and frozen. He'll be sorry he cast me out
of the family then.

> *Ah, come not, write not, think not once of me,*
> *Nor share one pang of all I felt for thee.*

In the rhythm of the rain he could not keep the snatches of
poetry from his mind. Every self-pitying verse that he had ever
learned came back to him.

> *In each low wind methinks a spirit calls,*
> *And more than echoes talk along the walls.*

Charlie prayed for the rain to stop, and it came down harder.
He prayed for the wind to stop, and it chilled him subtly even
between the gusts. He prayed for his family to find him, and
he heard a voice above the wind, calling, "Charlie, Charlie!"
He did not move; he was dying, he knew, and only heard his
name in the rain as a taunt from the devil before the end.

In the rain Dinah walked all the faster. Every night after
work she had come here to look for Charlie, and now she knew
by habit the way to walk to see everywhere that Charlie might
be. She was not a fool; she knew each time she came how
slight was the chance he might be there. But that did not
diminish her search by a single step. If he was not found, it
would not be because she had not looked for him.

Even so, she almost didn't see him. His shirt blackened by
ash, his body curled against the piles, the rain so thick and
swirling, the night so dark—she only came closer because she
felt, in that part of her that knew truth from falsehood despite
her best reasoning, that there was something different about
that pile, something that required her to come near. And there
he was, his hand up to his mouth, his whole body shuddering
every now and then with the cold.

"Charlie, Charlie!" she called, and ran to him, and took his
hands and turned him to face her. He moved sluggishly; he did
not open his eyes. "Charlie," she said. She took his face between her hands and kissed him. "Oh, thank God, I've found
you."

And now he saw her, and smiled. "She came vested all in white, pure as her mind. Her face was veiled, yet to my fancied sight, love sweetness, goodness in her person shined so clear, as in no face with more delight." Then he wept.

He walked only stiffly, but with Dinah's cloak wrapped around him he began to recover somewhat from the cold, though Dinah suffered a little from it. They splashed steadily through the puddles and did not slow for the turning wind. Only once did Charlie speak, to ask her, "Is it all right?"

She understood. "We all want you home, Charlie. Things are better now. Robert has more money, Mother's well and working still for Mr. Hulme, and I've even had a rise in wages. There's plenty at last. We never needed to send you away, and we're all sorry for it."

"You didn't *all* send me away," Charlie said. It was an accusation of Robert, of course, and Dinah could not argue with it. Not because Robert was guilty of wanting Charlie gone, for he wasn't; rather she judged Robert guilty of the crime of thinking he knew best what others ought to do, and then making them do it against their will. For that she would not forgive him. Charlie was her true brother, her good brother. She did not let herself recognize in Charlie the one trait of Father's that Robert did not have: weakness.

As for Charlie, he knew now that God loved him after all. The bad things had been a trial, like the fire that softens the iron only to make it into steel. When, like Ishmael, he lay close to death, God had sent an angel to him, for he, too, would be a mighty man, despite his brother's enmity.

When they got home there was rejoicing for an hour, and then sleep. No one would mar the happiness of Charlie's return with accusations; Robert did not know how much it all had cost him until all was done, and they were lying down to sleep, and Charlie wouldn't take his place beside Robert on the bed. Instead Charlie took his pillow and lay on the floor. No one spoke, no one argued. Grim-faced, Anna got up and took a blanket and helped Charlie wrap himself in it. So in silence Charlie made it clear that he and his brother would not again be close, if in fact they ever had been. Their bodies would not touch in the night, any more than their hearts would touch in the day. Bitterly Robert lay awake denying the accusation that no one made. I did the right thing. I did what had to be done.

I'm glad the boy is back, but at the time there was but the one course and I took it and I have no regrets at all. Despise me all of you, but trust this, too: when the hard decisions must be made, I will make them. You may hate me for it, but it will keep us all alive, and happier than if I let you have your way.

Anna also lay awake, but for another reason. The quarrels of Robert and Charlie were trivial, she was sure. They would pass. They had always passed before. All she cared about was that her child was back. God had given her seven children and taken four away forever; this fifth time he had relented and let her keep Charlie, the jewel of her crown. She had grieved for him, had said and believed it, "Farewell, thou child of my right hand, and joy; my sin was too much hope of thee, loved boy." God had brought her to the lowest day of her life, and now had lifted her out, out of the direst poverty, out of illness near death, and most of all out of the grief of the loss of her dearest child. Quarrel, my little ones, if you like. Robert, rule us all, if you can. Dinah, be cold, be frightening to all of us, if that's the only way you see to live. It is enough that you live, that you all three live, I ask for no more. I have lived with Job, and though I bitterly cursed God and wished to die, I have been restored. From now on every day of my life I will bless God and follow gladly every path He opens for me, for He has found me lower than the grave and lifted me up, and I am alive again.

➤➤➤ BOOK TWO ◄◄◄

*In which Providence acts to provide
a grown man's trade for Robert,
an education for Charlie,
and a husband for Dinah.
As usual, Providence gets
mixed reviews.*

🌿 First Word 🌿

Dinah Kirkham seduced me. I had no intention of writing about her. She was peripheral. Trivial. Let some feminist historian celebrate her, I said.

After all, *she* wasn't my ancestor, Charlie Kirkham was. The book was half written. It was all about the rivalry between Charlie and Robert. In *that* book, you would have read about the irony that if Charlie hadn't hated Robert so, he might not have tried to compete with him, and so might have been happy. Robert was like his Mother, resourceful and ambitious, and Charlie was like his father, a dreamer, an artist. Charlie would have been a fine scholar or poet; instead he broke his heart trying to surpass his brother—who was wealthy and powerful and prestigious and is only forgotten because he died before Gladstone made room for him. It would have been an interesting study in frustration. But Dinah seduced me.

I didn't even like her, I must tell you that. She was charismatic, and that annoyed me: visions, prophecies, speaking in tongues. The Prophetess, they called her; the priestess. I didn't have much sympathy then for spiritual gifts. Worse, she was an ardent feminist who submitted

to polygamy and preached for it, which in my mind made
her a puppet of the patriarchs, a tool, a hypocrite. She
annoyed me when she didn't talk like a feminist, and
she annoyed me even more when she did. For instance,
in one speech in 1881 she said:

> Why do you think that women wear skirts and
> men wear trousers? In ancient times men and
> women all wore gowns, but when the tailor's art
> improved so that comfortable trousers could be
> made, why is it that only men were able to profit
> from the discovery? There can be no doubt that
> women continued to wear the less convenient gown
> because men preferred them in skirts; and there
> can be no doubt that men preferred their women
> in skirts because they are more conducive to ef-
> fortless ravishment. The hoop skirt is merely a
> refinement, to keep the gown conveniently out of
> the way and to interfere with a woman's efforts to
> defend herself.

This sort of feminist rhetoric really offends me—I
not only have never desired rape, I could not imagine
intimacy with a reluctant or disinterested partner. To
generalize and say "men want this" and "men want that"
strikes me as sexism of the worst order—worst, I admit,
because it is directed against my sex.

That was how I felt about Dinah Kirkham—baffled
by her spiritual gifts, offended at her feminism, skeptical
of her sincerity when she preached for polygamy.

I was reading her journal only because of the information it might give me about Charlie and Robert. She
began her journal as a diary just at the time that Robert
became an apprentice engineer and Charlie began his
education with Old Hulme. I was writing a chapter about
how suddenly things were looking up for the Kirkham
family. Instead of poverty, they had money, and Charlie's need for education was miraculously being satisfied.

Then I realized that I was ignoring something rather
curious. Even though Robert was making enough money
to support the family easily, Dinah kept working at the

mill for mere pennies. I could understand that—the desire for independence and all that. She deliberately annoyed Robert by refusing his support. Every week she noted her pay, and then wrote, "Gave to Mother. Robert angry." Feminist, of course.

The curious thing, the well-known fact of her life that I could not reconcile with this, was that in the midst of her insistence on independence, she suddenly married Robert's friend and brother-in-law Matthew Handy, a man infinitely beneath her in ability and intelligence and so weak that a woman of her strength could only despise him, I wondered: Was this part of a pattern? Insist on freedom, and then leap into utter surrender, just as she did when she embraced polygamy?

The question intrigued me. I thought I finally understood this strange woman. This is why I say she seduced me. I was enticed into studying her journal in order to prove that she was secretly a frustrated Happy Homemaker, and then found the cryptic journal entry in 1836 that changed my whole view of her: "Today Mr. Uray gave me the gift of his love. Ruin but no despair. God forgive my fraility."

For Robert and Charlie things were at last going well— their dreams of the future looked possible at last. But for Dinah, at that very moment, a man undid her and forced her into submission to the world of men. Rape? Attempted rape? Seduction? I ruled out the last because she was no fool. I ruled out the first because the morning after her wedding night she wrote, "Matt found a virgin in his bed. So surprised." And at that moment I knew— not without regret—that my book about Charlie was gone. It would be a book about Dinah, for now I knew that she was not spouting rhetoric when she talked about rape, and I also knew—knew without reason—that she was no liar when she preached for polygamy, no hysteric when she prophesied and spoke in tongues and healed the sick.

Her whole life unfolded to me in that journal, and I could not tell Charlie's story when hers remained untold. After all, Charlie's tragedy was that he always wanted greatness and had to settle for happiness instead; Dinah's tragedy was that she always wanted happiness and had to settle for power, fame, and adulation. Charlie had many wives and children and lived surrounded by love all his life; Dinah never loved anyone that she did not lose too soon. And yet Dinah never wavered. She never bent. A whole people leaned on her, trusted in her, and she never let them down. And I found myself wondering how she could continue to love her God if He never gave her anything.

Of course, I was wrong. She said it, in a letter to her niece LaDell that she died without completing: "Though you live all your life in pain except one day of joy, if it is enough joy, on the right day, it makes up for all the rest."

—*O. Kirkham, Salt Lake City, 1981*

🌱 10 🌿

Old Hulme
Manchester, 1830-36

ONCE CHARLIE WAS HOME, once the Kirkham family was all together in their new cottage, it seemed that at last God was on their side against the world. As if they had passed some test, and were judged worthy, and now the Lord would raise them up to their proper place in the world.

It did not come all at once, but in little changes that each made life a bit easier. One day the butler at Hulme's house, who had never let up persecuting Anna whenever he could, was suddenly dismissed for having got a neighbor's maid pregnant, and Anna found herself free in the house, so that she could come to work quite happily; she could, in fact, almost forget the shame of being a servant in the pleasure of having no fear. The family rejoiced, and the burden lightened a little on their backs.

Then Robert, young as he was, got a promotion because he was learning so well, because several times he had improved the design of a machine as he worked on repair. Several times a fellow worker would say, "Ought to be an engineer." And Robert decided that he would, indeed, become one; he secretly bought a book on steam engineering and began to learn.

So it went for three years, until in 1833 their lives were lifted up again. Robert was promoted to engineer, after insisting that they let him compete with the applicants for an engineer's position. In all the tests he beat every one of the trained men easily. He was still only seventeen, but because the head engineer already liked him, the position was his.

Things were going so well that Anna and Robert decided that Robert's wage was enough to support them entirely. It would be a momentous change, but to have Anna cease to serve in another family's house would raise them up to the class where they properly belonged. Anna went to work prepared to give notice. And yet all the way there she felt a vague misgiving, as if she ought not to do it. It annoyed her, this feeling, for she should be rejoicing at ending her servitude, and she was not. It plagued her all day, so that she could not bring herself to go to Hulme and give notice. At last her time was done, and she hadn't spoken to the master. She almost gave up on it, but then thought of facing Robert without having acted—it would seem to him like an insult. So she swallowed her doubts and went to the library.

Hulme looked up at her in surprise. "Already?" he asked.

Flustered, Anna wondered how he could already know her errand. "It's been near four years now, I think, sir."

"More like two minutes since I sent Barton to look for you. Well, here you are, and quicker than I could have hoped for. You have a son."

It took a moment for her to realize it was a question. "I have two sons."

Hulme raised an eyebrow. "But one who stays at home."

"Charlie. He's eleven."

"That's the one. A bright lad, Barton tells me."

Barton could only know from the stories Anna told about how well Charlie read and recited. "For one who's never been to school, he does well, sir."

"Well, then, I have a proposition for you, or rather my father has one." For the first time Anna realized that old Hulme was sitting in a corner of the library, watching sharply all that went on. "My father here still fancies himself a clever man, though you have to remind him to take his meals and he drools occasionally. He once knew a good deal, however, and there is a library here, and he thinks—and he may be right, for all I know—that it will be good for him and good for the boy if he tutors him."

"Tutors, sir?"

"Don't be misled by his senile appearance. Father has his Latin and his Greek, and more important he knew the world of business and numbers better than any man of his generation. I'm sure it's no secret that our money isn't old. Father made it all. Bought the house, damn near got a title for me during the late war through his financial contributions to putting Boney on his arse, and in short he's a man of accomplishments, which I'll never forget, despite the inconvenience of having him about to remind people that our money is definitely too new to be respectable."

Anna suddenly felt the world turn around. A chance for Charlie to have education, even from senile old Hulme, was more than she could have hoped for. And gratis—for surely the master would never expect his servant to *pay*. But one must be sure. "I couldn't afford such a thing, sir—"

"There's no charge, of course. You can bring your son with you when you come in the morning, and take him home with you at night. He can take luncheon freely with the servants, and in the afternoons he may take exercise on the back lawn, provided he doesn't tear any divots from the turf or trample the plants."

"He's a very well-behaved boy."

"I have no doubt of it. And, of course, if he does well enough we'll endeavor to find a place for him, perhaps in an accounting house, or even studying for the bar. No promise, mind you. Just a prospect, if he does well."

She practically sang all the way home. A tutor for Charlie, a chance for her brilliant younger son. The bar! A solicitor or—yes, she could hope it—a barrister, perhaps someday a judge, the possibilities were endless. She shouted out the news as soon as she got home, embraced Charlie, and danced around the cottage with him.

Robert didn't take the news so brightly when he got home from work. "What does he need a tutor for? He reads better than he'll ever need to as it is."

"He's a fertile field," Anna said, "plowed but fallow, and now I have a chance to plant and cultivate."

"There's never any reasoning with you when you talk in parables. Charlie's old enough he ought to go to work."

Anna was annoyed that Robert wasn't excited. "Work? You argue with Dinah every Saturday that she *shouldn't* work."

"If you can't tell the difference between a daughter and a son, Mother, you ought at least to try. Charlie needs a trade."

"Why, if I can get him a profession?"

"We're not professional class people."

"We *are!*"

"How, if Charlie's mother is a servant? That'll go well when they're looking for a judicial appointment, won't it? Even the ministers don't get such extravagant hopes when they talk of heaven, though you wouldn't know about that."

At that Anna fell silent. Robert used that as a weapon against her, that he was the only one in the family who went to church, now that Dinah had pretty much stopped going. He always brought it up when she spoke to him of the Commandments. The worst of it was that she knew he didn't believe in the Establishment any more than she did. Hirelings, that's all the pastors were, and no closer to God than any other avaricious or lazy men. But Robert went to church, and it was a cudgel he used to silence her whenever they argued.

Charlie saw in his mother's silence the beginning of defeat, and he knew that here was his only chance of becoming what he ought to be in life. His only chance, and of course Robert was trying to block it. "What is it, Robert?" Charlie asked. "It won't take money out of your pocket—Mother said it was for free."

"For free? Do you call it free?" Robert towered over Charlie, for puberty had divided them. "Your mother continues to labor in another man's house, a servant so that *you* can study numbers and your damned philosophy, and no doubt Greek and Latin, too, so that you can become even more useless to the family than you already are."

Charlie heard his mother gasp, and well she might. For three years now there had been a wary silence between Robert and Charlie; both had backed away from any confrontation. But now, for the first time, perhaps because Robert was so cocksure of himself as the head of this fatherless home, Robert dared to open an argument. Well, let Mother fret, Charlie was glad of it. He had held his tongue too many times as he heard Robert lording it over Dinah and over his own mother, had kept the peace because it wasn't his quarrel, and he was the youngest after all. But now it *was* his quarrel. And Charlie had a tongue for this sort of battle.

"What is it, Robert? I'll only be useful to the family as a chimney sweep?"

Ah, yes, that's all it took, and Robert was retreating. "I don't mean that, you know I don't. I thought that was all forgotten—"

"*I'm* the one who was sold. Of course I remember better than the one who did the selling." Robert tried to protest at the unfairness of that, but Charlie knew victory when he smelt it. And he had another weapon, a treasured snatch of conversation Charlie had overheard between Robert and his friend Matthew Handy. "So I read better now than I ever need to. I guess I'm not the only one who wastes time. Why do you go to church so much, unless it's because you know you have to be a good Anglican if you ever plan to stand for Parliament?"

There it was, Robert's dream, so private that he had never shared it with the family, now laid out in the open to look pathetic and ridiculous by Robert's own view.

"You hear too much, little boy."

"If you think you can get into Parliament, what's wrong with me thinking I can maybe make good at the bar?"

It was such a pleasure to see that cocky bastard sputter that Charlie nearly laughed aloud. Robert had no answer for him, and so could not speak at all; Charlie saw how his brother clenched his fists and wanted to strike. But Charlie knew that he was safe, for Robert would never let himself look such a fool as he would if he struck his little brother simply for besting him in an argument.

And then Dinah came home, and calmed it all down.

Dinah saw at once, of course, that there had been an argument, and from the fear in her mother's face she knew it was the long awaited quarrel between Charlie and Robert. From Robert's fury and Charlie's scarcely hidden smile she knew who had had the better of it. So she turned to Robert and asked him, "What is it?"

Robert turned to her. She smiled at him, to reassure him.

It soothed him. She reached out and touched his arm. "It must be important, Robert."

"No," Robert said. "Only that Charlie's found an old man mad enough to tutor him. Nothing important at all."

Even before Robert got the words out, Dinah had turned to Charlie and was touching his cheek, soothing him so that he would make no answer. Let Robert have his last gibe, let him save face, her hand said; it costs nothing and gives us peace. And so Charlie smiled at her, and she squeezed Robert's hand, and the tension in the room abated. "Charlie, will you tell me about it while Robert goes out to see Matthew? You know Matthew's waiting at the pub."

And so it was done, as only Dinah could have done it, the argument gone as if it hadn't happened. Or almost, for of course the words had been said and wouldn't be forgotten. But Anna knew as she watched Dinah listening so excitedly to Charlie's news that as long as Dinah was at home, there would be harmony. God help us when she marries. And at the thought of Dinah's marriage Anna felt a shudder of dread. Immediately she was ashamed of it. A good mother looks forward to her daughter's happy marriage. And Anna sat and watched her daughter and her younger son, hardly hearing their conversation, and she thought of her own marriage and wondered if Dinah would marry a man she could love as much as Anna had loved John. Unimaginable that she could do better; unbearable to think that she might marry someone just as weak and untrustworthy. Don't think about John. Don't miss him. He's gone as sure as if he had died. I never, never want to see him again, I'd slam the door in his face if he came; don't think, don't think about him, think only of Charlie and the hope that has come to him at last.

The next day she almost cried with joy when the old man doddered into the library and Charlie, trying to look confident, followed him. God may have great blessings for her children after all. If things worked out, she might even go to church again, and put up with the ministers for the sake of their reputed Master. God might well be Love after all.

"He beats me."

Dinah raised her eyebrows. She knew about beatings, and the way Charlie said it she was sure it could not be much.

"Such an old man, I'm sure he nearly breaks your ribs."

Charlie shrugged and smiled. "Well, not a beating then. But look at my hands." He held them up. The palms were red.

"Ah," Dinah said. "Cruel. You'll never use your hands again."

Charlie laughed. "It's not so bad, I guess. But it was the first thing he did. He had me sit down and lay my hands open and *whack* with a ruler. I nearly wet my pants."

It was Dinah's turn to laugh now, and she watched as Charlie also came to enjoy the memory. "I remember you and Robert used to get caned at school, now and then, didn't you?"

Dinah nodded. School. Aeons ago. She had almost forgotten. "I hardly remember," she said.

"Did you like it? School? I learned so much today. About numbers. He has a trick way of adding up whole columns."

"How does he do it?"

And so she didn't tell him her memories of school. Instead she listened while he taught her the technique. She learned it quickly—so quickly that it annoyed him. "It took him all morning, and here you've learned it before going to bed!"

Dinah shrugged. "I haven't really got it down well yet," she lied. Of course she had it down. But she had long since learned that it annoyed men—it had annoyed her masters at school, for that matter—when she learned quicker than any of the boys did. Charlie was no different, of course. So she lied, and then realized that it felt good to have learned something again. Something that wasn't a spinning jenny, that wasn't the endlessly winding bobbins and the belts humming by and the asinine gossip of the other girls. "Charlie, will you teach me?"

"Teach you?"

"When you come home at night, and on Sundays, teach me all there's time for."

"But—why?"

She knew the reason for his doubt. What would *she* ever do with learning? She could already read and write, which was more than most women ever needed.

"A foolish notion of mine, Charlie, but I mean it." And suddenly she found herself gripping him by the arm, gripping hard, and he looked a little afraid. "If you love me, Charlie."

He looked at her wide-eyed. "Of course I will, if you want it so much."

She released his arm, and he pulled it away. He's only eleven, she reminded herself. We're all still children, and yet I refuse to admit that my wants are childish. I refuse. But to dissemble: "I might have a son like you someday, and how would I teach him?" Ah, yes, that eased his worry, he could understand *that*, and so he grew cheerful again, and taught her a bit more, even though it was getting late and she'd pay for this with excruciating weariness at work in the morning.

At last he realized that she could ill afford the loss of sleep, and he stood to leave, only glancing at Anna where she lay sleeping with rasping breath. Dinah saw it, though. "She doesn't mind staying a servant, if you learn well, Charlie," Dinah said. "She'd do far worse to give you a chance in life."

"I know it." He smiled at her ruefully. "If I'm ever rich, I'll pay it back to her."

Dinah shook her head. "Only to your own children. It's a debt you can only repay to your own children."

He did not leave, not yet; he had one more thing to say. "Dinah," he said. "Whitesides hurt me, and I thought his was the face of the devil. But when Old Hulme hurts me, I look at him and I see—I see that he—"

"That he means well for you?"

"I see the face of God."

Dinah nodded and smiled. "Perhaps so."

Charlie shook his head. "He's only a crazy old man. But he was once great. And he wants to make *me* great, too. He said so."

"And he will."

Charlie stepped out and closed the door behind him. Dinah sighed and undressed and climbed into the bed beside her mother. To her surprise, Anna was not asleep.

"To him you talk," she murmured.

It took Dinah a moment to realize what Anna meant. Dinah was not conscious of how silent she usually was, nor of how loquacious she had been tonight. She said simply, "I had something to say."

For three years Charlie studied with Old Hulme, and came home and taught Dinah, sometimes at night, but always on Sunday. There was no Latin or Greek, but the numbers made up for it. The numbers were infinite, and he drilled and drilled every day until he could manipulate ridiculously large sums and columns in his head, never needing to touch a pencil to paper. Dinah couldn't keep up with him in that, though she did well enough, practicing the calculations as she ran her spinning jenny. What she loved were the other lessons, the ones that Old Hulme threw in almost as an afterthought, because he meant Charlie to make his way in the world, and a man of the world must know more than money. So it was that Charlie came home on weekends with books of verse. For months they read *Paradise Lost,* and pored over Pope and Dryden, Gray and Shakespeare and Spenser and Sidney and Jonson until the verse fairly sang in her. When the numbers forsook her and the belts were near to driving her mad, then came the memory of Charlie's voice reciting, for his voice had a melody that spoke of true understanding of the verse, and it kept her from madness, that voice, kept her still when she wanted to throw herself into the belts and be free. Free of what? She didn't know. She couldn't speak of these feelings to anyone, for they would only say, Why don't you simply quit your work? Robert makes enough now. Robert makes plenty. And indeed he did. So much that the pittance she earned as an operator was almost embarrassing when she gave it to Anna and Robert glared. Why did she do it, when she hated every moment that she spent at the factory? And yet she knew that if she quit she would despise herself, that if she gave up the slavery of the spinning mill, it would only be to trade it for another sort of slavery: being subject to Robert's rule. At rare moments she admitted to herself that that was what kept her in the factory. Robert. And yet he was no tyrant. He was gentle, and though he worked hard he made no unreasonable demands. I'm a fool, I'm proud and I'll go to hell for it, she admitted to herself. The one thing she could not admit was that she couldn't bear the thought of being subject to any man's power. And so to avoid her kind brother, she kept herself under the watchful eye of Mr. Uray, the overseer.

Mr. Uray. He had been a figure of terror when she had begun as a doffer three years before, for he was the one who wielded the strap and liked to lay it on. But recently it had changed, her fear of him. He did not strap her now, or not so often, anyway. Now she only felt him watching her as she worked, watching and watching, so that she felt constrained and stiff and awkward as she moved to run the machinery. Because he was watching her she was keenly aware of the way her growing breasts fell forward within her dress when she leaned to loop the thread; because of his unblinking gaze she felt that even under her skirts the movement of her legs was visible. And yet at fourteen years she wasn't wise enough to put a name to his gaze. It took a friendly older girl to whisper to her, "Watch out for the overseer. You're too pretty."

Pretty? That was the one thing that had never occurred to her. Oh, she used a mirror and she wasn't blind, she knew she was unblemished and she was neither fat nor undernourished-looking—thanks, she knew, to Robert and his ample income, which put fresh fruit and even occasional beef on the table. She was strong and she kept clean so she wouldn't stink and when she smiled people smiled back. But pretty? It was a new thought, and vaguely disquieting. Mr. Uray watched her because she was pretty. But if he knew that she could do sums far more quickly than he, and that she had poetry in her head that he hadn't sense enough to understand, would he stand and watch her *then?*

So she thought little about her face and body, and studied whatever Charlie brought to her to learn, and refused even to wonder what would come of it, what good this learning would ever do for her. She only knew that it was the hours on Sunday with Charlie drilling her on numbers or testing her on the nations of Europe and their commodities and shipping or chanting "The Rime of the Ancient Mariner"—it was those hours she lived for, and could not do without.

For the three years of Charlie's training with Old Hulme she lived for the crumbs from the table of education, knowing all the while that it would do her no good, knowing all the while that it would end; yet still the end could take her by surprise.

Perhaps Charlie understood something of that, for he broke the news to her gently when the years of his schooling were up. "Dinah, I'm sorry, but I can't teach you anything tonight."

She looked at him in surprise over the supper table where her bread and cheese lay untasted.

"Because," he said, "I had no schooling today. Old Hulme and Young Hulme together took me into the city, to the firm of Coswith, Royal and Clay, Solicitors."

"You've gone to work."

"He said it was time for me to have experience in the world. He's tested and tried me, but there's only one proving ground that matters. They're paying me nine and six a month."

Nine and six a month! No wonder Robert stood glowering in the corner. Nine pounds six shillings! It was a higher wage than Robert earned! Oh, Charlie would work for it, Charlie assured them. There every morning at seven, and not home until six, and he must bring his dinner for there'd be no hour to come home at noon. Dinah thought of what it would be like to come home at six, and with so much money. Why, Charlie was wealthy—just like that. And Robert had doubted Charlie's education would come to anything.

"That's more than a bookkeeper should be getting," Dinah said.

"I'm not just a bookkeeper," Charlie answered. "Old Hulme had me examine the company's books. All these years I've thought that every bookkeeper trained as I've been trained, but there were mistakes all through the books, and they didn't even have a cross check to protect them against errors. I set it all to rights in front of them, the week's books, and Old Hulme was a marvel. He looks to be an old fool, but my new masters, they know better, I should guess. He says to them, 'Since he's worth any two of the bookkeepers you have now, you should put him in charge of them all.'"

"In charge of grown men?" Dinah asked. She heard Robert begin to pace the floor, though she didn't look at him or call attention to his discomfiture.

"That's what Mr. Royal said. 'How will I get grown men to take instruction from a boy of—good Lord, thirteen!'"

"Now Charlie, watch how you take the Lord's name—"

"Mother, I'm only saying what *he* said. And Old Hulme says, 'Simple. Just *pay* him more than you pay them.' He asked for ten a month, but they settled on nine and six."

At that Robert could bear no more, and he blurted out, "They're only doing it to keep Old Hulme happy, he's such a client of theirs!"

Dinah could see rage instantly flash into Charlie's eyes, and she quickly reached out and touched his arm, and said with a laugh, "Well, of course, that's the beauty of it—Charlie had a teacher who could make sure his pupil got a good place at

the end of his education!" The tension eased a bit. The telling
and the excitement went on awhile, Dinah taking great care to
bring Robert into the rejoicing. And finally, when it had gone
on so long that Robert was beginning to be snide despite her
efforts, Dinah said the one thing that she knew would silence
him—but happily.

"And best of all, Robert, your money won't be needed in
this house—you can spend it in another."

"Another! And what other house is that?"

Dinah laughed at him. "Why, yours and Mary Handy's!"

That did it; the conversation turned, with Dinah and Anna
teasing him as he denied any thought of marriage. "And why
not!" Anna said, laughing. "It's plain you don't think she's so
ugly you won't talk to her—"

"She's not ugly!"

"Well, then, why do you deny you want to marry her?"

"She's far too young."

At that Dinah laughed nastily. "She's only a year younger
than I am, and you told me only last week that I should have
been married a year ago!"

A bit more banter, and at last they separated, the women
to their room, the men—for Charlie had become at last a man
today—to theirs. But Robert did not stay long in his room; he
came to Dinah after she was in bed and knelt by her and
whispered, "Dinah, may I talk to you?"

"Mm," she agreed.

"Dinah, why does Charlie hate me so?"

"He doesn't," she said.

"Then tell me why it is I hate *him?*"

The words made her tremble inside. They were brothers,
and here he could speak of hate. "You don't, either."

"I'll tell you this. I won't take Mary to wife as a favor from
Charlie, you can be sure of that. His money won't get me
married."

"Don't be a fool, Robert."

"I don't give a damn if I'm a fool—"

She touched his lips to hush him, though she knew that
Mother was undoubtedly awake and silently listening. "Robert,
you're not the father in this house. For all these years you've
kept us, and kept us well. And at last God has opened up a
door for you to be free."

"I don't mind supporting the family."

"And neither will Charlie. Your money should be going into the home where you're the husband and father, not here. Charlie's giving you no gift. He's finally making up for all the years of food and shelter that we all owe to you."

"I don't want to be repaid."

"Don't quibble, Robert. Take Mary before she gets tired of waiting. Who cares if it's Charlie or the devil, just so you can be happy."

It was enough to make Robert content, and he left.

Dinah thought to sleep then, but it was not done, not yet. Mother began to whisper beside her in the darkness. "I have to tell you."

"Tell me what?"

"I said nothing, because I didn't want to rob from Charlie's glory."

Dinah waited, still not sure if it was good news or bad.

"This morning, before Young Hulme left with Charlie and the old man, he called me into the parlor and dismissed me."

"Gave you the sack!"

"Oh, Dinah, he stood up when I came into the room as if I were a lady, and he said, 'No one knows better than I the sacrifice you've made all these years, to remain a servant when you were born to better things, all so your son could have his start in life. Madam,' he said to me, 'you've served this household well, but you're not a servant, and as of this moment the days of your humiliation are over. I honor you.' He said that to *me*. 'I honor you.' I memorized the words all the way home, I can still hear him saying them."

Mother wept to be free, and Dinah embraced her, and finally Anna fell asleep.

Dinah lay there, weary but too unquiet in her heart to sleep. Charlie was joyful, and Robert was free, and Mother's servitude had ended, but where would it end for Dinah? She was not blind; she saw how they had all told their tales to her, how they all came to her to grieve and to rejoice, how she was the spindle that wound them all together into a single thread, even when they threatened to fray apart and break. She was at the center of them all, and held them all—but who held her? Who would set her free?

I am seventeen years old and know no course in life that

interests me at all. My life is bound about by machinery on one side and my brothers on the other. There is no escape for me in either direction, for if I touch the one it will catch me up and kill me, and if I lean on the other, they will also take me and hold me and rule me and if that happens it will be worse than death for I would despise myself without relief.

The factory was nearly unbearable. Surrendering to her brothers' desire to care for her and control her—that would be worse. And so she finally slept, praying silently for something, anything to happen that would set her upon the course her life should follow, the path that would lead to a destination worth arriving at.

After all, she was tired. If she had been more alert, she might have thought twice before praying such a thing. She well knew that God has a way of granting our most foolish prayers. And this prayer was no exception. God will rarely let slip an opportunity to play one of his uproarious practical jokes.

◥ 11 ◤

Mr. Uray
Manchester, 1836

AS LUCK WOULD HAVE IT, Old Hulme died only four days
before Robert's wedding. It was the perfect touch, to have
Charlie grieving in the cottage while Robert fairly danced with
excitement. They both tried to be decent, of course. Charlie
would smile and laugh at times, and Robert at times would be
somber. But there was no life in Charlie's laughter, and too
much mirth behind Robert's sobriety. Even now when harmony
should have been possible, Providence had assured that the
division in the family would only widen.

The funeral was on Sunday, so Dinah went with Charlie.
Robert and Anna had offered to go, too, but Dinah had quietly
said, "Charlie learned from the old man's lips, and in a way
so did I. We're the ones who have a part of him in us, and
we'll go alone." When she spoke that way, her family rarely
argued with her. It was better that way. It gave Robert a chance
to bring Mary to the house for a time of merriment. And Dinah

111

was also secretly glad that she did not have to be there when Mary came. Not that she didn't like Mary—the girl was sweet, if a bit daft about Robert, and she had become something like a friend to Dinah. No, it was Mary's brother, who came with Robert and Mary as inevitably as a shadow, it was Matthew Handy that Dinah wanted to avoid.

What was wrong with Matthew? Nothing, really. As Dinah walked to the funeral, silently holding Charlie's hand, she tried to decide why she was so glad not to see Matthew. Certainly she had no reason to dislike him—she *didn't* dislike him, really, she told herself. He was shy around her, he tended to stammer with her, or make boorish jokes that were laughed at only out of charity. She was not so naive that she didn't know he had eyes for her. Not like Mr. Uray, who was making life harder and harder for her at the factory; Matthew didn't measure her bosom or her buttocks with his gaze. Rather he worshiped. That was, in a way, harder to take. Lechery could be ignored. But adoration—that laid upon her an obligation she did not know how to pay. At least, not in any coin she was willing to offer him. And then she condemned herself for her pride. Matthew was a good man, and it was a sin for her to despise him merely because he admired her.

At the cathedral Charlie broke down and cried, and Dinah realized for the first time how much his teacher had meant to him. It surprised her, for it reminded her that Charlie's fourteen years were so very few; he was still a child. She knew him well enough not to put her arm around him there in the church, where others would see. She let him wear his grief with dignity. After a while, Charlie went to the coffin and kissed the coffin. Dinah came with him, and heard him clearly say, "Two million four hundred thousand, at fourteen percent." It was such an odd thing to say, especially with his cheeks tear-stained, that Dinah almost laughed. But she did not. He would tell her soon enough what it meant.

Outside, on the way home, Charlie was full of speech. Memories of the teaching. Even the many times his hands were slapped he spoke of with affection. "And the Hulme and Kirkham Company." He sighed.

It was plainly an invitation for her to invite him. "Go on— what was that?"

"I never told you because it was so silly, but—when I first

started with him, he gave me a thousand pounds in imaginary capital, and advised me in the investment of it. All imaginary, everything we did, but we followed the offers of stock and the sales of land, and I wrote down what I would have done with the money. At first he corrected me when I made a bad investment and told me why, and then after a time he let me learn from my own mistakes. But in the last year or so I made no mistakes. If the money had been real, Hulme and Kirkham would now have control of investments and properties worth two million four hundred thousand pounds, with an average return of fourteen percent. He would have been—" And then he could not go on.

It struck Dinah as touching and yet perverse that Charlie's love for Old Hulme was so linked with an imaginary sum of money. It disturbed her vaguely to discover that Charlie measured his own worth in pounds and shillings and percentages of return. It was not that uncommon a measure of personal value, as much among the poor as among the rich. A man *was* how much he owned or earned, and the greatest division of all was between owners and earners. In his heart Charlie was an owner; in his life he could only earn. She had not, until now, realized how Charlie's life centered around money. It was the scholar and poet in him that she most loved, and yet he valued this aspect of himself least of all. She had seen in him the seeds of his own unhappiness and knew it, though she could not name her fears.

At home again Charlie said his courtesies to Mother and Robert and the Handys, who were obviously merry with beer in the front room; then he retreated to the bedroom. In short order Robert announced that it was time he and Matthew went to the pub to drink to his bachelorhood "and give a speech to my friends deploring virginity and enlisting their support in the abolition of it!" Anna feigned horror and hurried them out the door.

The talk among the women followed the inevitable path— Dinah herself would later guide many such discussions the day before a wedding, though now she had a curious feeling of detachment, as if she were standing outside the window, looking and listening as Anna, Mary, and a stranger named Dinah discussed matters of marriage.

It began with talk of the wedding itself, congratulating themselves on all that they had planned and what a fine affair it was going to be and how it didn't matter that there wasn't enough money to really do it *right*.

Then the talk turned to what life after marriage was going to be. Here Anna turned it into something of a monologue. To Dinah it sounded as paradoxical as a sermon or the Gospel of St. John. You must keep your home impeccably clean for him, but never be so absorbed in housecleaning that you forget to listen to him when he talks. You must have meals ready for him when he needs them, but never let him see you tired or unbeautiful. You must always be there for him; you must never be in his way. You must obey him always; you must not wait to be commanded in anything. You must never argue with him; you must keep him from making mistakes that he will regret. You must never bring up problems and worries; you must have no secrets from him.

Dinah could finally bear no more. She laughed aloud and said, "Mother, it would take at least two wives to accomplish all of that."

Immediately she regretted having said it, for Anna's face became rueful, and she nodded wistfully, and the talk turned again, into realms of pain from which Anna had tried to emigrate years ago, but never quite succeeded. "It's true. *I* never succeeded in any of that, nor any woman I know. Though *you* may, Mary—you're such a glad girl, it'll smooth many a quarrel before the first word gets spoken."

"We'll never quarrel," Mary said. "I'll give in too quickly."

Dinah could not account for the strange anger that came to her then. But she held her tongue and said nothing.

"John and I never quarreled," Anna said. "But still he left me. There's more than that." She sighed and looked at the wall, where imaginary paintings hung. "I've thought about it often and often during these years, I've thought why did he leave me."

"He left because he was weak," Dinah said coldly. She was afraid of what her mother would say.

"No, he wasn't weak. He was strong in his own way. But the needs of others weighed on him. Think what a man goes through. When he goes to work, he doesn't carry just the labor of the job with him. He also carries on his shoulders all his children, and his wife, all the bellies he has to fill—all his

days are spent satisfying others. When does he satisfy himself?"
Anna hesitated, for it was not an easy thing for her to say. "He
satisfies himself in his wife's bed. No, don't blush or get silly
when I say it. We're only women here, and I'll speak frankly,
as much for my daughter as for you, Mary. When there is nothing between your husband and you but your own flesh, what
he needs is to satisfy himself, and no one else. My mistake was
that I loved his body more than he loved mine. My mistake
was that I desired his love. I took more pleasure from our
embraces than he did, and he knew it, so that even in our bed
he was satisfying me more than himself. Even that became an
obligation for him, instead of a release. Do you understand?
It's a great pleasure, the love of a man and a woman, and the
preachers who tell you about the carnality of lustfulness between a husband and a wife are liars. It's a glorious thing that
God gave to Adam and Eve as their greatest comfort in this
lone and dreary world. But it isn't good for the woman to show
her pleasure too much. Don't cry out for joy. Don't clasp him
hard or urge him on. Act as if it were only a gift you gave to
him, and then he will be satisfied. Take your pleasure, but
secretly."

Dinah could not understand why this made her so upset.
She was a virgin and had hardly talked of this with anyone,
only the joking comments among the women at the factory.
Yet she could not hold her tongue. "I still say it was Father
who was weak. A real man would rejoice in the pleasure he
gave his wife, and not begrudge her any of it."

Of course Mother smiled patiently and nodded. Of course
Mary blushed and looked at her lap. "There's time enough for
you, Dinah," Anna said. "You're still so young."

Dinah laughed in embarrassment. "I'm a year older than
Mary."

"Forgive me for saying it, Dinah, but a mother must say
such things. All married women are older than all unmarried
girls, regardless of their years."

"Mary isn't married yet."

"Even the day before a wedding, a woman's heart changes.
She begins to know things that a woman who has not given
her life into a man's hands can never know."

Dinah longed to make a sharp retort to that, because it hurt
her to be made to feel so childish, and by her own mother.

But she held her peace as she had known from infancy to hold her peace. Things were simpler that way, and anger soon faded. Besides, for all she knew her mother might be right. And she was jealous of Mary and contemptuous of her: jealous that she would be initiated into the mysteries of passion, of conception, and of birth; contemptuous because Mary was too small for him. How could a woman not despise herself, to marry so unworthily a man who deserved an equal partner? Or the opposite, as Mother did, to marry a man who needed someone small-hearted and weak, who could not hold his own with a woman who had something of the strength of Ruth in her?

Ruth: The woman who knew only one man in Israel was worthy of her, and so went to Boaz and lay at the foot of his bed, not waiting for chance to bring them together, because she knew that only she could make him happy, and only he could give her joy.

I would rather stay a maiden all my life than marry a man too great or too small for me. She meant it when she said it, or at least the second part; even now she suspected there might not be a man who was too much for her, for she had never met one, not even her brothers.

Of course the other women misinterpreted Dinah's silence; people usually did. Mary tried to reassure her. "You'll marry, too, Dinah, and soon. Though I may have taken the last good husband in the world."

Dinah smiled. "Probably. But I'll make do." Lies made conversations go so much more smoothly.

For once, perversely, someone saw through her lie. "You're not so easy as you pretend, are you?" Mary said. "*Is* there a man, then?"

"Not for me."

Of course when Dinah told the truth she would not be believed; Mary was too clever for that. "Oh, you can't fool me. There's a man. But why is your face so sad? Look at her, Mother Kirkham. Oh, she denies it, but her heart is breaking for someone. It's a tragic love—someone hopelessly above her station that she cannot wed."

The histrionic tone in Mary's voice was infuriating. She was turning Dinah's life into a ridiculous romance. And yet Dinah said nothing, for the only thing she could think of to say was, "*I'm* not the one who's marrying above her station," and it would never do to say *that*.

Mary took silence for consent, of course. "It's like Romeo and Juliet! Who is he? Dinah, you must tell us!"

"My heart isn't breaking."

"See how she suffers in silence, Mother Kirkham? Oh, we won't tell anyone, not even Matthew, though it would break his heart." And then Mary put her hand to her mouth and giggled. "I shouldn't have said that, should I? He'd just kill me if he knew. But it's true, and I'm glad I said it, so there." Her voice dropped to a whisper. "He's dying for love of you."

"People don't die for love," Dinah said.

"Perhaps not. But sometimes they suffer so much that they wish they could."

"Mother, perhaps it's time for us to go to bed."

But Anna would be no help to her. "Don't be rude, Dinah. You know Mary's welcome here as long as she likes."

"I didn't mean to offend you," Mary said. "I wouldn't offend you for the world. But it's true. Matthew said so. He said he's so jealous of Robert, marrying the woman he loves. And so jealous of me, to be taking a Kirkham into my bed." Mary blushed, but clumsily stumbled on. "Matthew's a blunt one, plainspoken, if you know my drift. He thinks you're the most beautiful woman in the world."

"His perspective would improve if he stopped going to pubs with Robert and saw more women instead."

Mary was so caught up in her own enthusiasm now that she was incapable of knowing when she was being told to shut up. "Oh, Dinah, wouldn't it be lovely if we could be sisters?"

At last Mother saw that things had gone too far, and she interrupted the grotesque conversation. "Mary, dear, tomorrow you and Dinah *will* be sisters."

"Oh, yes, of course, I forgot. Robert and I will be one, as the parson says. I'm to *be* Robert, in a way, we'll be parts of the same person, and so we *will* be sisters, won't we!"

And on that cheerful note the conversation turned to other matters until Robert and Matthew came tipsily home, singing bawdy songs until Anna threatened to throw both of them into the street and let Mary stay with them tonight. Finally all was calm; Mary and Matthew were gone, and Robert snored heavily, filling the bedroom with the smell of celebratory beer.

In the dark, returning from the private house to the cottage, Dinah paused for a moment in the courtyard. The air was smoky, so there were no stars; it was not for contemplation that she waited. It was something else. She wanted something, wanted it very specifically, and yet could not think what it was.

In the darkness she heard Charlie pass her, heading for the private house. She said nothing to him; he did not see her. She tried to think what had made her so unsatisfied. Was it all the talk of love? Was she longing for a man's touch on her body? The moment she thought of it, she remembered Mr. Uray, whose touches were becoming less subtle and far more frequent. Because they were done with the pretense of discipline, to call her to her work when her attention wandered, she had been able to ignore them. But now she knew what the pokes and pinches really were; now she understood why the other girls were getting colder to her. Mr. Uray had long looked at her in the wrong way; she was so used to ignoring it that she hadn't realized that the other girls might think more of it than she did. They must pity her for it, and yet feel so ashamed they couldn't speak of it. Or no—could some of them even be jealous, wishing the overseer would try to touch *them?* Welcome to him, I'm sure, Dinah thought, laughing silently. If that's what Mr. Uray thinks is love, pinches that leave a bruise, he can take his love to someone else and welcome to it. What did not occur to her was the truth: that the other girls believed that in her very silence, in her very ignoring of Mr. Uray's provocation, in the fact that she had not quit her job long ago, they believed that she was encouraging him. They believed that she was getting special favors from him; some were even sure that he was paying her extra on the side. The only thing that was really debated was whether he had actually had her yet. The majority still held that Dinah was a virgin who was playing with fire, not a harlot who was already well scorched. Of course none of them spoke of it to her, as her reputation slowly deteriorated though she was innocent of any of the sins assumed for her.

Charlie saw her on his way back to the cottage. It turned out he had come out less to use the privy than to find her. "I heard," he told her.

She looked at him calmly.

"I mean—what you and mother said." He was resolute—embarrassed to speak, but determined not to stop. "I couldn't help hearing. I just wanted you to know that I agree with you. And when I marry, I'll be as careful to please my wife as to be pleased by her. I'm not like father. I'm not like him at all."

It touched her that he was so eager to have her good opinion. "Of course you aren't. And when you marry, Charlie, you'll be a good husband. But not too soon, please."

He laughed. "I guess not. I'm only a boy." But the way he said it, she knew that he thought of his youthfulness only as a disguise for a fully grown man inside.

"You're taller."

"You noticed."

"You'll be as tall as Robert soon."

"I'll be taller. He's built wide, like an ox."

Ah, yes. Robert was animal-like, in Charlie's view. While *he* would be a man. Let be, let be. "Better go in now, Charlie. There's the wedding so early tomorrow, and then a day's work afterward. Only Robert and Mary get the whole day."

"Oh, they'll be working far into the night."

"Enough of that, Charlie. I'm only your sister, but you should still think of me as a lady."

"I'm sorry—"

"Go on in. I'll come soon."

"I'm sorry."

"Your sins are forgiven."

They laughed, and Charlie left her. She stood in the darkness and touched her lips, wondering what it would feel like to have a man do that. And then she felt a terrible, trembling fear that no man ever would, that like Matthew all men would be afraid of her, would adore her but never want to be one with her, to be part of her, as the parson said.

The wedding came and went in the weak light of smoke-blocked dawn, at the chapel a few blocks away on Canal Street. Mary was pretty and Robert was handsome in their rented finery—and Charlie was fiercely proud of the fact that his gift to them had been a rented coach for their trip from the chapel at Canal Street to their new home at Ravald Street. There had been some argument on that, Anna insisting that Charlie should spend his gift money on something that would last, and Charlie equally adamant that he wanted his brother "to have the best." Privately Dinah was sure Charlie's motive was not so selfless: Robert would know whose carriage it was when he took his bride away, and though he had the manners not to refuse the gift, he hadn't the charity to forgive it.

Dinah's gift had been the rent of Mary's dress. It was the

only secret Dinah knew for a fact that Mary had ever kept; between the two women, Mary was profusely grateful, but she had readily consented to Dinah's request that she tell no one who paid for the dress, so that Mary's family wouldn't have to suffer the embarrassment of having it be known they were too poor to rent the gown themselves.

At the moment of the vows, Mother squeezed Dinah's hand tighter, is if to say, "Someday you." Dinah did not squeeze back. Instead she thought of her mother's marriage, and silently resolved that if she ever married a man who wanted to leave her, she would make him leave her in daylight, not lie there in the dark passively while he took her money and walked out the door; she would kill him first before she would let him be so cowardly. Then she realized that God might construe her thought as a wish for the death of her own father. Forgive me, she said to God. The prayer was not answered. Never was.

It was November when Mr. Uray tired of his subtle pinching and poking and decided that the time had come to win the beautiful young operator who obviously didn't mind his advances but never did anything to come halfway with him.

He began his direct approach by slipping two extra shillings into her hand on payday. The idea was not his own. The women who worked in the factory had told the men there about their speculation that Dinah was getting extra pay; the rumor had reached men on the same level as Mr. Uray, and they had teased him about keeping his own private payroll for work done after hours. Mr. Uray liked the idea of the other men thinking him something of a rake; he did not contradict them. And now he had decided that the strategy of extra payment might raise those skirts.

He was wrong. Dinah immediately noticed the extra coins and stepped back to drop them on the table in front of Mr. Uray. Uray looked dumbly at the money. "You must have miscounted," Dinah said softly, and then she hurried out the door. Mr. Uray was furious, sure that he saw ridicule in the faces of the other men and women as they passed to get their money. Now they would know that the rumors weren't true, and he had not had Dinah after all. It was humiliating, and he would not bear it.

All Sunday he fretted about it, burning with shame that

Dinah was too proud to take his money, that she would dare to humiliate him in front of everyone. It did not occur to him that she had never heard the rumors about the extra money and that she could not have known that anyone would think that his overpayment was anything but an accident. He knew better. The way she moved more slowly and liquidly when she knew he was watching her; the way she breathed faster when she saw him coming toward her; the way when he pinched her she blushed and said nothing, but only worked faster, pretending that she hadn't noticed it—it was obvious to him that she desired him, that she wanted him as much as he wanted her. And why not? He wasn't young, but some women prized the wisdom of a mature man over the flightiness of youth. He knew well enough from his discreet inquiries that she had no man, that she never kept company with any of the fellows at the factory. The poor wench was obviously dying with desire for him, but she was too proud for his money. All right, then. She might think the money would turn her into a whore—he should have thought of that, she was better than that sort. He would not try again to appeal to her purse; now he would appeal directly to her heart. But since her heart was so well-concealed behind bodice, blouse, and bosom, he decided that the best persuasion would be to give her a taste of what his love could be like. It wasn't money she wanted, it was the ecstasy of love, and Mr. Uray was the man to give it to her.

Monday morning was icy, and the women all came to work bundled in whatever warm things they owned; raggedy clothes, mostly, though a few had had the spare coins to buy something still in fair condition. But Mr. Uray was adamant about the washing. The master insisted on cleanliness, because he was concerned for his employees' health. He was an enlightened man and took some pride in the fact. So his overseers did his bidding and whatever the weather, warm or cold, the sinks like horse troughs were filled with hot water and the soap and towels were set in their bowls. Men and women alike had to wash arms to the shoulder and faces to the neck and feet to the knee. But enlightenment was not carried to extremes. Real estate costing what it did, there was no sense in having men and women wash in separate rooms. Poor people had no modesty anyway—that was plain from the holey, scanty clothes they so often wore. So never mind what clothing might have to be removed. Men and women would wash each morning and each night, wash to the neck, to the shoulder, to the knee, and quickly, too. And of course it was Mr. Uray's job to watch closely and be sure that all washed as thoroughly as they should. Dinah Kirkham had such a graceful leg.

All day Mr. Uray thought of nothing but Dinah. Though he was often tempted, by both habit and desire, to come and catch her idling and pinch her to alertness, today he restrained himself. He deliberately did not watch her, did not speak to her, did not so much as notice she existed. He imagined her worry, for of course she would think he was angry about her having refused his money. Of course she would be afraid that he no longer cared for her, that her chance with the overseer was lost. Well, let her fret, let her fret. He murmured it to himself as an incantation. It did not occur to him that, far from fretting, she was gratefully thinking that he had at last realized that she detested him and had therefore ceased his crude advances. After all, he thought, there were so many rumors that she was his paramour, and how could such rumors persist if there wasn't at least some underlying truth to them?

Work ended. Dinah was tired. She filed with the other women into the washing room. Men from other parts of the factory were also coming in, and the children. Men and boys rolled their trousers up and took off their shirts, some shyly, some wearily, but most with their backs to the women as the women turned their backs to the men. To wash their legs, however, the women had to lift their skirts and pull down their hose, and if most of the men did not look, some had no compunction, and stared frankly at the calves and ankles that could not be hidden. Mr. Uray solemnly did his duty and watched them all.

Afterward Dinah would wonder if, in her weariness, she had been careless of her modesty, if perhaps she had done something to provoke Mr. Uray beyond his endurance. But she did not think of such a thing when, as she reached the door to be checked off the list of those who had done a full day's work, he looked at her sternly and said, "You must wait."

Now she realized that his ignoring her today was not courtesy but anger—she would be punished. It made her afraid. Would he dismiss her? He didn't even need a pretext. But worst of all was that he might be angry enough to pass the word among the overseers in other factories that Dinah Kirkham was a troublesome woman, and then she'd never get another job. It filled her with terror, the thought of being able to find no work, even though she knew that Charlie made plenty of money and that she could stay home or even go to school if she wanted to. She needed her job, and Mr. Uray had the power to take all work away from her—it had been done to other girls, she knew. So when the last of the other women filed past Mr. Uray, pausing only to cast a dark glance at her— of pity, she thought—she was trembling and eager to apologize, to humiliate herself if it would placate Uray and keep her employed.

"To my office," he said coldly. He gestured for her to go ahead, and he followed her to his tiny cubicle. She knew that her hand trembled on the railing up the steep stair to Mr. Uray's door. Later she would wonder if that trembling, if the slowness and uncertainty of her step had led him to believe she was anticipating what he meant to do.

She said nothing when he came in after her and closed the door. He did not lock it, of course, for the master did not allow any of his employees to have locks on their doors. What did any of them have a right to hide from *him?* But the door was nevertheless locked as surely as if there had been a latch to throw. No one would come into Mr. Uray's closed room, and Dinah knew she would not leave the office without his consent, unless she chose to leave it without her job.

She waited for him to speak, but he did not speak. Instead he removed his coat. She was surprised. A gentleman did not appear in public in his shirtsleeves, and Mr. Uray had pretensions to gentility. When he removed his waistcoat, however, she began to be afraid. Not that she completely understood yet. She only feared that he meant to beat her so severely that he had to free his arms for the labor.

"I'm sorry if I offended you," she said, her voice shaking. She hoped to forestall his violence; he was sure, however, that she was only trying to encourage him to overlook her pride and take her as a man should take such a beautiful woman.

"I'm a married man, a happily married man, but as Adam himself learned to his sorrow, women are a temptation a man cannot resist, God forgive us both." And he threw his arms around her, backed her to a wall, and began to kiss her.

She struggled, and his lips only occasionally found hers, but he also did not let go of her, and her arms were helplessly pinned to her sides as he kissed her neck and groped behind her, pulling up her skirts and reaching into her drawers to knead the soft skin he found there.

In the silence Dinah frantically tried to think of what she could do. What she could say that would make him let her leave this room without dismissing her from her job, how she could persuade him that he had misunderstood her somehow, that begging your pardon I must get home to my mother. "My brothers are meeting me outside."

"Then we must be quick." And he bent his knees so his hands could reach lower, could play between her legs, and suddenly she remembered that in such situations women were accustomed to screaming. Dinah had no such custom—she was not a screamer. But custom could change at need. "You mustn't. I'll scream."

"No you won't."

But she would, for now she found her body responding to him whether she loathed his touch or not; responding strangely and frighteningly, and she did scream, and it worked, for his hands came away from her and he backed off. For a moment she was relieved, but then she saw the rage in his face and his hand came up and down again and there was a terrible pain in her nose and she felt the blood stream down to her chin, down to her neck.

"You'll not scream," he said. She cried frantically as he roughly unbuttoned the bodice of her dress, pulling off some, unfastening others; then, the job half done, he got impatient and bent to raise her skirts in front. She did not think, only knew that she must not scream or he'd hit her again, and yet she must stop him. So she brought her knee up into his face, hard. But not hard enough; her blow was tempered by her fear of him and her fear of the act of violence she was committing— she remembered, for some reason, a man crying out and falling backward down the stairs and the terrible fear that he might be dead, that she might have killed him. The fear of doing murder held her back. Too late she realized that she should have hit him harder or not at all. His face twisting and his mouth uttering obscenities he hit her in the head, twice, and when she turned away and sank to the ground to try to avoid his blows he kicked her, his boot catching her once in the side and twice in the thighs. She wept with the pain, and her body was too limp to struggle as he seized her and pulled her out supine on the floor. He threw her skirt high over her head, hiding her face, and pulled down her drawers. She was naked and could not bear that, and despite her weakness she drew her knees up, thinking to curl out of his way in the corner; but he took her knees and roughly opened them.

And then there was a pause, and in the pause she decided that she did not have to submit to this, that she would not submit to this. It was nothing so melodramatic as a decision to die before letting him take her, though in fact she would have thoughtlessly done so had it been necessary. It was more a decision that she would not let any consideration stand between her and getting out that door. No fear of hurting him; no fear of losing her job; no fear of any pain it might cost her.

With the decision came a great clarity of mind. She felt her drawers still around her ankles. That would hamper her, so with her feet she got them off. Whatever Mr. Uray was doing, he saw and giggled. "I knew it," he said. "Must have our little show but I knew you'd come round." Then she pulled the skirt down from her face and saw him on all fours, kneeling over her, his hands straddling her body and his legs between hers, and him naked except for his long shirt, which he had pulled up high under his arms. She screamed again. He looked surprised—wasn't she willing now?—and then her hands flew out and jabbed at his eyes; she felt her fingers as they found his face, and one finger did strike the eyelid, closed over the eyeball. It gave a little, and now it was his turn at last to scream and recoil from her. He held his face, but she cared not at all whether he was blind or not. She struggled to her feet and limped to the door.

She had it open and thought she was free when he caught her skirts and pulled her back into the room. A hand under her dress caught her ankle and pulled her off balance, but instead of falling she only spun toward him. He was kneeling upright, his legs widespread, his hands reaching up under her dress. She did not even have to think. She kicked him harshly, and the boot he had not bothered to remove from her made a perfect fit, nesting his groin like a ball in the curve from toe to shin. She felt his fragile organs yield and slip sideways as the force of her kick lifted his knees from the ground. He opened his mouth but did not shout, only gurgled and then fell unconscious to the floor.

Have I killed him? The thought was tinged with hope: that she hadn't, that she had. She took up her drawers where he had tossed them on the table, but did not stop to put them on, just tucked them inside her bodice and ran to where her coat waited for her, the last on the racks save his own topcoat, and she clutched the collar around her instead of trying to fasten her bodice. She took no time for anything but to get out of the factory decently covered, and even then she could not stop running, she did not even think of direction or destination; she reached home only because her feet knew the way.

❧ 12 ❧

Dinah Kirkham
Manchester, 1836

SHE BURST INTO the cottage, exhausted and weeping and
unable to speak. Poor Charlie, sitting there reading a book,
was absolutely stunned and could only think to call, "Mother!"
until Anna came in and helped Dinah to her room, saying,
"Poor thing, poor thing, poor thing." In the room with the door
closed, there were questions. "Who was it? How did you get
away?"

Charlie was the one who fetched Robert. Later Dinah would
be amused to think of that: Charlie, so determinedly free of
his brother, still knew that when there was real danger he must
get Robert, that only Robert would know what to do. And
Charlie was right. Robert was icy but calm, and took immediate
charge. And he knew, of all questions, which one was most
important.

"Did he get in her?"

Dinah shuddered at how near it had been, and cried out,
"No!"

"She got away in time," Anna added quietly.

"Is she hurt?" Robert asked.

"Bruised ribs and legs. He beat her. A bloody nose."

"Did you scream?"

"Yes," Dinah said. "But they were all gone."

"They'd all gone home! Then why the bloody hell did you stay?"

Anna started to remonstrate against his language, but he brushed her off—no time for that. Dinah answered, softly. "I didn't know what he meant to do. I thought he was just going to reprimand me."

Plainly Robert was skeptical. "Come now. He has you stay, and you *do* it. What did you expect him to think?"

"Nothing!" But even as she shouted her denial, she was uncertain. Now she found dozens of uncomfortable things in her memory. Her mousy words when he first had her closed in the office; her carelessness, perhaps, in washing in front of him; her having endured his touches for months before. I did it, I'm to blame, she thought in despair, God forgive me but I know you won't—

"Of course she did nothing!" Anna said angrily. "How dare you suggest it!"

Robert was instantly ashamed, but it was not in him to apologize. Instead he asked, "Did you get him back?"

"With any luck," Dinah said fiercely, "he's lost an eye and got nothing left at all between his legs."

Robert whooped in delight at that. "Old Mr. Uray finally got his comeuppance, the fud-grabber!"

Anna was not pleased. She took her oldest son by the jacket and forced him to look at her. "You knew this man was evil and still you let her go every day to work for him!"

"*Let* her!" Robert was outraged. "I've been trying to get her to quit from the start! I tried to keep her out of the factories altogether! *You* stop her from something when she wants her way! By God, Mother, even the old bastard himself couldn't stop her when she decided she was coming home!"

Anna had no answer to that. And so she surrendered, left the matter up to him, and concentrated on the only thing that she could do, comfort her daughter, weep with her daughter. Dinah heard her mother's soft keening and clung to her while Robert enumerated the consequences of what had happened. "Everyone knows that she stayed after, but no one saw what actually happened. *They'll* know why he kept her, even if she's such a fool that she did not." Robert paced up and down, growing angrier and hotter by the minute. "Doesn't matter what she says, doesn't matter even if she could prove anything, which she can't. She's ruined. They'll all know her for a whore, and you can bet the old bastard won't give a hint that he didn't get what he was after. All Manchester will know her for Uray's quean. I'll kill him."

The threat was rhetorical, but Anna was too distraught to realize it. "Oh, no, Robert, you mustn't! They'll surely put you in jail, or hang you!"

It flattered Robert to have his mother assume he had the courage for vengeance and the strength to succeed. "Me in jail! I don't care!"

But he allowed Anna to persuade him with arguments that in fact he had already thought of. He might have done something violent if he hadn't a wife who was already pregnant, but he had no wish to leave Mary the widow of a man hanged for murder. And besides, Dinah hadn't been raped, she was only *thought* to be a whore, and you might hate a man for that, but you didn't sacrifice your own life to kill him for it.

"Take him to court," Anna said. "Let the magistrate do for him."

Robert laughed at that. "The court? And the owner of the factory comes in and tells the magistrate—who himself owns three factories—he says, 'Are we going to let these working women put any overseer they happen not to like into the clapper, just by crying rape?' And the magistrate, he says no, and they slap a fine on Dinah and she loses her job and nothing happens at all to the overseer. That's the way the law works in Manchester, in case you hadn't heard. It's happened a dozen times before. Dinah's lucky—she won't get a baby out of the bargain. I'm not wasting any time going to the law on it."

In the morning Dinah awoke in pain. Bruised ribs, bruised thighs, an ache in her nose and forehead. The nose wasn't broken, but it was still swollen and bruises had formed under her eyes. Worse than the pain, though, was the knowledge that her future, already dim before, was bleaker still today. Oddly, she wanted to go home, even though she already *was* home. Where did she belong, if not here?

Still, there was some quiet relief in the change. She did not have to hurry to get out of bed, because she was not going to work today, here or anywhere. She could smell potatoes frying—her breakfast would be hot, not cold. To her surprise, she was hungry. She resented her body's opinion, so frankly stated, that life should go on. But she obeyed all the same, got up and dressed slowly, learning that some of the pain was mere stiffness and would go away, while the rest of the pain was bearable and could, with care, be ignored. Her body would heal.

And so would her soul, she suspected. Already she found it hard to think of Mr. Uray at all, let alone to remember the terror or the rage. She thought it was an encouraging sign. She was even able to write in her journal about it, albeit cryptically; it gave her some satisfaction to have it down in letters, for the writing of it put it in the past, where it belonged, where it could be dealt with.

Robert and Mary were in the kitchen, waiting for her. Mary looked a little wan from morning sickness, but still she was all touch and tenderness with Robert. They bent toward each other, the husband and wife, leaned into each other's words, leaned back on each other's silences, as if a part of each was controlled by the thoughts of the other. Yet they spared a little of their attention for her.

At first, as Anna put food before Dinah and she ate, Robert was apologetic. He was sorry for yesterday, for even hinting that any fault lay with her. Of course that was absurd, he should know his sister, he was just crazy with anger.

"It's all right," she said. "I had already forgotten."

And it stopped the flood of apology, for when she spoke like that she was believed. When she told her brother that he was not guilty, the load lifted from him as surely as if Jesus himself had forgiven him.

But now he began, for no reason that she could detect, to talk about marriage, about how happy he and Mary were. How the first few days were all joy, and then the little fights and irritations that so quickly passed, and now Mary was participating with God in creating new life. That last phrase almost made Dinah laugh, for she knew that if Charlie's God was money, Robert's only deity was well-made machinery. Robert misinterpreted her smile, of course, and thought she was sharing their delighted contemplation of the wedded state. "It's marriage that makes a person complete," Robert said. "Man or woman."

"It's true," Mary said. "Robert says it so beautifully, and it's even true."

Finally, however, Robert came to the point. Dinah could see it by the way he looked at Mary for courage. "A life as an unmarried woman would be miserable for you, Dinah, and you deserve better than that. But the word's got round cruelly fast, that's the way of it. One of the girls in our row has a niece in your factory, and the word's got round that you stayed with Mr. Uray last night. They all know it, and they're saying worse things that I won't repeat."

"Repeat them," Dinah said.

"I won't. I tried to tell them the truth, but you know how much good that'll do, they nod, they smile, oh yes, of course, we know, we believe you—but I'm your brother, and they wouldn't expect me to say anything else, it makes no difference what's true."

"But it *is* true."

"I know that, and so do you, and in this house there's no shame to you at all. But out there—where do you think your husband's going to come from, if not out there?"

Dinah did not want to think of a husband.

"And you can't go away anywhere else. They'll all just think you're going away to—to—"

Robert was unaccountably shy to say it. It was Mary who came to his rescue. "They'll think you're like I am, only not married."

Robert nodded gravely. Dinah noticed the way he drew Mary tighter to him and she almost invisibly smiled and was satisfied. They were still talking more to each other than to Dinah. From the secure fortress of their marriage they were going to shout down directions as to how she should fight her dragon.

"Dinah, there's only one way out of this, so you can hold your head up and be known pure and good and not have any more of this nonsense."

Dinah waited.

"Damn, but you make it hard, you're so silent!"

Ah, Dinah thought, you are *not* so safe as you thought.

Anna spoke from beside the fire. "Robert, it grieves me to hear words like that in my home."

"Sorry, Mother." He dismissed her with his unmeant apology and went on with Dinah. "You must know what I mean.

You've got to wed, and you've got to wed right away."

She had expected it, and liked it all the less for having had some time to anticipate it. "I wonder," she said icily, "whether Mr. Uray would have me now."

"No, Dinah, you're hearing me wrong on purpose!"

"And he does have a wife who might object to the arrangement, particularly if I've done any lasting harm to his connubial powers."

"Damn!" Robert stood quickly, moving the table a little and upsetting his stool. "Mother, I'm sorry, but there's not a man in the world who can hold his tongue when this woman speaks!"

"If I remember, Robert, you swore last because she *wouldn't* speak."

"She gets it from you," Robert accused. He paced toward the window of the cottage. "Dinah, it's not Mr. Uray we're proposing, as you know perfectly well. There's a man who loves you dear, who knows about these stories but knows they're not true, and he wants to marry you, and he's happy to marry you quickly. He counts it as his good fortune and not as a favor he's doing you."

"Tell this Christian soul that the offer will get him blessings in heaven, but not me for a wife."

"I'll tell him no such thing. I'll tell him that I talked to you and proposed his name, and that you're thinking, and you'll damn well think today and by tonight you'll damn well have an answer of yes for me."

"But you haven't proposed his name," Mother said from her ineffectual place near the kitchen fire. "You haven't told her *who*." Dinah heard with irritation the note of excitement and happiness in her mother's voice. I have no allies here, she realized.

"Of course she knows," Mary said. "It's Matthew, my dear brother, who already loves Robert as his good friend and wants to make a home for you."

Dinah was silent. She could think of nothing to say. She kept thinking, better Matthew than Mr. Uray. But it was not the right thing to remember now, for when she thought of Mr. Uray she pictured him kneeling over her, and "better Matthew than Mr. Uray" was no consolation for the desolate prospect of marriage and facing a hot and irresistible intruder night after night. She knew that it was surely not that way in marriage;

Mary's joy in it was proof enough of that. But it was too soon after her encounter with the overseer. She said so.

"It has to be soon," Robert said. "That's the whole point, it must be *soon.*"

Dinah only shook her head.

"Hold off on her," Mother said. "Give her a few days. It's only yesterday it happened, and she just woke up this morning, the world's wrong side out for her today. Like you said, tell Matthew she's been asked and now she's thinking."

Robert sighed. "All right. You women make up your minds so slowly, it drives me mad. Come on, Mary. I'm late enough to work, and so's Matthew, waiting to hear her word."

Mary followed him to the door.

"Robert," Dinah said.

He turned to her, obviously hoping she had already changed her mind and would consent. It annoyed her, but she said what she meant to say anyway. "Thank him for his kindness. And I thank you for yours. But please—tell him not to come here. Tell him not to visit."

"I can't tell him that," Robert said.

"You certainly can," Mother said. "After what Dinah's been through, it's perfectly natural if she wants just to be with her family. Get on, Robert, you've done what you meant to, you've done it well, now give the girl some room to breathe! Her food is getting cold. Get out, go on, get to work, earn money, get rich!"

Finally they were gone, and Anna stood at the door watching Dinah push potatoes back and forth with her spoon.

"Do you want to know what *I* think?" Anna asked.

"No," Dinah answered. She knew what Anna thought, and hated the idea. Anna was hardly the one to talk about the joys of marriage—hadn't her husband left her, and only luck had kept them all from starving to death or being split up since then? No, Dinah had no wish to hear her mother spout foolishness. She sat and ate her potatoes in silence; in silence her mother watched her from the door. It took very little time for Dinah to be ashamed of herself for having hurt her mother so. But Dinah could think of no apology that would not also invite her mother to go ahead and offer her advice after all. So Dinah ate her potatoes, got up from the table, went to her room, and lay down.

In a few moments she heard the door open, and knew her mother was watching her. Dinah would not look. Her mother spoke anyway. "You'll know what I think whether you want to or not." Dinah said nothing. "I think your brother loves you."

"Too much," said Dinah.

"Yes, too much indeed. He's as bad as Charlie, they both think they can run other people's lives. So here's what I think you should do. I think you should make your own decision, and whatever you decide I'll back you up."

Dinah heard the door close. Her bruises suddenly hurt worse, and her nose suddenly throbbed, but for a moment she felt less homesick, and she could lie there peacefully enough to sleep again.

When Charlie got home for dinner and heard what had happened that morning, he was furious. His shouting woke Dinah in the other room.

"She doesn't even like him!"

Anna's answers were softer, but still clear. "Liking isn't everything. A husband's better than not. And Dinah's ruined otherwise." Dinah felt a stab of bitterness at that. Mother might be willing to leave the decision up to her, but she did have a firm opinion, after all. Dinah knew her mother well enough to know that Anna would find many small ways of letting Dinah know what she ought to do.

"How is Dinah ruined!" Charlie demanded. "She's as clean as any girl could be." Dinah noticed that Robert, married, called her a woman; Charlie, still half a child, called her a girl. They see themselves in me.

"She has the name of it, anyway, and that's what ruined is, having the name of it. What other husband will she get?"

"Better than him, or none at all."

"None? You don't know what you're talking about, Charlie, you're only a boy. It's better to have a bad husband than none at all. I should know. I've had both."

It was an argument that silenced Charlie, even if it didn't convince him. He couldn't answer such appeals to adult knowledge. He knew he was still outside that world, and his ignorance humbled him a little—one of the few things that could.

Later, his dinner done, Charlie came softly into Dinah's room. She didn't pretend to be asleep.

"How are you?" he asked.

"I'll be fine. Don't be late to work."

"Mother told me about Robert's and Matthew's little plot. I'm against it."

"I overheard."

"Don't do it. You don't have to, you really don't. I'm due for a raise, they like my work, we can save the money and you can leave here, go to another city, start over. And even if you stay here, you'll be free. I'll pay for you to go to school. You can be a scholar, and never have to worry about a husband until you want to."

He went on about his plans for her; she let him. But as he talked she realized that he had no better alternative for her, really, than Robert had. Either way she was to be dependent on someone, unfree and owned by someone, forced to accept someone else's decisions in her life.

"Charlie," she said at last, "I don't want to take your money or Matthew's home. I just—want to get a job and live my life."

"But you can't get a job here. There's no overseer who won't have heard of you, only the way Uray'll tell it, there's not a one who'd hire you. He'll tell them you're a bad worker and when he called you in to fire you, you threatened to tell everyone he raped you. And so he gave you a good licking and bravely said, 'Say what you like, girl, I'll have no truck with baggage like you!'"

"Who'd believe that?"

"Not many. But they'd know that you were trouble—and anyone who hired you would risk the suspicion of wanting to have you for a paramour. I may be only a *child*, Dinah, but I know *that* much."

"How do you know it?"

"Because that kind of thing happens where I work, too."

"There aren't any women there."

"Doesn't always take women," Charlie said. "I've got to go back now."

Dinah was horrified. "Charlie, what do you mean? What's happened at your place?"

"Nothing. I was lucky, I came in high, the owners know me and when a man tried it with me I got round him. He leaves me alone now, hates me but I'm safe enough. You're helpless, though. Nothing you can do without connections."

That was no news to her. But another idea struck her. "Charlie, I know my numbers, I know all you've taught me. Can't you get me work at your firm?"

"As a *bookkeeper?*" The thought was obviously absurd to him. That was all the answer she needed. If her own brother, who knew her ability, could not imagine her there, no other man would consider her for a moment.

"You'd better go now, Charlie."

"Don't even consider marrying that woodenhead. We'll find another way around this." He patted her shoulder and left.

She thought it ironic, almost funny that even though Charlie understood her better than the others and knew the idea of marrying Matthew would appall her, he was the one who inadvertently convinced her to say yes to Matthew's proposal. But he had made the choices clear. Either wife to Matthew or wife to no one, and if wife to no one then bound to Charlie's generosity all her life, for she'd get no decent work. She did not doubt the permanence of Charlie's generosity, of course. But as a wife, even Matthew's wife, she would have a place in the world, a stature among women that she would never have as a maiden. And food and clothing would be her right, as a wife; she wouldn't have to be damnably and eternally grateful for every crumb that fell to her. She would not be despised by the world. And, perhaps, she would not even despise herself.

Matthew. After all, he wasn't a bad man, just bad for her. It was not her privilege to be choosy now. Matthew or worse— the only alternatives. So she would take Matthew and be for him as good a wife as she could, and she would have this consolation: that whatever problems marriage with that well-meaning oaf might mean, her marriage would be happier than her mother's had been.

When she announced her decision that night, Charlie wanted to argue, but Dinah silenced him with a look. It's my life, and I've chosen it, she said. He confined himself then to one snide comment about family members being sold into slavery, a reference back to the chimney sweep episode that Robert magnanimously ignored. Soon Matthew came to ask her formally. He was even more shy than ever, and managed to say everything as clumsily as it could possibly be said, but Dinah made it easy for him. She noticed, however, that under his words there was more than a hint that he didn't believe her story about Uray, that he was sure Uray had succeeded and she was no longer a virgin. Most disturbing was the fact that this seemed to make her even more attractive to him: she was the woman that the overseer could not resist, and now he was getting her with no resistance at all. The allure of the fallen woman who forsakes sin to marry the charitable man who will save her from hell. Matthew was even more dismally stupid than she had thought. But she smiled anyway, for he was really the only choice she had; she said yes with all the tenderness she could muster.

Afterward Matthew and Robert manfully finished off a jug of beer to celebrate and left singing, with Mary scolding behind them. In the ensuing silence, when the song had at last faded, Dinah kissed Charlie and her mother, smiled as if she were happy, and went off to bed, where she did not sleep for hours, just lay there with her arms crossed over her breasts like a gate that should not be opened or all the griefs of the world would surely come in. Come in? No, escape. For they were already in her, held deep, and she did not want to know them any better than she did.

They married three weeks later, and though there were loud whispers about her daring to wear white, they carried it off well, and Charlie borrowed from his employers to give her a gift: seven books and a small cabinet to keep them in, a precious gift that she valued more than any other. Charlie—he had the mind and the heart to be a good man, and she loved him.

After the ceremony, despite the many people shouting and clapping Matthew on the back and kissing Dinah and crying, Charlie managed to take her aside and say, "I'm sorry."

"Not now, Charlie," she said, turning away.

"No! I just want to tell you that this has taught me something. That nine pounds a month is nothing. Ten times that is nothing. If I had been rich I could have had Uray's head for this, and whatever story I told the world would have believed. It's too late now, for you. But I just want you to know. Whatever it takes, whatever comes in the future, Charlie Banks Kirkham is going to be so rich that no one will ever be able again to bend the life of someone that I love."

"No, no, no, Charlie," she whispered, taking his face between her hands. "Don't talk like that. Don't you love me?"

The question hurt him, and young as he was the tears came easily to his eyes. "You know I do."

"Then be happy for me. Please, so I can do this well."

It was a confession; she was inviting him to take part with her in a conspiracy of truth. "I will," he said, and immediately he made a pathetic attempt at a smile. "Can I visit you?"

"You have to," she said. "We have books to read together." She hugged him and went back to her wedding.

Matthew was waiting for her, not hiding his eagerness very well. The sooner the dinner was done, the sooner the wine was all drunk, the sooner the late-staying guests were gone, then the sooner her clothes would come off and he would achieve the goal he had damn well earned by now. She smiled at him prettily, and she knew he thought she was as eager as he. She still believed that a good marriage could begin with a lie, and after all, this lie was not so hard to tell, for he was so eager to believe it that it would never occur to him to question it.

➽➽➽ BOOK THREE ⬅⬅⬅

*In which debts are incurred
and accounts are called due,
and some find themselves bankrupt
when they thought they were rich.*

❧ First Word ❧

The more I immerse myself in the nineteenth century, the more I value their vices. Especially hypocrisy, I am grieved that we have lost the art of lying decorously to each other.

Cultured people were all actors then, playng exquisite roles, creating themselves with every word they uttered. Parties were improvisational plays, with scenes and acts, with curtains and encores. Even home life was lived as high drama. Not the low comedy we rustics act out now. *Our* conversation is modelled on the inanity of the talk show host; *our* thoughts are created for us by pollsters and journalists, who do not respect the role we *wish* to play, but instead distill us into percentiles or cast us as good guys and bad guys in a melodrama in which the journalist himself is always the knight in white armor, the man in the white hat.

We are still actors, but the play is melodrama now, out of our control, acted by amateurs who are such fools as to believe the parts they play. Give me again the days of glorious hypocrites—they knew they were artificial, but the artifice was beautiful.

—O. Kirkham, Salt Lake City, 1981

↘ 13 ↙

Robert and Charlie
Manchester, 1838

ROBERT GOT BORED EASILY in meetings. He always had. But now it was getting worse, so that the meeting had scarcely begun when he got up and left the room and went out the back into the courtyard. Matt looked at him questioningly when he got up, but Robert only grinned and Matt kept his seat. The speaker droned on.

Even outside, Robert could hear him. Rights of man. Free association. Trades unions. The national federation of labor. God-given dignity for all men.

Well, Robert thought, if it's God-given, why the hell hasn't God taken some steps to spread it around?

The courtyard was fairly clean, but that only meant that the stench was barely endurable. A child came out of one of the inner-facing cottages and squatted in a corner of the yard, unperturbed at Robert's frank observation. This is the common man, Robert thought. Give them all the rights they clamor for, and what will they do with them? He tried to imagine Anna letting him shit in a corner, even when he was a child. Unthinkable. Some people were born low, Robert knew, for all that the theorists shouted about equality. Most people, perhaps. Most people are exactly where they belong in life. Only a few of the rich deserve to be low—those who squander their fortunes, as Robert's grandfather had done. And only a few of the poor deserve to be rich—those with the courage and drive to achieve wealth.

He looked up and saw no stars. In Manchester there were no stars to be seen, the smoke loomed over the city, preparing to pounce. At times like this it felt heavy and oppressive.

But it was different in the factory. There the smoke was closer tied to the fire, and Robert tended his steam engines and gave power to the machines. Smoke was only a sign that the power was coming. It was the dark face of the fire, and Robert breathed in the smell of it as other men drank their liquor.

Other men drank their liquor; other men sat in political meetings and believed in all the talk of votes for the workingman, power for the people. In America, maybe, the common man might have some strength; but then, America was a land of savages. Robert had hoped once that when the Parliament was reformed, some of the power might filter down to the people. But of course that could never happen. Now instead of boroughs being in the pockets of great lords, they were in the pockets of substantial business interests; great money had taken the place of great names, that's all. Workingmen could get together all they liked. They could make fiery speeches and talk rashly of strikes and whisper cautiously of revolution, but it would come to nothing.

I will not come to nothing, Robert whispered. I have the power of coalfire in my blood, and I am as fit to run the gears of England as any man alive. Why should I destroy myself to keep fellowship with these pitiful supporters of a doomed cause? If the power goes to the men with money, then what I need is money. And so I'll get it.

"You're taking a long time plucking daisies, Robert," Matthew said from behind him.

Robert was startled, but he only turned calmly and said, "Didn't come for that."

"They don't like the way you leave so much these days during meetings."

"Don't they now?"

"Makes them think you're off with the police."

"Neither the police nor the militia could find their arse with their hands tied behind their back."

Matt laughed. It was what Matt was best at. Robert found himself getting irritated. Matt never knew when a thing wasn't really funny.

"So what *do* you do out here?"

"Plan what to do with my second thousand pounds."

"What happened to the first?"

"If I had the first thousand, I wouldn't have to sit out here dreaming, now, would I?"

"We're both dreamers, Robert."

Maybe you are, but I'm a maker.

Matthew thought for a moment. He always did that, Robert reflected, before he said something unusually stupid. "We ought to be more like your brother Charlie."

"Charlie! And how should *we* be like a little boy?"

"Well, he makes good wages, Robert."

"He makes clerk's wages. If he's very, very good, when he's fifty he'll be a partner in the firm and he'll earn only five hundred in a year, maybe even a thousand, if he's very lucky."

"You're right. I'd be ashamed to have so little."

"Mark me, Matthew. Five years from now I'll have more than enough to buy Charlie's little counting house out of my household budget."

"And when you've bought it, you'll sack him?"

Robert was appalled. "My own brother?"

"Oh, don't get your Kirkham face on, it's what I like least about you—and Dinah, too. When she gets her Kirkham face I know there'll be no peace until I give in to her. Yes, your own brother. You know you detest him."

"A brother's a brother."

"So you don't sack him. So you give him a big raise in wages. He'll know it came from you, and it'll gall him all the more."

Matthew was getting uncomfortably close to Robert's unspoken wishes. For a fool, Matthew was sometimes wise. Never, though, when it was convenient. "Who gives a damn for Charlie? It's Parliament I'm after. Not these silly meetings."

Matthew grinned. "Parliament? To bomb it, Mr. Guyfawkes?"

"To sit in it," Robert answered testily.

"You, a common engineer with greasy hands, *you* sit in Parliament? While you're at it, why not wish to be king?"

"The king's an old fart who loses power every day."

Matt looked terrified. "My Lord, Robert, what are you trying to do? Get us transported? I hear Australia isn't heaven, you know."

"I'm just telling you, Matt. It's time for me to move on. Move up. The meetings are getting me nowhere. I've been to the last of them. I won't be back."

"I thought you believed in the rights of the workingman."

"The workingman will have rights when the rich men give it to them. When I'm rich, I'll fight to give the vote to the poor. But while I'm poor, I can't do a damn thing for anybody."

"I didn't know you had a rich uncle who was leaving it all to you."

"Out your nose, Matt. You're still my friend, whether you believe in me now or not. In six months, if you want a piece of what I'm doing, you just say so and you're in. And in five years I can promise you there isn't a rich house in Manchester we won't be welcome in."

"Go on then, Robert. I thought you were being serious."

"When I walk into the Exchange the price of cotton will rise."

Matt laughed, punched Robert in the arm. "Come back in, Robert. Everyone has dreams, but you can still keep fellowship."

"I'm not going in, Matt. Never again."

"Well, for all that, you'll have to go through the cottage to get home from here."

"Maybe *you* will." Robert walked across the court and began climbing up the drainpipe. The pipe was old and most of the water circumvented the drainage system anyway, but the pipe held well enough and in a few moments Robert was sitting on the edge of the roof, regarding Matthew with a smile.

"Come down, you silly fool!" Matt was laughing, of course.

I have ascended out of hell, and you're laughing. Robert got up and began going over the roof.

"Where are you going?"

"To the railroad, Matey! Coming?"

"No! Come down!" But Robert did not come down. So

Matthew also scrambled up the drainpipe and joined Robert on the roof. "Hope the constables don't see us here," he said, out of breath. "They'll have us as dancers sure enough."

"I don't plan to stay up here long." To prove his point, Robert went to the street side of the roof, let himself slide out off the edge of the roof, dangled for a few moments, then dropped to the ground and rolled.

He looked up at Matthew, who was standing near the roof's edge, shaking his head.

"Good God," Matthew said. "Didn't you break your leg?"

"Just roll when you hit bottom, and you'll come up fine."

Matthew tried it, much more awkwardly but well enough that he broke no bones in the fall. "At least I think nothing's broken."

"If you can think about it, nothing's broken."

They made their way to the railroad, then. It was the Manchester-Birmingham line. It came in as far as Store Street and stopped. The left track was empty; on the right track a train was standing idle. It was half-loaded with cargo. Because they were both engineers, they went at once to the steam engine sitting on its little platform and wheels.

"Pitiful little thing, isn't it?" Matt said, stroking the boiler.

"Hasn't enough guts to push a cow out of the way. But it moves. And pulls a load."

"There's no future in them," Matthew said. "Hauling coal, maybe. But the canals are cheaper and can carry more."

Robert said nothing. He just fondled the engine, measured the gauge of the track with his step, compared weights and tolerances with the huge steam engines at the factory.

"And it's impractical," Matt went on. "Has to carry its own fuel with it. The farther you go, the more coal you have to bring, and so if you go any distance at all, you can't carry any cargo above the engine's fuel supply."

Robert only nodded. He knew better. He knew in his mind the shape of an engine that would be light enough to move yet strong enough to pull a train three times the size of this one, and probably go faster to boot.

"There'll come a day," Robert finally said, "when a train will go twenty-five miles an hour, carrying more load than a canal boat."

"And what difference will it make? People will still be

starving in Manchester, no matter how fast the trains move."

Robert looked at Matt, wondering how his good friend could be such a fool. "You're married to my sister, Matt."

"And you're married to mine."

"Do you plan for Dinah to be an engineer's wife, always? When you're done fighting for the six points of the charter, when the Grand National's formed and taken over England, she'll still be an engineer's wife, won't she?"

"There's nothing finer than to be the wife of a workingman."

"Do you believe that?"

Matt nodded defiantly. "With all my heart, Rob."

"Start using your head, then. When *your* sister is a rich man's wife, then by God my sister had better be, too."

"When God leaves us money in our boots, then our wives will be rich."

"In a year you'll come to me. You'll want a part of what I have, Matt. And do you know what I'll say to you?"

Matt tried to take it as a joke, and laughed as he said, "No."

"I'll say yes. But not for your sake, Matt. For Dinah's."

"Well, just so I live in comfort all my life." Matthew laughed, but soon realized that Robert didn't share his mirth. He fell silent. They began to walk home together in darkness. Up Store Street to Great Ancoats, then up Jersey to Prussia. They talked about a lot of things; about nothing. When they neared Matt's cottage, he started talking about Dinah.

"She's not lively, you know, Rob," he said. "Not lively at all."

Robert could not figure what Matt meant by lively.

"She's cheery enough with little Val, of course. And she's glad enough about expecting another. You knew that she was that way again, I expect."

"I knew."

"But she doesn't seem to like it, you know?"

"Like what?"

"The blanket hornpipe, man, must I spell it for you? She avoids me. I thought when I married her that she'd be lively."

"It's not a thing a brother ought to talk about," Robert said.

"For a freethinker you're a bit of a prude, Robert. I had just thought that what with the overseer and all, she'd be glad to have a younger man in her bed. But do you know? I think she was a virgin when I married her."

Robert stopped in the road. "She damn well *was* a virgin."

"So I said, Rob. So I said."

"I mean she damn well was. I told you so at the time."

"Well, a brother has to say such a thing, so I didn't quite take you at your word." Matt saw immediately that it was the wrong thing to say. "I don't know what you're so upset about, Robert."

"Go home to my sister, Matt, and treat her kindly. The girl you married was clean."

"I don't beat her, you know."

"She's a lady, Matt. You treat her with respect. You don't go thinking evil things about her."

Matt turned resentful. "She's *my* wife, you know."

"She's my sister, Matt, and she was *that* before she knew you."

Sarcastically Matt answered, "Oh, yes, I know how thick you Kirkhams are. No one was ever a family except you. Well, Rob, if you're such a loving hutful of happiness, why hasn't your brother set you up for your railroad scheme?"

"My brother! Charlie's earning a wage, he doesn't own the money that passes through his books."

"But Hulme does. And Charlie knows him."

"He knew the old one. The old one's dead."

"I'm sure Charlie has a thousand excuses. But he knows young Hulme, and he could introduce you if he wanted."

"I haven't asked him."

"That's what I figured. Oh, you Kirkhams are such a lovey crew, but you can't even ask your brother to introduce you to his friend. Or is it that you don't believe that your ideas are really good enough to get capital?"

Robert knew how Matthew was manipulating him—Matthew was too clumsy to be subtle—but Robert also knew that he was right. Why *hadn't* he asked Charlie? It simply hadn't occurred to him, that's all. But why not try now? If Hulme was at all clever, he'd know the value of what Robert had to offer. A simple introduction would be enough. Taking anything from Charlie's unforgivingly generous hands would be galling—but he'd put up with a lot more gall than that if it let him build the engines he dreamed of.

"I see," Matthew said. "You're afraid of Charlie."

"I am," Robert said. "Afraid that someday I'll lose control and go to hell as a fratricide."

"You aren't afraid of Charlie and you don't believe in hell,

Robert Kirkham. But you'll never talk to Charlie about it."

"I'll talk to him tonight. See if I don't end up talking all this through with Mr. Hulme."

"I was joking, Robert. There isn't a hope in the world of Hulme going into business with the son of his former servant."

Robert refused to let himself get angry at the slighting reference to his mother. Much of Matt's value as a friend was that he didn't always say what would please people, that he sometimes said the truth. So Robert let the insult pass, and then invited himself into Matthew's cottage for coffee.

They found, to their surprise, that Charlie was there visiting Dinah, with a book of poetry in his hands and a slightly embarrassed look on his face. "Stopped by on my way home from work."

Matthew grinned, but Robert saw that he was not pleased. What, Robert thought, is Matt jealous of Charlie?

"Two hours is a bit of stopping by," Robert said.

Charlie's eyes flashed at his brother. "I had a book of Wordsworth, and we've been reading together."

Dinah sat in her chair, Val asleep on her shoulder, the boy's legs cast over the broad abdomen that held the next child. Robert did not like looking at his sister pregnant, perhaps because he held so near in his memory the conception of his own children, and could not see Dinah's growing belly without also thinking of Matt covering her in his clumsy way. It embarrassed Robert. He was not responsible for everything, he knew, but for this he partly was, as if he had placed on Dinah at least some of the great weight she carried, and not the lightest part of it, either.

Dinah smiled up at Robert. It came to him as a relief. Benediction. She still loved him, despite Matthew. And why despite him? Why shouldn't she love the fellow? Robert loved him, after all, and forgave his inadequacies because he was such good company—why should he feel sorry for Dinah, who had the same good company? No, Dinah did well, Dinah was happy. Wasn't she smiling?

"You should read some poetry, Robert. It would do you good."

No doubt Matthew felt himself left out of a Kirkham family conversation; he insisted on making himself a part of things—even, apparently, a quiet argument. He reached for the book.

"Let me have a read, then. Maybe poetry can do us *all* good."

Reluctantly Charlie handed the book to him. Robert was amused at that, to see Charlie handing a sacred book to the infidel. Poor Charlie—such a hoity-toity fellow about learning, it never occurred to him that someone like Matt might read poetry, too.

Matt opened the book and awkwardly began to read. "She dwelt among the untrodden ways," he declaimed. "Do you want to hear it?"

Who could say no? Dinah tried, saying gently, "Perhaps this isn't the best time for poetry."

"It's a good enough time," Matt said. "'She dwelt among the untrodden ways, beside the springs of Dove, a maid whom there were none to praise, and very few to love.' Now there's a nice rhyme, I think."

Robert cringed a little. Perhaps Charlie had been right when he wanted to withhold the book. Matt read it like a nursery song. Jack and Jill went up the hill, to fetch a pail of water, pause at the end of every line, beat the accents with your body as you read. Like a child. Mercifully, Matt didn't finish reading. But mercy goes only so far, for now Matt said, "Well, now, was that all right? You read it, Charlie—the same poem! I'd like to see if you could do any better."

Didn't Matt know what he would do to himself in the eyes of his wife and his best friend? And Charlie would have no mercy, he wouldn't read woodenly or make mistakes in order to leave Matt some pride. No, of course not. Charlie took the book and read with his sweet and expressive voice, bringing the poem to life, so that the rhythms were not the main thrust of the sound of it, but rather an accompaniment to the meaning.

> A violet by a mossy stone
> Half hidden from the eye!
> —Fair as a star, when only one
> Is shining in the sky.

And then Charlie's voice grew softer, and there was a hint of emotion in it, not like an orator pretending to weep, but as if Charlie himself were the poet, a little ashamed to let his emotion be seen, yet unable to quite contain it.

> *She lived unknown, and few could know*
> *When Lucy ceased to be;*
> *But she is in her grave, and, oh,*
> *The difference to me.*

Against his own will Robert felt tears smarting at his eyes. It wouldn't do to let either Matt or Charlie see that he had been moved, so Robert looked away. Looked toward Dinah, and saw that she, too, was touched. But oddly so: she did not weep, but rather looked away toward the door of the house, her eyes full of reflection, as if she longed to escape through the door, as if she were imprisoned here, like Lucy in her grave; as if she dreamed of a lover who would say, "Dinah's in her gaol, and, oh, the difference to me." But no—that was just the mood of the poem, just the sort of thing Charlie would want Robert to think of. It was Charlie's voice, the actor in him that brought such melancholy thoughts to Robert's mind.

As for Matt, Robert need not have worried. Matthew was oblivious to what happened to the poem when Charlie read it. "See? I made no more mistakes than Charlie did," he said.

Dinah smiled patiently. "You read very well, Matt."

"So what I want to know is, why do you always have Charlie over here reading to you, and you never ask *me* to read?"

Oh, Matthew, hold your tongue, Robert wanted to shout. Yet he could think of no civil thing to say to forestall such a question; Dinah, too, held her tongue; and for once it was Charlie who eased someone else's problem.

"How would *I* get any practice reading it, if she never let me read to her?"

"Practice! What's to practice?" Matt demanded.

"It's that I want to write some poetry," Charlie said, "and reading aloud helps me learn how the thing is done."

Unaware of how easily Charlie could have humiliated him, Matt blundered on. "Write poetry! What a thought! And to think grown men do it, too. Poetry's for ladies and fine foppish gents, not men like us who have strength in our arms. You, Charlie, you're a clerk, and that's womanly enough that I suppose poetry suits you."

Charlie might have exploded at that, and the night would have ended in a bitter quarrel in which Robert would have been bound to take his brother's part, but Dinah mended it. "That's why I never ask you to read to me, Matt. I know you have better things to do, and I'm just womanly enough to need it now and then. Charlie humors me, don't you, Charlie? But that's enough for tonight. Robert's here, and perhaps you can walk together for a ways in the darkness."

It was an excuse that both Robert and Charlie jumped at —a chance to avert a quarrel with Matthew tonight. It was plain Matthew had been displeased to find Charlie here. Not that Matthew had ever ordered Charlie not to visit when he was away from the house. But Matt had a crazy streak of jealousy. He feared no lusty paramour for Dinah—what he feared was someone who would make her dissatisfied with her unintellectual husband. Rather than rejoicing that she found her satisfaction with someone as harmless as her brother, Matt resented her for needing anything at all that he could not provide.

So Charlie and Robert said their good-nights and left Matt and Dinah alone together with baby Val and the squirming animal that inhabited Dinah's womb. Out on the street, they were silent awhile. Then Robert realized that if he were ever going to enlist Charlie's help in getting capital from Hulme, there would be no better time than now, when they were temporary allies on the side of poetry against Matt the Philistine.

"You read well," Robert said.

"Not so well," Charlie answered.

Robert chuckled. "Better than I had heard it read before, though I'd never heard the poem before tonight."

Charlie laughed, understanding Robert's oblique way of comparing him to Matt without directly speaking ill of their brother-in-law.

"It's only Wordsworth, and not at his best," Charlie said. "You should hear Lord Tennyson. I've been memorizing 'The Lotos-Eaters.' It's Dinah's favorite."

"Well, then, let's hear it."

Charlie was startled, and tried to beg off, but Robert insisted. Robert was not being insincere, either. Hearing someone else read so badly had given him at least a fleeting appreciation for his brother's gifts, for that damnable voice he had so often cursed for reciting endlessly while Mother worked. And certainly Robert's enthusiasm was increased by realizing that he and Charlie were, after all, brothers, two of a kind however different they were in some ways. Charlie could read, but

Robert had enough ear to know good reading from bad. Likewise, Robert could build, and Charlie would certainly know that Robert's gifts were worth investing in. So Robert insisted, and Charlie recited the poem as they walked along, speaking in a fine voice that interrupted the few nighttime passersby and brought many people to their windows to hear what man it was who walked along in the night, crying out poetry in a powerful and fervent voice.

> *Surely, surely slumber is more sweet than toil, the shore*
> *Than labor in the deep mid-ocean, wind and wave and*
> *   oar;*
> *O, rest ye, brother mariners, we will not wander more.*

The words hung in the air, full of wistfulness and relief and rejoicing. Robert was strong with the liquor of the words, feeling something of an Odysseus himself. He did not care that the words were in praise of the sweet release of death; there was too much life in Robert for him to care much for the melancholy of the fashionably romantic poet. What he took from the poem was what he took from every good thing: hope.

The words had not quit echoing in the street when someone's voice came loudly: "Just a couple of drunks." Then a window slammed shut. Charlie and Robert burst out laughing at once, drunken on poetry and even more on the heady wine of brotherhood. They were inexperienced at it; they trusted it too much, thinking their momentary affection was stronger than it was, and would last longer than it could.

"Charlie," Robert said.

"Mm?"

"We're brothers, man. Why shouldn't we profit together?"

Robert did not notice how Charlie immediately began walking a few inches farther away from him.

"I have a plan, Charlie. An engine to pull a train that I know will be profitable, both to run and to sell. I'm a good engineer, and even more I think I could be a good businessman."

"How much do you need?" Charlie asked.

This time Robert heard the lack of enthusiasm in Charlie's voice, and he understood it. It annoyed him that Charlie assumed he wanted a handout. "No, I don't want to borrow money from you, Charlie. I'm talking about five or ten thousand pounds over the next few years, and I think that sort of investment is still a bit beyond you."

Charlie immediately relaxed. "Not that I wouldn't mind investing in your scheme," he said. "I think you know your work—Matt says you do, and he'd know—and if you can raise the capital I'll be glad for you and I'll expect to see you succeed."

"I was thinking, though. Ten thousand pounds is a bit more than a bank is likely to lend me."

Charlie laughed. "A bit."

"But there are plenty of rich men in Manchester who might be willing to risk capital on a venture like this."

Again Charlie misunderstood. "There are lots of men with money, but I can tell you where it goes—into the tried and true factories or into fine homes and fine clothing; it's that way on all the private accounts we handle. Besides, they're all in strict confidence—I can't tell you about any of them."

"That's all right, Charlie. I don't want you to violate confidence. You don't know any of those fellows personally, anyway, I expect." The words came out against Robert's will, for even as he said them he knew that Charlie would take it wrong, Charlie would take it as a slight, a reminder that he may handle lots of money but he was only a clerk, not regarded as worth knowing by any of the great men. Not that Charlie argued or even answered; Robert was habituated enough by now to know when Charlie was angry and keeping still about it. Robert cursed himself for the blunder, but went on, hoping that Charlie would take it as a minor offense.

"You see, Charlie, there *is* one man that you *do* know. And he does have the money, and if he's as clever as word has it that he is, he might just be glad of a chance to be part of what I plan to do."

"Who's that?"

"Mr. Hulme, of course."

"I haven't seen him more than once or twice since the old Mr. Hulme died."

"But when he comes into the office, he still speaks to you."

"Well, of course, and asks after the family. He's a gentleman, that's all. But he doesn't ask my advice on financial matters. He had the same teacher I had, after all, and there's nothing I know that he doesn't know."

"I'm not asking you to advise him, Charlie. I'm asking you to give me an introduction, for you to arrange for him to give me half an hour. In that much time he'll know whether he's interested or not."

"I can't do that," Charlie said.

"You haven't even thought about it."

"I don't have to," Charlie said. "You're not the first who's thought of asking a rich man like Hulme for capital. They come to the firm every day, men with schemes, men with inventions. Rich men spend half their time avoiding such men. Don't be angry, Robert. I know you're not one of the crazy ones. But *they* won't know. And Hulme will simply tell me, very politely, that you'll have to make an appointment with his secretary."

"That would be enough."

"Secretaries only exist to keep people from talking to their employers. I tell you I can't do it, Robert. I have no influence. Not when it comes to that kind of money. It's a good dream, Robert, but ten thousand pounds!"

"Ten thousand pounds to make ten times that in a few years."

"Of course. But what if it fails, Robert? Will you work the rest of your life to repay even half of the losses? Why should Hulme enter into a partnership with you, when you have no money?"

Robert hated hearing discouragement; hated worse hearing it from Charlie. "And how did Old Hulme make *his* money, find it in the streets?"

"He worked and saved, Robert, and started small, not with a railroad, not with manufacturing train engines. Take my advice and forget it for now."

Take his advice indeed! Charlie, a mere boy, only sixteen years old even if he was taller than Robert by now. "For now? And in five years, maybe I've saved thirty pounds—what good will *that* do?"

"To start a shop, it's good enough."

"A shop!" Robert said the words with contempt.

"Father was a shopkeeper, after all."

"And look what good care he took of his family! I'm not going to be a shopkeeper, Charlie. You watch—in five years I'll be your precious company's biggest client. You'll be doing my books for me, Charlie, and giving me credit, and watching me walk into offices where you can't even get an appointment."

Charlie went stiff and formal. "You may think that way if it pleases you, Robert. I'm sorry if you resent my moderate success. I've had the wisdom to plan for things within my reach, and I'm doing well. If you hope to succeed in life, you'll not waste any more time dreaming of great wealth. That's what Father did, and Father never found it."

"How do you know what Father did and what Father thought? He was gone before you were old enough to keep your pants dry."

"Be that as it may, Robert. I'd help you if I could, but I can't do that."

"You mean you won't."

They were in front of the cottage where Anna would be waiting for Charlie's return. Charlie stopped at the door and faced his brother. Robert was keenly aware, was sharply annoyed by the way Charlie looked downward at him from his greater height, as if by conferring a few more inches God also gave a man more authority.

"Yes, Robert, I mean I won't. I mean that your dreams are fine for you, but why should I risk my own reputation in business by trying to promote my working-class brother in his mad schemes for getting rich without labor?"

If Robert had not such perfect self-control, he might have struck Charlie for that—but supercilious as the boy was, he had not said anything crude, there was no reason to strike him except that Robert feared that he was right, that his ideas were worthless after all. It stung him deeply to have his own brother characterize his plans as madness. "I'm not afraid of labor, Charlie. I think I've proved that to anyone's satisfaction."

Charlie shook his head. "You misunderstood me."

"No. I understood you well enough. When I speak to Hulme—and I damned well *will* speak to him—I'll make it very plain to him that you told me I shouldn't. That way he'll know that the madness is all my own, and you by God know better."

At that moment the door opened, and Anna peered out with a worried look on her face. "Boys," she said. "Are you quarreling?"

"No," they both said quickly.

"I just walked Charlie home," Robert added.

"I listened at the door before I opened it," Anna said. "I'm not deaf. I wish you wouldn't argue."

"I'm sorry, Mother," Charlie said, but he never took his gaze from Robert's face.

"I'm not," Robert answered. "Charlie's such a fool he can't recognize opportunity when it comes to him."

"He's your brother, Robert," Anna said.

"That's your own damned fault, Mother, don't try to blame *that* one on me."

"I also wish you wouldn't swear so much," Anna said.

Robert looked at her in silent consternation. She insisted on bringing irrelevancies into the discussion, like family relationships and polite language, instead of arguing to the point. He turned away and walked down the street, making a point of saying, and not softly, "God's bloody wounds! Jesus' bleeding feet!" Let the cocky little prig look down on me, let him call my dreams crazy. I may be a lunatic, but by God I'll be a rich one.

He walked by an empty cart standing at a curb and shoved it with the heel of his palm, pushed so hard that the cart rocked on its wheels and clattered noisily on the cobblestones. No one will cheat me out of my future, Robert insisted to himself. I will believe no lies. And whoever agrees to finance me, *he'll* be the one who's lucky to have such a partnership, not me.

❧ 14 ☙

Hulme
Manchester, 1838

THE BUTLER KNOCKED POLITELY on the library door. Peter Hulme knew Terence's knock—it had more confidence in it than would the knock of any other servant. Hulme set down his book and murmured for Terence to enter. He knew that even if he answered not at all, Terence would still enter, because even though he was a relatively young man, the butler had lost almost all his hearing and usually read lips. That made Hulme's "enter" quite superfluous; but still he said it, because he could not leave it unsaid. It was the way of things with Hulme, and he knew it. He could not leave a morsel of food uneaten—that was how he came to fill chairs to overflowing until he had to order new furniture just to hold his bulk. He could not leave an acerbic remark unsaid—that was why he had no friends, except those who are friends to money regardless of the mannerisms of the money's owner. If something *should* be done, and God only knew how Hulme decided which

159

things were necessities—Hulme would do it or go mad with anxiety until he did. He called it his superstitious nature, sometimes; other times he blamed it on his father for inflicting on him a damnable sense of sin that plagued him whenever he did not do what ought to be done. It made him so predictable that Terence could be sure that no matter what else happened, when a door was knocked upon Peter Hulme would say, "Enter."

The butler entered. "My apologies, sir."

"Quite all right. The book was positively moribund. A man could damage his intellect trying to make sense of Rousseau."

"There's a young man to see you. He has no appointment."

"Then send him away. Why do you bother me with such trivialities?" Again, Hulme only showed annoyance because he knew annoyance ought to be shown. Actually, he had been hoping for some sort of diversion or interruption. The duty of the rich was to serve the public, go to fine parties, and become educated. The parties were painful, the public had no gratitude or honor, and as for education—Hulme had no taste for the great writers. He missed his account books; he missed the bustle of business. But he was a rich man, and he was going to live the life of a man of leisure or die trying. That's what money was *for*, and Peter Hulme would do his duty. "Is he someone I should know?"

"I think not. His name, he says, is Robert Kirkham."

"Kirkham. I don't suppose he's a relative of the Mrs. Kirkham who used to be a part of our household."

"He would have said so, I think, sir."

"What does he want?"

"He has a business proposal."

Hulme sighed. Nothing interesting, then. Just some other ambitious young fellow wanting to ally his young energy with Hulme's aging fortune. They always had the same notions. Buy this, buy that, and watch the money pour in. As if Hulme were incapable of conducting his own investments wisely; as if the Hulme fortune were not already increasing at an excellent per centum every year.

"I told him you wouldn't be interested."

"You were quite correct."

"But he said that you might be interested in hauling nails from Manchester to London at seven pence the ton."

"Seven pence?"

"That's what he said, sir."

"Not seven shillings?"

"Pence, sir."

"He's a liar. Any man can make such numbers up. Seven pence! Send him up—I want to see such cheek before I have you throw him out on his arse."

Terence smiled—smiled the exact half-inch wider in the lips that was protocol. Hulme nodded at him, and Terence left the room. Ah, how good to have a servant who knew how things ought to be, and kept them just so. How good—and how utterly dull.

The young man came in with several rolls of paper under his arm and a timid look about him. Not a promoter, then, not one of the young men who went into debt for a suit of clothes before they bothered with spending a shilling on a book to decorate their minds. More than that, Peter Hulme was sure he recognized the fellow. Had the look about him.

"Robert Kirkham," Peter Hulme said. "Do I know your family?"

"I think not, sir," the young man said stiffly.

Coincidence, then, Hulme decided; or perhaps hearing the Kirkham name had made him think there would be a resemblance. Well, then, he owed him no debt of courtesy.

The young man could not keep his eyes away from the two stories of shelves rising almost out of sight in the haze from Hulme's pipe. "I'm glad you admire my library. However, I will not lend you any books. I'll tell you right now, young man, that I need no help or advice in my business. I have retired from direct involvement and am inactively pursuing a life of leisure. Or rather, letting a life of leisure envelop me. You have interrupted my languor, and I resent it."

Kirkham looked, if possible, even more stiff and awkward. Yet, to Hulme's surprise, there was neither an immediate rush to the door—Hulme's favorite outcome—nor the more common flood of asinine verbiage designed to convince Hulme that *this* was the chance of his lifetime. The young man only said, stiffly, "Sir, I ask only for five minutes of your attention."

"Good God, man, that's more than I ever gave to my wife before she died." Ah—there it was, not the look of horror that some got when he spoke that way, nor the forced laughter that the glad-hands always insulted him with. Instead the boy let a

slow grin come to his face, which quickly faded. Peter Hulme
was delighted. He knew a kindred mind when he saw one,
even when it masked itself in the sort of costume that a workingman was likely to think appropriate for calling on a rich
man. He began to like this Kirkham, a little.

"One minute," Hulme said. "Renewable if you aren't completely asinine."

Kirkham nodded, and immediately untied one of the rolled
up papers, letting the others drop to the floor, as if the library
were a common shop. "Would you hold this end, sir?" Kirkham
asked, and without waiting for an answer slipped the curling
edge of the paper under Peter's hand. Then he unrolled an
unusually well-drawn engineering sketch of a train engine.

"Why are you showing me this?"

"It's a steam engine, sir. To pull a train."

"It's identical to the locomotive that now provides the pro-
pulsion for the trains on my Manchester-Birmingham Railway.
When I need pictures of my own possessions, I'll order them
done."

This time the fellow *did* look shocked. "The Manchester-
Birmingham is yours, sir?"

"I own more of it than anyone else, that pretty much makes
it mine." Hulme waited for the man to roll up his drawings
and retreat, caught in his theft of another man's engineering.
Instead, young Kirkham only looked at him steadily and said,
"So you own a railway already."

"Why? Did you think to sell me another?"

"Perhaps you'd like to improve the one you have."

"Improve it? Mr. Kirkham, I subscribed to the railroad proj-
ect as my civic duty, so that Manchester would not be lacking
in the latest toys for the public awe and titillation, and because
the stock was ridiculously cheap. But I see no point in putting
more money into a mode of transportation that can carry scarcely
anything beyond the weight of its own fuel."

"Exactly," Robert said, and before Hulme could demur, he
was unrolling another paper. This time the engine was unlike
any Hulme had seen before.

"You have conceived of an even uglier locomotive, Mr.
Kirkham. You have my congratulations."

"My uglier locomotive can pull three times the load yours
can, and twice as fast. Yet it's lighter, and uses only a little

more fuel than your engine, so that almost all the gain in power means more freight, and therefore more income compared to expense, and therefore lower prices per ton and more profit per pound of investment."

"You speak as if your engine exists. Does it?"

"It could, at a cost of three hundred eight pounds. For the prototype, of course—later, the locomotives could be made more cheaply. And sold for a little less than you paid for the engines you're using now, without depriving us of a decent profit."

"In other words, these are all plans."

"You can't be making a profit on the trains you're using *now*."

"I can't recall making my profits a matter of public record."

"Mr. Hulme, look at this." And now the young fellow opened a sheaf of drawings, showing details of his engine. He went over point after point, explaining how the design was improved, how it would cost less to make or work more efficiently or allow more capacity. He also pointed out relative drawbacks, but explained why they were unavoidable. At first Hulme was annoyed at being bored with details of engineering, a subject about which he knew little and cared less. He quickly noticed, however, how deftly Robert was explaining his points, never sounding condescending about having to clarify things for someone uninitiated in the rites of steam engineering, yet always making sure that Hulme could easily grasp the significance of the changes he had made. There was no effort to overawe Hulme with technical expertise; rather, Kirkham's effort was all to explain, clarify, and persuade. An appeal to reason, and Hulme responded. He listened. And when after twenty-five minutes young Kirkham at last said, "There it is, and that's why it'll work," Hulme felt he had just been taught a full course in a school of engineering. Now as he gazed at the overall drawing he appreciated the simplicity of Kirkham's design and saw the awkwardness of the engines he now had in use. He also, to his own surprise, believed that Kirkham was the man to build his own designs. Kirkham spoke clearly and well, but so did many fools. The thing that most impressed Hulme was the man's intense reasonableness, his determined yet unabrasive advocacy. It was precisely the mixture of deference and leadership that Hulme longed to find in the men who worked for him, and had never quite found.

"Well, sir," Robert said, rolling up the papers again, "I've taken thirty minutes when I asked for five. I'll leave my address with your butler, in case you wish to send for me."

"No."

"Very well."

"I mean no, I don't want to see you *again*, I want to see you *now*. Half an hour? An afternoon yawns ahead of me, filled with sedate walks around the gardens and, later, visits from my bilious and loquacious acquaintances who, if they understood only half of the subjects on which they have opinions, would be able to replace whole faculties of colleges and lecture endlessly without notes."

To his surprise, young Kirkham did not take it as a compliment. "I didn't come to amuse you, sir," he said. "I came to offer you a share in my engine."

"Mr. Kirkham," Peter said, "when a man is as rich as I am, even the prospect of fantastic profit is merely amusing. Don't roll up your papers, don't leave your address with Terence, stay here and agree on the terms of our partnership, so that I can have my solicitor draw up the papers and arrange for the line of credit that will begin the new company."

Kirkham kept rolling up the papers; as he finished tying them, he said, "Aren't you going to have the Manchester-Birmingham Railway do it?"

"The Manchester-Birmingham is a joint-stock company and I only own a third of the stock. I see no reason why we shouldn't enter into partnership in a new firm, to build your engine. How much capital do you suppose it will take?"

"My best estimate is two thousand pounds, to build the prototype and set up a minimal shop to build more."

"And if the shop is better than minimal?"

"With four thousand pounds, I could hire the best men in Manchester to work with me, and enough of them to build the engine quickly. Competitors are bound to come up with some of these improvements in the meantime, and the more quickly we produce a working engine—"

"*Five* thousand pounds, then, Mr. Kirkham, and you will have three locomotives in production by the time the prototype emerges for trial. As for the partnership, I'll offer you one-tenth ownership and participation in profits."

Kirkham's answer was immediate. "No, sir."

"One-fifteenth, then, but no more."

"I want half. Equal partnership."

Hulme laughed at the audacity of it. "You forget, Mr. Kirkham, that I am putting up all the money."

"And I'm providing all the intelligence."

An acid tongue, then, to go along with the rest of his wit. Hulme smiled. "If the company fails, Mr. Kirkham, you will still have your intelligence, but I will have lost all my money. Since I'm bearing the greater risk, I think it only fair I have the greater return."

Kirkham began gathering up the papers and tucking them under his arm. Hulme was very surprised. The fellow had seemed so diffident when he first arrived, not at all the sort of person who would actually walk out on five thousand pounds of capital over the matter of shares of profit.

Kirkham paused at the door. "Thank you for your time, sir. Should I leave my address with the butler, in case you reconsider?"

"Name of heaven, young man. One-fifth for you. Anything more and you'll go to hell for greed."

Kirkham set his face in an expression that Hulme recognized. He had seen it before, yes, many times. Seen it on young Charlie Kirkham when he was arguing with the old man over some point of mathematics. Seen it on Mrs. Kirkham many a time in a dispute with one of the servants. Robert had lied about his family relationship. Pride, of course—but which kind? Was he too proud to use his family's acquaintance as a means of gaining entry into Hulme's house? Or too proud to admit he was related to a servant? The latter was impossible— he could not imagine this young man being ashamed of his family's past suffering. He simply didn't like to use influence. It made Hulme admire him all the more.

"Mr. Hulme," Robert said, "I'll work with you for twenty percent."

"Good."

"However, all the patents on my inventions will belong to me. I will charge our firm only a nominal royalty, but on a fixed lease. I will sell my next engine where I please, and I assure you, it will be better than this one."

"Nonsense," Hulme answered. "If this engine works as well as it looks like it will, *any* man would want to fund your next one."

"Would *you?*"

"Of course."

"Then you may bid on it like anyone else."

"I won't be bartered with as if this library were a common marketplace!" Hulme shouted.

People usually got frightened when Peter Hulme shouted. This young man did not. "It became a marketplace," Robert said, "when you offered me less than my work is worth. If I own half our company, it will be foolish of me to take my new engines anywhere else. But if I only own a fifth, I'll have no great stake in making the company succeed."

"I can see that working with you is going to be an interesting experience," Hulme said, knocking the ashes out of his pipe in annoyance.

"You'll give me an equal share?"

"I will," Hulme said. "But on conditions of my own. All the patents belong to the firm. Your next three engines belong to the firm. And, if the company should fail, you will work for me for five years—at a good salary—in whatever part of my business holdings I want you to work in."

"Why would you want me, if my engine doesn't work?"

"Because I want a thoroughgoing bastard like yourself working *for* me, not against me, whether this pile of iron you've designed pulls cars or not."

Robert grinned and dropped his papers as he stepped forward to extend his hand to Hulme. Hulme paid him the ultimate compliment—he arose from his chair, at great cost in effort, to shake hands with him.

"I'll have my solicitor draw up the papers, and tomorrow you and I will select a location for your factory. The next day you may begin hiring, though I insist that you advertise for men and not just hire your friends. And tell me, Robert, why did you deny your family?"

For the first time Hulme saw Robert utterly nonplussed, unsure what to say or do. Finally he decided that further denial would be pointless. "I didn't use my mother's name because I didn't come here to ask you for favors for her sake."

"And Charlie?"

"I promised Charlie that I'd tell you he had no part in my coming to you."

The way Robert said it conveyed more than the young man probably realized. So Robert and Charlie didn't get along. "Too bad," Hulme said. "Charlie's the best mind for business in this city, if he keeps learning. I was going to suggest we have him manage your accounts."

"I don't think," Robert said stiffly, "that Charlie would be pleased to work for me."

"Ah." Nor, thought Hulme, would you be pleased to have him working with you. "That is all to our loss. My father loved that boy. Charlie had the mind and heart to learn the lessons that my father taught. If the old man had been as kind to me, had taught me with such patience and delight as he taught your brother, I might have loved the man. But sometimes we are blind to the virtues of those nearest to us."

Robert smiled wanly. "I'm not the one with the blindness, I think. But I must be fair. There are things I did in the past that gave Charlie cause not to love me."

"If all of us were truly known, Robert, all our past acts, no one would love us. And yet God knows us and loves us anyway. Which is a great deal of comfort, if you happen to believe God takes much notice of us. I think I have ample evidence, however, that God pays little heed to this world. If God were just, a scoundrel like my father and a lazy man like me would never have been rewarded with great wealth. Never mind. There are other bookkeepers we can hire. Come here at nine o'clock and breakfast with me. That will give you ample time to take leave of your current employer."

"Yes, sir."

"And if we're to be equal partners, you must call me Peter. And you must also buy a new suit of clothes. Go to Humphrey and Randall and tell them you want a suit very much like the last one they made for me. Except, of course, for the size. Do it this afternoon and pick up the suit tomorrow."

"Can they make it so quickly?"

"Tell them that I would be most grateful if it were ready by half-past eight. I can't take you to negotiate for a proper building dressed like a workingman. The landlords would never treat you with respect. Especially considering that your name will be on the sign above the door."

"Hulme and Kirkham?"

"Lord, no. Kirkham Locomotive Works. It's one thing to own a railroad—that's a public service. But I can't have *my* name associated with *manufacture*."

"That's where your fortune comes from, I thought."

"Indeed it does. My father was a common weaver who happened to have the foresight and the money and the credit to buy a steam engine and a spinning jenny back when no one thought they'd be worth a damn. He was a brilliant man of business, and I've spent my whole life trying to live it down. You see, wealthy people like to pretend their money came from God. They detest reminders that it was earned by wit and labor, and not by superior virtue."

"Why are you going into this business with me, then?"

"I *am* my father's son. And I believe that you and your locomotive may very well bring me more money than spinning and weaving ever have. Not that I know what I'd do with more money than I have now. But it seems like something that I ought to do. My father, I know, would approve."

The statement was full of more truth than Hulme usually allowed himself, and he wondered why he had such confidence in this boy. Certainly not because Robert wouldn't understand his confession. On the contrary, Robert was looking at him with a cool intensity that seemed to see far into him. Why, Hulme asked himself, do I feel a desire—a need—to burden this young man with my ancient bug-bears? Why should I tell him about my feelings toward my father?

"How old are you, Robert?"

"Twenty-two."

"I warn you. I'm getting older and in the morning I have an unusually crabbed disposition. Try not to be too youthful around me before noon, or I shall be rude."

Robert smiled. "For you I'll age a few years."

And then he was gone, drawings and all, the library door pulled shut behind him before Hulme even had time to summon Terence. Another gift that Hulme had long looked for and never found—a man who knew how to leave when a conversation was ended. In workingman's clothing he had come at last, a true gentleman, a true equal. Only twenty-two. Well, that youth was a forgivable sin. Besides, he'd grow out of it. Indeed, he had already grown out of it, already had more confidence, more wisdom than most men. That's why I want to surrender responsibility to him, Hulme decided. Because he looks like the sort of man who can bear it.

❧ 15 ❧

Dinah Kirkham Handy
Manchester, 1839

DINAH MOVED INTO HER new prison in March. Matthew had started working for Robert three weeks before, and soon decided that if Robert was moving to a better part of town, so would he. The new place had six rooms, and Dinah watched, darkly amused, as her mother exclaimed again and again, "If only we could invite our old neighbors to see us now!" What, isn't it enough that we have more than enough for our needs, Dinah wanted to say. Must we also gloat over those less fortunate? But no, I am being uncharitable. To Anna the new prosperity was not so much good fortune as the restoration of the proper order of things. For Anna all was as it should be now, people in their proper class, money in the right pockets. She had had to live among the poor, but she had never *become* poor. It was a precious difference to her.

But not to Dinah. What was rich and poor to *her?* The money was Matthew's, and the only way Dinah could influence the spending of it was by persuasion, not by right. She hadn't

even the few shillings she had once earned from the factory—
every penny that she spent had to be accounted for. It was
agony for her, though to his credit Matthew never questioned
a single purchase that she made. She was not grateful for his
kindness, however. He never criticized her because she scru-
pulously avoided buying anything that he would not certainly
approve of. She did not buy clothing for herself unless he gave
her money specifically for that purpose. Only then did she have
any freedom, for the dressmaker would conspire with her to
write a receipt for a bit more than the dress actually cost. The
money Dinah thus saved she kept hidden away; not that Matthew would begrudge it if she told him, but Dinah needed
desperately to have money that he knew nothing about. It was
not the amount, it was the privacy that mattered.

It was a sign of their prosperity that this time there were
three carts, and the carters willingly carried in the trunks and
furniture. Dinah, holding baby Honor, only had to tell the
carters where to put down the various items while Anna made
suggestions and little Val ran under everyone's feet, until finally
he was knocked down by the corner of the divan as it swept
into the parlor. Crying, the boy allowed Anna to comfort him
until the men were gone and all was safe. Then he ran through
the house, looking into every room, opening and closing every
door. At last he came to his mother and shouted, "Are we
home? Are we home?"

"Yes," Dinah answered, "we're home."

But the answer satisfied him no more than it did her. She
had to go through the house with him and tell him who would
sleep in each room, what each room was for. Anna kept smiling
and patting the boy on his head until Dinah wanted to shake
her and say, Do you think Charlie would have grown up as
fine and intelligent as he is if you had spent his entire childhood
patting his head? Dinah held her tongue. Mother was merely
learning how to be a grandmother, just as Dinah was learning
how to be a mother; Anna was certainly doing no worse a job
of it than Dinah.

"What a lovely, lovely home," Anna said at last, her benediction upon the home as she left it.

"It's a pretty place," Dinah answered.

Anna looked at her sharply. "You certainly are mopey for
a woman moving up in the world."

"Am I?"

She had meant: Am I moving up? Anna heard it the other way. "Yes, you can't smile at anyone, and you even get impatient when you see me patting little Val's head. For your information, my dear daughter, *you* had the same curly hair *he* has as a child, and I patted you until you yelled at me to leave you alone. Val isn't old enough to yell at me yet. Don't begrudge me your children. I shan't have any more of my own."

"I'm sorry, Mother. I'm tired."

"Always tired, and yet working less than ever you did before you were married."

That was a nail driven home in one blow. But deny it, deny it, Dinah told herself. "Having babies takes the strength out of me."

Anna immediately softened. "Oh, I know. You're so frail, Dinah. You have a body like your father's sister, your Aunt Alice, who died a maiden at thirty-five. She could never put any meat on her bones at all. It frightens me, sometimes, the way you hardly get fat at all when you're carrying a baby, and then lose all the belly within a few weeks. It's not natural. It's not healthy."

Dinah smiled thinly. "My body seems not to want to have babies."

Anna reached down and picked Val up and squeezed him until the boy yelped and insisted on freedom. "But yours live, Dinah. Weak as your body is, your babies live."

It reminded Dinah of all that her mother had lost over the years. Husband, many children, her proper social station, all security of home and family. It was petty of Dinah to criticize her now, to think ill of her at all, and even more childish for Dinah to feel sorry for herself. In case she ever wondered what real grief and pain looked like, she had only to call upon her mother and see the way the lines grew upon her face. If my six rooms are a gaol to me, what was Mother's hovel by the River Irk? Hell, that's what it was. Anna had been gnawed by Cerberus, and still knew how to rejoice. Dinah forced herself to smile. "Yes, mine live."

Anna reached for Honor. The baby was getting old enough now to know whether she was being held by her mother or not—it would be only a moment before she started bellowing. But in the meantime, it felt good to have her arms empty; the weight of a baby in her arms was such a constant pressure that now her arms felt light, as if she had to hold them down or they would rise. Dinah walked to her window and looked out.

"Daughter," Anna said.

Dinah felt an inward cringing: Anna only called her *daughter* when she was about to teach a lesson.

"Daughter, I see you looking out the windows, I know what you long for."

"Do you?"

"You want to be a child again," Anna said.

"No." Why would you think that, Mother? I was never very happy as a girl.

"You want to be able to walk out the door and come back only when you want to, not when you know you have to prepare a meal or wash a diaper or give your breast to a screaming baby."

Dinah said nothing.

"All women feel that. Do you think men are so different? However much they love their work—and few do—they stare out the window now and then and wish they could lay down their tools and wander where they want, without care for children crying to be fed, without a wife to scold for being late. The good men and the good women feel those things, but they know where virtue is. They do their duty, and come to love it."

"How is such a miracle wrought?" Dinah asked bitterly.

"It isn't, always." Now Anna stood beside her at the window, looking out. Dinah knew what she was looking for. But he would never come back—she knew that and was glad of it.

To Dinah's surprise, Honor was asleep in Anna's arms instead of crying for her mother. She should have been glad of it, but instead she felt a flash of resentment. What, did Honor now love someone else? Dinah stifled the feelings, however, for she knew that it was silly of her to want so much to possess the heart of an infant.

"Dinah," Mother said softly.

Dinah raised her eyebrows as if to say, Go on.

"Dinah, how content is Matthew in your bed?"

It was a question that had never occurred to her, one she did not want to think of even now. How content is *Matthew!*

Do you ask the cup whether the drinker's thirst was slaked? He drank from the cup whenever he wanted, didn't he?

"It's not my business, I know. But Robert left a hint with me a while ago that Matthew was unsatisfied."

Just thinking of the matter made Dinah feel uncomfortable. Suddenly she felt as if she were lying on the bed with Matthew sweating at his work, only now Robert and Anna were standing nearby asking each other, Is she satisfying him? "I've never denied him anything."

"I know it's a delicate thing to talk about, Dinah, and women of our class are above coarse conversation. But I must tell you this—sometimes a man needs to have your desire as well as your consent."

"I remember once, Mother, that you told Mary and me quite the opposite."

"I warned you against too much passion. It didn't occur to me to warn you against too little."

"You were a passionate wife."

"All wives should be."

"You loved your husband."

Anna looked at her fiercely, with the expression that Matt called the "Kirkham face"—it was not Kirkham at all, of course, but Banks, that sharp and heavy axe-like gaze that could not be endured. "Look at what I hold in my arms, Dinah."

Honor was asleep, drooling placidly on the bosom of Anna's dress, making a small dark stain on the dress. Those soft lips, slightly apart, now and then made a sucking motion that recalled the pleasures of giving life to the child. Upstairs Dinah could hear Val's feet clattering on the wooden floors—the boy could never walk if there was room enough to run. Dinah felt what her mother wanted her to feel, an overpowering tenderness for those who depended on her for life and the meaning of life. All that these little ones did and thought was centered around her. All she thought and did was shaped to fit them. Suddenly, seeing Honor in Anna's arms, Dinah could feel herself there, could feel in a certain position of her neck, her head, her arms that once her own body had known that soft place, the shape of it; Dinah knew where she could lay her head nestled between the hard collarbone and the soft swelling of the bosom. As I feel toward my mother, they will feel toward me, my children will. Impatient sometimes, angry sometimes, but never indifferent, for their hearts will always beat in rhythm with my own.

"Look at the little ones," Anna said, "and remember that they are half Matthew."

And suddenly there was Matthew's curling lip in Honor's face. Dinah shuddered.

"More of me than him."

"Half."

"He is half of their bodies. I am all of their lives."

"Think as you like, Dinah. If you love the children, you can never hate the husband, however ill-used you feel."

"Don't tell me that you don't hate Father."

"I don't."

"You should."

"I know I should, but I can't. Not for more than an hour, even the first few days after he left. Now not even for a moment. I think of him and feel only sad. Don't pretend you hate your husband. Don't harden your heart against him, Dinah, don't make him feel like an invader in your bed. You think you don't want him now, but when he despairs of you and goes hunting affection with the whores, then you'll know that what you despised in the having, you crave in the lack."

Dinah turned on her mother. "Whores! What are you saying! What have you heard?"

Anna laughed softly. "You *do* care."

"Whores have *diseases!* I'll kill him if he ever gives me such a loathsome sickness!"

"Dinah, my darling, it's not the disease that provokes you. Mark my words, that's all I say. Make him welcome, or you'll pay for it. And disease is the first and smallest price." Anna gently handed the baby back to her. "Charlie will be home soon, and I have supper to prepare. If he comes here on his way home, send him away quickly, or the meat will be cold."

Despite all her heavier thoughts, Dinah could not help but notice how proudly her mother said "meat." Yes, meat whenever she wanted now, because Charlie earned so well. And Dinah's children would never grow up, as she did, knowing only potato, with onion as a delicacy. We are truly rich. And I am ungrateful to the Lord to cast up small dissatisfactions against great blessings.

"Mother," Dinah said, stopping Anna in the door. "Thank you for helping me."

Anna smiled grimly. "I helped you fill up a house with furniture."

"Thank you also for what you said. I'll try."

Mother's smile softened. "Will you? That's all that anyone can do."

Through the rest of the afternoon, Dinah put things away in the kitchen, filling the cabinet that Matthew had bought for her. Then she prepared dinner, knowing that Matthew would want it hot and ready, a perfect meal to celebrate his being such a good provider. Dinah tried to keep herself from thinking how profitable Robert's friendship had been for Matthew. Matt would come home from a job that Robert had arranged for him and eat a meal prepared by the wife that Robert had provided. Even Matt's own children, in whom he took such silly pride, had been given to him by someone else. Was there nothing Matt could do for himself? He is weak, Dinah said softly. I am stronger, and he rules me. Where is the justice in that? Val cut himself on a knife and Dinah cleaned up the blood and comforted him. Val clung to her and kept saying, "I'm sorry, I'm sorry," as if the cut of the knife had been a punishment for his sins. "It's just an accident, Val. No one did it to you." But Val would not believe it.

It was near nightfall when the front door opened. Dinah was weary, and the meal wasn't ready yet—Matthew was home early. Dinah wiped her hands on her apron and went into the parlor. Instead of Matt, however, it was Charlie. He was carrying a vase of flowers. He looked at her sheepishly. "I was just going to duck in and out, but I couldn't find a place to put the flowers."

Dinah laughed and hugged him quickly. She carried the vase into the dining room and placed it in the center of the table.

"A dining room," Charlie said. "How you've come up in the world. Ah, the miracles of steam."

His voice had a strange edge to it, and Dinah guessed at what caused it. "Do you feel bad that it's Robert's money that pays for this place?"

Charlie shrugged. "Robert had the courage to get it, and the good ideas. I wish him well, I don't resent it at all."

"You don't?"

Charlie smiled. "I refuse to, anyway. No, what bothers me

is that I could have helped him, and I didn't. Do you realize that? A simple introduction, and he would have owed a part of it to me. It would have drawn us together. But I couldn't do a simple thing like sending a note with him to Mr. Hulme."

"It's hard to believe in your own brother."

"I suppose so. But it wasn't so much doubt as—as fear. Of the cost of it. That's what I'm ashamed of. My own brother, and I was too afraid of Mr. Hulme to do well by my own brother."

Dinah noticed how determinedly Charlie still called him "Mr. Hulme," as if to draw more clearly the line between him and Robert, who always called his partner Peter, even to his face, something not a banker or solicitor in Manchester would dare to do. It was a point of honor with Charlie not to presume on his brother's intimacy with a man who once had known Charlie better than Robert. Just another wall between Robert and Charlie.

"Oh," Charlie said. "I didn't mean to be dismal. I brought you this." He handed her a package wrapped in plain paper, but with a short poem on the outside. "For your birthday."

Dinah looked at him in surprise. "My birthday?"

"It's not till tomorrow, I know—this is only April third, but I wasn't sure I'd see you tomorrow. It's a book."

"I would never have guessed."

They both laughed. Charlie always gave her a book.

Val ran into the room, calling loudly, "Charlie! Uncle Charlie!" Charlie lifted the boy to his shoulders, laughing, then as quickly set him down again to dance around him, occasionally clutching at Charlie's knees.

"Hush, Val," Dinah said.

"He's all right. Open the package."

"But this verse on the outside—who wrote it?"

"Do you like it?"

She knew then that he had written it himself. "It's lovely. Would you read it to me?"

"If you like," he said. He was carrying off quite well the pretense that it was by someone else.

The shepherds counted in the twilight. One was
    gone.
Too dark for searches, lightning flashing in the
    hills,

The evening drove them inside, leaving the
　　sheep alone.
Only the shepherdess went splashing through the rills
Until she heard the bleating, answering her call.
She lifted him and bore him on her shoulders home,
Saying, Look! See what I found in the lee of the
　　ruined wall!
The one who had the will but not the wit to come!

"It's lovely," Dinah said, remembering well the rainy night when she found a younger, smaller Charlie shivering in the rain beside the piles.

"It's not the best of verses," Charlie said. "It has six beats to the line, and the rhymes slant too much, and the meter's far from right."

"You read it beautifully."

"I hoped you'd like it."

On impulse she reached out to him. Charlie embraced her. She was surprised at how tall he was, and how thin compared to her more massive yet shorter husband. She realized that she had not held him so since—since Old Hulme's death? Or had she even embraced him then? Sweet Charlie, who would turn seventeen this year, each birthday making him less of a prodigy in his bookkeeping duties. You're in a prison, too, aren't you, Charlie? It's time for your next step, time to rise, as your brother rose. And you could do it, just by asking Robert to support you as you study law or go to the university—you could do it, except that how can you ask Robert to believe in your dream, when you didn't believe in his? So you write a poem on the paper that will be torn off when the gift is opened, creating yourself in words that are bound to be torn and burned.

"Good God," said Matthew's shocked voice from the door.

Startled, Charlie and Dinah turned around. Matthew was leaning, stricken, against the doorjamb, his face red. It took an instant for him to recognize Charlie.

"Oh. Oh, it's you. Gave me a start."

Immediately Matthew pretended that it had been nothing, that he hadn't been surprised at all. But Dinah and Charlie both knew exactly what he had thought, coming into his own home and seeing Dinah and a young man locked in an embrace. Dinah felt an unaccountable rage. How dare he even suppose such a thing! How dare he immediately *assume* her unfaithfulness. But because he said nothing, she could say nothing. "Welcome home, Matt," Dinah said. "Thank you for this new cottage. It's beautiful."

"Daddy's home!" Val yelled as he launched himself at his father.

"No more than you deserve," Matt said, picking up his son.

"I like it," Charlie said. "Nicer to think of you in this place than shut away in the dismal old place."

Matt still had suspicion just under the surface. "The old place wasn't so bad."

"But six rooms, I mean," Charlie said, refusing to quarrel. "Why, you'll be like small shot in a bucket!"

"That we will," Matthew said. "Will you stay for supper?"

"No, thanks," Charlie said. "I should get home."

"Yes," Dinah said. "Mother asked me to hurry you home if you happened to stop by here. Matthew! Look at this package Charlie brought me. A birthday gift."

Matthew looked worried. "But Robert said your birthday was tomorrow."

"Oh, it is," Charlie said. "I'm early."

But all Dinah heard was that Matthew still had to be reminded of her birthday.

"You haven't opened it," Matthew pointed out.

"Tomorrow," Dinah said. "There's a poem on the outside that I want to keep and copy down. It's by a new poet whose work hasn't been much published yet."

Charlie grinned. "I can't fool you, can I?"

Of course Matt didn't understand. "Why would you want to fool her about a poet?"

"It's just a silly joke," Dinah reassured him. "Good-night, Charlie."

Charlie said his good-byes and left. Matt carried Val into the kitchen. "But Daddy, we're eating in *there*," Val protested.

Matt laughed. "I'm too used to being poor and eating in the kitchen." When they were all seated at the table, the food ready to eat, Matt decided to make a show out of it. He insisted on walking around the table and kissing Dinah, then shaking Val's hand and welcoming them to their new home. Then he actually said grace. It so startled Dinah that she nearly laughed during the prayer. Matt was so solemn that she could hardly contain herself. It would be more appropriate, wouldn't it, to offer grace to Robert than to God? But she didn't say it, and Matt didn't notice her near laughter, so all was well.

Matt watched her undress Val and prepare him for sleep, talking constantly about progress on the new locomotive, which was going to be the wonder of the decade. At one point, though, he spoke to Dinah about herself. "You work too hard, Dinah."

"Do I?"

"You look weary. Too thin. In six months, if all goes well, I can get you a servant to do this sort of thing."

"What sort of thing?"

"You know. Bathing the children, cleaning house, cooking."

"I don't want a servant," Dinah said.

"Of course you do," Matt said. "Don't worry, I won't hire one until we can really afford it."

"I say that I'd rather take care of the house myself."

"Not another word, Dinah. I know you feel it's your place to care for me, but Robert says that with servants a woman can finally come into her own. More time for you to read, that sort of thing. You forget, we're going to be rich, and rich people have servants."

"I know," Dinah said. They heard Val say his night prayer and then went together to the bedroom they shared. In the crib in a corner of the room Honor was breathing with a soft snore. Dinah stood a moment by the garderobe, watching her husband undress. She thought of what her mother had said, and wondered if that, too, was indeed part of her duty, to not only give him her body, but pretend that she wanted him to have it. As he shed his clothing, revealing his white and softening body, she realized how pitifully small were his demands of her, really. She had heard of worse husbands than hers. He was kind enough, and rarely angry, and though she worked hard to keep house, there were times when he might have complained and didn't. He deserved well from her.

She crossed the room to him and reached him just as he turned around to take his nightshirt from where it was folded on the bed. Wordlessly she embraced him, pressing her hands against his naked back. He murmured a slight exclamation of surprise, and another when she kissed him.

"What is this?" he asked.

This is all sham, she wanted to say. This is a woman doing

her duty as she has been taught to do it. But what she really said was, "Thank you for our house."

He grinned. "You like it *that* much? I'll get you a new house every week."

"This one will do." She smiled at him. He smiled back. Why don't I like him more? It's my failing, my weakness. He's a good man, and I should love him with all my heart. I *do* love him, she told herself as he roughly undressed her and hurriedly took her on the bed. Instead of being more affectionate this time, the very fact that she had initiated it made him more eager, less considerate than ever, so that for the first time since she had healed from Honor's birth it hurt her, and she moaned in pain. Of course, he took the sound as ecstasy and worked all the harder at it, hurting her even more. She bit her lip and was still.

Suddenly Honor started crying in the corner. It was time for her to nurse again. "Let her cry," Matthew said. Instead, Dinah gripped his buttocks, knowing that when she did that he would finish immediately. He swore softly in frustration, then rolled off her. She got up and took the baby from the crib. Honor hunted eagerly for the nipple, then fastened on and drank greedily. Dinah returned to the bed, where Matt was lying naked, watching her.

"Would you turn down the covers, Matt?"

He got up wordlessly and pulled down the featherbeds. She sat on the edge of the bed and slipped her feet down under the covers. Matt also crawled into bed as she leaned against the headboard, nursing the baby. Matt slid close to her, and began stroking her breast near the baby's lips. It was annoying. She wanted him to leave her alone as she nursed the baby.

"Let's move the damned crib into another room," Matt said.

"I have to hear her when she cries."

"Sometimes I'd rather you didn't hear her." Matt meant it to sound clever, but to Dinah it only sounded crude. She endured his probing, tickling finger for a while longer, then pried Honor's lips away with her finger. Honor immediately protested sleepily, but Dinah only turned her around and lay beside her on the bed, facing away from Matthew. Then Honor began suckling on the other side, content again, dozing again. Matt stroked her arm and her hip for a few moments, but when she didn't respond he tired of it and finally left her alone.

"Damned inconsiderate greedy baby," Matt muttered.

Suddenly Dinah felt terribly ashamed. He had only meant to be tender. Was it his fault that he never thought to be gentle with her until he was satisfied? And he blamed it on the baby, when it was all her, when she was the one who turned him away. This is what Mother meant when she said it was my fault. I'm cold to him, and turn him away, not his body but his heart. Perhaps he even loves me. I think he really loves me. I should rejoice at that, and yet it feels like just another bar in my cell, another manacle that ties me to the walls of my gaol.

Honor slept again. Dinah carried her to the crib and laid her gently in it. The baby muttered something deep and unintelligible and then returned to contemplative sucking on her hand. Dinah went to the garderobe and took a nightgown from it, pulled it over her head. Relieved to be covered and protected again, she returned to her bed. Matthew was already sleeping, but when the bed moved with her coming, he stirred and reached out to her.

"Love you," he murmured. His hand lazily caught her wrist and held it tight, pulled it toward himself, tucked her hand under his body as if it were a treasure he was guarding against thieves. She looked at his face in repose and felt an infinite pity for him. She kissed his cheek, then lay down to begin an uncomfortable hour of sleeplessness before he finally released her hand. Even then she could feel his grip on her as she dozed in that near-sleep that fills the nights of mothers until the last of their children leave home. Twice in the night Honor cried out, and once Val, and each time Dinah arose like a spirit and, without quite waking, cared for their needs and returned to bed. Once in the night Matt, too, cried out, and she whispered to him and soothed him back to sleep before he was ever quite awake. My children, all of my children, you are why I am alive, the only purpose left to me.

And, to her surprise, tonight at least that purpose seemed enough. It was the work of God she did, caring for these mindless creatures until they were old enough to go away and take care of themselves. Then she would be free. Surely then they would set her free. "Ma ma ma ma ma," Honor called sleepily in the night. Let me sleep, Dinah whispered. The voice fell still, but Dinah heard the sound ringing in her ears as she drifted back into sleep. That is my name now, and all the rest of my life, my name till death do us part, till only death do us part. God help me, I wish I knew whether or not I'm glad of it.

➤➤➤ BOOK FOUR ⬅⬅⬅

*In which God sends a rustic angel
over the sea,
a destroying angel with good
intentions,
to tear brother from brother,
husband from wife,
and a mother from her children,
all to suit his grand design.*

ॐ First Word ॐ

One of the most annoying things about Mormons, right from the start, was that they didn't subscribe to that gentleman's agreement among the Christian churches that said it was all right to compete with each other for the souls of the unbaptized heathen, but not at all acceptable to raid each other's congregation for members. And it was downright offensive to insist on *baptizing* those stolen converts. Why, that was a slap in the face to say that that even their baptism wasn't good enough for the Mormon God.

Of course, Mormons were far from being the only group breaking that unspoken code. What made the Mormons conspicuous was the sheer number of their missionaries. Every reasonably faithful Mormon man could expect to be ordained to some office of the priesthood before he was quite dry from his baptism. Then, without any preparation beyond a few sermons, and without any text other than a few tracts and the Book of Mormon, the new convert was frequently called upon to leave his family and go out preaching the gospel, as best he could, to whomever would listen.

The result was a lot of desperately eager missionaries,

preaching while the first excitement of conversion was still on them.

Even more remarkable than the audacity of the attempt is the fact that it worked. Why didn't these new, inexperienced converts get *discouraged* with the arguments and snubbings and occasional mobbings and tar-and-featherings that were their almost certain lot? Why didn't they get sick of traveling with no money, sleeping in beds and eating good meals only when people were charitable, and sleeping in the open and eating nothing at all when people were close-fisted? Why didn't they just quit?

Some of them did, of course, and never quite came back to the Church from their missions. Most held firm, however. There's something in human nature that says that if someone is going to abuse me for being a Mormon, I'm damn well going to be Mormon till the day I die.

And they never lacked for an audience. In an age before television and movies, when books weren't cheap and radios couldn't be switched on for background music, the latest Mormon missionaries were an interesting diversion, and a good argument about religion was better than sitting on the stoop watching the dogs mate.

The gentleman's agreement among the Christian churches had been a survival mechanism. It ended the terrible wars that had periodically ravaged Europe and the Middle East; it brought peace at the price of a loss of fervency.

The Mormons were proof enough that the religious peace was fragile. When the agreement was breached, the religious wars and murders began again at once. In the land where religious freedom was supposedly the cornerstone of the Constitution, the Mormons found themselves on the receiving end of the American version of pogroms and crusades. Informal mobs gathered on the spur of the moment to burn out the local Mormons; when the Mormons were too much for the mobs to handle, they were likely to be joined by official state and federal troops, called out because the Mormons, by preaching and living their religion, had become an intolerable threat to their neighbors.

So Mormon blood was spilled in many states, and Mormon graves dotted the landscape of Missouri...

And still the missionaries left their wives and children and crossed mountain, desert, and ocean to take their message to anyone who would hear it.

What was the message that they were beaten or killed for, the message that so many thousands believed and followed to Zion? Simply this: God had spoken again to man, after centuries of silence, and his word was alive again in the world.

Of course it annoyed the Christians. They had finally got their speechless God under control. How dare these uneducated bumpkins rouse him up again, to undo all their comfortable theology?

—*O. Kirkham, Salt Lake City, 1981*

🢃 16 🢂

Heber Kimball
Manchester, 1840

HEBER LEFT CLITHEROE BRIMMING with the Spirit, in a mood to fairly fly to Manchester himself. Practical considerations prevailed, however; no need to bother the Spirit with miracles of transportation when there were wagons and coaches going all the time. He jingled the coins in his underfilled pocket and decided he'd just as soon preach to a generous farmer as contribute to the wealth of a coach company. So he walked to the edge of town and hailed a farmer whose load was produce and not goods; bound to a town, not back home.

"I warn you," said the farmer the moment Heber had clambered aboard, "I'm not much of one to talk."

"I'm delighted," Heber declared. "For *I* am, and you're going to hear the greatest news you'll ever hear in your life, Brother."

"I'm a Methodist," the farmer said. "What are you?"

"An apostle of the Lord Jesus Christ, sent by the prophet

of God to preach repentance to the people of England, including you."

The farmer grunted, and Heber set to his task with a will. The man's face might have been set in stone. It bothered Heber not at all. He'd preach to the devil himself and enjoy it—the gospel sounded as good in his own ears as it had the day he first heard it ten years before, and whether it pleased the farmer or not, it pleased Heber Kimball.

Not that he was without hope of converting the man. Miracles of conversion happened all the time. Oh, the first time Heber had come to England back in '37, with Orson Hyde and Willard Richards and Joseph Fielding, they had baptized quite a few people, and when Joseph sent them back with the promise that the field was ripe and ready to harvest, Heber had expected to do some baptizing. But not on the scale they found! Wilford Woodruff had baptized the whole congregation of United Brethren down in Herefordshire, including fifty lay preachers. Hundreds were joining the church all over the West Midlands, and even as they put dozens of people under the water in a day, the apostles marveled to each other about the miraculous fulfillment of Brother Joseph's prophecy. Indeed, Heber himself had reached a conclusion that surprised him. The Lord may have chosen America, the promised land, for the restoration of his gospel, but it was here in England that the people were readiest for it. "They're jumping in the water faster than we can ordain priests to baptize them," Orson Pratt had complained at Preston. And if this farmer seemed to have no more wit than his potato crop, that stolid face still might conceal a soul hungry for the gospel.

If it did, however, the farmer was able to conceal it from himself and Heber both. In Whalley the man turned west for Preston; Heber cheerfully got off the wagon and searched for transport south. He ended up walking through Accrington and Haslingden, but he didn't mind. It was a fine May afternoon, his boots were reasonably comfortable, he had a delicious biting hunger in his belly that sharpened his attention to the countryside, and it was a brilliant opportunity to practice his hymn singing. He hymned his way thirteen miles to Edenfield and, it looking to be a warm night, bedded down in an uncomplaining haystack a hundred yards from the road.

The next day, however, the hunger had turned from sharpness to a definite physical disorder that had to be remedied.

But it was friendly farmland here in the west reaches of the Forest of Rossendale, and he was fed two breakfasts by farmers who didn't suspect when they invited him in that they'd be getting angels and apostles and the millennial reign along with his tremendous appetite. Still, they were good-natured about it, and while they confessed that they had too much affection for the vicar to want to offend him by hearing any more, they didn't begrudge him the biscuits he tucked into his coat pockets for the road. "If you feed me, you feed the Lord," Heber Kimball proclaimed, and they didn't doubt it—the man, for all his rough American manners and bent for profanity at odd moments ("Joseph Smith is a damned fine man!"), could charm the shingles off the roof in a rainstorm.

And he knew it. But he didn't think it was any virtue of *his*. He was just an ordinary potter, among other trades, until Joseph Smith touched his life and woke up within him all that he really was—and more. An apostle of the Lord Jesus Christ: he was still awed by the responsibility of it, even though he had become quite reconciled to it now. Well, these were perilous times, the millennium was only a few short years away, and the Lord was using the weak things of the earth to confound the self-anointed wise men who were running the whole she-bang to hell. If people smiled at Heber, he took it as a smile to the Lord, a reaching out of their spirit to find comfort in the gospel. If people pressed food on him, he accepted it as if they were lucky to have the chance to give it to him, because they were: it would be counted much in their favor in heaven, and for only small cost to them on earth.

Another farmer took him on in Edenfield right after his second breakfast, and Heber knew the Lord would be with him today. They began the descent through Bury into Manchester, Heber's first visit to the great coal-burning, steam-driven, cotton-manufacturing heart of the industrial revolution. There was a congregation there already, he knew; he had the address of the branch president, William Clayton, a man he had baptized himself in another city three years before. He even knew that the industrial cities were going through hard times these days— there had been a taste of it in Liverpool and Preston. But nothing had prepared him for the abject poverty that worsened as they rode along Red Bank Road. The stink from the River Irk was offensive, of course, but his eyes suffered more than his nose, for he cared only for the people who sat or squatted in the early afternoon shade that narrowly fronted the buildings on the east side of the street. The farmers might have stone faces, but these people were made of ash; a breath could break them; their hearts were gone. Heber suffered with pity for them.

"My good friend," he said to the farmer, "you have a wagon full of food and these folks are hungry."

"I have a family back home gets hungry, too, so don't start giving me milk of human kindness charity sermons or you'll get off and walk."

Actually, walking sounded like a good idea; the farmer had been unreceptive and as long as Heber stayed on the wagon there'd be no one else to preach to. He thanked the farmer for his generosity, urged him to think about the welfare of his eternal soul, and stepped out among the poor, who watched him incuriously. That is, until he began producing biscuits from his pockets; then he found himself surrounded by silent reachers, who did not touch him but jostled each other for place; he was hurt but not condemning when he saw little children pushed out of the way by some of the grown-ups; he took care to give food first to those who pushed least, where that was possible.

It took only a minute or two to shed the excess weight of bread from his pockets; in another minute he had distributed all the coins that had been given him by the charity of the Saints in Clitheroe. If their donations were turned from missionary work to feeding the poor, it would hardly lessen the value of their gift. Besides, it was as Joseph said: "Feed them first, then preach. A hungry man is all belly; feed him and he has a spirit again." So Heber passed out all his worldly possessions to the poor, confident that these were spiritual gifts he gave them; and equally sure that the Lord would return his generosity fivefold.

He passed the new mills near Scotland Bridge, where he held his breath and walked briskly over the Irk, wondering how anyone could work near such a place, let alone live there. Then he followed Long Mill Gate to Todd Street and Hanging Ditch, carefully observing how the fortunes of the other pedestrians improved. It was in St. Ann's Square that he finally found his spot. Plenty of people who seemed in no hurry; plenty of space for a crowd to gather; and a church a hundred years away, a very nice illustration for the remarks he intended to make about the Great Apostasy.

He used the colorful condemnations of the Great and Abominable Church, the Whore of the Earth, to draw a curious crowd. Then he began telling them the glorious story of the angel that brought the golden plates to Joseph Smith, the first prophet on the earth since the last of the ancient apostles was slain. He made it as exciting as he knew how—it was still early and he had a lot of energy. As he spoke, he carefully watched the faces to distinguish the scoffers from the listeners, the doubters from those whose eyes got brighter with excitement the more they heard.

A fair crowd, a dinnertime crowd, full of food and not too eager to get back to work. The rich, of course, passed by quickly; Heber Kimball personally doubted the Lord's ability to get camels through needles' eyes. And the poorest of the poor were begging surreptitiously and illegally on the fringes of the crowds, not listening either. It was workingmen and clerks who heard his message, and so, he knew, it would be workingmen and clerks who could come with him into the water to be baptized.

As he preached to and studied his crowd, there was one young man who kept catching his eye. The fellow was tall and thin with a face as pretty as a girl's; doubtless still in his teens, yet dressed smartly and bearing himself with the dignity of one who was accustomed to dealing in the world of men, not of children. Heber especially liked the way he seemed to have to chew an idea a little before swallowing it. Heber foresaw in his interest the possibility of a conversation that might lead to a chance of holding a meeting in this man's home.

The crowd began to dwindle as the dinner hour ended; Heber saw the young man start to drift reluctantly away. Quickly Heber testified that Joseph Smith was a true prophet, passed out a dozen tracts to people as he passed through the crowd, and caught up with the young man as he was turning the corner onto Bank Street.

"Young man, do you like to read?" Heber asked.

"I—yes sir, I do." But the young man looked hurried.

"Here's something for you to read." He pressed a tract into his hands. "I know you're late to work but it'll take just a moment for you to tell me your name and invite me to your home for supper."

The young man looked surprised, but then laughed. "You

must be one of the Americans I heard were preaching here."

"An apostle of the Lord Jesus Christ, and I feel inspired to say that while you can feed my flesh, I can feed your soul tonight, and I will hunger again long before you do. My name's Heber Kimball, at your service because I'm at the Lord's."

"I'm Charlie Kirkham. But I'm not very religious."

"Only because you've never heard the true religion. The light of Christ is in every heart, and it made you reject the false doctrines taught by false churches. But your heart awakens to truth, and I prophesy the Lord holds greatness in store for you, if you have the courage to serve him as his true disciple."

Charlie laughed. "You must be a prophet, friend—only God could get a word in edgewise. I live at number 80 Bradford Street. I'm not interested in religion, but my mother'll want to hear you. Get on Canal Street from Great Ancoats, and Bradford bends off to the right. Mother always has supper ready at seven sharp. Or do you stop talking long enough to eat?"

"I have no compunction about doing both at once." Heber gave him a second copy of *A Timely Warning to the People of England*. "For your mother," he said; then he let the young man go. His mother indeed. Heber knew damn well the boy had felt the Spirit and was a prime prospect. Heber had seen that look a thousand times before. It always meant the Lord had led him to one of his own.

Three more sermons that afternoon in other places downtown, and then the tower clocks told Heber it was time to start searching for Bradford Street. William Clayton's address was still in his pocket, but Heber figured that the already-baptized could wait another day to receive an apostle into their homes; it was the lost sheep the Lord sought first, not those already safe within the fold.

❧ 17 ❧

Sister Dinah
Manchester, 1840

MATTHEW WAS OUT TONIGHT. It would be late. He would come home with beer on his breath, full of politics and lust. Usually Dinah bore it stoically, making sure the children felt no upset in the rituals of evening; tonight, though, was one of those times when she could not bear it. To sit alone in the house after the children were asleep, waiting for the key to touch the lock. Or to lie in bed, unable to sleep for fear that fumbling hands would waken her in the dark.

So tonight Dinah took Val and Honor and set out for Mother's house—for home, thought Dinah, for Matthew's house was not home. As always, she opened the door without knocking. And then stopped on the threshold, for a great bear of a man was leaping to his feet and rushing toward her, his hand outstretched.

"Come in!" he cried enthusiastically. "Glad to have you! I'm about to preach to this good family, and they're terribly

195

afraid I'll bore them, so the added company will help them stay awake."

He spoke in a harsh American accent, and he shambled when he walked, as if he had never worn a suit that fit. Yet he was acting the host as if he owned the house. Dinah was angry that he would invite her into her own home. Dinah was angry at his coarseness in a home that had always been filled with grace, even in poverty. Dinah was angry that he was so strong and that Charlie and Anna shrank weakly into the background behind him. Most of all, she was angry that on a night when she needed her family, a stranger should be there. Dinah raised her eyebrows and met Heber's grin with a look of such aloofness that it stopped the American cold.

"Beg pardon," the man said. "We haven't been introduced. I'm Heber Kimball. I'm an apostle of the Lord Jesus Christ."

Dinah did not answer him directly. Instead she spoke to Anna. "If I had known you had company, Mother, I wouldn't have come to call."

"Come in, Dinah," Charlie said. "He's an American."

"That explains his accent, but it doesn't forgive his boorishness."

"Don't be cross," Heber said. "In America we believe in being friendly."

"It's all right, Dinah," said Anna. She held out her arms and took Honor from Dinah.

"This is England," Dinah said. "Charlie, will you introduce us?"

"Dinah, this is Heber Kimball. Heber, this is my sister, Dinah Handy."

"*Mrs.* Handy," Dinah said, holding out her hand. "A dose of formality can only do us good."

"Well," said Heber, "I hope you won't mind but I mean to call you Sister Dinah. And I'm Brother Heber. We're all brothers and sisters, because we're all children of God. At least I know *I* am."

"If I had known you came from such an exalted family, sir, I would have done a curtsy," said Dinah.

Heber grinned at her again. It got under her skin, the way he looked at her, as familiarly as if he had known her for years. What does he see when he looks at me? Everyone in her life knew who she was, knew the story of her life, more or less, and looked at her in a certain way, as a certain person. But Heber Kimball looked at her as if he knew the secret history of another life that no one else had seen. It made her feel at once violated and glad.

It was the gladness that won. She could not help but answer his grin with a smile. She regretted it at once, when he crushed her hand in his and shook her. She managed to pull away before he could bruise her, and the four of them pulled chairs near to the fire.

"Heber thinks that I'm a good prospect for religious conversion," said Charlie, winking at her. "He wants me to become a Mormonite."

"Actually I don't think you're such a good prospect for Mormonism," said Heber. "I just think you're a good prospect for hell if you *don't* become a Mormon."

"Heber ate dinner with us," Anna said. "And we'd like him to sing for his supper. We want him to tell us about his America and his religion and—whatever."

Ah, thought Dinah. There'll be no privacy tonight. This stranger will be here until I have to leave. As soon as she knew what the inevitable course of the evening was, Dinah resolved to bear it well. And hearing to this man preach couldn't be worse than staying home waiting for Matthew in the silent six-room house. Besides, she didn't have to listen. She could sit and let the words pass through her while she watched the fire and felt the heat of it on her skin, using up her senses so she didn't have to pay attention to *anything*. That was good, that was the next best thing to not existing, when she could glide along without having to care.

But Heber Kimball would not let her do it. He spoke as if Dinah were the only person listening, constantly referring to her, asking her questions, making sure she understood.

The tale he told was not of strange dogma. It was the story of a farmboy who saw an angel, and suffered much from the abuse of his neighbors, but finally managed to translate the sheets of beaten gold that the angel had given him and publish the translation as the Book of Mormon. He told on: How Joseph Smith and Oliver Cowdery received the priesthood of God, not from any man, but from St. Peter, St. James, and St. John themselves, resurrected beings who came to earth especially to do it. How Joseph Smith was beaten, tarred and feathered, poisoned, chased, tried, imprisoned, but never convicted of a crime by a lawful court. How the Saints in Kirtland had tried to live with all things in common among them, like the early saints, but the world was too wicked for it right now. How they were driven with blood and terror from Missouri, and now were building the city of God on the banks of the Mississippi River, the Father of Waters. "Someday all the nations of the world will flow to Zion and sing the praises of the Lord in the gates of the city," Heber said, and his eyes glowed.

"You sound as if you expect the Second Coming of Christ," said Anna.

"Joseph Smith will probably greet the Lord himself, provided we can keep him out of jail for a while."

"Your prophet has been in jail?" asked Anna. She had nothing but contempt for criminals.

"You don't have to be a criminal to go to jail in America," said Heber. "Just like you don't have to be lazy to be poor in England."

Anna would not be sidetracked that easily. "What was he convicted of?"

"He's never been convicted of anything. They put him in jail because he's a prophet of God. They keep sentencing him to death, too, but they might as well try to stop the tide as kill Joseph Smith, at least until the Lord decides his work is through."

"Governments don't sentence people to death for their religious beliefs," Anna said. "This is the nineteenth century, not the seventeenth."

"Is it? Well, then, you go explain it to the men and little boys who were shot down in cold blood at Haun's Mill with the blessing of the Missouri state militia. You go mention that to the governor of Missouri, who issued a proclamation that the Mormons were to be exterminated or driven from the state. You tell it to the women who were raped on the road to Illinois, or the children whose corpses were covered only one inch deep in the dead of a Missouri winter, you tell it to them that this is the nineteenth century. I think they'll tell you that the same spirit that put Jesus on the cross lives on in the hearts of evil men in this century. I think they'll tell you that the lions that tore the Christians in ancient Rome are still alive, dressed like human beings and regularly elected to the legislature."

"They really killed children?" Charlie asked.

"Blasted off one little boy's head, and then he laughed and said, 'Nits breed lice.'" With that, Heber launched into the bloody tale of the Saints' expulsion from Missouri back in '38, while the Prophet and his closest friends languished six months in prison under sentence of death. Heber was a master story-teller. By the time he wrapped the stories up with the defiant words, "We don't figure to get driven out again," Dinah felt as if the *we* included her.

"We're building the city of God on the banks of the Mississippi, Nauvoo the Beautiful," said Heber Kimball.

We are building the city of God, said Dinah to herself. She stared into the fire and wondered why she was not there, building with them.

"God speaks to us," said Heber Kimball, and Dinah wondered why she could not remember the sound of God's voice.

Dinah was vaguely aware of Charlie smiling at her now and then, whenever Heber said a particularly outrageous word, like *discombobulated* or *skewompus*, but Dinah did not want to share jests with Charlie at the American's expense. She did not want to return to reality just now. Reality was Matthew, was leaving here with no more hope than she had when she came. Far better was Heber Kimball's storytelling. Whatever the Mormons suffered, they could bear it because it had a *purpose*. What Dinah suffered had no purpose at all, unless God had something up his sleeve. God didn't play surprises on the Saints. He told the prophet what was going on, said Heber. It was the safest world that Dinah had ever heard about; to know God's purpose would arm her against despair. Joseph Smith taught a sermon the very morning he was tarred and feathered. He could bear the pain because there was a reason to have suffered it.

Without realizing it, Dinah did what Robert and Charlie had done years before. She discovered the face of God. Where Robert had found God's visage in the hot ovens of the steam engines, in the whirring belts and rocking machinery; where Charlie had learned to pray to the face of Old Hulme, leaning down to open his mind to learning even as he chastised him stingingly with a ruler on the palms; that was the place in her mind where Dinah put the face she imagined for Joseph Smith. It was nothing so simple as supposing that the man Joseph Smith were perfect—she was not such a fool as to trust any man, especially one she had not met, with such faith. Rather she quite unconsciously found in Joseph's story those things that she most valued in a man, all the things that her husband and her God should have before she could love them, and created a face that stood for all that, and began to believe in that face as an ideal. It did not occur to her that such perfection could not exist. The ontological argument was enough for her: if she could conceive of him, he lived, and all other men were merely flawed attempts to represent him in the flesh.

It grew late. Honor was asleep and Val grew more and more whiney. But Dinah made no motion to end the evening by going home. Anna finally said something about Charlie having to work in the morning and Heber said, "Good heavens, so late at night, and I haven't even thought about finding a room at an inn!"

Of course that led to insistence that he stay the night, and he didn't even bother to pretend to be reluctant. It was Dinah who would leave, and the stranger who would have the solace of her family. But Dinah did not mind as she had thought she would. She went through her good-byes as if she were in a trance. Charlie offered to carry Val home for her, but Anna glared at him and said that she wasn't staying alone in the house with a strange man, even if he *was* an apostle, and so *she'd* go with Dinah and Charlie could help Mr. Kimball to his bed.

Anna carried Honor while Dinah carried Val. "I hope you're not too annoyed," said Anna, completely misunderstanding what Dinah felt. That was all right. Dinah wasn't quite sure herself. "Charlie's never brought a stranger home like that before. And such a man. He ate as if he had just learned how, and was proud to show what he could do."

"And he talked as if God had taught him all the words," said Dinah. She had meant to sound flippant, but she couldn't bring it off. She didn't feel flippant tonight. The mood on her was more akin to reverence. It was a bright moonlit night, and there was no difficulty picking their way through the alleys, along the paths, and over the footbridge between the Kirkham and the Handy houses. The moonlight was at such an angle that at one moment, as Dinah stood at the crest of the footbridge, she could see not the dark faces of the shabby buildings, but only the roofs shining brightly. The city on a hill, she thought, and when they see it men must come to dwell there.

That was where Dinah wanted to be—a place where no one could possibly starve because their neighbors would share freely with them, without interference from pride or shame. She wanted, most of all, to be in a place where the men who controlled her life were not selected for her by other men, as her husband had been, but by God himself. That would be her true home, not the six rooms where Matthew ruled, not that empty place. She had long felt homesick for a home where she had never dwelt, a home that she had looked for in poems and almost found sometimes; a home that now she knew existed, that now was being built on the shores of a vast river called the Mississippi, where a prophet had said God wanted his people to come. To come home.

They paused at the door of Dinah's house. Valiant grumbled sleepily about being forced to stand while his mother fumbled with the key.

"Dinah," asked Anna quietly, "can it be true that he has the power to wash away my most terrible sins?"

The words took Dinah by surprise. "Mother, if there's ever been a woman without sin, it's you."

Anna smiled wanly and looked away.

"What sin could *you* have?" asked Dinah.

Anna gazed down at Valiant. He was young enough and sleepy enough that the truth could be at least hinted at in front of him. "The one that brought all my woes upon me, all our suffering upon us all."

The idea appalled Dinah. Had her mother, all these years, blamed everything that had gone wrong in their lives on some fancied sin in her past? "Mother, what can you be talking about?"

Anna turned toward Dinah then, with all her fear and shame upon her face, and said, "I loved my husband's body far too much and far too soon, Dinah, and because of my covetousness God took him from me, and with him all my hope."

Dinah saw in her mother's face, for just a moment, the young girl who was not taken—no, she gave herself to young and beautiful John Kirkham upon the banks of the Medlock thirteen days before their wedding. Dinah saw how every crease and line in the aging face that now fronted the same soul was tinged with that guilt. Dinah saw, and she embraced her mother and whispered, "Whatever sin you might have committed, Mother, you've already paid for."

Anna wept then, for she had never confessed her secret crime to anyone before, and had never thought she would. In a few moments she told the whole story of it, and told how she knew right away that she would be punished all her life, would never be clean. "Why else would four of my seven children die within a year? Why else would I lose the husband I had wanted too much? Why else would my dream of real education for my children be destroyed, my daughter be brutally used by a man, my sons be enemies to each other?"

In vain Dinah tried to assure her that it would hardly be fair of God to punish her children for some sin of hers. Anna only quoted the scripture that said, "I will punish the children of them that hate me unto the third and fourth generation." Then Anna gripped Dinah fiercely with her free hand so abruptly that Honor awoke and began to squawl, and defiantly said, "I believe this man, Dinah. I believe him when he says he has the power to make me clean and pure before the Lord, white as new snow, as if I had never committed a sin in my life. He isn't a venal vicar like the ones I've known, he isn't after his salary from the government, he's simple and pure and he received his power from a man who was touched by the hands of the ancient apostles. I know you think I'm a fool, but I want so badly, Dinah, I want so badly to be *clean*."

Dinah thought of the face of God, the face of the imagined Prophet. Not like Matthew, forever sweeping with the wind; not like Robert, full of plans and machinations without ever knowing how they would end. He had the power to act, and the wisdom to do good, and God would not despise Anna Kirkham.

"Yes," Dinah said.

"Yes what?"

"Yes, I think he has that power," Dinah said. The words were utterly inadequate for what she *wanted* to say. It was enough for her that her mother also believed, for whatever reason. Enough for her that though they both desired something different from this American preacher, they both believed that he could give it.

Anna looked at her in wonder. "You believed him?"

"Yes," she said, "I believe him."

"When you sat, when you looked into the fire, I thought you were angry—"

"I was thinking—if only I were with them, and could see this prophet, and live my life for the sake of something important."

She opened the door, bent down and picked up Val. They brought the children in and put them to bed, then talked for only a few minutes more. They decided to wait for several days, to make sure they weren't caught up in the enthusiasm of the moment, to make sure that they weren't doing something foolish. Besides, as Anna pointed out, Matthew might resent it if his wife changed religions.

That was a whole realm of problems that Dinah refused to think about. She hurried her mother on her way and shut the matter of Matthew out of her mind. It was *her* soul, not his, she said to herself as she closed the door. I won't conceal it from him, but I won't ask his permission, either. Why should I? Does he ask my permission about his ridiculous political meetings, when any one of them could have him arrested if the authorities started suppressing them again? Did he ask me if I *wanted* a new house? Does he even ask for my consent when he wants to use my body as a dumping ground for his reservoir of passion? Why, then, should *I* ask *him* when it's a matter of my relationship with God, a matter of what I choose to believe in my own soul?

The words of her argument came to her formally, not in a rush of thought but in ordered sentences, logical patterns like a sermon or a speech. And she began to let the words come to her lips as she walked up the stairs to the room she shared with Matthew. She uttered no sound, merely let her lips form the oration, which she presented as carefully as if a thousand ears were listening.

She was not aware that she was doing it, of course. She only listened to her thoughts and did not realize how close they were to being audible. Certainly she did not realize whom she was speaking *to*. And yet it was no coincidence that this sermon came to her lips for the first time in her life the very night that Heber Kimball had shown her a vision of the face of God, the perfect Man. It was to this person that she spoke, he was the one who heard her. She was not teaching him, she was justifying herself to him, and she knew that with *him*, if her arguments were clear and ordered, if she spoke pure truth without dissembling, he would nod and say, Yes, Dinah, that's correct, that's true, I accept you, your choice is right.

Her lips moved with the silent monologue as she took off her shoes and unlaced her bodice. It occurred to her that she ought to pray, but she rejected the thought, in part because her sermon *was* a prayer, in part because she had so often in her childhood knelt in futile pleading, talking to bedpost or a wall of brick.

Instead, she walked to the window and drew open the curtains. From this room she could see the moonlight streaming into the court, the well-kept garden below with small trees reaching up to the bedroom story of the cottages. The garden was painfully empty. There was nothing living it it; if ever a bird or squirrel were tempted to set up house there, the children who played daily in the garden would have killed it within a week. And now, grey in moonlight, even the trees looked unalive, as if they were only the empty image of life, waiting for dawn to make them pregnant with light and upward-thrusting power. Dinah stood on the brink of creation; below her God was first putting form to the world, and she was watching. She was part of it. She herself could reach down and touch the tree and it would spring green under her hand, and from her fingers would come sunlight. It was a giddy feeling, that in all this darkness the sun still shone within her, held in place only by her flesh. Her body was a curtain that concealed her glory, and if she could once open it completely, all the world could look to her for warmth and vision and be satisfied.

She felt herself being watched. She stepped back from the window, but not in alarm. She wanted to be seen, but not by some neighbor going to the privy. She wanted to be seen by the very Man who listened to the words that still came eloquently to her lips. The room was already so full of him that it would burst, and as she spoke silently she reached out her hands to touch him, not knowing who it was she wanted to find under her hand. Her fingers closed on emptiness; the light within her could find no release; she would surely burst if he did not come and see her shine like a star, hear her speak like scripture. She must break the enclosure around her and let him in; unable to pierce her opaque flesh, she opened the only thing she could open: the door to the bedroom.

Matthew was standing there, his hand outstretched to the latch.

"Good God," he said. "You startled me."

Dinah was quite used to the idle use of God's name. But tonight, feeling holy, she resented it as a mockery of the Man she spoke to. Her silent monologue instantly ceased; the room at once became empty; and she knew as Matthew glanced down at her open bodice that there was no hope of avoiding his intimacy tonight.

So be it. If it must be, let it be quick. He hardly stepped within the door when she began pulling his shirt from his trousers. He laughed softly and unbuttoned his waistcoat and his shirt; she stood behind him unfastening his trousers, clumsily pulling them down. "Let me," he said. "I can do it quicker."

"Hurry," she said, and undressed as he did, resenting his eyes on her but forcing herself to smile until she was naked and lay on the bed, waiting for him impatiently. He looked at her in awe, not smiling now. She did not care if he thought she was acting the whore; it was not his thought she cared for tonight. Like a whore, she wanted it to happen and be done with so she could get on. He crawled up the bed to her and she wrapped her legs around him to draw him close.

To her surprise she was as aroused as he was, as if her body were translating spiritual excitement into carnal. She found herself responding to him as she never had before; or, rather, interpreting the strong passion of her body as pleasure instead of shameful loss of control. She cried out softly, panted as he did, and she did not mind after all that tonight of all nights he did not simply turn over and go right to sleep, but instead lay facing her, kissing her, letting his hands play over her. She did not mind that the blankets were not pulled up modestly to hide them, that Matthew was warmly covering a part of her when he finally fell asleep. She felt an affection for him that she had never thought would be possible; her body's release was, for once, satisfying to her, and she felt a marvelous contentment.

But the ideas began to flow back into her mind as the emptiness of Matthew's love retreated. Her lips began to move again in silent speech; she felt the evening begin to grow chilly, and she slid out from under Matthew, put on her nightgown, and pulled a blanket over them. Matthew murmured and reached for her in his sleep, but his hand, finding only cloth, retreated again. He rolled away from her and the lovemaking was past; she had got through Matthew's return without losing the fervor of this new religion. She had increased it, in fact, and she began to hear music as she silently spoke, a drone of harmony softly in her ears, a hum that retreated when she became aware of it and returned as soon as she no longer tried to hear it.

Father, she said softly. Father, Father, Father. She was a young farmboy lying on a bed in his father's house in America, longing for something, knowing it would not come, expecting it to arrive any moment.

The feeling grew and grew until she could not bear it. The light also grew within her, until at last she could see it, a whiteness spreading from her to fill the room. She heard her words become audible, and she finally realized that the angel would not come and stand outside her in the air, that the angel would be within her, and her own lips would speak the message she was meant to hear. "I love you," said her lips, and only her own ears heard. "I love you, I hear you." And then the whiteness grew too bright and she closed her eyes and almost immediately felt herself drift toward sleep, felt the whiteness drowse over her like endless sheets and blankets to warm her, and she heard her own voice fall silent and the other voice at last speak in answer, speak from those perfect lips only one thing: "I am," said the voice so slowly, and Dinah lay in wonder all night, sleeping but feeling herself awake forever, the sun and moon and stars all within her body, the leaves of the trees so large that she could stand between them and watch them grow to infinity so that she could touch the stars that dwelt within them, too. "I am," said the voice. So slowly. And Dinah answered, silently, "I know."

◆ 18 ◆

New Saints
Manchester, 1840

SOMEHOW CHARLIE ENDED UP volunteering to sleep on the divan so Heber could have a bed. He tried to see how he had been maneuvered into it, but Heber hadn't done anything obvious enough to catch. Oh well, hospitality was hospitality. The only thing that really, annoyed Charlie was how affected Dinah seemed. It was as if the two of them had been listening to different men. Charlie heard only an American with outlandish speech. Dinah apparently heard something else.

"I don't want to belabor it," said Heber from the doorway, "but would you do me one last favor?"

Charlie shrugged and smiled. "Gladly, of course."

"Two favors, really. The first one is, would you mind if I read you just a short, short passage from the Book of Mormon?"

"Please," Charlie said.

"I mean, the Book of Mormon is kind of the linchpin, don't you think? If it's true scripture, then everything Brother Joseph said about how he got it must be true too. And if it isn't true scripture, why, it's all as false as a goose egg in a chicken coop."

Heber began reading in his halting, half-literate way. It drove Charlie crazy to listen to the mispronunciation, the halting pace, the stammers. Then in midsentence Heber paused and said, "I don't read worth a bucket of horse manure. Why don't *you* read it to *me?*"

Charlie had the book in his hands before he could get the words out of his mouth. Heber pointed to the paragraph, and Charlie read it aloud, hardly thinking about what he was saying, only wanting to show this American how things *ought* to be read. It was in a high-flown language that sounded like scripture, a promise that anyone who read the book with a sincere heart would have the Spirit of God come and tell him it was true, if he prayed about it. The whole thing, Heber and the book and the story of the suffering people in America, it all came together then for Charlie, for a moment, and he saw them as at once a pitiful people duped by a charlatan into meaningless sacrifice, and a chosen people ennobled by their faith, laboring to prepare the world for the Savior to come again. The first was what Charlie knew they really were; the second was what they believed themselves to be. But for a moment Charlie wasn't sure whether the fairer measure of a people was the way others saw them, or the way they saw themselves.

"Well, you're a *reader*," said Heber.

Charlie couldn't help but smile. No matter how ignorant Heber was, he could at least tell good reading when he heard it.

"I reckon you could read that whole book in a month," said Heber.

Charlie laughed. "I could read the whole book in a day."

Heber handed it to him. "Then if I lend you this, you should be able to get a few pages read before you go to bed."

Trapped. "I'll read some of it tonight," Charlie said. "I like reading."

"Good. Now, that second favor I needed."

"Yes?"

Heber grinned and bounced up and down a little on the balls of his feet, like a little boy taken short. "Would you tell me where the privy is?"

Charlie laughed. "In the courtyard. Through that door."

While Heber thumped out of the house, Charlie opened the book.

He had thought to read just enough to satisfy himself that the doctrines were childish or the writing immature. To his own surprise, however, it was no parallel Bible. Instead it began with the story of the youngest son of a prophet, living in Jerusalem just before the Babylonians would come to destroy it. The youngest son, Nephi, believed in his father and tried to serve God, but he had oppressive and unbelieving older brothers, Laman and Lemuel, who tried to tie him up and abandon him for wild animals one time, then tried to kill him outright another. Always Nephi had the power of God with him, and once an angel came to stand between him and his brothers. Charlie knew all about cruel and heartless older brothers.

When their father, the old prophet, had a vision that even he didn't understand, the youngest brother prayed and not only saw the same vision but got an angel to interpret it for him as well, which made his brothers hate him all the more, even as it became clear that Nephi was obviously the only true son of his godly father. When their hunting bows were broken or sprung, it was Nephi who got help from the Lord in learning how to make a bow. When they reached a seashore and could go no farther, it was this youngest son who built a ship, even though his brothers mocked him and said he couldn't do it. And then as they sailed across the ocean toward the promised land of America, his older brothers tied him to a mast and starved him while they got drunk with some of the women they had brought along. Then the Lord sent a great storm that nearly sank the ship, until the brothers got frightened and untied him. And what did Nephi do? Did he rage? Did he strike them down? Did he curse them? No. He forgave them freely, even though they obviously weren't really sorry they hurt him, and then he calmed the storm. Yes, Charlie thought as he read it. Yes, that's the truth. That's the way the world is, or ought to be, by heaven.

Then he turned a page and several sheets of paper fell out. For a moment Charlie was afraid he had spoiled the book. Then he picked up the papers and discovered it was a letter. "My dear Vilate," it began. But then it collapsed into the most absurd

combinations of letters Charlie had ever seen. He could make
no sense of the words until he realized that he should simply
pronounce them as they were spelled. *Jest* for *just*, and he had
Heber's pronunciation preserved in ink. *Opertunity. Enuph.
Hous. Ware* instead of *were. Inhabitance* instead of *inhabit-
ants. Piana* for *piano, presents* for *presence.* The man was a
gold mine of information about the incompetence of an American education. He couldn't help but smile at the most ridiculous
words.

He didn't know how long Heber had been watching him
before he cleared his throat and said, "Beg your pardon."

Charlie looked up in surprise. Immediately he folded the
papers closed and stuffed them back in the book and closed it
quickly. "Sorry," he said. "It was just here, it fell out of the
book and I was afraid it was pages. I didn't mean to read so
much, just glance at it is all."

"No doubt you were admiring my interesting spelling."

Charlie felt himself blush with embarrassment, something
he almost never did. "I didn't mean to give offense, I—"

Heber grinned. "That's all right. Parley says I spell worse
than Brigham, and Brigham spells worse than anybody. But I
figure"—and here Charlie mentally spelled the word *figger*—
"that if the Lord wanted a good speller he would have called
one. Instead he's got me, and I've got better things to do than
learn which words get extra *E*s and which ones don't. Vilate
reads my letters out loud anyway. If I started spelling it right
she'd never make head nor tails of it. And it really isn't my
fault. It's you folks here in England made up the way to spell
these words, not me."

Charlie handed him the closed book with the letter inside.
Heber opened the book, removed the letter, and handed the
book back to Charlie.

"I loaned you the book so you'd read it," Heber said. "But
you were turning the pages so fast, I wondered if you were
really reading. You kind of slowed down when you got to my
letter."

It was forgiveness, of course—Heber was telling Charlie
that he knew he was really reading the Book of Mormon, not
trying to pry. It was praise, too, of Charlie's speed as a reader,
and Charlie didn't mind taking it as such. "I read quickly," he
said, "but I read every word." And to prove it he recounted
the tale he had just read.

"Sounds like you've been paying close attention, all right." Heber measured him with a look. "You've read that much of it—what do you think?"

Charlie was at a loss for words. He was afraid to tell this man how much the first few chapters of the book had meant to him, for fear he'd think Charlie was becoming a Mormon. So he tried to think of some sort of comment. It was late at night and he was tired: the best compliment he could come up with was "It's very inventive." The word sounded limp even to him, when applied to a book that was capturing him the way this one did. But to Heber it obviously sounded worse than limp. He stepped forward and took the book out of Charlie's hands.

"Thank you kindly, and I'll be going now. I'll have to hurry if I'm to find a place to sleep tonight."

Charlie was horrified. "What do you mean? You're sleeping here!" What if Mother came home and asked where he'd gone? Oh, I just read his letter to his wife and then insulted his Book of Mormon and he left—that would sit less than well with Anna.

"I don't mind sleeping in a house with those who hate me, but I don't stay with those who take me light."

"I don't take you lightly, you or your book!"

"Inventive! Mr. Kirkham, there ain't one invented word in that whole book. What do you think this whole business of religion is, a game I play? Do you think I'd come over here to this stinking damn city to talk my jaws off to people who mostly think I'm a curiosity, if I didn't know—not *think*, Mr. Kirkham, *know*—that the word of God is in that book? By God, and I say that not for blasphemy but because by God I'm speaking in the name of Jesus Christ, that book ain't *inventive*. It ain't no little toy for no pretty-faced little English bookkeeper to look down his nose at because it was brought here by an American who can't spell his own name without asking. You're damn lucky to have had a chance to look at that book, there's been prophets who would have given their lives for a look at it, but to you it's just a bunch of funny names and a lot of preaching."

Charlie tried to interrupt, to explain, but Heber wasn't one to let anyone cut him off before he was through.

"My wife's been sick, and my children, too, and when I left them I didn't know if they'd have a roof over their heads but I trusted in God to look after them because I know that the most important thing in the world is that book you're reading and the prophet who got it and the gospel he's teaching and the kingdom of God we're building and if you think I'm going to let you call it *inventive* then you don't know me, because I sure as hell ain't going to cast no pearls before *swine!*"

At last, out of breath from the force of his speech, Heber fell silent. Charlie looked at him in awe. "Mr. Kimball," Charlie said, "I'll tell you the truth. I like that book, I like it a lot."

"Liking is nothing."

"The whole truth. I *want* that book."

Suddenly, as if he had torn off a mask, Heber's face went from wrath to pure delight, and he handed the book back to Charlie and clasped the hand Charlie reached out to take it with. "I wish I had another copy, so I could give you one. But since that's my only one, I'm afraid I'll have to have it to take with me in the morning."

Charlie didn't know what to say. He had never been forgiven so fast in his life.

"Charlie," said Heber, "I spoke to you sharply a minute ago, but that's part of my work, too. If you really *want* that book, don't you go lying to me or to yourself with words like *inventive*. OK?"

Charlie smiled sheepishly. "I'll leave the book here on the table before I go to sleep. You can take it in the morning."

Heber shrugged. "As I said, it's there to be read. But let me give you two warnings."

"Warnings?"

"That part you just read is easy, it's all as exciting as a romance. But pretty quick they get into some heavy sermonizing. Some long passages that are bound to be above the head of a young fellow like you."

"Do you think so?" Charlie asked. He resented the idea that Heber considered him to have only the capacity of a "young fellow."

"Well, most young folks generally skip right over the book of Second Nephi and pretty well take up with the little books that come after. Lots of quotes from Isaiah in there, and Isaiah's as tough as going up the Mississippi without a paddle."

"I've read the Old Testament twice, and I particularly liked Isaiah."

Heber grinned at him. "Beg pardon, then. You're going to like Second Nephi just fine."

Heber turned to go.

"Wait a minute. You said there were two warnings."

Heber turned and leaned against the door frame. "The second one you'll like even less than the first."

"Well?"

"Well, reading the Book of Mormon is dangerous."

"How is it dangerous?"

"What if you find out that you think it's true? What'll you do about *that?*"

"Why should I do *anything* about it?"

"Well, Charlie, if the book's true, so's the prophet who translated it, and so's the angel who gave it to him, and so's the apostle of the Lord Jesus Christ who lent you the book to read, and so is the baptism that I offer you, and so is the church the Lord expects you to join. You can't have just part of it. If any of it's true, it's all true, lock, stock, and barrel, and once the Spirit tells you that it's true, why, kick against it all you like, you'll either become a Mormon or go to hell."

Then Heber stamped into Charlie's bedroom. Charlie heard the clump clump of the American's boots as they hit the floor; then he heard nothing more until his mother came home. By then he was well past the Isaiah sections, and if truth be known he had skimmed those, seeing how he had already read them before. He was caught up in the story of how once they got in the promised land the wicked older brothers rebelled and the Lord cursed them by turning them into Red Indians, only they were called Lamanites, and there was war constantly. It wasn't so much that it was exciting reading—there were a lot of sermons, and the language was stiffly scriptural. What kept Charlie fascinated was that it all felt important, it all felt true. Not true the way arithmetic was true, or the way things he saw with his own eyes were true. It just felt right, it felt like all this happened in a world where God knew his children and cared for them.

So when Mother came home, Charlie barely grunted a goodnight. Anna contemplated him for a few moments, then reminded him that work came at the same time in the morning no matter how late he went to bed. He muttered his usual "I know" without really hearing her. He was reading about how

Alma and Amulek, a prophet and his friend, were forced by the enemies of God to stand at the edge of a pit while men and women and children whose only crime was believing in God were cast into a fire and burned alive. "Why doesn't God strike his enemies down?" Amulek asked, and Charlie echoed the anguished question. Alma said, "The wicked must be allowed to do their wickedness. The ones who die find that death is sweet to them." True, true, Charlie cried out silently, that's how it must be, our enemies are cheated because however they try to hurt us, the pain is sweet to us for the sake of our faith!

He did not recognize that sometime during the night he had stopped thinking *they* and started thinking *we*, just as Dinah had done while Heber was speaking. He also did not notice the passage of time, only the passage of the tale. After the wars, which Charlie's imagination let him experience virtually in the flesh, there was terrible destruction—earthquakes and fires from heaven and huge waves and awful storms. Then silence, and darkness, and Jesus Christ spoke from the heavens. He had just been crucified in Jerusalem on the other side of the world, and where was he going? Why, straight to America to visit his people there. It was so far from the standard sermons about the harrowing of hell and the mystic, unintelligible union of the Father and Son and Holy Ghost in an indistinguishable trinity that Charlie found himself nodding and whispering yes, yes, for this was surely what it meant when the scripture said that Jesus came to *all* men, not just to the Jews in Jerusalem.

After Christ left, the people lived in peace for two hundred years. Then the wars began again, all because some people had to be rich when others were poor; they couldn't stand to share. All because of ungenerosity and greed, and finally the Lamanites were allowed by God to destroy the Nephites entirely, except for one lone man, Moroni, who finished writing on the golden plates and then buried them so Joseph Smith could find them and translate them a thousand or so years later. Charlie closed the book and couldn't bear for it to be over. He had lived in the world of the book and didn't want to leave it. He had been Nephi and Alma and the brave young sons of the Ammonites. He had touched the wounds of Christ's crucifixion and wept when he blessed the children. He had grieved with Mormon for all that the Nephite people had lost through their own sins.

And finally, when Moroni told his readers to ask God if the book was true, Charlie found himself saying: I don't need to ask, I know already. This was not written by a man. It was written by God, who knows the truth about the sufferings of children and younger brothers, who knows that those who have more money through luck or inheritance or profits are really just stealing the things of the earth that should belong to all men equally.

It was not all joy, finding something that sounded true to him. There was pain, too: the shame of realizing that he had never really forgiven Robert the way that Nephi forgave his brothers for even worse crimes; the frustration of knowing that by the time Nephi was Charlie's age he was already a prophet, writing scripture and calling upon angels. Yet what had Heber said? The worthy Saints all had the priesthood, the power of God. They all could speak and, if they had the faith and the need, the very elements would obey them. There were mighty works to be done, great works of faith, and Charlie wanted to be part of them. Wanted to be at the heart of them. Wanted to act without getting the counsel of any other soul. This time, God himself has called to me, and I don't need Robert's ridicule or Dinah's advice or Mother's worried glance.

Charlie got up from the divan and walked quietly into his bedroom. Heber was snoring softly, sprawled not under the blankets but atop them like a vast, untidy dog. Charlie went to him and touched his shoulder.

It startled him how quickly Heber awoke, how alert he was when he did. "It's not morning yet, Charlie," he said. "What do you want?"

"Heber, if I become a Mormon, will you give me the priesthood?"

Heber suddenly gripped Charlie's arm. "I was dreaming, Charlie, when you came in here. I dreamed I saw you sitting beside the Prophet Joseph, and he was dictating the words of the Lord and you were writing them down, and when you were through Joseph put his arms around you and said, 'Charlie, the Lord surely loves you.'"

The words coming the way they did, like prophecy, with Heber's voice husky with sleep—it sent chills along Charlie's back, and he shuddered. "Will it come true?" he asked.

Heber shrugged. "I don't know. It's hard to tell a vision

from a dream this early in the morning. If it comes true, it was a vision. Now go back to sleep."

"No. I've got to be at work in three hours. We'll have to hurry."

"It isn't morning yet."

"It's four-thirty."

"Charlie, have mercy on a man who walked from Clitheroe!"

"You can sleep all morning after I go to work. But you won't get any more rest tonight until you baptize me."

Kimball sat bolt upright, swung his legs off the bed, and began pulling on his boots. "I knew it!" he said. "I knew it, Charlie, I knew it the moment I saw you in the square, I felt it like a fire in my heart. That young man has been chosen for a great work. Did you finish the book?"

"Every page."

"It ain't exactly a short book, Charlie. You must be just about the fastest person ever to read enough of it to be converted."

As Heber put on his coat, Charlie chewed the word. *Converted.* Was that what had happened to him? He didn't feel any different. Just a small change, really. Just the feeling that God knew his name. Just the feeling that Old Hulme had reached out of heaven and touched him, opened up his heart and said, This is who you are, Charlie Kirkham—now what are you going to do about it?

Charlie opened up his palms in front of him, as if waiting to have a ruler strike him sharply, wake him up and tell him what to do. But there was no stinging slap from a slender piece of wood. Just Heber Kimball's large, strong hand gripping him and pulling him to his feet. "Before we leave the house, Charlie, I figure we ought to say a prayer together." Without waiting for Charlie to agree, Heber bowed his head, still holding Charlie's hands, and said, "Lord, yesterday Charlie Kirkham was so proud and stiff-necked he wouldn't know a mule if it kicked him. Well, it looks like you kicked him hard enough to wake him up. Now give him the strength to endure the trials and temptations that Satan will put in his way, to block him from performing the mighty work you have prepared for him, in the name of Jesus Christ. Amen."

Charlie didn't lift his head for a moment: he wasn't used to such brief prayers.

"It's early in the morning, Charlie. I don't get warmed up for long prayers until noon. Now come on, Charlie. If you still want to get baptized, the water's waiting for us."

Five minutes later they were standing in the cold water of the Rochdale Canal hoping that no barge would come along till they were through. Brother Heber said the words and dunked him under the water. Charlie came up sputtering and Heber laughed and said, "By damn, Charlie Kirkham, I'll bet you're the first man ever to come out of *this* water cleaner than he went in!" Then Heber wrapped him in a great bear hug. "Brother Charlie," Heber said. "Welcome to the fellowship of the Saints." Then they climbed out of the water together and went home to warm up and dry off. "And I hope we can talk your mother into a few inches of medicinal wine," Heber said. "Water's so cold it damn near cut me in two up the middle."

It hadn't been half an hour since Charlie set down the Book of Mormon; it hadn't been eighteen hours since he first saw Heber Kimball preaching in a square in Manchester. And here Charlie's whole life was changed, turned right around without him ever suspecting it was going to happen till it came. But there was no doubt in his mind: The Lord had sent Heber Kimball to Charlie. The Lord cared what happened to Charlie Kirkham. Charlie was his own man now—let the others do as they liked.

Old Hulme's face kept dancing before Charlie's eyes until Charlie said to him, "I belong to you now, I'm yours now, I'm your true son." Old Hulme smiled and nodded at him. He had done it right. He had answered all the questions right.

Dinah's madness of the night before was gone by morning, but in its place was an unaccustomed feeling of peace. She awoke looking at her husband's naked back, but instead of forcing herself not to resent him she felt the memory of her affection for him the night before, and she kissed his shoulder before she got out of bed, forgiving him for being so far short of what she needed her husband to be. For a moment she was even grateful for those good things that he actually was, and she even felt she knew him, and, knowing him, could love him.

She sang cheerfully as she prepared breakfast, and Val and Honor caught the mood and did not quarrel. It occurred to her

as Matthew happily gorged himself that she ought to mention
something about Heber Kimball and the new religion, but she
did not want to spoil the happiness of the moment by mentioning its cause. Matt kissed her passionately and said, "Good-
bye love," and she saw with pleasure that his eyes were a little
dazzled as he gazed at her a moment before leaving. We might,
she realized, make a happy marriage of this yet.

By the time the children were dressed, she no longer felt
the languid contentment of her first waking. She was more
vigorous than that. She wanted now to get out into the warm
morning sunlight, to talk to someone. Mother, of course, since
she did not know if Charlie shared her belief in this American
apostle. It was not until she had the children out of the house
and they were nearly at the footbridge that she remembered
that Heber Kimball would probably still be there, that he had
spent the night, that she might actually have a chance to speak
to him today. She quickened her step, hoping he had not got
an early start.

He was there at the table with his hair wet and sticking out
every which way as he made short work of cheese and toasted
day-old bread. She stood at the door; the children ran from her
straight to Grammum, laughing and talking about the birds they
had seen on the way. Dinah only stood there. Heber Kimball
looked up at her and smiled.

"Good morning," Dinah said.

Abruptly the smile left Heber's face. Or no, did not leave
it, but intensified to more than a smile, and he rose slowly
from the chair and reached out a hand to her. She walked to
him and took his hand. His eyes were very bright.

"Elect lady," he said softly, "the light of God is in your
face."

She did not understand the words, but did not care about
that; she knew that without her having to say anything, he knew
all about what she had felt the night before. He had seen it in
her face, and so she knew that it was real after all, that it was
not just madness or the afterglow of her husband's love; the
God that Heber had brought to her the night before was real.

As quickly as it had come, the feeling faded, and the touch
of hands became a handshake. "Your hair's wet," she said.

"Took a duck in the canal this morning," Heber said.

Anna came to the table, trailing children, and took Heber's

empty dish away, saying, "He baptized Charlie this morning."

Dinah could not speak. In all her life she had not known Charlie to make a decision like that on his own. Charlie, baptized already. It should have made her more confident of her own decision, but instead it frightened her a little. How much power did this Heber Kimball have over them?

"You look surprised," said Heber.

Dinah shrugged as if to deny it, then nodded slightly to confirm. Or thought she did—usually when speech failed, her gestures also became so slight that no one noticed them. But Heber noticed.

"I was confused, too," said Heber. "Last night he kept smiling a little at my best words. I figured he thought I was pretty funny, and so I did most of my talking to you, because you weren't laughing. And now here is a believer, and you—"

"Mr. Kimball, will you baptize me today, too?"

Heber made a face. "I wish you and Charlie had planned this better. My clothes are finally getting dry."

It was only then that Dinah realized Heber wasn't wearing his own suit. He was wearing some of John Kirkham's clothing, left behind when he had quit home years before. It fit Heber no worse than his own clothes, but that was not praise.

"I didn't know Charlie was going to be baptized," Dinah said.

"Well, at least you and your mother could have the consideration to do it at the same time. Your mother had a notion of waiting a few days."

Dinah looked at her mother, and Anna smiled. "I suppose there's no need to wait, if you and Charlie are so certain. But it's all so quick."

Heber laughed. "Quick! Why, you've been waiting all your lives for this. Before you were born you knew the gospel was true, and all your lives have been spent trying to see through your disguise and discover who you really are. Well, that's what the waters of baptism do—strip away the disguises and let you see yourselves whole. Though in fact I hope you won't mind my asking if we could choose some water cleaner than that canal. I don't think I'll ever smell sweet again."

Dinah was glad enough to avoid the canal—it was too public, and she did not want the eyes of strangers violating the event. "The River Medlock is clean upstream of Holttown, and it gets to be open country up that way. No one to see or—"

"Interfere."

"Will that do?"

"How deep is it?"

"I don't know."

Anna spoke from the hearth. "I know a bathing place on Medlock. I've picnicked there before."

"Well," Heber said, "sounds fine to me. But you're not just being baptized, you're joining a whole church, and it might be nice to meet some of the Saints. Besides which, I haven't so much as tipped my hat to the other brethren here, which some might think is rather rude."

Dinah did not want any delay. "I want to be baptized this morning."

"Won't take more than a half-hour. And don't dilly-dally. I've just eaten half the town of Manchester for breakfast and I'm ready to baptize the other half by noon!" With Val perched on Heber's shoulders, they set off.

The English headquarters of the Church of Jesus Christ of Latter-day Saints was installed in a dingy flat above a shop on Oldham Road, in one of the flimsy new buildings that Heber said would "not be around to see the Millennium unless the Lord hastens His coming." Dinah and Anna followed him up the stairs, carrying the children; Heber fairly bounded to the top, and they heard him bellow, "Brigham, Parley, it's good to see you!"

The office was furnished with one table, six stools, and a half-dozen packing crates, all stuffed with pamphlets like the ones Heber had given Charlie in the square. Stacked in one corner were bales of a journal, the *Millennial Star*. Heber had a copy of it and was sitting on the table poring over it, saying, "Wonderful! Wonderful! That'll wake 'em up!"

The two men in the office were both as American as Heber, sprawling back, hands behind heads, looking lanky and comfortable as pigs in a wallow, their hair just a little unkempt, their suits just a bit wrong for them. They were all fairly young men, too. Dinah had assumed that at least some of the apostles would be old, or older than Kimball, anyway. But both these men looked to be under forty, and their faces seemed more accustomed to grinning than to the sober mien most preachers cultivated.

It was Brigham Young, the one with the roundish face and light-brown, almost golden hair, who saw them first. Immediately he stood. "Heber, did these ladies come with you or find their way here on their own?"

Heber turned around, wrinkling some papers in the process, and looked very embarrassed. "Of course they came with me." He got up from the table and strode to them, ushering them into the room. "Sister Anna, Sister Dinah, and Dinah's children Val and Honor."

The jut-jawed man in the black suit offered his hand. "I'm Parley Pratt, apostle of the Lord Jesus Christ, and the only man in the room fit to recognize real beauty when I see it. Are you sisters?"

Anna laughed and allowed him to flirt a little. In the meantime, Brigham Young quietly introduced himself to Dinah. "I've learned," he said, "not to try to cut into Parley's conversation when he's performing for a lady. He takes it as a challenge and talks twice as long to put me in my place."

"I hear you maligning me," Parley said. Then he immediately returned to his flirtation with Dinah's mother.

Brigham grinned. "You see?"

"Beautiful, beautiful," Heber said, thrusting the *Millennial Star* at Brigham.

Brigham continued to grin at Dinah. "So I see."

"I meant the paper, Brigham. Sister Dinah is married to a man much better-looking than you."

"Impossible," Brigham said. Without looking at Heber, he took the journal and offered it to Dinah. "Here it is, the first issue of the first journal of the only true church of Jesus Christ in the British Isles. What do you think?"

Dinah was used to Heber's exuberance and rough American manners; she didn't mind Parley's rustic gallantries with her mother. But there was something about Brigham Young that annoyed her. A cocksureness about him. A hint that when he jokingly pretended to have a high opinion of himself, it was no joke at all. This is a man who's used to being obeyed, Dinah decided, and just as she had always defied her brother Robert when he had such a mood on him, she could not resist putting a small needle in Brigham's inflated pride.

"The quality of printing is quite good," Dinah said, "but it would not be harmed by a bit of attention from someone who knows how to spell." Deliberately she selected an article that had the initials "B.Y." at the end and said, "For instance, this article is virtually unintelligible to someone who actually knows how to read and write."

Heber whooped and Brigham smiled, but Dinah could see a slight hardness form around his eyes. He knew what she was doing.

"Sister Dinah, I agree with you completely. Just this morning we prayed for someone to come along and help us on that very matter. Here's my article for the next issue. I hope you'll be kind enough to correct it."

He held a sheaf of papers before her. This had gone too far, she knew—the game was becoming real, and she didn't want to make an enemy. "No," she said, "I'm not good enough myself to do it."

"I assure you," Brigham said, still smiling, "that it would be a great service to the work of the Lord if you'd fix up our writing. After all, we don't want to give the impression here in England that the Mormons are nothing but a bunch of country bumpkins who haven't the brains to spell *cat.*"

"I didn't say that," Dinah said.

"I didn't say you did."

There they stood, the papers between them, both of them smiling cheerfully. Dinah had challenged Brigham Young's authority, however slightly, and he was determined that she yield to him. Dinah had never bowed to Robert or, for that matter, to any man, and she certainly wasn't going to bow to Brigham Young. At the same time, she didn't want to make a quarrel of it—only Joseph Smith and his two counselors had more responsibility in the Kingdom of God than he.

She almost said—the words formed clearly in her mind— "I couldn't correct your writing without a translator to tell me what it said." Instead she used Brigham's own tactic. She could out-humble him easily. "How could a mere woman hope to do justice to a man's ideas?" she said, and grinned right back at him.

Brigham was beaten and he knew it—she could see it again in the hardness at the edges of his eyes. He held that expression for just a moment, and then laughed aloud, the corners of his eyes crinkling with genuine mirth. "You haven't been a Latter-day Saint long enough, Sister Dinah," he said. "All the sisters in America, at least, know perfectly well that God only gave the priesthood to *men* to even up the odds a little."

It was all so jovial. But underneath the conversation Dinah knew that the true dialogue had gone another way.

Don't cross me, woman, Brigham Young had said, for I'm much stronger than you.

And Dinah had answered, Watch your own step, Brother Brigham, for I'm your match.

They were baptized in a place on the River Medlock far enough from Manchester that the city was only a pall of smoke in the distance. The only spectators were sluggish cattle and a misanthropic squirrel who cursed them and vanished in the grass. There were a few trees along the banks of the stream, and on the other side of the fields the poplars stood as a windbreak wherever oaks and ashes hadn't deigned to grow. It was a place of peace, and Heber spoke Dinah's feelings when he said, "By damn, if heaven looks this good all over, I can't wait to die."

Parley told them, speaking of dying and heaven, how Brother Somebody-or-other had been absolutely certain the Millennium would come on April sixth, 1840. "Why, I think he was downright disappointed when he woke up that morning and the world hadn't ended."

"I remember," Heber said, "but I remember Brother Joseph telling him, 'Brother, if you really believed, why didn't you go and borrow a thousand dollars on a note due and payable on April seventh? And why did you buy a week's worth of groceries just the day before? If you'd had enough faith, why, the end might have come right on schedule.'"

"Now, Heber," Brigham said, "you know that Brother Joseph didn't say any such thing. It was *you* that said it."

"I know that, Brigham, but the story sounds so much better if it's him."

They had a laugh at that, but Dinah noticed that it was Brigham who damped the levity a bit, refused to let the tall tales get out of hand. The others never particularly deferred to him; they talked as if each man was free to decide to do whatever he wanted. But in fact Brigham was firmly in control, and things went his way. Dinah had to admire the subtlety of his leadership even as she resented the fact that he exercised it at all.

"I'm not sure, sisters, how I ought to broach such a delicate subject," Brigham said, "but you need to decide how modest your underclothing is, because there's no need to get your dress wet if your underclothing would not offend decency. Heber has promised me that his long shirt has no holes in it."

Dinah saw at once the sensibleness of it and refused to blush. "That will do very well, provided that you are circumspect while Mother and I help each other with our dresses."

The word *circumspect* was new to Brigham. Parley shrugged, but Heber snorted and said, "Look at the clouds, Brother Brigham, she wants you to look at the clouds!" Brigham and Parley decorously looked the other way, and Heber plopped himself on the grass to take his boots off.

A few minutes later Dinah stood at the water's edge, feeling very white and conspicuous in her petticoats. Heber was already in the river, his long shirt billowing out on the surface. He was discreetly conversing with Brigham and keeping his gaze away from the ladies, but at last he grew impatient and said, loudly, "Do hurry, Sister Dinah, since this river still thinks it's winter and wants to freeze over with me in it."

Dinah glanced at her mother, who smiled tightly and squeezed her hand. Then she stepped into the water. It was very cold indeed, and she gasped when the water reached her chest on a sudden step into deeper water. She stumbled forward. Heber caught her, laughing. "Sister Dinah, it does you no good to baptize *yourself*—I've got to say the words first."

He showed her how to hold her nose and grip his arm, too. They were both trembling in the cold, and he reassured her. "I never heard of anybody catching cold from a baptism. What's your full name?"

"Dinah Kirkham. Handy."

In an instant all the humor vanished from his face, and he raised his hand and said loudly, "Dinah Kirham Handy, having been commissioned of Jesus Christ, I baptize you in the name of the Father, and of the Son, and of the Holy Ghost. Amen."

The words were no sooner finished than he bore her backward into the water. She had expected him to hold her up, to keep her from sinking, but the water did that, catching the pockets of air that made bubbles in her petticoats. Heber pushed her down instead, farther and farther down, and for a few seconds she wondered if he meant to push her clear to the bottom. The cold was heavy; she needed to breathe.

Then, as suddenly as it had begun, the immersion ended

and she rushed upward to the surface of the river. Brigham and Parley were standing on the water's brink, nodding. "It's all right," Brigham said. "She was completely under."

Heber grinned at her. "You're lucky. If we don't get every speck of you under the water, we have to do it again."

Dinah's teeth were chattering as she struggled to shore. Now with her clothing wet and heavy on her, the current of Medlock seemed stronger, and it was harder to make headway. The current wanted to carry her off, now that she had given herself to the water. Brigham seemed to see her difficulty, and without hesitation he stepped into the water, boots and all, and helped her get to the bank. She sat there shivering in the sunlight while Heber baptized her mother.

When it was all over, the men walked back to the road while Dinah and Anna stripped each other of their wet petticoats. The sunlight was bright and warm on Dinah's naked shoulders as she helped her mother with her dress. She had never felt so healthy. As for Anna, she was weeping softly, but tears of joy. When they were both dressed again, they gathered up their wet underwear into a bundle, which Dinah insisted on carrying; but they did not go immediately to join the men.

"Sister Anna," Dinah said.

"Sister Dinah," Anna said, and they laughed and embraced each other. "I'm clean," Anna whispered. "I'm forgiven. John can come home now."

The words sent a shudder up Dinah's spine. "Mother," she said, "whatever gave you the idea that baptism would bring him home?"

"I prayed last night. I asked God for a sign. I told him that I'd be baptized if it meant I was completely forgiven and John would come home. And I asked for a sign. If two of my children were baptized on the same day, then I'd know it was all true. I didn't dream that Charlie would be baptized before I even woke up in the morning, and when you said that you weren't going to wait another day, I knew my prayer had been answered."

"Mother," Dinah said, thinking to help her see reason.

"Dinah, my dear, I know I'm being perfectly unreasonable. I don't care. It doesn't matter whether you believe in it or not. The Lord heard my prayer, and sooner or later, he'll bring my John back home to me again."

Dinah could not bear to argue with the joy in her mother's

face. But neither could she help hoping, as they walked through the grass to the road where the apostles waited, that of all the miracles God might work the return of John Kirkham would not be one.

✎ 19 ✎

Charlie and Dinah
Manchester, 1840

CHARLIE'S HAIR WAS STILL damp from the baptism when Mr. Royal called him into his office. It was a summons that would have filled most men in the firm with dread. Charlie knew better. He made few mistakes, and Mr. Royal had no reason to censure him; in the years he had worked there, nothing but good had come to him in Mr. Royal's office. It wouldn't have mattered—Charlie was still so elated from the events of the night and morning and so giddy from lack of sleep that even if Mr. Royal had sacked him he might well have thanked him effusively and laughed all the way home.

It would be no sacking. Mr. Royal was all smiles.

"Charles Banks Kirkham, it occurs to me that your eighteenth birthday is not far off."

"A few months, I think," Charlie said.

"Have a seat, my good fellow. Nearly eighteen. And doing a damn fine job here, a boy with promise, with real promise. You're not meant to be a *bookkeeper*, boy."

Charlie had long harbored that opinion himself, of course. Still, it didn't do to admit discontent. "Oh, I like being a bookkeeper well enough, sir."

"You won't in fifteen years, I can promise you, Charlie. No, you have the gifts to follow another path in life, and soon you will take your first step along that path. I shall not meander any more, good fellow. We have arranged with our London solicitor, and *he* has arranged with a noted barrister, for you to begin the study of law in the autumn. In London. Entirely at our expense. Do I surprise you? Don't let your jaw gape, boy, it's unbecoming."

Charlie's jaw had not been gaping, of course; it was all Mr. Royal's good humor. And now Mr. Royal arose from his chair and strode around his desk, took Charlie by the hand and drew him up into a hearty, back-slapping embrace. "You know what it means, Charlie? We don't mean for you to become a mere solicitor, like ourselves, lad. We mean you to achieve the bar, and then to come home and be a most junior but most worthy partner in our firm. How's that, lad? Study in London, and come home to part ownership of the finest, most prestigious, and I must say the most lucrative firm of solicitors in Manchester. Think of it! A man who knows both law and money! And what will there be to stand in your way then? In ten years you stand for Parliament—Tory, of course. In twenty years bewigged as a judge. And in thirty years, why not Charles Lord Kirkham, I ask you? The world is open to you. What do you have to say?"

Say? "Thank you, sir!"

"That's the closest to speechless I've ever seen you, Charlie. Do I take it that I have your consent to make arrangements for your housing and study in London in September?"

"Oh, yes sir," Charlie said. "I hope to be able to deserve this honor, sir—"

"Yes, yes, of course you do, and of course you will, never mind all that. Of course, you *will* have to make some changes in your personal habits. I did a bit of asking around, and I'm relieved you've never acquired the habit of loitering in public houses. So far as I can discover your record in the matter of women is perfect. You are exemplary in all the necessary traits but one. The matter of the Establishment."

And now the first wedge was driven into Charlie's joy. The

Establishment. Of course a barrister and a partner in the firm had to be a good Anglican.

"Mind you," Mr. Royal said, "no one expects you to become *fanatic.*" Charlie inwardly cringed at the word. *Fanatic.* Exactly the word that a man like Mr. Royal would apply to a Mormon. "It would be almost as bad if you attended service too often," Mr. Royal said, "as it is now, with you attending not at all. Moderation in all things, lad. Twice a month, that's all, you ought to be seen in services. Prominently seen in services, in fact—it is definitely expected. And since I follow my own advice and attend twice a month myself, I invite you to come with me. I'll introduce you to our honored pastor, and from that time forward you will be known as a godly man. You see, it's quite simple to establish a decently religious reputation, and to maintain it you need only limit yourself to the more customary or fashionable sins, and be discreet." Mr. Royal winked.

Charlie managed a smile. A few days ago, this cynical attitude toward religion would have struck him as amusing. Now it seemed almost atheistic. It repelled him. He wanted to say, Sir, I am a believing member of the Latter-day Saint faith. I shall attend services *every* Sunday, and will commit no sins at all, fashionable or not.

But he did not say that. Instead, he said, "Sir, I shall not disappoint you in any particular."

"You never have, boy, and I believe you never will, which is why we are extending you this considerable opportunity."

Mr. Royal exuded pride as he took Charlie through the firm, announcing Charlie's wonderful prospects to everyone. Charlie did not have to pretend—he relished every moment of it. The bar. It meant a real chance to amount to something, not just in Manchester but in *England*, and not just in England but in the world, for didn't England lead the world? It was everything Charlie had ever dreamed of, and God surely meant him to do it. It was God's plan for him. The signs were clear: Hadn't this good news come the very day of his baptism? Charlie repeated it to himself over and over. God wants me to do this. It is the will of God. He told himself this most particularly whenever he thought of the fact that he had been baptized into one church and had just agreed to be a faithful member of another. It was only a small hypocrisy. God surely wouldn't mind him holding his new Mormon allegiance in abeyance for a few months or years. This was plainly, plainly the will of God. Charlie was *sure* that it couldn't really be, was *sure* that there wasn't a chance in the world that Mr. Royal's offer was, in reality, a temptation from the devil to lead him away from the true church. The devil never tempted you with something *good*, only with nasty things—if he had learned nothing else of religion in his childhood, he had learned *that*.

Anna and Dinah knew it wouldn't be easy to tell Matthew and Robert about their baptism. Anna suggested telling Mary and letting her tell her husband and brother, but Dinah dismissed that suggestion as cowardice.

"They'll be angry anyway," Anna said. "If *she* tells them, they'll have time to calm down before talking to us about it."

"I'm not so sure," Dinah said, "that they'll be angry."

Anna looked askance at her daughter. "My dear child, don't you know anything about men? They think they own a woman's conscience when they only own her heart."

Dinah did not mention that Matthew didn't even own *that*.

In the end they decided that they would gather all the family at Dinah's house for supper that night. They left a note for Charlie, then stopped by Mary's house to invite her, telling her only, "Mother and I have something very important to announce to the family, so we hope you and Robert and the children will come."

It was still bright evening outside as the family ate together. Dinah watched with pleasure the friendly way that Robert and Charlie spoke to each other. Matthew wasn't quite so jocular and happy, but then he was prone to surly moods, and at least he wasn't rude. Robert's three sons—one every fourteen months since the marriage—managed to make a healthy amount of noise with Val and Honor, and Anna kept saying, "We must do this more often, it's so good to have us all together like this."

Finally, when the meal was through, Anna began the announcement. "Something has happened that I think will bring us more happiness than anything else that's happened in our lives before." She hedged around awhile more, but Dinah let her do it. It was a measure of her innocence that Dinah was much more interested in Charlie's response than in Matthew's.

After all, Charlie still had no idea that he wasn't the only member of the family who had believed Brother Heber's message. His surprise would surely be delicious to watch. And Anna and Dinah had agreed not to tell about Charlie's baptism—they'd let him break the news himself.

"So today, this very afternoon," Anna finally said, "Dinah and I went to the River Medlock and were baptized."

To Dinah's surprise, Charlie did not burst out in delight with the news of his own earlier baptism. If he had, things might have gone differently; but instead of adding to Dinah's and Anna's enthusiasm, he stared glumly at his plate, avoiding anyone's eyes.

The silence became heavy very quickly. Charlie had not done his part; Anna could not think of anything to say, and Dinah could only watch in silence as Robert and Matthew traded eloquent looks.

"Good God," Robert finally said. Dinah nearly laughed aloud, the words were so ironically appropriate. "Good God, Mother, I thought you had more wit than to run off after the first fine-talking American frontiersman who reads your fortune and forgives your sins."

Dinah watched her mother grow angry. "I haven't run off after anyone."

And so it went, bad to worse, and yet never loud, never furious. It was all the more horrible because of that, Dinah felt; Robert saying terrible things to Mother, and Anna doing her best to answer, neither of them raising their voices, all said in such an oppressive calm. If they could only shout at each other, Dinah thought, then they would realize what they were doing and stop themselves. Instead they went on, and in the back of her mind Dinah kept hearing a relentless tearing sound, like the ripping of heavy velvet. The fabric of the family was coming apart now, and she had not even known that it was frayed. For so many years now Robert had acted in the family as if he were the father, but only because he had never tried to rule, only because Anna had willingly given place to him. Now he was asserting authority at the very moment his mother had withdrawn it; this cannot end well, Dinah said silently. Something will be irremediably broken before the night is out.

Charlie, too, felt the heat of the argument and the weight of his own silence. Who would have dreamed that Dinah and

Mother would be baptized, too? He had thought he was alone, the only one, that no one would mind much if he pretended to be Anglican for a while. Now he knew that the women expected him to speak, needed him to speak; and he also knew that if he spoke now, his whole future was undone.

In the end it was not Anna's and Dinah's needs that made up Charlie's mind for him. It was Robert. Robert, who knew so much about the Mormons from having heard a bit of asinine talk from the half-witted fools in the shop. Robert, who sneered and asked if the religion could be any good if they couldn't find fools enough to fill their churches in the wilds of America? Robert, who again and again said, "I won't have my family members making idiots of themselves like this. I forbid it."

Charlie could see that every time Robert forbade it he made Anna and Dinah angrier than before, more determined to pursue their faith. He could almost see the wall growing between Robert and the women. And as the wall grew he stopped thinking about his promise to Mr. Royal, stopped thinking about studying for the bar in London. All he could see was that the family was being split apart tonight, perhaps never to be healed again, and when the split was complete, Charlie knew where he must be: on the other side of the wall from Robert. When Charlie had been baptized this morning, it was an act of exuberant faith; but faith could fade. It was hatred and envy that lasted. Now if the family divided between Mormons and unbelievers, between Saints and cynics, it would shut Robert out forever. All that would be left would be Charlie and Anna and Dinah. The three of them, as they had always ought to be, without that strutting cock to say, I forbid it. Forbid all you like—you will not change *me* with your forbidding, Charlie declared silently, never realizing that in fact it was Robert's very forbidding that had changed him. Temptation had made him waver in the faith; but if Robert was against Mormonism, Charlie would be a Mormon forever.

Yet Charlie began his answer calmly enough. After all, he was a martyr now, like Christ saying, Forgive them, for they know not what they do. He was sacrificing future wealth and honor for the sake of God and the true religion, and it behooved him to speak with the proper Christian mildness. "I guess it makes all the difference whether you believe in Mormonism or not. Whether or not you've been touched by the—the Spirit of God." Ah, yes, that was just right; and Charlie completed the effect with a beatific smile.

Robert turned slowly to look at him. "From those words am I to assume you partake of their insanity?"

Charlie's voice stayed soft and gentle, but his eyes now turned his words into javelins. "If what we learned last night is madness, I would to God all the world were mad."

"It would give you company, I expect," Robert said contemptuously. "If you had the smallpox, you'd probably wish for an epidemic."

Charlie only smiled more broadly. Yes, Robert, attack me all you like. The more you argue the more I know that God is on my side. With an accuracy born of years of practice, Charlie found the words that would hurt the most. "I understand why you're so upset about it, Robert. You're afraid that if we keep this up, we might discover that you aren't God."

All pretense of civility ended here. Dinah had wished for shouting; soon enough she would wish for whispering again. Robert shouted that he had no such pretensions; Charlie answered, "You always think that you know better than God what's best for other people. When we don't do what you say, it always leads to misery. Why, if I had followed your fine plans for me, I might be a journeyman chimneysweep today, instead of settling for mere bookkeeping." The perfect touch. It always worked. The argument would have ended right there, probably, or at least begun to weaken, except that Charlie could not resist adding one more accusation. In the heat of the argument, he had forgotten that Matthew was even there. "I'm surprised you didn't end up getting Dinah married to Mr. Uray— but you did your best, didn't you!" He had meant only to attack the way that Robert had controlled his sister's life; but Matthew took it another way.

"Watch your tongue, you little bastard!" Matthew shouted. "No one had to force a girl to marry *me!*"

Charlie immediately realized what he had done, that this was a point of pride with Matt, but he was too angry and felt much too righteous to back down now. "May God strike me if I've said anything that isn't true tonight!"

"I've half a mind not to wait for God!" Matthew bellowed, leaping to his feet. "Let's see if your Mormon God will save your head from breaking open!"

Charlie immediately stood up from his chair, though he knew that a fight with Matt was not much different from walking into a den of lions. It was an apt occasion for a martyrdom, and Charlie was ready and willing for the matter to come to blows. Dinah, without thinking, acted at once to prevent unforgivable violence between her brother and her husband.

"Matt," she said, "you'd be wise not to speak about things you know nothing of."

It worked this far—it drew Matthew's wrath from Charlie to Dinah. "I see that you're determined to make your husband out a fool for your brother's benefit."

"Angels," Robert said coldly. "Golden Bibles. It's not worth hitting the boy, Matt. He's never had any sense at all."

The fire of faith was in Charlie's eyes. "It's not a matter of sense, Robert—you're right that far. But I swear to you in the name of Christ that every word of the Mormon religion is true. And now that Mother and Dinah are with me, I'd gladly die for it."

"No doubt of that, Charlie," Robert answered him. "You've always had to borrow your courage from women."

It was a vicious remark, and Anna gasped.

"Never mind, Mother," Charlie said. "I'll freely admit that I've learned courage from Dinah and you. God only knows where else I would have learned it."

Stiffly Robert got up from the table and reached for Mary's hand. "Come, Mary, we're going home."

Mary, who had looked on in horror through the entire quarrel, made a few feeble efforts to patch things up. Robert would have none of it. He gathered up his sons, gave the baby to Mary, and was out the door without another word to anyone. The children sensed something of what was going on; they were all silent, watching the adults, and when Robert's children were gone, Val and Honor retreated to a far corner of the parlor, out of sight, their eyes wide and watching. Matthew stood near the wall, looking at the door that had just closed behind Robert.

"I think," Anna said quietly, "that it would be best if we went home now, Charlie."

Charlie glanced at Matthew, whose face showed less than nothing. Dinah whispered, "Please, Charlie."

Charlie walked around the table and took Dinah by the shoulders. "It's all bearable, knowing we're together in it. I'm glad, I am, with no regrets." When he said it, he meant it. Yet under his anger at Robert there was a part of him shouting that he had made a terrible mistake, that he had traded a sure and marvelous future for an uncertainty, and all just to make sure he was in the opposite camp from his brother. Was it worth it, to give up all this, just to shut Robert from the family? But the answer was, and always would be, Yes. Robert stood forever between Charlie and manhood. And with this day's work, Charlie had shunted him aside.

Anna kissed her daughter. Her good-bye to Matthew was unanswered: Dinah's husband just stood by the wall, his fists clenched, staring at nothing.

"Is he going to be all right?" Anna whispered.

Dinah nodded. It was just the surprise. He was angry, but given time it would all smooth over, it would be all right.

The latch clicked; they were gone; only Matthew and Dinah remained, with the children quietly watching from the corner, invisible. Dinah turned to face her husband. Now he moved, coming away from the wall toward her, his face dark, his fists clenched. She steeled herself for the flood of abuse, for the accusations, for the recriminations. She was not prepared for him to raise his fist and swing it furiously at her face. She saw what he was doing, but she could not believe it, she could not respond to it, she could only watch the fist coming until it came.

The pain exploded in her head, and she found herself on the floor, leaning against the wall. She lay stunned for a moment; then the pain in her jaw struck her, and she felt her mouth filling up with blood, tasted it; she tried to spit it out, but she hadn't the strength to spit. She could only open her mouth and let the blood flow out. With it came something hard. She could only think, thank heaven it wasn't a front tooth, no one has to know my husband knocked my tooth out. No one has to know what we've sunk to.

She became aware that Matthew was screaming at her. His voice was very distant, and she could only make it out now and then, but it was full of fury, and it frightened her. Make a bloody ass of me in front of your family, will you? Leave your husband to go off chasing after some American bastard! On and on, until the accusations became monstrous. How often has he had you? Answer me! You've had the American preacher here in my own bed, haven't you! Answer me!

She would have liked to answer him, but she knew her body could not make the shout she needed, knew her lips could not form words strong enough to express her loathing for his filthy mind.

He grabbed her by the jaw and throat and yanked her forward. She gagged. "Answer me, you filthy bitch! Pretending to be my wife and running around behind my back, I want words from you!"

To her surprise her mouth would open after all. She did not know what she was going to say until she heard herself saying it, and even then her mouth was so clumsy, her tongue so sluggish that she could barely understand herself. "Compared to you, Mr. Uray was a gentleman."

But Matthew understood her, understood that she regarded him, not with anger, not with fear, but with contempt. He roared with anger; it was more provocation than he could bear. She saw his boot coming at her body. There was nowhere to move, no way to hide or protect or cushion and the blow came, yes, there, and it drove out even that slight self-control that had let her hold still to try to minimize the pain. She screamed, and her jaw popped out of joint with a hideous crack; the boot hit her again, this time in the belly, and she vomited instantly.

She lay in the pool of vomit wondering when she would die. But she didn't die. And vaguely she was aware that the door had opened and someone had come in, it was little Val leading someone in, saying, "Uncle Robert, stop him, please." Oh yes. It was Robert. He had come back, Val had brought him back, Robert would take care of things, Robert would make everything all right. Mr. Uray won't dare hit me again, because I have a brother. I don't have a thing to worry about, nothing to worry about at all.

❧ 20 ❧

John Kirkham
Manchester, 1840

IT TOOK THREE WEEKS for the bruises on Dinah's face to heal enough for her to go out; Matthew's bruises took even longer to heal, but he hadn't the luxury of being able to stay indoors as Dinah could. He had to go to work every day with Robert, who had, with only a few well-placed blows, blacked both his eyes, bruised his ribs, and broken his nose. For the first time Dinah believed that Robert might have been sincere when he threatened to kill Mr. Uray—she had never known Robert had such a capacity for violence.

Nor did she suspect her own capacity for forgiveness. Certainly she had feared and hated him at first, as she tossed and turned in an impossible effort to escape from the pain. Her mother nursed her for three days before she was able to get up and care for herself, and even then speech came only with difficulty through her aching jaw. Her tooth had only been broken off—a dentist had to come and pull the rest of it, and during the agony of his wrenching and tearing she hated Matthew again. But that, too, passed, and Val and Honor looked up at her from faces that were as much Matthew's as her own, and she began to remember all the pressures that had pulled at him that day; her pain faded, and so did her fear and anger, and when he came to her abject and sincerely ashamed of his brutality, she did not feel the loathing she expected. She found, to her surprise, that she wanted to go home again, out of her mother's house, back to the routines that she had so detested before, but now missed.

Dinah had no fear of the incident happening again. Matthew was not habitually violent, and now they lived in an uneasy truce. Robert had been plain about it: If Matthew ever raised a hand against his sister for any reason, Robert would take it upon himself to provide for Dinah, Val, and Honor, for he'd see to it that if Matthew lived he'd be divorced and disgraced and discharged from his job. Dinah could not help suspecting that it was the job that held Matthew under control better than the threat of disgrace or divorce. Robert held Matthew's pursestrings, and Matt was too used to living well now. He would not do anything that would force him back to a common engineer's wage.

Yet the humiliation of obeying Robert's orders told on Matthew, hurt him deeply, and Dinah grieved for him. Glumly he would come into the house after work, and speak, when he spoke at all, only of common household matters. He ate, he thanked her graciously for the meal, and then off he went to Chartist meetings or the pub. The political meetings were his one gesture of independence, yet it was feeble enough: Charlie had already refused his firm's offer and was going to Mormon meetings regularly, so the need for Matthew to avoid indiscretion was gone.

He found small ways to punish Dinah, however. He gave her money of her own now, for the first time, but in a way calculated to offend. He never made love to her anymore except on the nights when he got paid, and after he satisfied himself he would get up and take ten shillings from the pocket of his pants and put it on her dresser. She knew he meant to make her feel like a whore; oddly enough, however, now for the first time she didn't. She could not forget what had happened the night of her conversion, and she took more pleasure from his body now than she ever had before. If he sensed the difference, he probably attributed it to the money, and despised her for it. He would never believe it if she told him that her new faith had healed the scars in her that had kept her from the pleasures of the bed. He would more easily believe that it was the beating that had taught her to be less cold during the act of love.

The beating did still loom between them. It had left no permanent disfigurement on her, and Dinah, understanding how provoking that night had been, allowed the memory of fear and pain to recede, almost to be forgotten. Forgiving him was easier than she had expected—for her. It was the children who kept the memory of that night alive. Val would wake up screaming in the night, "Father, don't! Uncle Robert, help me, help me!" Dinah would get up and take him from his bed and walk up and down the hall, holding him and singing softly to him that it was all right, that no one was hurting anyone now. At such times Matthew would pretend to be asleep, but she knew it was a lie: more than once she came back to bed after getting Val to sleep again and saw tears reflecting candlelight at the corners of Matt's eyes. Matthew grieved to hear the terror of his son; Matthew was ashamed. It was that more than anything that led Dinah to forgive him, and yet it was also that which kept Matthew from letting the wounds heal. He was so sure that she hated him as she walked the floor with their crying child that he could not admit the possibility that now, for the first time in their marriage, she might be willing actually to love him, not *because* he had been cruel to her, but because he was so ashamed of it.

When her face no longer showed the visible signs of the beating, Dinah began attending the Mormon meetings. That was part of the settlement Robert had imposed. His family may have gone mad for this foolish religion, but by God if she wanted to take her children to these meetings Matthew had better not try to stop her. Dinah suspected that if Matthew had *not* beaten her, but merely forbidden her to attend the meetings, Robert would have gone right along—it was his rage at Matthew's violence that made Robert so solicitous of her religious freedom.

Life at home was so tense and bleak that Dinah began to live for those hours with the Saints. She was not the only one who had suffered for the sake of the Church, she knew, and more than one of the sisters sneaked into the meetings after they had begun and left early, obviously stealing precious moments of fellowship against the will of their husbands. Dinah made a point of sitting with these women and whispering to them now and then; she was one of them, and hoped to give them the strength that would come from knowing they were not alone in their sufferings. It began with Dinah squeezing a hand, whispering a word, smiling at a face worn grim with discouragement. After a very short time, Dinah found herself always surrounded by sisters. One of them even spoke to her about it. "Sister Dinah, I thank God for you every night."

"Why?" Dinah asked in genuine surprise.

"The Brethren are all good men, but *you* understand."

Understand what? I understand the need of a woman to know that she is not utterly alone in the world her husband creates for her. I understand that side by side with the brotherhood that Brigham and Heber and Parley sermonize about, there is a sisterhood also. Of course the apostles give no comfort to these lonely women—how can *they*, who are husbands, really sympathize with disobedient wives?

She began to feel that this sisterhood was what the Lord wanted of her. As she came to care more and more for them, Dinah felt the light within her growing, so that although it never was as intense as that first night, she often felt life and power just under the surface of her skin; she often felt that God was honing her like a fine and sturdy knife to cut through the veil that hid his face from the world.

On a Sunday in June, at Carpenters Hall, Brigham Young announced to a conference of all the Saints in England that the Lord commanded the faithful to come to America and help build Nauvoo, the city of God. Many of the Saints were filled with fear at the idea of crossing the ocean, but Dinah heard it with joy. It was what she had wanted from the start. The place where there would be no poor, for the Saints would all uphold each other plenty and in want. The place where God walked among living men.

But cheap as the voyage to America was, it was far too expensive for most of the Saints. Brigham was pretty plain about that—the rich Saints would be forbidden to go to Nauvoo unless they had helped as many of the poor Saints make the voyage as they could. Charlie was the next speaker. He set aside his prepared text and spoke from the heart. "I'm not rich by any measure, but I know what real poverty is, and I think I can speak for my mother, too, when I say that we'll gladly live as we lived when we were poor in order to save the money for our own passage—and for the passage of five other people before the summer's out!"

There were cheers at that, and before Charlie could go on talking and weaken the effect, Brigham came to the pulpit and put his arm around Charlie and said, his voice breaking with emotion, "If every Saint in the Church had as much faith as Charlie Kirkham, Zion would already be standing, and the Savior would already have returned to the earth!"

Perversely, while the rest of the congregation was encouraged by Charlie's words, Dinah worried. Gathering to Zion posed a greater difficulty for her than mere money. There was the matter of Matthew. He would never go with her to America, still less to the city of the Mormons. Did that mean, then, that to fulfill her vows to her husband, she had to disobey God's commandment to gather with the Saints?

"We can't go," Anna said bluntly as they walked home from the conference.

Dinah said nothing, only hefted Honor higher on her shoulder. Val had stayed home with Matt this morning; the conference would only have bored him, and Sundays *were* the only days Matt had to be with his son.

Anna took her silence as argument. "I know that we're supposed to obey the Lord's commandments, but you have a husband, Dinah! And so have I."

"Do we?" Dinah asked.

"Yes we do," Anna said vehemently. "Till death do us part, if you recall."

"A marriage can die while both its members are still breathing."

"Do you mean that you'll *run off* from your husband?" It sounded ugly; Anna meant it to.

"I would never leave my husband for another man," Dinah said quietly. "I would never leave my husband, even if he beat me, even if he falsely accused me of terrible sins, even if he hated me. But if God commanded me to go to Zion, and my husband wouldn't come, then yes, Mother, I would take my children and *run off*."

"You've never reared children without their father. I have."

"You survived."

"There were many days when I prayed that I wouldn't."

They walked in silence for a few moments, watching a desultory game of ball going on in a square, the workman far too tired to put much vigor into the competition. What an empty land this England is, Dinah thought. "We're foreigners here, Mother," she said at last. "I want to go home."

"So do I," Anna said softly. "But *I* won't go without my husband."

Dinah sighed. Anna still believed that John Kirkham would come home. How could she even *want* him? Mother had loved her husband; Dinah had no experience in that.

Charlie caught up with them, calling out to them from a hundred yards behind. They stopped and waited. Dinah watched him running toward them. Seventeen years old. What was it that drove him to seem so much older?

"You were there, weren't you? You heard what Brother Brigham said, didn't you?"

"Yes, and we're proud of you," said Anna.

"Not proud of *me*," he said. "What do *I* matter? America! Zion! Of course, Dinah, I know you won't be able to go at once. But someday soon we'll bring Matthew round to see the truth. And in the meantime Mother and I will be there, and we'll write to you and tell you all about it. I'll write you hundreds of pages, a book's worth—who knows! Maybe I'll really *write* a book! And I'll meet the Prophet. Brother Heber prophesied, or at least he had a dream—but you know about the dream, don't you, I already told you."

A dozen times. "I'm glad for you," Dinah said. "But of course Mother isn't coming with us."

"Dinah," Anna said.

"Mother won't leave unless Father comes with her."

Charlie looked at his mother oddly. "What would you even want him for? Bloody lot of a husband he's been to you. And I might as well have been an orphan for all I ever knew of him."

"Mind your language, Charlie," Anna said. Angrily she took Honor out of Dinah's arms and strode on ahead of them.

"I didn't mean to make her angry," Charlie said. "But has she lost her mind?"

"Now she's been baptized, she thinks God will bring her husband home."

"If we're lucky, he'll never come back. If I didn't kill him, Robert would."

"You don't sound like much of a Saint when you talk like that."

Charlie immediately sobered. "No, I don't, do I? I'm sorry. Of course I'd forgive him. Seven times seventy, the Savior said." He didn't sound too happy about the prospect. They walked in silence for a while, and then Charlie suddenly brightened. "I haven't told you yet, have I!"

"Told me what?"

"I'm to be ordained an elder."

"At your age!"

"Oh, don't give me that nonsense, Dinah! At my age." He playfully elbowed her and laughed, looking for a moment even younger than seventeen. "The Prophet was my age when he saw an angel."

It startled Dinah to think of that. To Brother Joseph's own family, he was just a boy like Charlie. *Would I follow Charlie if he started his own church?*

When she got home she served Matthew his dinner, and was so determinedly cheerful that he also smiled, though she knew he resented her having gone to church even if she had left Val with him. *Could I leave you?* she wondered as she dished him more potatoes. *Could I take your children from you, could I take your son and go off to America where you'd never see them again?*

Yes, I could.

That realization filled her with a cold hard light that was at once frightening and exhilarating. *Have I no heart? Or too much spirit to be bound by old and already-broken oaths? Love, honor, and cherish, he had promised, and then beaten her for following her conscience. Surely that released her from her oath, didn't it?*

No, it didn't. The oath was not conditional, it didn't say love, honor, and obey until you decide to go to America or until you get angry. *I can't leave him, I can't steal his family from him, I'm lying if I say I can.*

After dinner he groaned and lay on the floor and tussled

with Val, who didn't believe that his father could really want
to rest. Dinah held Honor on her lap and told her a story while
they watched their menfolk at play. For a while she believed
that she really had a family after all, that one reason she couldn't
leave Matt was because she loved him. That was possible,
wasn't it? God had changed her heart in so many other ways,
mightn't he also have changed it in that? And when the hour
came to go back for the testimony meeting in the afternoon,
she kissed her husband with real affection, carried Honor and
took Val by the hand, and set off fairly dancing with joy.

As always, Dinah wasn't allowed to hold her own children
during the meeting. Val was a great favorite with the young
unmarried women. He could flirt audaciously and never offend—there were advantages to being three. And there were
several older women who either never had children of their
own or missed their babies who had grown up and left home,
and one of them always ended up jealously cuddling Honor,
refusing to relinquish her until the meeting ended.

So Dinah was left without the burden of the children as she
sat in the midst of the sisters who gathered to her. It was a
testimony meeting, the Saints rising to their feet to give little
impromptu speeches about their love for God. The words were
so often the same that Dinah only occasionally listened. Then
a sister arose whose husband had threatened to have her put in
the asylum if she continued her madness of being a Mormon.
The sister spoke of how nothing would stop her from associating
with the family of God as long as she was able, and the emotion
in her voice and the story behind her words were profoundly
moving. Here, touched by real faith, surrounded by women
who depended on her, Dinah's momentary affection for Matthew faded. Here is where I am at home, thought Dinah. Here
is my family. How could I have thought otherwise? When the
boat leaves for America, I will be on it. I have put my hand
to the plow and I will not look back.

As that surety grew within her she felt the light also grow,
with a fire that burned behind her eyes. It grew so hot and
bright she thought she would burst with it, and she longed to
leap to her feet and cry out—what, she did not know.

Suddenly the woman stopped speaking in midstream. Dinah
realized that the woman was looking at *her*, and Dinah was
sure she could see the light coming out of her eyes. The woman
paused for just a moment, and then she began to speak again.

But now the words did not come in the accents of Lancashire. They were a rush of syllables that sounded like no language Dinah had ever heard, sounds cascading from her lips and filling the room. It was the gift of tongues, which Dinah had heard of but never seen before, someone so caught up in the Spirit of God that English would no longer contain her feelings.

Suddenly Dinah realized that she understood her, that playing about at the back of her mind were the words the woman was really saying, only the words were swords of light, and they could pierce the veil that bound them, they could be expressed. Without thinking, Dinah leapt to her feet and began to translate, saying the words that formed themselves within her. She hardly understood herself; all that mattered was to speak. For five minutes it went on; it went on forever. Dinah and the woman who spoke in tongues looked steadily at each other, noticing only the tears that flowed from the other's eyes, not their own.

Finally the woman stopped speaking and slowly sat down, and Dinah felt the words fade within her. Physically spent by the experiences, she sat and trembled as the women near her touched her. Dinah saw that her own mother was weeping. What had she said? She couldn't remember. She only knew that it had happened as she knew it must. She had been a mouthpiece for the Lord; the light within her had been born, had come alive for all to see. It frightened her, it thrilled her, it gave her peace. I have chosen aright. I am acceptable to the Lord. It is my validation, my assurance. Father, she said silently, I will follow you forever, across the sea, away from my husband if need be, over the mountains of death, through whatever storms of suffering. The face she had imagined for Joseph Smith smiled at her.

And at the front of the room, standing at the pulpit, Brigham Young was also smiling. "Brothers and Sisters, the Lord has been gracious to us today. Remember that the gift of tongues is given as encouragement to the Saints, to strengthen our faith, and not as doctrine." And with that he announced the closing hymn and sat down.

Not as doctrine. What did he mean by that? Dinah resented it; she had only said the words that came to her from the Lord. Brigham made it sound as if she had been trying to usurp the role of a prophet.

She soon forgot him, however, for when the hymn and

prayer ended the meeting, she was surrounded by Saints, and this time not just sisters. Bit by bit from the things they said she gathered enough to remember most of what she had said. She had promised that no barrier would stand in the way of Saints who wanted to gather to Zion, as long as their faith was pure. She had promised that there were some in the room who would be present at the second coming of Christ, though whether or not in the flesh she did not know.

What must have annoyed Brigham Young was when she said that they would see St. Paul's promise fulfilled, when he said, "What do they who are baptized for the dead, if the dead rise not at all? Why then are they baptized for the dead?" The widows kept asking her what she meant; did she mean that their dead husbands would be baptized? The women who had lost children unbaptized asked her if it meant their little ones could receive baptism and be saved. And she understood why Brigham had given his warning. She had to repeat again and again that she didn't know what her statement meant—she had only said what the Spirit gave her to say, and it was the business of the apostles to interpret scripture, not hers. Yet still they clung to her, and some wept, and now what had been unspoken before became plain for all to see: Dinah Kirkham was the first among the women, and had their hope in her keeping. For the first time she heard the word, whispered softly in a conversation behind her back, that she would hear again and again through her life, and always deny: *prophetess*.

She did not know herself how powerful her words had been until at last she gathered her children and began the walk home with Charlie and Anna. For Anna, too, had been touched by some of the words she said.

"You promised that children would be restored to their parents, and brothers to sisters. And husbands who were lost would be returned to their wives. Don't deny you said it, Dinah. I heard every word of it, and it's written in my heart. Husbands who were lost shall be restored to their wives. It was the Lord speaking the truth to me through you, even though you doubted it yourself."

Dinah didn't try to argue with her mother. She cared very little, really, for *what* she had said. What meant most to her was the saying of it. I am acceptable to God. I made up my mind to go to America regardless of the cost, and only then did God choose to speak through me.

They were almost home before Dinah noticed how quiet Charlie had been all the way. Poor Charlie! she thought. Ordained an elder today, and all we've been able to talk about is my gift of tongues. She put her arm around him and said, "Charlie, I'm so proud of you. To have the power of the priesthood in my own family."

It was a small thing, but it was enough to soothe his envy. He smiled and talked until they got to Anna's and Charlie's home, where they planned to have supper.

They were all so involved in the conversation that none of them noticed the man who followed them from the meeting. He was so close behind them that he knocked on the door before they had even had time to lay the sleeping Honor on Anna's bed. With the women in the bedroom, Charlie opened the door. The man was a stranger in filthy, shabby traveling clothes, covered with dust and stained with unnameable liquids. He looked to be about sixty, and there was a smell of alcohol about him. Charlie was afraid—the smell reminded him of dark nights in foul places in his childhood.

"What do you want?" he asked.

"Don't I even get a good afternoon?" The man cocked his head oddly. "But then I don't look too lovely, do I?"

"If you're hungry," Charlie said, "I can give you some bread and cheese."

"I'm hungry indeed, but it's not food I came for. Would you be Robert?"

Charlie's eyes narrowed. What business had a man like this to know one of the family's names? "No," he said.

"Charlie, then. Won't you invite me in, Charlie?"

He had known audacious beggars before, but this man talked as if he had a right, as if he had some claim on Charlie. "I think not, sir." But hadn't he seen this man earlier today? Lurking about the meetinghouse, yes, standing outside the meetinghouse when he went inside. "Did you follow us here?"

"I've been searching for you for a week. Seems you've moved around a bit. I even thought of asking at the Kirkham Locomotive Works, but then I remembered that Robert wouldn't be more than twenty-four, and you wouldn't yet be eighteen, and so it had to be another Kirkham. Still, I finally found you from the Mormon handbills, advertising the conference you had today. Said that Brother Kirkham was to be a speaker, and I thought that was possible, though I supposed it would be Robert, and not you."

Now Charlie knew who this man was, though he dared not put it into words. "Let me give you some money, sir, and then go away. We don't want you here. Do you understand that? It'll be better if you just go, now. Will twenty pounds do it? Come to the firm tomorrow, I'll give it to you—"

"You don't understand, Charlie. I didn't come for money."

"Leave. Now."

Behind him he heard footsteps coming into the room. "Who is it, Charlie?" Anna asked.

"Charlie," said the man, "I'm your father."

Charlie heard Dinah gasp, and Anna murmured, "John." Charlie turned and saw the look of pathetic hope in his mother's eyes, the sadness in Dinah's, and he turned and with his right hand pushed at the man, driving him back from the door. "I don't have a father!" he shouted. "Go away!"

But Anna clawed at his arm and pulled him back, and Dinah walked out to the John Kirkham and touched him as if he were a dream.

"You're not my father." Charlie spoke quietly and intensely, more frightened of his mother's and sister's strange reactions than of the vagabond threatening them with his imposture. "In the name of God, if you were going to leave us, couldn't you at least have profited from it? I've seen better men than you lying in their own piss outside the pubs, and you dare to call yourself my father?"

But Charlie's words made no difference to the women, and John Kirkham knew it. He looked at his daughter and said, "Dinah, will you deny me, too? I don't ask for love. I only ask you to say you know me."

"You're my father," she said, "but I don't know you."

"No, I daresay not. Nor you, either, Anna?"

Anna's answer was to cry out his name and run into the house.

John stood for a moment, not looking at either Charlie or Dinah, just at the door where his wife had fled from him. Charlie looked at him with contempt, but the longer he studied him, the more he wondered how much of his misery was real and how much a pose. The clothing was old and frayed, but it had been neatly patched by someone with a good hand with a needle. His face was wrinkled beyond his years, but he was not gaunt with hunger or disease. He was dirty from traveling, but his hair had been cut, and not more than a month ago, by competent hands. Why have you made yourself seem worse than you need, when you came to us? Did you hope to win by pity what you once could have had by love?

Then Anna appeared again at the door, her eyes red-rimmed but not weeping now. "Come in," she said. Immediately she vanished again, and her husband ducked his head sheepishly and followed.

Charlie and Dinah stood outside for a few moments, until Charlie said, "He found us because my name was on the hand-bills for the conference. He followed us from church."

"I saw him outside the meetinghouse," Dinah said. "I didn't recognize him. Or perhaps I did, without knowing it." She did not say, Perhaps that's why I prophesied his return.

"I don't want him here," Charlie said.

"Mother does," Dinah answered.

"I hoped that he was dead."

"If God had been merciful," Dinah answered, "he would have been." Then she walked into the house, and Charlie, after a moment, followed.

To his credit, John Kirkham seemed determined to spare himself nothing. He insisted on hearing every detail of their suffering after he left them, and his tears, however beery, seemed sincere. He made no excuses, he dodged none of Charlie's recriminations and accusations. Once, when Charlie said, "I only have one regret, that we didn't change our names so you couldn't find us," John's eyes caught fire for a moment and he said, "Charlie, I've been cut by masters until I'm good at bleeding. You want my blood? I'll shed it for you." But other than that he made no resistance, only accepted the burden of guilt that was heaped upon him.

"Why did you come back?" Charlie asked again and again. "For your wife to throw her loving arms around you? For your little ones to run to you so you could bounce them on your knee? What are you here for?"

Dinah looked around at her family and silently asked the same question. Why would God actually grant Anna's prayer

and send the old bastard back? For it brought no one joy. Even
Mother, with her tears of joy, didn't know what to do with the
man, and was now sitting as far from him in the room as
possible, as if now that he had returned she regretted her many
prayers. He was back, it was the final sign that her sins were
forgiven, but now what in heaven's name was she supposed
to do with him? As for Charlie, he raged, he was snide and
cutting, but mostly he was afraid; Dinah could see the uncertainty in his eyes whenever he wasn't speaking. What was he
afraid of? Many things that Dinah could not hope to understand,
she was sure; but one thing she did understand. Charlie had
just been ordained to the priesthood, he was a man in his own
right now, but if John Kirkham returned to their home, Charlie
would be a child again. He was unskilled in having a father.
There was no hole in the family now to hold a father. After
all the years they had needed him, why did he come now, when
they did not need him at all?

"I'm worse than you ever thought," John said abjectly. "I've
failed at everything. Even at leaving you. I've done every black
sin in the book and some not, Anna. Charlie's right, you ought
to throw me out, though I beg you not to. I don't deserve any
goodness at your hands." Anna watched him through red-rimmed
eyes, fearing what he would say next. He said it. "Anna, in
these years I've kept company with other women. I thought
that was the only sort of woman a man like me deserved. But
I finally reached the end of that road, and I couldn't face it, I
said, Sweet Lord Jesus, how can I stop, how can I undo all
this, where can I go? I thought of dying and it looked good to
me, but then I heard it like a voice, it said, Go home, John,
that's where they loved you once, and where you hurt them
first, and if there's any forgiveness for you in the world it's
there. I don't expect forgiveness, Anna, I don't have a right
to it, if you threw me out of the house it would be better than
I deserve, but in the name of God, can you give me peace?"
His voice ended in a whine that turned to sobs; his body shook.

"He's drunk," Charlie said contemptuously.

Dinah looked at her father and understood at last why he
had come. God sent him back as the final test of their faith.
He had tested Dinah with her husband's brutality, had tested
Charlie with the temptation of the riches of the world, but those
were little trials compared to this. Here was the man who had

caused them more misery than anyone else in the world, the man who had most bitterly betrayed them. How strong was their faith? Strong enough to forgive this man, their father, their enemy? Val came to her, reached for her, and she held him on her lap. The child held her tightly around the neck, staring at this stranger.

Dinah knew what she was doing when she told him, "Val, this is your gramfer."

She nudged Val, and the boy slid down from her lap and walked across the room to the shabby man who was weeping, his face buried in his hands. Val touched John Kirkham's knee, and watched in wonder as the sagging, tear-stained face rose from the abyss of grief and smiled at him. Val knew what to say to someone who was crying. Hadn't Dinah said it to him over and over again, when he awoke from his nightmares? "Don't cry. It's all right now."

You must forgive your father and forget your fear of him, Dinah had taught Val, for however much he hurt you, he helped make for you the body that feels the pain. Forgive the sins of your parents, child, for in time you will beg your own children to forgive yours.

"It's all right, Father," Dinah said. "You've come home."

Dinah's decision was the final one; she knew it as she said it, for Anna looked at her with unspeakable relief, and even though Charlie raged, she knew he'd come around. Or at least she hoped he would.

"God in heaven!" Charlie shouted. "Am I the only one who remembers what this man has done? This isn't *his* home, it's my home, and I bloody well won't have him in it!"

Anna's voice was thick with emotion. "It's my home, too, Charlie." And at that Charlie stormed out of the cottage, slamming the door behind him

Charlie didn't know where he was going when he left the house, but he was not surprised to find himself at the apostles' office on Oldham Road. He ran up the stairs and then stopped, unsure of what he was there for, what he wanted to say. The apostles were all there, and William Clayton, the branch president, and several other men from other branches who had come for the conference. Plainly it was a meeting of the church leaders, and in other circumstances they might have told Charlie politely that he ought not to be there and could he please come back later. But there was something in the expression on Charlie's face that said this was something important. Heber and Brigham glanced at each other. Brigham nodded, and Heber got up and took Charlie down the stairs and outside.

Charlie poured out the whole story to him. The whole branch had assumed that Anna Kirkham was a widow, and the family had never said anything to disabuse them of the notion, so the whole thing came as a surprise to Heber. He listened quietly, now and then prompting Charlie with a question, but hearing the whole tale through without judgment. Charlie finally finished by saying, "I know I'm supposed to forgive my neighbor, but how can I? He's been the poison of my life, everything I've ever hated and feared came from him. I can't forgive him for that. I can't, Brother Heber, even if I go to hell for it." He was crying, of course, and so far gone in his anguish that he didn't even bother to wipe away the tears.

When it was clear that Charlie was through, that he had no more to say, Heber began to speak, softly and reasonably, his arm around Charlie's shoulder so that Charlie felt very young and small and safe, even though he was taller than the American apostle.

"Charlie, you don't have to forgive him for the chimney-sweep putting needles in your feet. You don't have to forgive him for your not having proper schooling, or for your family's poverty, or for your mother being a servant, or for the man who attacked your sister. You don't have to forgive him for any of that, because he didn't do it. If he hadn't left you, he might have lost his job anyway, right? You might have had to go live in the same filth, your sister might have had to work for the same foreman, you might still have been apprenticed off to the sweep, your mother still might have been a servant in a rich man's house."

"But I would have had a father through it all."

"Yes," Heber said, "yes, that's the one sin you can lay at your father's door, the one thing you must forgive him for, that he left you fatherless through all those years. But the other things were not in his control. You can't blame your own sins on Adam, Charlie, and you can't blame all your suffering on your father. Lay at each man's door only what he did himself."

Charlie didn't answer, and they walked on in the darkness.

"Charlie," Heber said. "If you're going to blame him for every bad thing that happened in your life, at least be fair about it. If your mother hadn't had to be a servant in Mr. Hulme's house, then would you have ever been tutored by the old man? Would you have your fine position where you work now? And would you have been in St. Anne's square that day at noon and heard me preach and looked at me with such a brightness in your eyes that I knew I should go to you and invite myself to your home? Would you have ever read the book, would you have come to the day when you heard your sister speak with the voice of an angel, would apostles have ever laid their hands on your head and given you the power of God, if it hadn't been for your father?"

Charlie stopped walking then, for Heber had led him to the front door of his own house, and inside the door he knew his father was waiting for his answer.

"Don't think I belittle what you feel, Charlie," Heber said quietly. "But I can't help remembering that I left my wife and children hungry and penniless and homeless in Illinois to come on this mission. I'd like to think my children will understand and forgive me for walking off and leaving them in a time of trouble. I reckon I'm waiting for your answer, too."

Charlie's answer was to embrace Heber and kiss him on the cheek as the Brethren were wont to do to show their love in Christ. Then he left him there in the darkness, walked to his own door, opened it, and went inside.

They were still there as he had left them two hours before, Dinah and her children, Anna, and John Kirkham. They all looked up as he closed the door behind him. "You can stay," Charlie said. "Father."

And so it was done. Or almost, anyway. For after Dinah and the children had gone home, there was the matter of going to bed. Anna went first into her room. John Kirkham started to follow her. But Charlie was there, blocking his way.

"That's not your room, sir," Charlie said softly. "You'll be sleeping in *there*." He pointed to his own door just across the hall.

John's eyes looked sadly up into Charlie's. "I thought after ten years I'd sleep with my wife tonight."

"You have the smell of another woman's sweat on you."

Forgiveness for abandonment Charlie could give; forgive-

ness for adultery was out of his reach. After all that had passed,
it would offend decency too much for them to share a bed so
soon. John Kirkham opened his mouth to speak and Charlie
cut him off curtly. "I'll see you in hell first." After that John
Kirkham made no argument.

Anna came out of her room then with an armful of John's
old clothing. "Yours," she said.

John smiled ruefully and fingered the clothes he was wearing. "I suppose there'll be no point in even washing these."

"Oh, we'll wash them," Anna said. "And then we'll give
them to the poor."

John pointed to the clean clothes she was carrying. "Why
didn't you give *those* to the poor?"

Anna did not need to say a word. They all heard the answer
anyway. Because I knew that you'd come back. I saved them
all these years for you.

Then Anna returned to her room and closed the door. If
John had had any lingering hope of entering that room tonight,
that was his answer. He looked at Charlie and smiled in surrender. And then, almost as an afterthought, he said, "Charlie,
this religion that you and Anna and Dinah have joined. Your
mother said they baptize for the forgiveness of sins."

Charlie nodded. "I'll bring them to preach to you, if you'd
like."

"Yes, I'd like that."

John smiled again, trying to establish some bridge between
them. But Charlie didn't smile back, just left the room and
closed the door. And tonight he made up his bed in the hall,
so John could not possibly leave the room without Charlie
knowing. Not until the old man was clean in every way would
Charlie let him pass that barrier in the night.

❧ 21 ❧

Corey Kirkham
London, 1840

ROBERT HAD NO KEENER eyes than Charlie or Dinah, but his memory was sharper: he knew John Kirkham instantly, the moment he saw the man loitering outside the factory gate. Days before John made his way to the Mormon conference and followed his family home, Robert saw him and knew him and gave him an answer that would never bend.

"Man here to see you, sir," the office boy said.

"Did he give his name?"

"Said he was a man you'd want to see."

"He was wrong."

The boy knew his duty then, and started out the door of the drafting room. Robert stopped him.

"Wait."

"Yes, sir?"

"Don't tell him I won't see him. Tell him to wait. And then talk to him. Find out all you can—where he's from in London,

255

what he's doing here, what he wants. As much as you can. But don't so much as give him the name of my wife. Then come back to me."

Robert had longed for this day. Once, when he was younger, because he loved his father and missed him; then, for many years, he had hoped there'd come a time when he could repay the old cruelty. Now he stood leaning on the drawing table, feeling so weak, trembling so much that he dared not let go. The man was here. After all these years, why had he come?

And then Robert's gaze fell upon the newspapers stacked on the table—London papers of a week ago. Hulme's solicitor had brought them back with him from London only last evening, because they had articles on the new engine. And in the articles there was a paragraph that explained why John Kirkham was here:

> The young inventor, Robert Kirkham, carries himself like a gentleman. One would never supposed that he arose out of poverty. Born in a decent family, he was orphaned at an early age; since then he has set an example for all the lower classes, for instead of trying to seize what did not belong to him, he has risen through his own effort and genius to the forefront of his trade.

Of course John Kirkham read it. So young Robert was saying he was orphaned, was he? So young Robert was at the forefront of his trade, was he? The smell of money was powerful enough to be detected as far away as London. And from the look of him, John Kirkham needed money.

"He wouldn't say much," the boy reported. "But he's a cheerful fellow."

"No doubt."

"Said he was from London, that's all. But he did mention a pub he was often at—St. Vine, he said."

"A pub or a church?"

"That's what he said. St. Vine."

"And nothing more?"

"Just that he's hungry."

Robert dug into his vest pocket and took out a guinea. "Give him that and tell him he's not wanted here."

The boy's eyes widened. "He's a kind enough man, sir."

"Say as I said it. Tell him exactly this: The place he wants is no longer available."

The boy paused a moment, trying to make sense of the message, then gave up and went to do the errand. In a few moments Robert could see the shabby man walking away from the factory. He had understood well enough. Whatever else Robert's father was, he was no fool. He knew he had been recognized; he knew he would not be forgiven.

It was only later in the day that Robert realized he would not be shut of his father so easily. As Robert went to take his dinner with two railroad men from Bristol, he saw a man passing out papers to those who walked by. Robert recognized him as a Mormon, one who was often at Mother's house. Ordinarily he would have passed by, deliberately paying no attention, but he happened to hear his brother's name. "Charlie Kirkham," said the man, "so it won't be just Americans speaking—you'll hear the gospel of Jesus Christ in English, too!"

There was some laughter at that, but Robert was not amused. He took a flier out of the man's hand and read it as he walked to the restaurant. Charlie was going to give a speech. John Kirkham would surely see the notices. He would go to Mother and Dinah and Charlie. And, fools that they were, they'd believe whatever lies he told, believe his tales of repentance and love and suffering and whatever else he said to win their pity. But Robert knew better. John Kirkham had accepted the guinea. The man was a beggar without pride. Whatever he might say, it was Robert Kirkham's money that had brought him to Manchester. But failing that, John Kirkham would surely settle for Charlie's money. It wasn't nearly as much, but it would do.

The dinner went well, despite the fact that Robert's mind was busy with worries about how to protect the family from this dog returning to his vomit. By now Robert could handle railroad men with ease. Of course they did not want to buy—they wanted to steal. So Robert accurately told them everything his engine could *do*—and amiably lied about how his engine did it. Go home and try to build *that*, he said silently as he smiled at them over the wine. Go home, build what you think I've taught you to build, and your customers will all come to *me* for an engine that delivers on its promises. They laughed and told stories and for all the world might have been friends dining together for the first time in years; but the dinner was a battle in a long war, and as usual Robert won. He might be fooled, but not so easily as *that*.

After the meal, Robert went to his solicitor. Since Charlie worked in the firm, Robert did as he always did: he entered by the back stair and slipped into Royal's office without passing through the counting room where Charlie ruled and Robert would be viewed as an interloper.

"I thought you said there was no urgency on those papers!" Royal said with surprise.

Papers? Oh, yes. Royal was doing research for him on the question of the powers of a husband over a wife. Not for him to use against Mary, of course, sweet Mary who was all a man could hope for, loyal, hardworking, and uncomplaining. A wife like that needed no compulsion. "I'm here on another matter."

"Matters do have a way of proliferating, don't they?" said Royal with a chuckle. "Therein lies the profit in the legal profession."

"When are you going to London next?" Robert asked.

"In a month, I expect," Royal said. "It's a city I do not love, I will confess it."

"Then have you a man there who can do me a service, in your name?"

"Of course." Royal looked interested. "Investments?"

"Information. I want to find out all there is to know about a recent resident of London. All I have is the man's name, his occupation, his appearance, and the name of a pub."

"Not much, you know. What sort of information do you hope to find?"

"Everything that can be discovered about him. I'll decide what's important and what isn't. And not a word of this inquiry breathed to anyone."

Royal looked pained. "When have I ever been wanting in discretion?"

"It's the people you confide in who might be indiscreet."

"I won't even tell the other members of the firm."

"I wish," Robert said, "that there were a way for you to avoid even telling yourself."

"My ears shall not hear what my lips pronounce." Royal grinned. "Who is the man?"

"John Kirkham."

Royal wrote it down. "Last name spelled the same as yours?"

"Yes. And the pub is called St. Vine."

"A pub or a church?"

"From the look of him, definitely a pub. But tell your friend not to ask about him *there*. This fellow's friends might be primed to tell a false story. Instead he should locate that pub, and then go to all the pubs in the vicinity *except* that one, and ask about John Kirkham, the painter."

"What does he look like?"

"Like me. Only older, dirtier, and poorer."

Royal did not ask; he did not have to. Robert had found his father.

A week later, Robert came home from work to find Dinah there, visiting. He was always glad to see her, but there was an awkwardness now. Not because she had become a Mormon. The strain was because of the incident with Matthew. It should perhaps have brought them closer together, but the very fact that Robert had intervened in her marriage made him, now, her superior; they both felt it. And Robert felt something else, too—that every blow Matthew had struck was Robert's fault. After all, he had forced her into the marriage, hadn't he? It had been the best way, the only alternative, but Robert knew that Dinah would never see it that way, any more than Charlie would ever forgive him for apprenticing him to the chimney-sweep. It seemed that the family always depended on Robert to save them from disaster, but then hated him for whatever that salvation cost. Nevertheless, Robert would not shirk his duty, just because he went unthanked for it. Robert was not John Kirkham. He would fulfil his responsibilities whether anyone liked it or not.

"Father's home," Dinah said.

"Such as he is," Robert said. He had received one letter already from the London solicitor, and the mere thought of his father made him angry.

"You knew?"

"He came to me first."

She looked surprised. Of course John wouldn't have mentioned it.

"I gave him a guinea," Robert said, "and he went away."

Dinah's face went cold. "A guinea?"

So it had already progressed so far that Dinah would be

angry at *him* for demeaning the man by treating him like a beggar. "He'll have no more from me than that."

"It isn't money he wants," Dinah said.

"No doubt he came for love and forgiveness."

"Strange as it may seem to you, yes."

"And he's probably told you that he wants to become a Mormon, like you."

Dinah raised an eyebrow. "And why not? It *is* the gospel of Jesus Christ, and the only way a man can receive forgiveness."

Robert could not help but laugh a little. "I thought you had a better mind than that, Dinah, religion or no religion. Don't you see that he's doing exactly what he would do if he were trying to get your money?"

"He's also doing exactly what he would do if he had had a true change of heart."

"That is a problem. Did you know that he was an adulterer in London?"

Dinah pursed her lips and nodded. "So you've been spying—"

"I've been making inquiries."

"He is your father, Robert."

"I grew up as an orphan and did rather well. He should have stayed in London and been grateful that we managed to survive his crime against us."

"And how would he have known it?"

Robert showed her the London newspaper articles. She was unimpressed. "You don't know that he saw those, Robert."

"These articles appear, and a few days later he's at my factory gate. It is difficult to believe it was just chance."

Dinah got up and began walking toward the door.

"Dinah!"

She stopped and waited, but did not turn to face him.

"In the name of God, Dinah, don't you know I only want to protect you?"

She turned around, her face softer now. "I know it, Robert. But just because you've chosen to hate your father doesn't mean that I must choose to hate him, too."

"Dinah, he hasn't changed. He was drunken scum in London, and he'll be the same here."

Dinah smiled. "And you, you're a doffer in a sweatshop."

"If you'd only listen to me when I warn you, Dinah, I wouldn't have to step in and save you later, when you're in trouble."

"You don't have to save me."

"What, will *Father* protect you now?"

She knew—he could see that. She knew he was right about John Kirkham. But she wouldn't admit it. It was that damnable religion of hers. She had to forgive him, because Jesus would have. Well, Jesus ended up dead. That was the way it was with all gentle, weak people. And damn few of them got resurrected, either. It was only beneficent power—law, money, prestige—that kept trusting fools alive. Only people like Robert. And damn little thanks he got for it, either. Well, he didn't do it for the thanks. While Dinah and Charlie were going around being godly, Robert would reach out his hand and set a few things straight in the world. A few things straight, and then the world would be better because Robert Kirkham had lived in it.

Dinah heard Robert's carriage outside, saw through the window as it slowed to a stop. She reached for her teacup to finish drinking it before Robert came in. It would be a nasty little meeting, but she knew she was more than a match for Robert—he always resorted to shouting, and she could always defeat his shouting with her silence.

Then she saw through the window that Robert was not alone. He had a small boy with him. For a moment she tried to recognize him as one of Robert's boys. He had the family look, after all. But it was not one of Robert's sons. Dinah was not a fool. Robert had asked them to be there so he could call upon them. Robert wanted a battle—and he had brought a weapon. There was no doubt in Dinah's mind who the child was. Robert was armed for war, and Dinah wondered how she would fend his attack.

Anna opened the door. "Robert," she said. Then she saw the child, and thought she recognized him. Thought she recognized him, realized that she had never seen him before, and then knew she recognized him after all, and did not want to.

"What are you here for?" she asked.

"May Corey and I come in?"

Anna backed up, opening the door. Robert led the boy into

the cottage. The boy hung back, stood behind him. Robert looked around. Dinah sat placidly at the table, sipping her tea. Robert's eyes met hers for a moment; then he looked away. The battle would be between the two of them, at the end. But for now he would pretend that the fight was between him and his father.

John Kirkham also sat at the table—but not at the head. Robert noticed that at once, with rueful pleasure. Charlie sat at the head of the table. He might have accepted his father home, but he would never relinquish place to him. For once Robert felt a bit of respect for his younger brother. There were ways, after all, that they were alike.

"What did you come for?" Charlie asked. The tone was so belligerent that Robert's good feeling melted away.

"I came because I thought it would be good for all of John Kirkham's children to be together." And he pulled Corey forward, put his hand on the boy's shoulder, and looked squarely into John Kirkham's eyes.

"Corey," John said. "Thank God." The man got up from his chair and came to the boy, arms outstretched. "I was so afraid for you."

It was a gamble. Robert depended on Corey's pride, on his loathing for the man who had left him a few weeks ago, without a word or any means of living. And Corey did not let him down. When his father reached him, Corey shrank back, clung to Robert's leg, and turned his face away from the man who had sired him. John looked at him with the face of failure.

"I have the papers," Robert said. "He's *my* son now." Robert looked at the others gravely. "His story is a sad one. His father, who never bothered to marry his mother, abandoned him only a few weeks ago. Not a word did he say, not a penny did he leave. The boy was hungry, and his mother was desperate. But I promised to raise Corey as my own child, with education, with every advantage he could possibly have. I promised that I would never abandon him. And I never will. What would you think of me, sir, if I abandoned him now, after such a promise?"

John Kirkham looked him in the eye. Robert tried to imagine what was going on in his father's mind. Tried to imagine the calculations. How much damage had this revelation done? How should he respond to this discovery of his second abandonment of a family? And, as Robert expected, he chose the best of all possible responses. He turned away from Robert, flung himself to a chair, buried his face in his arms, and wept loudly, piteously crying, "O God, I should have known you wouldn't let me hide my sins from thee!"

John knew his audience well. By accusing himself, he forestalled their accusations; by calling upon God, he reminded them to be forgiving. But Robert was determined not to let him get away with it.

"He saw in the newspapers that I was rich. He came to me first, came to my factory gate. Did he tell you that?" He saw from their faces that he had not. Only Dinah had known it, and only because Robert had told her. "And what did he confess to you? Adultery, yes? For that you could forgive him, apparently, God knows how; it happened far away. But he told you he repented of his sins, didn't he? Told you he was a changed man, that he would never abandon a family now, right? What kind of change is it, when he abandons the family that needs him, to come back to a family that long since learned to live without him?"

John arose from the table, his face a mask of righteous indignation. "I was weighed down by the sin of my adultery! I could bear no longer living in sin!"

"You could bear no longer living in poverty."

"You have reason to hate me and be cruel to me. I understand, Robert, and for Jesus' sake I forgive you for it."

"By God you'll forgive me for nothing. You no more believe in Jesus than you believe in fatherhood. Here we stand, John Kirkham. Your sons. Look at us—we wear your face, we bear your name. But behind the name and the flesh there's no part of you in us. Because *we* value honor above any other thing, Corey and I. And you'll never trick *us* into forgiving you, however you play the penitent."

"All I know," Anna said in a husky voice, "all I know is that I prayed for God to bring him back, and back he came."

"And too bad if he let another child starve to do it."

"But don't you see?" Anna said. "God provided a way for the child to be cared for."

"I beg your pardon. *I* provided the way."

"Who are you to judge your father!" Anna shouted.

"There are many low things a man can do, and still remain

a man. But lower than manhood are these: To rut with a woman when he already has a wife, and to abandon the children of his body."

"There are worse sins," Charlie said quietly.

"How would *you* know?" Robert asked. "You've never had a wife, you've never had a child. If you had, you'd feel as I do."

At that Charlie fell silent, but Robert regretted every word of it. He knew then that he had made a mistake. Yes, he had silenced Charlie by telling him he was not yet fully a man—but he had also assumed that Charlie would oppose him, and that meant Charlie might, after all, forgive the old bastard. And yet Charlie wasn't the only one there. If he could at least get Dinah to side with him, if he could at least awaken her to the truth, then John Kirkham wouldn't have his victory. If Dinah wasn't for the man, he'd never truly have his place in the family—such was her power there, and Robert knew it. So he spoke to her, only to Dinah, desperate to keep her unbeguiled.

"Remember this, when he tells you he repents. Didn't he seem sorry before? Didn't he confess his sins before? And yet it was all a lie, because he didn't tell you this. And wouldn't have told you this, if I hadn't forced him."

Dinah was looking at John Kirkham, studying her father's face. And John studied her in turn, trying to think of some way to save his comfortable place in this house. For a moment Robert thought he couldn't do it, that with Dinah his cause was lost.

But he had underestimated John. Suddenly he groaned, a powerful cry of agony that came from the heart. "God will not be mocked!" he cried. "Oh, God, I can't bear it! Destroy me! Annihilate me! I cannot bear to live in thy presence!" And he flung himself backward, crashing to the floor, smacking his head loudly on the boards.

Anna screamed and rushed to him, crying out his name. Charlie also came to lift his father and carry him to the divan. But Dinah sat at the table, staring at nothing until she looked at Robert and at Corey. Then she smiled wanly. She was not fooled, was she? No—she saw through the old bastard.

But the others didn't. Or chose not to. For whether John really knocked himself unconscious or not, he certainly revived with his wits about him. "Cleanse me," he whispered. "Take me into the water and let me be clean." Then he opened his eyes. "Charlie, my sins are darker than I can bear! Will you baptize me? Will you make me clean before the Lord?"

"Yes," Charlie said. "I will."

"Wash manure," Robert said, "and it's still shit."

Dinah walked over to her father, took him by the hand, helped him up. "Come, Father. Robert's leaving now."

Robert looked at her in amazement. She smiled at him. "You just don't understand, do you, Robert? It is the weakest soul who needs help the most."

"Dinah, *you* know what he is!"

"I also know what he *can* be."

"He'll never change."

"There's always hope." She touched him gently on the arm, then touched young Corey on the cheek. "My brother. Remember this—there's always hope, even when there isn't any faith. And sometimes, without hope or faith, there must be charity."

Corey looked up at her dumbly. Robert was no less speechless. He turned and left the house, beaten. Beaten by Anna's love for her husband, Charlie's hatred for Robert, and Dinah's damnable patience. She could wait for anything. There was no helping it, then. As always, they wouldn't trust in Robert until it was too late, until John Kirkham had betrayed them again. And, as always, Robert found himself cut off from the rest of his family, not because he had done them harm, but because he had tried to do them good. That is the way of the world, isn't it—if you want to be hated, be kind.

❧ 22 ❧

Charlie and Sally
Manchester, 1840

CHARLIE WAS NOT ABNORMAL: he thought about women about as often as any young man was likely to. So it wasn't that Robert's taunting words put the idea in his head. Rather Charlie realized that he wasn't really a man, wasn't really one of the full-fledged brethren until he had a wife. He would not be adult until then. And he was certainly ready to be adult.

So now instead of merely appreciating a well-formed bosom or a lovely gliding step, instead of comparing the relative virtues of a heart-shaped face or dark, flashing eyes, he began to consider what he must have in a wife. Charlie was sure of one thing—his wife would have to know how to comport herself in elevated society. He would have money, of course, and *his* wife would not be an awkward homebody like Robert's Mary. She must have grace, refinement, and above all an accent more redolent of Middlesex than of Lancashire. Of course she would be beautiful, have an unbounded admiration for Charlie's accomplishments and abilities, and be content with a reasonable wardrobe.

And one other requirement. She must be a Saint. That narrowed the field considerably. He studied the unmarried sisters and despaired. None of them would make a proper wife for the sort of man he was destined to become. Least of all Sally Clinton. He decided that right at first. It was well known that she was the most beautiful girl in the Manchester Branch, but it was the wrong kind of beauty. Her face was pretty and soft, but not refined and delicate; she was small, but her body was too sturdy and strong. She was made to endure love and hard labor; Charlie needed a woman whom poems could be written about.

Once he had decided that Sally was definitely not fit to be the object of his affections, he was free to be friends with her. She was good company after church meetings. She had a quick mind and they could argue cleverly for the entertainment of the other young people in the Branch. Inevitably, whenever both Charlie and Sally were in the room, they were together, with everyone else gathered around them, laughing. Not always laughing, though. They could slide easily from cleverness to quiet, serious conversation about the gospel, their ideas building on each other until they were sure that the Spirit of God must be inspiring them. Good times, with the excitement of being new Mormons and young all at once.

And best of all was the fact that Charlie and Sally were just friends. Charlie even mentioned it to her when they were, for once, alone in a corner of the meetinghouse. "We have something very rare between us," he said.

"We do?" asked Sally.

"We're a man and a woman who are friends without the slightest romantic interest in each other."

"Yes," she said, "isn't it wonderful?" Such was Charlie's innocence that he didn't even suspect irony.

They were not *completely* alone at that moment, of course. They were never *completely* alone. Always off in the middle distance was Sally's forbidding elder sister, Harriette. At first glance it was impossible to believe they were related. Harriette was as cold and withdrawn as Sally was warm and outgoing. And yet when they were together it was hard to discover why Sally was pretty and Harriette most emphatically was not. Their bodies were not unalike; their faces were similar. Harriette had no unpleasant features; she kept her hair as carefully as Sally did. And yet Harriette was plain. When she and Sally were together, no man could look for more than a moment at Harriette before his gaze would slip away to Sally. If sometimes Charlie thought of Sally as the epitome of woman, albeit lower class, he also thought of Harriette as the quintessential chaperone. After a while, though, quiet Harriette simply disappeared. She was there, but she was not there. Sally, however, was unquestionably there.

But the untangled idyll ended when Caroline Crane was baptized. Charlie didn't see her until the actual baptism ceremony. From the first moment Charlie knew she was what he had been waiting for. Delicate and lovely, graceful of step and gesture, her voice soft, her eyes deep and sentimental. In the swirling waters of Medlock, it seemed a miracle she was not swept away like a leaf.

Charlie determined to do everything correctly. At his request Anna met her and then after a church meeting she introduced Charlie to her. Charlie spoke quietly and at once turned the conversation to matters of some sophistication. He quoted lines from Wordsworth; Caroline finished the quotation. He used his most elevated vocabulary; she answered in kind. He asked if he could walk her home, and she accepted.

This is my destiny, he thought as he guided her out of the building. He was careful not to touch her except, tremblingly, upon the elbow; then he offered his arm and her fingers pressed gently upon the back of his hand. It was ecstasy.

It was also the high point of the walk home. He did not notice it at first, but after a while he realized that Caroline Crane had nothing to say that was worth hearing. She gave correct, polite answers. She knew all the right poets. But she did not seem to *care* about the poetry the way Charlie did. She did not understand when he joked with her. And when the conversation lagged, she kept questioning him to start it again. But her questions were not piercing, like Sally's would have been. There was nothing to prove that she had listened to what he said before.

So he said his good-byes at the door and walked home. Nothing is what it seems, he told himself. What frightened him was the suspicion that he was the one who did not measure up to his appearance. Perhaps Sister Caroline was not shallow, she was simply uninterested in him. He was, after all, the son of a woman who had scrubbed floors in a rich man's house. He was a man of trade, wasn't he? And he despised himself for not fulfilling his own dream.

The day was not destined to get any easier. When he got home to his cottage, there outside his door waited Sally Clinton, of all people, and her older sister, Harriette.

"Why, Sister Sally," Charlie said.

"Good evening, Brother Charlie," said the girl. There was no pertness now, however, and even in the dusky light of early evening he could see that she was upset.

"I'm glad to see you," Charlie said.

Sally made a face of skepticism. "Are you?"

"I said I was," Charlie said irritably. He had faced his own unworthiness today. He couldn't deal with Sally's anger, too. "Why didn't you go inside?"

"We didn't want anyone to see us inside your cottage, for fear it would interfere with any alliances you might be pursuing elsewhere." So it was jealousy brought her here. And of course they had waited on his doorstep in the very hope that they would be seen, and word would spread, and any budding romance with Caroline Crane would be harmed. If you only knew, thought Charlie bitterly.

"Well, will you come in now?"

"I'd rather walk," Sally said. "I'd rather talk to you as we walk. Or do you only walk with ladies?"

"I only walk with ladies," he said, but offered his arm as he said it. There was no reason to accept Caroline's judgment of him. He could at least pretend to be a gentleman. Yet the touch of her hand on his arm annoyed him. She was not like Caroline; she put her arm through his, held closer to him, so that they looked more like a common laborer and his girl.

She must have felt him retreat from her, for she suddenly withdrew her arm and with elaborate care placed her hand delicately over his wrist in a parody of Caroline. Had she watched that closely when he left with Caroline?

"You're so graceful at that," Charlie said. "You must have practiced."

He immediately regretted saying it. Because of his dismal mood it didn't sound like a joke. She stopped walking and snatched her hand back from him. "I'm sorry," she said. "I made a mistake. I thought you cared for me, at least as a sister in the gospel. Now I see that you don't even consider me worth treating with respect."

Because she accused him of not caring for her, he found himself protesting that he did. He did not know how to deal with Sally when she was angry—they had never quarreled. After a few placating words she was holding his arm again, though she seemed to be no less angry. In a moment they were on Pott Street, arm in arm, and Harriette had fallen about ten paces behind. Clearly the sisters had planned this so Charlie and Sally could have a genuinely private conversation without any scandal because of a lack of chaperone. Sally led them a ways up Pott Street toward the canal, but a football game was still in progress on the field there, and in a huff she turned around, passed her sister furiously, and continued the walk another way. All this time, growing angrier and angrier, she had hardly said a word, and Charlie had dared not breach such a formidable silence. And yet she clung tightly to his arm.

At last he could bear no more. "What's this about?"

"You know perfectly well what it's about."

"As a matter of fact, Miss Clinton, I do not."

"Don't *Miss Clinton* me, Charlie Kirkham. What do you mean by walking that prim little Miss Snot-nose home today?"

Hearing Caroline referred to so crudely made him furious. "I won't hear a lady referred to in such language!"

"So you *do* love her?" It was an accusation.

"Nothing of the kind!"

"Then why did you walk her home *without* a chaperone?"

"On Sunday many couples walk without chaperones, Miss Clinton."

"It isn't any of my business, anyway, is it?" And then her face grew sad. "But I thought I had cause to think it my affair. I thought we were friends."

"So did I." In his coldest voice he emphasized, "Friends."

"I see," she said. Her tone was even colder, and it made Charlie uncomfortable.

"What do you see?"

"That I mean nothing to you after all. I was clearly misunderstanding your feelings toward me."

She was in love with him. She was not just being possessive or resentful of a more elevated woman. All this time she had really cared for Charlie, and dreamed, as he had dreamed, of love. She sounded so miserable that Charlie could not bear to leave her uncomforted; he felt a responsibility to comfort her—no woman should feel utterly unrewarded for having found Charlie worthy of love. "Sally, it's not that you mean nothing to me."

"Oh, please," she said, avoiding his gaze, "tell me again how you love me as a sister in the gospel."

That was precisely what he had been planning to say. Once again today a woman was too deep and quick for him. "How *should* I feel toward you, then?"

"If you can't see that I'm a woman, I would rather you didn't notice me at all."

"Of course I see that you're a woman—"

"Well, you don't show that you see it!"

"Sally, I—"

"When did I give you permission to call me by my given name?"

"You didn't."

"Then kindly don't take liberties with me."

"Liberties! For God's sake, Sister Sally, I—"

"And don't take God's name in vain!"

Charlie was about to answer in rage when he realized that she was crying. He stood facing her in silent consternation. Then he looked back at Harriette, fearful of her stern disapproval; but Harriette was discreetly looking the other way. It was nearly dark, and Pott Street was deserted right here, with fields on either side. Still, a passerby might come along; word might spread that Charlie Kirkham was seen out with Sally Clinton, and Sally was weeping. It wouldn't do. Charlie took her by the arm and led her off into the field. It was an untended one, with high grasses and the foundation of an old building that had once stood there. A farmhouse, it looked like, from the days when Manchester was a small town amid fertile fields. Now it would serve as a perfect place for this miserable conversation, for it was sunk into the ground a ways, and if they went down into the foundation the weeds would hide them completely.

"Where are you taking me?" she asked through her tears.

"Where no one will see you crying."

"You're ashamed to be seen with me."

"Not at all. I just didn't want you to be embarrassed."

"I'm already embarrassed. What do I care what anyone else thinks? You're the one I wanted to think well of me, and now you think I'm just a witch, just angry and crying and—"

"I don't think that," Charlie said.

"What *do* you think?"

"I—I think you're a lovely girl, and I like you very much."

"A girl. But you think Caroline is a lady, don't you?"

"No more than you, Sister Sally—"

"Oh, won't you please call me Sally, do we have to be strangers?"

"Sally, then."

"Do you really think of me as a lady? As a woman?"

"Of course I do," Charlie said. He was not sure how, but the meaning of the conversation had changed subtly; the tears were forgotten as if they had never been shed, and she was looking up at him eagerly, almost passionately.

"Couldn't you love me, Charlie?" she asked. She didn't wait for an answer, just put her hands on his chest and pressed herself to him in a most startling way; he had never had a woman's full body pressed against him, and he lost balance and stepped backward.

"Oh, you hate me!"

"I don't," he said, catching her by the arm before she could run from him. "I was just—I lost balance, that's all—"

"Charlie, I thought you cared for me, and today you were ridiculous, waiting on her like a dog on his master. At first I was jealous because you had never fawned on *me* like that. And then I was glad. I'd hate to have a man like you demean yourself for me. I don't think love should make a strong man be weak."

"Was I weak?" Was that how Caroline, too, had seen him?

She saw his dismay. "No, Charlie," she said. "Not you!"

Suddenly her arms were around his waist and her lips were on his, and it was no pristine little child's kiss. Her lips were open and she clung to him passionately. Not for long, of course—with his lips closed it wasn't much of a kiss. But she barely gave him time for a breath before she kissed him again, and this time he was readier. He knew he ought to push her away, ought to make things clear once and for all, yet he kissed her back and embraced her as tightly as she embraced him. It left his head spinning, and even when the kiss ended she still pressed her hips against his and held him tightly.

"You must think I'm a slut," she said coarsely.

"I don't," he denied. He only vaguely sensed that by accusing him she was forcing him to deny every single thing he really felt.

"You're the first man I've ever kissed," she said.

He doubted it.

"You don't believe me."

"Of course I do. It's just—you kissed me so—"

"I kissed you like my mother kisses my father, because that's how much I love you! Charlie, can't you love me, too?"

"Sally, this is so quick—"

"It's only because I was afraid I was losing you! Charlie, we're going to America and I don't know anybody there! Won't you take care of me?"

"I—of course, I—"

"I'm not asking you to promise anything. Just don't ignore me, please!"

No, not promise anything. But even being here with her was betrayal of his promise to himself that he would marry wisely, marry well. He could not entangle himself with a girl like Sally. She was too coarse for his future. Or was she? Perhaps the lesson God meant him to learn today was that his future would not be special. That his proper mate was a sturdy girl with the hips to bear a dozen children and the strength in her back and legs and arms to plow a field. He could not decide which was harder to bear, the knowledge that he was only fit for a working-class marriage after all, or the fact that at this moment, with Sally's kiss fresh on his lips, the impress of her body still strongly felt, at this moment he could not think of anything more important in his future than Sally Clinton.

"Charlie, are you promised to Caroline?"

"Of course not."

"Then you do care for me?"

"Yes."

"I'm a proper lady," she said. "I'm not what you think."

"I think you're a proper lady."

"Charlie, you'll be my friend forever?"

"Of course I will."

And their interview was over. Charlie had a terrible feeling, helping her out of the old foundation, that he had promised her much more than he could possibly have meant to. He felt that he had betrayed himself, but what could he do? As he walked through the field his knees were weak from the passionate embrace. He felt guilty; he felt exhilarated. He braved Harriette's stern look of disapproval and squeezed Sally's hand in farewell.

"In America," Sally said. She smiled shyly in a half-successful effort to hide her triumph.

Charlie watched the two sisters on their way, then walked back home, feeling unsatisfied and ashamed and blissfully happy. What an incredible, miraculous day. He had lost a few illusions, but he had also conquered a fear that he hadn't ever named: that no woman could ever love him.

When he got home the house was still. At first he assumed that his parents were out. Had there been an evening meeting scheduled at the hall? No—even love could not make Charlie forget his responsibilities. Perhaps they had gone visiting, then, though it was unlike Mother not to lay a supper for him. He took off his jacket and hung it on the peg by the door, then began undoing his waistcoat as he walked to his room. It was not until he was naked and began looking for his nightshirt that he realized what was wrong with the room. There was nothing of John Kirkham's in it. For weeks now it had been a constant annoyance, John's clothing here and there, his unmade bed, his poor-man's habits. And now it was all gone. For a moment Charlie thought his Father had gone; to his surprise, it was not a joyful thought. He had come to rather like the man, though loving was out of the question. Then he realized that John would not have gone any farther than across the hall.

Charlie strode to his door and flung it open. Across the hall the other door was already open; John Kirkham stood there, regarding him placidly. He was in trousers and shirtsleeves, but his rumpled hair spoke of his being recently in bed. In Anna's bed. They regarded each other without words, until Anna emerged from the bedroom, John moving aside to make way for her.

"We thought since he was baptized," Anna said, "that what God had made clean was worthy of my love. I'm surely no better than God."

Charlie said nothing. There was no answer. When he had set himself in Father's favor against Robert's attack, Charlie should have known it would end with the old man in Mother's bed. He had thought, however, that the permission would come from him, that only his consent would allow John back into Anna's bed.

"You're naked, Charlie," John pointed out gently.

Yes. Naked, that was it. His authority, his power was only

clothing that could be stripped away in a moment. Charlie turned away and closed the door to his room behind him. He lay on his bed, staring up into the empty gloom that hovered just under the ceiling. He heard his mother knock softly on his door, but he said nothing. The door might have opened a crack—he thought he heard the sound of it. If she did open the door, his nakedness drove her away again, and he was alone.

At first he tried to think of anything else, but it was impossible. So he allowed himself to conjure the scene. John Kirkham, dissipated and weak-eyed, yet still manly; Anna Kirkham, heavy with the residue of so many pregnancies, and yet all the more voluptuous in her lingering beauty. Each knew the paths of the other's body so well that trespass was inevitable. And as Charlie thought of his parents doing what he had so long prevented, he forced himself to believe that it was all right, that John was clean now, forgiven now, worthy of her after all. That his mother was still his mother, despite her unfaithfulness to him.

He slept at last, and the scenes he had not been able to avoid awake pursued him even more vividly in his dreams. Only now it was not Anna Kirkham who sluttishly accepted what she ought to have refused—it was Sally. And in John Kirkham's place, the animal of lust was Charlie. In his dreams he had no self-control at all. He woke in the darkness, panting from his imaginary passion, ashamed of his nakedness and of his dream. He got up in the darkness, dampened a cloth and washed himself, then pulled his nightshirt over his head and crept under the covers. Like a child he pulled them up to his neck and curled his knees up near his chest. The more he remembered the ecstasy of his dream of Sally, the more guilty he felt, until he found himself praying and weeping, damning himself and pleading for forgiveness. And yet all the time he knew he was a hypocrite. Even though it was a dream, it was a powerful experience, not to be quickly erased from his memory. And once again before morning he dreamed the dream again. It terrified him, for what you dream three times comes true. He lay awake for hours the next night, and the night after, praying and struggling to keep his mind from evil. It was the sorest trial of his life so far, he was sure; the war in his heart was between God and Satan, and he did not know what weapons he could array on God's side.

❧ 23 ❧

Matthew Handy
Manchester, 1840

MATTHEW WAS NOT A FOOL, whatever Dinah might think. He knew, for instance, that Dinah meant to go to America. There had been enough hints. Charlie's remarks about his and Anna's plans to emigrate; Dinah's frequent wistfulness about favorite places in Manchester; her occasional unaccustomed tenderness with Matthew. A blind man could read those signs.

The question, of course, was when, and how she'd broach the matter with him. He had confided his worries to Robert, but regretted it at once, for of course Robert became cold and businesslike and told him not to worry, it would all be taken care of. Matthew did not want it taken care of. He wanted it avoided entirely. He wanted Dinah to be changed. He wanted her to love him, so that she would not think of leaving him. But she was thinking of leaving him. Perhaps not desiring it, but it was surely one alternative she was considering.

He toyed with the idea of going to America himself. That

would silence her, he suspected. "Good morning, Dinah. How would you like to go to New York with me? Robert and I want to manufacture our locomotive in America." How close was New York to Nauvoo, or whatever the place was? Couldn't be far. Wasn't America just a string of cities along the coast, with mountains, forests, and Indians only a few miles inland from the sea? She could go visit her Mormon friends as often as she liked. They would stay together. But of course he couldn't do it. Not now, anyway. In a few years, they might be ready to reach out to other places, but right now it took all their capital and all their attention just to stay ahead of competitors. They had already had to fire three employees for revealing secrets to other manufacturers. And America would be even worse. Yankees were notorious sharpers. It was said a Yankee could steal the wings off an angel and then turn around and sell him the boat passage home. Besides, Matthew wasn't altogether sure that Robert would trust him to head an operation in America, so far from supervision. Robert didn't have much faith in him. No one did, really.

He couldn't help the way it preyed on him, that Dinah wanted to leave him. He could tell himself that she had gone mad, that she was following her damnable prophet. Made no difference. He still came home and saw her so beautiful and wise, so much above him; he desired her more than anything else in the world, and yet she did not want him. She was courteous, but they were only in a truce. She despised him, and every time he loved her in her bed, he felt ashamed, as if it had been a gift bestowed on him by someone who was wondering the whole time if he had bathed. So he had taken to visiting whores.

The first time was almost by chance. He was feeling low; it was midmorning Sunday, and Dinah was gone with the children, and he happened to sit in a park near an off-duty whore. He suspected what she was from the start—the painted lips don't come quite clean, and the habits of walking don't disappear because it's forenoon Sunday. Yet he did not get up and move away. I'm a bit of a whore myself, he thought. I stay where I'm not loved because of the money. If I left Dinah I'd lose my place with Robert, that's certain. And I don't want to lose it. God's name, it's all I have. That's how he felt that day. And so he stayed there, and even struck up a conversation with the girl. She wasn't much older than Dinah, anyway, and though she wasn't pretty, she reeked of desire. Here's one that wouldn't find me too dirty and low for her. Here's one that considers herself lucky to get a man like me, usually has to make do with the low sort, she'd be glad for me. And one thing led to another, until she smiled and said, "You wouldn't have three shillings I could borrow, would you?"

He fumbled in his pocket, that's how innocent he was; this wasn't a factory girl, she was talking another language and he just didn't understand. But she only touched his arm and said, "You're supposed to say, 'What will you give me for security?'"

So he said it, and she answered, "My crinkum-crankum." Then she giggled.

"What?" He understood, all right. He just didn't know what to say.

"Look, for three shillings, you can do a grind. Unless you want a perpendicular." She giggled again, but then sobered. "I don't do nothin' else."

He should have got up and walked away. He even thought of it. But he wanted her after all, and when he got up he did not walk away; he reached down and offered her his arm.

"Oh, no," she said. "We might be seen. My place is only three blocks from here." She told him the address. They walked separate ways. He thought of just not keeping the rendezvous. He thought of going home. He thought of Dinah, and decided it would serve her right. The whore pretended much more passion than she felt, but when it was over her smile was genuine enough. "I don't usually do it in the morning," she said. "But you was so sad."

Pity. It should have made him angry, but instead he only laughed at her and made arrangements to meet her at the same time the next week. It seemed an appropriate thing to do during the Mormon meetings.

Did Dinah know? Matthew feared she did, and hoped she did; it was the only pleasant tension left in his home life. Would it hurt her? Would she be angry? Or would she only nod complacently and say, "One expects a hog to wallow in the mire— that's his nature." That was like her, that was possible—but even that gave him the pleasure of comtemplating a quarrel that he would surely win. In his imagination he was a much better arguer than he was in fact.

And whenever he was with a whore, he imagined it was

Dinah, her so lovely body yielding to him completely, enslaved by his ardor. I would be so masterful, if only she would let me rule her.

"Matthew," she said one night, after the children were in bed. "Can we talk?"

"Mmm," he said, looking up from the drawings he had taken home to study during the night.

"It's important."

Slowly, unconcernedly he rolled up the papers. He felt an ecstasy of tension inside, for her tone said that the time had come at last. She was going to precipitate a change. Had she found out about the women? Would she rage?

No. She was very calm, and she said nothing of the women. "My family is going to America. Did you know?"

So it was America, not the whores. He knew this scene; he had played it out a hundred times in his silent imaginings. She would say, Let me go with them. And he would answer, I am not an unreasonable man. I understand that a woman can have desires that are different from her husband's. So in a year or two we will take a voyage to America, and you may see your family and visit your prophet, and perhaps then we can decide whether to move there for an extended period of time. She would see his magnanimity and love him for it. He would turn this issue of religion to advantage after all. "Yes, I knew," he said.

"I'm going."

He waited for a moment, for her to finish her statement. But that was it. Name of God, what did she think she was, his brother? No, by heaven, she was his wife! *I'm going* indeed. Didn't she know that he had the power to restrain her? He could lock her up if he chose, or commit her to a lunatic asylum, there'd be no trouble with that; not a judge in the world would move to block him. How dare she announce it, as if it were her right! "Oh," he said. He heard his own calm voice with surprise. Surely he had meant to speak more forcefully than that.

"If you wanted to come, I would be glad of it."

Her tone was so complacent, as if she cared not a bit whether she ever saw him again or not. The woman had no justice in her, and no mercy. He found words to say now, but they were grotesquely inappropriate to his feelings. "I thought I had kept my part of the bargain. I do not think I deserve to be deserted."

She had not noticed the enormity of what *she* said, but she seemed now to take offense at the word *deserted*. "I think if you may follow women into bawdy houses without blame, I may without sin follow the Spirit of God to Zion."

This was not how the whores were to have been discussed. It was to be a tempest, not a quiet freezing of the air between them. He was supposed to bow before her rage and penitently explain that it was because she made him feel so unworthy, so unloved that he went where affection could be purchased. Now such an explanation was impossible. She was not furious at him; she did not weepingly accuse him. She only sat there using his whores like a wager in a game of cards. He had bet on her guilt; she countered with his own, as if she was not hurt by it at all. And that made his visits with the whores seem even filthier, to know that his wife did not even mind, that Dinah only regarded it as a means to get her own way. He wanted to shout at her, to accuse her of being cold and unfeeling. But when he opened his mouth, he quietly said, "I don't want you to leave." He had meant to command. Instead he pled.

"If you came with me, I wouldn't have to leave you." And then she broke her perfect posture, leaned forward a little, and came as close to passion as she would come in the whole strange conversation. "Matthew, when one has communed with God, one cannot bear the thought of losing him. I'd gladly die before I'd stay here, now that God has made plain the course I'm meant to follow." Matthew heard the trembling in her voice; she meant it, and he knew that she was capable of martyrdom. No ancient saint had anything on her.

"You won't have to die," he said. He did not plan to say it, and only realized after it was said that it constituted permission. Had he meant to grant permission? Surely not.

The words were spoken, though, and suddenly Dinah brightened. Suddenly she was effusive, more excited than he had ever seen her before. "You won't have to pay for passage. Charlie's already paid it. In fact, you know, the Apostles are making those who have money pay the way of those who don't, or none will go to Zion; it's a way of keeping all the Saints equal so that no one gets to Nauvoo just because he has more money than anyone else. So Charlie's paid for seven people besides us to go—saved all his money." Then she bent over him, embraced him, kissed his cheek. "Oh, Matthew, you'll never regret this. You'll see—we'll prosper there, and within a year or so we'll come back to visit. And you'll visit us, surely there's business for the firm in America; you'll visit and it won't be long before we're together almost all the time. Just because I love God doesn't mean I can't love you, you'll see."

So Dinah, perfect Dinah, could be bought. Give me my way, and I'll love you then—he felt cheapened because he wanted her love so desperately, and now it was so mercenarily given. He turned away from her embrace, he stood and walked away from her. It did not occur to him that this show of love was the truth, and her prior coldness was because she had been afraid of him. He forgot how he had earned her fear. So he felt justified in rebuffing her, felt a delicious thrill of revenge at the quiet pain in her voice.

"You are generous," she said behind him. "I will teach the children to love you, and of course when Val comes of age I'll send him back to England to go to school." Then she left the room.

Name of heaven, she meant to take his son and daughter on a voyage that killed as many children as survived it. She meant to strip him of his family all at once. What, was she so happy being reared in a fatherless home that she aspired to such an abomination for her own son and daughter? Well, she'd discover how much he was willing to bear. He stood up, thinking that he would go directly to her and tell her what she could and could not do. But instead he found himself outside, heading for Robert's and Mary's home. Robert would know what to do. Robert would solve it.

Robert's answer was impatience. "I told you I'd take care of it. Your children will stay in England, and if I know Dinah, so will she, and willingly, too."

"May I not know how you plan to work this miracle?"

"If you knew Dinah as well as I do, you'd know the plan without asking. And if I told you, she'd guess it from your face before the week was out."

"So I'm to put my future in your hands."

"It has been for years."

Matthew left angrily, but the visit to Robert did make him feel better: it made things easier, to know that all the money of the firm would be behind him, that and Robert's wit and determination as well. Let Dinah plot to widow him and leave him childless all at once, like Job; he had an angel now to intervene. In this battle, God and Robert were both on Matthew's side.

Dinah was already in bed asleep when he got home. She looked so peaceful—why shouldn't she? She thought that she had won. As he watched her sleeping, he realized that he felt love for her quite apart from his passion. All these trials would lead to a good end. Robert would work the miracle and keep her here. Matt wanted more than life itself to truly be one with this woman, who was nobler than anyone else he knew. She was beautiful, yes, but also she knew beauty. *Was* beauty, in fact, and if he could make her truly a part of him, he too would be beautiful.

It was time for him to go to bed. On his way out to the privy, he stopped in each of the children's rooms. Perhaps it was unnatural in a father, but he positively doted on the children, and often spent long minutes dreaming of their future, planning how he'd love his daughter and his son when they were old enough to know they had a parent besides their mother. Already, in fact, Val watched him, often did what he saw his father do. He is not ashamed to be like me, Matthew thought at such moments, despite his fear from that one terrible night when I lost control of myself and did the unthinkable, struck down Beauty because I could not own it. Val, at least, has forgiven me.

Somewhere between the privy and the cottage, his decision was made. Before he would let these children out of his home, he'd do something terrible. Yes, that was a resolve that would not flag in the face of Dinah's iron will. He would not bend on that. Dinah had never been his, not in her heart. But these children—they were the part of her she could not withhold from him. Before he let her take them, he'd see her dead.

Upstairs, she heard him walk away from the door as she dozed; it woke her enough that she thought to pray. It was a clumsy, sleepy prayer, and she fell asleep halfway through, but to the face of Joseph Smith that she had learned to worship, she prayed for this: that before she and her children left for America, God might work a miracle and make her husband also come with her. And as she prayed she felt this certainty: that in America she would have a true marriage, that at last she would love a man she could not rule, and yet who would not rule her. It did not occur to her that it would be anyone but Matthew. And so she fell asleep content.

➷ 24 ➴

Joseph Smith
Nauvoo, Illinois, 1840

"I HAD THE STRANGEST DREAM."

Emma did not seem to hear him, just continued dressing in the scant morning light through the oilcloth window.

"I dreamed," Joseph said, "that I was walking in the marshes and a squirrel came out to the end of a limb and spoke to me."

Emma laughed abruptly. "When did the Lord start sending you squirrels in your dreams?"

"I'm not saying it's a revelation, I'm just saying it might mean *something*." Joseph sat up and slid his legs out from under the sheet—all that he could bear to have covering him on summer nights.

"What did the squirrel say?"

"I left behind my children for you. Have you no inheritance for me in the beautiful city?"

"Mm."

"I didn't say I understood it."

"The children will be wanting breakfast." She walked out of the room. Joseph sighed. Not going to be a good day with Emma today. He had given up trying to understand what caused her moods. Sometimes they came at her time of month, and then he understood why Moses had commanded the women of Israel to stay away from men during such times. It was doubtless to limit the incidence of murder. But today was definitely not Emma's time—*that* had been last week—and so of course he thought as he always did of his feeble attempts at initiating plural marriage. Had she heard rumors? Despite the strict oaths of secrecy, had someone hinted once too broadly? Or worse, had he been seen going into the wrong house at the wrong time?

Not that he hadn't tried to tell her. One night as they lay in bed he started talking about how all things were to be restored—*all* things, including the ancient practice of marriage the way Abraham did it, the way Jacob did it; even polygamy on the grand scale of David and Solomon. She lay there in silence until she finally asked, "And when will you restore murder, the way Cain did it, or even on the grand scale of Joshua and Samson?" Ever since then, whenever he broached the subject she got angry and began questioning him about his relations with the young unmarried women of the neighborhood.

Sometimes she even accused him of being false to her, and what could he say? He always confessed some little sin, some minor indiscretion, for Emma would recognize hedging if he tried getting around it by saying, "I have never slept with a woman who was not my wife," or even, "I am innocent of adultery." Better to satisfy her suspicion with a repentance that was genuine enough, even if he lied about the offense, than to say anything that would fuel her suspicions. In short, he was afraid.

He laughed at himself. He had been beaten, poisoned, tarred and feathered, imprisoned, sentenced to death, hunted by murderous mobs, and it had only made him more determined to bind the world to the law God had taught him. But tell Emma the truth? He thought of what Sidney Rigdon had said about Socrates; no wonder he spent his life out of doors, conversing with anyone he could find rather than go home to Xantippe. Not fair, not right. He cursed himself for such an unjust thought. Emma's tongue was sharp because her wits were keen and her afflictions many. In all their years of marriage, when had she had a home of her own? When had she even had a husband who would surely be back tonight, or even this week? Half their marriage she had lived on the charity of the uncharitable, the other half on the pittance he could eke from whatever business he was in at the time. Well, this time things would be different. In Nauvoo she'd have a fine home, the best in the city. No one could begrudge the Prophet that vanity— he had for so many years made do with far, far less. But he knew that she would rather live in a pigsty than let her husband have another wife. He understood her feelings. If she loved another man, he'd seriously consider killing the son of a bitch, and to hell with eternal damnation.

Of all the things God demanded of him, celestial marriage was the hardest, for it smacked of adultery even to him. And hiding it from Emma made it feel yet more like a sin. It *was* a sin, in fact, for celestial marriage was only to be practiced with the consent of the first wife. Hadn't Sarah given Hagar to Abraham of her own free will? Hadn't Leah and Rachel asked their husband Jacob to go to their handmaids and conceive children? But what wife would Emma ever give to him?

He could tell her that God would damn him if he didn't obey the commandment, but he knew that Emma would not be swayed by that. "Then go to hell," she'd say, "but I'll give you no wives but me." So to obey the larger law, he broke a lesser one, and denied his wife the choice that was hers by right. He knew that he could never teach polygamy to the Saints if he weren't living it himself; and yet he was also setting an example of deception and faithlessness, because he had not yet taught the law to his own wife. Telling her, though, might well be the end of their marriage, and he could not imagine life without Emma. Yet the longer he waited, the more deceived and betrayed she would feel when she finally learned. Emma, my love, I have already seven wives besides you, and in heaven they will be mine forever. No, he could not tell her, not for fear of her sharp tongue, not for fear of her rage, but for fear that she would leave him, and that he could not bear.

In the meantime, he told himself that during the passing months the Spirit of God would doubtless prepare her heart to receive the principle of celestial marriage. Surely that would be no harder than parting the Red Sea or raising the dead. And then came the most optimistic of his unbelievable dreams: What if Emma already knew all about the Principle, and the only thing that made her so angry was that he hadn't trusted her enough to tell her? When he told her, why, she would rejoice and embrace him and say, "Why didn't you ask me to do this before?" It's *possible*, he told himself. When hell freezes over.

Downstairs she was even colder to him, and scolded the children unmercifully for the mildest offenses. To spare the little ones the anger that was meant for him, Joseph fled the house without his breakfast. He went down to the wharf, where all day rafts and little boats pulled up and put out—arriving always full, leaving always empty. It was the bane of his labor in this place. Nothing was yet manufactured here except houses and babies. All the money drained away from the town as quick as water through a sieve, and precious little came back to make it up. Something would have to happen soon, or there wouldn't be a hope in the world of paying their debts. And no one around him seemed capable of helping. Joseph's older brother Hyrum did his best, of course, but he was only one man, and not one for fresh ideas. Sidney Rigdon, who was either ill or shamming, was off in Pennsylvania or some other such place, waiting until all the real work was done. And the Twelve—they were in England. Well, the Lord wanted them there. Now if the Lord expected anything to get done, the Lord had better send some-one capable to do it—the strain would kill *this* man, at least, before winter.

Of course Joseph knew perfectly well that the Lord probably already had help on the way. The Lord had a way of answering his prayers before he even said a word. It didn't occur to him that it might not have been the Lord who sent small and beau-tiful John C. Bennett to help him in his time of need.

Bennett was elegant, that was the word for him. He rode his horse with energy along the muddy road; he was no dandy, fearful lest he be spattered with mud. And yet the mud seemed not to touch him, and when he dismounted gracefully, tossed the reins over his horse's neck, and thrust out his hand toward Joseph Smith, he seemed to fill the space of a man twice his size; people stepped back to make way for him, though there was plenty of room.

"President Smith!" Bennett said. "I think if the City of God is ever built, it will be built at this place and no other!"

A clever one—that was the first thought that crossed Joseph's mind. Bennett had weeks to devise the first words he would say to the Mormon Prophet, and from the few letters they had exchanged Bennett had understood him well enough to know that the way to Joseph's heart was to flatter, not the man, but his dream. And yet Bennett's expression was so genuine, his tone so sincere, that it made Joseph a bit ashamed to suspect him, even for a moment, of guile. "We mean to do it," Joseph said, "if we can keep our enemies at bay long enough."

There wasn't even an introduction. It was as if both men assumed from the start that neither of them needed one. Joseph noticed that it made them equals, and that bothered him. The man took liberties. Soon, however, Joseph had his mind on other things. For Bennett was a man of ability, and if his deeds could match his talk, he was the answer to prayer.

"It strikes me that your worst enemy right now is disease."

"Disease? Half the city has a fever and the other half has the chills. I heard of a man who had the chills so bad he shook all the shingles off his roof. And then had a fever so hot his wife set the teapot on him to bring it to a boil." Bennett laughed, as Joseph wished him to. But it wasn't a matter that could be cured with a joke. "I'm not Jesus," Joseph said quietly, when the laughter was done. "I can't heal them with a word, and when they touch the hem of my topcoat, they die anyway. Some even say the land is cursed, and if an idea like that takes hold, good-bye to our chance of building anything here."

"Well, then, I'm your man. I'm a physician, and though my specialty is the ills of women and children, I've made it a point to use my office as Quartermaster General of the Illinois Militia to investigate this river fever. It's endemic to this whole area, and if you can fetch a horse, sir, I propose we ride out and I'll show you how to make this infirm land whole again."

The horse was fetched, of course, and in a few minutes they were riding alone together away from the people gathered near the stable. It all happened so quickly—things happened quickly around John Bennett. It was not until they were alone together that Joseph realized that he, the most hated, hunted man in Missouri, an escaped criminal there with a bounty on his head, was now riding alone near the edge of the river, a ripe target for capture or murder. He was relieved when he saw, in the distance, Porter Rockwell galloping hard to catch up. "Whoa up, now," Joseph said. "We're in no hurry." And he slowed his horse to a walk, to wait for Porter.

Bennett wheeled and returned to him. "My horse always runs when I feel urgent, President Smith." Then he cast his gaze back along the route they had followed, and he looked alarmed. "There's a man riding hard toward us who looks like a bandit."

Joseph didn't turn around. He had never asked Port to be his bodyguard, but he didn't mind in the least the frightening impression he made. Porter Rockwell was small, had a game leg, and talked in a high-pitched voice that was almost comical. But he decked himself out with as many pistols and carbines as a cavalry troop, and those who had seen him shoot knew that the guns weren't there for show. Joseph took pleasure watching Bennett's face. For when he first saw Porter, Bennett's face showed only curiosity, and by the time Porter arrived, Bennett was the picture of courage and confidence. But in between, for a fleeting moment, Joseph saw that the man could wear a fear that wasn't pretty. Not a cowardly kind of fear. More like the face of a boy who's just been caught stealing again, and knows there'll be no mercy in *this* whipping.

"Mornin', Brother Joseph," Porter said.

Joseph offered not a word of explanation to Bennett, just said, "Mornin', Porter. Well, now, let's have a look at the cause of our fever."

They rode on. Much of the swamp was firming up now, with the drainage ditches carrying the standing water away to the Mississippi so there'd be room to build, but Bennett seemed determined to seek out the foulest spots. The insects droned around them, and the horses sloshed water all over their boots and trousers; Bennett seemed not to notice. "Look at this," he said. "Wet as a cuspidor at closing time. See that fallen log? Last year's leaves rotting on the water? The air here has death in it. Malaria, we call it—that's Latin for 'bad air.' You won't be rid of that fever until every last bit of this swamp is dry land, firm enough to draw a cannon across it with a slow mule. The standing water causes the rot, and the rot causes foul odors to rise in the air, and those odors are poisons that attack the body and start the decay going inside a man. Of course, it takes brave men to dig ditches in places as foul as this—but I see you've already done some ditching, so I expect you'll have it done before long."

"Drain this, and it'll cure it?"

"Try me and see. President Smith, I can be a useful man to you—but only if you use me. Try me now. Dig those ditches. If the disease doesn't clear up within a month, then you'll know the only malaria around here comes from *me*."

"Bad air."

"It's the latest scientific discovery, President Smith. And in the meantime, I happen to have brought with me a supply of the drug quinine, which is extremely effective against this disease."

Porter Rockwell's piping voice interrupted. "How much you plan to sell it for?"

Bennett looked at him in surprise. "Sell it? Good heavens, man! I'm not a patent medicine dealer, I'm a medical doctor and a surgeon, the Quartermaster General of the Illinois Militia and a brigadier general. I have been a professor of medicine and a member of the board of regents of universities in West Virginia, Ohio, and the fair state of Illinois. I do not sell life-saving drugs for profit."

Properly abashed, Port looked away and watched the birds diving through the swarms of gnats and mosquitoes.

"It has to have cost you some money, General Bennett," Joseph said.

As Joseph had supposed, Bennett was a man who loved titles. Well, so did Joseph, for that matter. Bennett grinned and extended his hand. "President Smith, here with you I'm just plain John Bennett."

Joseph was quite capable of answering, "And you may call me President Smith," when someone presumptuously asked for first names. This man, however, was clearly not a charlatan. He had offered a plan and was willing to accept the judgment that would come if he failed—such confidence was a rare thing in this rough country, where few men were willing to stand to a tenth of what they said. "I'm called Brother Joseph by the Saints. And I hope you won't misunderstand me if I call you Brother John."

"I'd be proud to have a man like you call me brother," Bennett said. "Not that I'm a believer, mind you, I've heard something of your doctrine and while it sounds sensible it doesn't incline me to change preachers. I'm here for something else."

"And what is that?"

"I'm a visionary man, I suppose. As soon as something is built up, I lose interest in it and go on to something else. Nothing I like better than to sink a plow into virgin land, lay brick on brick, and watch civilization rise from the wilderness. Here you are on land that was swamp till you reclaimed it, with a citizenry of what, ten thousand souls?"

"Not that many, and certainly not here yet."

"The potential for it, though. All believing alike, all willing to work hard, all obedient to the same authority. If ever there was a chance to build something fine, it's here and now. So I saw that, and I said to myself, John Bennett, what the hell are you doing here in Springfield counting chickens in the army chicken coops, when somebody's out there making history! And here I am."

Porter, his courage returning, spat a good squirt of tobacco juice on the ground and said, "Don't look like you'd measure much against a plow."

Bennett didn't show any anger at the gibe at his size. He just grinned and said, "If you're pulling it, my small friend, I think I can handle the other end."

Joseph couldn't help himself and whooped with laughter, though he was sorry immediately, since Port plainly didn't like the man turning his own joke back on him. This John Bennett— he was a man of wit as well as wisdom, and that was almost enough to win Joseph's heart by itself.

"I was sayin'," Porter went on quietly, "that anyone can tell a hundred men to dig a ditch. What're you good for?"

"Sometimes I don't know myself," Bennett answered candidly. "There are days when I think I could do anything in the world, if I set my mind to it. And days when I wonder why God bothers to let me keep on taking up space on this good earth. But you're going to want a doctor here, at least. And maybe when you set up your town, you'll want someone to organize the militia—I could do that, and I've got friends in Springfield to ease that along. In fact, I might even be able to help when it comes time to petition the legislature for a city charter."

That was the moment that Joseph decided this man was sent by God. "Brother John, I don't know how I'll get a legislature to do it, but I want a charter that'll keep us free from any of the harassment we've put up with these last many years in Missouri and Ohio both. I mean I don't want outside judges trying our cases, I don't want outside generals ordering our militia, I don't want outside politicians making our laws, and I sure as hell don't want my people to stand unarmed and defenseless before a mob in military uniform, never again. As long as I'm alive, I want the power to take care of my people and keep them safe. Can you get me such a charter, Brother John?"

Bennett smiled. "I can if you take my advice."

"On what?"

"A simple matter, Brother Joseph. Elections are coming up this fall. Don't submit a charter until after that's done with. And during the election, vote wisely."

"I don't tell my people how to vote. They're free citizens."

"But I hear they take your advice pretty seriously, most of the time."

"When I give advice at all."

"Now I know you don't have much love for Democrats, what with the Missouri governor and that do-nothing President Van Buren both Democrats. It's the opinion of the good folks of Illinois—and of the politicians, too—that you Mormons would burn in hell before casting a vote for any Democrat. Now, that makes every Democrat in the legislature your enemy, and it *doesn't* make the Whigs your friends, since they'll figure they've got your vote no matter what they do."

Joseph knew a thing or two about politics, and he understood. "I have a friend, James Ralston. He's a Democrat, running against a fellow named Lincoln for the legislature."

"Excellent. One Democrat will be better than half a dozen. Where you Mormons are, you swing the vote, if you all vote together. And when they count up and find Mormons electing all Whigs *except one—*"

Joseph saw how it ended. "They'll all take notice of the fact that Jim Ralston is a friend to the Mormons."

"Hell, you won't even have to bribe anybody to get your charter through. They'll be standing in line for the privilege of voting for you."

Joseph laughed and slapped the shoulder of Bennett's horse, causing the animal to dance away, startling Bennett and nearly losing him his dignified posture on the saddle. But Bennett understood exuberance, and only laughed in return.

"Come along, Brother John, and let's see what your quinine does for the, uh—"

"Mal, aria. Latin for *bad air.*"

Joseph turned and faced the flat where the city was laid out and the hill beyond it where a temple would rise. He made a grand gesture. "There it is, Brother John. To you it's mud flats and scruffy grass, but I can already see the city it will be, a jewel in the crown of God."

"I'd like to think I have a glimpse of that city myself," Bennett said. "But I sure hope you aren't going to keep the name of Commerce, just because those scruffy houses on the shore are pretending to be a town."

"The name of my city is Nauvoo," Joseph said.

Bennett looked at him dumbly, and Joseph winked at Porter Rockwell. Rockwell grinned and took the opportunity. "That's Hebrew, Mr. Bennett. For *city beautiful.*"

One thing about Bennett. He could take a joke. He laughed harder than either of them, and told the story a dozen times, even though the tale was a poke at his own vanity. Within a few days practically everyone in Nauvoo had met John Bennett, and the longer he stayed the more the people saw that Joseph liked him. Liked him a lot. Bennett was baptized after a reasonable amount of time to allow for a proper conversion, and no one was taken by surprise that even though he didn't hold any official position, he managed to get invited to the meetings of practically every governing body of the Church. The only reason he didn't attend meetings of the Twelve, some folks said, was because the Twelve were in England. And a few even muttered that if Brigham and Heber and the rest of the Twelve were here, Bennett would find out that he wasn't the second tallest man in Nauvoo after all.

Joseph noticed the resentment. He had seen it before, when other men rose higher in the Church than some who had been Saints longer. But the jealousy of weak people would never stop him from using every able man he could find to build the Kingdom of God. Besides, there was Joseph's dream. John Bennett was little like a squirrel, and he had won Joseph's heart among the trees at the river's edge, just like the dream. And so Joseph tested him one day, when the two of them were alone.

"Brother John," he said, looking Bennett in the eye, "where's your family?"

Bennett smiled. "That's a bliss that God has not seen fit to grant me."

"Mr. Bennett," Joseph said, "where are your children?"

Bennett looked at him sharply. He caught the change in Joseph's tone, and the change in the way the Prophet addressed him. "It's something I don't much talk about. I guess I've got in the habit of lying. But it doesn't do much good to lie to a prophet, does it?" Bennett turned away, as if to hide the pain of recalling such bitter memories. "Brother Joseph, I caught my wife in bed with another man, back in Ohio, years ago. I was like to kill them both on the spot. Thank God I wasn't armed, or I would have. But I prayed for wisdom, and I prayed and prayed, for hours, until finally my heart was at peace. I knew then that it was the will of God for me to forgive, to just walk away and forgive. I wanted to take my children with me, but that was during the Black Hawk War, and I was going to be a surgeon there. So I left, meaning to return. The war wasn't half over when I started getting my letters back. She hadn't the decency even to tell me where she'd moved my children to."

Bennett's voice went high, and the urge to weep was plain, but he manfully held back the tears in spite of his grief. "I searched for a year, until I had no medical practice, no money, no home, and no hope. And then I woke up one morning and knew that it wouldn't do my children any good for me to ruin myself trying to find them. God had given me certain gifts, and it wasn't my right to waste them. I was needed. To do things like—like what I'm doing here." He touched the table where the plans for the Nauvoo charter lay. "Brother Joseph, I abandoned my children. Do you think you could pray to the Lord and find out for me where my wife has taken them, or even just tell me whether they're alive or not!"

Joseph embraced him and let the man weep against his shoulder. This was his little squirrel, all right. He had abandoned his children, all because God needed him here, in Nauvoo, to do a mighty work among the Saints. "Brother John,"

Joseph said, answering the plea of the little beast in his dream. "Brother John, here among us you will always have an inheritance."

"Thank you," Bennett whispered. "As God is my witness, I'll never let you down."

❧ 25 ❧

On the Ship North America
Liverpool, 1840

IF EVER A TOWN was calculated to make a man glad to leave England, it was Liverpool. It lacked most of the smoke of Manchester, though it had enough to keep you well in mind of the taste of coal. But what was missing in effluent from the chimneys was well made-up-for in the sheer squalor, the brazen poverty that flaunted itself instead of hiding in the shade of buildings. The only sign that God had a hand in the creation of Liverpool was a dismal little cathedral that hardly deserved the name. It was a seaport town, John Kirkham told himself, forgiving the place for being itself; all sorts of foul things are brought to shore by the lapping of the waves.

John Kirkham was a forgiving man. He forgave Liverpool for being Liverpool; he forgave his family for giving up safety and security in Manchester and dragging him off to a land of savages—if he didn't win a soggy grave on the way; most of all he forgave himself for his whole life. He had tried anguish, and it worked for a time. Then he tried self-justification. That worked not at all. Now he merely accepted. Accepted himself as a weak man who hadn't talent or drive to succeed at anything. Forgave himself for the lies that had won him a sinecure in his discarded home. And last of all endured easily even the humiliation of his son Charlie treating him like a child.

Now he stood on the dock in Liverpool where the Mersey was devoured by the sea, listening to his son haggling with a carter; he felt like a canopy of seaweed, contouring himself with the waves, rising where the water rose and sinking where it fell, and, because of that flexibility, holding together and staying alive. He was content. Life or death, America or hell, it made no difference to him. All the burdens had been lifted from him. No one looked to him for food and shelter; no one looked to him even for advice. Anna expected ardor now and then, which he willingly supplied. Other than that, he might as well have been a tree.

"I agreed in advance to a shilling one-and-a-half pence and that's what I'll pay!" Charlie was angry. It made his voice go high and weak.

"*I* didn't agree to that!" It was obviously a cheat: John had seen it often enough in London. The carter agrees on a price, and then at the destination the "owner" of the cart shows up and demands some outrageous fee, refusing to accept the earlier agreement. "You might as well kill my horse, you'll put me out of business in a minute that way!"

"You can't be doing too badly," Charlie pointed out. "After all, if you can hire a carter, you've got a bit to spare."

John cringed. If you started trying to be logical with these thieves, they'd have you every time.

"Well," said the owner, "I won't argue with you. I don't mean to be robbed on the open streets of Liverpool. We've had a bit of trouble with out-of-towners like you, and when I fetch a policeman you can plan on a day or so in the lock-up, and then a word with the magistrate."

"And *I* think the law will look more kindly on my agreement with *this* fellow than your claim for five times that amount. Shall we try the experiment? There's a policeman! Ho there! Officer!"

"Now don't go trying to cause me trouble—it'll go harder with you. I'm willing to meet you halfway."

"And your carter here, he'll back me up in court, won't you, fellow? Under penalty of perjury?"

The carter would, and the owner instantly backed down, accepted the lower fee, unloaded the cart and quit the dock before anything worse happened. John smiled at his son in approval. The boy hadn't backed down before the threat after all. Charlie saw the smile and pretended not to notice it, but John was no fool. He knew that it made Charlie proud, to have his father—even such a father—approve of him.

Val and Honor were tired and out of sorts, and Dinah's patience had run out somewhere between the train station and the pier. Now the children were sitting on a box, their backs to each other, their hands folded, keeping quiet until their mother released them from the punishment. That was the theory. In fact they were squirming and crying and shouting at each other and their mother and the world at large. It was going to be a long voyage. Of course, a little seasickness would calm them down. It calmed a good number of children right to death, as everyone knew, vomiting their lives out and dehydrating before their parents' eyes. After that thought John was willing to endure their noise. Nothing justified the deaths of little children. If anyone had asked him, which of course they hadn't, he would have said that it's better to leave your children behind than drag them off to die in a stinking little ship. But then, he was the expert on abandoning children, that's what they'd say to him if he tried to interfere. He knew the sound of contempt— he had no desire to hear it again in their voices. So he held his tongue.

"Here comes the boat," Dinah said, and at that the children jumped up and ran to the edge of the pier. Anna screamed. John caught Honor six feet from the edge and Dinah took Val by the jacket right at the brink. Children were such damn fools it was a wonder any of them lived to adulthood. It was proof there was a God after all.

Everyone was in a flurry of fear, scolding the children and thanking God loudly that they had been quick enough. John said nothing. He usually said nothing these days. But it amused him. Their reaction was so out of proportion. This was just an excuse for them to let out the fear they had been keeping in for days.

How could they do it? he wondered. He was used to owning

nothing—this was nothing new to him, he liked it this way. But in their last few weeks as they sold off Anna's china and half Charlie's books, all their furniture, everything they could convert into cash, John had seen their anxiety growing. This was too much like poverty. They kept looking at John covertly, talking especially cheerfully when he was around. He knew what they said when he wasn't there: This is just like it was after Father left us. We're losing everything again. And yet they went ahead. One thing John had to admire them for— they really had faith. Why, they were so damned Christian they had even forgiven John and taken him back, and that was a test he had never really believed they'd pass. Mormonism had made the difference. It was a sure bet that gentile Robert would never forgive him.

Dinah held her children tight, the scolding done. Val was writhing to get free, but John knew he wouldn't make it. Dinah clung to those children like a drunk to his cup. She was so afraid. John got a bit of pleasure out of that. Served her right, for thinking that she didn't need her husband.

The boat pulled up against the dock and the sailors started manhandling the boxes aboard.

"Careful," Charlie said.

The sailors stopped in mid-throw, long enough to glare with loathing at him, and then treated the boxes rougher than before. How interesting, John thought. There may be murders aboard this ship before we reach New York.

Their things were loaded on the boat, ready to be ferried out to the ship at anchor in the river, and they were just about to board themselves when another family of Saints arrived, Brother and Sister Corbridge from Thomly. They were farmers and had little luggage, so they were loaded aboard quickly. Val at once took possession of their oldest child, a two-year-old girl, Mary; they also had a babe-in-arms that squalled constantly, a boy named John. Plain names for plain people. The salt of the earth. The scum of the earth. All depended on your point of view. John Kirkham took a scanted view of mankind. He leaned a bit toward the scum opinion, and willingly included himself in that category.

There was a lot of terror and shouting and impatience as they clambered down into the boat. The tiny vessel rocked alarmingly as they got in, and from the pier it looked like they were being expected to jump into a bucket from a second-story window. The Corbridges were the worst—the adults, not the little ones. When they were finally aboard, James Corbridge turned to John Kirkham—apparently under the misconception that he was the head of the family—and apologized. "Can't swim, you know, nor the missus."

"Neither can I," John said merrily. He could afford to be fearless. He didn't really much care at this moment whether the boat stayed afloat or not. All one to him.

"Only water I've ever been in was to baptize me," Corbridge went on. Then caught himself. "Oh, and bathing, too, but that don't count."

"No sir," John agreed. "Don't count at all."

The boat reacted seismically to every undulation of the water. Mrs. Corbridge looked a little ill. Her husband was quite solicitous. "Not so bad, Elizabeth. The little ship rocks but the big one'll stand still in the water."

When they got to the ship, it was harder than it had been at the pier—the dock had at least held still. Dinah became quite timid about climbing up the ladder, especially holding Honor, so Charlie made the trip twice, once with each child. John was amused that it didn't occur to any of them that *he* could carry a child. But the Corbridges gave him their little John to carry—strangers, he noted, valued him higher than his own kin. Well, he could forgive that, too. It was the Corbridges who were too trusting, not his family too suspicious.

Their boxes were winched aboard and dropped with a resounding thud on the deck. Anna grimaced. "I'm glad I sold my china after all." Then they manhandled the boxes down the hatchway, down the steep stairways, into the deepest, dankest portions of the ship.

Steerage. It was the only way most of the Saints could afford to travel, and Charlie and Anna had decided they would go steerage even though they could afford second-class cabins, because they belonged with the Saints. John might have offered advice to the contrary, but he went unasked. So he helped Charlie stack the boxes, leaving the ones full of food atop the pile, and then calmly accepted Charlie's decision that Anna would sleep with Val and Dinah with Honor, while Charlie and John shared a bed. It made no difference. In this unprivate place Anna would not expect any conjugal bliss for the duration.

And Charlie didn't snore. He'd make a good husband someday.

When the Corbridges got their things down, it turned out there wasn't room for all their boxes to be in easy reach. So there was a general reshuffling as both families repacked their belongings to keep food and most-needed clothes in the accessible boxes. When it was done, everyone sat down on the edges of the lower berths and looked at each other.

"I've seen gaols with more room than this," John said. The joke fell flat. The family reacted with quiet disdain. The Corbridges laughed, but *they* didn't assume that John had really been in gaol.

John looked down the rows of berths, which were officially regarded as being wide enough for two persons. The berths were bunked two levels high, and the beams of the ceiling hung low enough that Charlie, at least, had to duck. John noticed that before Charlie learned to bend over all the time when walking, he bumped his head fiercely several times; and as was his wont, John cheerfully forgave the ship for doing it.

It took Charlie an hour or so of poking around and making himself obnoxious to the sailors, but by day's end he felt he knew the ship. Knowledge was ownership for Charlie, so the *North America* was *his* now; he was in charge. He presumptuously made friends with Captain Lower, and without anyone asking him to, he became the liaison between the Saints and the ship's officers. When Brigham Young, Willard Richards, and John Taylor arrived to hold services on the ship, it was Charlie who arranged permission to hold the meeting on the main deck. Charlie was brazen enough to ask Captain Lower to attend, and even though he politely declined—he would be ashore at that time—there was a palpable warming of relations. It was Charlie's greatest gift: strangers could not help but find him likeable.

At the meeting, Brother Brigham made official what Charlie had already done, and appointed him clerk of the company. Obviously this was going to be a fine and successful voyage.

Charlie even loved the gentle rocking of the boat. He quickly learned to walk on the swaying decks without lurching, and writing the official journal for the company of Saints he prided himself on the fact that his handwriting showed not a sign of the movement of the ship.

Others did not fare so well, though. More than one Saint complained of slight nausea and headaches. "You'll get used to it quicker than you think," Charlie encouraged them. "It could be much worse." For once Charlie was being prophetic. None of the Saints yet had a notion of the difference between harbor and open sea. It was a figure of things to come when the little Corbridge girl became sick with the sway of the boat at anchor, and vomited in the night. The acrid smell was annoying, but Charlie said nothing, just listened as Val complained to Dinah, "It stinks." Dinah hushed the boy, but for the first time Charlie realized that children might really have it worse than adults on the voyage. No adult had vomited, at least, and he heard the next day that two other little ones had been sick in the night.

"Fresh fruit, that's what we need," Anna assured Sister Corbridge. "That'll have you little girl fresh as a daisy in no time." Of course that meant Charlie would go into Liverpool— there wasn't a chance in the world that Dinah or Anna would climb the ladder from the ship into that miserable little boat until they got to New York. Father looked bored, so Charlie invited him to come along. Without a word John got up and put on his coat. There wasn't a chance of him doing something so polite as saying, "Thanks for inviting me," or even, "Splendid idea."

The ladder was harder down than up, but Charlie handled it well and then shouted advice to his father as he climbed down after him. In the boat Charlie felt like an old sailor, and he asked the rowers questions, using ship's terminology as much as he could—lots of *fo'c'sle* and *mizzenmast* and *starboard* and *aft*. He only quit when he finally realized the suntanned men found him somewhere between amusing and annoying.

The market wasn't far from the wharf, and they had little trouble getting a fair price, once they made it clear they did not intend to be cheated. The Liverpudlians made a good deal of their living by stealing from those who passed through the port never to be seen again; but business was apparently good enough that they did not feel obliged to cheat *everyone*. Charlie and John indulged in a pear each for supper as they walked back to the dock. "I hope they have pears in America," Charlie said.

"That all depends on the dealers, don't it?" John answered.

Charlie got the pun and, feeling charitable, he laughed at it. No reason why he and his father shouldn't be friends of a sort, anyway. John took it a bit farther. "Why not step in for a pint?" he offered.

"This once, why not?" Charlie said. The Word of Wisdom said for Mormons not to drink alcoholic beverages, but for special occasions the brethren often made exceptions, and surely the last trip ashore in England for heaven knows how many years was a special occasion. So they pushed their way through the crowded street toward a pub. Charlie leaned close to a window and looked in. It was dark enough inside that he could see little, and that only through the portion of the window made transparent by his shadow. The place reminded Charlie of the dingy holes where Robert and Matthew always used to go. Charlie had only rarely been inside such pubs, but they still held a fascination for him, as if entering conferred true manhood. He was pulling away when he glanced down at the table just under the window and found himself staring into the surprised face of Matthew Handy.

Charlie stepped back in surprise, and of course the window became opaque as a mirror in the sunlight. By the time he got back to the window for another look, four men were walking away from the table. They were moving too quickly to be sure, but two of them were in uniforms. One was a constable, while the other was a ship's officer. Indeed, for a moment Charlie thought it might be Captain Lower of the *North America,* but then they were out of sight from the window, and Charlie could not be sure.

"What is it?" John asked.

"Could have sworn I saw Dinah's husband."

"Here! In Liverpool!"

Charlie didn't answer, just pushed his way to the door and went in. The table by the window already had a couple of new drinkers now—it was getting on toward evening. And there was no sign of the four men who had been sitting there. Charlie looked around and saw a back entrance leading onto another street, but the alley was empty when he got there. Whoever the men were, they left in a hurry. But Matthew!

"What would Matt be doing here?" Father asked.

"How should I know?"

"He has a common face."

That was true. Charlie only saw him through a window,

anyway. And yet the thought plagued him. What if it *was* Matt—*and* Captain Lower? There could be only one meaning for that.

"Do you think Matt might try to stop Dinah from coming?"

"Dinah said he gave permission."

"Dinah said he didn't mind. What if he's decided that he *does* mind?"

John laughed. "The way he lets her lead him about by the nose? The man has no spine."

Charlie thought it was odd for Father to criticize another man for being spineless—but it didn't differ from Charlie's own assessment. Yet there was that side of Matthew that had led him to beat Dinah, and that wasn't all that long ago. A constable, the captain of the ship, and Matt. And another man. A solicitor? What was the law on a mother taking children away from their father? "I'd better tell Dinah," Charlie said.

"That's right," Father said. "It'll worry her sick, and you only *think* you saw him through a dazzled window, and it's as unlikely as pigs flying, but you ought to tell her."

"I will if I think it best."

"And if I advised you not to jump into the sea, would you jump just to prove you know better than me?"

Charlie looked at his father, willing enough to quarrel. But John Kirkham did not look quarrelsome. He was grinning, in fact. "Am I just being ridiculous, then?" Charlie asked.

"I think that it's natural to think you saw what you most fear."

"What I most fear is dying of thirst," Charlie said, and paid for two mugs of beer. That did a bit to help settle his fears. Charlie drank so rarely that one beer was enough to keep him cheerful for hours.

It was a cheerful night aboard ship anyway. The first mate came into steerage just after suppertime and announced that they'd sail with the tide in the morning, within a few hours after dawn. It was welcome news, and the night was spent in reveling. They began by singing hymns—after all, there were three apostles spending this last night in harbor with them aboard the ship—but along about eight o'clock Brother Brigham said, "I think we'll make the Lord weary of us with so much worship. Isn't there a fiddle in this company? Isn't there a lady willing to take a step or two with me?"

So the celebration moved to the deck, and the sailors stood around watching the reels and corners. Charlie was a good dancer, and Brigham chose him three times for his own square. It was doubtless an accident, but all three times both Sally and Harriette Clinton were in the same square.

When Harriette was his opposite she said, "My sister thinks you must be angry at her." Then she spun away before he could answer. Charlie looked over at Sally, who had been gazing at him; she soulfully looked away and then fell into the hand over hand of the allemande, which brought her to Charlie in a few steps. He looked at her questioningly, but she wouldn't meet his gaze.

Charlie could not bear thinking that she thought he was angry. He *had* avoided her, he knew, but not because of anger. It was because his dreams of loving her were too vivid in memory; he was ashamed to be near her, knowing he had had such lustful and unworthy thoughts. Yet it was not fair that she should be punished for his sin. In the next square, when Brigham brought them together, Charlie insisted on being her partner.

He had learned a lesson from her book. Accuse your accuser with her own accusation. "Why are you angry?" he asked, then went off to swing his corner.

"I'm not," she said when they got back together. "I thought you were."

"Pay attention," Brigham barked. Charlie flung Sally toward the Apostle and took a turn with Sister Featherstone.

"You two make such a darling pair," Sister Featherstone said.

The promenade was next, and Sally bumped him with her hip. "What did she say?"

"That you deserve a better-looking partner," Charlie answered.

"You're such a liar."

"Don't tell Brother Brigham, or he'll disfellowship me."

"Don't you wish you could kiss me?"

Charlie only had time to blush before he was off with his corner again. He saw to it the dance ended without another word.

He sought out Dinah and took her out to step the next dance. Dinah was laughing at him. "You and Sally aren't making any secret of things, are you?"

Dinah could not know about their stolen kiss, could she? "If there's anything between us, it's a secret to *me*."

"Sorry." Plainly Dinah didn't believe him.

"I haven't met the woman I want to marry."

"Well, make do the best you can. The voyage will be long, Charlie, but good company will pass the time."

The dancing ended and the company went back below decks to sleep. Charlie of course sat down and wrote copiously in the company journal. He paid little attention to the others until he heard Val crying.

"I want to go home," he said.

"We're going to a *new* home," Dinah said.

". . . 'Ome," said Honor, testing the word.

"Where's Daddy?" Val asked.

"He won't be coming to America until later. On another ship."

"I want Daddy!" Val wailed. Charlie wanted to shake the child and say, Aren't things hard enough without you torturing your mother like this? But of course Val was just a child, and didn't understand a thing.

Val would not quiet down until John Kirkham took him on his knee and looked him in the eye. "Listen, little man, your father would be ashamed if he saw you acting like this."

"I want Daddy," Val said.

"And your Daddy will come along presently. Don't you think he misses his little boy already? You be happy and smile, and go to sleep like a good boy, and your Daddy will come sooner than you think."

Charlie felt annoyed at his father. Couldn't the man comfort the child without lying? Charlie refused to admit to himself that part of what he felt was jealousy. He had once sat upon that knee, no doubt, but he had no memory of it. He should have had a memory of it.

Charlie was the last to bed. So the others could have relative darkness, he finished his entry by the light of a lamp well down the corridor between berths; it strained his eyes a little, and he was tired. He had thought to write a glowing rhapsody about the glory of departing England and leaving it for Zion. Now the words came painfully, and he finally gave up and rapidly wrote in plain language how worried everyone was about the voyage, and yet how they felt lifted up by the Spirit of God and no one was willing to complain. It wasn't beautiful. Just true. But he reread it and decided there was a certain elegance to that as well.

He closed the journal and put away his pen and ink. Before he could climb up to the berth he shared with his father, however, he heard Dinah whisper his name. Immediately he knelt on the floor beside her berth and quietly said, "Yes, Dinah?"

"Charlie, you heard Val crying for his father tonight."

"Yes. He's just a child."

"Am I right to do this?"

"Can you doubt it?"

"For myself, no." Her voice sounded husky with emotion. "But how can I make my children live without their father?"

"Better than making them live without their God."

"Oh, Charlie, are you sure of that? Are you certain?"

Charlie had never known Dinah to have doubts. It frightened him a little. "Aren't *you?*"

"What is it like, to be a boy with no father?"

"It's different for Val."

"Yes. His mother is stealing him away."

"He doesn't understand now. But he will."

"Do you think so? Will he forgive me?"

Charlie thought of his own father. "Anything can be forgiven, Dinah."

Perhaps she also thought of him. "Can be forgiven—but *will* it be?"

Charlie thought of the dangerous voyage ahead. If either of the children were to die at sea, Dinah would condemn herself forever. And perhaps rightly so. How would Charlie feel if instead of Father abandoning them, Mother had taken them away? It was a terrible responsibility to take on. Charlie could not advise her to bear it, though he also could not imagine going to Zion without his wise and compassionate sister. "If you have doubts, Dinah, it's not too late to go home."

"I *am* going home. This is no idle voyage for me, Charlie. I've felt it all these days, a fire within me. When I think of England I get no answering flame, but my heart leaps to think of Zion. I've been in exile all my life. But it's nearly done."

"Then be at peace."

"If Matt had done this to me, I'd hate him forever."

Charlie toyed with the idea of telling her then what he thought he had seen during the day. But she was worried enough as it was—and what would she do even if it were true? And it wasn't true. It had just been the way the shadows worked in the window of the pub. It was nothing. It was not Matt. "Will you miss him?"

"Don't you see, Charlie? Whether I miss him or not doesn't matter. The children miss him. For me this voyage is all joy. It's the little ones who are paying the price. It isn't right for them to suffer for my sake."

"You'll make it up to them."

"Give me a blessing, Charlie."

It was a strange request. It was not as if she were ill and needed anointing with the consecrated oil. He did not answer, uncertain what it was she wanted of him.

"Never mind, darling Charlie. Just pray with me. I need some comfort tonight."

So he prayed, not sure what he ought to ask for. He just thanked God for the trip ahead of them, and asked God to bless Dinah, that her heart would be reconciled to his will. It was the first time anyone had asked him to act alone in a spiritual matter. Baptizing Father was one thing, and easy; clerking came to him as naturally as sleeping; but to pray on someone else's behalf, that actually required him to be in tune with the Spirit of God. Maybe he was and maybe he wasn't—he wasn't altogether sure what it should feel like.

It occurred to him as he knelt there that even though Dinah held no office in the Church, she was closer to God than he was. After all, she had had the gift of interpretation of tongues, she had spoken almost like a prophetess. She had so much faith, in fact, that when the prayer was finished she murmured *amen*, smiled at him, and went instantly to sleep, an expression of contentment on her face. It was strange that a woman should have so much more closeness to the Spirit than he. But he decided, before finally drifting off to sleep, that she was not really more spiritual. It was just that, being more emotional, a woman was better able to express her feelings.

When his mother shook him awake, he was not aware that he had even slept; the single lantern still shone far down the row of berths, and no one else was stirring. "Charlie," she said. "Charlie, wake up."

"What is it?"

"Charlie, the first mate came down and woke Dinah and

told her to take the children on deck."

Charlie sat up and slid off the upper bunk. "What for?" he asked, pulling on his trousers.

"Didn't say, and Dinah told me to stay here, but Charlie—"

"I thought I saw Matt yesterday."

"Matt! Oh, Charlie, why didn't you say something?"

"I thought I was mistaken." He didn't bother with his waist-coat or even his shoes, just pulled on his coat as he hurried down the corridor. It was Matt, of course it was Matt, and he had seen him yesterday meeting with Captain Lower. Captain Lower, who couldn't attend the Mormon meeting the day before because he had his damned treasonous business ashore.

When he got to the deck, the first light of dawn was showing in the east, but it was too dark to see easily. The sailors were about their business. Charlie had not realized there were so many seamen in the crew. They had never been all together on the decks before, but the wind and tide would wait for no late sleepers among the crew this morning. The breeze was cool as it ruffled Charlie's hair; he shivered. Had they taken Dinah ashore, too, by force? But no. There they were. Dinah and the two children, with Captain Lower and a constable. No doubt about it, then. They had got some sort of legal way of forcing Dinah to come back with them. The sight of Dinah clinging to her children, surrounded by men who could easily overpower her was intolerable. Charlie ran along the deck, dodging sailors and getting roundly cursed in the process. He reached Dinah and stood behind her. She was holding both children in her arms.

"Dinah," Charlie said.

She turned and looked at him blankly.

"Let me hold Val."

She shook her head. She was not letting go of the children for any reason.

"Good morning, Charlie," Matthew said.

Charlie looked contemptuously at his brother-in-law. "It was kind of you to visit us, Matt."

But it was not Matt who answered. "You're up early, Char-lie. But not early enough to stop us." It was Robert, and he was smiling.

Perhaps because he was not fully awake, perhaps because Robert's smile, in these circumstances, was an unbearable provocation, or perhaps because he knew this was the last chance in his life to do it, Charlie pushed his way past Dinah, walked directly to Robert, and struck him with the heal of his fist, a hammering blow with all his strength, square in the nose. Robert did not so much as raise a hand or turn his head aside to protect himself from the blow. After all, violence from Charlie was a complete surprise. Robert had long since categorized his brother as a man of words. Now he learned that words do not always satisfy a clerk. And perhaps Robert unwittingly welcomed the blow. It unburdened him of one of the gravest debts of his life, the guilt he owed to Charlie, even as he was in the act of taking on another, even heavier load.

The blood gushed from Robert's nose as he stood there, stunned and unbelieving. The constable laid hands on Charlie immediately, and Captain Lower called for some of his sailors to restrain him, but Charlie made no resistance to them. He had done it. He had drawn Robert's blood. He should have done it years ago, it felt so satisfying.

"You'll be in gaol within the hour, lad," the constable said.

"No," Robert said.

"This is a savage, unwarranted attack, and we'll have this boy in prison until he grows a beard."

"No!" Robert said. "I won't have him arrested."

"But Mr. Kirkham, look at you, all over blood!"

"I won't have my brother arrested! He's going to America, and that's far enough away to suit us both."

Captain Lower daubed at the blood on Robert's shirt and jacket with a handkerchief as Matthew tried to stanch the flow from his nose. "I don't think it's broken," Matt said.

The constable turned to the sailors. "Take him below decks, then," he said.

Charlie spat his words at Robert. "That's right. Make sure Father and Mother and I are all out of sight while you do it!"

"Let him stay and watch," Robert said. "It's all one to me."

The constable shrugged, annoyed at Robert's seeming lack of resolve. "Then let's get on with it." And he unfolded a paper and began to read.

Dinah watched almost as if she were not a participant. She had been wakened suddenly, knowing at once what was happening, but strangely unafraid. She had given no alarm to the children; Honor was still dozing on her shoulder, and Val had only sleepily said, "Hullo, Daddy," when they reached the main deck. The fear did not come until she realized that Robert was not there to make sure Matthew did not get out of line. Robert was there because it was Robert who was her enemy. It was Robert who had brought the legal papers, Robert who was giving the orders to the constable. Weak Matthew was merely a spectator. And if Robert was against her, there was no sanctuary. It was Robert she had run to after Mr. Uray attacked her, Robert who had saved her from Matt's murderous blows. But this time he was the one with the terrible look of purpose on his face, the one who would break her if he could. And of all the people in the world, if anyone could break her, it was Robert. Now she was afraid. Now she trembled.

Poor Charlie, she thought as the sailors held him roughly, apart from the group. Always wanting to help, yet never having quite the tool needed.

"Do you understand?" the constable asked.

Dinah could not remember hearing a word of what he had just read from the papers. She shook her head.

The constable looked at her in exasperation.

"Explain it plainly, Matt," Robert said.

Matt looked confused. Obviously he had expected to get through this morning without having to take any action *personally*.

"Dinah," he said. "We've come to take you home."

She said nothing, only held the children and tried desperately to penetrate her own fear deep enough to find the words she could say, the act she could perform that would end this, that would return her to her berth in the ship, the children with her, the ship putting out to sea. Surely God could arrange it—such a little thing. Surely this could turn out to be a dream.

"Dinah, did you think because I took it calm, I'd let you do this? A man's family is his own, that's the law. The law won't let you steal my family from me, Dinah."

At the times of trouble in her life, why was it so hard for her to find speech? "Then come with me, if you want your family so much." Yet the words came from her lips as a whisper, not with the force she thought to use. And Matthew didn't even understand her.

"What did you say?"

Robert spoke in pain, the handkerchief to his nose. "Matt won't go with you, Dinah. A man stays where his work is, and a wife stays with her husband. I made Matthew wait to do this until the last possible moment, in the hope that you'd come to your senses. I'll put it plain, Dinah. What you're doing is as bad as what Father did to us, and I won't let it happen. Do you understand that? It will never happen again, not to any of mine. No child without a father, without a home, so don't think of persuading us, don't think of resisting, it'll do no good. You'll come home, you'll be a wife and a mother. And don't think you'll sneak away again. I'll pay for servants to stay with you, and you won't be allowed near the children except in the presence of a servant. You won't be able to take them outside without two servants. You won't be allowed to associate with the Mormons who put this insanity in your mind. In short, Dinah, you have proven yourself to be dangerous to the welfare of these children, and they will be protected. In time, in a year or so, if you show yourself to have come to your senses, these restrictions will be relaxed. On the contrary, if you resist or rebel in any way, your access to the children will be limited even further. I hope you understand that this is not harsh but merciful. You could have been gaoled for this. You could have had the children taken from you. We found in the law the kindest way of protecting your family from your madness."

Dinah heard his words and understood them, but all she could really feel was Honor's breath against her neck, Val's wriggling in her arms.

Robert studied her face and nodded. "Matt, Mr. Simpson, I suggest you take the children first."

Dinah knew there was no hope of resistance before Robert said it. She hadn't the strength to hold these children, not if these men were determined to take them. So for the children's sake, to keep them from having memories of being torn from their mother's arms, she stepped forward and yielded them into her husband's arms, avoiding the constable entirely. Val hugged his father and said, "Why didn't you come before?" But Honor cried at being wakened out of her mother's arms.

Matt held the children gratefully. "Thank you, Dinah," he said. "I hoped you'd see reason. And it won't be so bad. You'll see. In no time things will be as they should be, no more of this bitterness. All forgotten in such a short time, you'll be surprised."

"Come along then," the constable said. "This ship will need to sail soon, and the Captain has other business."

Dinah saw their relief, the relaxation of tension. They had won, they were sure, and without a real struggle.

"I'm not coming," Dinah said.

The mood of relief was gone in a moment.

"It's not a matter of choice," Robert said.

"Put me in irons, then."

"If we have to."

"I'll take you to court. I can fight you with your own weapons."

Robert shook his head. "You don't understand, Dinah. The way that we avoided divorce, the way that we kept you out of gaol, was by having you declared mentally incompetent. You are legally a lunatic, and all your legal rights are vested in your husband and me jointly. You haven't the power to so much as sign your name without our consent."

"You've had me judged mad," she said.

"It was the best of bad alternatives. Don't blame us, Dinah. In a few months of not seeing any of these damned Mormons you'll be back to your senses and thank us for this. You'll be angry at me then for not doing as much for Charlie and Mother as I'm doing for you."

"You're doing this for me?"

"I have no other motive than love for you and your children. If you had done this, your children would have hated you all their lives."

Robert's righteousness, his sincerity in destroying her for her own sake, it was too much for her to bear. A floodgate cracked within her, and her anger began to seep quietly out. "May God damn your soul to hell forever."

"I'm willing to endure your hatred now for the sake of your love later."

She thought of the future they planned for her. Living politely in a home where she was a prisoner, asking permission to see her children, forbidden to leave the house alone, totally in submission to her husband's will. And Matthew would be so kind about it. "Of course you may go to the park with the children, my love," he would say, and then call the servants to go with her. "That's my dear wife," he would say when she came home, and then he would climb aboard her and she would smile and pretend to be pleased so that he would do her favors. She saw in her mind the face of God, the face of her imagined Joseph Smith; she remembered with her whole body how it felt to stand in the presence of God, alive from the skin inward, hot at the core. That was her true self. If she bowed before Robert and Matthew, that part of her would die. They were right. If she ever lived as they wanted her to, docile and compliant, she would so loathe herself that within a only a few years she would have become what they wanted: a perfect wife and mother, her mind empty of will, her heart devoid of hope, for she would have forsaken her God and lost herself.

"How neatly you have it planned," she said, and the hate tasted strong in her mouth. "But I have a better plan. You'll like it, Robert—it'll save you money and you can still feel just as righteous. Instead of hiring servants, Matthew can just bring some of his whores to live in the house with him. He'll get from them all he ever wanted from me, with variety to boot, and from time to time you can get a judge to declare them insane and throw them out for new ones. You can live gay as a goose in a gutter. And better to have the children reared by cheap carrion than by a woman who dares to believe in an inconvenient God."

Captain Lower blushed. "Madame, mind your language."

"Forgive me. I forgot we were being polite about this. You'll stand there, Captain, and let them do to me what they're doing, but I mustn't use crude language. Well, that's the truth of it. My husband goes to whores while I'm at church, and yet I'm insane to take my children and leave him."

"Not in front of the children," Robert said.

"Maybe if I charged you money, Matt, you'd like me better."

"Dinah, please," Matt said.

She was trying to hurt them, but they only looked embarrassed. There were no words that would serve her as weapons. In despair she screamed so loudly that it ripped at her throat: "Have I no friends here! Is there no deliverance!"

Her words reached from bow to stern, and in the highest rigging the sailors fell silent. And in that silence, which no one dared to break, she felt herself fill with light. There was one deliverer that would come when no one else could help her.

He burned her, but she knew his touch within her flesh. He was the one who had called her to cross the ocean; he called her still. And because he wanted her, she must go. Must go, but not without a price. Not without a sacrifice, and the sacrifice was a broken heart. The sacrifice was to give up her children for God. If she stayed in England, it would be a decision to reject that inward light; it would leave her and never return. And what then would she have to give her children? What sort of mother could she be? Hating herself, there would be no love left in her. She would be a stranger in her own house, an alien in her own body. She would not stay in England. Rather than do so, she would suffer her life to end.

"Matthew," she said to him, her voice a painful whisper. "As God is my witness, I would rather lie in a grave than live with you. No matter what you do, no matter what you say, I'll never forgive you for this morning. I'll fill your home with hatred. I'll weep when you're happy, I'll rejoice when you fail, and every hour of every day until you die, I'll see to it you know how much I despise you. It's the only weapon I have, my hate for you, but I'll drive it in you to the hilt, and deeper if I can."

"Good God, woman," the constable whispered.

"Let her stay," Matthew said. There were inexplicable tears on his cheeks.

"It's just the way she feels right now," Robert said. "Bring her home, she'll soon change."

But for once Matthew had understood Dinah. "I said let her stay. There's no healing this day's blood." He turned and walked away, the children in his arms. Honor cried out for her mother, and Val had understood enough to be afraid. "Come with us, Mama!" he called.

Dinah watched Matt walk to the brink. She was so filled with light that she could hardly see. Matt turned and faced her, and from that distance shouted back to her. "I'll teach them to hate you!" he cried. "I'll always tell them that you left because you didn't love them!" But her heart was so full of fire that she could not feel pain now, could only watch as mute as a deer being torn by wolves as the stranger carried off her little ones. This was the plan of her life. This was the way it was meant to be. She had surrendered herself to God, and this was the first gift he gave her. "I'll never divorce you!" Matt shouted. "You'll always be my wife!" And at that moment the sun broke above the western sea, and Matthew winced at the blinding light. The constable came to him and carried Val down the ladder. Matthew, his last hope of winning her gone, climbed down after him, holding Honor in his arms, looking weak and beaten and older because of the day's work.

Only Robert had not gone. He stayed to plead for understanding. "I've never meant anything but good for you," he said. She did not answer, and her silence goaded him. "You're truly Father's daughter, Dinah. You and he are just alike. If there were a God, he would have made you barren, for your children's sake." And then, those word said, her silence made him ashamed. "I swear to you, Dinah, if you ever want to come back, write me and I'll come for you, no matter what the cost, as fast as ships and trains and horses and my own two feet can bring me." And then he, too, broke against the coast of her indifference and weakly fled from her to the edge of the deck, down the ladder into the shadow of the ship.

Dinah did not move, did not watch them out of sight. She only stared inside herself at the face of a terrible God who seared her with a vision of hope. She saw a gentle young woman weeping, handing her an infant child; she felt her own arms reach out and take it, and draw the little one to herself; she felt the tiny, sharp-nailed fingers scratch her face and pierce her cheek. And as the blood flowed from the small wound the dream-child gave her, so the light seeped from her body. She felt it going, and in terror whispered, "You can't leave me alone *now*." But he could. God could do what he liked. No, no; God must do what he must. He had been there to help her at the moment of her choice, but now came the time of sacrifice. Now she must bleed.

So she let the light leave her, and let the grief come and brood heavily in a crooked place in her heart. She walked to the gunwale just as the little boat passed out of the shadow of the ship, into bright sunlight. That was the picture she would hold in her memory: the small boat like a stain on the dazzling water, the faces of two children bright with moonlight, both of them crying, both of them reaching toward her. She watched them until they were so far that she could not distinguish child from man. That was when they finally let Charlie go, and he came to her, and embraced her, and wept for her, and she comforted him.

Behind them the sailors resumed their work, but soberly.

Charlie and Dinah were only passengers to them, and so beneath notice as a general rule, but such a scene as they had witnessed transcended the barriers between them, and Dinah had their awe. Respectfully the seamen picked their way around Dinah, as if she were a mast, immovable in her place on the deck. Captain Lower had the tact not to offer condolences. And soon the ship began to move under tow from a harbor steamer, steadily out of the Mersey into the Irish Sea.

Word spread from the sailors to the company of Saints below decks. Dinah's choice had been a terrible and heroic one, and no one dared to talk to her, though to each other they spoke of nothing else. Anna came on deck and joined Charlie in silent vigil with Dinah; John Kirkham knew that the kindest thing that he could do was stay away.

At midmorning, the sailors drew up the cable from the steamer, and the harbor craft put alongside the *North America* for the last time. Captain Lower came to her then.

"Madame, if for any reason you'd like to forego this voyage, the steamer is the last opportunity. I'll gladly have my sailors carry your boxes for you, and we'll refund your passage money, under these circumstances."

Dinah managed a courteous thank you, and refused. The captain stood there helplessly. "They had a court order. I was forbidden to give you any warning, or the ship would have been impounded and I would have lost my place. There was nothing I could do."

"I don't blame you," Dinah said. She touched his arm, comforting him enough that he could go away.

Brigham Young and the other two apostles who had spent the night below with the Saints were going ashore now with the steamer. They had heard of Dinah's sacrifice already, and for fear that they would try to speak to her, Dinah walked away to the bows of the boat the moment they came on deck. She wanted no foolish speeches from them, no meaningless comfort from cocky Brigham Young or gaunt and distant John Taylor or even the fat little doctor, Willard Richards. Apostles they might be, but they had families waiting for them in America, and they would someday return. They knew nothing of what she felt, and their sympathy would be no help to her.

She could have guessed that Brigham would not be put off. He came to her just the same, so damnably sure that he knew best that even her desire for solitude meant nothing to him.

She found herself angry at him before he even spoke. Yet the anger was a sort of relief; it was better than the agony of grief that she was barely holding at bay through her rigidity.

"Sister Dinah," Brigham began. She was sure that he would say something foolish, like, "I know what you're feeling" or "you have our deepest sympathy," something to prove once again that he had all the sensitivity of a jackass.

But he did not say that. He took her by the shoulders and looked into her eyes. "You are not what I thought you were," he said. "I thought you were stubborn and rebellious, but by damn you're the truest Saint I've ever seen among women. It's little help to you now, but I tell you God has a work for you to do, and he's putting you through the refiner's fire to prepare you for it. With all my heart I honor you." He bent and kissed her cheeks, twice each, tenderly, almost worshipfully. Then he turned and left her, and to her surprise she found that he had soothed her last fear. It was not a lie. God had designed this, and truly wanted her sacrifice. The light was in her again, dim now but unquenchable, and all would be justified in the end, whenever the end might be.

And so her rigid posture bent. She sat on a coiled cable and embraced the grief that now took her; she wept in her mother's arms for an hour. When the weeping was done, she felt better. She could go on. There was hope ahead, and Zion would be worth the price of her dark passage there. In a way it disappointed her. Shouldn't true grief last forever? But it could not last, not without changing. Soon it became gentler, and she did not weep so easily or often, and gradually all those tears dried. This remained: In all her life she would never hear the word *mother* without feeling a tiny, almost unnoticeable prick of grief; and in all her life, if she were ever tempted to condemn someone, there would come to her mind that vision of two children in a distant boat, reaching for her, weeping, and she was compassionate, for she had also done evil in her time.

Before Dinah and Anna could come below decks again, Charlie repacked all their boxes to put the children's clothing deep in the least accessible place. He rearranged the bedding, for Dinah and Anna would sleep together now, and the Corbridges willingly moved to fill the place where Dinah had slept before with Honor.

He was just finishing when Elder Turley, the leader of the

company of Saints, came to him.

"You have our deepest sympathy," he said.

Charlie thanked him.

"I think you can see that this incident has cast gloom upon the whole company," Turley said. "I wondered if there might be something you could do to help cheer us up. We should be rejoicing to be on our way to Zion."

"Don't look in my family for a source of cheer," Charlie said coldly.

"Brother Charlie, what I'm asking is—would Sister Dinah mind if we had some celebration? If there was some rejoicing despite her grief?"

Charlie understood, and it was a gracious thing for Elder Turley to ask. In answer, Charlie dug into their box and pulled out a bottle of wine. "I brought this for us to celebrate landfall in America. But perhaps it'll be better used tonight. Should be enough for a sip for all the adults in the company, don't you think? And make sure they know it's from us, to wish them joy."

"Are you sure? This is more than I would have—"

"Tell them it comes from the Kirkhams, and tell them that we *all* are joyful to be on our way. No one should wear a long face for Dinah's sake, Elder Turley."

Turley clapped him on the back. "You're a good fellow. I couldn't have wished for a better as my clerk." And then he was off, bottle in hand, to prepare the celebration.

It turned out to be not much of a celebration after all. Too many of the Saints were queasy from the movement of the ship, even though the water was calm; too many children were whining or crying in the misery of seasickness. Still, the wine worked its warm effect, and there were jokes and laughter, and the mood was good.

The next morning Charlie went on deck as they rounded Holyhead, their last glimpse of British soil. He was feeling pretty good, not least because he had not yet felt the slightest twinge of nausea. That boded well for the voyage; he might be one of those who was born to take sea travel well. The voyage would be pleasant. He felt as if his whole life had been shaped to get him to Zion, and now his effort was over; just sit aboard the ship, eat when fed, write in the journal, be civil to others, and eventually Zion would come into view and he would be home. It would be his first extended period of idleness since Heber Kimball had first invited himself for supper. He rather looked forward to it.

"Brother Charlie," said a voice he knew. "Can we cheer you up?"

He turned. Sally Clinton smiled at him. Harriette stood right behind her, *not* smiling, but at least not looking quite so glum as usual.

"Just seeing you cheers me already," he said. He was getting pretty good at gallantry, and Sally beamed.

"It was kind of you to share wine with us all last night, especially after your poor sister—"

"Sally," Harriette said.

"No, it's quite all right," Charlie assured them. "It's not a thing I want to speak of, but I'm not afraid to hear it."

"We all love Dinah so," Sally said. "And that's why. None of us would have had such strength for the gospel's sake."

For the gospel's sake. Charlie wondered how much of her decision was for the gospel's sake, and how much because she was too proud to bend to Matthew's will. The others would have no such question. Dinah had acted out of faith, and so these people would honor her all the more. Well, there was truth enough in that, and no reason at all to try to change their opinion. "No one knows her strength better than I."

Sally touched the sleeve of his jacket. "Charlie, I'm so tired of seeing you hours and hours every day."

Her irony was plain, and he winced comically. "All the eligible women on this ship keep me so busy, Sister Sally—"

"Doing what?" she asked.

"Making them wish they had a better selection of eligible men."

Sally laughed at his joke, but then grew serious. "Why are you angry at me? What did I say?"

"Nothing," Charlie said. "I'm not angry."

"Don't tell me that," Sally said. "If you're not angry, it would mean that you've been avoiding me because you don't like me."

"I have responsibilities," Charlie said.

"To everyone but me?"

"Don't be foolish, Sally. You don't need me."

Her face went hot with rage. "You're right, of course. I

don't need you. And now you will not have to put up with my foolishness another minute." She strode away across the deck, lurching awkwardly with the rolling of the ship.

Charlie turned to Harriette. "What did I do?"

"You don't love her," Harriette answered simply. Then she handed him something—a small book wrapped in a handkerchief. "It's for your sister, Dinah. I thought this might bring her some comfort."

He started to thank her, but Harriette hurried off. Charlie wondered about her—she seemed so unpleasant and sober, and yet she had the kindness to turn her sympathy for Dinah into a gift.

Charlie gave it to Dinah before supper, so she could thank Harriette for it. Dinah wasn't even sure who Harriette was, until Charlie identified her as Sally's sister. "Oh, yes, she's like a shadow, isn't she?"

"A bit," Charlie answered. "But a kind shadow, I think."

Dinah took the handkerchief from the book. It was the second volume of a collection of Wordsworth, quite an old book and well thumbed-over. The book fell open to a certain page, and Dinah saw it and gave a small cry.

"What's wrong?" Charlie asked.

She shook her head. She handed him the book, and he knew from her look that she wanted him to read. So he sat on the boxes and began where she had pointed:

> There was a time when meadow, grove, and stream,
> The earth, and every common sight,
>   To me did seem
>   Apparelled in celestial light,
> The glory and the freshness of a dream.
> It is not now as it hath been of yore;—
>   Turn wheresoe'er I may,
>   By night or day,
> The things which I have seen I now can see no more.

It was a melancholy little stanza, but Dinah wanted him to read on, and to Charlie's pleasure a group of Saints began to gather, drawn by his voice. They crowded quietly into the aisle, and some lay or sat on the lower berths to hear.

The fifth stanza was the best. It seemed to speak to Charlie and the other Saints as a poet had no right to speak. Heber had taught them one of the Prophet Joseph's more novel doctrines, the idea that God did not create man at birth, but rather that man had always existed as an intelligence before the foundations of the world. Wordsworth spoke almost like a seer, almost as if God had spoken through a poet, though surely that would never happen.

> Our birth is but a sleep and a forgetting:
> The soul that rises with us, our life's star,
>   Hath had elsewhere its setting,
>   And cometh from afar;
>   Not in entire forgetfulness,
>   And not in utter nakedness,
> But trailing clouds of glory do we come
> From God, who is our home.

Charlie went on and finished the stanza, but he knew the reading should end; Dinah was in tears at this remembrance of her own children, and worse was coming: "Behold the child among his new-born blisses," the poet cruelly said, and spoke of "sallies of his mother's kisses." That would be too much for Dinah to bear. He closed the book. There was some mumbled protest from those who had gathered to hear, but he shook his head with a small smile, and said, "If I read it all tonight, what will we do tomorrow?" They laughed ruefully at the reminder of how many weeks they would be together, and dispersed.

As the Saints were drifting away, Charlie saw Harriette and Sally well to the back, and Sally waved at him. He smiled at her, wishing insanely that he could go with her wherever she was going tonight. That lustful desire passed quickly, though, when he saw Harriette also lift her hand to him. Charlie touched his brow to salute her and smiled, in thanks for her gift to Dinah. Harriette actually smiled in return. Then, to Charlie's delight, Sally quickly drew her sister away. I earned a smile from Harriette, and Sally's jealous of her sister. I'm not the only one mad with love.

A bit later the first mate clumped into steerage and loudly announced, "Storm comin' up, and captain says all's to be tied down fast. We're in for a good rocking tonight." There was an hour of bustle as the unprepared borrowed rope from those who could spare it, and then supper was cold bread and little of that, because fires were forbidden and many of the Saints had forgotten and tied down their food boxes. Charlie didn't mind. Hunger now and then was a sort of pleasure, and the prospect of a storm was exciting. He came alive in wind, and had long suspected that the pagans might have been right about God dwelling in sheets of rain and lightning. Snug inside the ship, the rainstorm should be invigorating.

Soon enough, however, he and all the company discovered that a good rocking was not the same as sitting indoors a tight little house listening to the howl of the wind outside. The ship did not sway, now it lurched from side to side, and you could never be sure which way it would move next in its incredible wandering through pitch, roll, and yaw. Being two decks down, they could not hear any rain or wind, just the agonized shrieking of the timbers and the whine of the rigging like a dream of hell. For Charlie, it was more excitement than he would have wished, and now for the first time he felt a touch of queasiness. However, many others who had already been ill were now violently sick, and soon the stench of vomit had Charlie cursing the first mate for not warning the Saints not to eat any supper at all.

Anna and John were sick enough that they had to lie down, but Charlie and Dinah were both much better off, and soon they were moving among the Saints, mopping up vomit, soothing the panicky, and carrying water for washing and drinking. The children had it worst—there was not a one under the age of five who wasn't sick, and in their fear they had no patience. They screamed in terror until they vomited, then choked on it until they were able to start screaming again. There would be little sleep in steerage that night. It was not until well toward morning that the storm eased off enough that the exhausted, fevered children could sleep, and then the groaning adults began to doze. Charlie made Dinah lie down then, while he and Elder Turley and William Clayton drew seawater and brought it down into steerage and washed the vomit from the deck.

At dawn, Elder Turley ordered the whole company on deck to wash. If they were to survive the voyage, they would have to stay clean, and it was all the more vital when many of them were ill. The sky was still lowering, but the sea was calmer in the grey light. They washed in seawater, of course, since fresh water was for drinking. The men stripped down and bathed entire, but the women soon realized there was no preventing the sailors in the rigging from having a look at anything they did, so the women had to content themselves with washing face and hands and mopping at their dresses. The seawater took care of the sweat and oil and dirt, but it left behind its own residue of salt, which so itched and irritated that some of the Saints had to use some of their precious rations of fresh water to dab it off their faces. Then the men regretted that they hadn't followed the women's practice, for they hadn't fresh water enough to rinse their whole bodies.

By noon, however, the storm came up again and no one cared much whether they itched or not. The first mate brought them the dismal news that they were pretty much pacing the gale—it would be with them for some days. Elder Turley led them in prayers for the health and strength of the company and the protection of the ship, and they went below again.

The second night was worse than the first. And now the condition of some of the children became serious. The Corbridges' infant son John, in the berth right across from Dinah and Anna, cried without ceasing all day and all night. He couldn't even keep water in his stomach, and retched in dry agony when there was nothing left in him. He had a high fever by evening. Dinah stayed with the Corbridges most of the night, trying to give the child water from her own ration—and Anna's and John's and Charlie's as well. Charlie even had a turn standing in the aisle holding the boy, trying to outguess the movement of the ship to give the child something close to a steady berth. Little John did not sleep, did not drink, did not eat, and his fever did not break.

It was not just steerage that suffered. They heard at dawn that a little girl in second-class had gone insane from fear, screaming constantly; she died before morning, though whether from fear or the extreme vomiting could not be determined. The storm abated the next day, and the girl was quickly buried at sea. But now several children were very ill, despite the calmer waters, and Charlie watched as Dinah became something of an angel, always at the berth of a crying child, comforting the parents, who knew that some children were bound to die on the voyage and were terrified that their own would be among that number. And when in calmer moments the children had some peace, Dinah still did not rest, but brought water and thin broth to the many adults who lay helpless and groaning in their stinking berths. Some of the adults could not bring themselves to leave their berths even to make water or move their bowels, and so new stenches were added to the smell of puke. And pouring seawater across the floor would not be enough now—some had defecated in their clothing, and many had left night soil in their berths.

The worst of it, to Charlie's mind, was that many of the Saints were not behaving like Saints at all—there was a good deal of grumbling, and some who even said quite openly that they doubted God would have commanded them to bring their children out to die. Elder Turley called the Saints together and tried to smoothe things over, but some refused to cooperate. One man said right out that he expected the Corbridges' son to die. Sister Corbridge began to cry; it was a dreadful night, and Charlie was hard-pressed to find anything uplifting to write in the journal. So he wrote about Dinah, who, despite near sleeplessness night after night, still held little John Corbridge until at last, fevered and frantic and utterly worn out, he finally cried himself to sleep. Then she laid the infant in Sister Corbridge's arms and all were asleep in a few minutes.

The child died in his sleep before morning. At dawn Sister Corbridge held the little body while Anna and the child's father sewed a length of sail cloth to hold him. The captain ordered that all dead were to be put into the sea within the hour—it would do no good to have corpses around to cause worse gloom, and perhaps spread disease. It was very wise of him, but the hurry of it made the poor Corbridges frantic with grief.

Dinah embraced Sister Corbridge as they watched the child being committed to the deep, as Captain Lower called it. The sea was so rough that they couldn't even hear the splash. Sister Corbridge wept bitterly, and Dinah held her as her husband looked helplessly on. Charlie went to the man, if only because no one else did. "I'm sorry," he said.

James Corbridge managed a little smile in return. "I have no lack of faith," he said. "And it says in the Book of Mormon, doesn't it, that little children who die unbaptized are taken straight to the arms of Christ?" Charlie nodded, marveling that the man could take such comfort from words in a book, even if the book *was* true.

After the burial, going down into steerage again was a shock. They had known it smelled bad before, but not *how* bad until now, when they came from the fresh air of the deck. "It's unliveable," Elder Turley said to William Clayton and Charlie. "They've been shitting in the berths."

"Well," said William Clayton, "if they won't take care of themselves, *we've* got to take care of them."

Turley pondered for a moment, and then said, "All right, William. Boil some seawater. Some folks will have a bath this morning on deck, and while they're up here, we'll have their berths scrubbed down. We won't become animals, and that's final."

Charlie and Elder Turley went down to steerage and began following their noses, an infallible guide to those who needed washing. There were protests, of course, as they carried grown men and women onto the deck, where others stripped them and washed them. But those too weak to get up and put their night soil where it belonged were generally too weak to struggle much. Clothes were washed, berths were scrubbed out, and by nightfall, though the storm was still with them, it became clear that the worst was over. The sheer activity had helped those who did the work, and the cleaner air helped all the rest. Sailors came through steerage burning oil to clear the last of the odors, and then Elder Turley insisted that they have a prayer meeting and sing all the cheerfulest hymns they could find.

There wasn't much to be happy about—two children had already died, and others was deathly ill—but the singing perked their spirits and reminded them that they were on God's errand. And in the prayer meeting, Brother Corbridge got to his feet and bravely told the company that he regretted nothing about the voyage, and never would. "I chose to follow the Lord, and the devil can rock the boat all he likes, he won't break *me*." There was anger in Corbridge's voice, and tears in his eyes, but he had drawn the battle lines properly: This wasn't a struggle of men against a cruel God, it was a struggle of Saints against the forces of sin. They saw their afflictions in a different light, then. Those who died were martyrs, not victims of fate, and God was accepting their suffering as sacrifice, for which they would be rewarded in time to come.

That night, Charlie and Dinah took a moment's rest together on the ladderway leading up to the second deck. There were some groans, but things were quieter than they had been in some time.

"The Lord's a harsh teacher," Dinah said.

"With sometimes a vague lesson at best."

"For me it isn't vague," Dinah said. "Tonight my children are alive and warm and safe. They have all their lives ahead of them, while little John Corbridge lies at the bottom of the sea. I have nothing to complain of."

Charlie wondered if she really believed that. But he would not argue. Whatever comfort could be taken in a difficult time was welcome. And sometimes it did not matter if the comfort was a lie or an illusion—it was true because it had to be true, and to hell with anyone who insisted on facts or logic.

"Charlie," Dinah said, closing her eyes and leaning back on the ladder, "do you remember the Tennyson? 'The Lotus-Eaters'?"

He did.

"The very beginning, before the choric song."

He began to recite, from memory, with few hesitations— he had lost none of that gift. And finally he came to the end of the part she had asked for, and realized why she had wanted to hear it.

> *They sat them down upon the yellow sand,*
> *Between the sun and moon upon the shore;*
> *And sweet it was to dream of Fatherland,*
> *Of child, and wife, and slave; but evermore*
> *Most weary seemed the sea, weary the oar,*
> *Weary the wandering fields of barren foam.*
> *Then someone said, "We will return no more";*
> *And all at once they sang, "Our island home*
> *Is far beyond the wave; we will no longer roam."*

Dinah sighed deeply when he finished. "Have no doubt of it, Charlie. We're going home now. And no one will ever bar the door and turn us away."

"Zion," Charlie said, and it was a question.

"Worth every cost," Dinah said, and it was the answer.

⇒⇒⇒ BOOK FIVE ⇐⇐⇐

In which people think they understand each other.

◥ First Word ◤

People get used to things. Good or bad, if they go on long enough, people just don't notice them anymore. I don't mean that they forget. Nobody on the *North America* said, "Hey, you know? This isn't so bad after all." They knew it was terrible. They just stopped being surprised about it.

It was the same thing when they got to Nauvoo. Charlie had heard all the glowing reports of Zion being built, the city of God, Nauvoo the beautiful. So what was he to think of row after row of miserable mud-chinked cabins? Weeds wherever there weren't wheel tracks? He wasn't used to so much sunlight all in the same day, especially getting on into fall. The first day there his eyes were full of tears all day, usually because of the dust in the air. A horse riding by would raise more of a cloud than a steam locomotive. And then next day it rained. No dignified shower, either, it was what the old-time Mormons were calling a frog-strangler. Main Street was so wet that you could have got to the end of it and walked right on into the Mississippi and never known the difference. And everybody dressed poorer than even the poorest people of Manchester. Even men who should have known better would come out in public in shirt-sleeves, like factory hands; he even saw a few men stripped right to the waist, chopping wood or wrestling stumps, and people would talk to them like normal. He didn't know that here in the West people weren't so picky about wearing coats all the time.

But it was only the surprise of it, really, that had him worried. Within a week he stopped caring that the four of them had to live in a mud hut. After all, *everyone* lived in mud huts, or almost everyone, or at least all the newcomers, of whom there were plenty. He still noticed the weather was disgusting and the air was as wet as fog even when the sun shone, and he even complained about it, but he complained like a native, not like a stranger. He stopped comparing. He made friends, even if they had accents like slow-witted Yorkshiremen. Heber Kimball had talked that way, after all; it was part of his charm. He found some people who could read, and had a taste for his kind of humor. And one close friend: the prophet's own brother, Don Carlos Smith.

It began with Charlie stopping by the editorial office of the *Times and Seasons* to offer to correct spelling errors for them. Young Don Carlos was the editor, and he laughingly confessed that the spelling errors were his own. "I think of my spelling as an interesting reorganization of the English language." There would be no income in working for the Nauvoo newspaper—it barely supported Don Carlos. But the two young men liked each other immediately, and Don Carlos saw to it that they were together often after that. He made Charlie teach him stanza after stanza of Wordsworth while Don Carlos taught Charlie how to milk a cow, how to watch for chuckholes in meadows because the horses were too dumb to notice, and how to chop efficiently through a thick log without losing a foot. Charlie would get along fine in this frontier town. He decided, in fact, to forgive Nauvoo's shortcomings. As he told Anna and John, it was a new city, wasn't it? Just springing up out of nothing. They shouldn't expect too much of it. Things would be fine.

But Dinah—hers was a different story. She hadn't been so starry-eyed as Charlie. Dinah had listened closely to the Brethren, noticed that they talked a bit vaguely whenever they described what Nauvoo was actually like *now* rather than what it would be in ten, twenty years. The mud huts, the vile roads, the mosquitoes, the filth— that didn't faze her. She settled down to her work, and in the process helped all her fellow immigrants cope with the shock of it all. Of course the houses are only huts, she said, of course the fields are rough and weedy. What did you think we were coming for, if it wasn't to build Zion? And why would God need you to build Zion, if it was already done up in brick and clapboard with cobbled roads? She was a great comfort to them all, without particularly noticing herself doing it. But it wasn't that she had no expectations. It's just that all her expectations were tied up in the Prophet, in Joseph Smith, and it took a while before she got to know him. Took a while before she could be disappointed.

Which is why I'm not going to tell you any more about the voyage and the overland trip and the first few weeks at Nauvoo than I already have. A better writer would have made you feel every roll of the ship, every miserable moment of rail and lake steamer and log raft getting across America, and probably would have broken your heart with disappointment over Nauvoo. But I can't bring it off. I tried. There are a hundred pages of Getting To Nauvoo that you'll never see—because it bored me. It was dull. Frightening things happened, there was enough angst for Henry James to write a thousand commas— but everybody took it in stride. It didn't change anybody. So I'm telling you it happened and then skipping it. And picking up where life gets interesting again. And, as many people found out in Nauvoo, everything interesting happened near Joseph Smith, or because of Joseph Smith, or whenever his back was turned.

                                        —*O. Kirkham, Salt Lake City, 1981*

⤸ 26 ⤷

Joseph Smith
Nauvoo, 1840

JOSEPH WATCHED FROM THE window as Don Carlos capered in the store yard, swinging an ax above his head. He charged like a bloodthirsty soldier and savagely embedded the steel head in a thick log, spattering wood chips in all directions. Then Don Carlos turned, pretending to be exhausted. His friend, a young new convert from England, applauded. Suddenly, as if he had heard a noise from the log behind him, Don Carlos whirled and let loose a flurry of chops at the log. At last, satisfied that the thing would pose no further threat, he stood in triumph on the log, whirling the ax over his head, holloing. Through the window Joseph could faintly hear his shout. And he caught himself being jealous.

"What are you watching?" Emma asked.

"Don Carlos."

"Mm." Emma came and stood beside him. "If he spent

more time selling advertising, maybe the paper would earn his little family a decent living."

"He's so young," Joseph said.

"Don Carlos forgets he has a wife and three daughters. He plays like a boy." Emma looked at him piercingly. "You love him too much. We should never have named the baby after him. You think they're both your sons."

Joseph's laugh was half a sigh, but he felt neither amused nor sad. He was really a little afraid. Emma read his emotions so easily sometimes—how much, then, did she know about the secrets he kept from her? But mostly he was afraid because he wasn't as young as Don Carlos anymore.

"You're only thirty-five yourself," Emma said. So Emma understood that, too.

"Halfway through my three-score and ten."

"You'll live forever."

"So will everyone."

She touched the hair that curled a little at the nape of his neck.

"Emma," he said. "Will anything stand to say that I once lived?"

"You are the greatest man in a thousand years."

It touched him, and so he teased. "Why only a thousand?"

She did not laugh. She had a disconcerting way of knowing when his jokes were not jokes. "Don't wish for Don Carlos's youth and beauty, Joseph. Everyone gives a smile to him— but they'd give their lives for *you.*"

"Sometimes I'd rather have the smiles."

"Then stay home more with me and the children." She laughed, but she could not hide from him behind humor, either.

"Abraham's wife Sarah became a sharp-tongued woman in her loneliness," Joseph said. "I'm glad that you have not."

"I was born a sharp-tongued woman," Emma said.

Well, it was true; Joseph had no argument. "Why else do you think I enlisted your sword on *my* side?"

Outside, Don Carlos had seen Joseph in the window. He waved. Joseph beckoned him inside. Don Carlos glanced at his Englishman, and Joseph beckoned again.

"They're up to their knees in mud," Emma observed.

"Tell them to take their boots off."

"May I tell them to take their pants off, too?"

Joseph laughed. "If you like. But that Englishman looks like he might just think you mean it."

"I *do* mean it." And Emma retired to the kitchen to receive their visitors.

Joseph watched the two boys as they came in. Boys, he thought, though at that same age Joseph had fancied himself a man. How did he ever expect anyone to take him seriously at such an age? And yet they *had* taken him seriously. They even let him ruin their lives, some of them. What is it like to be young, without the weight of prophecy on your back? For ten years I've dragged a church behind me, like an over-full sledge. Would I have a spring in my step like Don Carlos's, if I had been free at his age? No. Never like that. For if I hadn't had responsibility, I would have had the worse burden of not knowing what to do. I was too serious at heart, like that English fellow. Except that I didn't let it show, the way he does.

Emma really didn't want them in the kitchen, so Joseph quickly maneuvered them into the drawing room while she prepared the dinner. Don Carlos stood with his backside toward the fire, telling some extravagant story that Joseph knew would end nowhere—Don Carlos always forgot where he was going with a tale. Usually it didn't matter—Don Carlos loved to hear himself talk, and everyone else loved to hear him, too. But this time Joseph hadn't the time. "Introduce me to your friend," Joseph said, interrupting.

"Was I being dull?"

"Dull as a rock in the road. I don't know how your friends can bear having you around."

"This is Charlie Kirkham. He's the worst woodcutter in Nauvoo."

"I'm pleased to meet you, sir," Charlie said. He gave a slight bow.

Joseph, by main strength, didn't laugh. Instead, he bowed back. Why make the lad ashamed of his dignity? And yet Joseph couldn't stop himself from putting on his best back-country manners in response. "Howdy-do," he said. "Right proud to have your acquaintance."

"I'm sorry to be so ill-dressed for a meeting I've—hoped for—"

"I'd rather meet a man with mud on his pants than any high-toned hypocrites, I can tell you. The only thing I can see wrong with you is that you have no judgment about the company you keep."

The Englishman's eyes went wide, as if he were searching his memory for some unfit acquaintance.

"He meant me," Don Carlos said. "Charlie can read and write, Joseph."

"A scholar?"

Charlie demurred. "A bookkeeper."

"Around here that makes you a mathematician. I should hire you to run my business affairs, maybe."

Don Carlos whooped. "Change all the minuses to pluses and you'd look right prosperous."

Annoyed at his brother's indiscretion about his finances, Joseph turned his back on Don Carlos and excluded him from the conversation. "Brother Charlie, there's things for a man good with figures to do." He smiled. "We're all here to build up the kingdom of God. If God has given you talents, it's not to keep them to yourself. So don't be modest, lad. Tell me what you can do when you're not stunting around with the village idiot."

"I—I read and write, that's all. I write a fair hand, and spell rather well."

"He's been helping a bit at the paper, in his spare time," Don Carlos said.

"And no doubt being underpaid for it," Joseph said. One barb about finances certainly deserved another.

"I enjoy it," Charlie said.

"What else could you do, if you weren't doing Don Carlos's work for him?"

"I can do correspondence. I'm best at financial matters. I can figure in my head faster than—" He paused, aware that he was being immodest.

"Faster than me, no doubt," Joseph said.

"I meant to say, faster than most bookkeepers can do it on paper. I think it's my only real gift."

Joseph looked him in the eye and felt something, some unease. Was it in the boy, or in himself?

Behind him, Don Carlos softly said, "He's more than he looks."

Joseph ignored him. "Do I know you, Charlie?"

"I—don't think so, sir—we've never met—I would have remembered."

"You say 'figure' and I say it 'figger.' Is yours the right way?"

"I'm English, sir, and you're—"

"I know what I am." Joseph watched how the boy struggled to say the right thing, tried not to offend. "You don't like the sort of work you're doing for a living, do you?"

"I have no complaint," Charlie said, glancing at Don Carlos.

So he doesn't like it, but doesn't want to say so, Joseph thought. It's unnatural, how good he is at being careful. And with that Joseph decided to push him, to see when he would forget how much he wanted to be liked and speak his mind. "Come on, now," Joseph said, letting a taunting tone into his voice. "You're meant for better things than we have to offer in Nauvoo. How could you possibly like sweaty work when you're used to working in a nice clean suit?"

"I don't think it matters much whether I like it, does it?"

To Joseph's delight, behind his dignity Charlie was getting a little angry. "Not to me, anyway. I have enough to worry about without wondering whether everyone is content with his lot. Do you have any strength in you at all?"

Charlie flushed, then looked desperately at Don Carlos. Joseph did not have to look to know that his brother was wearing a simpleton's grin. Don Carlos knew from experience what was happening, and knew to keep silence till it was over.

"Come on," Joseph said. "What kind of man *are* you? I'll bet I can throw you in three seconds. Can you stand against me?"

Joseph reached for Charlie, to grip his arms. Of course there'd be no honor in wrestling this slightly built young man, but Joseph had long used wrestling as a way of finding what a man was made of. Few men refused him; no man had ever beaten him. Joseph didn't expect the Englishman to be a challenge; he only hoped for the boy to show his courage.

Charlie did not back away, but he did not make a move to join in a contest, either. "I didn't come to stand against you, sir. I came to work beside you."

Don Carlos laughed quietly.

"I've heard all kinds of excuses," Joseph said. "Don't want to muss the furniture, these are my best clothes, it isn't seemly,

I hurt my wrist yesterday—but you're the first man I've met who out and out admitted he was a coward."

At last the fire flashed in the boy's eyes. "Call me what you like, sir, but I think any man looking at your body and comparing it to mine would say it wasn't a match but a human sacrifice. Still, if you find pleasure in defeating someone who has never wrestled in his life, go ahead and throw me. But when I hit the ground, sir, I won't be your friend."

"I told you," Don Carlos said softly. "He's more than he looks."

"I think I have a job for you," Joseph said.

Charlie still waited for Joseph to wrestle him.

"Put your arms down," Joseph said. "I have a work for you to do. John Bennett is in the state capital at Springfield, trying to get us a city charter that'll keep us safe from our enemies. His work's getting ahead of him, he needs help, I want you to go."

"But I don't know anything about city charters—"

"I thought you said you came here to stand *with* me."

"I'll go, sir."

"Are you my friend, Charlie?"

"I'd like to be."

"Then call me Brother Joseph. I'm not so old that I like a young man calling me *sir*. We're having something of a party here tonight. I think I'd rather have you come to that than stay to supper. There are people I want you to meet. Do you have a wife?"

"I'm eighteen, sir. Brother Jo-Joseph."

"Then don't bring her."

"I have a sister. Older than me, may I bring her?"

"Of course. And tomorrow morning you and a companion come here by seven. I'll have you take letters to Springfield, as long as you're going."

"I don't have a horse."

"The Lord will provide. Don Carlos will tell you how the Lord usually does it."

"When should Don Carlos and I be back?"

Joseph was startled. "Don Carlos? Where is *he* going?"

"I thought—you said he should come with me—"

"To get a horse. You'll have to find someone else to go with you to Springfield."

Don Carlos walked to Charlie and put his arm around the Englishman's shoulders. "You see, Joseph's brothers have to work twice as hard to get anything interesting to do. He has to avoid charges of favoritism." Don Carlos looked at Joseph and winked. "There are two ways that one of Joseph's brothers can get something decent to do. You can either be very, very good—better than anyone else in the Church. That's what Hyrum's done. Or you can be very, very troublesome, so that you get a job to keep you busy."

Charlie chuckled at that. Poor lad, Joseph thought, he doesn't start laughing until after the jokes are over. "Which one are *you* doing?" Charlie asked.

"I haven't decided yet," Don Carlos said. "I keep hoping the Lord will open my brother's eyes to my obvious talents. Instead, though, Joseph prefers to give the good missions to strangers."

This had gotten out of hand, Joseph decided; even Charlie could see now that it wasn't a joke. So Joseph laughed, and said, "Among the Saints we're no more strangers, Don Carlos. I call those whom God has called."

"And has God called Charlie Kirkham?"

Such impudence in anyone else would have won him a stern rebuke, but Joseph loved Don Carlos to the point of patience. So instead of retorting, Joseph let himself be stung, and then examined the pain. It was, after all, a good question, one to which Charlie himself had a right to an answer. Was Joseph calling him because he liked the way Charlie answered the challenge to wrestle? Or was it inspiration from the Spirit when Joseph thought of sending him to Springfield? It was so hard to tell the difference; Joseph didn't bother to try very often anymore. This time, though, he tried. He walked to Charlie, took him by the hands, studied his face.

"Do you love me, Charlie?" he asked.

Charlie started to nod, and then shrugged apologetically. "I don't know. I—I love the gospel."

"Then you love me."

Charlie's eyes were awash with tears, and Joseph felt an answering heat in his own heart. It was the burning that he had long since learned to believe was the Spirit of God. Always alive as a spark within him till some wind fanned it, and then like a fire it burned him. People told him that at such times his face glowed as if the sun shone through his skin. He didn't doubt it. Even now he looked at his brother, sure that Don Carlos could see it, too.

He saw. "Like I said. I told you he was something."

"No, Don Carlos," Joseph said, his teasing mood on him again. "He's just another pretty face." The young Englishman was indeed a beautiful boy. But it was not the beauty of naivete. It was the beauty of someone who had endured the worst thing in the world, and was at peace with the terrors of his own heart. "Is your sister as pretty as you?"

"Much prettier," Charlie said. "You'd like her. *She* would have wrestled you. She would have won, too."

Joseph looked at him, appalled. How could a man say such a crude thing about his own sister?

Suddenly Don Carlos burst out laughing. "It's a joke, Joseph. He's having you, that's all."

Of course it was a joke. Joseph forced himself to laugh. It was a joke and Charlie had brought it off well, with a straight face. But even so, Joseph knew that it wasn't funny. That part of him that decided what to believe knew that Charlie had told the truth. Charlie's sister was—dangerous? No, that wasn't it, the Spirit wasn't *warning* him. What then? She was important, that's all. And she was a match for Joseph Smith.

Joseph couldn't let himself brood about it for long, though. As soon as Charlie Kirkham was gone, Joseph faced Don Carlos and asked, "What was that bullheaded nonsense about what my brothers have to do to get noticed?"

Don Carlos was grinning his I'm-too-sweet-for-you-to-yell-at-me grin. "Just joking."

"If you were joking then I've got a five-day-old fish in my pocket."

"Mostly joking, anyway."

"When you learn to keep your mouth shut, Don Carlos, then you'll get a responsible assignment."

"You can trust me, Joseph, better than you think."

"I think I can trust you with my life," Joseph answered. "It's whether I can trust you to take care of anything else that I wonder about."

The door opened and Emma came in. "I thought he was staying to dinner?"

"Who?" Joseph asked.

"Charlie, that English boy."

"No. He's coming to the party tonight, instead."

Emma pursed her lips. "You might have told me in the first place."

Joseph saw Don Carlos out of the corner of his eye, looking amused. The boy thinks he's too clever by half. "He's bringing his sister, too." As long as Emma's annoyed, let her have the full dose.

Emma immediately smiled. "Dinah," she said.

"You know her?"

Emma laughed. "When have I had time to go calling among the new Saints from England? But word passes. I hear she was a tower of strength among the people coming over on the *North America*. I hear she has visions, and the gift of tongues. I haven't talked to anyone who doesn't love her."

"Then I expect," Joseph said, "that we'll love her, too."

"I don't know," Emma answered. "You aren't famous for recognizing the true worth of a woman."

"I married *you*, didn't I?"

"There are those who reckon that's the final proof. I think the way they put it is, 'Let Brother Joseph buy a bull for you any day, but go yourself if you want to buy a cow.'" Emma laughed as she said it, but it did not amuse her. And when she told it, she glanced at Don Carlos.

Joseph had patience about many things, but not when it came to insults about Emma. "Who says that!"

Behind him, Don Carlos chuckled. "Not many. Usually they tell it with boar and sow."

Joseph turned on his brother. "I hope that every man who's said such a thing had his nose broken by any brother of mine who heard it!"

Don Carlos grew solemn immediately. "Just hearsay, that's all."

"From now on, you might start concentrating more on the hear, and less on the say."

"Make sure I meet Dinah Kirkham when she comes," Emma said. "I mean to make use of her."

"And I mean to use her brother," Joseph answered.

Don Carlos spoke so quietly that Joseph reckoned he didn't mean to be heard. "I only mean to love him." The words stayed with Joseph for more than a few minutes. Use him; love him;

were they such opposites? Joseph tried to think of a way he could truly love someone without working beside him; how he could work well with someone and not love him. Impossible, he decided. There is no difference. Only a child like Don Carlos would think you could love without using, give without taking. Even Jesus, who gave all, thought Joseph, even Jesus demands so much from me.

It was a rare hour when Joseph had nothing to do. In fact he had a dozen things to do even now, but he could not do them. While Emma hurried in the kitchen, cleaning up after dinner and preparing for the party, Joseph stalked through the house, rattling cupboards with every step. He was hunting, but had no notion what he sought. His quarry kept eluding him in the reaches of his mind. He felt the beginning of a struggle; the muscles of his arms needed flexing, needed someone strong to try against. He lacked only a worthy opponent.

Emma stormed out of the kitchen and found him in the parlor. "Go outside," she said coldly. "The good sisters helping me in the kitchen are convinced that all this pacing around like an angry stallion is because you're having a revelation of the end of the world."

As always, Emma's advice was excellent but unpalatable; Joseph left the house immediately, but feeling more disgruntled than before. The mud made it slippery going. He almost fell getting out of the dooryard. He was ready for a fight.

And a fight was not hard to find. Joseph lived near the shore, and soon enough he spotted a group of river rats. The thieves and pirates of the Mississippi, such men had long used these reaches of the river as a hideout. Now that the Mormon city was here, they were starting to gather. They had a habit of getting baptized Mormons, committing more crimes than ever, and then, when caught, rushing to the Church for protection. Joseph had little concern for their souls—those who defiled the waters of baptism like these unrepentant scoundrels were all the more sure to be damned, and good riddance. What worried Joseph was that half the crimes along the river would get blamed on the Saints if such men continued to find refuge in or near Nauvoo.

"You're just about the weakest, sickliest looking bunch of hound dogs that a farmer ever forgot to shoot," Joseph said cheerfully as he approached the men.

The river rats perked up at that. They began eyeing the Prophet carefully, to measure him as a fighter. Joseph knew how deceptive his frock coat and tie could be. It was always hard for men like this to believe what Joseph could do in a match.

"I seen cats died of starvation lookin' better than you," one of the men said. But Joseph had spotted the real fighter among them, big as a barn door with eyes like death. He wasn't saying anything yet. But Joseph's arms were tingling to get around that man's body and crush a little wickedness out of him.

Since Joseph still stood some ten yards off, they were talking loudly, and a crowd was forming. The streets could look downright empty, but let a ruckus start and the crowd would be there every time. Mostly Saints, of course. Joseph saw out of the corner of his eye that Port was there, armed to the teeth, and a few other Mormon boys who'd see to it that there wasn't any thought of five or six men taking on the Prophet at once.

"I'm disappointed," Joseph said reproachfully. "I called you hound dogs, and all you can call me is a cat?"

Still it wasn't the big man who answered. "You're just so slick-lookin' we couldn't figure what kind of creature you was."

"Well, maybe you guessed right after all," Joseph said. "Maybe I *am* a cat, and maybe I been trained to catch the biggest thieving rats I could find and give 'em a good shake so we didn't have to look at 'em or smell 'em around anymore."

Fighting words had been said, and now the fighter pushed his way to the front of his group.

"You said one damn thing too many," said the man.

"Well, what a surprise. I didn't think your master ever trained you to talk," said Joseph.

"There's a lot of dead men who talked a hell of a lot nicer to me than you. There's a lot of men walkin' around today with no noses who said howdy-do a little too insincere. There's a lot of men walkin' around with no ears who didn't hear me quick enough when I said step aside."

"Well, I can understand that. A man with no nose couldn't tell you were comin'," said Joseph.

Suddenly the man began to roar. "I am the meanest son-of-a-jackass ever walked across the Mississippi on the back of a buffalo! I can row the river in seven minutes with a broken paddle! I can throw a yearling bull over a fence, against the wind! If I piss upstream the Mississippi flows backward half a mile! If I piss downstream the tide don't come in at New Orleans! I can bite the nose off a charging buffalo! I can shoot the balls off a squirrel at twenty yards! There ain't a man alive can say he ever knocked me down, and there's two dozen men in graveyards with a stone that says, 'This damn fool picked a fight with Buck Rigley.'"

"I'm shiverin' so hard I can barely stand," said Joseph, smiling. "I'm terrified. But I wonder what you can do without a knife and without a gun, just man to man. I bet you're down in three minutes. I figure three minutes because I'm a little tired. My horse went lame about a mile from here and I had to carry the poor fellow home."

"You best take off your pretty coat and give it to some lady to hold," said Buck Rigley. He was stripping off his own buckskin shirt, and peeling down his dirty underwear. Joseph too off his coat and walked to the edge of the crowd. Instinctively he made for a group of ladies—he had found they took much better care of his coat than any men were likely to.

As he approached, several of the women, laughing, informed him it was their turn to hold his coat. But instead he was drawn to a pretty woman with deep and sober eyes. She was new in Nauvoo—he would have noticed her before this if she had been a Saint for long.

"Beg your pardon, Sister," Joseph said. "I'd be grateful if you'd hold my coat for me."

Without a smile, just those deep eyes looking into his face, she nodded. Her expression was almost insolent and her silence felt like an accusation. So you don't approve of wrestling, is that it, ma'am? Dignity first, is that it? Joseph was in no mood to be conciliatory. Instead, he stripped off his waistcoat and his shirt, too, and laid them both in the woman's arms. Then, like Rigley, he peeled his underwear down to his waist and stood there bare-chested like a prize fighter. Her expression did not change. She said nothing; nor was she embarrassed, for she frankly looked over his chest and arms as if she were evaluating the merits of a horse. But she was beautiful, and suddenly Joseph was glad to have her see his body, and something inside said, She is yours.

I know something about your future, Joseph said silently to her. You will marry Joseph Smith.

As if his thought showed in his face, her expression hardened. She looked him in the eye challengingly, and he could almost hear her say, I'll see you in hell first.

He grinned at her and then turned around to face the river rat. Rigley was already hunkered down, ready for the rush, the quick grab, the iron grip. Joseph knew the man would go straight for his eye—he was a gouger, Joseph knew the type. Took all the fun out of wrestling, to know the other man wanted to leave his marks on you.

Joseph tried to look as unready as possible, and Rigley smiled at him. He had lost some teeth, but probably not in a fight, Joseph decided, judging from the condition of the surviving teeth. Wouldn't be a tragedy if he lost some more. Rigley rushed. Joseph instantly leaned forward, so his feet would be firmly planted, and just as Rigley was about to reach him Joseph lunged forward, low, and grasped the man around the chest, pinning his upper arms against his sides. Just as Joseph had thought—all muscle, and not a bit of skill. Rigley clawed at Joseph's back, tried to stomp Joseph's feet, but there was no way he could break Joseph's grip on him. Joseph squeezed. Rigley tried to writhe his way free. Joseph squeezed harder and heard the man's breath come out in a rush. The man tried to bite Joseph's shoulder. Joseph responded, not by shying away, as most men would have done, but by butting him in the ear with his head. Rigley cried out in pain and relaxed momentarily, just long enough for Joseph to shift his grip lower on Rigley's body, at his waist. Then he picked the man up, kicking and cussing and gasping for breath as Joseph hauled him to a mudhole in the road.

"Which way is the wind blowing!" Joseph shouted.

"Over here," someone answered. Joseph got on the opposite side of the mudhole from the wind and heaved Rigley in. He made a fine large splash. The crowd roared with laughter.

"That was against the wind, too," Joseph told him. Then he turned his back and walked away.

"Look out!" someone shouted, but Joseph knew already that Rigley was out of the mudhole and running at him from behind. Again at the last moment Joseph shifted his weight, this time downward, forward, and Rigley's mud-slick arms and chest slid over Joseph's back and the man sprawled on the road, a fairly firm place, this time, so that the wind was knocked out of him.

"You have to watch your step in the mud," Joseph said. "You can take a nasty fall if you aren't careful."

Rigley roared and ran to the attack once more. This time Joseph was through toying with him. He avoided Rigley's head thrust, and gave the man his thigh hard against the belly and chest. While Rigley tried to regain his wind, Joseph again pinned his arms and chest, but this time over the back, so that they were locked in a four-legged arch, with Rigley helpless underneath. Joseph liked to use this against stupid men, because stupid men never figured out that the way to break the hold was just to go limp and stop supporting their own weight— both men would fall to the ground then, and that hold would be impossible. Instead, Rigley kept trying to break free by butting forward, so that he was bearing both his own and Joseph's weight, and Joseph could use all his strength in squeezing Rigley until he couldn't breathe at all.

It took only a few minutes until Rigley was gasping in tiny, quick breaths; only a few seconds more, and Rigley's ribs gave a little. He went limp then, and Joseph let him fall. Then he beckoned to the other river rats, who were looking a little sick. "Your friend pissed upriver once too often," Joseph said. "I suggest you take him on south. If I hear of any of you north of St. Louis again, I'll come after you. But next time I won't be so tired, and next time I won't be alone. You hear?"

They heard, and bore away their groaning champion.

Joseph's arms ached from the struggle, and the breeze was cold on his sweaty, mud-coated back. He felt good. The unnameable yearning in him was sated for the moment. He raised his arms above his head and shouted to his people gathered around him, "Don't you have just about the finest specimen of a Prophet in the whole world?" It was brag, it was a joke, and the people laughed even as they cheered. They knew that Joseph had been at some risk in order to affirm the public order. In Nauvoo, it was Mormons who were the old settlers and expelled unwelcome outsiders. In Nauvoo, it was Mormons who were strong, and the Prophet who had been jailed for six months in Missouri was powerful and free in this place. It was much, much more than a wrestling match, for the onlookers as well as for Joseph himself.

But the pretty girl holding his clothing, she did not cheer. Joseph smiled all the more broadly when he saw her icy expression. A new convert, no doubt, and offended that the Prophet did not comport himself with proper dignity. So many converts expected Joseph Smith to act like a minister. Well, if they wanted ministers they could have stayed with the pious old frauds who taught them lies every Sunday for a tidy fee. Come to Nauvoo, and you get the man the Lord called as Prophet, and no other.

"I'm obliged to you for holding my clothing," Joseph said. "I think a Prophet ought to keep his coat clean, don't you?"

She handed over the clothes without a word. It took Joseph back a little—few women would have kept their tongues at such an open invitation to comment on what a prophet ought or ought not to do.

"Well, what did you think of the little contest?" Joseph asked. How could he make a joke to ease the tension, if she said nothing, if she gave him no opening for banter?

She cocked her head a little, and spoke very quietly. "The Prophet Jacob wrestled once," she said.

Joseph could not answer her. He had expected an attack, and instead her words excused him for his breach of decorum. "That's right," he said emphatically.

Only then did she turn it to criticism, only after he had agreed, only after it was too late for him to turn it to a joke. "But *he* wrestled with the Lord," she said, "and he came away cleansed."

She gave him no chance to answer. Without ever altering the expression of her face, without so much as a flounce of her skirt to weaken her quiet triumph, she turned and walked away. She had the best of him. She had faced Joseph Smith in a contest of words, and had beaten him fair and square, and the watching crowd didn't know what to make of it. That sort of thing shouldn't happen. They were uncomfortable. So Joseph laughed aloud and said, "It was a good thing for that river rat that he only had to fight *me*."

It was enough. He had turned embarrassment into rueful, amused surrender: the tension was broken, the people laughed, and a large number of them escorted Joseph to the rain barrel where they washed him down before he went inside. Emma took one look at him, shook her head, and walked away. Joseph almost laughed aloud. I met another woman who felt the same way, he wanted to tell her. But *she* knew what to say.

Then he remembered that the Spirit had whispered that she was his. Well, fine and dandy, thought Joseph as he changed for the party. She may be mine, but what if I don't want her? The last thing I need is a woman who knows how to shovel me under in public. I'd sooner court a rattlesnake.

The party went well. There wasn't a band yet in Nauvoo, and the fiddler tonight wasn't very good, but any fiddler was better than dancing to clapped hands. Joseph had a grand time. He danced a few minutes now and then, because he was a fine dancer and loved the way the quadrilles all centered around his step no matter where he stood. Most of the time, though, he talked, moving from group to group, listening a moment to get the gist of the conversation, and then saying a few words to everyone in the group. In the poverty of this young city, it helped morale if a large number of people could say to their friends, "Why, Brother Joseph spoke with me just the other night, at a party at his house." Joseph was still the glue that bound all the pages into one book; the more people who felt an intimate connection with the Prophet, the stronger the Church would be. It was a fragile church, though, if one man was all that sustained it. What happens after I am dead? Who will make this work live after me?

So, as always, when Joseph was most cheerful, most outgoing, he brooded the most inside, where no one but Emma would see. You are weak, he said silently to all his friends. You still must drink so often from my well. What will you do when I am dry? Will your faith wither then, will you be blown away in the wind? And he smiled, and laughed, and joked, and the room was bright because of him.

Then he glanced away from a group and looked at the entry, where a tall young man was helping a lady with her cape. It was Charlie Kirkham, and the lady would be his sister, the one that Emma so wanted to meet. Joseph started toward them, to welcome them to the party and introduce them around. Then the lady turned and he recognized her. The girl who had held his clothing just an hour or so before.

Joseph did not break his stride. He gripped Charlie's hand warmly and pulled him farther into the room. "Charlie Kirkham, the ladies have all been longing to have a turn with you at the quadrille. I told them there was a young man coming tonight who was even handsomer than me, and now at last they'll see I wasn't lying." Then Joseph deliberately faced Charlie's sister and reached out his hand. "I haven't met your sister, Charlie," he said.

"This is Dinah Handy," Charlie said. "And Dinah, this is Brother Joseph."

She extended her hand, and her fingers were cool and dry in Joseph's as he bent to kiss them. No sign that she was flustered, or felt at all shy about having spoken so boldly to the Prophet only that afternoon. In the candlelight she was even more fragile and lovely than before, but Joseph knew that it was a lie. She was exactly as fragile as a thin and wicked blade. And now he put together all he had heard of Charlie's sister with all he knew of her himself. This was the woman who was regarded as the strength of the Saints on the voyage of the *North America*. This was the woman who had visions and spoke in tongues, the woman that Emma wanted to meet. And I have made her angry. I stripped to the skin to annoy her today, I provoked her into a public quarrel, and *she* is the woman whose influence among the Saints is strong enough that even though she's a newcomer, Emma wanted particularly to meet her.

And the Spirit said she was mine.

"Sister Kirkham," Joseph said, "a pleasure to meet you again."

"Again?" asked Charlie. "You didn't tell me you had met before."

"Just a few hours ago," Joseph said. "But I assure you, Sister Kirkham, that I usually wrestle with angels. It's just that there've been so few angels this week, and I wanted to stay in practice."

Of course the story had already passed through the party twice tonight, and so everyone knew what she had said to him today. The onlookers laughed, but again Dinah Kirkham did not so much as smile. She only bowed her head gracefully for a moment and withdrew her hand. "I'm so sorry," she said. "My brother spoke so softly. My name is Mrs. Dinah *Handy*."

She had done it again, taken the conversation away from him and embarrassed him in front of his people. What a knack. I'm going to adore this woman, Joseph thought angrily. "I beg your pardon," he said. "When will I have the pleasure of meeting your husband?"

Charlie spoke quickly. Obviously it was a sensitive subject. "He stayed in England," he explained. "It was a legal thing. He took her children away from her when she decided to come here and help build the City of God."

The other guests at the party were all listening now, and

they murmured in sympathy. They all knew about sacrifice for the Kingdom of God, and Dinah's loss made her one of them at once. But this had also changed the mood of the party, from good cheer to reflectiveness, the last thing that should happen this early in the evening. Yet he couldn't think how to turn the mood of the party back again without being boorish. The party was out of his control—for now, at least, it belonged to her.

"You make me ashamed to be having fun tonight," Joseph said to her.

She paused for just a moment, but in that moment she understood what he was asking her for. "If I wanted never to have fun again," she said, suddenly smiling, "I could have stayed in England."

The listeners laughed, relaxed, returned to dancing and conversing and telling jokes. The smile lingered on Dinah's face long enough to be convincing. Long enough for Joseph to want her to smile again, for when her face was bright and warm like that he could not imagine her husband letting her go for any reason.

But the smile was gone, and her steady gaze told him that she knew she had done him a favor by giving him control of the party again. Or did she know? Joseph could not be sure. It was so easy to read meanings and intentions into her impenetrable silence. It made him appreciate loquacious women for the first time in his life.

"My wife wanted to meet you," Joseph said.

"I would like to meet her," Dinah answered.

"Would you follow me?"

She nodded gravely, and as Joseph led her across the room he felt for all the world like a schoolboy running an errand for his teacher. He almost laughed aloud at the thought. What a schoolteacher she'd make! The boys would fall in love with her and live in terror of her all at once. But God help the man who married a girl who had once had this woman for a teacher.

Joseph led her to where his wife quietly supervised the punch. "I wish I could leave the table and talk with you," Emma said, when the introduction was done.

"But I was just going to ask you if I could stay and help you serve," Dinah answered. Joseph left her gladly then. And yet he could not keep from noticing her through the rest of the evening, now and then seeing her serving punch or talking earnestly with a sister or carrying something to or from the kitchen. Wherever she was, she was an island of solid purpose in the frivolity of the party. People who spoke to her were never laughing or smiling when they left, and Joseph saw that it took a while before they could rejoin the bright and laughing conversations, or return willingly to the dance. She does not fit into this group, Joseph realized. Instead she fits the group to her.

Near the end of the party, Charlie was still lingering, and Joseph told him he should go home. "You ought to make an early start tomorrow. It might take you all evening to find decent lodging at Springfield."

Charlie smiled. "I'd go in a moment, Brother Joseph, but it might not look right, to go off and leave my sister to find her own way home."

"Fetch her and go, then."

"But she's in the kitchen talking with your wife. I didn't think it was my place to interrupt."

Joseph laughed. "What did Emma say to you this afternoon, to make you so terrified of her?"

"Oh, I'm not terrified. I just think it a better policy to keep at least one wall or fifteen people between her and me."

So Joseph went off to the kitchen, chuckling over the way people seemed so determined to misunderstand Emma, forgetting for the moment how many times he himself had misunderstood; forgetting, too, how often people were offended, not for misunderstanding her, but for understanding her too accurately.

Dinah stood in the kitchen with her back to the door. She was talking seriously with Emma, and Joseph knew from the way Emma pretended not to see him that it would be better if he did not interrupt. So he stepped back through the door. But he stayed close, and unashamedly eavesdropped, for he heard Emma say, "You have to understand, Sister Dinah, that my husband is a man as well as a prophet," and he had to hear Dinah's answer.

"I expected nothing else," Dinah said. Joseph could hardly hear her.

"That's not true," Emma said. Joseph winced at how bluntly she spoke. "You expected him to be perfect. You put too much of a burden on him. It's as if you walked up to him and said,

'I left behind my children for you.'"

Dinah did not answer for a long moment. Then she said, "You are mistaken, Sister Emma. I left my children behind because the Holy Spirit came to me and said, 'I have an inheritance for you in the beautiful city.'"

Joseph had heard those words before. In a dream, a dream of the marshes, when a squirrel, of all creatures, had spoken to him. But that dream had been fulfilled, hadn't it? With someone else, the dream had been fulfilled. It had been a great proof of something. Was it wrong then? Or was it only coincidence now?

"We *do* need you here in Nauvoo, Dinah," Emma said. "It is you who will make it a beautiful city."

"You overestimate my gifts," Dinah said.

"No, Sister Dinah," Emma answered. "You underestimate my husband. You saw him today and he was less than you expected. Now you must understand that he is far more than he seems."

"Today I found it hard to tell the Prophet from the ruffian as they wrestled half-naked in the mud."

Joseph knew Emma so well that he could almost say her words along with her. Icy and harsh, that was Emma when someone attacked her husband. "Perhaps you have had a moment in your life, Sister Dinah, when you would not have wished to have someone watching you to judge your godliness."

When Emma spoke in that tone of voice she was so offensive that many a woman had wept and many a man had raged. Instead, Dinah answered softly, so softly that Joseph could not make out the words she said. Then there was nothing but silence. Whatever was going on in the kitchen, Joseph had delayed longer than he should have. He swung open the door and walked in swiftly, as if he had crossed a room to get there. "When you women finish solving all the problems of the city, there's a young man out here who wants to go home." By the time he was through speaking, however, he realized that he had misunderstood most of what he heard through the door. He had thought it was his wife attacking, and Dinah retreating under her verbal blows. Instead it was Emma whose eyes were filled with tears, whose face was full of pain. And Dinah, this stranger who said nothing and understood too much—Dinah Handy was comforting her.

"Thank you for a lovely evening," Dinah said quietly to

both of them. Then she was out the kitchen door and across the other room. Joseph wanted to call her back, to demand an explanation. But he wasn't sure what it was that needed to be explained. He was angry, that was all, angry and unsatisfied, for this woman had said no more than half a dozen sentences to him and yet in those few words she had undone him every time.

"I hope you were listening," Emma said.

Joseph nodded.

"You've shattered that girl," Emma said. "You broke her heart today."

Joseph almost laughed aloud. "Shatter *her!* She's made of stone!"

Emma looked at him and smiled grimly. "She's a strong woman, Joseph, but she isn't stone."

"What did she say to you? The last thing she said before I came in? I couldn't hear."

Emma raised an eyebrow. "I had asked her if she had ever done something she would be afraid to have judged. And she said, 'I wanted him to be the one who was fit to judge me.'"

"And I'm *not?* Because I wrestled with a river rat and ran him out of town?"

"That's the least of what hurt her, Joseph."

"And you, why were you crying?"

"Was I?" Emma reached up in surprise and brushed a tear off her cheek. "Oh, yes. Well, I don't know." She laughed at herself, a bit embarrassed. "I was crying. Isn't that funny?"

They saw all the guests to the door, and finally had the house to themselves. Because the spell of the party was still on them, they could not sleep for a while; they were not at a loss for how to fill the time. But afterward, when Emma slept, Joseph still lay awake, thinking about Dinah Handy, this woman so fragile he had broken her heart, this woman so harsh that she had condemned him on the evidence of one day. She had faith enough to leave her children for the sake of the Church, and yet was not afraid to criticize the Prophet to his face at their first meeting. She was dangerous and desirable, and her beauty stayed with him like a headache half the night.

"Read to me," Dinah said.

"It's near midnight," Charlie answered.

Dinah stood and held him by the force of her need. Read

to me, Charlie, she said silently, put some words into my head or I'll have no sleep tonight.

"All right," Charlie said. He shuffled through his box and came up with four volumes. He shuffled them, trying to decide which to read. "What do you want? Tennyson? Wordsworth?"

"Charlie, I'm afraid," Dinah said.

"Of what? How can you be afraid? We had a wonderful time tonight, I'm going to Springfield tomorrow on the Prophet's errand, the Prophet's brother is the best friend I've ever had in my life, this is the happiest we've ever been."

Dinah could not answer him. Charlie was too damnably content. Either he would not understand her, which would make her feel even lonelier than now, or he would, which would break the fragile crystal of his perfect day. I have two little children in England, Charlie, and I haven't embraced them in months, and today I saw the Prophet of God brutally embrace another man and break him, I saw the Prophet boasting like a street bully, I saw the Prophet of God look at me with eyes that wanted to own me—

"Read, Charlie."

"Coleridge? 'Recollections of Love'?"

"I don't care."

"How warm this woodland wild recess! Love surely hath been breathing here; and this sweet bed of heath, my dear!—"

"No! Not that!" Dinah knew she was baffling the boy, knew that he could not satisfy her tonight, what she wanted was beyond human power to give; that was the problem, she knew, that there was no living man who could be what she wanted. "Never mind, Charlie. Go to bed."

"I can read something else," he said.

Now I've worried him. He thinks I'm losing my mind. Well, I am. "Go to bed."

Charlie did not leave his chair. Dinah knew he was studying her, trying to understand her. You cannot understand me, Charlie. Understanding people isn't your gift.

And then, to make a lair of her, he began to read another poem. "It reminds me somehow of Nauvoo," Charlie said. "But I don't know why." He began to read about a strange city of beauty and pleasure beside the river Alph, with walls and towers, and blossoms on incense-bearing trees, and forests ancient as the hills. It was not by any means the shabby town of Nauvoo or the ragged woods that spotted the prairie land or thickly bent over the Mississippi. And the mud of that river was surely not sacred.

Yet as Dinah listened, her eyes closed, she began to hear Charlie's voice as if it came from Joseph Smith, standing there in the late afternoon sunlight slanting in under the clouds, his naked chest covered with mud and sweat, not hairy like animal men, like Matthew, but clean and strong as a god, and Joseph said to her, with those eyes that owned her,

> *A damsel with a dulcimer*
> *In a vision once I saw:*

and it was you, Dinah, I saw you, and on your dulcimer you played, singing of Mount Abora.

> *Could I revive within me*
> *Her symphony and song,*
> *To such deep delight 'twould win me,*
> *That with music loud and long,*
> *I would build that dome in air,*
> *That sunny dome! those caves of ice!*

Beware! Charlie cried to her as he read the poem. Beware his flashing eyes, his floating hair! Weave a circle round him thrice, and close your eyes with holy dread, for he on honeydew hath fed, and drunk the milk of Paradise. . . .

"Are you asleep?" Charlie asked her.

Dinah said nothing. Let him think that I'm asleep. Go away now, Charlie. Thank you, Charlie.

"Go in to bed, Dinah," Charlie said, gently shaking her shoulder. "You can't spend all night on a chair."

"In a minute," she whispered.

Because he was Charlie, he did not argue, even though he slept out here in the front room, and couldn't go to bed until she left: "All right," he said. And then, because he was Charlie, he had to ask, "Was it a good poem?"

She answered his real question. "You read it beautifully, Charlie. I thought I was in Xanadu again."

He chuckled. "Again? You've been there before?"

Today, Charlie, and it made me afraid, because I did not

come here for a pleasure dome. I came here for sacrifice. I knew the Prophet would be a man, I was prepared for him to have human failings, but I did not know he would own me with his eyes as if he had a right, that he would be strong enough to break a man in his arms, and that I would want— that's not what I came here for. That's not what I left my children for. A prophet of God should make me want holiness. To deny the flesh and live in the spirit. To be caught up by God to dwell in light.

"Do you know why I love that poem, Dinah?"

Not now, Charlie.

"Because Xanadu is the secret city of Nauvoo. Within that flowing sea of mud they call a river there's another river, the clear, sacred Alph, and the muddy dooryards are gardens bright with sinuous rills and within every filthy shanty in Nauvoo there's another building, the dream building, the walls and towers—"

"They must be very tiny walls to fit inside these cabins."

"Not even inside the cabins. Inside the mind of every man and woman here. That's why people are happy in this place. They know what they will turn it into in ten years, in twenty years. And Brother Joseph is Kubla Khan, he hath drunk the milk of Paradise, beware of him."

Dinah trembled, as if Charlie had discovered her secret understanding of the poem.

But Charlie did not suspect what Dinah was in her own unspeakable dream. He was too caught up in his own. "Do you know what *I* shall build, Dinah? What this cabin is already in my mind? A factory. A clean, new building, painted glorious white, and men will come here to sweat and make something where it was not before, and I'll sell it outside Nauvoo, and bring money back to the city. And this cabin is just a corner of the true house, the new house where we'll all live. I shall make it happen, Dinah. All I lack is money."

All I lack is money.

Dinah got up from her chair. "Thank you, Charlie," she said. "Go to sleep."

"You don't believe I'll do it," Charlie said.

"Of course I believe you," Dinah answered.

Charlie smiled happily. "If you believe in me, Dinah, then I know I can. It'll be a factory as fine as any we saw in Manchester."

A factory as fine as Robert's, Dinah thought, and sighed inwardly as she closed the door to her tiny room. She undressed half-ashamedly, as if Joseph Smith himself were watching her. I am surely out of my senses, Dinah thought. I've just been too long away from a husband, and so a man's body—

She changed her line of thought, could not bear where that led. She was merely disoriented, she told herself. She had lost her sense of direction in this new place. The other English-women all depended on her like the centerpole of a tent, but she herself stood in a mire. The light of God had burned within her, but she could not find it now, it was spattered with mud, it was shaped like a man, and it could not dwell within her in this place. She had to find some purpose. Charlie had a purpose, and he was happy.

She sat on the edge of her bed with a board on her lap and tried to write a letter to Val. I am in Nauvoo. This city is so new that it won't even be on the best and newest map you can find, and we are building it from nothing. All we lack is money.

She crumpled the paper and started another. Darling Val, I cry every night when no one can see me because I can't put my arms around my boy. Do you cry for me, too? Someday we shall see each other again. Perhaps your father will let you visit me in this new city of Nauvoo. Or perhaps I have made a mistake coming here, trading one vain man for another, and losing you in the bargain.

She crumpled that paper, too, and set aside the lap board. She could not speak to Val through paper, for the words would also be read by Matthew. Could not speak to her son because she must tell Val the truth and could not bear to let Matthew hear it. Perhaps if she wrote a letter to Robert, he would speak to Val privately sometime. That's what she would do, write to Robert tomorrow, and give him a message for little Val, and have him tell her children how their mother loves them even though she is far away.

She wrote the letter, baring more of her hear to Robert than she ever meant to, begging more than her dignity would ever allow if she had to speak the words aloud. When the letter was done and sealed, she felt a little better, felt as if she had done something to reach back into the past and touch her children, who after all had been herself for years.

As she lay in bed, finally letting sleep come at her from the edge of the room, she began to dream of the same fine house that Charlie dreamed of, only she cared most for the knock at the door; she opened, and there were Val and Honor, older now but still as glad as little children, crying out, "Mother, Mama," and embracing her, then running through the house saying, "Is this my room? Oh, I shall play here! And here is where we shall have school, isn't it, Mama!"

Then, because it was all made of ice, it melted, and the children melted, and Dinah wept in her sleep. I must make it real, she thought. All I lack is money.

🖐 27 🖐

John Kirkham
Springfield, Illinois, 1840

SPRINGFIELD WASN'T MUCH OF a town, but to John Kirkham anything was better than Nauvoo. It had been hard enough keeping everybody happy back in Manchester; in Nauvoo he was hemmed around with righteousness till sometimes he wanted to say something disgusting just for the pleasure of hearing the words. There's a devil in me, John Kirkham figured, but God made me as I am so it isn't my fault. That particular line of reasoning freed him to estimate the town of Springfield through the eyes of a calculating Londoner. He knew the street women for what they were, even though they shunned anything so obvious as paint in broad daylight. He knew the legislators, too, knew which ones were hungry and which already had their share of power and bribes and pleasures of the flesh. John was amused at how innocently Charlie misunderstood everything, how he kept talking about the excellence of democracy and how things were obviously so much better here in America where power was with the people. Power with the people? But John didn't bother correcting him. Charlie wouldn't understand. Like any child, Charlie could read people's clothes and tell rich from poor, but he had no notion of what their manners meant, what the look of a man's eyes told about the condition of his heart.

And yet, John had to admit to himself, Charlie was not an utter fool. The lad might not know *why*, but sometimes he could tell when a man would be useful. As soon as they had reached Springfield and tied up their horses, Charlie looked around and pointed straight at a short fellow in a fine new suit. "That's our man," Charlie said. And with that Charlie marched right up to him, lifted his hat, and said, "We're from Nauvoo, sir, and we're trying to find John Bennett. Could you help us?"

He could. His name was Stephen Douglas, and John liked the look of him. Hungry, but not for money. Small though he was in stature, this man was above corruption. He wanted power. In large draughts. "Not only can I tell you where he is," said Douglas, "I'm going right now to the same hotel—his room is down the hall from mine. You have news from Mr. Smith?"

Naturally, Douglas looked to the elder of the two for an answer, but John Kirkham deferred to his son. That, at least, was no longer painful—Charlie liked being at the fore and John was much happier standing back, watching. Charlie and Mr. Douglas conversed about this and that, Douglas pumping Charlie for everything he knew, which wasn't much, and Charlie talking away, oblivious to how he was being used. John walked beside them, pretending to care what they were saying. He was studying Douglas's face. Douglas was one of the few men John had met whose portrait might be worth painting. But the little man would no doubt resent the way John would paint him. It was no accident that John Kirkham had never made money in London. People liked to look like heroes in their portraits. John Kirkham's eye was too honest. His brushes were too frank. He had never known a man who could look without some pain at his own portrait as John Kirkham drew him. Douglas was not so remarkable as to be an exception to *that*.

As they stepped onto the sidewalk in front of the hotel, a tall, spindly-legged man with a face like a gnarly tree tipped his hat at them. John and Charlie responded, but Douglas stared straight ahead and walked on into the lobby of the hotel as if he hadn't noticed. Charlie looked at his father in surprise, and John winked. "They must be friends," John said.

Charlie didn't take the hint—he wasn't good at letting things lie. "Who was that?" he asked their guide.

"Oh, that's 'Honest Abe' Lincoln." Douglas said the name without love.

"He seems a pleasant fellow," Charlie said. John winced. Charlie had neither tact nor a sense of proportion.

"He's not a friend to the Mormons," Douglas said coldly.

John was delighted at this little politician's lack of subtlety. Did he really think the Mormons divided the world so easily into friends and not-friends? Of course, John remembered, the Mormons might very well see the world in just that way. Americans were so simple about these things. "He *seemed* friendly," John said, putting a bit of regret into his voice.

Douglas knew the value of sounding magnanimous. "Oh, he'll support your city charter. Democrat or Whig, they'll all help you in this legislature. You Mormons've got enough votes to swing this state. Just remember that *we* believe in the same principles as you. *We* were your friends before it was smart."

John nodded as wisely as he could. "And you're Whigs?"

"Democrats," Douglas said testily.

"He must be a remarkable man," Charlie said.

Douglas looked puzzled.

Charlie glanced back toward the door where Lincoln had passed them. "He must be remarkable, if people call him 'Honest' as if it were part of his name."

Douglas hooted. "That's rich. Part of his name! Don't you know, he probably thought of that himself? Probably invented the stories that go along with it, too. No, out here in the West a man's name is whatever he says it is. Though for all I know it might be his Christian name. I can picture his mother, a-rocking her little baby, singing Tooraloo, Tooraloo, go to sleep, Honest Abe. I heard of a man named Doctor Philastus Hurlbut. That was his name—Doctor. It got him all kinds of respect, and saved his parents the cost of providing him with a college education."

Douglas's penetrating voice filled the hotel lobby, and dozens of men laughed with him at the joke. John looked at the crowd, sized them up. Not a hard group to convince of anything, he estimated. If this was a fair sample, America was the greatest argument against democracy that could be devised. If pigs could vote, the man with the slop bucket would be elected swineherd every time, no matter how much slaughtering he did on the side.

But that judgment didn't mean John Kirkham wasn't happy to be here. He had already made quite sure that this hotel was exactly what he hoped: it did a little whoremongering on the side. The ladies in pleasant conversation here and there were discreet enough, but John knew their trade—they had the look about them that was advertising enough among people of the world. Would Charlie be clever enough to catch him at it? John doubted it. Charlie would have to see them in bed before he'd suspect. That was the charm of the virgin boy. He could stare at sin and never notice it.

It turned out Bennett wasn't in and hadn't left word. The sky was darkening outside, and Charlie was willing enough when John suggested they find a hotel less dear than this one. A couple of horses the Mormons could provide their messengers—a decent traveling allowance, however, was beyond their means.

John waited until Charlie was lying on his bed, well buried in a book, before he got up and stretched and said, "I think I'll take a walk. The air is close and I need to work my legs after such a ride." Charlie barely mumbled a reply, and John was out the door and free of his son in the darkness. So easy.

The smell of liquor on his breath would be too plain; with regret John passed the pubs—no, saloons—without doing more than breathing in the alcoholic air. He knew what he was after and made no pretense to himself. He had long ago learned that while lying to others was his Christian duty, so that they could be happy, lying to himself was dangerous. And so he didn't pause a moment, didn't deviate from the course that led to the ladies he had seen earlier in the day.

There were none in the lobby of the hotel when he arrived— just a couple of amateurs who probably told themselves they were looking for husbands. So John bought a newspaper and waited, holding it in front of him but not bothering even to glance down at it. Within the quarter-hour he had caught the eye of a lady who carried herself almost as if she believed her own costume. Her eyes, though—it was the eyes that drew him. She looked like she could see through anything with those eyes. Such a woman would be worth the depletion of the little sum he had managed to squirrel away out of whatever money his family left carelessly within his reach. She smiled at him. He fancied it was more than a professional smile. It pleased him to pretend she saw his true worth.

An hour later, as he left her room, full of her laughter and empty of love, a grand young man swept by through the hall with all the airs of an earl at least. He grinned at John's lady, and the lady smiled back. "Good-night, Doctor," she said.

John watched the man go by and open a door well down the hall. "Doctor?" he asked his lady, cocking his eyebrow.

"You have a filthy mind," she said. Then she shrugged. "Well, somebody has to clean up, or we'd all be out of work in a few months, you know. And anyway, he *is* a real doctor, too. A specialist in women's ailments." She laughed. "I like to think of it, sometimes. In the same day he goes from examining a fat rich lady to cleaning up for us. There's some fun in that, isn't there?"

John grinned at her. Better than saying anything. He knew that to the whores such men were as useful as blacksmiths were to cavalry, but John could not be philosophical about abortionists. Not just because they were usually swinish men, but because they went about removing the inconvenience from corruption. John did not see anything hypocritical about this opinion. He knew that he was corrupt—but he expected to bear the consequences of it, too. This abortionist had obviously never heard of consequences; he did not act as if he had ever heard of shame. That was America for you—a man could be in every social class at once. No sense of where people *belonged* in the world.

"You'd like him," she said.

"Do you think so." He did not let his tone of voice encourage her.

"You're two of a kind." Perhaps she saw that this did not please him, for at once she corrected herself. "In some ways, I mean. He's got education, like you." She tweaked surreptitiously at John's thigh. "And he does a right fine hornpipe on his middle leg."

John kissed her again and left her quickly. He'd been out more than an hour now, and if Charlie was awake he'd wonder why he had been out so long in such cold weather. As for that, John wondered why he had come here himself. He wasn't starved for love—Anna saw to that, the woman was not cold. Why then did he hunger so for a woman of this sort? Perhaps because with a whore he did not have to pretend to be a decent man. They throve on indecency, they lived off it, the world's decay was their aliment: here he was needed, not for what he should be, but for what he was. It was a little ache he had, and for a price they physicked him. That was it. He could couch himself in such ladies, let his burden down, leave his sins behind. Surely there was a hymn in that somewhere. I am a very holy man, he told himself as he opened the door to the room where Charlie's breaths were whispering. I am a holy, holy man. And he laughed himself so quietly to sleep.

Charlie went early to meet with Bennett; John Kirkham stayed behind to do some sketching. It was a good day for it, sunny and cold and the air crisp and still. John liked the way winter gloves on his hands distorted what his pencil did. It wasn't like nature—but sometimes it seemed truer. He sketched a few legislators and they came out like newspaper cartoons. John wondered for a moment if that might be a place where he could sell some work. Then he thought of seeing his name in one of these miserable rags, attached to a jest base enough for these people to understand it, and he shuddered. There was a bottom limit, after all.

At suppertime John got hungry, and figured Charlie ought to pay for a meal about now. He went looking for an hour, and finally found his son at a dining table in the best hotel in town. Alone—and so, as always, caught up in a book.

"I didn't know you were so flush," John said by way of greeting.

Charlie looked up, startled. "Oh! Yes! Did you get the note I left in the room?"

John shrugged. "Didn't see it when I left off my papers. Can we really eat here?"

Charlie was embarrassed. "Actually, we can't. I was invited here. And now he's late—I think they're wondering if I plan to eat or just use their table as a study."

John sat down opposite his son. "Did you get much done today?"

"I took near forty letters for him." Charlie flexed his fingers. "The man has more words in him than I had ink—had to buy another bottle halfway through."

"But your work is done?"

"He had a meeting with the secretary of something. State. Commerce. Army. I think Army. The one person in America he didn't write to, and so he had to meet with the man so he didn't feel slighted."

John laughed harder than the wit deserved, but the boy's humor was so rare that it sounded funnier than it ought when it finally came. He was laughing when a hand touched his shoulder.

"Are you still waiting for your meal, or have you already finished?"

Charlie looked up at the man. "General Bennett," he said.

John Kirkham turned in his chair, already smiling a greeting. He expected to meet a stranger. Instead he looked up into the face of the abortionist from the hotel corridor. For a moment he was afraid—this man had seen him coming out of a whore's hotel room. But he calmed himself immediately. Bennett was vulnerable, too—John Kirkham had nothing to fear from him. Of course he allowed none of this to show. John had lived in a part of London where it didn't do to let people know your feelings from your face—there wasn't so much as a pause in his turn or a slackening of his smile. And Bennett was just as poised.

It was Bennett's poise that was so provoking. The man was not abashed at all. Even though he could not know that John Kirkham had heard he was an abortionist, Bennett should have been at least a little reticent about his supposed religious faith. Instead he sat down and immediately began to discourse fervently on theology. It was all about some idea he wanted to discuss with Joseph Smith when at last his work in Springfield was accomplished. John Kirkham watched in awe at the utter confidence of the man. Even without a conscience, surely he felt some fear of being discovered—yet if he did, he showed no sign of it. John wondered whether Bennett believed in a God. No doubt he would claim he did, but John was pretty sure that Bennett was his own Creator, and his own Savior, too.

It was not possible, John learned, to remain detached for

long. Bennett was too strong a man to be at table with you and merely be observed. Several times John found himself almost believing what Bennett said; more often, he genuinely liked the man. It only became too much for John when Bennett started praising the joys of married life; too much for him when he realized how Charlie was hanging on every word the hypocrite was saying. Not that John minded a lie. John Kirkham could stand and lie with the best of them. But he didn't try to pass himself off as a great divine. And so John was provoked.

"I just realized why you look so familiar," John said.

Bennett, interrupted in mid-sentence, looked at John in mild surprise. "I didn't know I did."

"Last night I saw you." John paused a moment, searching Bennett's face for some sign of fear. Ah well; it was too much to hope for. Enough to have stopped him from spouting pieties and making a fool of Charlie. "I was on my walk. We both had made some use of one of the most trafficked roads in Springfield."

Bennett smiled winningly. "Even the biggest streets of this town must be cowpaths compared to those wide-open roads of London."

"London's roads," John said, "are only good for getting to the end of the journey. In Springfield, the road itself is worth the trip."

"You are an admirer of the beauties of America?"

At this, poor Charlie, who understood nothing but the bare surface of what was being said, intruded himself into the conversation. "I don't think my father has a very high opinion of anything American."

"It's a shame if you don't," Bennett said to John. "There's a lot around here to make a man stand right up." Then he turned the conversation to safer ground. "I hear you met our local secretary of state, Stephen Douglas. Clever little fellow, isn't he?"

"Didn't get a chance to know him very well," Charlie said.

"All we know is that he doesn't much like Honest Abe," John added.

"Abe Lincoln? Well, I wouldn't expect him to. Lincoln stole the little man's woman, took her right away. Mary Todd."

"What a choice for the lady," John said.

"Between a stump and a beanpole. I reckon she's betting

on size over vigor." Then Bennett grinned to show that all
innuendoes were intentional. It was plain that Charlie didn't
get it, but John did, and laughed aloud. He couldn't help it,
Bennett simply could not be disliked. He was a criminal of the
most contemptible kind, and yet John could only chuckle and
watch the man in awe as he did whatever he wanted with
Charlie—and, for that matter, with John himself. Well, then,
if Bennett could not be frightened and would not be antago-
nized, John might at least reach accommodation with him.

The conversation soon turned to Bennett's dream of Nauvoo. Here, at least, there could be little doubt that Bennett was
sincere. He wanted Nauvoo to be the Boston of the West.
"There are cities and cities," he said. "New York is a cesspool
with aspirations of someday, with luck, becoming a sewer. But
Boston—it was founded by people of God, and they've never
forgotten. Nauvoo can do that. It's not in a place where trade
will corrupt it. I see a city of universities, of churches, of
museums, of grace and beauty. Carriages on cobblestones."

"And all of it yours," John said.

Bennett grinned. "As much of it as possible, anyway. A
man's a liar if he says he doesn't want to possess things. But
I at least want to possess beautiful things, and if there aren't
any, why, I'll build them. And find others who can help me.
Like you, Charlie. If I had ten like you I could build another
Paris. A hundred like you, and I could build another Rome."

Charlie went bashful for a moment, unsure what to do with
his face while Bennett smiled at him so paternally. Looking
on, John found himself getting angry. He didn't much like
Charlie most of the time, but the boy *was* his son, and while
that was a relationship that held little advantage for Charlie, it
was better than letting the boy be under the influence of a
bloody abortionist. "It's too bad," John said, "that Charlie's
already taken."

"Oh?" Bennett asked.

"Well, he didn't come here on his own. Charlie's been
helping Don Carlos Smith with the newspaper, and you recall
that it was the Prophet who sent him."

"Oh, I hadn't forgotten. Brother Joseph asked me to have
a look at him, to see if he was of any use. Joseph and I have
the same dream, you see, and whoever helps me, helps him."

John wondered, fleetingly, if it was true—if there really

was no difference between Joseph Smith and this man. It raised questions, certainly. If Smith was a prophet, why didn't he know what Bennett really was? And if Smith was not a prophet, then Bennett could well be right—he and the Prophet might have been cut from the same cloth.

"There are a thousand ways that Charlie can be a great man in a great city," John said quietly. "But you should count on this, Brother Bennett. Charlie won't belong to any man. He stands on his own."

Bennett lifted his glass; just before sipping, he said, "Like you?"

The blow struck home. John saw the absurdity of what he had been saying. He avoided looking at Charlie, out of shame at having played the father's part so ineptly. Instead he only raised his own glass, and offered his bargain. "I'm my own man, yes. What I am is what I made of myself. I'm only a painter, and if there's a public for my work, God knows I've never found it. But Charlie has his mother in him. And he *will* be great, by any measure."

"Well, Brother Kirkham, you don't have to worry about Charlie. He's proved his value already, and he won't go unnoticed. My guess is that once he gets well acquainted in Nauvoo he'll be too busy to fasten his pants after pissing."

They all laughed at that—though, to John's amusement, Charlie was a little offended at the crudity. Be offended, my virgin son, my young Galahad, be offended but use this man for every advantage you can get from him.

"So you're a painter," Bennett said.

"After a fashion."

Charlie, who had been silent when the conversation was about him, spoke now. "I remember," he said, "that father painted woods and meadows that made you believe in heaven."

Startled, John looked at his son. "I didn't think you were old enough to remember."

Charlie was talking to Bennett, however. "And he put people in them that made you believe in hell. I remember a painting of a boy prodding a cow with a stick. I always thought the boy was trying to kill the poor animal, he had such hate in him."

"It sounds like you're a remarkable painter," Bennett said.

"Charlie last saw it when he was only four or five. Memory changes things." Still, though he denied it, John was deeply touched at this. Charlie remembered. Charlie, who had never really known his father, Charlie remembered a painting, and not just a pretty scene. He remembered it as a thing of power. To John's surprise, he realized that he just might love his son.

"Are you doing any painting in Nauvoo?" Bennett asked.

"They've had me doing carpentry. I'm a damned bad carpenter."

"Would you do my portrait?" Bennett asked.

You wouldn't like what I'd do to you, John said silently. I know too much about you. There would be casual murder in your face.

Bennett saw his hesitation. "Oh, don't worry about it now. I'll tell you what." He paused, leaned back, and gazed steadily into John's eyes. "Since it's plain you're a quiet man, and don't go about telling people all that you might tell them, I'll just have to do it *for* you." It was the bargain. He had understood what John Kirkham was asking, and he was going to do it. "I reckon by the time I get through talking you up, Brother Kirkham, you'll have a hundred people begging for your services as a painter. Can't build the city I dream of without artists, can I?"

"I'd be in your debt," John said. And so the bargain was sealed: John's silence about Bennett, in exchange for Bennett's help in establishing him as a painter. Not bad, for one night's work. Perhaps Providence even likes me, John speculated, letting me get a hold over Bennett.

The conversation went innocent again, without the hidden meanings; the food came, good coarse American food with far more bulk than flavor; and at last Bennett declared the supper over by getting to his feet, patting his waist, and then offering his hand to Charlie. "Would you come by my hotel in the morning on your way out of town? I'll have a letter or two for you to take to Brother Joseph."

"Of course," Charlie said.

"We'd better call it a night, then," Bennett said. "I have three more meetings tonight, and you'll need to get plenty of sleep for an early start tomorrow." Then Bennett cocked his head and smiled at John. "Of course, at your age you probably get to bed pretty early *every* night."

John laughed in recognition of Bennett's parting shot, and then he and Charlie got their coats and headed out into the night. The wind was sharp, and they hurried through the cold-hardened dirt streets.

They were near their cheap hotel when Charlie suddenly asked, "Do you really think I can stand alone, Father?"

"Mm," John said. "Do you really remember that painting?"

"I sometimes see it as clearly as when I was a child. I always see it very high, way out of my reach." Charlie laughed.

"Funny. I don't remember that one at all."

Charlie shrugged. "You've painted so many, I suppose." What he didn't say was, "So many that I never saw." That easily, and the moment of affection could have been turned into a reproach, a reminder of the years of abandonment. It meant more to John than he would have expected, the fact that Charlie stopped short of reminding him of his past sins.

Then they were inside, shedding scarves and coats. "What do you think might come of this, if Bennett recommends me?" Charlie asked.

"Perhaps they'll hire you to help Don Carlos."

Charlie laughed. "There's not much money in the newspaper."

"There's not much money anywhere," John said. "Except banks and rich men's pockets."

Charlie shook his head. "No, Father. That may be where the money ends up, but it comes from dreams and work. Nauvoo is all dreams right now. And the money will grow out of the ground in wheat, or come out of factories covered with laborers' sweat. But it's a circle. If we're going to build the dream of Nauvoo, we need money. And to get money, we have to *make* something. Make something exist that never existed before."

Then, because it was a night for frankness, John added, "It has to be something that other people want."

Charlie shook his head. "The only thing people want from me is clerking. I've always been just a clerk to them. I don't mind, though. I can't think of anything I'd rather do than be the Prophet's secretary. Write his letters, keep his journal. run his messages. That would be building Zion, too."

"What about working for Bennett?" John asked.

Charlie grimaced.

John was genuinely surprised. "I thought you liked him."

"Oh, I do. He's a great man."

"But you don't want to work for him."

Charlie shrugged. "It wouldn't be so bad. But I came to America for the Prophet's sake, not John Bennett's."

"Bennett doesn't think there's much difference."

"I think there is."

John could not help but be pleased that Charlie knew it. "Bennett's as religious as the next man, I would think."

"Bennett? No. Not really, Father. Maybe I'm making it up, but it strikes me that Bennett—that he's only *wearing* the gospel, and it isn't quite a fit." Charlie smiled sheepishly at his father. "Who am I to judge? He's working miracles here. But they're all—"

"All what?"

"All political miracles. He has a smile that would bring coons right out of the trees."

John laughed aloud. Maybe Charlie was quicker-witted than John had thought. Maybe he had better eyes than it sometimes seemed. Even this aberration of being such a damnably pious Saint—maybe even that was smarter than it looked to John Kirkham. It's the young who have the gift of believing. We older ones, we lose faith and think that makes us wise.

As if to disprove all his father's new opinion of his wit, Charlie completely misunderstood why John was laughing. "Coons out of the trees! I can't believe I said that. I've been spending too much time with Don Carlos, I even talk like him now. You don't think I'll become an American, do you?"

He said it with mock horror, but John understood how much the idea really appealed to the boy. "You're more than half there already. What are Americans, anyway, but Englishmen with brains enough to leave?" And for once, John almost believed his own opinion.

In the morning, before dawn, they stopped at Bennett's hotel. Bennett only left one letter at the desk for them to take. He hadn't sealed it, either, just folded it over. It was an open invitation to read it. Of course, Charlie would never consent to such a thing. So John made sure the letter ended up in his own coat pocket, an easy enough thing to manage, since Charlie was pretending he didn't much care about the letter anyway. Charlie was so sure it was a letter of recommendation that he had even talked of not bothering to pick it up, all as a show of modesty. John argued that it was their duty, however, and Charlie acquiesced willingly enough.

As John expected, they weren't halfway home when Charlie became completely lost in his own thoughts and drifted ahead on the frozen road. You could always count on a dreamer to dream. John remembered that once he, too, had walked or ridden along so oblivious to other people that he could have been robbed and wouldn't have known it. All John's dreams had been pictures, though, and he had watched the scenery. Charlie watched nothing at all. Probably he dreamed of words and numbers, riding along endlessly adding or conjugating or whatever it was a clerk dreamed of. There's much of me in Charlie, John thought, but too damned little of my art.

While Charlie dreamt, John ungloved his hands and pulled Bennett's letter from his coat. He nearly froze his fingers, holding the letter so tightly in the breeze, but it was worth it to know what Bennett had to say. It *was* a letter of recommendation, of a sort.

Brother Joseph,
 You askt me to tell you what I thoght of Charlie Kirkham. I think you will have your answer by the fact that I do not mean Brother Charlie to read this, and yet I have not seeled it. He is in evry way satisphactory, even his spelling is good, and he works harder then many twice his age. I urge you to get him in your close imployment as fast as posible before sombody else notises him—like me, if I had funds to salery him.

 As for his father, I must be frank. I do not trust him and I think you shoud not. I do not think that his convertion is sinsere. The boy plainly takes after his mother, for the father has little to reccomend him. Maybe if the fellow sticks to painting he will be harmless, but if I may be frank I must say I think he is probally the worse liar I ever heard. My own feeling is that a liar is pretty low on the ladder of Gods creation, but you be the judge, I am just
 your servant and brother
 Gen. John C. Bennett

John sat ahorse for some time, holding the letter in one hand. It was only when a wagon came along the other way that he finally came to himself and put the letter away. Wouldn't do to let himself be seen reading it, if Charlie should turn around when the wagon passed.

That sly devil, John Bennett. He was soaped all over. He'd make a bargain to promote John's painting, he'd advance Charlie's career, too, but at the same time he'd protect himself by naming John Kirkham a liar, so that if the day should come that this old man turned against Bennett, why, no one would believe the tale he told.

John wondered if that was why the letter hadn't been sealed. Probably was. Bennett knew that John would read it, and knew that Charlie would not. Maybe Bennett thought that John would squirm. Well, John admitted to himself, no man likes to hear such things said about him, even when they're true. But I'm also quite used to having things not be the way I want. Let the Prophet look at me and think me low; what's that to me? Let him pity Charlie for having a father who's unworthy of him; it's true, isn't it? And when the time comes—and it will come—when I want to undo John C. Bennett, to name him as the criminal he is, I'll know how to make myself believed. I'm no such fool as to expect them to take my word against his. I'll paint you in strong colors, Bennett, not in any crumbly charcoal grey, and when I'm through they'll know you.

John Kirkham sent his horse forward, picking up the pace and drawing Charlie along more quickly behind him. It was time for this journey to end, time to get back to Nauvoo. For Bennett's letter had spurred John Kirkham in a wholly surprising way. "Maybe if the fellow sticks to painting he will be harmless." Not the strongest recommendation in the world. The only one that would count would be the work itself. It was time for John to paint again in earnest. There was no taste in America, that was plain, but it wasn't taste that sold paintings, it was vanity. And of vanity there was no shortage, least of all in the Mormon city at the river's bend. I'll stick to painting, Bennett, and then let's see a few years from now how harmless I am, and how I do at telling truth, if once I set my hand to it.

❧ 28 ❧

Dinah Kirkham
Nauvoo, 1840

DINAH HAD TO EARN money again, that was the solution. It had worked before, given her a sense of strength, of knowing who she was and what she was supposed to do, until Mr. Uray destroyed it all and forced her into Matthew's bed. But the work itself had been good for her, working for money, because when the coins fell into her hand at week's end she had a measure of what she had done, she could change that portion of her life, those hours and days, into food, into house, into clothing, into *things.* It was the alchemy she knew would work: Time transformed into gold.

And it wasn't as if the family didn't need money. What savings they had were nearly gone, there wasn't enough coming in to make ends meet. Charlie and Father were off to Springfield on the Prophet's errand, which was all well and good except that it meant three days in which they didn't even earn the pitiful wages they had been able to earn doing odd jobs and making a botch of carpentry. Worst of all, she couldn't get her mother interested in the problem. Dinah spread the money on the table, but Anna only looked away and said, "I know, Dinah."

"Well, what can we do?"

Dinah clearly remembered the day, many years ago, when Anna had grimly set herself to make things work: selling paintings, taking the children out of school, moving to a cheaper cottage, finding work, whatever it took to stay alive. But not now. Too much had passed since then. "The Lord will provide," Anna said.

Well, perhaps He will, Dinah thought, but it wouldn't hurt to help Him out a little.

The trouble was finding any paying work to do. This city was too new, its growth too unnatural. People didn't come to Nauvoo because there was opportunity; they came because of religion. But religion wasn't a sound base for an economy, and as a result even carpenters were underpaid, though it seemed building was the only steady work around. Even bookkeepers like Charlie, whose skills were desperately needed, could not find work because there was no cash for salary. Where, then, would there be work for Dinah?

There were no factories here, where a woman with ten fingers and reasonable wit could get a few shillings a week. The women were all wives or daughters, and their work was all at home. Dinah had never done such work: kitchen gardens for vegetables on the table, ashes saved for soap, milk from the cow in the yard, eggs from the chickens they tended. What they couldn't make alone, they made together. If one woman had a spinning wheel and another had a loom, then both had a wheel, and both had a loom. If a quilt was too large for one woman to make in a month, a dozen women would frame it up and make it in a day. Where was there a place for a woman to make *money?*

She needed advice. She was too new, too English to know what a woman could do for money in America. Emma would know, of course; and as she thought that, she realized that she was already out in the road, walking toward the Smith house. The Smith house. Joseph would be there. Dinah at once turned and walked westward. She shouldn't impose on Emma, anyway. Poor Emma had enough to do without an immigrant woman adding to her burdens. But whom else did she know?

Brother Heber had often talked about his wife, had often told Dinah to meet her, talk to her, bring her word of how much Heber missed her. That would surely make Dinah welcome in Sister Kimball's home, at least long enough to ask advice. Dinah would impose on her for no more than a few minutes of talk.

It was easy to find the Kimball home—everyone seemed to know where the apostles' families lived. The house was an anthill of children, despite the cold weather. They were shouting and laughing and quarreling so that Dinah had to smile just to see them. Yet she noticed that except for the very youngest, they were not playing. They were chopping wood, hauling water, loading hay into a shed for the cow. No one seemed to notice as Dinah opened the gate and walked into the yard. Apparently visitors were common, and the children ran by her, shouting or laughing without so much as a howdy. Dinah tried to remember Val's face, and if he had ever run and shouted like that. But she could never conjure his face, except in nightmares, with his face covered with tears. As she stepped to the door, a girl bounded out with a basket in her arms. "We're going to Sister Landen's!" Then she saw Dinah and stopped. "Good morning," she said. "You're early." Then she leaped from the porch and went galloping across the yard, calling out for her sisters to come with her to Sister Landen's. Dinah knocked on the door.

Two children brushed past her into the house before someone finally came to let her in. It was a lovely, bright-faced woman who looked to be in her thirties. She was covered with flecks of cloth and small strands of yarn. "Good morning. If you want to be heard around here, don't bother knocking, just open the door and call."

"My name is Dinah Handy," Dinah said. "I was wondering if I might see Sister Kimball."

"*I'm* Sister Kimball," the woman said.

Dinah apologized for her surprise. "There are so many children, I expected someone older."

"I *am* older. I'm a hundred and five, in fact, but I sold my soul to the devil so I could pass for fifty."

"You could pass for thirty."

"I love you already, Sister Dinah. Come in. Don't count the

children. A good two-thirds of them aren't mine. But there's a good dinner here at noon, and if they work hard they can eat with me." Sister Kimball led the way into the parlor, where some yarn was strung on a strange wooden machine that looked like a sawing tackle gone mad. "Are you too English to lend a hand?"

Dinah didn't know what to say. "I'm English, but my hands aren't made of glass."

"I'm skeining some yarn here, and I've also got some women coming by for these squares. They've got to have them to make quilt tops for the quilting bee we're going to have in my drawing room all winter long, and this morning being the way it is I haven't been able to get them all counted out, so if you could run the husband-saver for me I could count the squares and you'd've made yourself useful enough to hug."

"I've never used one of these before," Dinah said.

Sister Kimball nodded. "That's what I mean by English. English ladies never used *anything* before, I get to thinking. Well, do you have the brains of a three-year-old? If you do, you can learn in about thirty seconds."

"Let's give it a try."

"You turn this crank."

Dinah took hold and turned. The yarn wound easily between the rotating posts.

"When the weasel pops, we cut the yarn, tie it off, string it again, and go to it. The Lord sent you to me, Sister Dinah. I was just praying for help, and here you are. My husband didn't baptize you, by any chance, did he?"

Dinah cranked away as Sister Kimball began counting colored squares of cloth into stacks of thirty. "He asked me to tell you that he thinks of you all the time."

"I'm glad to hear that," Sister Kimball answered. "I was especially worried since he broke his fingers."

"Broke his fingers? I heard nothing about that!"

"Neither did I. But it's the only reason I can figure why he doesn't write. Is there an ink shortage in England? Have all the westbound ships sunk into the sea? Did they stop selling paper for six bits a ream?"

"He probably means to write more often than he does. We kept him busy there."

"What does he look like? I can't even remember the color

of his hair, it's been so long." A child ran past and Sister
Kimball called out. The boy stopped. "Is your hair brown or
just dirty?"

"Brown, Ma."

"That's Heber's color, isn't it, Sister Dinah? Tell me it is,
or I won't have any way of knowing which of these children
are mine."

Dinah laughed. Just then a little twig of wood was sprung
by the husband-saver, making a sound as loud as a gun going
off nearby. Dinah gasped and backed away, afraid that she had
broken the machine. Sister Kimball just got up and cut the yarn
with a knife that was lying nearby. "Pop goes the weasel," she
said. "Can you figure how to string a new skein on it?"

"I used to thread the spinning jennies—I think I can manage
it with yarn, Sister Kimball."

"My name's Vilate. You used to work with all those big
machines?"

"Every day for years."

"And a little thing like a husband-saver makes you jump
a yard. Oh well. What you aren't used to is what gives you a
fright. Heber wrote me that you were the second most beautiful
woman he'd ever seen. Near drove me crazy trying to figure
out who was the first. He also said you're worth your weight
in beaver skins. That's a compliment. What'd you come for?
I'm pretty sure you didn't come for yarn-skeining lessons."

"Maybe I did," Dinah said. "I came for advice."

"Well, that's free. Tell me everything, Sister Dinah, only
don't expect me to answer till I'm through with my count."

So Dinah told her dilemma while Vilate counted. It was
disconcerting to have Vilate triumphantly announce "thirty"
from time to time; once or twice Dinah almost decided that the
older woman wasn't listening at all, that coming to her had
been a mistake. But she was here, and so she asked her question. "So what can a woman do to make money?"

"Thirty." Vilate set down the squares. "I can't talk and count
at the same time. So you do the squares now, and I'll do the
yarn." With that they traded places, and Vilate began her response as if it were an oration. "In these hard times when
everybody's a bit hungry except the dishonest and the dead,
it's hard enough to find work for a man, let alone a woman.
But there's some things that you can do, if you're not too proud

and don't expect to make more than a pittance at it. If you're out to get rich, you joined the wrong church and came to the wrong city. But I figure you to be in the right church and the right city, so here's what you do. It just so happens that there's a shortage of shirts in this town, and an oversupply of men who need wrapping. There's also a shortage of money, and cloth is none too plentiful. So if you're clever with a needle, you beg old shirts from big men, rip out the seams, cut good smaller pieces out of them, and come up with good new shirts for smaller men and children. Then you sell them and you've had no cost except labor."

A few moments of silence.

"Thirty," Dinah said. "Is anybody else doing that?"

"I doubt it. I just thought of it. Keep counting. The drawbacks are that old shirts are likely to be dirty, faded, thin, and worn. Also, the poor are just as glad to take an old shirt, holes and all, without nobody fixing it up. Gladder, in fact, because they don't have to pay for it. In fact, just about the only people who'd buy the shirts are people with only a little bit of money and a wish to look respectable."

"Is there anyone like that?"

"Did you lose count?"

"Twenty-two, twenty-three."

"Just don't want any stacks to come up short. Yes, I'd say just about half of Nauvoo has a few cents here and there and wishes to look as if they had more. I'm ashamed to say we have never overcome our love of looking wealthy. Why, you walk around Nauvoo and find nothing but sham. The ones who look real poor are probably better off and just pretending, so that they can live off the charity of their neighbors. The ones who look like they're doing decent are probably really poor, only they keep up the looks of money. The ones who look downright rich are probably so deep in debt it takes three days for sunlight to reach them."

"And what about those who are really rich?"

"Why would a rich man live here? In three days Brother Joseph would have talked him into loaning the Church all his money so we can buy land for the immigrants, and then the Prophet'd get him to borrow ten times that much to help the Church pay its debts. Rich people don't last long here. They either stop being rich or get out quick as they can."

Vilate's humor had a sting in it. Dinah heard the sting too

well, the humor not enough. Vilate had come as such a relief after this morning of anxiety that Dinah assumed too much, believed that Vilate would answer *all* her fears; believed that Vilate would also answer her doubts about the Prophet. So she plunged in and began to tell her fears about Joseph Smith. But because she dared not confess what disturbed her most, the fact that he had stood half-naked before her and owned her with a look, she began with what she knew was petty criticism.

"You can't blame people for wanting to look better than they are when they see the Prophet himself doing the same thing," Dinah said. "I suppose I shouldn't have expected any better than the sham I saw yesterday, when he bullied a man out of town and then boasted to the crowd about what a fine—"

The husband-saver stopped. Startled, Dinah looked up.

"What number are you at?"

From the dread she felt at knowing Vilate was offended, Dinah realized how much she liked this woman. "Seven."

Vilate stood up and took the stack from her. "Thank you kindly for your help. I'll manage just fine from here."

"I can finish. I'm in no hurry."

"Sister Kirkham, I'll gladly feed you if you're hungry, clothe you if you're naked, and nurse you if you're sick, but I won't be friends with anyone who talks against the Prophet."

Dinah could not think what to say. She had not meant to talk against Joseph Smith, she had meant to ask for reassurance. Now she could not argue, for she knew Vilate was right. So she fell back on the habit of childhood and said nothing.

With Vilate Kimball responses were merely optional anyway. "A man who has walked and talked with the Savior is not a sham in my book, Sister Kirkham. Others may talk him down, but not where I can hear, and certainly not in my house. I don't know how to make myself plainer."

Dinah got up from her chair and started for the door, feeling so humiliated and confused that she made a wrong turn in the hall. Vilate caught her by the arm and steered her the right way. "Mind you, I'm not saying you don't have a right to your opinion. There are plenty of folks in town who'd be glad to hear any mockery you care to make. I'm just not one of them."

At last Dinah found a few true words. "I wasn't mocking," she said.

"Well, whatever you call it, you said it and I heard it.

There's much to correct in Nauvoo, but where Brother Joseph is concerned, it's us that need to line up with him, not him who should line up with us."

It was only a matter of seconds since Dinah had said the offending words, and now Vilate was firmly guiding Dinah onto the front porch. It was frightening how quick and irresistible the eviction had been. One moment Dinah was sitting there feeling as if she had found a true sister among the American Saints, and the next moment she felt as if she were being cast down to hell. It wasn't fair. And so she stopped cold in the doorway and stared Vilate in the face. "Sister Kimball, I think you are being unjust to me."

Vilate stared right back. "I don't have to hear a whole hymn to know which one it is, I can recognize it from the first line. You are singing apostasy, and I've heard that one too often already."

"I am as faithful a Latter-day Saint as you are likely to find."

"Oh, I know. That's what they all say. 'I'm the faithful one, it's the Prophet Joseph who has fallen, the Lord has refused that man because he changed a word in the Book of Commandments, or because he spelled my name wrong in a revelation, or because a prophecy didn't come true just the way I wanted.' I've heard it so often I near puke whenever it comes again. Excuse me for not talking like a lady, but I say what I think, and I'll tell you this—if you think you can love the gospel and despise the man who the Lord chose to give it to us, well, you're as dumb as they come, and that's a fact."

This time Vilate's hand against her back was not to be resisted. Dinah stepped onto the porch and Vilate stepped back into the house. The door began to close. "Wait!" Dinah cried out.

The door stopped a few inches ajar.

"Please. How can I be your friend again?"

She waited for Vilate to say, "You can't," or worse, for her just to close the door. Instead, the door opened a few inches and Vilate peered out quizzically. "Now that's something I never heard an apostate say before," Vilate said.

"I said it all wrong. I'm not what you think. I'm just trying to find out why I'm *here*."

Vilate cocked her head and then nodded slightly. "You just go back and meet Brother Joseph again, and this time don't look at him like a farmer glaring at a stump in his field. When you look at him, just keep thinking, the gospel is true, and the Lord gave it to *him* first."

"How will that help me understand him?" Dinah asked.

"What do you want to understand him for? Either you love him or you hate him, but I never heard of a soul who understood him. Now you run along and make shirts, and come back to me when you've figured out whether Brother Joseph is real or a sham, and whether you love him or hate him. If he's your friend, then for sure I am, because I must say you're a likeable woman. Besides, Heber thinks the world of you, and he's sometimes right about people."

With that the door closed. Dinah looked at it empty-headedly for a while as the children raced around in the yard. Then she made her way to the road. She wasn't sure whether she was angry or ashamed, but about one thing she knew Vilate was right. Dinah was a fool if she thought she could separate Mormonism from Joseph Smith. The whole church was like him, wasn't it? Cocksure of itself, sure that all of history was only prelude to this moment, and unable to understand how anyone could disbelieve. That was the very thing she hated worst about Brigham Young. It was also the very thing she liked best about Heber Kimball. But Brother Joseph—why did he have to stand so large? Everywhere she walked in Nauvoo today, she saw his shadow across it. She'd never know who Dinah Handy was in Nauvoo until she decided who Dinah was to Joseph Smith.

All day she went from door to door, calling at the biggest houses in town. And when she got home she had seven old shirts, a spool of thread, and a headache sharp enough to whittle stone. Instead of eating dinner she ripped seams and cut and patched. Anna found her in the morning, asleep in a chair, holding a nearly finished shirt in one hand. In the other hand she held a needle, and in her sleep her hand had closed a little, enough to drive the point of the needle into her palm. Dinah looked so peaceful in her sleep and her headache had been so bad the night before that Anna could not bear to wake her. And yet the needle could not be left like that. So Anna gently opened Dinah's fingers, then pulled on the needle. It slipped smoothly out of Dinah's skin, pulling at it only a little, drawing a thread of blood after it that trailed loosely down Dinah's palm and onto her apron. Anna winced to see it, but because Dinah

slept on with no sign of pain, Anna said nothing and let her
sleep.

Dinah was drifting through an unintelligible dream when
she felt something passing through her hand as gently as a fish
drifting through a pool. It roused her a little, enough that her
dream changed, took a shape that she knew. She was opening
and closing her hand on emptiness, reaching to find something.
She could see it: it was the face of God, the face that she had
seen so often in dreams before; he stood just out of reach,
holding out his hand to her, reaching for something she held,
flowing with light. She reached, but she had nothing to give
him. Seeing that, he pulled away, shaking his head. No! she
cried in her dream. You can't go now that I've finally seen
you! But he turned away. He reached down and drew to him
something that hung limp as cloth from his hand. Then, legs
and hips and arms and chest, he donned it like a suit, concealing
his glory within it so that the dazzling light was gone. It was
a man's body, ordinary flesh, strong and tangible and inglorious, and on his face he wore a man mask, too, and it was
the face of Joseph Smith. Now the naked hand reached out to
her. Timidly she touched it, and it was there, she could feel
it, feel it so sharply that it hurt and she cried out in the joy of
it.

"Hush, Dinah. You shouldn't fall asleep with a needle in
your hand. You could get blood poisoning from it." Anna was
daubing vinegar on Dinah's palm with a rag. "I'm sorry to
wake you, but if you leave a wound like that it can fester."

"It's all right," Dinah said.

"Were you dreaming? I thought you were awake, you were
humming and nodding, but then you didn't answer me."

"Yes. It was a—just a dream."

"A true one? Or just indigestion?"

"I don't know. I haven't eaten."

"You've got to eat. It's one thing to decide to work for
money, but you don't have to do all these shirts in the same
day. You especially shouldn't stay up all night doing them.
The night air isn't healthy if you breathe it sitting up, it causes
the phlegm to fill your lungs."

"Or an incubus to press you."

"What?"

"One of Charlie's books. Incubus, succubus—demons that
come to you in your sleep."

Anna stared at her aghast. "Did a demon come to you?"

"Don't bind my hand so tightly, Mother. I have to be able to hold a needle."

"Let be for a day at least."

"I haven't a day. I haven't an hour. I have work to do."

"Oh, Dinah, the Lord will provide."

Dinah looked away from her mother. Anna was getting old, as if coming to America were the end of her life, not the beginning, as if she had died and could rest now.

But perhaps Anna was not wholly wrong. The Lord would provide, yes; not necessarily food for the table, but that was not what Dinah needed most. Things kept happening to her, and only God knew why; God could take the madness of events and give them meaning. Perhaps the dream was a true one, as true as what she felt the night she was converted. Perhaps Joseph Smith was wearing a disguise. He masqueraded as an ordinary man to allow him to touch ordinary people; if he revealed to them who he really was, it would blind them all. The man of brag and bullying was just a role. It was not his nakedness that had disturbed her, it was the fact that even his flesh was a disguise. But when his eyes said, "You are mine," then it was the light of God that spoke to her. Despite his flesh, he was still as holy as she had so long imagined him to be.

She finished two shirts in two days. Anna grumbled at having to do the housework alone, but Dinah ignored her. The needle leapt through the seams. The pieces clung together almost by themselves, it seemed, and when she was done the iron was hardly needed, for the seams were flat and smooth as if the shirts had been woven whole.

"Back already?" Vilate Kimball asked when she opened the door.

Dinah held out the shirts. "Are they good enough to sell?" she asked.

Vilate pulled one up by the collar, letting the folds fall open. She studied it for a few moments and then looked at Dinah with wide eyes. "Oh, you're a marvel with a needle, aren't you? Yes, you can sell these. Though I expect you'd prefer not to offer them door to door. If you like, I can show them to ladies who come by. These'll sell in a day." Vilate raised her eyebrows. "Is two bits price enough for them?"

Dinah had no notion what "two bits" meant.

"A quarter," Vilate said. "Twenty-five cents."

It was pitiful. "It was a whole day's work on each."

"New ones cost much less than a dollar. Yours are so good, though, that I haven't the heart to sell them for a dime. That's what used shirts go for, by and large, if they got no holes." Vilate studied the shirt again. "Keep this up, Sister Dinah. The pay isn't much but it'll be steady, and it's more than a lot of folks is getting anymore. Will you have another done tomorrow?"

"It'll be done by suppertime tonight."

"Bring it by tonight, then. I'll wager these'll be sold already. Now if you'll excuse me, I have to go to Sister Cline's. She just lost her youngest girl, and it'd be a shame if there wasn't someone there to help her dress the baby for the burial."

Vilate tossed Dinah's shirts onto a chair just inside and then was off down the path toward the street, her hoop skirt flouncing over the icy ground. Then she stopped and turned. "Oh, Sister Dinah—Sister Emma mentioned yesterday at the quilting bee that she hoped you'd drop by her house sometime soon."

"What for?" Dinah asked.

"If she'd wanted to tell me, I reckon she would've tole me." And with that Vilate was into the street and gone.

Twenty-five cents a shirt would be a dollar fifty a week, with Sunday for resting. With the little bit that Charlie earned, it might just be enough to get by. But this wasn't Sunday, and so she dared not get behind. As for Sister Emma wanting to see her—that could only mean that Vilate had told the Prophet's wife what Dinah had said. Dinah had no wish to go and be ashamed before that good woman, or to run the risk of meeting Brother Joseph again. Dinah did not know which she feared most: that Joseph would know what she thought of him two days ago, or that he would look at her and see what she thought of him today.

Oblivious as Charlie often was to the world around him, it was three days after he got home from Springfield before he realized that Dinah was remaking shirts and selling them. "Don't you think I'm doing my best?" Charlie asked.

"Of course you are," Dinah said.

"I can't bring in the kind of money I had in Manchester; it isn't fair for you to expect it!"

"I don't expect it. Why are you so angry, Charlie? Our

savings were getting low, that's all. I've worked before when times were hard."

"This isn't Manchester! This is America, and in America decent women don't work for pay. Not like this, begging shirts from door to door. You might as well walk down the street calling out, 'Charlie Kirkham can't provide for his family.'"

"Charlie," Dinah said impatiently, "no one even knows who Charlie Kirkham *is*."

It was the wrong thing to say. Charlie jammed his hands into his jacket pockets and turned his back on her.

"Charlie," Dinah said softly. "Charlie, what harm does it do if I work for money? It's not as if I had a husband to care for. And what will we do if you get married? We need to be self-sufficient, not always depending on *you*."

"If I were dependable, you wouldn't be thinking about that."

"Charlie, we all do our best."

"You could have told me, at least. Don Carlos spent ten minutes strutting in his new shirt and teasing me about how he was milking my cow before he finally realized I didn't know you had sold him the shirt."

"I don't know who buys them. Sister Vilate sells them for me."

"And when he found out I didn't even know you were doing it, you could hear him laugh clear to Iowa."

"Charlie, it's been no secret. You've seen me sewing every day since you got back from Springfield."

"I thought they were my shirts."

"You don't own that many shirts."

"I don't care! I want you to quit doing it, that's all!"

"I'm sorry. It's something I can *do*."

"Why can't you be like other women? Why do you have to keep trying to be a man?"

That made Dinah angry, and so she said something cruel. "The last person to say that to me was Robert." The mention of their older brother's name stung Charlie into silence. Dinah at once softened her tone. "If it's going to bother you to see me sewing, Charlie, then I suggest you stay out later at night and leave earlier in the morning."

"You can bet that I will."

"And try not to be so quarrelsome. It's a hard time for everyone, not just for you."

"Is that *all*, Sister Handy?"

"You're truly Robert's brother, after all," Dinah said.

Charlie glared at her and left the house.

Dinah's hands were trembling so that she could hardly thread the needle, and she had to unpick the seam she had been working on during the quarrel. She shouldn't have let it make her so angry. It was absurd to have a quarrel at all. Why was it that whenever a man was failing, that was the one time he couldn't bear to have a woman help him? What was she supposed to do, starve so that he wouldn't be embarrassed?

This place has twisted us all. Surely Saints should be most holy when among their fellow Saints; yet when all your neighbors, good and bad, are Mormons, you no longer think of them as precious friends. They can be unmannered, their children can have snotty noses, and you half suspect them of stealing from your garden—and they are the Saints you are supposed to love. In Manchester, being Mormons was itself so unique that they needed no other name to know they were important. Here, they had to struggle for other ways to name themselves. Charlie was working incompetently at odd jobs, dreaming of being the Prophet's scribe and an industrialist all at once. Father was smelling up the house with his paints. Anna was drifting, waiting for God to make things right.

And I, Dinah thought. What am I doing? She didn't know. When she tried to name herself all she could think of was the Prophet clothed in disguising flesh. She wondered if she, too, were in disguise, What would I be, if I could shed this veil of flesh?

A knock on the door. Anna answered—she loved the chat of neighbors who had likewise given up on improving themselves. Dinah plied her needle without looking up, but soon became aware of a woman coming to her, standing before her. She realized, to her surprise, that the visitor had come for *her*.

It was Emma Smith. "Good day," she said.

Dinah got up, letting pieces of the shirt she was assembling fall to the floor. "Sister Emma! Sit down! If I had known you were coming—"

"You would have found some way to avoid me."

"No," Dinah protested. "How could you think it?" But it was true, though Dinah could not understand why she felt so ashamed of herself before this good woman.

"I asked Vilate to invite you to my home, and you didn't come."

"I thought your invitation was only—courtesy."

"Even if it were, does that make it less of an invitation? May I sit down?"

"I'm forgetting all my manners—please, yes." Of course she was embarrassed to have the Prophet's wife visit after what she said about Joseph. That explained Dinah's confusion. "Forgive the clutter, I'm sewing—"

"That's what I came about, Sister Dinah. I brought a snatch of linen. I wondered if you could make my husband a couple of shirts." Emma pulled a good length of cloth from the basket she carried. "Is it enough?"

"Oh, of course. But I'm not really a seamstress, I just remake old shirts."

"Your work is meticulous and you are grossly underpaid. I offer you sixty cents for each."

"I would do them for free—"

"Nonsense. Everyone in town is Mormon. So if we all did favors for fellow Saints, we'd starve in perfect harmony."

Dinah did not know what to say. Emma sat upright in her chair. Her cold way of speaking had good feeling in it—unlike some people, Dinah had known that from the first. Yet today her coldness masked even more coldness. Dinah knew what was coming, and dreaded it. Well, she would face it squarely and soon.

"Sister Vilate told me that you wanted to see me—even before I had sold a single shirt."

"Yes," Emma said. "Yes." She looked toward the window, as if her next words were inscribed in the sky. "You are a well-beloved woman, Dinah. There are hundreds of English-women who look up to you. One of them told me the other day that you were—a sort of prophetess, she said."

"She did me no kindness to say so."

"She loves you, Sister Dinah." Emma stood suddenly and walked to the window. "Whether you know it or not, you have influence among a large number of the Saints." Then she turned back, and Dinah was shocked to see that in those few short moments she had wept enough that her cheeks were shiny with tears, her face somewhat reddened and twisted with grief.

"Sister Emma," Dinah said, rising.

"Do you know how many people there are who want my husband dead? Six months he was in jail under sentence of death, and do you know who delivered him up to his enemies? Saints. Good, loyal Saints, who thought they knew better than he did. They've turned on him so often, the ones he loved and trusted best. He loved no one better than Oliver Cowdery, and he's gone. David Whitmer, and he's quit us. Thomas Marsh and Orson Hyde as much as called for his death. Time after time, the people who have done him the most harm are Saints who found he did not measure up to what they thought he ought to be."

As suddenly as the crying had begun, Emma visibly got herself under control. She sat again in her chair. Immediately her voice was steady. Immediately her face set back into its icy repose. Only the glistening tears remembered her emotion. "I thought when we met that you were a woman of understanding, that you would be such a help. The problems are so great, and you have such promise. But how can I depend on you, if you turn against Joseph like the others?"

So Vilate had reported the whole conversation. Well, what else could Dinah expect? If they saw her as a woman of influence, it mattered if she seemed to have spoken against Emma's husband. Dinah would bear the burden of her own mistakes. "I said something other than what I truly meant. I am not good at choosing words."

Emma almost smiled. "On the contrary. Joseph said you have a gift for saying exactly what ought to be said. Which always means, he said, exactly what people least want to hear." Emma looked out the window again. "And perhaps your words were justified. There are times when Joseph gets in an odd humor and he must grapple with someone and take him down, he must joke and brag and have the Saints adore him. Perhaps it's even a fault in him, though *I* love him for it. But speaking against him, Dinah—that's no little thing. Someday it will cost him his life, when enough people have said enough little things. Perhaps you don't know how a wife lives in her husband— you didn't love yours."

It was a terrible accusation for one woman to make against another. And yet Dinah realized that now in the middle of what should have been a painful conversation, she was filled with relief. It was not her *words* about Joseph or her problems with

Matthew that Dinah had been afraid to discuss. *This* she could handle with trite phrases and easy poses. "I think," Dinah said, "that I am not glad to learn that my miserable marriage is such common knowledge."

"Oh, no, not at all. I had it from Joseph, and he had it in a letter from Brigham Young. Brigham is something of a gossip—he wrote to warn Joseph that you were headstrong and spiritual."

Dinah could tell from her tone of voice that Emma wasted little love on the senior Apostle.

"But don't fear that it's common knowledge," Emma said, "because it isn't. I only mention it because you cannot possibly know how I fear you."

Now Dinah was faced with what she really dreaded: that Emma had discovered what Dinah really felt about—about— what she could not name. "Fear *me!*"

"You're one more person who will have the power to harm him. Because he'll trust you—he's never learned to be suspicious. And if you, too, turn on him, then you have done nothing good, Dinah, because he is the heart and mind of this Church, and if you undo him you have undone God's work."

"Then let me assure you, Sister Emma, that I will never lift a hand or speak a word that will harm either him or you."

Emma searched Dinah's face for truth. Her gaze was so piercing that Dinah wondered if Emma's eyes had found the secret that Dinah herself could not name. But no. What Emma saw made her eyes soften. "Then you *are* my friend, as I thought the night I met you?"

It was a moment when with other women Dinah would have felt a need for an embrace. With Emma, though, embracing wouldn't have felt right. They leaned forward in their chairs, clasped each other's hands, looked into each other's faces and read the love there. Distance remained between them—but then, without some distance you cannot see. And yet even as they touched, Dinah felt herself trembling with shame. I am doing you an injury that even *I* have not discovered yet. I am lying when I promise friendship, and yet I cannot understand why it's a lie.

It is *not* a lie, Dinah told herself. I love this woman, and if I can help it she'll have no truer friend than I. And to make sure of it, Dinah said it aloud. "Sister Emma, I love you. And you can trust me as much as any other woman."

Emma bowed over their clasped hands a moment before arising to leave. She made an appointment four days off for Dinah to come and measure the Prophet for the shirts. Then she left. Afterward, Dinah tried to go back to work on the shirt she had been sewing, but she couldn't keep her mind on it. First Charlie came home, wanting to talk about how he would raise money to build a factory. She nodded and agreed without listening, until Charlie went away and told it all to Mother, and then again to Father.

"What do you mean you'll build it *here?*" Anna's voice was angry and too near; Dinah found that the hem had slipped. She started picking it out. "I thought when you said a chandler's shop you meant you were buying one that already stood somewhere else—"

"This is the only land I have," Charlie said. "I didn't borrow enough to lease land, only enough to get up a decent shed to do the work."

"Charlie, have you ever *smelled* a chandler's shop?"

"It won't smell half as bad as when I start in making soap."

"Why do you want us to live in foul smells and filth?" Mother was starting to cry. Dinah thought it was a terrible sound—she was too old for this petulance. "Didn't we work hard enough to escape the factories, and now you have to bring them right back in our own garden?"

"Haven't you heard of money, Mother? It's what people live on. And you don't get more than a damned scant trickle of it if you work for someone else. Well, I'll have *them* working for me. Dinah's not going to have to go out and solicit work like a street peddler." Of course, thought Dinah. It's because of me, never because he wants to be rich. Yet she said nothing as she sat and undid her work.

"What do you know of making soap?" Father asked.

"I know how money works, and how you use it to get more. What do I care for soap? Or candles? It's going to be done, and that's it. I'm doing it all for you, aren't I? And after a few months of stinks and smells we'll be able to build a decent house and move away from here. A house of our own, down closer to the rest of town." Charlie saw that his promise of a rosy future was not convincing them. "What is it that's making you so angry? Would you be happier starving?"

And on and on and on. Dinah tried not to hear it, pretended

that she was not listening, until she discovered she had unpicked the entire hem, not just the part that was badly done. Her mind was not on this work. She picked up her sewing to take it to the other room, where it would be quieter. She stopped when she found herself reaching for the linen Emma had brought. Suddenly that linen was hot as fire; she dared not touch it. Don't be a fool. She picked it up and took it into her room.

Even with the argument muffled by a door, she could not concentrate on remaking the old shirt. The needle was rebellious in its track; it did not want to stitch this shirt. And so she laid the shirt aside, and took up the linen.

She laid it on the table and began to draw. She took the pattern from the shirts she had remade the last few days. She took the size from her memory of him standing just so far away, his shoulders this wide, his chest this broad and deep, his waist so narrow, his back so long when it bent over the man, his arms hanging easy this long, his arms extended that long. She knew her memory of him was so true that she did not hesitate when it came time to cut; the shears bit into the linen in great swooping lines. She finished one, she finished the other, her needle flying through the work, until in two days they both were done.

Only then did she lay out the shirts across her bed and think, God in heaven, what have I done? She was not afraid that the shirts would not fit. She was afraid because she hadn't the slightest doubt that they would. How could she know his body so perfectly from that quarter-hour in the late afternoon sun? Why had she held the memory so well, when already she had trouble picturing Honor in her mind, or remembering Val when she wanted to? Who am I, that I know the Prophet's body better than I know that faces of my daughter and my son?

And when she had carefully folded the shirts and put them in a basket to deliver them, she realized that she could not possibly bring them now. She had never measured him. If she brought the shirts now, Emma would surely know.

Know what? Dinah rebuked herself. I have no terrible secret. I happened to see the Prophet wrestling shirtless in the mud. I have a keen eye, he stood right in front of me and so of course I can measure him against myself. It means nothing. I have nothing to conceal. She carried the basket out the door and into the windy street.

She knocked at the door of the Smith house. There was no

answer. She knocked again, and it fell open a little before her. Remembering how Vilate Kimball had told her just to come in, Dinah wondered if she could at least look inside, in case the wind had been so loud that she simply hadn't heard someone bid her enter.

The hall was empty, and there wasn't a sound within. Perhaps Emma was back in the kitchen. Bringing the door just up to the jamb, Dinah went around back. Again no one answered to her knock. All out somewhere, of course. Her measuring appointment was tomorrow—she should have waited till then anyway. Yet she did not go home. Instead she went into the parlor and sat on a chair. Emma would not mind if she came in and sat awhile. And Dinah needed the money.

She held the basket on her lap, and because there was nothing else to do, she opened it and took out the top shirt. Laying it across the basket, she toyed with the button at the neck, examined the tiny seam that she had done so perfectly, even though it would be hidden by the collar and no one would ever see.

"It's a sin to love what your own hands have made."

The Prophet stood in the parlor doorway. His hair was disheveled, and he wasn't wearing his coat or even a waistcoat—just his shirt and trousers.

"You were asleep," Dinah said. "I didn't mean to wake you."

"I heard the door open. I came down to see what the burglars had taken."

Dinah blushed. "I did knock, and when I thought no one was home, I came in to wait."

"I thought your appointment was tomorrow. Did you come to show me samples of your work? Don Carlos already did."

"Don Carlos advertises too well for me already."

"Let me see it." He reached out, and she handed it to him. "Who is this for? This is new linen."

"Yes," Dinah said.

"And the size of it. There aren't three men in the city besides me who could wear it."

She was afraid to tell him the obvious. He did not need to be told.

"Let me try it on," he said. He began unbuttoning his shirt. "Did Emma give you my measurements? I don't know how she could. She hasn't made me a shirt in years. I keep her too busy at the domestic slavery here."

Dinah didn't answer. She was too busy studying the sky framed by lace curtains. She was afraid that if she saw his body again she would discover things about herself that she did not want to know.

"It fits," Joseph said.

She turned and looked. The linen flowed over his body, smoothly across the woodchopper's chest, slackly down the wrestler's belly, to where it bloused at the waist. Yes, it was right, it was a good fit.

"Tailors always manage to get the arms too small."

She had know to lengthen the sleeves. And make the shoulders more copious than the pattern. And the breast of the shirt broad enough for a man who could crack a man's ribs with a flex of his arms.

"You didn't have my measurements, did you?" Joseph said.

She shook her head.

"You only saw me once."

"You stood close," she said. "I could remember."

"Charlie didn't tell me that you were a seamstress. Still less one who works miracles."

"It's not a miracle," Dinah said. "I—have an eye for that sort of thing."

"Charlie's a marvel for ciphering, adds up the columns faster than I can read the numbers. He says you're the smarter one. Is it true?"

"It isn't."

"Charlie's a liar, then?"

"Will the shirts do?"

"Haven't I made it plain? They're the best shirts I've ever owned."

"I'm glad." She got up from the chair and handed him the other shirt. "I should leave now. I've interrupted your rest long enough."

"Don't go," he said.

"It's snowing. I should go home."

"When Emma gets back I'll send you in the carriage."

"I can't."

"Sister Dinah, I want to talk to you."

But Dinah was afraid to talk to him. Afraid because the

shirts had fit; afraid because by chance he was home alone, which never happened; afraid because his eyes still looked at her and said, Mine, and because somewhere in her was something that answered, impossibly, Yours.

"I'm looking for a schoolteacher," Joseph said.

"Oh," Dinah said. It was so anticlimactic that she almost laughed. That was what he saw when he looked at her—a schoolteacher!

"For my children. I'm starting up a school. The children are learning nothing right now, they don't like their master, I thought a clever woman rather than a man—men always get too impressed with themselves for teaching the Prophet's children. They start trying to make friends with me so I'll give them a *good* position. I don't suppose you want to do it, though. Cooped up like a hen in a cockfight, the little demons'd have you up the walls in half an hour."

Suddenly her fears seemed absurd. He wanted her to teach school. She had to laugh. "Brother Joseph, I never went to school. Not beyond the first few years."

"You read and write, don't you? You spell, don't you?"

"I don't know the American system. Your Mr. Webster seems to have forgotten how to make a 'u'."

"Then teach them the English spelling, do you think I care for that? Just so the children don't spell like *me*, that's all." As an afterthought he added, "Emma was a schoolteacher once. She wasn't very patient, though. I think that you'd be patient if they don't learn quickly."

She wasn't sure how to answer. She had lived for years for the sake of Val and Honor, but she had left them. It seemed somehow indecent to abandon her own and then take on someone else's children for money. And yet she was hungry for the sound of small young voices, eager to answer again those impossible questions, those unreasonable demands.

"Or are you too much in love with stitchery to change your line of work?"

"Stitchery!" Dinah said. "No, I'm not in love with it."

"The pay can't be much. A tuition of fifty dollars a year, fifteen or twenty students—rent shouldn't be more than twenty dollars a month—could you live on that?"

Dinah instinctively performed the calculations as he gave the numbers. It might be a thousand dollars a year, with expenses of at least four hundred, counting books and slates and chalk and—

"What about tables and chairs?" Dinah asked.

"Well, to start with we could split a few logs and varnish the smooth face. A few splinters don't do any great harm to little backsides. You'll do it, then?"

"I need the money."

Joseph shook his head. "I don't want a teacher who does it for the money."

"I'm afraid." She had not meant to say it. But he waited for her to go on, and so she did. "That I might come to love them too much."

"Sister Dinah," he said softly. "You can never love children too much. Even the ones who are gone."

The tenderness in his voice spoke of remembered pain. There was no brashness now. The light was bright behind his eyes, and she felt a fire leap in her heart. He knows my sorrow, she told herself.

"I know your sorrow," he said. "And I promise you, Sister Dinah, that your children will forgive you."

It was a promise she had never dared to ask for. And yet coming as it did so close behind her hope, she had no way to refuse it; she believed the promise and wept for joy. He stood there, watching her, but she did not care. He had seen her greatest need and answered it truly.

He brought her a handkerchief and she daubed at her eyes.

"Blow your nose, too," Joseph commanded. "Ladies always pretend their noses never need blowing, as if God made them dry."

She blew her nose, and then laughed at herself for crying when she was so happy. "Thank you," she said. For the handkerchief. For the promise.

"Oh, don't thank *me* for the job. If you can keep my children from growing up fools I'll be thanking *you*. And so will the parents of the other children. We may all be ignorant Americans, ma'am, but we know the value of education. We aim to have our children smarter than we are."

"I don't know how they could," Dinah said. "You are— very wise."

"Like Solomon?" asked Joseph.

"No, not Solomon. For terrifying a woman by threatening

to kill her child? For marrying a thousand women and forsaking the Lord for their sake? If you ask me, Solomon is one of the classic fools of the Old Testament."

She had said too much. He was silent, just as Vilate had been the other day when she had burst out with ill-considered words. She was always better off when she said nothing.

But Joseph wasn't angry. Just thoughtful. As if he were somehow measuring her before he spoke. She held her tongue, though, until he decided to speak. "Do you think," he asked, "that Solomon had all those wives for venery?"

"I never heard that he was celibate."

"No, no," Joseph said, shaking his head. "But those wives were given to him by the Lord. And so were David's wives, except Bathsheba. That was his sin, that he took a wife given to another man, and that he killed to get her. But there was no sin in the plurality of wives."

Dinah could not understand why he was telling her this. And yet he said it carefully, as if it were very, very important.

"I want you to understand Solomon," Joseph said.

"I never think of him at all," Dinah said. "I was just babbling."

"No, no, you weren't," Jospeh said. "I used to think as you did. I've always had a hard enough time being a decent husband to one good woman. I couldn't understand why a man could want a thousand wives."

Dinah thought of Mr. Uray and shuddered. "I've known men who probably wouldn't be satisfied even with that many."

"But not men who were chosen of God," Joseph said. "Not the man that God chose to build his temple."

"No," Dinah said. And then she realized that Joseph, too, was a temple builder, and that when he spoke of Solomon he was also, somehow, speaking of himself.

"It was when I was translating the Old Testament," Joseph said. "There was so much I didn't understand. David and Solomon—I didn't understand why God kept blessing them when they were bigamists a hundred times over. And Abraham, and Jacob, wives and wives and wives."

"Maybe God didn't mind then."

Joseph ignored her. "It was in thirty-one. I remember asking Sidney Rigdon about it. Sidney was so wise, I thought. But he hemmed and hawed a little and said a few things that boiled down to the fact that he hadn't the faintest idea. So I figured I should ask God."

"Did he answer you?"

"He sent an angel."

His tone was too bright, too cheerful. A man should be solemn, talking about such things. And yet couldn't it be such a commonplace to him that he felt no need to get solemn? Or was it something else? He seemed—yes, timid. He was acting the way Charlie did as a child, when he was trying to get away with doing something he knew he shouldn't have done. Too cheerful, as if to forestall anger. "What did the angel say?"

"That it was the order of marriage in heaven."

Dinah thought he was joking, his tone was so light. "I thought that in the next life there was neither marrying nor giving in marriage."

"Those whose marriages have been sealed by the power of God will be married forever, and they'll have posterity and create kingdoms, worlds without end. In fact, it's impossible for a man to be exalted without a marriage sealed by the Holy Spirit of Promise, and the same for a woman. When Paul said the man is not without the woman, nor the woman without the man, he was speaking in the eternal sense."

She thought of being in heaven forever with Matthew. It seemed like a better description of hell.

"When your husband refused the gospel, he became unworthy of you. The Lord won't bind a woman to a swine, Sister Dinah."

"Then I will be a woman without a man, Brother Joseph. He'll never divorce me."

"Don't you know that a wicked man can never stop the Lord from doing righteousness? That man is *not* your husband. He divorced himself from you in the eyes of God the day he forced you to choose between your children and the gospel."

She looked to him with hope. "He is not my husband?"

"In the eyes of God. In the next life, *you* will have the children. Mr. Handy was unworthy. His wife and children will be taken from him and given to another."

This was no jest. The cheerful tone was gone, and he stood now in the middle of the room. She looked in his eyes and the light was now ablaze there. She knew now where his promises were leading, and yet she could not put it into words. Wanted it, but could not name it. And so she answered him with questions. "Given to another! Who? And when?"

"You have been given to me, Sister Dinah."

She could not move, could not speak. Suddenly all she could see was the perfect stretch of white linen across his chest, knowing what lay under the shirt. He had named it, and it was exactly what she had wanted the moment she first saw him, exactly what she had so feared from that moment on. It was not the light of God in his eyes, it was the light of desire, and it was a perverse, criminal desire. It was her own desire, too. The very shirt he wore was proof of that. Her dream was a lie. It was not the light of God disguised in flesh that she desired. It was flesh pretending to contain the light of God. "I must leave," she said.

"Please stay." Stay? She had played this scene before, with Mr. Uray. Then she had been innocent, but now if she stayed it would be consent. Even to hesitate would be a betrayal of Emma, and worse, a betrayal of Val and Honor, who might forgive their mother if she left them for God, but could never forgive her if she left them for adultery. He could not be a prophet and ask for this, she had nothing to gain by staying, she had nothing to lose by going that was not already lost, and yet her feet did not move. She could not understand why she wasn't already at the door, why she was still listening to him.

"Sister Dinah, I will do you no harm. You're as safe with me as with your mother. It's as a wife I want you, honorably, not like a whore."

"You have a wife," Dinah said.

"If you were the sort of woman who would accept this eagerly, you wouldn't be worthy to be asked."

"You wife is my friend."

"My aim is not to corrupt the weak, but to exalt the strong."

She should not have looked at his face again. For he, his voice, though quiet, had power, and the light burned too fiercely in his eyes to be denied; it held her; she could not go. It was not lust: she had seen that in Mr. Uray's dead, inhuman face.

"Sister Dinah," Joseph whispered, "when the Lord first told me that I must do this, I felt as you do now. My wife had sacrificed for me, had lived in wretched poverty, had borne me children. I love her dearly and would never hurt her. I had no desire for any other woman. But the angel of the Lord came to me and told me that all things must be restored or my work would not be complete. If I refused this, the mantle would be taken from me and given to another, and I would be cast out of the Kingdom of God."

She had to answer him, or she would be swept away. And she dared not say the terrible things that she desired. So she put as much contempt in her voice as she could manage. "Does your wife know you do this sort of thing?"

"When I saw you a few days ago, the Spirit whispered to me, This woman will be your wife. When that Spirit speaks, I have learned to obey. Don't you see how the Lord has brought you here today? Don't you see how the Lord has already bound you to me?"

Desperate to end the conversation, desperate to leave, she challenged him on the very ground where she herself was weakest. Witheringly she said, "And of course you had no lust for me at all."

She waited for him to deny it, for him to protest that he was just doing his duty. But instead his face went pale and his gaze went distant, and he whispered, "I could have answered any other woman truthfully. But I can't think of any answer now that wouldn't be a lie." He looked at his hands. They were trembling. "Emma is my wife and she will be forever. If I have to go to hell to fetch her I'll have her with me. I don't want you to take her place. You couldn't do it if you tried."

His tone was so insulting that she was speechless in disbelief. He was the one who had asked for the impossible, and yet now he spoke accusingly, as if she had offended him. But his face immediately softened. "How could I expect you to take this, Sister Dinah? An unmarried man would have courted you, but I can hardly do that. A clever man might have found a way to do this gentler, so you wouldn't be taken by surprise." His eyes glazed with tears. "God has given me no harder commandment to obey. Nothing could be more against my nature. Or against yours, I think. I'm sorry."

"Then let this be the end of the matter," she said.

"I'll not mention it again, if that's what you mean. But it won't be the end of it. The Lord has commanded it, and you *will* marry me. Of your own free will, you'll come to me and tell me that it's time."

"It will not happen," Dinah said.

The tears spilled over his eyelashes. "I wish with all my heart that it would not." Then he turned from her and left the room quickly, as if she were the seducer and he the virgin fleeing from the mere suggestion of a sin. She wanted to scream at him to come back. But what would he do then? He could not unsay what he had said. And she could not change the fact that she had never been more certain of his truthfulness than at the very moment she had proof that he was false.

She took her basket and left his house, terrified that at any moment Emma would appear before her, and know where she had been, and know what had been said. Terrified because Dinah knew that she should confess to Emma, tell her at once exactly what her husband had done, and yet she knew that she would not. Dinah would keep silent about it, would conspire with Joseph that far at least, to keep Emma ignorant of it. In her heart she was already a traitor, even though Dinah was sure that she would never accept his unspeakable proposal. For she also knew that her very silence was the first step toward accepting it, and to her shame, deep within her she was glad.

❧ 29 ❧

Charlie Banks Kirkham
Nauvoo, 1841

CHARLIE'S FACTORY WAS STILL only a naked frame, but Don Carlos pointedly walked through the door. "I want to see it the way it's going to be," Don Carlos explained. "You can bet it ain't worth seeing the way it *is.*"

It was the respect that was true, not the joke. Charlie spread his arms and asked, "What do you think of it?"

"I feel a draft."

"Putting on the walls may cut part of that."

Don Carlos strode to the fireplace. "I suppose this is where all the soap will be made."

"And the candles."

"Then I suppose you'll want your own office as far from it as possible."

"Of course."

"And you'll spend as little time there as possible."

Thinking of the possibility of someday serving as the Prophet's scribe while living off the income of the factory, Charlie nodded.

"A man after my own heart, Charlie. I know men who work all their lives just so they can get enough money that they don't have to work anymore. Hell, I've got that *now*."

"You don't have any money at all."

"I'm better off than *you*. This place must have you up to your ears."

Charlie shrugged. "If you don't have any capital, you have to borrow some."

"What I can't figure out is how a mere child like you could get a rich man to lend to you."

"I know what I'm doing," Charlie said. "I'm a good credit risk."

"Of course you are," Don Carlos answered, pushing a knot through a plank. "You're not nineteen till summer, you haven't got a dime in the world, you're living in a house you can't possibly pay for, you have no job, and you've never worked for a chandler or a soapmaker in your life. Of course you're a good credit risk."

Charlie didn't understand why it was funny, but went along, as always, with the joke. "Brother Ullery recognized my true worth, that's all."

"Old flint-heart Ullery. They say the only man he's ever lent money to before is the Prophet Joseph, and even then he let it be known he regarded it as a contribution—he didn't expect to get it back."

"He'll get *this* back," Charlie said.

Don Carlos grinned and turned to the half-built stairway. "Is this place going to have a second story?"

"An attic room, at first. But someday there'll be another floor, depending on business."

"You really have your eye on the future, don't you, Charlie?" Don Carlos balanced his way up the stringer. "Lovely home, mum, but the stairway's a bit narrow. Could do with a banister. Oh, look here, what a view! I can see the entire ground floor from any point in the second story."

While Don Carlos clowned, Charlie made connections in what he had said before. Flint-heart Ullery never lent money to anyone except Brother Joseph. Charlie was a poor credit risk, after all. It didn't take a fool to figure it out. "So Brother Joseph got me the loan."

"He believes in you."

Charlie understood. Brother Joseph believed in Charlie Kirkham, but not in his own brother. Don Carlos would never have got the loan. "I'm sorry," Charlie said.

Don Carlos dropped suddenly from the rafters down to the floor, rolled and came up half-sprawled. "Oh, Charlie, why can't I be more like you? I work hard—sometimes, anyway. The paper comes out, doesn't it? The children are never very hungry, they're decently clothed, most people like me well enough. Even my wife. But I'll never amount to anything."

Charlie knew that what Don Carlos said was at least half true. But there were other ways to measure a man besides money, Charlie knew. "He loves you more than he loves anyone. Everyone knows that."

Don Carlos leaned back his head and looked straight up into the roof. "Winter is a hell of a time to build a factory."

"I know. I'd rather clerk for Brother Joseph at no wages. But he won't take me."

"Because there are enough beggars in Nauvoo. Make this place prosper, Charlie. Employ some men and pay them decently. Get rich. Then Joseph can afford to have you beside him. He likes you." Don Carlos let his head hang farther and farther back, until he could see through the frame to the house beyond. "Your house has a certain charm to it, upside down. Like a boat. Does it leak?"

"A little."

"You can bail. And look! There's part of your menagerie. Two by two. Only they're going out instead of coming in."

Charlie looked where Don Carlos pointed. Two women were emerging from the house. He grimaced. "The Clinton sisters."

Still upside down, Don Carlos intoned, "Like blossoms, they turn their skirts upward to the warm face of the ground."

"They visit whenever I'm not there. Conspiring with my mother to get me to marry."

"Not necessarily a bad idea. Do you get to choose which one you want?"

"I have things to do before I get married."

"Who scrubs your back in the tub, Charlie?"

Without thinking, Charlie blurted out the truth. "My mother."

Don Carlos laughed, then rolled over and looked at Charlie with an earnest, comical expression. "Those Clinton sisters, they look like they could bear fifteen children each and not hardly notice it."

"That's what I'm afraid of," Charlie said.

Don Carlos got quickly to his feet. "Are you now, Charlie? Do you think this factory makes you a man, because you can sign your name and walls go up? Well, let me tell you a secret. You aren't even *here* until you have children. You don't even *exist*. But when you've got them, when they love you with their whole hearts and trust you with their very lives, Charlie, then you could watch a hundred factories like this burn, and you could walk away whistling." Don Carlos jumped through the wall onto the ground outside. "I don't know what you think you've got to do before you get married, but whatever it is, it isn't worth a damn." He grinned and tipped his hat. "If I've offended you, sir, it makes me very glad." Then he turned around and loped away down the road toward home.

Charlie stayed in the building for a while, deliberately not thinking about Sally Clinton. She was all wrong for him, whatever Don Carlos said. He didn't need a baby factory, he needed a rich man's wife because by God he was going to be a rich man. Sally Clinton, pretty as she was, had the manners of the working class. Charlie had been around enough moneyed men and ladies to know the difference. Sally simply wouldn't do, not in the future Charlie had planned for himself.

He tried to admire the factory to take his mind off Sally. But Don Carlos had taken away the pleasure of it. The wind picked up a little. Charlie cursed the weather and went into the house.

Mother was ready for him when he came into the house. "It's apparent, Charlie, that for all your good judgment about other things, you are not a good judge of women."

"I take it that Sally Clinton came to call."

"You know she did," Anna said. "I saw you and Don Carlos notice the Clinton sisters when they left. You didn't even have the courtesy to wave. Charlie, why do you suppose Sally and Harriette come only when you're not at home?"

Charlie knew why. Because Sally didn't want to burden him with her affection if he didn't want it. So instead she burdened him with his own mother's remonstrances.

"Charlie, a man needs a wife who is strong where he is weak, and who needs him where he is strong. That way they can face everything together. There are hundreds of women in Nauvoo who have just the strength you need. But none loves you more than Sally Clinton."

"What is it that Sally Clinton has that I don't have?"

"Practical good sense, that's what. An eye for what is possible. For the cost of things."

"I have been figuring costs and income and profits and losses since I was little."

"I wasn't talking about money."

"Mother," Dinah said from the cluttered nest where she sewed every day. "You're doing your cause more harm than good."

"Everyone is wiser than I am," Anna said.

"Except me, of course," said Charlie.

And now, from his easel and paintpots by the window, John Kirkham spoke. "I'm not the best one to give advice on marriage, Charlie, but will you listen to me a moment?"

"No," Charlie said.

"Yes he will," said Anna.

"There are two kinds of women that a man can marry," said John. "The kind that's stronger than he is, and the kind that's weaker. I've lived with both, Charlie. It's hard to live with a strong woman, because she makes you afraid sometimes, and sometimes you feel like you aren't in control of your life. But let me tell you, boy, it's a damn sight better than living with a weak woman, because many a man isn't as good as his woman, but I never knew a husband who was *better* than his wife."

"I don't need advice on marriage from you, sir," Charlie said coldly. "Or from any of you. There's not one of you who was particularly good at choosing a mate for yourselves, and it takes some gall for you to presume to choose a wife for me."

It was a rebuke his parents had no answer for, Charlie knew. Only after a few moments of painful silence, however, did he remember that Dinah was in the room. And when he looked at her, the expression on her face told him that he had unwittingly hurt most deeply the one that he would never wish to hurt at all. "Dinah, I'm sorry, I didn't mean—"

She shook her head and looked at her sewing.

"Dinah, I know you never chose your husband, I didn't mean *you.*"

She looked up at him with eyes full of tears, and spoke with a voice husky with held-back pain. "Damn you if you don't marry her, Charlie. Damn you for thinking you're better than her."

Charlie looked at his sister in shock for what seemed like several minutes. Then he fled the room, fled the house, and ran. Uphill, cross-lots, the most difficult path he could find, all the while thinking how unfair it was, they were all against him, Don Carlos and Mother and her husband and even of all people *Dinah* and what possible right did they have to try to push him into marrying someone who was beneath him just because she was good and strong and pretty and loved him more than he deserved—

And when he came to that thought he stopped cold. She loved him more than he deserved, that's what he was running from. Any woman who actually loves me can't be good enough. He remembered that evening in Manchester, when he had desired her. He desired her still. Be honest, Charlie, admit it to yourself. You watched her closely all the way across the Atlantic. You knew every time she smiled at someone else, and even though you were saying to yourself, That's just the sort of lower-class man she should marry, you were jealous as hell.

Charlie looked around and discovered that he had run to the temple site. He studied the flagged and posted ground where the temple was to be and he imagined it being built, the rising stone of the walls grey in the overcast light, the scaffolding climbing it like winter ivy, looking dead. But it was still only a dream, and the vision would not stay. He turned from the place, gazed down at his own hopeful factory, the new wood still bright, and understood something he had not really seen before. The shacks and cabins of Nauvoo were scattered like dirt clods across the frozen ground. But the place was full of seeds. He was one of those seeds. Yet it was as Don Carlos said, he didn't really exist until he bore fruit.

Suddenly, as he looked out over the city, it changed. The pitiful curling threads of smoke from kitchen fires thickened, became great belches from furnace stacks; the greyish, weathering cabins became red-brick factories and row houses, or graceful mansions like Hulme's; the streets were cobbled, were edged with tame trees, and carriages clopped noisily along. He could hear the laughter and the energetic talk of the business-men, the cries of tradesmen. It was the hidden city, the one that would grow from the ten thousand seeds here. Didn't they see that he was more than just a common man? Didn't they know that the voices in the future city were speaking to *him*, the laughter was at his jests? People craved his advice—should we invest in the railway, Brother Kirkham? Or the textile mill? Should we bring the Pennsylvania coal down the Ohio, or ship it the longer, cheaper way, round the lakes? Will you sign with me so I can get my start, Brother Kirkham? Here's the interest on your loan, Brother Kirkham. I can repay you the money, Brother Kirkham, but never the faith you showed in me when no one else believed.

I am needed here. My flame can ignite this city. Why else did Joseph get Ullery to invest in me? It's industry, it's business that this city lacks to come alive, and I can do it, because I have seen the vision of the smoky, bright-faced, laughing City of God, and I know how to build it. There's more to life than just fathering babies. If that's all I care about, I'll end up a failure like Don Carlos.

It was a cruel judgment, and it wasn't true. Don Carlos wasn't a businessman, but somehow he still wasn't a failure. There was something wrong with Charlie's reasoning, but he couldn't think what it was.

"I'd say he looks more like a sentinel who dozed off standing up."

It took a moment for Charlie to realize that these voices were not part of his vision. In that moment the woman spoke, and her voice explored him as deep as the fountains of desire. "I'd say he's more like a tree that grew up overnight."

"In this cold?" asked the man.

"Blossomed in the morning with frost on his limbs, bore fruit this afternoon, and now shines ripe, with golden fruit and golden leaves."

"I don't know about him being a tree, Emma, but I'd say he's deaf as a post."

Charlie recognized the voice now, and the vision fled away west, over the Mississippi into the haze of the far shore; the shanties were back, with only his new factory bright as a spark in the cold grey ashes of Nauvoo. He turned around. Joseph

and Emma were not twenty feet off, with a few dozen others
trailing away up toward the temple site.

"Don't move, Charlie," Joseph said. "You make such a
pretty figure there."

"I'm sorry," Charlie said. "I didn't know that you were
here."

"I know. We were so quiet." The people behind the Prophet
laughed at that. They all looked so small and uncertain behind
Brother Joseph.

"I was looking at the city," Charlie said.

"And which city did you see?" asked Joseph. "The one *I*
see, or the one that's there?"

So Joseph knew that Charlie had been transfixed by vision.
"The one *you* see, I think."

Joseph threw an arm around his shoulder. "It's a rare man
who can see the true city in spite of the buildings. Everything
you need for happiness is here."

Against his will Charlie thought of Sally Clinton, who also
burned, who also was alive in this grey winter. If I have not
quenched her, Charlie decided, I will warm myself at her fire.
"Should I get married, Brother Joseph?"

If Joseph was surprised at the non sequitur, he did not show
it. "By all means, Brother Charlie. Don't put it off until you
find the perfect woman. *She's* already married." He gave Emma
an affectionate squeeze, and cold-faced Emma loosed a smile
of surprising warmth—it was brief, though, like a flash of light
from a distant lantern. Charlie compared this distant woman
to Sally, and thought that his own home would be a happier
place than Joseph's. Sally Kirkham. The Prophet had said, "By
all means." So after all the advice he had rejected, it turned
out to be the will of God on this day of vision.

"Will you come see the plan of the temple with us, Charlie?"
asked the Prophet.

Charlie shook his head. "I've left my own work too long
already, if you understand me." He couldn't help smiling.

Joseph nodded. "Don't be shy. Ask her right out. If it's the
will of God, she'll say yes without so much as a breath."

"Yes, sir," Charlie said. He couldn't keep himself from
grinning now, and Joseph laughed back.

"Does he remind you of anybody, Emma?"

Emma also smiled. "I can't decide if he looks like the man

I ran off and married, or more like a silly-faced pig in a wallow."

"It's the same look, Emma," Joseph said.

"I know."

Joseph winked at Charlie, then turned and led Emma and the troupe of disciples back up toward the temple site. The afternoon sun picked that moment to come under the clouds and light up the posts and flags that marked the building's dimensions. They seemed to grow in the light, rise tall and golden, as if the temple already stood there—one more sign in a day filled with signs. After so long a silence, God was fairly shouting at Charlie today. On the one hand, the damnation Dinah promised if he failed to act; on the other hand, the Prophet's assurance of happiness if he acted. He watched the Prophet and the fiery temple a moment longer, then bounded down the hill in great, leg-breaking leaps; he had no fear of hurting himself today.

The Clintons lived in a mud-chinked split-log cabin in the poorest part of Nauvoo. There were some snowflakes getting tossed about in the unsteady breeze by the time Charlie got there—they caught sunlight and looked cheerful to him. That was the last cheerful thing he'd see for a while: it was Harriette who came to the door when he knocked. Some expressionless women looked placid as cows, but Harriette seemed more austere than that. More dangerous. Charlie tipped his hat and greeted her. Coldly she invited him in.

Inside, the single room was virtually bare—just straw ticks on the floor for beds, a single trunk that served for wardrobe and everything else, and a chimney in one end of the room that warmed not at all ten feet from it. A few snowflakes drifted in under the ill-fitting roof, and there were patches of mud on the packed-earth floor, a witness to what real weather did to the inside of the house. Harriette was wearing her warmest cloak. In a corner near the fire sat Sally, holding her youngest brother on her lap. Their mother was cooking at the fire. "How do you do?" Charlie said. No one answered. "Is Brother Clinton working?" he asked—it was always a good sign when a man wasn't home during the day.

It was Sister Clinton who answered. "My husband's across the river, Brother Charlie, on the Iowa side, in Zarahemla. They have a wee farm there, he and the boys, but we're to stay here this winter because the cabin's more snug."

It must be a hell of a cabin on the other side, Charlie decided, if this one was better.

"River's freezing over," Mother Clinton added. "If it freezes hard enough, they say we can cross like a road."

"That would be nice," Charlie said. He turned to Sally. "I've been told when the river freezes, there's skating. Would you like that?"

Sally said nothing. Her little brother said, excitedly, "I would."

"Then we'll have to go sometime," Charlie told him. At least someone here was glad to talk to him. But it was Sally he would have to win over, and he refused to be parried. "Sister Sally, I saw you visit at my house today." He glanced at Harriette. *"Both* of you."

It was Harriette who answered. "We didn't think you saw us. If you saw us, we thought, you surely would have waved or come to see us."

Charlie looked at his hands. "I'm sorry. I should have. I should have come to see you here, long before today."

"I wish you had," said Mother Clinton. "We've missed you."

Sally and Harriette immediately glared at her for having proved the weak spot in their uniform hostility. It was all the proof Charlie needed that their coldness was not genuine.

"I stayed away," Charlie said, "because I was afraid."

Sally looked hurt. "Am I so terrible that you have to be afraid of me?"

Charlie knew from long experience in talking with women and hearing women talk that if a man once started defending his motives, he was lost. So he changed the subject. "I was walking on Temple Hill today, and who do you think joined me there?"

Sally looked away, feigning indifference. Mother Clinton, however, could not resist a story. "Who?" she asked.

"Brother Joseph. I was standing there, looking out over the city, and I think the Spirit was with me, and I think he knew it. He came up and said to me, 'Everything you need for happiness is here, Charlie.' It was as if he heard my thoughts. Do you know what I was thinking of then, Sister Sally?"

"I'm sure I don't know," she said.

"I was thinking of you, Sister Sally. And do you know what Joseph said then?"

"I'm sure I—don't—"

"That's what you said before, Sister Sally, but it isn't quite true, is it? You know what he said—because what he said gave me the courage to come here."

Sally turned to him, and the coldness was gone, replaced by uncertainty and, yes, hope. It did Charlie's heart good, to see her so hopeful of him. "Why should you need courage to come to me?" Sally asked.

"Because of what I've known I would do, next time I saw you, even though I have no reason to hope you'd say yes."

Charlie heard Harriette breathe quickly at the door, and now Sally's expression changed to one of quiet repose. She was sure now why he was there. "What did Brother Joseph say that—gave you courage?"

"'Don't be shy,' he told me. 'Ask her right out. If it's the will of God, she'll say yes without so much as a breath.'"

Sally could barely stop herself from smiling now. "What do you mean to ask?"

"Maybe I just don't have enough faith, Sister Sally. I'm still afraid. What if you answered no?"

"I'm a good Saint, Charlie. I'd never make a liar out of the Prophet."

Impulsively, Charlie took a step toward her. She stood then, and Charlie could not help but notice how her bodice moved quickly with her breaths. Charlie reached out, and slowly, carefully she walked toward him and rested her hand on his. She was trembling slightly. So was he. It was not her answer that he feared, however. It was his own changeable heart. Only this afternoon he had been annoyed at the way everyone pushed him toward marrying Sally. Now he not only was proposing to her, but also was indecorously glad of it.

And yet he could not doubt his desire for Sally, nor his gladness at the happy way she looked at him. It made him proud to think this woman could want him so. Only a fool would think he had chosen unworthily; nor, he thought proudly, would anyone doubt that she had married well. He smiled at her. "Sister Sally, will you—"

"Yes," she said.

"Marry me?"

"Not even a breath, the Prophet said." She smiled.

He took her hands in his and kissed them. "I expect I should ask your father," Charlie said.

Mother Clinton spoke from her place at the fire. "I don't think you'll have much trouble there, Charlie. Only a week ago he said, 'I wonder what's taking that boy so damn long.'"

"I had to be sure I could support a family. We'll be married as soon as my factory's built and started running."

Sally looked dismayed. "How long will that be?"

"Depends on how fast I push the men to work."

"Day and night," Sally said. "Build it in a week!"

"Sally!" Mother Clinton said.

Charlie only laughed. "Don't worry, Mother Clinton," he said. "She can't be more eager than I am. We've put this off too long already, haven't we, Sally?"

In answer she clung to him. Yes, he knew how that body felt, pressed against his. Charlie held her shoulders gently— more passion than that would not look right, not with others looking on. A bit embarrassed, he looked away from Mother Clinton, away from the little boy, toward the door where Harriette watched, watched distantly, as if from the wrong end of the glass; and for the first time she did not seem frightening to Charlie. Rather she looked afraid. It was loneliness she was foreseeing now, and her sister gone. It's you I'm hurting, Charlie thought, watching her. But I don't mean to. I'm just doing the will of God. There's none of us can resist *that*. Even if I wanted to.

Harriette broke the silence. "Will you stay to supper, Charlie?"

"Oh, Harriette, there's nothing fit to serve company," Mother Clinton said.

"But Charlie isn't company now, is he?" Harriette looked pointedly at Charlie. He understood. Take my sister, Harriette was saying, but take her family, too. Charlie would have the roof fixed. Charlie would see to it there was enough to eat, and warmth enough in the house. Responsibility was not an unwelcome burden. He was a competent man, and would gladly prove it to anyone.

Charlie got home soon after supper, and after letting his mother complain at him for coming home late without sending word, he told his family what had happened that day, from his conversation with Joseph to Sally's saying yes. Mother tried hard not to gloat over what she regarded as a victory. Father had the wisdom to give no further advice about marriage. There was no wine for celebration—they toasted Charlie with thin tea. "May you have a dozen children," Anna said. "May you never hunger," John said. "May you be glad of Sally every morning, and may she be glad of you every night," said Dinah.

In the quiet light of one steady candle, after John and Anna had gone to bed, Charlie and Dinah talked.

"We'll find our own house now, of course," Dinah said.

"Of course not," said Charlie. "Sally and I will move into a cabin, that's all."

"When your factory's up, we won't want to live here anyway. We can afford it, I think. I'm making some money. And Father has his first commission."

"For a portrait?"

"Hyrum Smith's wife, Mary."

"How much?"

"Enough for a few months' rent on a cabin."

"I won't have you living with dirt floors. I won't have it said that Charlie Kirkham lived in luxury while his family starved."

"We won't starve, Charlie. And this house isn't exactly luxury. Besides, you can't afford to support two houses."

"I can."

Dinah looked at him sharply. "Where do you suddenly come by all this money? A factory, and still enough left over to marry and keep two households?"

"I'm going to prosper. Sally and I won't marry until the factory's going."

"And if you fail?"

"I won't."

"Failure is not impossible for a Kirkham," Dinah said. "There *are* precedents."

"I'm not Father."

"But you are Robert?"

"I'm a capitalist, not an engineer. What I'll create is money, not *things*."

"Soap and candles aren't things?"

"You know what I mean."

"Yes, I do. *I* believe in you. Why does Mr. Ullery?"

Charlie saw no reason not to tell Dinah how the Prophet had helped him. "Because Brother Joseph does."

At once Dinah became suspicious. "The Prophet arranged your loan?"

"I think so. Don Carlos hinted. Brother Joseph believes in me, too."

Dinah could not help but wonder if it was faith that prompted Joseph or if he was, in the only way possible to him, courting her. See what advantages come to your family when you are bound to the Prophet. It made her angry to think that he thought her such a whore. Then she caught herself, and reminded herself that it was also quite possible that Brother Joseph believed in Charlie. How arrogant was she, to think that she was the only person in her family that the Prophet might love?

And then she was ashamed at how she trembled at the thought that Joseph loved her.

"What's wrong?" Charlie asked.

Dinah shook her head. "Nothing," she said. "Finish your factory quickly, Charlie, and get that woman indoors. She's the wife you need. You're good enough for each other—that's a rare thing."

With that, Charlie thought he understood. Of course Dinah was upset. Charlie's marriage was a reminder of Matthew, and, worse, of Val and Honor. "How can I be glad, when you're suffering, and I can do nothing to relieve you?"

Dinah laughed and patted Charlie's hand. It was an old woman's gesture, and her voice was not young when she spoke. "Rejoice again and again, and I'll be gladder for you than you are for yourself."

With that she left her sewing and went off to bed. Charlie sat there after she left, thinking of how poor Dinah never deserved anything but happiness, and now, with neither husband nor children, with no possibility of marrying again while Matthew lived, now happiness seemed completely out of reach for her.

Feeling, as he had all day, that God was especially close to him now, Charlie generously put in a good word for Dinah in his prayers. Lord, I pray you, remove all the obstacles that bar her now from happiness. It's time that things went right with her, if goodness is to be rewarded at all in this world. Dinah is still young, could still bear children and make a home if only she were free to marry.

And suddenly Charlie wondered if in fact Dinah had fallen

in love with someone. That would explain her virulence when she commanded him to marry. It would explain why she seemed so upset when Charlie was marrying, and marrying exactly as she had advised. Dinah was still young. She was beautiful and good. It would be surprising if some man had *not* desired her, surprising if she did *not* respond. And yet, because of Matthew, she was forever barred from the very happiness that Charlie would achieve. It made her tragic, made their lives seem poetry to him, like star-crossed lovers in a play of Shakespeare's, the brother marrying in bliss, the sister grieving in her solitude.

Of course he knew it was probably nonsense. It didn't take an unrequited love to explain odd behavior in women. Yet he was so pleased with the poetry of it that for days, whenever he saw his sister in a group that included men, he watched, he studied the way she was with them and they with her, hoping to notice some man who seemed unusually eager, around whom Dinah was particularly shy. But there was no such man. Indeed, she was rarely around men at all. Just as she had done in Manchester, she ministered among the women, until Charlie was sure that he had fooled himself, and she had no thought of love at all.

❧ 30 ❧

Dinah Kirkham
Nauvoo, 1841

"AND OF COURSE YOU'LL come with your father when I sit for him," Mary Smith said, and though Dinah tried to resist, she could not, in the end, refuse. So here she sat in the home of the Prophet's brother, reading the Book of Mormon to the Prophet's sister-in-law as she sat rigidly in the light slanting through the south-facing parlor window.

"You needn't sit quite so still," John said.

"I wouldn't want you to spoil it," Mary answered.

"It would take more than you twitching now and then to cause me to get you wrong on the canvas. Besides, if I have to listen to one more 'And it came to pass' I'm going to burn that book."

"Brother Kirkham," Mary said, looking shocked. "That's the Book of Mormon!"

"That's it!" John cried. "At last, you have an expression on your face!"

Mary turned to Dinah in surprise. "Didn't I have an expression before?"

"Like a stump," Dinah said, and the women laughed.

John was delighted. "You're good for something after all, Dinah. Keep her laughing and she won't look like a corpse in the painting."

So Dinah set aside the book and talked. She did not know Mary well. The hierarchy of women in Nauvoo paralleled the hierarchy of the men; the wives of the Prophet and his counselors were at the pinnacle of society. To such women one did not speak until invited, and Mary simply had not made that invitation until now. Not because Mary was snobbish, Dinah realized, but because she honestly did not know her own social dominance. "I wish you had come before," Mary said when they had talked for more than an hour, almost forgetting Dinah's father was even there. "I had heard so much about you from Vilate and Emma and—oh, everyone."

"Nauvoo must be desperately short of things to talk about."

"Some of the women call you a prophetess."

"I'm nothing of the kind."

"And Vilate calls you a true Saint."

That opinion *did* mean something to Dinah, though she knew how little she deserved it. "Vilate is too generous."

"As a matter of fact, Vilate has a way of saying exactly what she thinks. If she says you're a Saint, it's pretty likely to be the truth. She's a hard one to fool."

"I know," Dinah said. But I am fooling you all. The Prophet wants me in his bed; I have rejected him; and none of you knows a thing.

"Not like Brother Joseph." And Mary smiled.

Dinah almost lost her composure. But it was just coincidence, she realized. All conversations in Nauvoo turned to the Prophet sooner or later. Besides, Dinah told herself, she had done nothing to be ashamed of.

"Now *he's* generous to a fault. If *he* were the only one who spoke well of you, I'd pay no attention."

So Joseph was speaking of her—at least to his family. A suspicion entered Dinah's mind. "It wasn't the Prophet who recommended my father to you, was it?"

"As a matter of fact, yes. How did you know?"

A loan for her brother; a commission for her father. It

couldn't be coincidence. It angered her that he would use his influence as Prophet to try to get a woman in his debt. But I don't mind, thought Dinah. It will also make it easier to despise him and keep from desiring him. Not that I need help for that, of course.

"What's wrong?" Mary asked.

"Wrong?"

"You're so quiet," Mary said.

John chuckled. "Dinah's had silent spells since she was a baby. Back then they could last for weeks."

"I was only wondering," said Dinah, "how the Prophet could recommend my father when he's never seen his work."

To Dinah's annoyance, John answered. "John Bennett recommended me. He said he would, when I met him in Springfield."

"That's right," said Mary. "Joseph said as much. Hyrum was asking if he knew a painter, and Joseph said—"

At that moment Hyrum Smith leaned into the room. "Good afternoon," he said.

"Oh, Hyrum, you're home!" cried Mary.

But he only had eyes for the painting. "May I see?"

Dinah watched him as he examined the canvas. He wasn't so tall as his brother, nor so open-faced; he was quiet, his face more serious than Joseph's. The Prophet's older brother, and yet willingly in his service. Dinah marveled at that—she tried to imagine Robert serving Charlie that way, and almost laughed aloud at the thought. Hyrum was either a weakling or something quite remarkable, to bear taking a place below a brother he once thought of as a child.

"It's very rough, of course," John explained. "It takes shape gradually."

"Oh, I know," Hyrum said. "But you've caught her all the same."

"Has he?" Mary asked from the window. "And welcome home, my love."

"Me?" Hyrum asked. "Were you referring to me?"

"Oh, no," said Mary. "I didn't mean to call you that. The secret's out. Now all the world shall know I love my husband."

"No one heard but these two. If we kill them immediately— or just cut their tongues out—"

"Oh, Hyrum, now you're getting gruesome." Mary studied

the painting. "It doesn't look like me at all. Just a spot like a crushed bug for my face."

"I thought that was the best part," Hyrum said. Dinah was unnerved by the way he and Mary bantered. Mary was cheerful enough, but Hyrum never so much as tried *not* to smile—from his face and voice you'd never know he was anything but sincere. "You're treading on my foot, Mary."

"And I will, until you tell me how you think this 'captures' me."

"Torture me all you like, I'll still tell you. It's just the way he has you standing, and the way your hand is held, up like that—you do that when you laugh."

"I do?"

"He noticed it, that's all. It'll make me glad whenever I see that painting." To John he said, "You're as good as I had hoped."

During the conversation, John had gathered up his materials and set them aside, affecting unconcern with the conversation. "Tomorrow?" he said now. "The same time?"

"The house is going to fall to ruin if I lose so many hours a day," Mary said.

"I'll divorce you if it does," Hyrum said. And then he caught Mary by both hands and looked into her eyes. "Mary Fielding, now that you're rid of that monstrous husband of yours, will you marry *me?*"

"Do you smoke or spit?"

"I'll give it up for you."

"Then I'll go get the children from Vilate's. Brother Kirkham, will you walk me to Vilate Kimball's house on your way home?"

"Of course we will," Dinah said.

Hyrum and Mary were both silent a moment, and glanced at each other before Hyrum spoke. "I had hoped to have a chance to talk to you alone for a moment, Sister Dinah," Hyrum said.

It all came clear now. Mary's insistence that Dinah come along for the sitting had been Hyrum's idea, or rather Joseph's. Well, I'll not be strung like a puppet. "I wish I could, but I must get home, actually," Dinah said. "I've taken as much time from my work as I can."

"Joseph wanted me to talk to you about the school," Hyrum said.

"Tell Brother Joseph that I've decided not to be a school-teacher."

"Oh, no!" Mary said. "And there are a dozen of us who've been counting on it! Imagine, a woman who can read and write, making over shirts while our children wallow in ignorance! You can't be so heartless as to refuse us."

"I'm no scholar," Dinah said, flustered.

"Talk to Hyrum, please, Dinah," Mary said. The woman was so genuine; it annoyed Dinah how Joseph was manipulating the friendship of women to bend Dinah to obedience, even in as small a matter as meeting with Hyrum.

"What's this about a school?" John asked.

"Brother Joseph wants me to teach. He thinks I'm much cleverer than I am."

"I just want a chance to explain some things to you," Hyrum said. Dinah looked him in the eye. He knows, yes, there's no doubt of it, he knows what Joseph wants from me. "Just thirty minutes, Sister Dinah, and you'll at least know what it is you're turning down."

"I already know what I'm turning down, thank you," Dinah said.

"I assure you that you know nothing of what you're doing."

"Hyrum!" Mary said. "She doesn't know that you're joking."

He was not joking. "Of course she knows I'm joking. Don't you, Sister Dinah?"

"I'll stay these thirty minutes," Dinah said, "if you promise me that then I'll be troubled no more about it."

Hyrum smiled—for the first time since he had come home. "Sister Dinah, I don't know how you could have been troubled *less*."

"Please give him a fair hearing," Mary said. "We'd love to think our children were in your hands."

So Dinah stayed with Hyrum, and John and Mary left.

"Convince me to teach school," Dinah said, knowing that he had no interest in doing so.

"I don't think I'll try. You're too damn proud to let anyone convince you of anything."

She had got so used to his ironic joking with his wife that it took a moment for her to realize that he meant the rebuke. But once she knew it, she answered in kind. "If I'm so damned proud, Brother Smith, why did you want me to stay?"

"To tell you a story."

"I think I've heard all the stories that I care to hear."

"It was while we were in Zion's Camp, a little army of us, traveling to Missouri to try to sustain the Saints of Zion against their persecutors—"

"I know about Zion's Camp."

"We found three rattlesnakes, and some was all for killing them when Joseph comes up and says, 'The animals will never lose their hatred for man until man stops killing animals. You have no business taking a life unless you need the food, and if you kill those rattlers you're going to eat them!' And so nobody kills the snakes, and we go on talking about that sort of thing, and then we see this squirrel up a tree, and we're watching him skitter about on whatever errands he had, when all of a sudden, Boom! a musket goes off behind us and the bullet whistles over our heads and that little harmless squirrel plunks down dead on the ground, shot right in the head. And when we turned around, who do you think we saw but Joseph, and he doesn't say a word, he just turns around and walks off." Hyrum nodded with finality.

Dinah couldn't figure out why he had told the story. "Are you trying to prove to me that Joseph Smith is a hypocrite?"

"That's just what some of them thought. I could see it in their faces, they didn't understand. What kind of prophet is this, who says one thing and does another? I know what's going on, but I says nothing, mind you, because it isn't *my* test, it's theirs, to see what they'll make of it. And lo and behold, down reaches Brother Parley and picks up the corpse of the squirrel, its head blown clean off, and Parley says, 'Didn't you hear the Prophet? When we kill an animal, it had better be for food!' And so Parley cleans the squirrel on the spot, and we skin it and cook it and by damn we eat the thing for supper. Parley said a blessing over it, and every one of us took a bite." Hyrum smiled. "We wouldn't've dared to say no, Parley would've skinned us, too."

"What is this story supposed to mean?"

"I don't know."

"Then why did you tell it?"

"Joseph said to me, 'Hyrum, would you mind telling Dinah Kirkham the story of that squirrel I shot in Zion's Camp?'"

"Is there anyone here who does anything without Joseph telling him?"

Hyrum looked at her coldly. "There's quite a few who do things because Joseph told them *not* to. But they're made of the stuff I scrape from my boot."

"Are you telling me that Joseph is just testing me, that if I say yes to him, he'll tell me it was just a test and I don't have to go through with it?"

"Parley *ate* the squirrel, Sister Dinah. We all did."

"And so you pander for him, Brother Hyrum, and he lends money to my brother and gets work for my father and I'm supposed to be so grateful I'll commit adultery with him?"

Hyrum walked over to a chair and sat, crossed one leg over his knee, and tilted the chair back against the wall like a schoolboy. "I figured you to be a right smart lady, Sister Dinah, but now I reckon you're as dumb as they come."

"Thank you, Brother Smith."

"Aren't you going to walk out of here and leave the Church and go around telling everybody how Joseph Smith is a fallen prophet and his brother's no better?"

"I think not."

"Why not? About three-fourths of the Saints have done that at some time or another. That's how we harrow in the spring, we just go around planting seeds in the footprints of the apostates."

"Well, don't follow *me* in the spring."

"Do you know why you won't leave? Because of two children you left behind you in England for the sake of becoming a child of God here. For the sake of visions and prophecies and a light that burns in your own heart. I don't reckon you'll change your mind about that."

I hate you for knowing my heart and using it against me. "No. I don't imagine that I will."

"Since Joseph asked you—what he asked you—have you ever let yourself think, even for a minute, that it might be true?"

"That is unthinkable."

"Begging your pardon, ma'am, but if Joseph is a prophet you ought to give some consideration to the idea that he might not be a lecherous, adulterous son of a bitch. That's all I'm telling you, Dinah. You're one of the great ones, you know that; Sister Dinah, the Lord has a great work for you, but not if you won't become what God means you to become."

"All I want is to be happy."

"Funny thing. That's all God wants for you, too. But you won't be happy if you refuse the husband the Lord has given you. Would you like me to walk you home?"

"I know the way."

"Good day, Sister Dinah."

"Good day, Brother Smith."

Dinah got no more than a hundred yards on her way home when her father came jogging up a side street and fell into step beside her. Dinah was not in a mood for smiling, and so, to punish herself, she smiled at him. "I thought you were escorting Sister Mary to Vilate's house."

"I did. But I didn't have a thing to say to either lady, and so I took my leave of them and came looking for you. And don't pretend you're glad of my company, because you're not."

John Kirkham was even more annoying when he was being clever than when he was being humble. Perhaps because he really *was* clever.

"My dear child," John Kirkham said, "you've been brooding about something for weeks. Charlie's commented on it. Anna's commented on it. You don't say much, but you can't hide it from your family."

I do not need to have the three of you prying at me, too.

"I, for one, do not really care what your dilemma is. I only want to put in a word of advice. Whatever it is you want to do but are afraid of doing—do it."

Dinah stopped walking and looked at him in disgust. "You don't know what you're saying, Father."

"I'm saying, my darling daughter Dinah, not to let fear stop you from anything. Not fear of pain, not fear of shame, not fear of God."

"Yes," Dinah said brutally, "you're famous for living that advice."

"I live with the consequences of what I did."

"And so do we all."

"You've all done rather well, I think. But what I could not have lived with, what none of us could have borne, are the consequences if I had not done it. What if I had stayed, out of duty, out of fear? I already hated my work. I already hated myself. I was beginning to hate your mother for daring to love me and need me. How long before I hated *you?* And what would you children be today if you had grown up with a father who filled your lives with hatred?"

"I would hate myself more," Dinah said, "if I did it." She wondered why she even bothered to answer his indecent philosophy.

"At least *I* hate myself for what I did, instead of for what I never dared to do."

"I don't meant to hate myself or anyone else at all."

"What a liar you are, Dinah. Hate comes off you like snakeskin wherever you go these days. Little empty Dinah corpses all over Nauvoo, pretending to be alive. Why don't you just figure out what it is you want to do and do it?"

"I think, sir, that I shall walk alone now," Dinah said.

"And a pleasant afternoon to you, too, madam." John tipped his hat, smiled, and let her walk away.

She did not get far. Coming down Mulholland Street from Temple Hill was a carriage that even the children of Nauvoo could recognize by now. Mud splashed up from the horses' hoofs and sprayed out from the wheels, but people still stepped closer, to tip their hats or wave and call, "Good day, Brother Joseph!"

Dinah saw the carriage coming to cross her path and waited. Like any other Saint, Dinah felt the excitement of the Prophet's coming. He was the heart of Nauvoo, and the beat of his horses' hoofs was the city's pulse. Dinah was keenly aware of the fact that he would pass and not see her; she told herself that she was glad of it. In fact, though, she hoped he would happen to glance her way, hoped that he would see her face and be stopped in his thoughts, wonder about her, even, perhaps, hope for her.

What do I *want?* asked Dinah. But it was her father's question, and so she refused to answer it.

Could it be true that God sanctions it? asked Dinah. But it was Hyrum's question, and so she tried to avoid it, too.

And yet in the asking she heard the answer; she wanted so badly for it to be true that she dared not trust her own belief in it. She had loved Joseph Smith from the moment she first heard of him from Heber Kimball, had belonged to him from the flesh inward since that night she prayed in her bedroom and discovered the light within her. Yet still she was afraid that it was not her conscience but her loneliness that cried out "yes" within her when she saw the Prophet's carriage. How could I accept him as my husband when I want him so? If only I hated him, then I could say yes and live this law as a sacrifice, suffering constantly so I could be sure I did not do it for pleasure. Only that way could I justify myself.

The carriage turned at the corner where Dinah waited, to head south on Main, but to her surprise it came to a stop. The Prophet himself swung open a door and leaned out to her. "Sister Dinah, will you ride with us?"

It surprised her how easily the word *yes* came to her lips.

The Prophet jumped from the carriage and helped her step up. There were two other men in the carriage. The one she recognized was William Law, one of Joseph's Counselors. The other was a stranger in a clerical collar.

"Reverend Hake, this is Sister Dinah Handy. Sister Dinah, Reverend Hake here's a visitor from Boston. He wanted a chance to speak to an ordinary Saint. I told him there's no such thing as an ordinary Saint, but he insisted."

This was not at all what Dinah was ready for. An emotional confrontation with Joseph, yes—but to have to be civil to a stranger, a visiting minister, no less, that was too much to expect of her, the way she felt right now. Still, she would do as well as she could. "I suppose I'm as ordinary as they come," she said.

"But her speech," said Hake. "She sounds English."

"She is," said Joseph. "She was baptized in Manchester and came here only a few months ago."

"Remarkable," said Hake. "And she seems a woman of breeding."

"If you think well of the Mormon women," Joseph said, "you should see the Mormon horses."

Reverend Hake raised his eyebrows in horror, but Dinah laughed aloud. Horses, yes, Hake had been talking about Dinah in front of her exactly the way men discussed their riding amimals. "I assure you," said Hake, "that I am making no such comparison. A good woman is the noblest creation of God."

"And Sister Dinah is one of the noblest," said Joseph. "She holds no office in the Church, but I doubt there's many offices Sister Dinah wouldn't be fit to hold."

Hake looked surprised. "Do you ordain women, then?"

Joseph only smiled. "And what would you think if we did, Reverend Hake?"

"I would think your priesthood a trivial thing if you devolve it upon the fairer sex, for whom God intends light burdens."

Dinah was annoyed beyond her ability to remain silent. "I can see that you've never been a woman, Reverend Hake."

"I am well acquainted with the ladies of the Church in Boston."

"They're quite lovely, I imagine," Dinah said. "They go calling and have teas. Well, God didn't create them. Money created them. God made the women you see here, and any other place where death is one bad harvest or one child-bearing or one sudden illness away."

Joseph raised an eyebrow at her, and Reverend Hake tried to pass it off as a joke. "You can't tell *me* you aren't a lady, Miss Dinah."

"After I lay the morning fire and help my mother get breakfast, Reverend Hake, I sew. All day, every day, I remake old shirts into new ones and sell them. I make a few dollars a week that way, enough to buy some of the food we eat, some of the firewood that keeps us warm in this cold. I work hours every day, and when I fall behind, as I'm doing right now, I feel it within days, because I get hungry. I'm no lady, Reverend Hake, because I know that the labor of my hands puts the food in my belly."

She could see on his face that he now agreed with her— no lady would say a word like *belly*. "Is it Mormonism that makes a woman like this?" Hake said, retreating to his former habit of talking *about* rather than *to* her.

"I'm proud to say it is," said Joseph.

"Well, sir, I say that it's against nature. God wants women to be treated better than this poor soul. After all, they *are* the weaker sex."

Joseph leaned close to Hake. "Reverend, I don't know three women in Nauvoo who wouldn't be a match for you in a fair fight, except they wouldn't be so unsporting as to take on such a measly specimen as yourself."

Hake stiffened. "I didn't come here to be insulted."

"No, you came to insult *us*. But we're generous—we try to give back even more than we're given."

"I don't understand your attitude, Mr. Smith. I have friends in the press in Boston. What I report will be printed widely."

"And what will you report? That when a man marries in Nauvoo he gets a helpmate instead of an ornament?" Then, suddenly, Joseph's voice changed. The smile didn't leave his face, but there came something powerful in his eyes, and Dinah found herself as transfixed by him as Hake was. For a moment, Joseph spoke like a prophet, and Dinah felt within herself an answering light. "Report this," Joseph said. "That when you looked into the faces of the people of Nauvoo, the spirit of God smiled back at you from every face. Because that's the truth."

In the face of Joseph's power, Hake's voice was weak, even though he tried to sound defiant. "I am perfectly capable of discerning the truth for myself."

As Joseph leaned over and warmly shook the minister's hand, his tone changed again; now he was charming and likeable. "We'll have the water ready by nightfall. You're a man who can discern the truth, and we're bound to baptize you within a day."

Hake could not help himself. Joseph was too much for him. He smiled and returned Joseph's handshake as warmly, saying, "As God is my witness, President Smith, I can't decide if you have the Spirit of God or the most devilish case of self-love I've ever seen."

"If God was your witness, Reverend Hake, you'd be able to tell the difference. Will you have supper with me and my wife and a few friends tonight?"

"Do you promise I won't be abused?"

"If you behave yourself, I'll be angelic, too. Open your eyes and see what's here instead of what you want to see, and then we'll treat you as a friend, because you'll be one. Isn't that fair?"

Hake was beaten. And as Dinah watched Joseph battle with the man, things became clear to her. Joseph had two kinds of power, and used them both willy-nilly. Now and then when he spoke it was with a power beyond a mere man, it stirred Dinah's inward fire; but most of the time, he was merely elusive, baffling the other man, beating him down with contradiction and charm. Even without the help of God, Joseph Smith would have been a dangerous man, nearly irresistible to those who hadn't the strength to be in his presence and remember who they were. For a few moments Dinah had been able to see both aspects of the man, and the difference between them. And she knew that it was not enough to decide whether to commit herself to this man or not. He could swallow her up in days, without even knowing what he was doing; like so many of the men who surrounded the Prophet, Dinah could easily become just another pair of hands for him, just another voice, so much under his control that without him she would not know who she was. Surely that could not be what God had in mind for her.

The carriage pulled up in front of Joseph's house. The Prophet swung open the door. "I'll expect you for supper, Reverend Hake. Brother William will show you around the rest of our city."

"But where are you going?" asked Hake. He sounded dismayed at the thought of being out of Joseph's presence.

"Why, Sister Dinah and I are going to discuss the school she's establishing."

Hake looked triumphant. "I was sure you were more than a mere seamstress!"

Dinah smiled sweetly back at him. "But you, sir, are exactly what you seem." She let Joseph help her from the carriage. As she expected, Hake did not understand that she had insulted him.

"Good day, President Smith," Hake called cheerily. "Till supper!" And the carriage rolled off, leaving Dinah standing with the Prophet in the road.

Joseph grinned at her. "Do you think we were too hard on him?"

"When a man insists on being an ass," Dinah said, "it's only polite to ride him as far as he wants to go."

"Are you ready to give up your needle and earn your living with your mind?"

"I'll teach your school, President Smith."

He impulsively shook her hand. "I knew you'd come round!"

"How far do you think I've come about, President Smith?"

He raised an eyebrow and gripped her hand tighter. "I think you've come all the way the Lord wants you to."

"If I were to agree to *all* that you asked me, do you know why I would do it, President Smith? It wouldn't be because you arranged for Charlie's loan. It wouldn't be because you found work for my father as a painter. And it most definitely wouldn't be because I have the slightest desire for you as a man."

He let go of her hand. "How much more pleasant for us all, then," he said, "since I haven't got the slightest desire for you, either."

"If I accepted you, it would be from pure obedience to the Lord."

"When I first learned this doctrine, I put off obeying it as long as I could. I delayed for years. And then an angel of the Lord appeared to me, holding a fiery sword in his hand, and said, 'Either obey the Lord in this, or be destroyed.' So I obey the Lord. I go to the women he has given to me, and I put my life in their hands. Do you want to kill me, Dinah? Go tell my enemies what I proposed to you. They'll believe you. They'll use it against me. They'll put me in prison, if they can—and I promise you, if I ever go inside a jail again, I'll not come out alive."

"I have no intention of telling anyone."

"Not even Emma?"

Dinah shrank inside. "Doesn't she know?"

"She knows the principle of celestial marriage. But she believes I won't practice it without her consent. She forgot that I'm bound to obey the Lord more than her."

Joseph regarded her with his prophetic eyes, and she felt again the light within her grow. You are, after all, what I left my children for, she said to him silently. But I will come to you as a sacrifice, not for joy. "I am also bound to obey the Lord," she said. "So I will accept you." She could see him brighten inside, could see how his smile grew truer. Wait, you who would be my celestial husband, and hear this all. "However, Brother Joseph, since we are both agreed that neither of us is acting out of physical desire, we have no need whatever to consummate our marriage in the flesh."

Still smiling, Joseph said, "This would all be easier if the Lord would only give me stupid ugly women. The marriage is not to be a sham, Sister Dinah. We are commanded to raise up a righteous posterity."

"I already have two children, Brother Joseph. I did not come to Nauvoo to get *more*." The anger in her voice surprised her. She forced herself to be calm. "It's as you said. They'll be taken from an unworthy husband and given to a worthy one. In the eyes of God, we already have a posterity. And they are a *good* posterity."

Joseph nodded soberly. "I'll not rob your children, Sister Dinah. Nor will I force my way into any woman's bed, even if it is postponing the Lord's will. But don't think you've fooled the Lord. Your struggle is with him, not with me. We'll take our vows, we'll have the seal of heaven, but I won't know you, woman, until you give yourself to me."

"You'll have a long wait before I ask you."

He smiled wickedly. "Sister Dinah, do you think that the man who sups at Emma's table needs to go begging afterward to be satisfied?"

The mention of Emma made her shudder. I am doing something terrible even to make a vow to Emma's husband. How can I fool myself that I'm clean because I deny him my bed?

"Dinah," Joseph said, "the Lord will bear you up, once you take the step."

She looked away from him, trying not to cry. "I am the worst traitor I know," she said.

"Hyrum is waiting in the house."

They went in the front way. Dinah could hear Emma in the kitchen, giving orders to the girls who were helping her. Dinah wondered if she could face Emma after this, and pretend to be her friend.

"I don't know you," she whispered to Joseph.

"You don't know anything," he whispered back.

Hyrum waited for them upstairs. Joseph's eldest son lay asleep in the room. They whispered so as not to wake him. Joseph and Dinah knelt and joined hands, and Hyrum administered a strange oath that spoke of kingdoms; she tried to follow the words but could not. She wasn't even sure when the oath had ended.

"Now you say yes," Hyrum prompted.

She turned to Joseph. "If I say yes, then am I truly your wife forever? And my children will belong to me?"

"To us," Joseph whispered.

"If you have lied to men, may God damn you to hell forever."

He made no answer, just gazed at her without expression.

Where was the light that she had so relied on? Why was there no witness that she was doing the right thing? She felt frightened, abandoned; Eli, Eli, lama sabachthani. What games was God playing with her life?

"Yes," she said.

Then Hyrum said the words that joined them for time and all eternity, in the name of the Father and the Son and the Holy Ghost.

She closed her eyes. What have I done? she asked. And then, in answer, the light erupted within her. It was stronger than it had ever been before. She dared not open her eyes, or it would blind her; she dared not speak, or she would be left mute. At last, when she thought she could bear no more, the light brimmed and flowed over, through her hand where the Prophet held her, rushed into him and left her exhausted and exalted and, for the moment at least, sure.

Now she could open her eyes. Joseph's eyes were still closed, and tears flowed down his cheeks. How could he contain such power, if she could not? Was he so much more copious than she? She, too, began to weep. In the blur of tears she thought she saw him dead, his eyes stitched shut, his face slack and sagging backward, his lips long in an imitation of a smile. She saw hands take a metal bowl filled with plaster, and press it against the face, and then withdraw, leaving the plaster to harden with the inverse of Joseph Smith contained there. But the deathmask was a lie, she knew—the man was not this face, the mask would show nothing of him. The man was made of light inside. She had passed her test, and God had given her an assurance.

"I know you now," he whispered. "You had another name, before you were born. Our Savior called you by that name, and touched your head, and ordained you to a great work. He called you Evening Star. He called you Daughter of Light."

He took his hand away from her. It burned and stung when he pulled away, as if the flesh had been grafted together as the light passed through. He doubled over and buried his face in his hands, elbows resting on his knees, his body shaking. She watched him, wondering why at the moment of their marriage she had been shown a vision of his death. She was certain that the death of his body should mean nothing to her, for he was not this body. He had grown far greater than the borders of his flesh: the whole Church was a part of himself, and anyone who thought *Joseph Smith* was the name of a man and nothing more did not know either him or the Church he had created. The whole shape of Nauvoo, of the Church in the far-off branches of England, that was all a part of him, and when they pressed the plaster on that stiffened face they would not be taking Joseph's shape. As long as the Church lived, Joseph would live and grow. She was the bride of something stronger and more beautiful and more terrible than a man.

"When you die," she said, "you'll get no tears from me."

And his weeping ended, and he knelt erect, taking his hands from his eyes and looking in her face. He smiled. "Then you know me, too."

Hyrum stepped to her, took her hand and lifted her from where she knelt upon the floor. "It's dangerous to stay any longer," he said. "We must go and plan a school."

"You don't need to salary me," she said. "I'm doing well enough."

"Dammit, woman," Hyrum said, "we want you for the school whether you marry him or not."

"Oh," she said, and followed him to the door. She glanced back at the man who was now, somehow, her husband; he was not looking at her. Instead he was stroking his son's forehead where the boy slept. Hyrum pulled her out just when little Joseph awoke. As the door closed, she heard the child asking, "Why are you crying, Papa?"

She and Hyrum went to the sitting room and wrote up the documents establishing the school. She had authority to buy as many as thirty books—a luxurious endowment, and she wondered if there were thirty books to be had here without going to Chicago. She had authority to rent a schoolroom and place an advertisement in the *Times and Seasons*. It was all very calm and businesslike.

At supper she amazed herself by acting and feeling perfectly natural with Emma. She did not feel shame at having taken vows with her friend's husband. She did not feel the contempt of a mistress toward the deceived wife. The sisterly love she felt before was stronger than ever, if it was changed at all. Hypocrisy was not so difficult an art as she had thought.

That night she wrote again to Val and Honor. I love you, she wrote, again and again. I love you, and it is not a lie. When you grow up you'll know that sometimes the right thing to do seems like the very worst, and then you'll forgive me, even if you are too young to forgive me now. You are my only children, and even though I can't be with you, I know you will be mine forever.

If the day's vows had accomplished nothing more, they had

accomplished that. The children would be hers forever. She had God's word on it. And wasn't she his Evening Star, his Daughter of Light? God would not let her believe a lie, surely. After opening so many doors in her life that led nowhere but to other doors, now surely she was home.

⇒⇒⇒ BOOK SIX ⇐⇐⇐

*In which fields are plowed,
seeds are planted,
and yet the ground is fallow after all.*

❧ First Word ❧

For a woman who wrote and spoke almost continuously for many decades, Dinah Kirkham remains annoyingly elusive. Right at the crucial time between Joseph Smith's proposal and the consummation of their marriage, she stopped writing daily entries and started putting poetry in her journal. For someone analyzing her role as the foremost Mormon poet in the nineteenth century, all this is very exciting, but I don't think her poems are all that good and finding page after page of them right when her life was at such crisis infuriated me. It was as if she could see me prying into her confidential writings a hundred-forty years later and said, "Snoop all you like, but you'll not get this from me."

So I snooped somewhere else. I'm not a folklorist,

but I like reading what the folklorists collect. And in one collection from southern Utah in the 1930s, I found something that may or may not explain anything to you—but it explains a lot to me. There was a peddler story that had several variants in Utah's Dixie, but the oldest variant was one told by a centenarian who had once been a student in Dinah Kirkham's school. And he claimed that he was telling the story exactly the way Aunt Dinah told it to him. It's thick with the accents of Mormon back country, but I had no trouble translating it into Dinah's crisp Midlands speech. To you, Dear Reader, this all may seem a digression. But then, you're always free to skip my little "First Word" sections and get on with the book. *I* think her story of a farmwife's choice is an explanation, at least in part, of the choice Dinah herself made.

Once there was a woman who had five children that she loved with all her heart, and a husband who was kind and strong. Every day her husband would go out and work in the fields, and then he'd come home and cut wood or repair harness or fix the leaky places in the roof. Every day the children would work and play so hard they wore paths in the weeds from running, and they knew every hiding place in two miles square. And that woman began to be afraid that they were too happy, that it would all come to an end. And so she prayed, Please send us eternal happiness, let this joy last forever. Well, the next day along came a mean-faced old peddler, and he spread his wares and they were very plain—rough wool clothing, sturdy pots and pans, all as ugly and practical as old shoes. The woman bought a dress from him because it was cheap and it would last forever, and he was about to go, when suddenly she saw maybe a fire in his eyes, suddenly flashing bright as a star, and she remembered her prayer the night before, and she said, "Sir, you don't have anything to do with—happiness, do you?"

And the peddler turned and glowered and said, "I can give it to you, if you want it. But let me tell you what it is. It's your kids growing up and talking sassy, and then moving on out and marrying other children who don't like you all that much, at least at first. It's your husband's strength giving out, and watching the farm go to seed before your eyes, and maybe having to sell it and move into your daughter-in-law's house because you can't support yourselves no more. It's feeling your own legs go stiff, and your fingers not able to tat or knit or even grip the butter churn. And finally it's dying, lying there feeling your body drop off you, wishing you could just go back and be young with your children small, just for a day. And then—"

"Enough!" cried the woman.

"But there's more," said the peddler.

"I've heard all I mean to hear," and she hurried him out of the house.

The next day, along comes a man in a bright-painted wagon, with a horse named Carpy Deem that he shouted at all the time. A medicine man from the East, with potions for this and pills for that, and silks and scarves to sell, too, so bright they hurt your eyes just to look at them. Everybody was healthy, so the woman didn't buy any medicine. All she bought was a silk, even though the price was too high, because it looked so blue in her golden hair. And she said to him, "Sir, do you have anything to do with happiness?"

"Do you have to *ask?*" he said. "Right here, in this jar, is the elixir of happiness—one swallow, and the best day of your life is with you forever."

"How much does it cost?" she asked, trembling.

"I only sell it to them as have such a day worth keeping, and then I sell it cheap. One lock of your golden hair, that's all. I give it to your Master, so he'll know you when the time comes."

She plucked the hair from her head, and gave it to the peddler, and he poured from the bottle into a little tin cup. When he was gone, she lifted it up, and thought of the happiest day of her life, which was only two days before, the day she prayed. And she drank that swallow.

Well, her husband came home as it was getting
dark, and the children came to him all worried.
"Something's wrong with Mother," they said. "She
ain't making no sense." The man walked into the
house, and tried to talk to his wife, but she gave no
answer. Then, suddenly, she said something, speaking to empty air. She was cutting carrots, but there
were no carrots; she was cooking a stew, but there
was no fire laid. Finally her husband realized that
word for word, she was saying what she said only
two days ago, when they last had stew, and if he said
to her the words he had said then, why, the conversation at least made some sense.

And every day it was the same. They either said
that same day's words over and over again, or they
ignored their mother, and let her go on as she did
and paid her no mind. The kids got sick of it after
a time, and got married and went away, and she
never knew it. Her husband stayed with her, and
more and more he got caught up in her dream, so
that every day he got up and said the same words
till they meant nothing and he couldn't remember
what he was living for, and so he died. The neighbors found him two days later, and buried him, and
the woman never knew.

Her daughters and daughters-in-law tried to care
for her, but if they took her to their homes, she'd just
walk around as if she were still in her own little
cottage, bumping into walls, cutting those infernal
carrots, saying those words till they were all out of
their minds. Finally they took her back to her own
home and paid a woman to cook and clean for her,
and she went on that way, all alone in that cabin,
happy as a duck in a puddle until at last the floor of
her cabin caved in and she fell in and broke her hip.
They figure she never even felt the pain, and when
she died she was still laughing and smiling and saying
idiotic things, and never even saw one of her grandchildren, never even wept at her husband's grave, and
some folks said she was probably happier, but not a
one said they were eager to change places with her.

And it happened that a mean-looking old peddler came by and watched as they let her into her grave, and up rode a medicine man yelling at his horse, and he pulled up next to the peddler.

"So she bought from you," the peddler said.

And the medicine man said, "If you'd just paint things up a little, add a bit of color here and there, you'd sell more, friend."

But the peddler only shook his head. "If they'd ever let me finish telling them, they'd not be taken in by you, old liar. But they always send me packing before I'm through. I never get to tell them."

"If you'd begin with the pleasant things, they'd listen."

"But if I began with the pleasant things, it wouldn't be true."

"Fine with me. You keep me in business." And the medicine man patted a truck filled with gold and silver and bronze and iron hairs. It was the wealth of all the world, and the medicine man rode off with it, to go back home and count it all, so fine and cold.

And the peddler, he just rode home to his family, his great great great grandchildren, his grey-haired wife who nagged, the children who complained about the way he was always off on business when he should be home, and always hanging about the house when he ought to be away; he rode home to the leaves that turned every year, and the rats that ate the apples in the cellar, and the folks that kept dying on him, and the little ones that kept on being born.[1]

Fortunately, Dinah's stories and poems aren't the only source we have for this time in her life. She did have a confidante. During the months prior to Charlie's wedding, Dinah became close to Harriette Clinton, Sally's forbidding older sister. Dinah had never forgotten that it was Harriette who gave her a book of poems to comfort her in her grief on the *North America:* now the woman

---

[1]Nels Heber Nelson, *Tales from Utah's Dixie* (Salt Lake City: Heritage, 1934), pp. 122–30.

was the strength of so many others turned to Harriette for buttressing. Harriette wrote nothing about it at the time, but years later, when she was writing to a friend in defense of plural marriage in the 1870s, she talked about Dinah's struggle. Though Harriette's version of events is colored by the fact that she was trying to defend polygamy, I think she is trustworthy when it comes to her plain recounting of events. That's where I learned about Dinah's arrangement with Joseph for a platonic marriage. And from some internal patterns in Harriette's letter, I feel secure in placing the date of the end of that arrangement at the same time as Charlie's wedding to Harriette's sister.

With that I am once again skipping several months in which nothing all that important happened. Charlie finished building his factory, and it made a great deal of smoke and stink and money from the first day. John Kirkham finished the portrait of Mary Fielding Smith, and it was such a great success that he was at once flooded with commissions. Though his Nauvoo clients paid nothing like London society, he made enough to support him and Anna in a little clapboard house on a half-lot on Parley Street just under the brow of Temple Hill. He would have made even more, but there were some portraits he refused to paint: John Bennett's, for instance, and Joseph Smith's, the one because he'd do too much justice to the subject, the other because he didn't understand him well enough.

And Dinah—Dinah systematically prepared herself to be Joseph Smith's secret wife in more than name. She rented a one-room cabin on Mulholland, four blocks east of the temple, a part of town so new that the streets weren't even pegged off yet, so isolated that she had no neighbors close enough to see her dooryard through the trees and bushes standing here and there. Even though she probably did not realize her own purpose, she had established herself in a place where even a man as well-known as Joseph Smith could secretly come and go in darkness without being seen. In the meantime she prepared her lessons and taught them, becoming a favorite with her students. And she continued her service as a ministering angel among the women, all the while struggling to find an adequate reason to do what she longed to do: invite her illegal eternal husband to her bed.

—*O. Kirkham, Salt Lake City, 1981*

❧ 31 ❧

Wedding Night
Nauvoo, 1841

HARRIETTE SEEMED TO LOOM over the wedding like a gargoyle. She never did anything; Charlie just felt her watching, constantly. Sally didn't notice it, of course. Harriette had been watching *her* all her life. On the morning of the wedding he tried to broach the subject.

"Oh, that again," Sally said.

"Again? I've never mentioned it before."

"You don't have to mention it. You keep watching Harriette all the time, with this silly little frown in your forehead. Honestly, if I didn't know you and Harriette better, I'd say there was something dishonest going on."

That turned the conversation to protestations of love and eternal fidelity, which always left Charlie exhausted, and yet eager to give Sally more tangible proof of his devotion. Tonight, he reminded himself; be patient. And then he grew ashamed of his indecorous lust; a true Saint would have nothing but holy feelings for his wife, he knew.

True Saint or not, however, Joseph Smith had volunteered to perform the ceremony himself, which immediately turned the wedding into an Event. People practically begged for invitations. Charlie was level-headed enough to know that it wasn't because he was so well-loved. The spring weather was good enough that at the last minute they resolved to have the wedding outdoors; Charlie had a platform built and they inserted a notice in the *Times and Seasons*, throwing open the wedding to anyone who wanted to come.

"That rather dilutes the thrill of getting an invitation, doesn't it?" Don Carlos commented.

"Good," Charlie answered. "Then only our *real* friends will come after all."

"They're both going fishing. *I* may not even come. I only serve as best man at the most exclusive weddings."

"Or any wedding that has free food."

"The truth is, Charlie, I'm the best man at every wedding I go to. If I weren't already married, the girls would never leave me alone. That's why I'm so rarely invited to weddings. Brides keep changing their minds after seeing me."

"Sally's already seen you, and she still wants me."

"Fine with me. I'd never marry a woman who can't pronounce her *r*'s."

Charlie took his bath at John's and Anna's house, not so much because he didn't want to fetch the bath himself as because Anna had pleaded with him to give her one last chance to perform that service for her son. He thought it was an odd thing for her to be nostalgic about; soon enough he discovered that it wasn't nostalgia at all. She wanted to give him a bath so he couldn't stand up and run away while she told him some things she thought he needed to hear.

He was naked and lathered up in the tub, feeling more than a little silly, when his mother, instead of scrubbing his back, walked around to the front of the tub and stared at him until he wondered whether she could see through the suds. "I think Sally's going to be pleased with what she sees tonight," Mother said at last.

Suddenly he wished he were dressed. "What a thing to say, Mother."

"Don't get shy with me, Charlie. I cleaned your diapers, you know."

"Not recently."

"Well, whether you like it or not, I have some words to say to you. There's two types of men in the world, Charlie. There's the type that takes and the type that gives. You're a giver, if I know you at all, Charlie. I want you to know that you'd better be generous with your Sally, and at night as well as in the daytime."

"The water's getting cold."

"It's still steaming. I had this same talk with Robert years ago, and he got just as silly as you, but it's good advice. There's men who hop into bed and please themselves, and not a care for the woman at all. Some of them even believe a woman takes no joy from love, and in fact they make their own belief come true by acting like animals. Your sister Dinah was married to such a man, poor ignorant Matthew, who was as far from understanding women as ever a man could be. But when a husband is a gentle lover, Charlie, and takes thought for what makes a woman feel loved, then his wife will always be eager to take him into her bed. You're blushing, Charlie."

"The water's hot, that's all."

"I know this is the sort of talk a man should have with his son, but your father and I agreed that you'd probably not take it kindly from him. Mind what I tell you. Be kind to Sally and she'll never be tired of you and always forgive you if you hurt her, and she'll love you more than she loves her children or her parents or God himself, if you treat her right."

"I'll treat her right, Mother. How about scrubbing my back before the soap dries on?"

Anna laughed all the way to the fire to fetch more water, and Charlie scrubbed viciously at his face with the harsh washcloth, embarrassed but still a little eased in his mind, knowing better what Sally might expect from him. Of course, Mother wasn't Sally. Mother could never have been so hot for kissing as Sally Clinton.

Dinah tore open the letter there in the store. Decorum mattered little, for the return address was Robert's house in Manchester. Ever since her first letter, so many months ago, all her letters to Val and Honor had gone to Robert's house, in confidence that Robert would find a way to let the children know that she was writing to them. And here, at last, was word from them.

The first thing she found in the envelope was the earliest

of her letters to Val. It had been opened and read, but she knew
at once that Val had never seen it. She stood and read her own
words to her son, the love she had desperately tried to put into
ink, knowing now that her effort had been useless.

"Are you all right, Sister Dinah?"

Yes, she assured the clerk, and thank you for the letter, and
good day to you. She fled the store, hurried around behind it
to the large room that she used as her school. There she found
the letter in the envelope. It was in Robert's hand, rushed and
scribbled, and it was brief and to the point.

> Dinah,
>   This decision was not lightly made. But I believe that
> you made your choice on the deck of that ship in Liv-
> erpool. The children have finally stopped crying all day
> and night for you. They have settled into a some sort of
> normality with their father, a very good nanny, and fre-
> quent visits with my children. Their lives are stable, and
> it would only upset them all over again to receive com-
> munication from you. The only communication I will
> permit you to have is a personal meeting, if you regain
> your senses and return to your duties as a wife and mother
> here in Manchester. Otherwise, you will remain entirely
> out of the children's lives. If you love them, you will
> see the wisdom in this plan and make no attempt to
> circumvent it.
>   Robert

She sat at her table and wished she could weep. Or better,
wished she could go to Charlie and tell him. In his clumsy way
he'd have some wisdom for her. In his rage against Robert he
would make her forgive him by his sheer immoderation. But
today was Charlie's wedding day, and so today she could not
go to him. Nor tomorrow, nor the next day, and for the first
time Dinah realized that with Charlie married she would be
almost entirely alone. Mother was no help anymore. Here in
America she was more like a daughter than a mother, caring
little for the future; all was in the hands of God, for her. Dinah
had no one, now that Charlie was marrying. Not parents, not
brother, not children, not husband. There was no one to go to,
no one to tell.

So she only read both letters, over and over, realizing that it had now been nearly a year, and as far as Val and Honor knew, their mother had not made the slightest effort to communicate with them. As far as they knew, she did not love them or think of them or even care whether they lived or died. And she knew, from the darkest places in her memory, exactly how much pain that belief would cause. Except, of course, that the wrong parent had stayed with them. It was the weakling father that they had, not the strong mother that had remained with Robert, Dinah, and Charlie so many years before.

Strong mother? Dinah examined herself, unweeping as she was, and realized that indeed she was strong. But not a mother. Not by any pretense a mother now. With no contact with her children, with no hope of budging Robert once he was certain he was right, she was strong but not a mother. She pressed her fists into her belly until she could not press harder. Not until I am dead are Val and Honor mine again. And in this life, how many years childless because Matthew will not let me have my children? What is this womb for, then? Why am I a woman if for God's sake I have lost all hope of bearing?

And now, when she thought perhaps she might be able to cry away the pain, the door burst open and two children burst in. Julia and Little Joseph, Joseph's and Emma's eldest children. Ten-year-old Julia was the adopted daughter, taken into their home as an infant to replace Emma's twins who had died the day they were born. She was quick-witted and had a way of lording it over the other children without their ever seeming to notice. Her Ladyship, Dinah privately called her. And eight-year-old Joseph Smith III, the first of Emma's natural-born children to live more than a day, he was his father's pride, like a little shadow of the Prophet, with his sweetness and his cleverness, but none of his strength. They did not see at first that Dinah was there. Instead they ran straight for the bookshelf at the back of the classroom, where Webster's dictionary always lay. "See!" Julia shouted. *"Luxurious* does *not* have a G."

Little Joseph looked at the offending page in bitter silence. Finally he flipped the dictionary closed in disdain and said, "Well, it *should.*"

Dinah could not help herself. She laughed aloud. They whirled around and looked at her in guilty fear. "It's all right," Dinah said. "It's all right if you come in when there's no school." And yet she was not glad the children were there. She did not want to see Joseph's children today. Did not want to

see anyone's children, for that matter, but least of all Joseph's.
For they were another reminder to her that she was the only
one sacrificing in this plural marriage of duty they had con-
tracted. He had children who adored him, had them any time
he liked. He came sometimes to meet them after school. Dinah
was always jealous of the way he tousled little Joseph's hair
and tickled Julia's ribs, resentful of the easy way he had with
Hyrum's children, with all children, so that they worshiped
him, every one.

"We thought you were at Brother Charlie's wedding, Sister
Handy," Julia said.

"Or at your new house," little Joseph added. "Mama said
you weren't holding school today because you had to move
into your new house."

"I just had—some work to do," Dinah said.

"Oh," Julia said. But the girl did not believe her, Dinah
knew.

"Is that why you're so sad?" little Joseph asked. "'Cause
you have to work today?"

Dinah smiled. "No."

"We just wanted to look up a word," little Joseph explained.

"I know."

"She *heard* us, stupid," Julia said.

"He is *not* stupid," Dinah said. "That is not a polite word,
Julia."

"Sorry, Sister Handy."

"If you have any other business, you'd best attend to it,"
Dinah said. "I need to lock up."

"No, we're through," Julia said.

Little Joseph continued to scrutinize Dinah's face. "You
look like somebody just died."

"No," Dinah said; and then, as if it were an easy thing to
say, she said, "I just learned that my children in England
haven't been getting my letters. And never will."

"Why not?" asked little Joseph.

"Because some men have decided not to let them."

Little Joseph took that easily, but Julia's eyes were wide.
"Do you still love them?"

Dinah nodded.

"They'll be all right," Julia said. "When Papa was in jail
in Missouri, and we thought all the time he was going to be
killed, we just prayed for them to let him go, and they did,

even though they were the wickedest men in the world."

Seeing the two of them there, concerned about her, trying to comfort her, Dinah realized that she wanted them. Wanted Joseph's children to be hers. And more: she wanted Joseph himself, wanted him to come like the answer to prayer, light in a dark place, and take her grief from her. *What stupid sacrifice is this, that keeps me childless when I could have children, that keeps me lonely when I could have a husband?*

"Julia," Dinah said, "could you deliver a note to your father?"

"Yes, ma'am," the girl said.

So Dinah quickly wrote to him, folded the paper twice, and gave it to Julia. "It's not really important, but if you could give it to him today—"

"Oh, yes, Sister Handy," Julia said.

Little Joseph lifted his cap: "Good day, Sister Handy."

"Luxurious," Dinah said.

"L-U-X-U-R-I-U-S."

"I-*O*-U-S," Dinah corrected him.

"Yes, ma'am." And they scurried off into the spring afternoon.

Joseph Smith was alone in the upstairs bedroom, dressing in his best for the wedding, when Julia burst into the room shouting, "Oh, Papa, she's like the heroine of a story."

She was holding out a note, and Joseph took it. "Who is?" he asked.

"Sister Handy. Oh, Papa, they don't even let her children read her *letters*. When you were in jail I would have *died* if they hadn't given me your letters."

Little Joseph walked soberly into the room.

"Well," Joseph said, "another visitor, too."

"He came with me," Julia said. "We went down to the school and there she was. She sent that note."

Plainly Julia wanted him to read it. But little Joseph had such a glum expression that his father could not put off asking what was wrong.

"Nothing."

"Tell me the truth, Joseph."

Little Joseph shrugged. Then, turning sideways and looking at the wall, he said, "Papa, if the Lord told you to go away and leave us, would you go?"

Joseph set down the note and took his son by the shoulders.

"Son, if the Lord told me to do it, I would. But it would break my heart."

The boy burst into tears.

"Well, for silly," said Julia. "Papa isn't leaving."

"Hush, Julia," Joseph said mildly. He embraced his son. "I always do what the Lord tells me, Joseph. And if you always do what he tells *you*, then no matter what happens, we'll be together in heaven forever. You'll always be my son, and I'll always be your father."

Little Joseph nodded. He pulled away from his father, signifying that he was through with tears for now and no longer needed to be treated as a little child.

"Go on then, both of you," Joseph said. Little Joseph took off at once.

"But the note," Julia said.

Joseph picked it up and read it. "She just wants me to dedicate her new house, Julia."

"Is it a very fine house, Papa?"

"Just a cabin, really, with a dirt floor. But the Lord can dwell in any house."

"I know that," she said. "I love you, Papa." And she, too, was gone.

Joseph read the note again.

> Dear Brother Joseph, I have a new house and I promised the Lord I'd have it dedicated before I ever slept there. It's important to me that I keep all my vows completely from now on. Will you help me?

He had almost laughed at her when she first proposed to test him. In fact he had not yet lain with any of his plural wives. Not that none of them were willing. Rather the oaths themselves were so difficult for him that he felt justified in postponing the other duties of a husband. After each of his marriages he came home and clung all the tighter to Emma. I'll obey you, Lord, he said inside himself, but I'll not *enjoy* it.

Until Dinah Kirkham. It annoyed him that continence was her idea, and not his. He had brooded on that awhile, in between the endless series of meetings, sermons, and ministrations. He saw her rarely, but was constantly reminded of her. The sisters who had come to him for counseling now came less, and when he asked they told him, "Oh, things are much better now. Sister Dinah prayed with me. Sister Dinah found work for me. Sister Dinah brought me into the most wonderful circle of sisters, Brother Joseph, I have so much to do now that I hardly ever think of my old problems—can it be that I was ever so selfish before?" Perhaps he had heard all this before, but now that Dinah had taken vows with him, now that God had taught him Dinah's true name, now he saw the effect she had among the Saints. In his own home, too. More than once Emma said, "I don't know what I'd do without Sister Dinah. She understands the gospel better than most of the men in the Church. And she lives it, too. I only wish she had a husband worthy of her, instead of that scoundrel off in Manchester, depriving her of her children. A proper husband cares for his wife," and Emma launched into a sermon on the duties a man owed a woman that left Joseph speechless at the irony: Was Emma teaching him how to deceive her?

That was the worst of it. The secret vows with plural wives were one thing, he could justify concealing that from Emma because she was not yet ready to live the principle of celestial marriage. But with her still doubting, if he consummated any of those vows it would more than smack of adultery to her. And yet Emma herself kept Dinah always on his mind. Dinah, the woman who, more than any other except Emma, loved his work and knew how to be part of it.

Of all the women God had given him, Dinah was the one he longed to take; yet she was the only one who still withheld herself from him. He told himself that he was glad of it, that it would be wrong for him to use the Principle for his own pleasure, that her very beauty and goodness were a snare to him. But still he saw her briefly in his own home, in the company of women, and he longed for her; he felt her in the city like the warm electric air before a storm, and he walked restless through his days, waiting for the lightning of her, and it wouldn't strike.

Until today. And his hand trembled as he held the note.

The wedding was fine. Hundreds of people came. Most were there in hopes that Brother Joseph would say something remarkable in his wedding sermon, and the Prophet obliged them, introducing the remarkable idea that if they only understood what God meant marriages to be, they'd grieve at ceremonies that part the couple at death. "They're a sign," he said, "that we've forgotten that God intends our best actions to last forever." Only a few hearers knew, as Dinah did, that he was trying to prepare the Saints gradually for the doctrine of celestial marriage.

The sermon ended by four o'clock in the afternoon, and within a few minutes Joseph had the wedding party in the house with the chairs pushed back and the table taken out of doors, so that those inside could dance while those outside finished off the food in fifteen minutes. Joseph was circulating from group to group, as always, when he came face to face with Dinah at the serving table. She was lithe and beautiful in her blue-flowered dress. He smiled and took a plate of cake from her hand. Yes, he wanted to say to her, but dared not speak. Do I dare come to you tonight? Even as he asked the question, he watched her as she laughed with her brother's guests, watched her greeting the shy ones, the ones who knew no one, the many hundreds of women who had come to the wedding only for love of Dinah, saw how she had bound them all together in webs of need and service, and he knew that he would go to her tonight, despite his doubts about his own motive in loving her, despite the danger of being seen and known, even if it delivered him into the hands of his enemies.

Inside the house there was no fiddler and no band—the couples danced to clapped hands. Charlie stepped solemnly through the quadrille, his eyes on Sally, admiring her apparent unconcern, the way she laughed and joked with all and still, annoyingly, flirted and looked beautiful. Too many men lined up for their congratulatory kiss, and Sally accommodated them all. Except John Bennett—just as he arrived at the head of the line, Sally excused herself abruptly and went into the bedroom, as if to adjust something in her clothing.

Bennett took it as a joke. "It's a good thing for you, Charlie, that your wife won't get a taste for *my* kisses. I have it on good authority that they're irresistible." There was a good round of laughter, and Charlie almost forgot the incident.

By dark most of the guests had already left; John Kirkham dismissed the others, and Clintons and Kirkhams shared a wedding supper. Charlie had decided to live the Word of Wisdom only three weeks before, and so John Kirkham and Sally's father had no help from him in finishing a bottle of claret that Brother Clinton had been saving for the first wedding in the family. Anna, Dinah, Harriette, and Mother Clinton quickly cleaned up and put away, and by nine o'clock Charlie and Sally were alone, with only the last distant strains of their fathers' lung-bursting song to keep them company.

Sally sat at the table, her hands folded, looking sweet and calm and determinedly virginal. Charlie had a notion that she wouldn't like it if he seemed too eager to get her into bed, so he made several abortive attempts to converse about the Prophet's sermon. Sally only smiled and answered with small words. It was impossible to get a conversation going. He was getting desperate when she reached out a hand and took his across the table. "Aren't you tired, Charlie? I am."

Gratefully Charlie admitted to a little weariness.

Sally grinned at him. "Oh, not *too* sleepy, I hope!"

Charlie wondered if he was blushing as he led her to the bedroom. They stood a moment at the door, and Charlie noticed that the room was not quite as he had left it. There was a Bible on the bed. Charlie walked to it and opened it at the ribbon. He as quickly shut it again. But Sally immediately took it from him and opened it and started to read.

"'Let him kiss me with the kisses of his mouth: for thy love is better than wine. Because of the savour of thy good ointments thy name is as ointment poured forth, therefore do the virgins love thee.'"

"I didn't know it was there," Charlie said.

"Harriette put it there. Of all the poems Harriette loves, she loves this one best of all."

Charlie didn't know what to think. Harriette and the Song of Songs did not belong in the same thought.

"Do you want to hear my favorite part, Charlie?"

He did.

"'My beloved spake and said unto me, Rise up, my love, my fair one, and come away. For, lo, the winter is past, and rain is over and gone; the flowers appear on the earth; the time of the singing of birds is come, and the voice of the turtle is heard in our land; the fig tree putteth forth her green figs, and the vines with the tender grape give a good smell. Arise, my fair one, and come away.'"

"Too bad it's still so wintry outside," Charlie said lamely.

"It isn't in here," Sally said. "Do you want to hear Harriette's favorite part?"

It annoyed Charlie that Harriette had managed still to be

present, looking on, even now. But he nodded, to be polite.

"'I sleep, but my heart waketh: it is the voice of my beloved that knocketh, saying, Open to me, my sister, my love, my dove, my undefiled: for my head is filled with dew, and my locks with the drops of the night. I have put off my coat; how shall I put it on? I have washed my feet; how shall I defile them? I rose up to open my beloved; and my hands dropped with myrrh, and my fingers with sweet smelling myrrh, upon the handles of the lock. I opened to my beloved; but my beloved had withdrawn himself, and was gone: my soul failed when he spake; I sought him, but I could not find him; I called him, but he gave me no answer.'"

"That's sad," Charlie said.

Sally shrugged. "Harriette is sad a good deal of the time. I think she likes it."

"I don't." He took the book from her and turned away, reading aloud, making fun of the scripture a little. Of himself a little. "Thou art beautiful, O my love, as Tirzah."

"Who's Tirzah?"

"I'll never tell. Thou art comely as Jerusalem, terrible as an army with banners."

"I do believe you're afraid of me."

He turned to her. "A little." He remembered his mother saying, Be gentle with her, go slowly.

She was holding the room's only candle. She smiled at him and blew it out. "Will I be less frightening in the dark?"

He could hear the swishing of cloth as she undressed; his own fingers were cold and trembled at the buttons of his vest. He finally got it off, and his boots, and his shirt, but by then the sound of her clothing had already ceased; too quickly he heard her climb onto the bed. "Are you still there, Charlie?" she asked.

"I'm—having trouble with the buttons in the dark."

"Which buttons, Charlie?"

"My, uh—pants."

"Maybe if I help you it will go faster," she suggested. She was right.

Harriette insisted on walking Dinah home from the wedding supper. It was not in Dinah's plan. Not tonight, anyway. What if he came, saw that Dinah had a visitor, and decided that he must have misunderstood her message? Or worse, what if he did not realize she had company until too late? I must be as careful as an adulteress, thought Dinah. I must be sure no tongues carry the tale to Emma.

And yet she could not refuse Harriette, not tonight, not with Harriette's younger sister being bedded by a husband, and Harriette still uncourted. Not fair, thought Dinah. No one sees, not even most women, no one sees that Harriette is worth ten of Sally, though Sally is better than most. It's bad enough that men can see no more of a woman than the arrangement of her face or the way hips and breasts ride on her—surely women should see more. Yet we judge each other, not as sisters, but as rivals.

"Since you're so silent, Dinah, shall I tell you what you're thinking?"

Dinah smiled, then let herself chuckle aloud because in the darkness a smile would not be seen.

"You're wondering how you'll get rid of me before he comes."

Dinah's chuckle died. She could think of nothing to say that would be neither a lie nor a confession.

"Don't be afraid, Dinah. I don't know who it is. But I know that you're no adulteress, and your secret is safe with me. I came tonight because I thought it was time you knew that you need not bear this burden alone."

"A moment ago," Dinah said softly, "I was thinking that women should be sisters, and not rivals."

"That's easy for me—I've never been a rival to any woman."

"How did you know?"

"You told me."

"I!"

"Don't be afraid. You've told all of Nauvoo, but I think no one will understand but me."

Told all Nauvoo—impossible. And then she remembered the few little poems she had posted anonymously to the *Times and Seasons*. Don Carlos had printed them. Yet those poems had said nothing of her secret husband.

"I knew at once that the poems were yours."

"How?"

"Because you were the only literate woman I know who did not praise them."

"Perhaps I merely had good taste."

"And because when I stood inside those poems to see the world the poet's way, I knew I was looking outward through your eyes."

"When *I* read them over, they seem as though a stranger wrote them."

"That's because your poems know you better than your own mind does. It doesn't matter. I didn't tell you before because I was afraid you'd stop publishing them if your name was known."

"I may do just that."

"But then I realized that there are two sad women in this world. There's the woman who can tell no one her inmost thoughts, because she is afraid. And there's the woman who is even more afraid, and so she does not even tell her inmost thoughts to herself, and instead publishes them for strangers because she knows they will not understand."

They followed the path that slanted across the face of Temple Hill. It was treacherous going, and the moonlight made deceptive shadows. Dinah took Harriette's offered hand.

"Two women like that ought to know each other," Harriette said.

Yes, Dinah said silently. Yet, afraid still, she said nothing aloud. They walked in silence for a few moments, struggling up the hillside with their hoops encumbering. Then Harriette began to recite Dinah's most recently published poem.

> *He will build his temple to the Lord;*
> *His tow'r will rise until the very heaven,*
> *The walls and windows all according to his word;*
> *For in this Godless world he is the leaven,*
> *And all he touches is exalted, all*
> *He loves is soon made whole.*
>
> *He will build his temple to the Lord;*
> *But, all unknown, he also builds in small:*
> *In me the light finds windows at his word;*
> *He raises up this daughter of the Fall;*
> *For as he teaches, I'm exalted, Heaven*
> *Opens to my soul.*

Dinah felt naked, hearing the words spoken aloud like that; and yet not defiled, for Harriette's voice, ungentle as it was, said the poem naturally, truthfully.

"I already knew," said Harriette, "that you loved a man and could not have him."

"Am I so transparent?"

"Sometimes, and only because I watch you. I saw how distracted you were some months ago. How people could speak to you at quilting and at prayer meetings and you'd not hear them. Silent you often are, but never inattentive, so I knew. And then, suddenly, around the time that Charlie and Sally got engaged, you changed again. I have never seen such calm. I'm not the only one who noticed it. Vilate said just the other day, 'Dinah is a well, so deep and pure that only God can drink from her.'"

"She said that?"

"Don't you recognize it? It's a line from your own poem. 'Let us all be wells of living water. Let us, sisters, all be deep and pure, so the Fount of all will know his daughter, and give his only Son to drink from her.' We read your poetry and quote it like scripture. Because you speak to women as the men so rarely bother to do. But *they* all think that you are writing about the Savior."

"I am."

"I wondered if you thought so, too. But those are all love poems, Dinah, and they're all written to Joseph Smith."

They were atop the hill now, with the excavation for the temple yawning open before them. Dinah felt giddy, dizzy, as if she would be sucked down into that shadow by the wind, if she leaned too far, if she didn't hold tight to Harriette to keep her balance.

"Don't be afraid, shh, shh, you have nothing to fear from me, don't you see that?" Harriette's arm was around her shoulders; Dinah was gripping the other arm as if she meant to wring it off. "It was only a few days ago that I understood it all— *you* didn't give it away. A man came to Sally, a man who knew she was getting married, a man who is trusted in this city, and he told her that God had commanded her to be his spiritual wife. That it was the will of God that the great men of the kingdom have many secret wives, and that even after she married Charlie, this man would come to her secretly so that all the children she conceived would be his."

Dinah was stunned. Put in those terms the doctrine sounded filthy, not at all like the celestial marriage Joseph had taught to her. Yet she didn't know how to name the difference. "That sounds," Dinah said, "like adultery masquerading as religion."

"It *is*. Sally told him to take a long stroll down the bottom of the Mississippi. He warned her that if she told anyone she'd be damned, and then he went away."

"But she told *you*."

"Sally and I are sisters. We have no secrets. And I went to Brother Joseph and asked him about it."

"You don't mean that it was—"

"No! Don't you know your husband better than that?"

Harriette's words burned her like lightning down a tree. Don't you know your husband? Dinah had not known how much it would mean to her, to have another woman speak of Joseph Smith and say those words.

"I assure you it was *not* Brother Joseph who came to Sally."

"Who was it, then?"

"I promised Sally that I'd never tell, and I keep my word. I didn't tell Brother Joseph, either. I only asked him if there was such a doctrine. And so he swore me to secrecy and told me all about celestial marriage."

Now it occurred to Dinah that perhaps Harriette had even more in common with her than she had thought. "Are you also his—"

"No. The Lord did not give me to him. Would it matter if I were his wife?"

"Of course it wouldn't." Don't lie to yourself. "Yes, it would. Isn't that stupid of me? I knew he had another wife when I married him, and yet I'd be jealous of you if—"

"Yes, it's stupid of you. But then, it's plain you didn't understand the doctrine from the start, Dinah. When Joseph was explaining that carnal pleasure was not the purpose of the doctrine, he told me that one of his own wives had refused to let him into her bed, and that he did not regard her as any less his wife because of that. It was at that moment that I knew: he was the lover you were writing to, and you were the wife so unbelieving that you denied your body to your husband."

"I was testing." It sounded even to her like a lame apology. Dinah had long been prepared to bear criticism of her accepting Joseph's offer of marriage; she had never imagined someone might criticize her for refusing him.

"You were testing the Prophet?"

Harriette insisted on looking at things so backwardly. "I was testing myself."

"Ah. Yes, I was afraid of that, too. That I believed only because I wanted to, and not because God wanted me to."

"How can you *want* to believe it?"

"Because, Dinah, only a man who already has a wife will look at this ugly woman and realize that she might be something worth having."

"You aren't ugly."

"I have looked thirty-five ever since I was thirteen. To a man, that's the same as ugly."

"Until you turn thirty-five." Log walls formed themselves in the moonlight. "There's my house."

"There's no light. Does that mean that he *is* there or that he *isn't?*"

"I don't know. Neither."

"Don't you have signals already planned?"

"How can we? We've never done this. He might not even come tonight."

"You've never done this? Dinah, do you mean that tonight will be—"

"If he comes."

"I wouldn't have come with you if I had known. I'll say good-night here—"

"No, come in with me."

"I'll no more come in with you tonight than I would go in with Sally." Harriette kissed Dinah's cheek and then hurried away into the darkness. Dinah watched her out of sight, which wasn't far, despite the moonlight; the bushes, still bare of leaves, were like a low fog, and Harriette was soon lost in it.

Dinah went to the cabin and opened the door, her hands cold and trembling. He was not inside. He was not sitting on the edge of her new bed, waiting for her. She was relieved; she was disappointed. It was not a new feeling, to be disappointed at the opening of a door. For all these months in America, she had opened doors now and then and been startled, grieved that Val was not just inside, playing on the floor, that Honor was not toddling to meet her, even though she had not been thinking of them until the door opened, even though she did not expect ever to see them again; the patterns in her heart were worn too deep, and she anticipated without knowing it, longing for that familiar, beloved sight. Joseph had never been behind the door, yet he, too, was anticipated, was familiar; she had dreamed him too often, had needed him so many times in years past, when it was Matthew behind the door. She had been disappointed then, too.

She closed the door and latched it, cutting off the wind; yet it wasn't that much warmer with the door closed, and for a moment she was afraid that the fire had gone out cold. But no, there were some coals. She nursed a flame to life with tinder and a few gentle puffs of breath; soon she had a blaze that filled the room with light. Then she slowly undressed, put on her nightgown, and then sat at the table for a few minutes to write in her journal. But when she tried to put down words about what she had done, what she had seen and felt today, she could not think of anything to write. "Charlie married," that was all. Then she set her pen aside and scanned through recent pages. She hadn't written more than two or three proper entries in months. Only poems. How could she baldly write the dilemmas that had torn her all this time? Someone might find this journal, and the evidence would be damning. The world would never understand that her marriage to Joseph was holy, not profane.

So holy that she wondered if perhaps she had waited too long. Harriette was wrong, of course. He would not come tonight. He might not come at all. Her note had been so cryptic; perhaps a clerk had intercepted it, and thought it not important enough to bring it to the Prophet's notice. Even if he knew she wanted him, why should he come at a woman's bidding? After she had refused him once, he might well feel it proper to repay one rebuff with another. No, he would not be so petty. Their marriage was pure. Maybe all his marriages were pure. Maybe that's how celestial marriages ought to be.

If so, then to hell with celestial marriages.

Dinah shuddered at her own thought. Forgive me, she thought. Come to me, Joseph. I've waited too long already.

But he did not come. No poem would come to her tonight, either, and so she put her pen away, closed up the inkwell, and blew out the candle at her writing table. Only the fire burned. She threw on a log, so it would last the night. Then she put off her slippers on the dirt floor, and slid under the cold and rough cotton sheets. She curled up, brought her knees to her chest, and prayed—it was too cold and dirty to kneel

beside her bed. The wind reached down the chimney and made
her fire flare out into the room, putting a little of the acrid
smell of smoke into the air. A thin film of dust skittered across
the dirt floor. And then, suddenly, she awoke, though she had
not been aware that she had dozed. There was a cold wind on
her face. The door was open. And a man stood in the doorway,
silhouetted in the moonlight.

As the night grew late, Joseph tried to think how he might
make his way to Dinah undiscovered. It was Emma herself
who gave him the excuse.

"Joseph, I wish you wouldn't wait till noon to go to Warsaw."

"The trip's been planned for a week," he answered. Little
Joseph snuggled into his neck and murmured, "Talk softer,
Papa, I'm trying to sleep."

"That's what I mean," Emma said. "You're getting careless.
You know that assassins from Missouri have crossed the river.
You should never let them know your comings and goings in
advance, it fairly invites them to try their luck with you."

"You make me sound like a hunted buck."

"It's what you are."

"Papa, shh. You'll wake me."

Joseph took little Joseph up the stairs and laid him in his
bed. Emma was waiting for him in the hall as he closed the
door to the children's room. "Leave at dawn, Joseph."

He didn't blush or stammer. Plotting to sleep with another
woman did not hinder his speech at all. "It takes till noon to
get things underway in the morning. I'll go tonight."

Startled, Emma protested. "But you need your sleep—"

"I have friends. I'll stay in a farmhouse overnight. Let my
murderers look for me by daylight and they'll have no notion
where I am."

"I have a better idea, Joseph! Don't go at all!"

Joseph shook his head. "If I can make a deal with Stephen
Douglas and his friends we'll have no hindrance in this state.
And they've made it clear they want to deal with *me*." He
smiled. "There are actually some people who like me better
than they like John Bennett."

Emma frowned. "I don't like John Bennett at all. I think
he's a liar."

"If he is, he's a very talented one. The whole state of Illinois believes our charter."

"He smiles too much."

"He's a cheerful man. Give me a kiss, love. I'll have Port hitch up the carriage. No need to waken anyone else."

"What shall I tell the Brethren?"

Joseph laughed. "*You* tell them nothing! I'll leave a note for Hyrum. The Brethren don't much like taking their instructions from my wife."

"The world would be better if more men took instructions from their wives."

"Too bad that I'm the only man who does," Joseph said. He kissed her again and walked down the stairs.

She called after him. "You don't either, except when it happens to fit what you already had in mind!"

"Quiet! You'll wake the children!" He laughed at her from the foot of the stairs, and she smiled down at him, and then he turned and went outside in search of Porter Rockwell, hurrying so that he could get to Dinah before she went to sleep.

Port stopped the carriage where Joseph told him. "Take the carriage on to Brother Simon's place, and tell him I want people to think I stayed with him tonight."

"Where *will* you be?" Port asked.

"I'll be at Simon's place by morning."

"But what about tonight?"

"If I wanted you to know, I'd tell you."

Port had his stubborn face on. "You're not just Joe Smith, you know. If the Church should need you, someone ought to know where you're to be found."

"It's my destruction if it's known where I am tonight."

"If you don't trust me by now, you're a damned fool," Porter said. "I wouldn't tell God himself if he asked me."

"God already knows." Why must my friends always test how much I trust them by asking me to trust them all too much? "I'll be at a new cabin on Mulholland, about a half-mile north of here, four blocks or so east of the temple."

Porter nodded. "Dinah Kirkham's place."

Joseph was annoyed. "How did you know?"

"I make it a point to know who lives in every house between Nauvoo and the nearest patch of wild country. If I don't know where you'll be safe, what the hell good am I as a bodyguard?"

"I'm on the Lord's business there tonight."

Port shrugged. "Whoever's business it is, it sure as hell ain't mine." He clacked at the horses and the carriage lurched off into the darkness.

It was a fair walk to Dinah's house in the dark. With the temple going up on the hill now, a good many people were building up here, and Joseph had to walk around several foundation holes. But there were no houses yet; no one saw him as he made his way northward through the night.

When he got there her cabin was dark. It surprised him. Surely she would be waiting for him—or had he misunderstood? What if the note wasn't from her after all? What if he had been so obsessed with her that he had read an innocent letter all wrong? He could not decide whether to go on to Brother Simon's house or go up and knock on Dinah's door. So he did neither, and was standing outside watching when Dinah and Harriette arrived.

He couldn't hear what they had to say. They talked only briefly, and then Harriette went off westward, alone. It was a good sign and a bad one: good because it meant Dinah wanted to be alone, bad because Harriette was no fool, and might guess why Dinah was so rude as not to invite her in.

As soon as Harriette was gone, Joseph started for the door. But he stopped short of it. Cold as it was he could not bring himself to knock and go inside. He was afraid, and had a thousand reasons for his fear; a thousand reasons, and only one that he believed: What if she wouldn't have him after all? He saw a candle lit near the oilcloth window; he told himself he dared not go inside when candlelight might reveal to a watching stranger his face at the door. The candle went out, and still he hesitated, not wanting to startle her immodestly as she undressed. But at last the cold breeze mocked him more than he could bear. Had he come as a husband or as a beggar to her door? If the latter, he should waste no more time, and go away. If the former, it was his right to go inside.

He came to the door, prepared to knock, and then saw the shadow of the latchstring in the moonlight. She had left the way clear for him to come in tonight. He had been a fool to wait. He pulled the string softly; the latch rose inside. He pushed the door gently, and it would not budge; pushed it harder, and it fell open suddenly, throwing a gust of wind into the room. He heard the leaves of a book turn in the breeze; he stood, trying to get used to the sudden firelight.

"Joseph," she said sleepily from the bed.

He couldn't think of anything intelligent to say, now that he was here. "I came to dedicate your house."

"Yes," she said. "Come in." But there was no hint of gladness in her voice. He was at such a pitch of expectation that her near monotone sounded like coldness rather than the timidity she really felt.

"He closed the door behind him, and drew the latchstring in. "It was careless of you to leave the door like that. You never know who might come in at night."

"I left it for my husband."

She sounded so distant. She didn't want *him*, he realized now. She didn't love him the way he loved her. She just wanted to obey the Lord. It would be torture to her, having to receive him in her bed, and he couldn't bear to know she felt that way. "I wouldn't do this if the Lord hadn't commanded it."

Her smile grew even thinner. "Be obedient then," she said, "and do your duty."

He turned away from her, faced the fire, and carefully undressed. He knew he looked brutish to her, coming in from the night for this purpose only. This wasn't how it should be between husband and wife; but how could he handle things any other way, without being discovered? He sat on the foot of the bed and pulled off his boots, took his feet from his trousers and put the clothing on top of a nearby trunk. He felt timid, embarrassed as a virgin, and so to deny that feeling he turned to her, the fire hot on his back. "You know that I'll never go to prison again. I'll never come to you if there's the slightest risk that I'll be caught."

"I know," she said softly, her eyes deep and red with reflected fire.

"Until the world is ready to endure the Principle, I'll have to deny you. If we conceive a child I'll never say it's mine. If a member of the Church should accuse you of adultery, I can't speak up in your defense."

"I wouldn't want you to," she said.

"Even if they excommunicate you, Dinah. Do you understand that? For the safety of the whole church, for my life's sake we can't tell."

"I can bear anything," she said. She opened the sheets for him, and he joined her on the bed.

He was angry at himself for having wanted her, and it hurt

him that she did not want him too. But he knew it was better this way, without illusion, without lies. He hated liars, couldn't bear to be one, though he knew as he took her that he was lying to Emma. It made him angry. It made him abrupt and quick, ungentle with her, so that even the way he took her made him ashamed. He could see in her face that his manner had caused her pain, that she regretted this night's work; he rolled to the side of the bed, turned his back to her, and hated himself for lying to Dinah even in the way that he had lain with her. Even if she did not want him, he wanted her now more than ever, for her body had been sweet and beautiful, her kisses fiery, and he loved her so much that he yearned for her even now, when he had just possessed her.

"Joseph," she said. "Don't you want to love me, even a little?"

Did she doubt *him?* "A little?" he asked. "Enough that I risked ruin to come. Enough that I think of you so often that I'm constantly afraid I'll say your name without meaning to. Enough that when I took the plate from your hand today I wanted to bend and kiss you in front of everyone."

"I wish you had," she said.

Did she love him, then? When the Spirit had told him she was his, had it been true after all. Tears came to his eyes in spite of himself, tears of relief that his love for her was answered. He could not think what to say, and so he said, "You're the first of my wives I've lain with, except for Emma."

She laughed gently. "Then you've failed in your duty, haven't you?"

He rolled over to face her. "I tried to do it for duty alone, but I can't."

She kissed the tears on his cheeks, touched them. "You are husband, brother, father, children to me now."

"All of those?"

All of those, and one more she did not name: for the face she touched now was the face of God, the light that she had followed across the sea. "If I ever lose you, Joseph, I've got nothing left. But if you lose me, what have you lost?"

His answer was plain, and comforted her much.

He got up from the bed in darkness, dressed quickly in the cold, and put another log on the fire for her as he left. They said nothing, just kissed once more; she tried to get up from the bed to see him to the door, but he gently held her to the bed. "I want to look back from the door," he said, "and see you there waiting for me." So she lay there and he looked back at her, and she was glad when he looked at her body with owning eyes: you, she said, this belongs to you, all those years of Matthew, but all along I belonged to you. And when he was gone she lay tingling under the sheet and blanket and comforter, as if the cotton were the touch of his hand. She prayed that she would conceive a child for him. She prayed that a miracle would happen, and Emma would embrace her and welcome her as a sister, and the two of them would stand beside Joseph in a public meeting, both equally honored as his wife, both surrounded by the children they had borne for him. She prayed for it, even pretended that it was a vision. But she knew that it was not. He would always come to her in secret, and go again; she would have to put a lifetime's marriage into a few hours each month, a few days each year.

She must have slept after he left, but she didn't remember it. It was still dark when she got up and dressed, still dark when she headed eastward in a thin rain to open up the school and ring the bell. Her students came in noisily, happy with their uncomplicated lives, resentful at having to surrender themselves again to their teacher's will. Dinah greeted little Joseph and Julia as calmly as ever, but she wanted to hug them for having helped her make her choice the afternoon before.

Today she was too happy to be stern. She tried, but her heart wasn't in it. The children knew immediately and soon were out of hand, quarreling and talking back to her, and finally slammed a book on the table so loud it sounded like a musket. The children were startled and fell silent. She laughed at their surprise and told them a story that she had heard from one of the older women at the factory in Manchester. Dinah changed details of the story so that it sounded as though it had happened in Illinois, and not too long ago—changed wishes to prayers, and told of a peddler and a medicine man instead of a curate and a libidinous monk. When the tale was finished, she had won the children back. And herself, too: she would not be impatient at the pain; life itself was change, and she could not live forever that one good night. It was day, and the children needed her, and no one in the world could share her joy, could share her grief.

Except for other plural wives. Let there be more plural wives in Nauvoo, she prayed silently as the day wore on. Let there be hundreds of women living the Principle of Celestial Marriage. Then we'll have a sisterhood to uphold us, women to know that our babies are righteously born. Then young girls won't have to watch in despair as all the men worth marrying are taken, one by one, forcing them to settle for the rest: the best of men can marry us all, and leave the swine to wallow with the whores.

Dinah and Harriette often talked about the Principle when they were alone, sharing the same dream of the City of God, where all the secrets could be opened.

"What I can't figure out," Harriette said one day, "is why the Lord is taking so long to get this under way. You have *your* husband, but mine's still blind as a bat."

"Yours?" Dinah asked. "Do you know who he is?"

"Why, don't you know yet?"

"How could I?"

"It's Charlie, of course."

"Charlie! My brother! Your own sister's husband!"

Harriette laughed. "I knew his worth before she ever set her cap for him. *I* was the one who pointed him out to her. He doesn't know it, but I'm better for him than any other woman in the world."

Dinah couldn't help but laugh. "No, I'm not laughing at you—just at Charlie. He doesn't suspect a thing, not a thing."

"I suppose the Lord is waiting for him to learn how to be a good husband to one wife, before saddling him with two." Harriette smiled her wise and frightening smile. "Or maybe he's just waiting until he gets over being afraid of me."

"He'll always be afraid of you. You're cleverer than he is."

Harriette shook her head and bowed over her tatting. "Not clever enough to learn to be happy alone."

"No one's that clever," Dinah said. "Be patient, Harriette. For Charlie to grow up is a full-fledged miracle. The Lord has to take time to do it right."

It was only later that it occured to Dinah how much her view of things had changed, not to be horrified when Harriette confessed that she coveted her own sister's husband, and meant to have him, too. Dinah tried to be ashamed, but couldn't manage it, for she hoped that Harriette would have her way.

❧ 32 ❧

Joseph Smith
Nauvoo and Quincy, 1841

EMMA GOT UP EVEN earlier than usual, and clattered dishes so loud down in the kitchen that it woke little Alex, who naturally felt it his duty to waken everyone else in the family at the impossible hour of five-forty-five. Everyone was out of sorts at breakfast. Except, by main force, Joseph Smith himself. He refused to let Emma get his goat. She was angry about something—he knew that last night when she fairly threw herself into bed before he was even up the stairs and pretended to be asleep as he undressed. Then she tossed and turned and thumped the pillow so often and so loud that Joseph thought he might prefer an earthquake. But he hadn't said a word then, and he didn't say a word this morning as she plopped bowls in front of everyone and slapped out spoonfuls of wheat mash as sullen as Joseph had ever seen her. She was angry, but she wasn't quite ripe yet, and Joseph knew from experience that when her wrath was ripe, there was no need to ask questions.

All would be explained, in detail with more than adequate repetition.

"What's wrong with Mama?" Julia whispered as soon as Emma took the pot back into the kitchen.

"Nothing's wrong with Mama," Emma said loudly from the kitchen.

Joseph just touched his lips with his finger and then said a long, long blessing on the food, in which he ironically thanked the Lord for the spirit of peace which constantly dwelt in his household.

After breakfast, the children were at a loss for things to do, being up so early. This led to five-year-old Frederick attempting to murder his older brother Joseph with a coat rack, which led to Julia getting kicked in the shin when she tried to intervene, which led to screaming and shouting until Papa got everything calmed down by telling the story all over again about how he got away from jail in Missouri.

"I wish you wouldn't tell them about jail all the time," Emma said sharply. "They have nightmares."

"Sorry, Mama," Joseph said meekly.

At last it was time for school. Joseph made sure Julia and little Joseph were presentable; Emma made a point of inspecting each of them again and finding something wrong, which required immediate remedy. Then Frederick started yelling that there was a spider on the wall above the baby. Emma rushed upstairs to commit arachnicide.

Taking advantage of her absence, Joseph opened the front door. "All right, off to school."

Little Joseph looked meaningfully up the stairs. "I don't know what you did, Papa, but it looks like you're really going to catch it."

"Maybe." Joseph pushed him gently out the door.

"Don't you wish you could come to school with us?" Julia asked.

Joseph thought of Dinah. He hadn't seen her in a week, hadn't even laid eyes on her. And after Hyrum and William left on their missions today, he'd have even less free time. I don't mean to be ungrateful, Father in heaven, but if you're going to give me a multitude of wives, you might also give me time to visit them.

"Where are Julia and little Joseph?" Emma asked.

"Gone," Joseph said. "To school."

"With their hair unbrushed, no doubt."

"You already brushed them, dear." It was seven o'clock. He had to get started for Quincy by eight. Whatever quarrel Emma wanted had to be over by then. So Joseph grinned at her. He knew that when she was upset that always provoked her beyond endurance.

It worked again. She got right to the point. "Spiritual wives," she said.

Joseph raised an eyebrow. "Yes?" he asked.

"Yesterday three separate people told me rumors about spiritual wives in Nauvoo. Two of them called it glorified whoring."

"How interesting," Joseph said.

"Don't play the fool with me, Joseph," Emma said. "How many people have you taught that doctrine to?"

"My love, I don't think that's any affair of yours."

"You *promised* me—"

"I promised you that you'd have the right to give consent to any plural wife I took. Nothing more."

"So you're going about wildly teaching this doctrine that could *destroy* the Church, without any thought of the consequences!"

"As a matter of fact, Emma," Joseph said, trying to remain calm, "as a matter of fact I can't think of more than five people who've been taught the doctrine, and I've commanded none of them to live it."

"*Someone* is."

"Not with my consent."

"Then obviously someone's disobeying you."

Joseph shook his head. "Not the people that I've taught. They'd never tell a soul."

"Joseph, I despair of you. Just because you trust someone doesn't mean he's worth anything. Who did you tell? Sidney? Now there's a sieve for secrets."

"Not Sidney."

"Bennett, then? He's famous for discretion."

"He is discreet about matters like that. Why do you always come down on Bennett?"

"I know, Mayor Bennett's sacred, Bennett is not to be criticized."

"He's done more for this city than any other man—"

"I will *not* be sidetracked! There's only one place where rumors of spiritual wives could possibly start, and that's with *you.*"

"I would never call them 'spiritual wives,' Emma, the term isn't even accurate."

"I thought it was a very gentle word for what they are!" Emma caught herself then. "I'm sorry. I know it's a doctrine—"

"I wondered if you would remember."

."Don't be snide with *me*, Joseph. The Church isn't ready to accept that doctrine—"

"Most of the Church—"

"And it's a sure thing that the world isn't ready. Wouldn't they love to have *that* to tell on Joe Smith and the Mormons. Harems, like the Turks. That'll do wonders for the missionary work. Join the Mormons so your daughter can go to bed with a married man—"

"Enough."

"It is *not* enough. Because I don't think it *is* a revelation, Joseph Smith. I think that one day a few years ago you saw a pretty young girl and compared her to this sharp-tongued shrew who's older than you and not very pretty anymore, and you thought, a prophet can't very well go around divorcing his wife, even if she *does* keep bearing sickly babies who die the day they're born, so I'll just—"

Joseph took her by the shoulders and brought his face close to hers and kissed her, hard. She resisted only at first. But when the kiss ended, she was only slightly assuaged. "I know you aren't an adulterer," she said. "And I know you're a true prophet, I don't doubt you for a moment—"

"But."

"But you shouldn't teach that doctrine to *anybody*. It'll be the end of this Church if you do. The end of *you*, Joseph. They'd kill you for that, you know they would."

"They don't need Celestial Marriage to convince them to kill me. Now when women bring rumors like that to you, you just tell them it's nonsense, that no such thing is going on."

Emma looked at him pleadingly. "Would I be lying, Joseph? Promise me that I wouldn't be lying."

"You can tell them that the Prophet hasn't taught any man to take any spiritual wives."

Emma nodded and embraced him, but Joseph knew she was not convinced. The pots still rattled noisily when she got back to the kitchen, and he wondered if one of his own wives had been indiscreet, had confided in a friend. Impossible. He had warned them all that when it came to the Principle, there were no friends. The only people to be trusted were the ones that the Lord commanded Joseph Smith to tell. No one else had the right to teach the doctrine.

And yet somebody was. Emma was right to be worried for the Church. The trouble was that Joseph knew she was far more worried for herself. And for the next few days she would be watchful, for she was no fool. She suspected, at least, that Joseph had already taken plural wives, if only because she knew he would not disobey the Lord for long, even if it meant breaking a promise to her. She was almost a madwoman on the matter. Sometimes she would test him by suggesting women he ought to marry, and seeing if he would rise to the bait and agree that some sister would make a good plural wife. He had a pretty good idea of what sort of hell the poor girl would go through after that, so he had never played along—but that didn't stop Emma from trying. After all, she had the evidence of their own elopement to prove that he was the sort of man who would run off and marry a woman secretly after promising he wouldn't. She was suspicious from the moment that he taught her the Principle.

I wish, thought Joseph, that all of Emma's children had lived, so that she wouldn't feel that God somehow judged her to be an unworthy wife for me. I wish that the years had been kinder to her, so that she would not feel so threatened by young and pretty women. And while I'm wishing, I wish we didn't live in the United States of America, a nation of hypocrites where lying, thieving, whoring bastards could do what they liked, but truly devout people could be mobbed and hounded and criticized for every move they made.

And above all, Joseph wished he had peace in his own home. Some respite from the struggle. But it seemed that the battle always worsened the nearer it came to home.

Joseph looked at the door, at the sunlight streaming in above it, and decided that one wish, at least, he could fulfil. If he couldn't have peace in this home, with this wife, he could find solace with another. Let Emma watch all she likes. I'm going to see how my children are doing at school.

Dinah was superb. She didn't even pause in her sentence when he opened the door and stepped in. She merely assigned twenty-five words in their spellers and walked briskly to the back of the room.

"Brother Smith, would you be willing to step outside for our conversation so we don't disturb the children?"

Once outside, she firmly closed the door and then led him twenty feet along the alley behind the store. "Speak softly," she said. "They'd love to listen to every word we say."

"Let them."

"No," Dinah said. "Because I intend to tell you that I love you rather often, and it might cause scandal if they heard."

"Tell me."

"I love you. And you're a fool to come here when I'm teaching."

"How are my children doing, Sister Handy?"

"Very well, thank you."

"And how is my wife."

"I love you."

He laughed and wanted to kiss her and dared not, which stopped his laughter. "I'm going to Quincy today. To see Hyrum and William off on their missions. And to meet with Governor Carlin."

"I hate it when you travel."

"We're hardly together even when I'm in town."

"But I can see you, and I can tell myself that part of you is mine. That part of you is me."

"I came to make an indecent proposal. Do you think you could find some excuse to get out of town today? I have in mind a ride in a closed carriage to Quincy, and I can make a big show of leaving Quincy this afternoon and then slip back into town tonight, and—"

Dinah was shaking her head. "I can't."

"You don't teach afternoons during the summer."

"I can't. I just can't."

He couldn't imagine Dinah would refuse without a reason. And it wasn't hard for him to guess what the reason was. It had been a month since last time, more or less, he supposed. "You aren't feeling well today?"

She was very, very relieved. "That's right," she said.

"Get back to your classroom, woman. The children will get suspicious."

"Joseph," she said. "I'm sorry. I wish—"

"No matter," he said. "Can't be helped." He brought her back along the alley, looked around to see if anyone was watching, and when he was sure no one could see he kissed her quickly on the lips, then turned and walked away. After a dozen yards he turned back to wave, but she was already inside, and the door was closing. It was a damn fool idea anyway, trying a rendezvous right in the heart of Gentile country. Perhaps that was what appealed to him so much about it. To meet this wife God gave to him right where the devil was so strong, that would have made it all the more delicious. But no matter. Just seeing her was enough to brighten him for the morning's ride. And to think the Lord went to all the trouble of bringing her from England to make his life joyful just when he thought he had forgotten what it felt like to be loved without criticism, loved without judgment, yet by a woman capable of both. Dinah doesn't love me because she doesn't know better. She loves me because she knows me better than anyone.

Hyrum was troublesome all the way to Quincy. Joseph tried to bear it without argument—after all, Hyrum *was* his older brother—but after a time it became more than he could stand.

"Joseph, if you're going to send me and William on missions, I wish you'd send Bennett on one, too."

Enough was enough. Joseph pulled his horse to a stop, wheeled and faced his brother. Dust rose from the road and stuck to the sweat on their faces. June in Illinois gave a fair preview of the torments of hell. Joseph was not in a good mood and knew it, so he tried to keep his voice gentler than he felt. "In the first place, Hyrum, *I'm* not sending you on this mission—the Lord is."

Hyrum glanced at William Law and grinned. "I think I made him mad, William."

William nodded gravely. "He shows signs of it."

"I'm reprimanding you. Please take it seriously."

Hyrum nodded. "I do take it seriously, Joseph. I wish you'd take me seriously, too."

"I can't send Bennett on a mission because he's mayor of Nauvoo."

"William's your Second Counselor and I'm the Patriarch of the Church. You're sending *us*."

"In the second place, I can't send Bennett on a mission

because the Lord hasn't called him."

"The Lord shows excellent judgment. Did the Lord call him to be mayor?"

"Mayors are elected, not called."

"Joseph, we're all grown up now. Bennett was elected mayor because you nominated him. They'd elect my horse if you said you wanted him in office."

William spoke up. "That's not a bad idea for next term."

"In the third place," Joseph went on, "I'm here to keep an eye on him, and so is Sidney."

"Sidney's a sick old man. He's no match for Bennett."

"Am I?" Joseph stared at Hyrum, warning him to be careful of his answer.

Hyrum stared back and made no answer at all.

"Joseph," William said, "you trust people too much."

"Maybe. I trust *you*."

"You trust our loyalty," Hyrum said. "I wish you'd trust our judgment."

"Judgment." Joseph said the word contemptuously. "This isn't judgment. This is pure jealousy." Joseph saw both Hyrum and William stiffen in the saddle—he was striking them deep. Well, that's how he wanted to strike. "Do you think I haven't seen it before? Whenever the Lord sends me a new man, a man of ability, my old friends hate him. Everyone's afraid that someone else's gifts deny their own. They said the same things to me when Sidney first came, ten years ago."

"Have you ever known me to be envious before?" Hyrum asked.

"Evidence, Hyrum. Not feelings, not resentments. Evidence. If you can prove to me that John Bennett is untrustworthy, then I'll discuss it with you again." Joseph waved off the clerks who were waiting behind them in the road—they were getting too close, and he didn't want them to hear the leaders of the Church arguing.

"I wish you'd trust me more," Hyrum said.

Joseph looked his brother in the eye. "You have the power to destroy me with a word, Hyrum. There is no more trust in the world than what I have for you. It isn't my trust you want. It's my presidency. You want to make my decisions for me." Deliberately Joseph raised his voice. "Well, Hyrum, that power isn't mine to give. Don't speak to me about this again, not without evidence!" He could feel his words hanging in the hot wet air. The clerks had heard enough to make this a public rebuke.

Hyrum knew that he had gone as far as he dared. He smiled cheerfully and swung his horse around to continue the journey. William, however, grew sullen. "A counselor's supposed to give counsel."

Joseph was weary of pampering wounded pride, and William Law required more of it than most; but Joseph smiled and pampered him again. "I know, Brother William. You're doing what the Lord wants you to do. Do you think I don't know that? But so am I." Mollified, but not willing to show it, William kicked his horse and moved ahead. Joseph followed behind him and Hyrum, watching them. For all his attitude of surety, Joseph was disturbed that both these men detested John Bennett. William—well, he was a child, he could be dismissed with the charge of envy. But Hyrum wasn't the jealous sort. It made Joseph wonder.

It was a good thing the Twelve were coming home. They had been in England too long. In just another month or so they'd be here to balance Bennett's power. Joseph knew that too much of the Church had been put in Bennett's hands. And yet Bennett could do the work; it made no sense to give the power to men who only botched it. Hadn't he rammed the Nauvoo Charter through the Illinois legislature in twenty-one days? Hadn't he arranged a charter for the Nauvoo Legion, and got Joseph Smith the only lieutenant general's commission in the United States? I outrank everybody, Joseph thought with a smile. They'll never be able to send a mere colonel of militia to order me to surrender or face treason charges. I can order *them* to surrender, and the treason trial will go the other way, for a change. Bennett gave me *that*. What standard can I use, besides accomplishment? Bennett gets things done.

By the time they got to Quincy, William and Hyrum were cheerful again. The clerks were riding right with them now, and they sang hymns right into town, which attracted more than a little attention among the passersby. Then it was good-bye to Hyrum and William as they continued eastward on their missions. Only one other errand on this journey. Governor Thomas Carlin was at home in Quincy now, and Bennett had advised Joseph that it was always good to pay respects to a politician. "Politicians have a way of forgetting who their friends are, if you don't remind them often," Bennett had said. It was one of the reasons Joseph disliked politics. The men he had to deal with all had the scent of rot about them. Only a few of them were decent men, and those were rarely powerful enough to make much difference.

Governor Carlin was glad—nay, overjoyed—to see the Prophet. "I've been hoping you'd come! I've wanted to talk to you for months!" But when they did talk for half an hour alone in the governor's parlor, Carlin didn't say a thing. Joseph marveled at how the man could speak for so long a time without once adding significantly to the amount of intelligence in the world. "And thank you for coming by! I'm always glad to talk with a man of God, sir, and you're welcome to come see me anytime." Joseph shook hands and said the same kind of silliness back to him.

They headed back to Nauvoo the same day, got to a town some thirty miles from Nauvoo by nightfall, and spent the night in a hotel. The next morning they were hardly in the saddle before Joseph began to calculate how he might get rid of the clerks so that he could visit one of his wives tonight. One of his wives, he told himself, but it was Dinah that he knew he'd go to. She was the one he missed most, and how long had it been now? Weeks since he had seen her last. Seen her privately, that is. They met in public all the time. Some of his wives he dreaded meeting that way—they'd blush or stammer, they'd get shy and retreat from him—nothing obvious to anyone but him, but still a sign that there was more between them than law or custom would allow. Dinah, however, never changed around him. Or if she did, only got brighter, more cheerful, moving among the Saints as an angel with a Lancashire accent. They would have listened to her for that alone, her voice was music, sometimes Joseph would like to lie on her bed as she read poems to him, listening to her voice, hearing no words, letting her give him peace like birdsong or rushing water. And yet when he did pay attention to the words, it was not disappointing. She was like Emma that way—when she spoke she made sense. Not like a certain governor. Maybe he ought to get Dinah elected to something. Alderman. Alderwoman. He laughed—the voters would never stand for *that*.

"Joseph."

He started from his reverie. Howard Coray was beside him, leaning over, tugging at the reins of his horse, turning his mount around. Joseph looked where the clerk was looking, back down the road they had just passed over. A group of armed men were approaching. There was a gentle valley between them, but there was little time.

"Let's run for it!" Howard said.

"They're too close. They could shoot us out of the saddle."

"Maybe they're not after us," one of the younger men offered.

Joseph knew better. He had learned over the years that groups of armed men at full gallop were either coming to get Joseph Smith or coming to save him—they never just happened along. "Howard, get to Nauvoo and tell them what's happened. Tell Mayor Bennett that a certain son-of-a-bitch Governor isn't worth the price of the perfume he soaks his hair in. You might mention that if once they get me into jail, the Brethren can bet they'll never see me alive again."

"I can't leave you, Brother Joseph!"

"What, you want to watch the hanging?"

Howard looked at him a moment, sick with fear, then wheeled his horse and galloped off toward Nauvoo. "Don't watch after him," Joseph told the others. The road took a turn, and with luck Howard would be around it before their enemies got up the road enough to see him.

"Are you Joe Smith?" a man called out.

"If I'm not, you gentlemen have worked your horses into a lather for nothing."

The leader wore a badge. "I'm Sheriff King and this is a *posse comitatus*. Governor Carlin has sent us to arrest you and turn you over to the authorities of the state of Missouri to stand trial for prison escape and other sundry charges for which you have already been indicted."

At the mention of the state of Missouri Joseph could feel death at his back. He had escaped once, but they'd never let it happen again. Hating Mormons was practically the established religion on that side of the Mississippi. But it wouldn't do to let this sheriff see his fear; Joseph smiled warmly. "You got that speech down pretty good," Joseph said, making it sound like sincere praise. "You must have been working on it all the way here."

Sheriff King almost smiled with pride. "I do my job."

"Well, arrest me, then."

King looked confused. "I just did."

"No, you just told me that Governor Carlin sent you to do it. Now you actually have to say the words."

"Joseph Smith, I have been sent to arrest you—"

"No, no, you're doing it again." Joseph brought his horse closer and whispered. "Say 'I arrest you.'"

King whispered back. "That's all?"

"Yes sir. I've been arrested a few times, and that's the proper way."

"Joseph Smith, I arrest you."

"What's your name?"

"I'm Sheriff King."

"Sheriff, I've been kidnapped by mobs, I've been taken captive by soldiers under a flag of truce, I've been arrested now and then, but I must say that I'm proud of the state of Illinois for the way you've handled this. No waste of ammunition on silly shooting off of weapons, no unnecessary shouting—why, you've handled it so peaceful, right according to law, that it's almost a pleasure getting arrested by you. So instead of calling on the Nauvoo Legion to bring ten thousand troops to blast you and your little *posse comitatus* all to hell, I'll proceed orderly, too. Let's go right back to that little town where I spent such a pleasant night picking fleas, and see if they have a judge in town."

"I'm supposed to turn you over to the Missouri authorities."

"This is the state of Illinois, Sheriff King. Nobody from Missouri has even a teeny little speck of authority here. *You're* the man with all the authority. Now I'm a citizen of Illinois— I must be, I'm a lieutenant general in the Illinois militia. And you know that every arrested man has a right to talk to a judge or a justice of the peace."

"What for?"

"To get a writ of habeas corpus for your *posse comitatus*."

"Oh."

"Well, I figure we've accomplished all we can right here in the road. Shall we go?"

"All right, let's get these men back to—"

"Wait a minute!" Joseph said. "These *men?* Show me in your warrant where it says anything about my clerks."

"Well, it doesn't, exactly. But I wasn't supposed to let anybody—"

"Now Sheriff King, I thought you were going to do this proper. You can't hold these men without a warrant. And frankly, I need to have them get back to Nauvoo and tell my wife and children—and my lawyer—that I have been properly arrested by the supreme authority of the state of Illinois. But if you take these men under arrest without a warrant, well, that's false arrest, and you'll not only lose your job as sheriff, you'll go right to jail yourself. That's how these things are done."

King looked around at his men, flustered and uncertain. Joseph knew to keep still while he made up his mind. He just sat gripping the pommel, pretending to be relaxed. Finally King sighed. "General Smith, they told me you was slippery as manure on cobblestones, but I figure a man's got a right to send word to his family. Let these other fellows go."

Joseph asked George Robinson to stay with him and sent the others on their way. It relieved him that King had made his final decision, not out of fear, but out of a sense of fair play. Joseph just might get out of this alive, if there was a decent judge in town—or if about a thousand men from the Nauvoo Legion could get here before he ran out of ways to stall Sheriff King. As for Governor Carlin, Joseph devoutly hoped that he'd be called on to testify against that lying bastard at the judgment bar of God. A half hour with him, and Carlin hadn't given a hint that the Missouri authorities were trying for extradition, or that Carlin meant to grant it to them. And they say *I'm* slippery. It's a wonder Carlin can keep his shoes on, he's so slick.

❧ 33 ❧

Dinah Kirkham Smith
Nauvoo, 1841

IT WAS AFTERNOON WHEN Harriette fetched Dinah out of the schoolroom with the news. Dinah was marking the older children's compositions, and was so disturbed when Harriette told her that she actually returned to her desk to continue, as if the papers couldn't wait.

"Dinah!" Harriette insisted. "Don't you know that you're needed?"

"What for?" Dinah asked. "What can I do?"

"All the men are sitting at Joseph's house, worrying and wishing that they could do something. Vilate sent me to get you. She wants you to set a fire under them."

"Vilate doesn't need my help to do *that*."

"Perhaps you haven't noticed it, but Vilate isn't quite so outspoken around the Brethren as she is with us. You act the same with everyone."

At last Dinah pulled herself together enough to get up from the table and head for the door. She had worried about this, as everyone in Nauvoo worried for the Prophet, but it was still terrible when it really happened. Only yesterday morning he had asked her to go to Quincy with him. If only she had gone. He would not have been with his men, he wouldn't have been found, if only she had gone.

Dinah needed to walk slowly. Though the baby she was carrying was only two months along, and Dinah had never got particularly sick with her pregnancies, this one had kept her frail for weeks. It worried her, for so many of Joseph's children had been sick or weak; so many had died young, or miscarried. And now, though Dinah had borne two healthy children before, her first pregnancy with a child of Joseph's was also plagued with nausea, with weakness. Why should the seed of the strongest man she knew be weak? It seemed a cruel trick for the Lord to play on him; but at least he didn't have to bear an unnecessary disappointment again. She had decided that until she was so far along in the pregnancy that she had to go into hiding, she would tell no one, especially not Joseph. If there was a miscarriage then he would never know. He loved his children so much that to know of another that died, even unborn, would grieve him deeply.

"Hurry," Harriette said.

"I'm sorry," Dinah said.

They rushed enough that Dinah was feeling more than a little nauseated when she reached Joseph's house. No one seemed to know who was in charge. Sidney Rigdon wasn't there—he was not well, and his wife refused to let him go out of doors. In his absence, William Smith, Dinah's least favorite of the Prophet's brothers, was the ranking authority. Dinah saw in a moment that he was not competent to do it. He kept announcing that a decision had to be made, a decision *must* be made immediately. With uncustomary modesty, he did not think himself the proper man to make it.

"When Bennett gets here, we can act," William said.

Dinah looked for the women. Emma sat in a corner with Vilate Kimball and Mary Fielding Smith. Dinah walked across the room. William Smith made a great show of standing and bowing to her, trying to make pleasant conversation about, of all things, the weather. Don Carlos took mercy on her and silenced his older brother. "Sit down, William, no one gives a damn about manners right now." Glowering at his brother, William sat and loudly made plans for what plans they would need to make once Bennett got there to make them.

"Why don't you do something?" Dinah asked Emma. "He was arrested hours ago. Who knows how long he has before it's too late?"

"I can't," Emma said. "If I told them to do anything, they'd do the opposite. We had that one out while Joseph was in Liberty Jail. The Church will not take orders from the Prophet's wife."

Dinah could see that Emma was right. Could see, too, that if Emma could make no decisions, neither could she. But at least she could speak—that was free for any Saint.

"Brother William," she said. "Aren't there a thousand soldiers in the Nauvoo Legion?"

"I'm not an officer," William snapped back. "It takes the mayor to order them out. Besides, Quincy's out of our jurisdiction."

"Why not make sure Joseph's alive first, and then quarrel about jurisdiction after?"

"Why don't the women keep to their own province, and leave the decisions up to those the Lord has called to make them?"

Dinah rose to her feet and walked to the middle of the room. With all the contempt she could muster—which was a fair amount of contempt right now—she looked at each of the men in turn. "If God should choose to judge you solely on the basis of your performance at this moment, brethren, you can all start right now packing your bags for hell." Then she headed for the front door.

"Where are you going?" Don Carlos asked.

"Since even the Prophet's brothers can't save his life, I'm going to the one man who can."

Vilate rushed across the room to her. "I'll go with you."

Don Carlos also got to his feet. "Let me come with you."

"Are you sure your brother William won't need you to help him make a list of things that Bennett must decide when Bennett comes?"

William glared at her and tapped his pen on the table. "I've been sending word to Bennett all morning, since the news came. He's probably on his way right now. You're wasting a trip."

"While you, sir, are wasting a morning." Dinah walked out of the house with Vilate, Harriette, and Don Carlos, leaving at least one enemy behind her.

It was not that far to Bennett's house, but Dinah felt every step of it. It was not just the exertion of hurrying so quickly; it was the fear of what might happen to Joseph, when the man didn't even know she was carrying his child; it was anger at how little these men who said they loved him actually cared for him. She winced with cramps, but kept walking; breathed deep, swallowed frequently to keep from vomiting, and walked on, faster and faster, not because she expected Bennett to do any better than the others, but because it was better to do something than to sit and wait as Emma and the others were doing. *If Joseph dies, it will not be because I sat and wondered what to do.*

They did not meet Bennett on the way to his house, and when they got to the door, his clerk refused to call him. "Dr. Bennett is unavailable at the moment," he said. "Some other time, perhaps? Or if your ailment is urgent, you can leave me your name and address and when he makes his rounds tomorrow, he'll stop by."

"We're not patients," Dinah said, pushing the door open and walking in.

The clerk followed her up the stairs. "He may be undressed, madame! This is not your house! You can be arrested for this!"

Bennett was lying on his bed, sipping tea and reading a book. He looked up calmly when Dinah walked in, panting from the walk, from running up the stairs. He smiled at her and said, "I was just lying here wishing for company."

"Why didn't you come when you heard the news?" Dinah demanded.

"Why should I go talk to men who have neither ideas nor the power to act on ideas? I notified Brother Joseph's attorney as soon as word came, and I rode with him before eight o'clock. I talked with Stephen Douglas—I knew him when he was secretary of state. It happens that now he's a judge, and he had a writ of habeas corpus out for Brother Joseph before ten. The extradition trial is set for the ninth of June, and Mr. Browning is quite sure we can win. Even if our case did not have superior merit, Judge Douglas is a Democrat, and the Democrats are our friends. I got back half an hour ago. I'm a little tired, and so I'm resting."

He had done it all, and now lay on his bed, smugly sipping at his cup, looking at Dinah with laughing eyes. Dinah could not understand why she was so angry with him. He had every right to be proud of himself—while all the other men, including the Prophet's brothers, had talked and fretted and done nothing, Bennett had acted—and saved Joseph's life before noon. She should be grateful. Instead she felt her stomach twist with anger, and she was afraid she might be sick. "You're mayor of Nauvoo. I would have thought you would take some care to calm the city."

Bennett swung his feet to the floor and sat up. "Good idea. If I hadn't been so tired I would have thought of it myself." He stood and headed for the door. "Do you think it would be immodest of me to tell the Saints who it was who saved the Prophet—and who did not?"

"He isn't saved till he gets back here," Vilate said.

"He's saved because he's alive right now, and because *my* friends in the state of Illinois are going to get him back, and not with any of the blood and thunder theatrics you talk about, not with the *Legion,* that useless collection of Sunday soldiers armed with sticks—he'll be back with a legal judgment against extradition, so that the charge can never be laid to him again. I did it *with* the law, not against it, so that we profit from it, instead of paying later."

"When did the news come to you?" Dinah asked.

"This morning. When I first got up."

Dinah turned to Harriette. "But didn't you tell me Howard Coray got here after ten?"

Harriette nodded.

Bennett smiled at her. "Do you think I have to rely on Howard Coray for my news?" Bennett started down the stairs.

Hadn't Harriette told her that Coray left the moment the Prophet first realized he was going to be taken? Hadn't Coray near killed his horse to get here when he did?

"You knew!" Dinah shouted. "You knew before it happened!" She ran down the stairs after him, but he was already going out the door. "You could have warned him, you could have prevented it all! You wanted him arrested!" She reached for the door, which was swinging shut behind him—she missed it, stumbled forward, fell to her knees. It was more than her body could cope with, the anger, the shouting, all the running, and now the fury of seeing the door click shut behind a man who had knowingly let Joseph Smith fall into the hands of his enemies. Her stomach lurched, and she vomited on the inlaid wood of Bennett's entry hall. Later she would remember thinking that it was strange that he should have inlaid wood when so many Saints had dirt floors and leaking roofs. She was not doing her best thinking then.

"Good God, and I suppose I have to clean that up," said Bennett's servant.

Don Carlos and Harriette helped Dinah get up. "Where are you hurt? Where are you hurt?" Don Carlos kept asking.

"I'm not hurt," Dinah managed to say. "I'm just sick."

"But all this blood," Don Carlos said.

Harriette gasped. "In the name of heaven, Dinah, you might have told somebody."

The last thing Dinah remembered before she lost consciousness was Vilate's voice saying, "But what do you mean she's pregnant? She left her husband in England more than a year ago."

Dinah recuperated in Vilate's house for several weeks. She was unconscious for the first five days, which gave Vilate time to sort things through, about how long it had been since Dinah had been with her husband, and what must have happened for her to get pregnant. Vilate was no longer confused by the time Dinah was conscious, and Dinah could see that she had planned and rehearsed her little speech.

"Are you feeling better?" Vilate asked.

Dinah nodded. She was vaguely aware that her head didn't move much when she told it to.

"Need anything?"

Just the answer to a question. "Brother Joseph?"

"Oh, he's all right. Word just came this afternoon. Judge Douglas ordered him to be released. Said the charges had no merit and that to release Brother Joseph into the hands of Missouri authorities would be tantamount to causing the murder of an innocent Illinois citizen. Mayor Bennett saw to the whole thing."

Dinah vaguely remembered being angry at Bennett, but could not think why. He had saved Joseph, hadn't he? That's all that mattered, wasn't it?

Vilate cleared her throat, sat upright in her chair to give her speech. "I want you to know, Harriette and I have told no one about—why you're so sick. Not even your father and mother. Far as anyone knows, you were already sick as a dog before you started running around all over. Bennett was willing to allow as how you weren't acting rational when you came to call on him, which he calls a sure sign of oncoming nervous prostration."

"So nobody"—she tried to make her lips form the right words—"thinks I'm—harlot—"

"Oh, Dinah." Vilate burst into tears. "Oh, of all women, Dinah, of all the women in Nauvoo, I would've thought you'd have *brains* enough not to get taken in by some man!"

It was bound to come sooner or later, Dinah had known that all along. Her regret was not that Vilate thought her guilty of adultery. Her regret was that she wouldn't have the baby to show for it.

"You've been—kind," Dinah said, "under the circumstances."

"Circumstances! I'm your friend, aren't I? Haven't we tended the sick together? Do you think because you done something dumb I don't remember what you're worth?"

Dinah tried to smile, but for some reason her muscles didn't want to respond. It was only then that she realized she couldn't even raise her hands, she was so weak. And as she spoke she heard her own voice as if from a distance, as if she were drunk, it was so sluggish and inarticulate. "Sister Vilate, do you forgive me?"

At that, Vilate looked away from her. "'Tain't mine to forgive or not forgive. That's between you and Brother Joseph."

It took Dinah a few moments to remember that she would be expected to confess her "adultery" to the Prophet—Vilate had not discovered who her supposed paramour was. She tried to nod.

"I won't bring your name before the bishop for an excommunication trial," Vilate said. "And Harriette says she'll shoot anyone who tries, she's that loyal a friend to you. But I tell you this. I'm still your friend. I'll quilt with you, I'll visit the sick with you, I'll even pray with you if you need me. But don't you dare get up in a meeting and speak, Sister Dinah. Don't you dare pretend to have a word of prophecy or tongues or give even so much as a little explanation of a scripture. The Spirit of God does not dwell in an adulterous heart, and if I hear of you doing even the smallest sort of preachment I'll call for a court myself and shout the accusation for the whole of Hancock County to hear it!"

Dinah nodded.

Vilate softened, looked for a moment as if she might weep again. Then she reached out and touched a cold damp cloth to Dinah's brow. "Oh, Sister Dinah, you were the best of all of us, the very best. I thought sometimes you were the only woman I knew worthy to stand beside Brother Joseph the way Hyrum or Brigham or my Heber do."

"I—never—I never tried—tried to—"

"Hush. Don't you talk, you're not strong enough yet. A miscarriage is every bit as hard on a woman as a birthing, sometimes. I only talked to you now because I knew you'd be fretting about what folks were thinking about you, and I had to let you know that you'll not be held up to public shame." Vilate stood up, leaned over and kissed Dinah's brow. She walked to the door, saying, "If you need anything, there's a little bell on the floor by your bed." At the door she stopped. "I'm your friend forever, Dinah, as long as you keep still in gospel things. Because if there's one thing I hate in all this world, it's a hypocrite."

Dinah lay there after Vilate left, wishing she could either sleep or get the strength to stand, to walk around, to do something, anything but lie here contemplating her future. Vilate had been kinder than Dinah had any right to expect. Not only to keep her miscarriage a secret, but to still be her friend, to care for her this way—when Vilate gave her friendship, she did not stint. But silence! To be forbidden to speak when the Spirit filled her, to keep her seat in the meeting when a few words could clarify a doctrinal point, not even to pray when the sisters gathered together—who was she in Nauvoo, if all that she did in public was to be taken away from her? And not even the child. That would have been her consolation, to have his child. Now all she could think of was Val and Honor. For Matthew I could bear children. Now John Bennett took my child away. No, that wasn't right. Bennett didn't do that, Bennett saved Joseph, didn't he? It was all that running that caused the—no, no, there was something else. Something about Bennett, but she couldn't remember. All she could do was sleep.

When she awoke again, Harriette was sitting by her.

"Awake?" Harriette asked.

"Mm."

"His child, Dinah. And you didn't even tell me."

Dinah shook her head. "I didn't tell him either," she whispered.

Harriette's eyes went wide.

"So many of his children have died," Dinah whispered. Talking was a little easier now than it had been when Vilate was here.

Harriette shook her head in consternation. "Well, what do you want me to tell him? When he gets back?"

"Nothing."

"I think he'd want to know. Why you're sick, at least."

"He'll know when I bear him a living child."

Harriette sat there, shaking her head. Don't tell me I'm wrong, Harriette, Dinah wanted to say. Tell me I'm right. Tell me I'm a good wife, tell me I'm a good woman, tell me that God still loves me and that Vilate is wrong when she says I'm unworthy even to speak, tell me—

"Harriette," she whispered.

"Yes, Dinah?"

Against her best intentions, Dinah started to cry. "I'm not an adulteress, Harriette."

At once Harriette's expression changed from judgment to compassion. "Oh, Dinah, no." Harriette fell to her knees beside the bed and took Dinah in her arms and held her, rocked her gently as she wept. "No, Dinah, you're the best woman in the world, you're the best woman I know."

She must have cried herself to sleep. She didn't remember, only wondered when she woke again is she had made the right decision. It would be so good to have him hold her, comfort her for the loss of their child. But why add one more coffin to those that already lay in the graveyard of his memory? She was willing to bear it for him—and she did not even have to bear it alone. God, in his mercy, had given her Harriette, who knew all, and Vilate, who knew at least some of her pain. She would not be forsaken.

Then, too tired to weep, she prayed that she could conceive

again, and soon. If she was truly to be Joseph's wife, she must bear him children. That was what it meant to be his wife, wasn't it? If she could do it for Matthew, then a just God must surely let her do it for the husband that she loved.

❧ 34 ❧

Wives
Nauvoo, 1841

BEFORE HE WAS HALFWAY down the stairs into the cellar, Charlie could hear Don Carlos coughing. The sound worried him. It wasn't the cough of a man who had just breathed wrong, or caught some dust in his throat. It was a deep cough, liquid with phlegm. Then the press began its rhythmic thump, clack, thump, clack, as Don Carlos pulled and lifted the handle, changed paper, pulled and lifted again. As so often before, Charlie said nothing when he came in, just read the front page. Usually Don Carlos spoke first, but instead he pumped at the press handle, changed the paper, and might as well not have noticed Charlie was there at all.

"What I can't tell," Charlie finally said, "is whether this paper is Democrat or Whig."

"Neither," said Don Carlos. He took a moment's pause before continuing—without the customary joke, Charlie wondered for a moment if Don Carlos could be angry. "This paper hates everybody."

Charlie laughed more than the joke deserved, perhaps because from the look on Don Carlos's face, he wasn't joking.

"You ought to do something about that cold," Charlie said.

"I am," Don Carlos answered. "I'm coughing my guts out. What can I do for you?"

Charlie was flustered. Don Carlos had never acted so unfriendly, not even when they were strangers. "I don't want you to do anything for me. I just wanted to talk."

"Talk then." Thump, clack.

"I just came to tell you—Brother Joseph asked me to clerk for him. Bookkeeping, some, and letters."

"I know." The printed paper clattered as Don Carlos set it aside. His arm brushed Charlie's waist, but if Don Carlos noticed it, he gave no sign.

For the first time it occurred to Charlie that Don Carlos might not be happy for him. That Don Carlos was angry *because* Joseph had asked him to be his clerk. "No great honor, really," Charlie said. "He only asked me because he couldn't afford to pay as many men as he needs, and he doesn't have to pay me a wage."

Clack. Don Carlos leaned on the upright handle, turned and faced Charlie. "Did you come to gloat?" he asked.

"Gloat!"

"*You're* the one with the independent income. *You're* the one who can spell and add and subtract. *You're* the one whose wife doesn't have to wonder whether the baby she's expecting is going to have enough to eat." Thump.

"You already printed that sheet."

Don Carlos lifted the handle. The paper was a blur of ink, completely unreadable. "Look what you made me do."

"I thought you'd be happy for me."

"It's not you, I'm mad at Joseph. I'm his brother, aren't I?"

"You're not a bookkeeper, that's all."

"I can do my ciphering." Thump. "I'm not mad at him, either." Clack. "I spent all day today bullying people into buying more advertising."

"Good!"

"I sold fifty dollars' worth. All on credit, but I can *do* it. I got up at five o'clock. The damn chickens weren't even up yet. I set all the type before nine. I didn't even come home for dinner. Near walked my butt off."

Charlie tried a joke. "You're right, it's half gone."

"Shut up, Charlie." Don Carlos tore up the overprinted sheet. "I hated it. Do *you* have to work like that? No. You have your soapmakers and your candlemakers and your wheelwrights but how often do you ever have to go ream out a hub yourself?"

"I wouldn't even know where to start."

"So where's my two-thousand-dollar loan from Flint-heart Ullery? I'm Joseph's own *brother*, ain't I? Oh, never mind. I had it out with Joseph yesterday, when he told me about you. He laid it out plain as a plow track. Charlie Kirkham is serious. Charlie Kirkham gets things done. Charlie Kirkham has already made himself near rich with his little homestead factory, at least compared to other folk here, and you haven't even got the *Times and Seasons* breaking even yet. *You* tell me why you have a right to compare yourself to Charlie Kirkham and expect to get treated the same as him."

"Don Carlos, I'm sorry."

"It's just time I grew up. That's all. I've been playing around the way I did when I was ten. My whole life I've been a little kid." He looked hard at Charlie. "You were never a little kid at all. I had to teach you how."

"I know."

"So now I'm trying to learn how to be a grown-up. My wife is very impressed with me the last few days, I've been so dependable. Damn dull, though. Stuck in this cellar all night. The place is so damp that I have to store the paper upstairs, carry it down every time I print. One good thing, though. I can leave the ink open, and it won't dry out." Don Carlos laughed.

Charlie tried to laugh, too. Don Carlos knew at once that it was forced. "I guess I've kind of wrecked things, haven't I? I guess we're kind of through playing, aren't we?"

Charlie wanted to put his hand on Don Carlos's shoulder, but he figured it would be too patronizing or affectionate or just silly somehow. So he didn't, just said, "I never had a friend but you, Don Carlos."

"Well, now you've got Joseph." Don Carlos turned back to the press and squared his shoulders to his work with a finality that said the interview was over. "Joseph's the best friend a man could have. You've just traded your mule for a racing horse."

"Didn't have a trade in mind."

Thump. Clack. Thump. Clack. Charlie gave up and went outside.

Joseph spent all morning counseling with a man who had just been excommunicated for adultery and wife-beating and he was worn out by the time Charlie slipped in with the morning mail. Charlie walked quietly and quickly, laid down the letters within easy reach but not where they would demand immediate attention. Deftly he slid one letter a few inches toward Joseph and said, "From Hyrum," then began immediately to leave. Joseph pretended not to be paying attention, but he reveled in the luxury of having an efficient yet unobtrusive clerk. I wish I'd had an English clerk years ago, thought Joseph. But he knew that Charlie wasn't just English. It was one thing to be deft with papers; it was quite another thing to understand money. And Charlie understood money. If I'd had *him* back in Kirtland our bank might not have failed and the Church might be prosperous today. But Charlie was only a little boy back then. It takes the Lord time to raise up the men and women who can help me. Women who can help me. Dinah.

Thinking about Dinah wouldn't do. He couldn't spend his days thinking about his wives. Though the truth was that Dinah was the only one who tempted him to reverie.

He was startled to realize that Charlie was waiting at the door.

"Charlie?"

"Brother Joseph, do you have a moment?"

It was hard to pretend he was busy when he had been leaning back with his eyes closed. "Yes."

"It's Don Carlos."

"Don't pay any attention to him. He's a little jealous of you but it'll pass."

"I'm worried about him. He isn't well. But to please you he's near killing himself with work."

"A little work won't kill him."

Charlie's voice grew insistent. "I'm telling you that I know him better than anyone, and he isn't *strong* right now. He'd die if he thought it would please you."

Joseph looked at Charlie and nodded. "It wouldn't please me, Charlie. But I'm glad if he's trying to do something. Even if it is out of envy. Even if I know perfectly well that just like a dozen times before he'll get tired of it and go back to just getting by. I'm also glad that you love him, Charlie, because so do I, more than I probably ought to, more than is probably good for him."

Charlie nodded and started to leave.

"Brother Charlie," Joseph said. "Would you mind staying while I read Hyrum's letter? I'll want to send an answer to him right away."

Charlie busied himself getting pen and ink and paper while Joseph opened Hyrum's letter.

"By the way," Charlie said, "Mayor Bennett is downstairs."

"Oh? What's he doing?"

"Sucking on a tomato."

Joseph laughed. Bennett had been trying to get the Saints to grow tomatoes, so of course he had to go around eating them to remind people. "One thing about Bennett. Whatever he's selling, he buys himself."

Then Joseph started to read, and by coincidence Hyrum was writing about Bennett, too. Joseph had heard enough nonsense from Hyrum against John Bennett; he skipped down the letter to find where the interesting things began. But the interesting things were still about Bennett. The whole letter was about Bennett. And it wasn't just vague suspicions now.

"Charlie, would you be willing to go down and invite Mayor Bennett up to my office?"

Charlie got up.

"No, wait. Is anyone else down there?"

"Brother Sidney's holding a meeting in the parlor."

"I'll go down." With Charlie following after, Joseph went briskly down the stairs. Sidney's meeting was droning on. They could do with a little excitement. So Joseph stopped in plain view of both the parlor and the drawing room, and in his loudest voice addressed John Bennett before he could finish his greeting.

"John Bennett, where's your wife?"

If there was one thing Joseph Smith did well, it was bringing off an effect. With that single loud question he turned Charlie and Sidney and everyone in the meeting into joint accusers of John Bennett, and Bennett, half-standing with a dripping tomato in his hand, was as cornered as a coon in a dogpack.

Only now, with all the people watching, did Joseph begin to let himself get angry. No sense wasting anger to no use. Now there was a use.

"I'm waiting for an answer, *Mayor* Bennett."

Joseph watched Bennett decide whether to lie or confess. It made him angrier, for Joseph had thought Bennett the sort of man who didn't have to decide. He had believed in John Bennett, and right now, in this moment of hesitation, Bennett was unraveling Joseph's trust. Plainly everything that Hyrum said was true. It would be—Joseph had never known Hyrum to tell a lie in his life except when Joseph asked him to.

Bennett's decision was made. It would be confession. Tears came into his eyes and he stood straight, poised to take his punishment manfully. "I see my youthful mistakes have come back to haunt me."

"Your wife, Mayor Bennett."

"I don't know where she is," Bennett said. The crowd murmured; it was well known till now that Bennett was a bachelor.

"Do you care?" Joseph asked.

"I hope—with all my heart that she is well."

"And your children, Mr. Bennett?"

"How are they? If you know, it's cruel of you not to tell me."

Suddenly Joseph roared at him. "How dare you speak to me of cruelty! There is nothing lower in the world than a man who gives his oath to a woman, fathers children on her, then abandons her to fend for herself, without money, without friends, while you have lacked for neither. There are animals who eat their own young—that is the species you belong to, Mr. Bennett."

Bennett withered, but his abject posture came a little too late, went a little too far to be believed, though Joseph realized that even ten minutes ago he would have believed it. Now that the lie was known, Joseph could plainly see that he was a habitual liar. No wonder Emma mistrusted him. No wonder Hyrum hated him. But so many times my friends have been hated, I have been hated for no reason but envy. I thought it was envy again. I thought God told me this man was true.

"Am I not to have a chance to justify myself?" asked Bennett.

"Justify?"

"Can't we suppose that some of the blame at least belongs to the wife?"

Joseph reached out his hand and slapped Bennett across the face—not hard, just enough to silence him, to humiliate him. "Don't make me despise you more than I already do," Joseph said. "Any word you speak against that good and injured woman is a lie, and doubles your guilt before the Lord. Do you think Hyrum and William did not verify that she was blameless before they wrote to me? Where you lived in Ohio it was public knowledge that you were an adulterer repeatedly, and she forgave you time and again before at last *you* left *her*. I owe you my life, John Bennett, but you make me ashamed of it."

That was enough. Here was where the scene should end. Let the word of this spread through Nauvoo, let Bennett have time to reveal himself through what he chose to do. Joseph turned to leave. Not upstairs, but out of the house, so he could close a door on John Bennett.

But Bennett wouldn't let the door close. He followed Joseph onto the porch and then fell to his knees, crying out as if in agony. "Oh, Joseph, I've wanted to confess it to you all along, but I hadn't the courage, you must know how I long for your forgiveness, for the Lord to—"

Joseph was furious. Bennett had broken the effect. He was crying his confession on the public street, and the initiative was taken from Joseph. It would be Bennett who was talked about now, Bennett at the heart of the story. Only now did Joseph realize that Bennett was his match in managing events. Well, Bennett, I will not let you turn this to advantage.

"Get him out of my sight and hearing before he adds blasphemy to his other sins!" Joseph cried.

At once the men from the meeting began to manhandle Bennett toward the street. He was spraying tears and spittle on them all as he writhed and wept and cried aloud in grief. Joseph stood clear of the scene, folded his arms and watched, letting nothing distract him. A few men came up to him and tried to ask questions, but Joseph ignored them, kept his eyes on Bennett. As long as Joseph held perfectly still, he would be stronger than Bennett in the way people saw this event. If he broke and talked to someone, he would immediately disappear into the crowd of onlookers, and it would all be Bennett's story.

Yet even as Joseph thought of this as a contest between him

and Bennett, he could not help but wonder if Bennett's repentance might be real. He had been too long in the habit of
trusting Bennett's advice, trusting Bennett's version of what
was happening. Hadn't Bennett been right, time and again,
when Joseph's other, more naive advisers had been wrong?
Hadn't Bennett given his all to the Church, loyally? Before
Bennett was out of sight, Joseph found himself hoping that
somehow Bennett would bring it off, that somehow Bennett
would make it possible for Joseph to trust him again.

Only after Bennett was out of sight did Joseph allow himself
to move. Still he talked to no one. He walked to his house.
Charlie opened the door and stepped in before him, smoothly
closed the door after him when he was inside, so that Joseph
did not have to touch the door at all. The scene had gone as
well as Joseph could make it go. Bennett had made sure that
what was talked about most in Nauvoo was the extremity of
his grief. But from this moment on, a picture would remain in
everyone's mind, Joseph Smith standing in judgment while
Mayor Bennett was led away weeping. Joseph might want to
trust Bennett again, but he wanted to make sure that there was
not the slightest confusion in the city of Nauvoo about who
was Prophet and who was not.

Emma was waiting for him in the parlor. Her eyes were
bright with triumph. "I was right," she said.

"You were right that he's a liar," Joseph said quietly. "But
you were wrong to think that's all he is."

"I know. He's an adulterer, too."

Her point was so telling that Joseph had to laugh. "Yes, he
even found a sin to commit that no one had thought to accuse
him of. He's a resourceful fellow, isn't he?"

Emma had not meant to amuse him. "How could you make
a man like that Assistant President of Christ's church?"

That was not an amusing question. It was still less amusing
that she asked it in front of his clerk. Charlie was trustworthy,
but he was also naive, and it was cruel of Emma to openly
question the Prophet's authority. "I don't always know what a
man *is*," Joseph said. "Most times I only know what a man
does."

"Why didn't you ask the Lord?"

"I thought the Lord had already told me. I reckon I misunderstood." He looked at Emma steadily, as if to say *enough*.

She didn't think it was enough. "For near a year Hyrum and I and half a dozen others have been trying to tell you that. But you trusted him and not us."

"Emma," Joseph said, "I trust you and Hyrum always to be *loyal*. But I'll never trust anybody to be *right*, because the minute I do that I might as well auction off my brains, I'd have no more use for them. The Lord didn't call me to be prophet in order to make *your* mistakes. He called me as prophet in order to make *my* mistakes. You were partly right and I was partly wrong. It's happened before, and it'll happen again, but it'll never happen on anything the Lord tells me direct. Do you understand that, Emma? Just because Joseph Smith Junior makes a mistake doesn't mean that God makes mistakes. It just means that I'm not a puppet."

"Neither am I," Emma said. "I'll say what I like."

"Say it to the walls, then. Come on, Charlie."

Joseph walked through the house to the back door, Charlie at his heels. Once they were well away from the house, Joseph stopped. "That's all, Brother Charlie. You might as well go home and tend to your own affairs for the rest of the day."

Charlie was surprised. "Didn't you want me to come with you? I had work to do in the house—"

"Charlie, if I left you there in the house you would have had a conversation with Emma. And in the course of that conversation, whether you wanted to or not, you would have had to decide whether you were her friend or mine. Whichever way you decided, your life wouldn't be very easy in Nauvoo afterward."

"Thanks, then. But I can go with you wherever you're going."

"Where I'm going now, you wouldn't be useful."

Charlie looked a little hurt as he went his way, but there was no helping that. Joseph couldn't very well say to him, Sorry, but I'm going to visit your sister in her cabin and you can't come along because there's a good chance we might spend part of the visit in bed.

Joseph saddled up a mare and was leading her out the stable door before Porter Rockwell reached him. "Howdy," said Port.

"Howdy," said Joseph.

"You gonna wait for me to saddle up, or are you gonna make me ride bareback?"

"Don't want you with me, Port."

Port walked up close to Joseph and in his high, piping voice said, "I know where you're goin' whenever you don't want me with you, Brother Joseph. Furthermore I know that these are not common whores. They are the finest women in the Church, and you are a man of God, and so I put two and two together. Or maybe I put one and about fourteen together, by my present count. With what I know, Brother Joseph, if you couldn't trust me you'd be readin' all about it in the Warsaw paper. But you ain't."

"No, Port, I ain't."

"Now if you'd just let me saddle my horse and ride along with you, I can do a lot to help you get to where you're goin' without a troop of people knowin' right where you're headed."

"Saddle up, Port. A man's a fool if he thinks he can keep a secret from you."

They rode north toward old Commerce, Illinois, passing through the shanty town where the latest immigrants all lived. A lot of people, mostly children, waved cheerfully from the most miserable homes Joseph had ever seen. We've got to get more money in this town before fall, Joseph thought, or we'll have real suffering from the cold.

At the place where the city plat showed Joseph Street, they rode down into a ravine. The spring rains had near filled it, but now it was just standing water with so many mosquitoes it has hard to breathe without eating them. They rode along the edge of the water, where the ground was firmest, until the ravine opened up to level ground, north and east of the city. Wheatfields and woods. They walked their horses south a ways; then Port stopped with the animals in a grove of trees and Joseph walked on through the trees and underbrush until the last patch of open ground before Dinah's house. I am a complete fool, thought Joseph. It's broad daylight, and who knows who might be hunting rabbits. But at least he had sense enough not to skulk. He walked boldly to Dinah's door and knocked. If anyone was watching, they couldn't guess he had anything to hide from the way he walked.

She opened the door and let him in. "You are the prince of fools," she said. "It's four in the afternoon."

"I asked all the Saints to look the other way."

With the door closed and barred, she put her arms around

him, and he bent and kissed her.

"That's what I came for," Joseph said.

"No it isn't."

"Don't argue with me today."

Joseph sat down on the chair by Dinah's writing table. Dinah stood where he had left her. Joseph pulled off his boots. Caked-on mud dropped onto the dirt floor. Still Dinah did not speak. "Emma's angry with me already." Still she did not answer.

I played too many scenes today. I walked too far, at far too great a risk. Bennett was a liar and I loved him. I came for refuge, and you are angry too.

Joseph wearily began to pull on his boots again.

"Going already?"

Dinah's voice was small and emotional. It only made Joseph wearier. I didn't come to you for this. And yet he could not leave, because she would be hurt if he left her, and he did not want to hurt anyone else today. How much before it is enough?

"No," he said.

"I can't," she said.

"Can't what?"

"I can't be the opposite of Emma."

Joseph bent over and wrapped his arms around his thighs, pressed his face against his knees.

"How can I know what she said before you left? If she was angry, then I have to be happy? If she was cold, then I have to be passionate?"

"No."

"If John Bennett is found to be a liar, then she can say I told you so and I have to pretend I never heard of the man?"

Joseph looked up at her, surprised.

"Do you think I live in a box? Charlie and Harriette have both been here with the story. It's been hours, how slowly do you think news spreads? Do you think the world stops when you aren't watching? Do you think I'm not *alive* when you're not here?" And then she stopped, and fingered her sleeve. "I'm not," she said. "But I'm not dead, either. I still listen. I still talk. I still think. Waiting for you."

Joseph got up from the chair, crossed the room in a single step, and lay down on the bed, his hands behind his head. "Don't wait for me."

"Oh, should I come visit you at home?"

"Why have you stopped teaching and talking in the Church? You used to have things to do besides wait for me. You used to be so busy ministering to the women of Nauvoo that I never found you at home unless we planned it."

He had never seen her so angry as when she answered. "And why don't you have revelations about how to solve the poverty here? Why isn't there a miracle to cure all the sick? Why didn't you know John Bennett was a liar from the start?"

He closed his eyes. "I don't hate Bennett even now," he said.

"Everyone thinks you should."

He laughed bitterly. "Isn't it funny how neither of us can do what everybody knows we should."

She laughed, too, and things were as they should be again. Of course he hadn't come to make Dinah perform for him. It was Dinah herself he came for, because he could say things to her that he had never said before, he could say thoughts that he had used to pretend he didn't think: the Prophet should say this; Emma's husband should do that. He wore so many faces and only now after all these years did he discover, not him*self*, but the face that he liked the best. The face that he wore with Dinah, for it never hurt to wear it, though removing all the others, *that* could be painful sometimes.

She knelt beside the bed, gently touching his arm, his face, and thinking carefully about what he said. She always thought about what he said before she spoke, which meant that she never answered from habit, which meant that her answers just might be true.

"How can I hate him?" Joseph asked. "He betrayed his wife with whores and did not keep it secret from her. I betray Emma with wives and lie to her every day. He had only one wife, and he abandoned her. I have many wives, and I abandon them all."

Dinah played with a fold of her skirt. "Sometimes, Joseph, I love you so much that I feel like an adulteress."

"Anything that pleases us this much must be a sin, is that it?"

She nodded.

"But when I hear myself thinking of you as my paramour, when I feel that I have been unfaithful to my Emma, I remember this: God gave you to me. And if my Father ever commanded me to leave you, I'd be gone without another word."

"I know you would." But she didn't like it.

"So would you, Dinah."

"No."

"If God commanded you, if you knew it was his will—"

"No."

"You think you wouldn't, but you *would* obey."

She put her palms over her eyes and then tipped her face upward, as though she were speaking to God but dared not see his face. "I'd obey Him, but I'd hate Him forever."

Joseph laughed. "It's a good thing He isn't vindictive. That remark would have tempted Him beyond endurance."

Dinah laughed, too. "So you and I are secretly no better than Bennett."

"I'm ten times the man he is."

Dinah began stroking his arm again. "And I'm not like him, either. For instance, I'd never let a friend go into a place where I knew he was in peril of his life, just so I could rescue him spectacularly, for the effect."

Joseph felt her fingers suddenly grow warm. Or was it his own skin growing cold? "Do you have a story about him, too?"

"Howard Coray brought the news of your arrest at ten. Bennett left Nauvoo at eight to save you. He thought the arrest would happen earlier in the morning, I suppose."

"John Bennett didn't plan the whole thing out." That was too much for Joseph to believe. "He didn't bring the men from Missouri. *I* chose the judge that I appealed to. *I* kept myself alive until he could pull the political strings to set me free. How could he know that I'd be able to do all that."

"And if you hadn't, I wonder who he thought would have succeeded you?"

She had named his fear for him. He trembled. "It's not enough for my friends to turn on me. They all start thirsting for my blood."

"But you still don't want to lose him."

"John Bennett does not want me dead."

"John Bennett scares me, Joseph."

"Who else is there? I can't govern this city without him. Liar or not, he's the most brilliant man among us."

"Then keep him to govern the city. But don't let him govern the Church."

"They're inseparable."

"Separate them."

Joseph shook his head again, with such force that he half-rolled back and forth, then rolled over against the wall, his knees drawn up toward his chest, and he shook with the cold. "I finally have the Church together, all in one place, secure from the world for a while, fenced around with laws, and now I have to break us down again, cut us into pieces again."

"Like the wise virgins and the foolish ones. Let Bennett be mayor of the outward Church, the city, the Nauvoo that everyone sees. And then within the city the True Church. Those who know."

"Who know what?"

"That I am your wife."

"I can't tell that to anyone."

"There are those who know, Joseph. No one had to tell Harriette—she knows. And your other wives—I've found four of them already. We who live this secret life, we know each other's faces, we know how a woman has to live, finding plausible excuses to be home all the time she can, in hopes her husband will come tonight. Or late one afternoon."

"Everyone who knows is one more who can betray me."

"Is the Principle the law of God or not? The more of us who live it, the more of us who can tell the truth to each other, the easier it will be to bear this life. You can have a public life, a public wife, children. Everyone in the Church is your brother or sister. Give me sisters, Joseph."

She was only asking for what he knew would have to come. The Principle could not be a commandment that only he and his wives obeyed. But he was afraid.

"When the Twelve come home," he said, "I'll teach the Principle to them. As soon as they come home." He felt her climb on the bed behind him; she embraced him, and in the stillness he could hear from her breath that she was crying. Or almost crying. "What's wrong?" he asked.

"Nothing. I'm glad."

He rolled back; she tried to turn away from him; he stopped her, took a tear from her cheek and held up the moist finger as a question.

"I was thinking of Vilate," she answered. Then she started

to laugh. "Joseph, we're so terrible. The Principle is the worst thing in the world, and I'm begging you to impose it on my friends."

He kissed her cheek. "The worst thing?"

"Yes," she said. "I've never been happier in my life than when you're here. But when you're not—"

"How can I make it up to you?"

"Let me bear you a child, Joseph."

He rolled her over and began unhooking the back of her dress. "I've been doing my best," he said.

"So have I," she answered.

She was still so new to him; yet as he discovered her again, he could not rid himself of the feeling that she, too, was keeping something secret from him. Protecting him from something. He almost asked her what it was, but then decided that if Dinah thought it better not to tell him, he would trust her judgment, and not demand to know.

It was well after dark when a knock came at the door. Joseph, dressed by then except his boots, leaped to the window to escape if he had to. But it was Port.

He was more embarrassed than Dinah had thought the dangerous little man could be. "Don't mean to disturb you," he said. "But it's after dark, and I've been doing some prowling around, and I ran into some men who were looking for you."

"A posse?" asked Dinah.

"No, no, loyal men, Sister H-handy. It's about Dr. Bennett. Mayor Bennett. He took poison, and he's dying."

Joseph was pulling on his boots. "I wanted to do many things to him today, but I didn't want him dead."

"He's a doctor," Dinah said. "Don't you think he knows a safe dose from a fatal one?"

She was only saying the obvious. They both knew now that Bennett could play his little play all he liked. And Joseph would publicly believe his tears and forgive him, and take him back, and use his gifts to benefit Nauvoo. But when the Twelve came home, it would be they, and not Bennett, who would learn the Principle and live it; they, not Bennett, who would be the true and secret Church.

"Since I've been seen without you," Porter said, "we shouldn't go back together. It's mostly clear south along the shore. Everyone's at Bennett's house, or gossiping wherever the houses are thick."

"The horses?"

"Where we left them."

Joseph started for the door, then stopped, returned to Dinah, and kissed her long and hard. Joseph watched with wicked pleasure as Dinah tried to find a reaction in Porter Rockwell's face. Porter never blinked, just stared her down with his emotionless face. Then they doused the lights, Joseph left, and Dinah was alone with the Prophet's bodyguard.

"You're an unlikely fancy woman," Porter said.

Dinah could not tell if he was being ironic, or what he really meant if he was. "You're an unlikely bodyguard, too."

"Rest your heart," Porter said. "Of all his wives, you're the only one *I* think might be worth dyin' for."

Dinah was deeply relieved, but angry, too. "He might have told me that he told you about the Principle."

"Never told me a damn thing," Porter said. "But you ain't a whore and he's a man of God. That didn't leave much else to guess from. I don't know if Emma's really Leah, but you're sure as hell his Rachel, unless I'm blind."

She clung to those words for a long, long time. I am Joseph's Rachel, his most-beloved. Please God, let me also bear his noblest son.

She thought of that desire many times when she taught Emma's sons in school. She loved little Joseph, and yet wanted her son to displace him in his father's heart. She was ashamed of herself, but could not change her wishes because of that. Could not change, either, the fact that two young children were growing up in Manchester believing that their mother did not love them anymore. Is there nothing adults can do that doesn't hurt the little ones?

John Bennett recovered from the poison, to no one's surprise. Joseph Smith forgave him publicly, upon his promise never to sin again, while Bennett's critics once again retreated into the background. Everything seemed back to normal in Nauvoo.

Except that two weeks later, on July 1, Brigham Young, Heber Kimball, and John Taylor returned to Nauvoo from England. Joseph didn't even let them go to their families before he brought them into an upstairs room and met with them in secret far into the night. He taught them the Principle, and wrecked their lives, and created the secret Church so there might be something strong enough to live when he was dead.

⤹ 35 ⤸

Joseph Smith
Nauvoo, 1841

IT WAS VILATE KIMBALL who had knocked so timidly on his door. Timidity wasn't like her. It must be a problem she came with, then. Joseph smiled at her to put her at her ease. It surprised him that it did not hurt to smile.

"Brother Joseph," she said, her voice too quick, too soft, "if there's anything I can do—"

"Now Vilate, if you have comfort you ought to give it to Emma, she's taking it much harder than I am."

"I know you better than that, Joseph. You named your son for your brother because you loved them both so much, and to lose the two eight days apart, it's cruel hard—"

He touched her lips with his fingertips. "Vilate, if a man who's talked with God hasn't the faith to accept the death of loved ones, who has?"

Vilate fell silent, then looked out the window behind Joseph. "There's so many dying of this fever that Brother Sidney's preaching a general sermon every day, for all who are being buried. They give him the list of names right before he speaks." With sudden anger, she turned to Joseph. "If you ask me, the Lord could better take some folks I might name than Don Carlos Smith, man or child!"

"I don't know, Vilate," Joseph said. "Maybe the Lord in his mercy is taking only those who are sure of exaltation."

"If he takes all the godly ones the Church will surely go to hell," Vilate said.

"This isn't what you came for," Joseph prodded. He didn't like to talk about his brother's death. He didn't like to think about it. It was better just to keep his mind on other things. Other people's problems. Whenever he thought of Don Carlos he feared his own feelings. It was one thing to lose his child. He and Emma had lost so many that Joseph hardly let himself love them now when they were still little—at least that's what he told himself, though try as he might he still had much of himself in every child of his that died. But his brother had taken sick in the damp, unhealthy cellar where Joseph had sent him, had practically ordered him to work day and night if he was to amount to anything—not my fault, Joseph reminded himself. Think of other things. Vilate has a problem. I must listen to Vilate.

"I have a friend," Vilate said. "And don't go thinking that it's me, because when I have a problem I won't come to you on little pussy feet pretending that it isn't mine. It's a friend."

"Yes, I understand that."

"She's a good woman. I know a good woman when I see one. I used to think she was the best woman I know. I felt the Spirit of God in her a hundred times this last year—and still, as recently as today, and I *shouldn't* feel that Spirit from her, and so I've come to you because I don't know if I've done right, or if I even understand anything—"

"I can't help you, Vilate, if you don't tell me the story."

"It's so selfish of me when you're suffering problems far worse than mine—"

"Tell me about your friend."

Vilate fussed with her apron. "She isn't married. Or rather, her husband is—she's had no husband for a year. But the day you was arrested, she was yelling at—someone—" She glanced up at him, looked back down. "Doesn't matter who she was yelling at. She got sick and had a—miscarriage, right on the spot, and she had no right to have a baby in her. I don't know a better proof of adultery than that. And she admitted it."

"Admitted adultery?"

"Admitted she was pregnant, and there's not much else to say after *that*." Vilate interlocked her fingers, then wrung her hands repeatedly back and forth. "But she was such a *good* woman, I didn't think she deserved—she was my *friend*, and only two of us knew what had happened, and so the two of us, we didn't tell anybody. We figured she'd come to you and confess it. But I warned her—if she ever tried to speak up in meeting or bear testimony, I'd denounce her before the whole Church, because if there's one thing I hate, it's a hypocrite."

Dinah. Silent in meetings, her ministrations suddenly stopped for no reason he could figure out. She didn't tell him. Dinah had been carrying his baby, and lost it, and she hadn't told him, and he hadn't guessed.

"Did I do wrong?" Vilate asked.

"No, no. You did right, I think."

"Maybe." Vilate suddenly trembled, as if she had a chill. "Today Heber told me to read the beginning of the sixteenth chapter of Genesis. Where Sarah tells her Abraham to lie with her maid Hagar—"

"I know the chapter."

"I read it, but I couldn't figure why Heber had insisted that I read it. And then my friend happened to call on me right at that time—and she doesn't call on anyone much anymore, she stays to home, which is proper, I thought—but her being there, I figured the Lord maybe sent her. Isn't that possible, that the Lord sent her?"

"The Lord sent her," Joseph said.

"So I broke my oath, and asked her to explain the scripture to me."

"And what did she say?"

"She wouldn't. She just said to ask my husband, and to believe everything he told me, because it was the most glorious—glorious principle of the gospel. And when she said that, sitting there like an angel, I felt a thrill like the first time a new baby sucks, it hurts so strong and feels so good, and I knew it was the Spirit of God in her, and she was speaking to me as a prophetess. And so I said to her, Did you repent? Were you forgiven? And she said to me, Vilate, I will never repent of that baby, or how I got it." Vilate was crying now, but whether from grief or from memory of the Spirit Joseph couldn't tell. "Brother Joseph, how can the Lord dwell in such a rebellious woman's heart?"

"Sister Vilate," Joseph said, "your friend is as pure as snow. She has committed no sin before God, though she would be judged a sinner by the unbelieving."

It was almost funny how quickly Vilate was laughing and hugging him. "I knew it! I didn't know *how* it could be, but I just couldn't believe that she'd—but Brother Joseph, how could it be? How can a woman do what she—"

"Sister Vilate."

She fell silent again.

"Go home to your husband and tell him that giving you scriptures to read is not enough. Every moment that he delays is disobedience, and his soul is in danger of damnation."

Vilate was stunned. "Why! What has he done!"

"It's what he hasn't done. But once he obeys, you'll understand everything you didn't understand today. Don't ask me any more—it's not for me to tell you, it's for your husband. Then both of you come to me here, tomorrow, and tell me what you choose to do."

She left, afraid of how serious this secret must be, but still eager to find out. It was a mark of godliness, Joseph knew, to be eager to know even what might hurt you. Those who were frightened of truth never amounted to much in the sight of God. Those who avoided truth weren't worthy to have it, and so they never did.

Joseph was frightened, too. Dinah couldn't know it, but it wasn't just the Principle that Heber was going to tell Vilate about. It was a far more terrible test than that, more terrible than Joseph would ever have thought of on his own, but the words just came to him as he was talking to Heber, teaching him about the Principle. Worse was knowing that no one could lightly pass this test, Heber and Vilate least of all. They had loved each other since they were children. They were the happiest, most utterly devoted couple he knew. Heber had been gone for more than two years, and they had only been together a few weeks since then. It was too much. They would fail. And Joseph didn't need to lose any of the few Saints he could utterly rely on. If anyone ever had reason to believe he was a false prophet, any reason to hate him and leave the Church, it was them, it was now.

It frightened Joseph, the way he could talk like a prophet without even meaning to. The way he could reach out and tear at people's lives, he had such power over them. Wasn't he supposed to heal them the way Christ did? He tried to remember if there was a time when Jesus ever caused anyone such pain. Why couldn't God let things go smoothly for a while? Let him have a whole month in which no one was tested, no one betrayed him, and no one died.

"Are you all right?"

Joseph almost cried out in shock, for it was Don Carlos's voice he heard. But it was only Charlie at the door of his office, carrying his ledger. Don Carlos's best friend. Charlie had sobbed out loud at the funeral. No one minded or thought it was unmanly—someone had to, so the rest could bear to put that young man's body in the ground. Charlie was needed then.

But now Joseph couldn't see him without thinking of Don Carlos. Of the way Don Carlos romped with this English boy who had a knack for doing miracles with money. Of the way Don Carlos had pled with Joseph to let *him* be a clerk, Let me be close to you, Joseph, he had said, how can you take my friend and leave *me*, don't you know I'm dying to be part of your work, don't you know I'm dying—and Joseph had sent him to the cellar to do a better job of the *Times and Seasons*, to prove that he was dependable. If anything killed Don Carlos, it was my trying to make him into Charlie Kirkham.

"Brother Joseph, what is it?" Charlie was staring at him in awe.

"It's tears, Brother Charlie." Joseph wiped his face on his coat hem.

"Is there something I can do, Brother Joseph?"

"Unless you can bring me my brother or my baby, no." He waved Charlie away, as if to say it was all right. "Go on, we'll go over the books tomorrow. I need to make a visit."

"Do you want me to go with you?"

"No." I'm busy, I have work to do, and having you with me would be like having a ghost walk beside me, blaming me. So today I'm going to try to think of a way to get you out of here for a while, out of my sight until I stop grieving every time I think of my brother. I can't just tell you to go away, that would break your heart. Mustn't break any hearts, must I? Or maybe that's the business I'm in. Getting power over people and breaking them, breaking all of them who don't try to break me first.

Long before Joseph could weave his way through the business of the afternoon and get to Dinah's house late in the summer night, Dinah had another visitor.

"Sister Emma," Dinah said.

Emma greeted her coolly, and Dinah dreaded some confrontation. But it was comfort Emma wanted today, which made her much more distant, for Emma did not like confessing need.

"I've come to see if you're not well," Emma said.

"Of course I'm well," Dinah said. "Your children came to school this morning for the summer reading class, didn't they? Didn't little Joseph recite the poem he learned?"

"I know you're well enough to teach the children, Sister Dinah. I only wondered why you seem to have forsaken the women of Nauvoo."

Dinah was used to questions like this, for the women she had once visited now came, in ones and twos and threes, to call on her, forcing Joseph to delay his visits later and later in the night, when he could come at all. And every woman who came asked the same question. Why don't you teach us anymore? Why don't you speak at meetings? Are you angry? Have I given some offense? Are you unwell? And always the same answer:

"I can only live as the Lord requires."

Emma's eyes narrowed. "They told me you'd say that."

Dinah smiled slightly. "I say it because it's true."

"I think it's cruel and selfish of you, and I've come to rebuke you." As always, Emma had to speak her affection in harsh words.

"Forgive me," Dinah whispered.

"Don't you know how much some sisters have needed you? There are sisters in Nauvoo who are in dire need of a friend, and can find none because the only friend who can help them stays hidden in her cabin like a hermit."

"But if a friend visits me, I greet her with the same love as always."

"Do you?"

Dinah walked to her, bent to where she sat, and pressed her cheek against Emma's. "Yes," she whispered. "The same love as always."

Dinah pulled away from the embrace, but Emma clung to her hand, so that Dinah had to kneel beside her on the rag rug that covered the earthen floor.

"Sister Dinah, I'm afraid that I'm driving Joseph away from me."

Don't speak to me of Joseph, Dinah said silently. On that one subject I am not your friend.

"He's hardly home anymore. He travels constantly, four or five nights a week, or visits around the city so late that I'm long asleep before he comes home."

"To avoid his enemies. And to do his work."

"To avoid *me.*" Emma whispered her dread: "He's punishing me."

"Why would he punish you? There's no wife in the world who's endured more than you, who's been more help to her husband than you—"

"I'm a cold and sharp-tongued woman, and when I disagree with him I speak the truth as I see it. It makes him angry, and he stays away."

"I've never known Brother Joseph to flee from the truth."

Emma touched her cheeks with the tips of her fingers, as if to contain her emotions. "I know. It's because I won't let him—because I won't bow to something that no wife could possibly endure, that no wife should ever be asked to do. He doesn't love me anymore."

There have been times, Dinah said silently, when I wished that it were true, when I wished that he didn't love you at all. But he does. "Sister Emma, if you think he could forget to love you, you don't know him. Part of him *is* you. All his past is tied up with you. His children are yours. Even the Church itself is so bound up in you that he hardly bothers to distinguish between what he's done with you, and what he's done without you. Have you heard him speak? *We* did this, he says, *we* lived above the store, *we* had a hard time of it in Kirtland, *we* were able to hold together after Missouri—and no one knows, least of all himself, whether he means you and him or him and the Church or whether it makes any difference at all. You are so much a part of him now that whatever he does, he feels as though you were with him. You *are* with him."

"I'm not. I'm home, alone in bed, listening to the children breathing, wishing for my husband's breath in the night."

Dinah ached with the knowledge that the fault was so often hers. "You're not with him, but he feels as though you were. He's busy doing what the Lord has commanded him to do. He knows that's what you want him to be doing."

"I don't. Not today, not these last weeks. I don't want him to be Prophet anymore. I want him home with me, belonging to no one else but me—" And she wept outright.

Dinah held her tightly, though her knees ached in her uncomfortable position. I can endure some pain for you, my sister wife; you've endured pain for me.

"Sister Emma, you know it isn't true. Whatever you think you wish for, if he even for a moment forgot his duty to the Lord *you* would send him back to his task again, and without wasting words, either."

Emma giggled in the middle of crying. Like a little girl—it was such a strange sound, coming from her. "I would, too. I'd send him right back out. But once he was gone I'd curse myself for a fool."

Dinah gripped her arms tightly and almost shook her. "He loves you, silly wife."

"I know he does. I never doubted it. Really. I just needed you to remind me."

They talked a few minutes more, to wind down, to become casual again. Then Emma left Dinah with a kiss on the cheek and a whispered thank-you in her ear. And Dinah closed the door behind her, already wishing for Emma's husband to come to her, feeling like a traitor as she did.

It was well after dark when he reached her cabin. Dinah let him in quickly, with no light on, and closed the door. She would have lit a candle then, but he wouldn't let her. In the darkness he led her to the bed and clung to her and said, over and over, "I'm sorry, I didn't know, you should have told me, I'm sorry, I'm sorry."

She did not ask him what it was she should have told him. There was only one secret between them, and he laid it to rest when he put his hand low on her belly and said, "Here. You had my child here. I had two babies die this summer, and I didn't even know."

"I didn't want to grieve you."

He kissed her hard, and held her so tightly that she could hardly breathe. "Don't shield me from grief," he whispered. "I'm not your son, I'm your husband."

But she knew he was not angry.

"Comfort me tonight," Joseph said. "For two children and a brother that the Lord took away from me before I could ever know them. And I'll comfort you for three children that you lost."

Later, as they held each other loosely in the bed, she said to him, "I wrote a poem for you. Harriette told me I shouldn't let it be printed, because people would think you wrote it."

"Anyone who can't tell your poetry from mine deserves to be confused."

"You may not even want to hear it. The title is 'Why the Prophet Grieves.'"

She took his silence for *yes,* and recited it softly, speaking to his chest as he pressed his lips into her hair and tried to hear it without pitying himself.

> *If I desire the Saints to think me wise,*
> *Why should I weep when son or brother dies?*
> *God only weeps for one cast down to earth*
> *Like Lucifer, denied his mortal birth;*
> *God greets the righteous dead with arms held wide,*
> *With tears of joy, and seats them at his side.*
> *In death be merry, or the gospel lies:*
> *Grieve for those who fall, not those who rise.*
> *(I know 'tis true, yet still I cannot sleep:*
> *Not for Don Carlos but myself I weep.)*

Until the last couplet, it had been nothing but a sermon, one well told but commonplace. But at the last two lines the meaning of the poem changed, and his grief became more than he could hold. It didn't spill over in silent tears as it had till now, it racked him with great gasping sobs so that for a long time Joseph was not in control of himself.

"I'm sorry," he said at last.

She kissed him and whispered, "That's what I wrote it for."

❧ 36 ❧

Dinah Kirkham Smith
Nauvoo, 1841

JOSEPH LEFT HER ONLY an hour before dawn. It was Saturday; Dinah would not be giving a reading class, so she had thought to sleep late. Instead she was wakened by a pounding on her door. For a terrible moment she thought it was them, the mob coming to take Joseph; they would find him in her bed and use her to destroy him. But then she remembered that he had left hours ago, before she slept, and she got up and stumbled to the door, pulling her nightgown over her head as she asked, "Who is it!"

"Vilate."

Dinah fumbled with the latch, lifted it. The door burst open almost at once. Yet Vilate did not rush in. She came in timidly, holding a shawl tightly wrapped around her though it was the middle of August and the night had been far from cold. "What is it?"

"I've come to ask your forgiveness."

Dinah searched the woman's face, but knew that penitence was the least of her feelings, if she felt it at all right now. "You've done nothing that requires my forgiveness."

Vilate looked at her with a face that spoke of agony. "I know where your child came from. Heber—explained."

Dinah was too sleepy to realize that the last thing Vilate wanted from her was rejoicing. "Oh, Vilate! Oh, I'm so glad!" And she embraced her friend.

When there was no response from Vilate, Dinah realized her mistake. Vilate could not hear the Principle with any joy. She was not like Dinah, a plural wife, viewing the Principle as a way to have the husband who would have been denied to her without it. Vilate was the first wife. Heber would be taking others, and Vilate was not rejoicing.

"Vilate," she said, "I know it's not an easy time for you." She meant to try to explain it to Vilate, to help her understand. But Vilate cut her off.

"It's a black time," Vilate cried, "a damned black time, with prophets fallen and husbands denied and the heavens sealed tight as the entrance of hell."

Dinah was at a loss; she had never seen Vilate like this. Usually when she had a mood on her, a jest would ease it. "I always thought the entrance of hell was wide open. I thought it was the exit that was sealed."

If Vilate knew it was a joke, she gave no sign. "Sealed up and I can't get out, I can't see any way out." Suddenly she looked up at Dinah with terrible eyes. "I did what I came here to do, I cleaned the slate with you, good-bye."

Dinah caught her before she reached the door. "Vilate, you mustn't weep alone."

"What should I do? Charge admission and hope for a crowd?"

"What prophets have fallen, Vilate? If it's Joseph you mean, I know that he has not."

"I *pray* that he has, that's what I'm saying, I *pray* that he's a liar and that God would never require this of me." Dinah took her arm, led her from the door. Vilate did not seem to know she was walking, or that she sat when Dinah brought her to the edge of the bed. "I've loved Heber all my life. Doesn't that count for anything?"

"It counts for everything."

"Nothing. Who considers it at all? I never thought of another man but Heber. I can't remember a time when I was so young I didn't know that he was my husband and I belonged to him forever. I don't look very pretty or young anymore, but it's true. You don't forget that sort of thing just because you get older and tireder. God took him away for two years. Did you ever hear me complain?"

"This isn't unbearable either, Vilate."

"For you. You hated your husband."

"But I love my husband now. And knowing he loves another woman, too—I can bear that, for love of him."

It was lame, Dinah knew it, and so did Vilate, shaking her head slowly, looking at the place where the wall sank down against the floor.

"What is it like," Vilate asked at last, "being married to him like that?"

Dinah could not bear to tell it truthfully. She could not lie, but she could color it, she could make it sound like as a plural wife she meant less to Joseph than she really did. She could help Vilate believe that the first wife lost little, so that she wouldn't be so jealous, so that she could bear to live the law. Dinah explained it as she wished for Emma to understand it. "He comes to me only rarely, months between, sometimes. He never pretends that he loves me more than any other—on the contrary, his heart is with his—his first. But I can bear that, because I think of myself as her handmaid, like Hagar—"

"Hagar was cast away by her husband, at Sarah's demand. It's not Hagar I fear. It's Rachel. The younger sister, but the favored wife."

"You can't compare. It was Rachel that Jacob meant to marry from the first, he was only given Leah as a trick. Think instead of Bilhah and Zilpah, who never usurped their mistresses' place, and yet served Jacob well, and bore him sons."

"I've borne enough sons."

"Don't you know Heber?" Dinah said, gripping Vilate by the arm. "You'll always have his love."

Vilate's only reaction was to shake her head and give one weak hiccoughing sob.

"Vilate, God will bless you for it. I promise you."

Vilate turned to her abruptly, and clutched at Dinah's hands and arms, scratching her as she tried to hold her hands. "Bless me, Dinah! Give me a blessing!"

If the words had been said to an elder or high priest, there would have been no doubt of their meaning. He would have put his hands out, touched the woman, and answered her petition with a declaration in the name of Christ and by the power of the holy priesthood after the order of Melchizedek. But to a woman, what meaning could the words have? Yet Vilate took Dinah's hands and lifted them, placed them on her own head. "Bless me."

"I can't!"

"God can't deny me, and no man can answer me! Bless me!"

"I'll pray for you—"

Vilate's answer was to hold Dinah's hands more tightly, pressing them to her head; so Dinah prayed for Vilate to have strength, to overcome her fear; prayed that her husband would be wise and kind, so she would be reconciled to God's will. When the prayer ended, Vilate stayed silent on the floor. Dinah leaned to her and kissed her on the lips, to give her courage; Vilate's lips moved slightly to return the kiss, but the older woman gave no other sign of knowing Dinah was there. She looked so frail and old, though she was scarcely in her thirties. Dinah was sure she hadn't eaten—no doubt she was fasting as she tried to bend herself to the will of God. It was too much, though, for her to fast; she was too weak. Dinah went to the fire, put the water pot over the coals so she could make a tea. But when she turned around from putting another few sticks on the fire, she saw the door closing; Vilate was gone, and Dinah had not helped her. It made Dinah afraid, to see a first wife react to the Principle this way. It seemed to tell her that Emma would be the same, that she would never bend, would never accept Dinah as her sister wife. If Emma knew, she would hate me: Dinah heard that thought in her heart and felt despair.

She went back to bed for a while and tried to sleep; got up at last and wrote in her journal, read the scriptures, tried anything she could to calm her fear. But she could not, and at last, as the afternoon waned, she put on her sunbonnet and went out into the hottest hour of the August day. She would go to Joseph. Not as a wife, but as any Saint could go to him, for counsel, for encouragement. She had never done it before; he would forgive her if she did it just this once.

Joseph was busy; she had to wait downstairs with Charlie. It was hard, for Charlie was almost laughing out loud every other moment with excitement over something. She asked him what it was, hoping that if he talked he'd not be so annoying as he was with his constant smiles and contented sighs. But he looked at her mysteriously and said, "I can't tell you. Joseph said to keep it private for just now."

So Dinah endured his unendurable good cheer until at last Joseph appeared at the foot of the stairs and said, in his formal voice, "Sister Handy? You wanted to see me?"

She went up the stairs decorously, keenly aware of her husband following behind. Emma was there in the hallway, holding a cloth that she was folding. Emma smiled and reached out her hand. "I'm glad to see you out of your house, Sister Dinah."

Dinah took her hand, pretending to herself that someday soon it would be like this every day, Emma greeting her with love in Joseph's home, not as a friend, but as a sister wife. But not yet. "Go on, Dinah," Emma said. "It's not good to keep Joseph waiting."

Joseph stood at the door of the room where he gave and took counsel. He smiled at her. Or was he smiling at Emma? Not at me, Dinah decided; he's surely angry at me for coming; he can't be glad to have both these wives together in his house today. What surprised Dinah was the fact that she felt a little jealous that Joseph was smiling at Emma. *I* am the interloper, Dinah reminded herself. I have no right to resent his love for *her*.

Joseph closed the door behind him. Dinah turned to face him. He did not smile. "What have you come for, Sister Dinah?"

Of course, Dinah told herself. The walls are not made of stone. Yet can't he so much as look glad to see me? Never mind. He's afraid I'm here for pleasure, and I'm not. "I came because of Vilate Kimball."

Joseph sighed.

"Heber taught the Principle to her, and she's taking it desperately hard. Maybe if you talked to her—"

"How much did she explain to you?"

"Nothing. She only said that she knew now where my— burden had come from." *Could* Emma be listening? "And she wanted me to forgive her. But the way she was acting, it wasn't hard to guess."

"You guessed wrong."

That was impossible. All the talk of how she loved her husband, the way that Vilate asked about what it was like for her, being a plural wife—"She must know about the Principle."

"Oh, she knows. But that's not what's bothering her."

"What is it, then?" Dinah asked.

Joseph shook his head. "If *she* didn't tell you, it's hardly *my* place to do it."

"She was talking of fallen prophets, Joseph."

"*Brother* Joseph," he whispered.

"Brother Joseph."

"Many people talk of fallen prophets, Sister Dinah."

"I'm afraid she may turn against the Church over this, whatever it is—"

"Perhaps she will." He sounded harsh, but she knew his voice well enough to hear that he, too, was afraid. "Sister Dinah, when you stood on the ship in Liverpool harbor, and chose between your children and the Church, was it hard?" He did not wait for an answer. "When the Lord sets a test to try the faith of someone, don't judge them harshly if they don't keep perfect decorum through it all."

"I wasn't judging her."

There was a knock at the door. Joseph was annoyed. "You shouldn't be here for this."

The door opened. Dinah saw such fear on Joseph's face that she was relieved to see that it was only Heber—Heber Kimball, with Vilate behind him.

"You'll have to excuse me, Sister Dinah," Joseph said. "I have to see the Kimballs privately—they came more quickly than I expected."

"No," Vilate said quietly. She was hoarse, as if she had wept all day, but her face was calm now. "Please stay, Dinah. I want her to stay."

Joseph and Heber looked at each other. They must have made a decision, for Joseph closed the door without making Dinah go through it first. He stood then with his back to the door, Heber and Vilate before him, facing him. "What did you choose?" Joseph asked.

Vilate whispered, "I'm the Lord's to do with as he pleases."

Then, to Dinah's shock, Heber took Vilate's hand and placed it in Joseph's and said, "Wife, here is your husband."

Of all things that Dinah might have thought of, this was the most impossible. Vilate, to *leave* Heber and become *Joseph's* plural wife? It was impossible that God could ask for such a thing, it was a perversion of the Principle; and now Dinah remembered the things she had said to Vilate just this morning, encouraging her to accept. I would never have urged her on to *this*. Dinah wanted to cry out for them to stop. But she did not. For at that moment Joseph began to weep, and she could see the spirit of God come on him. He stared past the couple, as if he saw something transpiring behind them; his voice, though quiet, became more penetrating, almost like a song. "And Abraham stretched forth his hand," said Joseph, "and took the knife to slay his son. And the angel of the Lord called unto him out of heaven, and said, 'Abraham, Abraham. And Abraham said, Here am I.'" Joseph looked Heber in the eye and changed the rest of the scripture. "And the angel said, 'Lay not your hand upon his wife. For now I know that he fears God, seeing that he has not withheld his wife, his beloved Vilate from the Lord.'"

It was a trial. Only a trial. God wouldn't require them to go through with it. Dinah watched as they embraced each other in relief. Then Joseph joined their hands and sealed them together as husband and wife for eternity. "Even the angels can't part you now," he told them when it was done. They clung to each other as they left the room, until Vilate suddenly remembered Dinah was there and ran to her and embraced her and whispered in her ear, "Oh, Dinah, without you I'd never have found the strength to do it." Then she was gone, and Dinah and Joseph were alone again.

To Dinah's surprise, she was angry. As Vilate and Heber rejoiced, Dinah had felt rage grow like fire in her. And now she whispered savagely, "What kind of God requires such things of people!"

With one hand he held her, his fingers in the hair at the nape of her neck. "Why are you angry? How is it different from the test *you* were given, when you gave up your children?"

"Where was the angel at *my* test! Where was God then! Why didn't someone put my children's hands in mine and say, They're yours forever, for time and eternity, nothing can part you—why doesn't God love me as much as he loves *them?*"

She wept and he held her to him and whispered, "I don't know." And then he said, even more softly, with some of her own pain in his voice, "The God who left your children alive— where was he when so many of mine died?"

Do you want me to be ashamed? "Do you want to compare the pain?"

"I'm not comparing," he said. "Father chooses for us what he knows we can bear, and what we need to go through to become what he wants us to be, if we have the faith for it. And not just once. Over and over again, that's what we're here for, that's all that life is, testing us again and again."

"Then the lucky ones are the ones who die before they're old enough to know."

"The lucky ones are the ones who know they have proved themselves in a wrestling match with the Lord."

"I surrender now," Dinah said. "I want no more tests. I have had enough."

Joseph laughed sadly and kissed her hair. "The one thing you'll never do, Sister Dinah, is surrender, to God or anyone."

Dinah was afraid of meeting Emma once she left the room; there was no way to hide the fact that she'd been crying, and Emma would want to know why, if not now, then later. But Emma was not upstairs, and when they got downstairs Charlie told them she had gone on an errand before Heber and Vilate came. Joseph didn't seem surprised. "These things work out," he said.

"Brother Joseph," Charlie said, "is it all right if I tell the news to Dinah?"

Joseph laughed. "It's not that big a secret, Charlie." Joseph turned to Dinah. "I'm sending Charlie to Washington. At his own expense, of course." Charlie was visibly proud that he was doing well enough that he needed to ask for nothing from the Church to pay his way. "I want him to work on winning support with Congress for our petition for redress of grievances from Missouri. At least restitution for the land that was stolen from us." Joseph slung his arm around Charlie's shoulders.

"Charlie's only just turning nineteen this week," Dinah said. "Even if he were a citizen, he couldn't vote in this country."

"Don't talk him out of it, Dinah," Charlie said. "I can do it."

"There isn't much that Charlie can't do," Joseph said. "A sister wouldn't know that, of course. My sisters never thought I'd amount to much, either."

Dinah smiled, but wasn't satisfied until Joseph playfully held Charlie at arm's length and said to him, "It's just the sort of mission I might've sent Don Carlos on."

Charlie soberly received the words as praise, as confidence, and Joseph meant them that way, at least in part. But Dinah knew as well that Joseph had found a way around the most painful of reminders of Don Carlos's death.

Charlie came to her and took her hands. "Dinah, are you glad?"

Impulsively she embraced him tightly. "Yes, I'm glad," she said. It startled the poor boy, but it felt good to her. He was the companion of her youth, and even though their marriages had drawn them apart, she still loved him as always, and when she was glad she needed to be glad with him, even if she couldn't tell him all the reasons. Couldn't tell him she was glad that there would soon be other families living the Principle. Couldn't tell him she was glad that the silence Vilate had imposed on her would end at last. Couldn't tell him she was glad that it would not be long before Harriette, too, would have the husband that she wanted. You, Charlie, if you only knew what God has in store for *you*.

❧ 37 ❧

Charles Kirkham
Washington, D.C., 1842

THERE WAS A WARM SPELL in January, and the First Lady, Mrs. Tyler, decided to pretend it was spring and have an orchestra perform on the White House lawn. Charlie was there, with writing paper and pencil so he could pretend to be using the time for correspondence, but in fact he was out to enjoy the weather and the company of other people, just like everyone else.

Charlie began a letter to Sally first, more out of duty than pleasure. He felt guilty whenever he had to think of her for long. He hadn't been there for the birth of little Alexandra in November. It was a much colder winter in Nauvoo. And the Prophet was in hiding much of the time, trying to evade arrest as the writs from Missouri came thick and fast. Charlie knew he should finish his business and come home, but the truth was, he wasn't that anxious to return. He *missed* Sally, and *wanted* to see his daughter, but he was in love with Washington.

There were people here who loved poetry, *men* who loved poetry. Old John Quincy Adams himself had lent Charlie more than one book of poetry, but when he copied some out and sent them home to Sally, she didn't understand them unless Harriette explained them to her. Cold as a corpse Harriette, but she understood love poetry better than Sally, even though Sally was as hot between the sheets as a woman could possibly be.

Too hot. Not like the cool Washington ladies in their lawns and muslins, always so distant and reserved. They had mystery; there was no mystery about Sally. She said what she thought, and what she thought was so common, so unpoetic that Charlie sometimes felt quite afraid to go home, for life in Nauvoo was swallowing up the last vestiges of refinement in him, his last hope of being a gentleman. Charlie looked around him at the people beginning to gather on the lawn. There had never been such a gathering at Nauvoo. It was not just that people had money; it was the grace of conversation when they spoke, the depth of thought when they touched on topics that mattered. Nauvoo seemed so boorish in comparison. Charlie hated telling people he was just a clerk. He preferred to tell them that he owned a factory. He liked to leave the impression that he owned three, in fact, a chandlery, a soap manufactory, and a wagon-making firm. He *meant* to make wagons soon, anyway, and he did make wheels, and wheels were what made the difference between a wagon and a box. You're in business, and only nineteen? Do you have partners? Oh, that's impressive, I wish *my* son were so ambitious. Charles! Recite the one, that Wordsworth one, Lucy—yes, it breaks my heart, you have to hear it recited by an Englishman. A pleasure to meet you; you have the soul of a poet, Mr. Kirkham. May I call you Charles? What are you doing out west? You aren't a pioneer, Charles. You're too civilized. Where you belong is New York. No, Boston—don't listen to him, New Yorkers can't tell a waltz from a waffle iron. You should come to Charleston.

But Sally wouldn't hear of it. He dropped a hint once, about how nice it might be to live on the coast. Sally's next letter fairly burned as she informed Charlie that she had married a Latter-day Saint and intended her children to grow up with Latter-day Saints and she would not for a moment be willing to live in *Babylon*, the *whore of the earth*; as the scriptures called it. Are you praying every day, Charlie? Don't forget me. Don't forget our baby. Don't forget the Savior. Come home soon.

Writing to Sally depressed him. He set down the pencil and watched the orchestra forming on a makeshift stand nearer the White House. Sally was right—*she* at least would never fit in here. In Nauvoo she was the perfect wife, bright, business-like, hardworking, fertile, strong, healthy, all that it took to do well in the rough life of the frontier. But here in Washington her movements would be too large, her emotions too obvious, her voice too loud, her words all inappropriate. A frog at a ball, that's what she'd be. With his choice of wives, Charlie had made his choice of career as well. He could visit Washington, but he could never belong here.

"And there is a true correspondent, lost in letters even at a concert."

Charlie looked up. Daniel Webster had decked himself out in his dashing blue swallowtail coat and buff trousers, the Whig colors, so that he would have looked like Whig Party bunting had he not also been an outrageously handsome man. His black hair recommended him from a distance; closer to, his voice required everyone to listen. Charlie noticed that already the inevitable crowd was forming around the Secretary of State and, therefore, around Charlie. In a way, Washington was as small as Nauvoo—it was possible to know everyone.

"Good morning, sir," Charlie said, getting up.

"But it's afternoon, my friend. What an engrossing letter you're writing, that it has held you so enthralled right through the dinner hour! I'm Daniel Webster, Mr. Kirkham—you may remember that we met at Mrs. Woodbury's soiree, an unfortunately Democratic affair at which I provided the only Whig of fresh air."

A man standing nearby—Charlie recognized him as an obscure new Congressman from Massachusetts or Georgia or some such foreign place—spoke up and said, "But the President himself was there."

"And you yourself, Mr. Colquitt, have been quoted as saying that poor President Tyler has no party, even when he attends one."

So the political wars continued on the White House lawn. Finding Charlie a good neutral foil, Webster stayed there some time, conversing with him for the entertainment and enlightenment of the onlookers. Charlie knew that his role was not to compete but to complement, and so he designed his answers and his questions to make him sound like a naive but fascinated foreigner. His Lancashire accent was indispensible at times like this.

Because Charlie was so good at conversation, it was still going strong after a quarter hour; Charlie wished it could last forever. But Webster began to break away, to move on—the concert was nearly over, and he had to make his appearance at the front before the affair broke up. "A pleasure talking with you, Mr. Kirkham."

Charlie had already learned how the famous love to be reminded of their fame. "A man of my age rarely gets to talk with men of fame."

"Fame!" Webster cried. "What is fame! Let me give you a striking illustration of how valuable a thing *fame* is. I was traveling in a railroad car a short time ago, and it so happened that I was seated by the side of a very old man. I soon found that this old man was from my native town in New Hampshire. I asked him if he was acquainted with the Webster family there. He answered that he and old Mr. Webster, in his lifetime, were great friends. He then went on to speak of the children. He said Ezekiel was the most eminent lawyer in New Hampshire, and his sisters, calling each by her Christian name, were married to most excellent men." Webster paused. "I then inquired if there was not another member of the family."

The crowd laughed. Charlie smiled.

"He said he thought not." At this Webster made a slightly woeful face, which drew more laughter. "Was there not one, I asked him, by the name of Daniel? Here the old man put on his thinking-cap for a few moments, and then he replied, 'Oh, I recollect now. There was one by the name of Daniel, but he went down to Boston, and I haven't heard of him since.'" The crowd roared with laughter. "There's your fame, Mr. Kirkham!"

Charlie thought then that Webster would move away, but Webster put his arm around Charlie's shoulders and brought him along as he walked toward Mrs. Tyler at the front of the gathering.

"A most delightful conversation," Webster said.

"I think I learned more from half an hour with you than in

all these months in Washington," Charlie said.

Webster chuckled. "You don't have *very* much to learn from anyone. If I were either more or less vain, I'd hire you to walk around with me, to converse with me so cleverly. It would enhance my reputation."

"Not to mention mine."

"You looked forlorn as you wrote. I cannot resist a sad story."

"My wife," Charlie said.

"A wife," Webster said sadly. "No wonder you're morose. There are ladies who quite openly set their caps for you, and you must ignore them most heartlessly. Of course, if word got around that you're married, as many as two or three of them might get discouraged. But don't worry—I'll tell no one your dark secret. How would I dare? The bearer of such news would be unwelcome in every Washington house that contains an unmarried lady."

Charlie laughed. "They never give me a second glance, sir, as you well know."

"Not while you're glancing at *them*, you may be sure. How can they give you a second glance, anyway, when the first glance lingers infinitely?"

The flattery was coming far too thickly. Charlie laughed, but he was becoming wary, though in fact he could not think what Webster might hope to gain by flattering someone as powerless as Charlie.

"You may have heard," said Webster, "that John Calhoun and I have had our differences."

Charlie wondered what Webster was getting at. "It's a rumor that I was not in a position to evaluate."

"It isn't a rumor, Mr. Kirkham. I'm telling you that it's plain fact. If I didn't hold the man's mother in such high regard I'd suppose him a son-of-a-bitch in the grand tradition; as it is, I can only think him a horse's ass. But both he and his moral twin, Henry Clay, may they share an appointment as ambassadors to Turkestan, have mentioned you favorably to me. Don't you think that odd?"

"I've met them both. I hope they remembered me pleasantly."

"I've never met this man you serve, your Joseph Smith. Is he really a prophet?"

"I wish you could meet him and judge for yourself, sir."

"I don't know. I'm not an expert on prophets, and I doubt he's ever met such a shameless demagogue as myself. It has been suggested to me that you might make an admirable secretary."

Charlie almost laughed. In a city swarming with office-seekers, Charlie was one of the few there who was not angling for an appointment. And now Daniel Webster himself was hinting at one. It tempted him sorely, but he was the Prophet's representative. "I'm a businessman in Illinois, when I'm not here on President Smith's affairs. I've been secretary to a law firm in England and to a prophet in Illinois, but I don't know that I long for a career at it."

Webster looked bemused. "At least they measured you fairly accurately. You really aren't looking for a position. I had thought there was not such a man in the world. Come see me, Mr. Kirkham. I want to have you about the house, if only so I can point you out as a curiosity. There is a man who is good enough to do well in office, and doesn't want one." Then Webster took his leave, and returned to being the center of a swarm of admirers as he went to greet the First Lady.

They said Webster wanted to be President. Well, thought Charlie, that was an easy disease to catch in this city. Every politician Charlie met was infected with it, or once had been, which meant that they were accustomed to making no clear statement of policy on anything. It made Charlie's official mission, to secure redress of grievances for the Saints' losses in Missouri, hopeless. Henry Clay had put him off with vague talk of waiting for an improved political climate. John Quincy Adams bluntly said that he was busy collecting citizen petitions on matters that had at least a bit of hope of success. But it was John C. Calhoun who explained things most plainly, though in his careful Southern drawl it sounded milder than it was. "Son," the Senator said, "I'd sooner see an enemy put Savannah to the torch than hear of a single federal officer interfering with a private matter in a sovereign state." That had been the enlightenment for Charlie. The Saints were asking the federal government to either guarantee private property within the states—anathema to anti-slavery Northerners—or forcefully enter a state to enforce the Constitution—an unspeakable idea to a Southerner.

But the redress of grievances was not Charlie's main purpose in Washington. Charlie's real reason for staying in Washington was to size up the men who were the most likely candidates for President, to see which of them was worth supporting. Because the Church was concentrated in one county of one state, the Mormon vote could conceivably swing a whole bloc of electoral votes; that potential power might be traded for future protection, if the right man won. So as Charlie made his rounds, petition in hand, from one Congressman and Senator to another, he would casually mention that Mormons tended to vote as a bloc, and how many they were, and where they all lived.

Within a month of beginning this ploy, Charlie found himself invited everywhere. Only Henry Clay was frank about it. "You're a charming fellow, Mr. Kirkham, but you got my attention the way you got everyone else's, by making me wonder whether Joseph Smith was a Whig or a Democrat. It's a clever game, and if you strike the right bargain you may do well for yourselves. But let me warn your prophet of something he may not know. After the next election, your influence will be *gone*. Once you decide to be Whigs, the Democrats will hound you until you drop; once you decide to be Democrats, the Whigs will drive you from the state at gunpoint. And if you don't deliver your votes solidly one way or the other, they'll figure you have no power at all, and despise you."

"So you won't help us?"

"Unbelievable as it may sound to you, Mr. Kirkham, there are still many men in Congress who put the public welfare above their individual good. But you Mormons are only a small part of the public. There are far greater issues than punishing the state of Missouri for crimes committed by a mob three years ago."

Charlie nodded and stood to leave. "Thank you for the interview, Mr. Clay."

But Clay stopped him. "That Smith fellow, your prophet. I met him when he was here, a couple of years ago. I didn't like him much. That sort of religion doesn't much appeal to me. But he has it, whatever it is that makes people lie down and die for a man. Has more of it than Webster, and Webster has more than anybody. But why are *you* taken in by it? It's still all humbuggery."

"You're getting politics confused with religion," Charlie said.

Clay grinned. "I suppose it's always easier to spot flimflam in the other man's argument. You tell Joe Smith he could have been President, if he'd only got himself an education or killed enough Indians, or if he'd kept out of religion. But as for getting the government on his side, he hasn't got a chance. Pleasure knowing you, Mr. Kirkham."

Charlie ate his last meal in Washington like a condemned man. He knew he wouldn't eat so well again once he crossed the Appalachians. The train would be fast, but that would only make the change to frontier living all the more abrupt. Sitting at the table, thumbing through the volumes of Herrick and Pope that he needed to return to Adams before he left, Charlie wondered if he really wanted to go back. Couldn't he make his report to Joseph by letter? Couldn't he send for Sally and Alexandra, and set himself up as a permanent, unofficial delegate of the Church in Washington? He could monitor the legislation, try to influence things, and in the meantime pursue a career that might bring him real power.

As he finished the meal, however, with his future mapped a dozen times over, he knew it would not be so simple. Sally would come if he told her to, but she wouldn't be happy here where the ladies would all despise her. And Joseph—he'd see through Charlie quickly, he wouldn't be fooled by any talk of being unofficial delegate. It was another temptation from the world, just like the one his firm had offered him in Manchester. It was Nauvoo where his home was, and so he would go back.

He had little time left when he reached Adams's house; he meant to leave off the books, thank the old man, and be on his way. But Adams wanted to talk a moment. "Tell me, was your stay in Washington a success?"

"My greatest success was in working my way through your library, sir. You were very kind."

"So your petition has accomplished nothing. Well, neither have mine. But that isn't all you were here for, was it?"

Adams had been President once, and now was back in the House of Representatives, finishing out his life as a sort of people's advocate—having once had the highest office, he was the only man in Washington who could say he had no ambition and hope to be believed. And he had been kind to Charlie without any hope of gaining from it. So Charlie told him his main purpose in Washington.

"Ah." Adams reached up and touched the bushy white fringe around his bald head, as if to make sure some hair still remained. "Like Socrates, searching for a wise man. Did you find one?"

"Many clever ones," Charlie said.

"Some men come here to this whore of a city, seduced by power or money or fame. But you and I, we are seduced by the undying faith that we alone, of all the men in the world, we will be the ones to accomplish something truly good."

"Does that make us fools?"

"It makes us unpleasant company. No one will ever meet your standards. Here, Charlie. Keep this collection of Pope. Whenever you start feeling that other men are too wicked or hypocritical to bear, read a little of his rhyming. 'The glory, jest, and riddle of the world,' that's all you are, especially when you're most certain that you're right. I'm making you late for your train."

"No—I have time. Thank you for the book."

"I hear you were wise enough to turn down all the offers that were made to you."

Charlie shrugged self-deprecatingly. "They overestimated my abilities."

"Don't pretend to be humble, Charles. You're as vain as anyone, and with much better reason than most. I don't care what reason you gave yourself for going home—I'm just glad you did it. Because you aren't strong enough for this place."

After all the flattery, Charlie was ill-equipped to enjoy this. "No, I suppose not."

"You don't like hearing it now, but I'm old enough that I can say it. You'd be a good teacher, but never a good politician or lawyer. Not really a top-flight businessman, either."

Not that Charlie believed him—but he wanted to know. "Why not?"

"Because you don't know how to kill, Charles. In the end, that's what it comes down to. You have to love the kill. It's life that *you* love. Never change. And never come back here as long as you live." Adams held out his age-knotted hand. "I like you. I'll miss having you ransack my shelves."

"Thank you sir. You've been kind."

Charlie walked to the railroad station through the cold and muddy January streets, feeling as dismal as the weather was now. Like the brief warm spell the week before, all Washington was a lie. Slaves everywhere in the capital of a free country; cowards in almost every office; animals in the streets; bitter old poverty and cruel new wealth competing for attention in the architecture, in the faces of the people. The monuments, the great documents, the rhetoric of democracy and justice— they were only a shared dream, not the truth of the place.

But that's the way it is in Nauvoo, too, Charlie realized. We call it Zion, the Kingdom of God, but it's a jealousy-ridden, poverty-stricken shanty town. And yet wasn't the truth either. The temple rising on the hill wasn't hypocrisy, it was hope. The Saints weren't pretending to be perfect, only intending to be. Like Washington, they just couldn't catch up to their own dreams. Yet if it weren't for the dream, neither Nauvoo nor Washington would exist at all.

And me, he thought on the train northward into Pennsylvania. I am no different from these places. I intend to be great, I dream of it, and yet I know that I'm not, and I think that I probably never will be. Is it so terrible, as long as the dream I try for is a good dream, is it so terrible if my life doesn't bring the dream to pass?

No, not terrible at all, he decided. I'll be perfectly content, as long as I tried my best.

Liar, whispered something inside him. Liar.

As the apostles had done when they returned from England, Charlie went to Brother Joseph's house before seeing anyone else in Nauvoo. Joseph wasn't there. No one was living there at the moment, in fact, for Joseph was in hiding and Emma was staying with Hyrum's wife while she recovered from the birth of a dead baby a few days before. William Clayton, who used to be their branch president back in Manchester, was caring for the house. Charlie glanced at the writing instruments and papers spread over the desk that used to be Charlie's. "I'm scribing and clerking for him now," Clayton said. "Brother Joseph knew you'd want to be with your family at a time like this. He'll be touched that you came here anyway."

"A time like this?" The tone of consolation in Clayton's voice made it plain that something must be wrong at Charlie's house.

"You mean you haven't been home yet?"

"I came straight here, to report to Brother Joseph."

"I wouldn't have wished to be the one to tell you, Charlie." Clayton had the look of death in his face."

"Who is it! Mother? Sally?"

"No, Charlie. It's your baby. Little Alexandra. They buried her this morning. They couldn't wait any longer."

Charlie felt numb inside. Clayton reached out a hand to steady him.

"No, I'll be all right."

"There are others besides yours, Charlie. It's been a hard winter on the little ones."

"I didn't even know she was ill."

"It's quick, when it takes the babies. That's a mercy sometimes, Charlie."

Charlie held out his hands in front of him. All the time in Washington he had thought little of his daughter—women hardly let fathers near the babies the first few months anyway. But he had never so much as touched her; the baby died without even a father's blessing, without ever hearing her father's voice. "I hardly knew she was *alive*."

"I didn't want to be the one to tell you. They won't be at the grave anymore by now. I'm sorry. I've lost little ones, too. You're not alone."

But he felt alone, and that made all the commiseration in the world worthless to him. He did not hurry—there was little point in that. He walked steadily homeward, not caring that his trunk was at the station, that he had left his papers in a box at Joseph's house. If he had only known. If God had let the baby live even another day. He didn't even know what the child looked like.

He opened the door. Dinah and Mother and Father were there, and Harriette and Mother Clinton, all red-eyed from crying. All except Sally. She was like still water in the middle of the stream; all the movement, all the grief eddied around her, but somehow she was miraculously calm. They all saw him as soon as the door opened, but no one spoke. Charlie realized that they were wondering whether they had to break the news to him. "I already know," he said.

Sally stood up and took a step or two toward him. "I spent the money for a tombstone for her," she said. She was shy, she was uncertain, as if she wanted very much for him to approve what she had done. "It wasn't that much, and I didn't want her grave to disappear. So many babies' graves seem to disappear, as if their lives didn't matter."

"Sally," Mother Clinton said.

"Let her be, Mother," Harriette whispered.

Sally came another step toward Charlie. "She was a very happy baby. She ate all the time, she was so strong. I didn't leave her hungry, Charlie."

"I know you didn't, Sally."

"She even smiled when she was sick. Almost to the end, she'd stop crying suddenly and smile. Do you think that little babies can see God?"

Charlie didn't know.

"I did my best, Charlie, but you just came home too slow."

He put his arms around her, held her close. He felt her body quake.

"Thank God," Mother Clinton said. "I thought she'd never cry."

"Crying's good," Anna said. "Took me a week to cry myself out when my Alice died. It's easier with the later ones. But it isn't healthy not to cry."

"I'm sorry, I'm sorry," Sally said in a thin, high, whining voice, over and over.

"It's all right," Charlie said. It's God's fault, not yours. "It's no one's fault." It's my fault.

"She was a good baby," said Harriette. "You would have loved her."

John Kirkham stepped away from the wall, where he had been standing when Charlie arrived. He looked awkward, embarrassed, as if he knew Charlie wouldn't want to hear from *him* at a time like this. "Charlie, I, uh—when it began to look bad for the little one, and we thought you might not come home, I sketched her. Three sketches, so you'd know how she looked. Later, when you want to."

"They're beautiful drawings, Charlie," Dinah said.

Charlie nodded, looking at his father, wondering why he felt so surprised. Ah, yes, now he knew. It was because he didn't hate his father. Not a shred of hatred left, none at all. Charlie had been away from home for the whole life of his first-born child. That was a match for any of his father's sins.

"No, Charlie," Dinah said, as if she could read his thoughts.

She came to him and touched his hair the way she had when he was little and afraid, and she had comforted him. "It's just the way of things."

Charlie shook his head. Not because he disagreed, but because he didn't even want to think. He had known just what his homecoming would be like. Caught up at once in the bustle of Nauvoo life. Received back joyfully among his loving family. He wasn't prepared for this. He led Sally carefully to the bedroom. "Thank you all," he said to them all from the door, without looking back.

As he closed the door behind him, someone said, "We love you, Charlie." Either it was that or the closing of the door, or maybe both that made him cry. He and Sally wept together wordlessly for a long time. It was only later that he remembered that it was Harriette who had said it. Cold Harriette who had known what he needed to hear.

Father's sketches were beautiful. Charlie had them framed and hung them on the wall. He changed the order of the pictures many, many times in the next few months. He wasn't sure why, except that there had to be some way to arrange them that would give meaning to her story. The smiling child, the girl sleeping, Alexandra in profile, reaching upward. Some way to arrange the pictures that would let her move, let him hear her voice, let her hand reach out to him. He tried every combination of pictures, over and over, but none of them satisfied him longer than a day.

➤➤➤ BOOK SEVEN ➤➤➤

*In which Providence at last
reveals the truth
to those who had illusions.*

❧ First Word ❧

The rumors of polygamy were impossible to quell. People sworn to secrecy had a way of figuring they could tell *one* particular friend or relative; even when they didn't set out to tell, they often didn't know how to slip around a direct question without giving something away. Those few who really were discreet still took some pleasure from leaving hints that they knew something that others didn't know. Pride in having special knowledge is an all-too-common trait. The trouble was, it let the curious know there was a secret lying about. They started searching for it and the facts were findable, if you searched enough. So the rumors spread through Nauvoo, invariably doing harm. Some who heard them didn't believe that the Prophet would counsel such a law—when they *did* find out the truth, they felt betrayed. Others believed in the Principle as soon as they heard of it, but didn't understand how rigidly Joseph meant it to be lived, and thought it gave license for promiscuity. Still others believed that Joseph Smith was teaching polygamy, but didn't believe that God had anything to do with it. And, slowly but surely, the enemies of the Principle became the enemies of the Church and, most particularly, the enemies of Joseph Smith. Polygamy, in the end, was in large part the cause of Joseph's death.

But the rumors seemed manageable at the time. Joseph Smith was most concerned about the select group of Saints who were commanded to live the Principle. Almost all of them came from a rigidly Puritan background, from old New England families whose ancestors had learned religion from John Winthrop and Increase Mather. They longed to be members of the original Church of Christ, the one they believed Jesus and the apostles formed at Jerusalem, the one revealed as much in the Old Testament as in the New. They had been weaned on the belief that the original church taught the only correct way to worship God. They accepted Joseph Smith's new church only because they believed it was old—the very gospel God had taught to Adam, to Abraham, to Moses, to Peter. They did not accept polygamy out of lust or sexual repression—that is the obsession of our post-Freudian times, and to interpret pre-Victorians in that light is to blind ourselves to who they really were. They had a deep-seated revulsion to adultery or anything that smacked of it. Brigham Young later said that when he learned the law of plural marriages it was the only time in his life that he ever envied the dead. Most of Joseph's followers lived polygamy either out of blind obedience or—and for independent-minded Americans this is much more likely—because it fit the pattern. If God had once given plural wives to Abraham, Isaac, and Jacob, to David and Solomon, then at the restoration of all the ancient gospel it only made sense that he would give plural wives to Joseph, Brigham, and Heber. They received the law as a commandment of a demanding God. It is no accident that the women who entered into polygamy were likely to be, not the weakest-willed, but the strongest, most gifted women of the Latter-day Saints.

Emma Smith, however, was slow to accept the Principle, and after Joseph's death she pretended that he had never taught it, that it had been invented after his death by Brigham Young, whom she detested. Perhaps she was actually able to shut those nightmare years in Nauvoo from her mind and truly believe that her husband never practiced plural marriage. But the fact remains that after years of bitter resistance, Emma Smith did give in, at least momentarily, to the Principle of Celestial Marriage. It is not hard to understand her reluctance. What is hard to understand is why she ever accepted it. It was not a godlike Prophet who taught the law to her, it was her husband. She did not learn it all at once, unfolded as an orderly doctrine—she learned it bit by bit, as rumors kept coming to her of her husband's apparent philandering. She could not hear another man command her husband to take another wife—she had only her husband's word that it was God's law. Besides, even if she believed the law she didn't think it fair to require her to live it. She had already given up more than most women. She never had a normal home, she and her husband were constantly at the beck and call of the Saints, and even when he was home Joseph was distracted from his family by the concerns of the Church. What little she had of him, she had no wish to share. Surely God had already required enough of her.

But the pressure to live the Principle was more than she could withstand. Joseph supplied most of that insistence himself; it was not proper that, with other men's wives bending to the law, the Prophet's wife would not. As more men and women entered the Principle, they too put pressure on Emma, until at last, whatever the particular reasons were, she gave in. Even then, like grass springing back after it is crushed, she rejected the Principle again, then surrendered again; refused once more, and probably would have gone on for some time in this pattern of compliance and resistance if her husband had not died.

If this were Emma's book, I would chart these vicissitudes, weighing the probable reasons for each change. Instead I must leave that for her biographers. It is Dinah's life that I'm writing about; Emma's problems matter to me only because Dinah Kirkham's life was changed when by chance—if you believe in chance—she was with Emma at the first of the times when the Prophet's wife bowed, at least for a moment, to the Principle.

—*O. Kirkham, Salt Lake City, 1981*

❧ 38 ❧

Dinah Kirkham Smith
Nauvoo, 1842

DINAH GAVE UP TEACHING school. She was pregnant again,
and at five months it was beginning to show.

"Why are you quitting?" Emma asked. "The children love
you."

"I love them, too," Dinah said.

"Julia cried all night. I think she wants to grow up to be
just like you."

"She'll come to her senses in a few days."

Emma touched Dinah's arm. "*I* want her to grow up like
you."

Dinah was touched—and, as always, felt unworthy of Emma's love. "Your children are clever, Emma. They'll learn
well with anyone."

Emma studied her, could find nothing to answer her questions. "How long have you been here, Dinah? And still you're
a stranger. Not only do you refuse to be my counselor in the

Relief Society, now you refuse to teach my children. Are you going into hiding again?"

In fact she was. Dinah didn't believe it was shameful for a pregnant woman to be seen in public, but a pregnant woman with no visible husband had to stay in deep seclusion. Yet, except for pregnancy, what possible excuse could Dinah give? She had lied too often to Emma. She did not want to lie again if she could avoid it.

"Isn't it enough that I say I have good reason?"

Emma walked to the schoolroom window. "Sister Dinah, are you going to have a baby?"

Dinah slowly sat down. It was the confrontation she had so long dreaded. "My husband Matthew is in England."

Emma pressed her hands against the window, as if she wanted to get out; yet her voice was still calm. "Perhaps you are aware that a righteous woman can marry a godly man for eternity."

She is not accusing me, Dinah realized. She is testing me about the Principle. She doesn't know for sure that I know. "I have heard of the Principle of plural marriage."

Emma turned around. "Did you think that something like this could be kept from the Prophet's wife forever? Vilate is my friend. She told me that Brother Heber has had plural wives for some time. You do not have to keep the secret from me anymore."

Dinah did not want to lie to her, but what if Emma chose to lie to herself? Let her believe my husband is Heber, and I don't have to hide from her any longer. "Emma, I'm so glad you know about the Principle."

Emma walked to her, smiling. But the smile still covered a great deal of pain. "I've known about the Principle for years," she said. "But I couldn't—bring myself to let Joseph take another wife. I was—weak. And Joseph was forced to command men to obey a law that I was keeping him from obeying. But Vilate's strength, and Hyrum's Mary—I couldn't hold back any longer, when these sisters were obeying. They tell me it is—bearable. So today, I'm going to—going to give my husband his wives, so he can begin obeying the Lord."

Emma was in such obvious pain that Dinah could not show her joy. Emma was accepting the Principle. It would only be a matter of time before Emma was ready to know the whole truth. "Who will you give to your husband?"

"The Lawrence girls, Sarah and Maria. They're like my daughters, I've cared for them since they were orphaned years ago. It's someone I already—love. And Eliza and Emily Partridge." Emma managed to smile again. "It would be—easier for me, if you were there. At the ceremony today. So I can look at you and think, This is the sort of woman that my—sister wives can become. You are my friend, and I know I can—lean on you a little, for strength."

"Of course I will," Dinah said. She rose from her chair and embraced Emma. "I was no more joyful than you, when I first learned of the doctrine." As she said it, she knew it was not true, that even now she was lying to Emma again. Soon, though, soon the whole truth could be known. In a year, perhaps, when Dinah's child had been born, and Emma had already learned to love the baby. Then we can become true sisters, with all things in common as no women outside the Principle can possibly understand.

"Dinah," Emma whispered, "is it truly from the Lord?"

Surely that was not a question the Prophet's wife should be asking me, Dinah thought. "Yes," Dinah said. "As I live, it's true."

Much comforted, Emma took her leave. Dinah could hardly concentrate well enough to remove her personal effects from the schoolroom. Emma was going to accept the Principle. Dinah wanted to go into the street and shout it. Instead she hurried to Charlie's house, to tell Harriette.

Harriette wasn't there. But Sally was, looking so distraught that Dinah at once set aside her own errand. "What's wrong, Sally?"

"Dinah, please come in. Please. Dorcas Paine was just here."

"The girl who's going to marry the Lipp boy?"

"I thought it was just the once, that he had only tried it with me, but he must do it constantly—"

"What are you talking about?"

"Dinah, have you ever heard of the doctrine of spiritual wives?"

Dinah knew there were rumors reaching the gentiles about some such doctrine, but Sally wouldn't be so disturbed about a rumor. "Where did *you* hear about it?"

"John Bennett." Sally said the name with loathing. "He

came to me the week before my wedding. He said he needed to speak to me alone, about spiritual matters. Mother took the children outside and he began to tell me that God had—God had commanded me to be his spiritual wife."

Dinah felt herself go cold. She already knew the end of this story, though she had never heard the tale before.

"He explained that I should go ahead and be married to Charlie, but that he and I would be husband and wife spiritually. He said it was a new and great commandment, that the men and women chosen of the Lord should be married in this way, so that the world would not realize that we were building great patriarchal familes like Abraham. It frightened me, and I turned away from him—I couldn't believe that God would want me to be unfaithful to Charlie. And then he came up behind me and held my bosom, he held me there and started kissing my neck and cheek and telling me that he was already married to me by the power of the priesthood and—"

"Sally, you can't mean that you let him—"

"No!" Sally looked horrified at the thought. "I was wearing my boots, and I stamped on his foot as hard as I could, and he let go of me. He told me that I'd go to hell, but I told him I'd rather."

"I wish I'd been there."

"I told Harriette, but she was so sure that I was exaggerating, until Dorcas Paine told me the same story today, everything almost exactly the same, and her wedding's on Friday. He told her that he'd be her doctor, and they could—when she came for him to examine her, they could obey the Lord's commandment to multiply and replenish the earth. He said that if they were righteous, the Lord would see to it that all the children she conceived were really his, even though for the sake of the world it would look like they were Billy's. She told him to—I can't repeat what she said she told him, but it wasn't vile enough for him."

So this was where the gentile rumors were coming from: they were true. Bennett had somehow got wind of the Principle, recognized an opportunity when he saw one, and invented a plausible sounding doctrine to go with it. Sally and Dorcas were smart enough to recognize a fraud when they saw one. Dinah was reasonably sure that at least a few other women weren't. If Bennett wasn't having success with it, he wouldn't still be doing it this many months after his attempt with Sally.

"Please, Dinah, it isn't really a doctrine, is it?"

If I deny it, then when you learn about the Principle, you'll hate me for lying to you. "I'll tell you this much, Sally. If there is such a thing as a man taking more than one wife, it won't be John Bennett who tells it to you, and it won't be your body that he wants first, and he won't ever counsel a wife to deceive her husband."

Sally was not dull-witted. "Then there is such a doctrine," she said.

"If there were," Dinah said, determined not to be too explicit, "you wouldn't be taught it until such time as the Lord required you to live it, and then you would have the witness of the Spirit. Don't even think about it now."

"If there is such a doctrine, how are you sure that Bennett isn't—"

"What Bennett said and did with you and Dorcas has no more to do with the Kingdom of God than does adultery." Dinah stood up. "Go to Dorcas, Sally, and tell her to be easy in her heart. You both acted righteously. And as for Mayor Bennett, I'm going to see Brother Joseph this afternoon. If I have my way, Bennett will leave town on a rail, wearing tar and feathers, and missing all the parts that might tempt him to approach anyone else as he approached you."

"And you'll tell me no more than that," Sally said.

"Be content with that."

"Just tell me—is Charlie—"

"Sally, Charlie knows less about these things than you do. And I suggest you not discuss it with him. Don't beg for grief."

"I'm more frightened now than I was before you came."

Dinah embraced her. "Don't be frightened, Sally. Anything that comes from God is good." And when you live the Principle, your sister Harriette will be your husband's other wife. Will that make it easier, Sally? Or unbearable?

"I'm not letting Charlie out of my sight again."

"If you think Charlie would deceive you, you're a fool." Dinah kissed her and left, feeling once again like a hypocrite. Anybody can deceive anybody, when it comes to this doctrine. The problem with all the secrecy was that it left the city open to a man like John Bennett.

As she approached Joseph's house, Dinah saw John Bennett

at the window looking out into the street. Surely he was not part of the ceremony today. Had Joseph taught the Principle to *him?*

But Bennett was merely lingering after a meeting of some city officials. Probably he noticed that more than a few important people were arriving for a meeting he had heard nothing about—and none of them had a plausible reason for being there. Bennett was not one to walk out willingly from a mystery, even though it was plain that he was not wanted in the house.

Bennett was his charming self. It alarmed Dinah that she found him likeable, almost by reflex, despite what she knew he really was. In revolt, she baited him.

"Sister Dinah, I hear you've been a bit under the weather of late. I hear you had to give up teaching school."

"Yes, Mayor Bennett."

"Glad to see you up and about, then. Does this mark a full recovery?"

"Actually, Mayor Bennett, I am quite sick to my stomach at the moment."

"Then you should be in my waiting room, so I could cure you." Bennett laughed self-deprecatingly, the way he did whenever he made a direct plea for patients, so that people would know that he didn't really need the business.

Dinah could hold her tongue no longer. She had mistrusted him since Joseph's arrest last summer; now she had cause to loathe him. She imagined his hands at Sally's breasts, and coldly said, "Actually, Mayor Bennett, I could cure my ailment immediately with a change of company."

Bennett's smile did not slacken, but his eyes went hard. "You have been rather frequently unhealthy of late, I think. Is this the same illness you had that time you got sick in my entry hall?"

She should not have provoked him. Bennett was intelligent, whatever his flaws. "Nauvoo is not a healthy city. I am only grateful that I haven't been afflicted as my sister-in-law was, just the week before her wedding day."

That dented Bennett's smile.

"And now I hear that Dorcas Paine had the same corrupting influence just yesterday. Odd how the disease seems to attack only the young and beautiful who are on the verge of marriage."

Bennett did not smile at all now. He knew that the truth

was finally in the hands of someone who could tell the Prophet and expect to be believed. Of course Bennett suspected at once that the reason he had not been invited today was because the meeting was about him. "Is that why you're here to see Brother Joseph?"

"My business with the Prophet is private."

Bennett glanced across the room to where William Clayton was watching them frankly from his writing table. "Brother Clayton, I'm in something of a hurry. If you could go upstairs and tell the Prophet that both Sister Dinah and myself would like to see him before his meeting, I'd be much obliged, and I don't believe that he would mind."

Clayton got up from his chair, looking questioningly at Dinah.

"Please, yes," Dinah said. "I would like to see him before his meeting, if possible."

It was not lost on Bennett that Clayton went at *her* instance, not at his. Once the clerk was gone, they were alone in the drawing room, and Bennett wasted no time. "Sister Dinah, I don't believe you realize that you are hardly in the position to be making accusations. I *am* a gynecologist, and I'm not so poor a one as not to know why there were bloodstains on my inlaid wood that day when you were taken ill. Nor am I so foolish as not to have a good idea about the particular discomfort that prevents you from continuing your school. In short, I think we both could profit by refraining from telling Brother Joseph all that we might know."

"If I had doubted that my information was correct, you would have damned yourself with those words, Mayor Bennett."

Bennett regarded her steadily. "You aren't afraid." Then he smiled again, but this time it was not a charming smile. "You goddam hypocrite. You've been taking in fancy-work and you dare to give me blame for getting some of my own, all because the Prophet gave you leave. Well, I don't need *him* to tell me when I may or may not plow my field—"

"It's not *your* field that you've been plowing."

"While *he* can play farmer wherever he damn well pleases, whether someone holds the deed on it or not. I'll bet *you're* one of his, too." Bennett laughed at the idea. And then realized it might actually be true. "No wonder you're so sure he won't mind that you have your little burden."

"You are mistaken, Mayor Bennett." She had been a fool to try to cross swords with him. He guessed too much, and she could see now that in a battle there was no weapon he would not be willing to use.

"I think I'm not. How did he free up *your* mortgage, Sister Dinah? What would your English husband do if he knew you were renting it out?" Bennett meant to go on, but then he glanced up over her shoulder. Dinah turned. William Clayton was coming down the stairs.

"Sister Dinah," he said. "Joseph says you ought to be upstairs with the others anyway."

"Allow me," Bennett said, offering his arm with a smile every bit as charming as ever.

Clayton rather boldly pulled Bennett back toward the drawing room. "I'm sorry, Mayor Bennett. Brother Joseph was quite plain. Dinah is concerned with the matter being conducted, but you are not."

"Put in a good word for me, Sister Dinah," Bennett said. "I'll be glad to wait down here till you're through and escort you home. Wouldn't want a woman in your delicate condition to walk all that way alone."

Dinah did not answer. She was already halfway up the stairs, pretending to take no notice of him. But her stomach was churning, and she was afraid. Bennett would not be docile if Joseph actually turned against him. Perhaps he'd try to face it down the way he did last summer with the poison, but if he didn't, if Joseph exposed and ousted him, Bennett could be dangerous. He knew enough truth to attack the Church for years in the gentile press, and Bennett was not one to restrain himself from adding to the facts. The danger was not just Bennett's tongue and Bennett's pen. A man who would use his privileges as a doctor and Assistant President of the Church to set up a system of mistresses obviously had few moral scruples. Dinah wasn't sure what he would do in vengeance, but she feared that he would find some way to do the Prophet harm.

Joseph was too excited about Emma accepting the Principle to want to talk about problems. Still, she tried to tell him. "It's about spiritual wifery," she said. "Charlie's Sally and Dorcas Paine have both—"

But he wasn't listening. "Is it so urgent it can't wait until afterward?"

"No," she said. "But right afterward, please."

"I promise." Then he went back where he belonged, with Emma.

The room was not large, and even though the furniture had been removed, there were too many people for the space. Heber and Vilate, Hyrum and Mary, other apostles, and their wives; it was a convocation of the Kingdom of God, the secret Church. And at one end of the room, Emma and the four young women she was giving to her husband. Emma looked tired, fearful, defeated. The ceremony began.

Emma led the girls one at a time to Joseph, took the girl's hand and put it in Joseph's, and Hyrum said the words that Dinah remembered from her own marriage to the Prophet. The girls were frightened and shy, and Dinah's heart went out to them. Yes, she knew that their husband was a kind man, but they could not know what kind of husband he was. They *did* know what kind of woman Emma was, and while she made a loving mother, they had every reason to fear her as a sister wife. They were not as strong as Dinah. They did not have her independence, her stature in the Church. I will soon be able to stand with Emma as an equal, Dinah thought, but it will be a longer, harder road for these children. She could see that Joseph felt more compassion than desire for them; but if Emma was giving him wives, he must certainly take the wives she chose to give.

Emma came to Dinah almost as soon as the ceremony was over. She was still on the verge of uncontrollable emotion. All around her the others broke into quiet conversations, but Emma was too on fire with feeling for any of the others to have the courage to approach her. Yet, seeing Dinah, Emma managed a smile.

"You're stronger than you ever thought," Dinah said.

"No, I'm not," Emma said, laughing a little, nervously. "This is only the first step."

"It gets easier," Dinah said. "Every day easier."

"You've never been the first wife," Emma said.

"No," Dinah said. "But I've loved a husband who had other wives. It isn't that much easier."

The others saw that Emma was smiling, conversing normally, and so the tension in the room eased. Eased so much that Heber Kimball got the courage to approach Emma directly. "Welcome to the fellowship, Sister Emma," he said warmly.

Emma took his offered hand. "I'm just learning," she said, pretending to be cheerful.

Heber nodded. "Dinah's been a help to more than one who entered the Principle. She was an old-timer when Vilate and I were taking our first steps. Vilate could never have done it without her." Then Heber, his duty done, cheerfully went on, not guessing the wreckage he left behind him.

How could he have known that Emma thought Dinah was his wife? But that was no help to Dinah now, watching Emma's face as she made the connection. "Oh," Emma said. "I thought— because because he baptized you, and because you and Vilate are so close, I thought—but then, who *is* your husband?"

I must lie to her, Dinah thought. A convincing lie. She isn't ready for the whole truth now, but what man can I possibly tell her, which of the Twelve?

The hesitation was too long. Distracted as she was, Emma saw it.

"Why won't you tell me? I thought we'd have no secrets now. Why can't I know who the father of your child is? Don't you trust me?"

"I'd trust you with my life."

"But you won't tell me."

"Of course I'll tell you. It's—"

"No, you've decided to lie to me. You're going to lie to me, even though you know that I accept the, accept the—" Dinah could hear it clearly now in Emma's voice. She was over the edge of hysteria now. No doubt if she could choose, Emma would choose to control herself, but she had been overtaxed today, and there was no power left in her, no force left that she could turn against herself. She must strike, and not inwardly, but out, against someone else. Against me, Dinah thought. She will hate me, and I can't even claim that she would be unjust.

Emma's face was crying, but her mind, her voice did not know it. "You didn't need to lie to me. You don't have to lie to me unless your husband, unless your baby, you didn't have to lie unless—"

Emma's voice was loud and harsh. Dinah could not look away from her, but she still saw the movement of people gathering at the doors of the upstairs rooms, watching. They will realize what is happening, she thought. They will call Joseph.

He will stop this, he will explain to Emma—I can't do this alone.

"You were my friend! I trusted you, I trusted you, he broke his word to me—*I trusted you!*" Suddenly Emma struck her across the face. The blow caught her brutally at the place where the jaw meets the neck, and she recoiled against the wall at the top of the stairs. Dinah panicked. The last time she had been struck that way was the night that Matthew nearly killed her. Terrified, Dinah's only thought was to run away, to get to Robert in time, to protect the babies or Matthew would take them away, she couldn't let him take away the baby—

Just as Dinah stepped backward onto the top stair, Emma's second blow struck. It was lighter than the first, a glancing blow. Perhaps in her terror Dinah would have stumbled anyway. Perhaps she was already falling, which is why Emma did not hit her squarely. The physical cause of her fall was impossible to know. But the real cause was unmistakable. It was the Principle that had hurt Emma so deeply, and it was God who gave it to them. Dinah would remember that afterward, would remember that it wasn't Emma who did it to her, that it wasn't any mortal soul, it was God himself, and God's will always has a good, a perfect purpose behind it. There was some eternal purpose that was satisfied when Dinah stumbled backward, flung out her arms to catch herself, spun around and landed with a sickening pain, not on her hip but on the soft flesh in front of it, where the baby was. She landed where the baby was, then somersaulted, crumpled, rolled, and finally sprawled on the floor at the bottom of the stair. She did not even feel the rest of the fall. The worst thing in the world had already happened. The stair of Joseph's house had struck at Joseph's baby in her belly, where it should have been safe; that's all she thought about, even though a stair-edge broke her nose, even though a place in the railing caught her foot and tore at it, spraining her ankle. She did not even hear Emma screaming at the top of the stair, "Dinah! Dinah! No!" She only lay on the floor and felt the ghastly cramping pain in her womb as the baby writhed, as the baby struggled against the pain, and that awfull stillness when the baby died. She was sure the baby died. Only then did she let herself faint from the pain, only when she was sure there was no hope. God had taken her child from her again, and she wanted to die.

⇜ 39 ⇝

John Kirkham
Nauvoo, 1842

JOHN WAS PUTTING FINISHING touches on a portrait of Sidney Rigdon when one of the Lawrence girls came pounding at the door. John knew at once from her wide-eyed look of dread that she had no good news for them. "Is Sister Kirkham here?"

"No, she's out visiting," John said. "I don't know where. A sick child, I think."

At that the girl turned to leave.

"What did you come to tell her?" John asked. "You can tell me, I'm her husband."

"Oh," the girl said. "Then you're Dinah's father."

"What's happened to Dinah?"

"She's took a fall, Brother Kirkham, at Sister Emma's house."

"A bad one?"

"She fainted. Dr. Bennett's caring for her. They're worried that she might lose the baby."

The girl was already a dozen yards away before John realized what she had said. Surely the girl did not mean it the way it sounded. If there was one sure thing in the world, it was Dinah's virtue—she wasn't the sort to be pregnant out of wedlock. She must have been carrying someone else's baby in her arms when she fell. That was much more plausible. Yet the thought of Dinah, pregnant, stayed in the back of John's mind as he rushed to the Prophet's house, along with a piece of information that disturbed him much, much more. Bennett was seeing her. Of course he is, John told himself, he's a woman's doctor, of course they'd call him. But John could not help but think of what the whore had told him Bennett really was, and the thought of those hands touching Dinah infuriated him.

The Prophet himself was downstairs, as white-faced as if it was his own daughter injured. John looked to him for explanations, of course, as everyone expected Joseph to speak, but the Prophet looked away, and it was William Clayton who explained. "She fell, the whole flight. She took a bad blow to the hip, we think, and her foot may be broken—bruises on her face—she doesn't wake up—"

"The girl who came to me said there was a baby in the accident, too."

Clayton went red, and stammered something unintelligible.

John could guess why as well as anyone. It was what the girl had said. Dinah was pregnant. Pregnant and upstairs alone with Bennett. "She's pregnant, and you're letting that bastard have his hands on her?"

The room went silent. Joseph looked at John distantly, as if he were puzzled about something. "He's the only woman's doctor in Nauvoo. He was here in the house."

"Whether she played the whore or not, I'd rather she saw no doctor at all than see him," John said. He headed for the stairs.

Hyrum reached out to stop him. "He said he wasn't to be disturbed, too dangerous—"

"I have no doubt of it. But the only danger he's worried about is danger to *him.*"

"What are you trying to tell us?" Joseph asked.

John had no intention of stopping to answer. He was halfway up the stairs when he heard Charlie come in. "Where is she?" Charlie demanded.

Someone started to explain, when a door opened upstairs

and John Bennett came to the top stop. "I've done what can be done," he said. There was blood on his hands. "There was no more clean water. Will someone draw me water so I can wash?" He brushed past John on the way down the stairs.

"Bennett!" John said, and Bennett turned to face him only a few steps down.

"How is she?" Joseph asked. John noticed how concerned he seemed to be. Was he somehow responsible for her falling?

Bennett was looking at the Prophet when he spoke, but John could see his face clearly, and it seemed to him that the man was gloating. "It's not mine to comment on whoever it was who got her with child. Providence apparently determined that the child should not live. The babe was too small to survive anyway, but no matter. It was already dead before I took it." A pause, and then, as if it should mean something to Joseph, "It would have been a boy."

Charlie still was waiting stupidly at the front door. "Dinah was going to have a baby?"

"Not now," Bennett said. "And it's tragic to say, but not ever. The injury was too great. I had to choose between her life and trying to save organs that could not be saved. She'll never have a child again."

The words hung in the air for a moment. Bennett sounded so convincing, so authoritative. There was no choice. He saved her life. And yet there was a hint of triumph in his voice, and John could not keep from hearing the harlot's voice saying, "Well, somebody has to clean up." Dinah's baby was dead, Dinah's womanly parts had been destroyed, and the man who had his hands in her to do it, the man who still had her blood damp on his fingers, Bennett was an abortionist. John did not *decide* to kill him; it was not the thing a man decides. He simply tried to do it, and if they hadn't stopped him, would gladly have finished the job. Standing three steps higher on the stair, it was almost effortless to kick out at Bennett. Bennett was off-balance, having turned to look at Joseph again. The heel of the boot caught him at the side of the face, just in front of the ear. The blow had force enough that Bennett's feet did not touch the three steps that remained below him; he sprawled on the floor, trying to raise himself to his feet. John did not wait to see if he had strength to rise. Someone was shouting the foulest language John had ever heard as he bounded down the stairs and kicked at Bennett's unprotected belly. Even when they grabbed him, began to pull him away, John got free enough to put a boot into Bennett's crotch. Bennett's cry of pain at last stopped the string of curses and obscenities. John realized only then that he had been doing the shouting himself.

"Brother Kirkham!" Hyrum was saying to him, "in the name of heaven, don't blame the doctor for doing his work!"

"Doctor!" John's throat hurt him when he spoke, and all he could manage now was a rasping sort of voice that he didn't recognize. "He's a butcher. He's an abortionist for the local whores, that's what he is!"

William Clayton tried to hush him. "It's not right to call such names—"

"I'm not calling names!" John cried out hoarsely. "I'm telling you what he is! One of the tarts told me so, and I've heard it again since then. He does the cleaning up when the whores get pregnant, he keeps them in business, he's *their* doctor, and you let him get his hands on my daughter!"

Someone was helping Bennett to his feet. "I didn't think you were the sort of man who visited prostitutes," Bennett said, his voice sounding sad.

The man could lie even after a beating. John wanted another try at killing him, but they were holding him too tightly.

"You knew I was, Bennett, from the time you saw me with the tart in Springfield. And you knew her, too; I saw you greet her."

"I don't know what you have to gain by lying about me, Brother Kirkham. I saved your daughter's life. When you're not so worried about her, you'll regret saying these things. But don't worry. You won't need to come apologize. I forgive you already. And the Lord will forgive you for adultery, as well, if you truly repent."

John looked around him, wanting someone to rebuke Bennett, to denounce his pose of righteousness, but the other men were embarrassed to meet his gaze. It was plain that whether they liked Bennett or not, they weren't going to take John's word. Except about his having been with a whore—they'd take his word for *that*.

"Brother Charlie," Hyrum said, "maybe you ought to take your father home."

"Not till I see my daughter," John said.

"No," Bennett said. "She's too weak, she couldn't bear to see him now. It would endanger her life."

"I'm her father," John said, "and she has no husband here, and I'll not have a bloody abortionist tell me not to see my daughter."

"I tell you it's too—"

Joseph interrupted. He spoke quietly, but Bennett fell silent when he spoke. "I'll go with Brother Kirkham myself," Joseph said, "to make sure he doesn't do her any harm. A man has a right to see his daughter—that's not a matter for a doctor to decide." Joseph reached out to John, and the men let him go. The Prophet took him by the shoulder and began to draw him toward the stair. His touch was firm and welcoming, and John wondered if perhaps the Prophet believed him after all.

Bennett limped to the stairs ahead of them. "I'll go too," he said, "to make sure she's doing well."

"No," Joseph said, firmly moving him aside. "I think you won't be needed with her anymore."

It did not take the murmurs from the watching men and women to tell Bennett what they all could see. Joseph believed John Kirkham, however unlikely his story sounded, and Bennett knew it now. He stepped back, letting them pass, and for the first time John could see an impression that might have been fear pass across Bennett's face. It lasted only a moment, however, before plain hatred took its place.

Charlie followed them up the stairs. The room stank of blood and sweat and vomit; Dinah was retching over a chamberpot, writhing in agony after every empty heave. John marked how Joseph ran to her at once, had his arm around her, supporting her as he took the pot and held it with his other hand. The action said more than any explanation could have done. There had been no hesitation. Joseph knew Dinah more intimately than John would have supposed.

Charlie, of course, didn't see it. "How are you?" Charlie said.

"Don't let him near me again," Dinah whispered after gasping for breath. "Don't ever." She retched again.

"Bennett?" Joseph asked.

Dinah clung to him and wept. "He was hurting me," she said. Her voice was almost too weak to hear. "I woke up. His hand in me." Joseph held her as she shuddered, tried again to vomit, twisted again in pain when she was done. "The baby's dead. I'm sorry, I'm sorry."

A woman whose husband was thousands of miles away when her baby was conceived might apologize to the Prophet for being pregnant. But she'd never apologize because the baby *died* unless the Prophet was the father.

"What's happening?" Charlie asked. "How could Dinah—"

Of course Charlie didn't understand. Or perhaps he did, John thought, but would not believe it unless someone put it into words. At any rate, he stopped with the question unasked. Joseph said, "I'll explain it to you. Tomorrow, Charlie."

"Don't let him near me," Dinah whispered.

"I won't."

"Spiritual wifery," Dinah said.

Joseph tried to lean her back on the bed, putting pillows under her. "Don't try to talk, Dinah. Try to rest. Try to sleep."

Desperately she tried to stay sitting up, but without his support she couldn't do it. "Listen to me."

Joseph stood up. "Later, Dinah. When you're stronger."

It was agony for her, but still she tried to shout it: "I don't want to die without telling you!"

"Listen to her," John ordered. Rest would do her no good if her mind was not at peace.

Joseph listened.

"Bennett. Telling women they're his spiritual wives. Just before they marry, telling them to let him—afterward—" She started to gag, then stopped and lay on her back, panting. "Sally was one. A week before the wedding. And Dorcas Paine. Ask them. He tells them you had a revelation."

"*My* Sally?" Charlie asked.

"Stop him, Joseph," Dinah whispered.

"I will," Joseph said.

"The baby's dead," Dinah said again.

"Sleep now, Dinah. We won't let him near you. Go to sleep."

She was crying softly, but it was so calm that it seemed to John almost as though she were happy now. She awoke with Bennett's hand in her. John wanted to spew the memory of the words out of his own mouth, though he had not said them; he wanted to drive the picture from his memory, but it stayed before John's eyes no matter where he looked, as he silently cursed his clear imagination and the way that strong pictures lingered with him. Bennett bowing over Dinah's naked body, unwomaning her with his delicate fingers as she awoke from the pain. "I wish I had killed him."

Joseph closed the door behind them. They stood at the top of the stairs. "No, Brother John. Vengeance is God's." They both whispered, so that they would not be heard downstairs.

"Don't tell me about God, Prophet," John said. "There's damned few men who could get a child on Dinah, damned few she couldn't say no to."

"Don't judge what you don't know," Joseph said.

"I'm no stranger to *that*, sir," John answered. "I know how little bastards come to be."

Joseph suddenly held him by the shirt front, in a strong grip that included a little bit of the loose skin of John's aging chest. "Your daughter is not a harlot, Brother John," he whispered, "and the child who died today would not have been a bastard. I'll take it out of the skin of the man who says otherwise." His voice was so quiet that John was sure even Charlie could not hear him. But Charlie could see the way that Joseph held him, could see that a warning had been given. John nodded, and Joseph let go of him.

"What will you do about Bennett?" Charlie asked.

"We were going to build the City of God together." He was speaking calmly, but John saw how his hands gripped each other too tightly, as if he were trying to hold himself in check by brute force. "I have to think. Give me time to think." Then, like a man awaking after talking in his sleep, he looked from John to Charlie and said, "We'll care for Dinah here, of course, until she's stronger."

Joseph started down the stairs. "John Bennett," he said. "I must have a word with you. We have something to discuss." He sounded distracted, unsure of what he meant to do.

It didn't matter. "He left," William Clayton said. "As soon as you went upstairs, he was out the door."

"Is it true?" asked Vilate. "He's an abortionist?"

Joseph nodded.

"But he was my doctor."

"Sister Vilate," Joseph said, getting control of himself because the others needed him to be in control, "would you go up with Sister Dinah? She needs you."

Vilate went quickly. Joseph then addressed the whole group. "It's too much to ask that no word of these things leave this room. I will say only this. Anyone who says that Dinah Kirkham Handy was carrying a bastard in her womb is a liar, and I will testify against him at the judgment bar of God." He did not shout, but the words had all the more power for that.

Joseph waited a moment, as if he meant to say something else, but he either forgot or thought better of it. Instead he walked into the parlor. Only then did John notice Emma, who was sitting on a chair facing a window. Joseph took her by the hand, and she arose from the chair and let him escort her out of the room. She looked as grim as a condemned prisoner.

"What happened to *her?*" Charlie asked.

John shook his head. He cared nothing for the periphery of the picture, what lay beyond the frame. All he could think of was Bennett and Dinah and the Prophet's baby. "I should have killed him," he whispered. If I'd been ten years younger I'd have done it. Killed him as he stood there with his hands bloody, like a wolf howling in triumph over the gory kill— even God would have congratulated me for that.

❧ 40 ❧

Charlie Banks Kirkham
Nauvoo, 1842

THE NEXT DAY, JOSEPH took Charlie to the river's edge where no one else could hear, and when the hour was over, had told him who the father of Dinah's baby was and why the Principle was not spiritual wifery.

"It will break Sally's heart," Charlie whispered.

"Don't be modest," Joseph said. "It will break yours, too. And then make you both again, more perfect than you ever were before. Happier."

"If I hadn't been there yesterday, if I hadn't known that Dinah was carrying a child, would you have taught me this doctrine?"

"Eventually. But the Lord chooses the time, not me. You're in the hidden Kingdom now, Charlie, and I'm glad of it. You're a man that should know my secrets, because I can trust you." Joseph embraced him, kissed him on the cheek the way he kissed the Brethren, and left him there on the shore to think.

The inner Kingdom. Charlie could not even exult. For he had to go tell Sally what the Lord required now. Let it be yesterday, Charlie wished. Let it be a week ago, when I knew nothing, when I was a child. Let it be last winter in Washington, when I lived in dreams. Let it be last summer, when Don Carlos was still alive and I was still his friend. Let it be years ago, when I did not love Sally, and so did not have the power to break her heart.

Sally was scrubbing the floor when Charlie came in. Her face was flushed from the exertion, from hanging her head as she ground the wad of rags into the boards. She didn't even hear him enter, and so he stood and watched her. It was scullery work, the way his mother had served in Hulme's house. Sally's arms were as strong as Anna's, and younger, and the play of muscles under the skin had a delicate grace to it that answered the gross flexions and extensions of arms and back and chest. Her hair was done up in a bun and wound with a rag, except for a few strands pasted across her face with sweat. She huffed as she worked.

At that moment Charlie loved her more than he ever had before—not out of gratitude, for everyone had work to do in this place and it was no surprise when someone did it, but rather because he felt the movements of her body in his own arms and back and hips, felt the shape of the house the way she felt it, because in this year—no, in these months since he came home from Washington—they had become each other. People spoke to him as if he were only himself, but he knew that hidden from them was someone else entirely, the Charlie that Sally had created out of him. Eve was made from the rib of Adam, Charlie thought, watching her scrub, but Adam was also made from the womb of Eve.

Sally stopped, hung her head and caught her breath, then laboriously got up to move the bucket to another place. Charlie saw that she was so caught up in her work that she would not notice him even now, so before she could set to work again he called her name.

"Oh, Charlie!" she said. Her first response was one of pleasure. Then she looked crestfallen. "I hate it when you take me by surprise, I look like such a pig." Charlie reached to embrace her. She refused. "I'm filthy all over, and I'd get a gallon of sweat on your coat." But Charlie embraced her anyway, and pulled her close until her face rested on the deep blue cloth, and when he had held her longer than any greeting could require, she said, "What's wrong, Charlie?"

He taught her the doctrine then. He was not one for breaking things gently to people, though he was not cruel about it either. He simply explained what the Principle was, how it was different from Bennett's spiritual wifery. She was shaking in his arms, searching his face for reassurance. "Charlie, is it true?" Tell me not, her eyes said.

"If Joseph is a prophet, then yes, it is. He always taught us that all things would be restored, everything that God ever taught."

"No one could live that way," Sally said. "Not today, these are modern times."

"There are many living it right now."

Sally looked at him in wonder. "Not anyone *I* know, though—"

"Dinah."

Sally's eyes went wide. "Your sister!"

"Is Joseph's wife."

She gave a little cry, stepped back from him, put her hands to her cheeks and sat on a chair. "Oh, Charlie," she said.

"The Lord has commanded us to do it too."

"I can't." Her voice was very small.

"Joseph told me, either you obey the Lord or you don't."

"So all our sacrifice is undone if we don't obey in this one thing? Well, if you take another wife you still won't be obeying the Principle, Charlie, because she'll be your *only* wife."

Charlie could not argue with her. There was no argument to make. "I love you," he said, "and I don't want another wife, and I'll never choose between you and any other woman." It wasn't fair that Joseph should require him to measure his loyalty to God against his loyalty to Sally, and it wasn't fair that Sally should make him choose between keeping her as his wife and living the gospel that Joseph taught. "I *am* your husband and I *am* a Saint, but I guess that I'm your husband *more* than I'm a Saint," he whispered. He could hardly see her she was such a blur, and he knelt before her and buried his face in dirty apron and clung to her and wept.

And as he held her, he felt the terrible rigidity of the muscles of her back and thighs give way, felt her slump gradually down into herself, and she began to stroke his hair. From a great distance he heard her speaking and tried to make out the words. "Your choice isn't between me and another woman, is it?" asked her small, small voice.

"No," he said.

"I'm making you choose between me and the Prophet. Between me and God."

"Yes."

Gently she pushed him from her lap, and stood. She looked around her, as if to find something, or decide what it was she had meant to do. Then she walked toward the door of the house. Without her hoops, in dirty clothes, looking like one of the river women, she was going out.

"Where are you going?"

"To see—to see Dinah, I think."

Charlie got up from his knees and started toward her.

"No," she said.

He stopped.

"I'm going alone. I—" She tried to smile. "I wonder if I can really make you choose between your woman and your God? I don't even know which I'd rather you chose. Would I love you as much if you were the sort of man who loved a woman more than God? But I wonder something else, Charlie. I wonder if I'd rather lose you entirely, or stay with you and know that you saw her every day, and saw me every day, and knew every difference between us, and found me lacking. I wonder which of my possible lives I'd hate the most."

She closed the door behind her. Charlie watched the door for some time, as if he expected it to move. Then he took a step toward it, turned, began to walk aimlessly around the room. He wasn't thinking of anything at all, wasn't even aware that he had no words at all going through his mind; all that was in his head was an endless column of figures—thousands, hundreds, tens, ones, tenths, hundredths, thousandths—and he added them and added them and added them. At last he reached a calculation and he could no longer remember the sum so far. That had never happened to him since he studied first with Hulme. He had never forgotten a sum. He looked around him and was surprised to see that the table was overturned, tilted half upside down against the wall; who would have thrown it so violently? He went to it and set it in its place again, laid the cloth on it, picked up the flowers and the fragments of the broken vase. Then he got the bucket from where Sally had left it, took off his coat and waistcoat, rolled up his sleeves and trousers, knelt on the floor and began to scrub, back and forth, back and forth, dipping into the bucket now and then, wringing the rags or changing them now and then, until the floor was clean from end to end.

❧ 41 ❧

Dinah Kirkham Smith
Nauvoo, 1842

DINAH LAY IN THE BED in Joseph's and Emma's house, trying not to listen to the buzzes of conversation here and there, trying not to think of all she might do if she were able to get up and walk. As long as she held still, the pain in her abdomen wasn't much, but when she moved she discovered exactly how much damage she had suffered in the fall down Emma's stairs. And yet she dared not complain or ask for help. Not that Emma ever came into her room—that would be too much for either woman to endure, and Emma had more tact than to think of doing such a thing. Dinah knew, however, that every time she rang the bell beside her bed to ask for water or food, to ask for company for a few moments, whoever came had to leave a task that Emma had set for her, and Emma would see what a burden Dinah was on her house, and would remember either shame for having injured Dinah or anger at how Dinah had deceived and betrayed *her*.

She heard footsteps coming up the stairs, tried to ignore them, knowing that it was just one of the Lawrence girls about her business in the house, fearing that it might be Emma, and she might have to talk to her. The footsteps stopped outside her door, and someone knocked.

"Who is it?" Dinah asked.

"Sally."

Family, of course, doing a dutiful visit. Dinah was not ungrateful; she was merely unused to being the recipient of kindness, and would rather have been the one being kind. But as Sally seated herself on the chair at the foot of the bed, Dinah saw that Sally was not coming to be kind to her at all. For she had never seen Sally look so distant, so upset, not even when she had brought the news of Bennett's attempts at seduction. Dinah was almost relieved that Sally had come with a problem. Dinah was good at other people's problems.

The conversation began as a duplicate of all the other courtesy visits: Are you feeling better? Much better thank you and how is Charlie? He's doing quite well and so are my sisters and brothers and parents and everyone else we both know and can I bring you anything next time I come? No thank you I am doing quite well and is there any news in the city? Rumors of this and that and we certainly miss you at Relief Society, all the women miss you, we've needed you so much. Oh that's kind of you but really I don't think people could miss me much in just a few days. Oh no Sister Dinah, we depend on you more than you think.

Dinah could see that Sally wanted only a little prodding to unburden herself. So Dinah prodded. "You, Sally. Why would *you* depend on me?"

"I shouldn't, I know. Ill as you are, you need no more worries—"

"Ill as I am, I desperately need someone else's worries to take my mind off my own."

Sally gave a wan smile, and then laid out her problem in a single sentence. *"Your* husband has commanded *mine* to marry another woman."

At once she had explained it all, and Dinah understood her dilemma. "But Sally, I'm a plural wife, and my sympathies might be with Charlie's second wife."

Sally shook her head. "You love Charlie, and you love me,

and you're the wisest person that I know."

"I'm lying in bed without my baby or my womb after my husband's wife struck me and an abortionist doctored me and you tell me you know no one wiser than me? You're worse off than I thought, Sally. "Tell me then—do you believe it's the Lord who has commanded, or Brother Joseph?"

"It makes no difference in the choice *I* make. Charlie believes it's from the Lord, and he won't be happy if he doesn't obey. Does God hate me?"

"What do you plan to do?"

"I told Charlie that I'd leave him if he married someone else."

"Will you do it?"

"No." Sally was looking all over the room, at anything but Dinah's eyes. "I can't leave him just because he wants to obey the Lord."

"But that isn't why you'd leave him."

"It was silly of me to come, it's something I have to figure out on my own."

"Why don't you look at me and tell the truth?" Dinah said kindly.

It took visible effort, but Sally let their eyes meet. "Now tell me," Dinah said, "what it is that you fear the most."

Now that Sally couldn't hide, her voice shook with the emotion she struggled to contain. "Losing Charlie." She had a catch in her throat and tried to look away.

"Look at me," Dinah commanded. Sally obeyed her. "And how would you lose Charlie?"

Sally's face was all atremble for a moment, and then her composure broke entirely as she wept and said, "He won't love *me* when he compares me to *her*."

As Sally cried quietly, her hands covering her face, Dinah realized that here before her was Emma. Here was the first wife, the one who had the most to lose from the Principle, and the one who held the key to making the lives of the other wives endurable. If Dinah could help this one young woman to find a way to live with the Principle, if Dinah could help her to avoid the mistakes that had poisoned Joseph's celestial family, she could prove that the Principle was good, that it could work. Dinah had no power now to change Emma, but she had power to change Sally.

"In twenty years," Dinah said, "a generation of daughters will have grown up knowing that in God's Kingdom no man is owned, nor any woman. They will enter into marriage, not caring who was first and who was second, not competing among the wives for mastery, but rather being sisters and upholding each other. I dream of a day when the first-married wife welcomes her new sister with joy, and watches with excitement to see what they all become together. Each wife will know her husband as if he were a different man for her, and the wives will know about each other the things no man can ever understand. You never knew, I think, how lonely I was married to Matthew, even when I saw him every day. Now I am often alone, but I know that when he comes to me he'll make me glad. And Sally, if only Emma would accept me as her husband's wife, if only she knew that his love for me robs nothing at all from his love for her, what friends we could be."

"I thought you *were* friends."

"Exactly. We were. But she forced her husband to choose between her and the Lord. The only way he could avoid such a vain and stupid choice was to lie to her. And because he had to hide his wives from her, he chose his wives without her. Tell me, Sally, do you think that Emma would ever have chosen *me* for her husband's wife?"

Sally shook her head, almost laughing. "It's hard enough that you're Charlie's sister, and to know he always compares me to you."

"He doesn't."

"He dreams of being a gentleman. But I'm not a lady, like you, Dinah. He tried to send poems to me while he was in Washington, but Harriette had to explain them to me, and now he shows the poetry to *her*. I know that sometimes he wishes—he wishes he were married to a fine lady."

"He is."

Sally dabbed at her eyes with her apron. "No I'm not. I even dry my eyes with my apron."

"Sally, a fine lady knows poetry and never has mussed hair. But a great lady is strong, and when her husband falters, he cannot fall because she's part of him, and when her children are afraid, they're comforted because she's in their memory."

"Like you."

"I was thinking of Sister Emma."

"I'd die for him, Dinah," Sally said. "But what good is it to be strong? If you're strong, God just makes you bear more suffering." She violently bunched her apron. "Why am I fooling myself. I have no choice."

"Oh, you have choices. You can run from it, Sally. Or you can bear it as a martyr all your life. Or you can let him marry her and then punish him for the next thirty years until he wishes he had died before he ever saw your face—there are wives who do that with far less excuse."

"That's a poor list of choices."

"There's another choice."

"I decided not to kill myself on the way over here."

Dinah could not help herself; she laughed at the thought of her actually doing such a melodramatic thing. "We'd have had to write a tragedy about you then. *Sally: The Martyred Mormon Woman of Nauvoo*."

Sally laughed, too.

"The other choice for you is to obey, not grudgingly, but with your whole heart."

"Oh, Dinah, tell me to do something *possible*."

"With your whole heart. Take charge of the thing. Make it go the way you plan. Not by dictating, but by being more eager for it than Charlie is."

"God would damn me sure if I lied and said I was glad."

"Choose your sister wife, Sally. Not someone that Charlie could not possibly love, but someone that you *could* love, or that you already love."

"I! Choose a wife for Charlie!"

"Why not? Let it be someone that you know that you can live with, and closely, too. Someone who loves Charlie with all her heart, and yet loves you at least as much, so that she wouldn't try to pull him away from you, but instead would pull you together—"

"Dinah," Sally said in wonderment. "Dinah, does Harriette love Charlie?"

"It's been nearly two years since Harriette learned of the Principle. She has prayed for you and Charlie to learn of the law and let her in."

"All this time she's wanted my husband."

"All this time she's wanted to be a part of both of you. But she will wait until you want her. Until you invite her, Sally.

If you're going to obey the Principle, could there be a better sister wife for you than your sister?"

Sally laughed. "Poor Charlie! He's scared to death of her half the time. He used to call her—"

"He doesn't now. He knows her now."

"If he marries Harriette," Sally said, "I think that I can bear it. Charlie was the first thing I ever had that I didn't share with Harriette."

Dinah knew then that she had succeeded. Sally was no longer resisting; she was coming up with ideas herself why it would work. They talked on for half an hour, thinking of what must be done. How the first wife ought to make it easier for the second, who would be just as scared. Don't try to rule her, or she'll be your enemy. Don't let her have her way in everything, or you'll become a little child in your own home. Don't ever ask your husband to compare you—he'll either lie to you or hurt you. Or both. Dinah thought of all the things she wished that Emma could have done, all the things she had dreamed of in her empty nights, waiting for Joseph. All the things she had been jealous of, all the mistakes that she had made, and she watched Sally grow interested in how it could be done, to make such a family liveable. At last, tired, she lay back on the pillows, and Sally took it as a cue to leave, despite Dinah's protests that she wanted her to stay.

Before she left, Sally kissed her hand, then sat on the edge of the bed and embraced her. "I still hate the thought of it," she said, "but I think that I can do it and not hate Charlie or Harriette or Brother Joseph. Maybe I won't even be angry at the Lord."

"He'll return the favor at the last day."

"Dinah, how can I become like you?"

"Barren? With my children in England and no hope of having more?"

Sally silenced her with a touch. "Once, when I first heard the gospel, the first time that I came to church in Manchester, when Brother Parley spoke, I felt an ecstasy, as if I were made of air, as if I were soaring with the wind. It only happened the once, but when I remember it it still is beautiful. I've always thought it was the Holy Ghost coming to me, just that once. But you, Dinah—that's what you feel like all the time, for the Lord is always with you."

Dinah wanted to laugh or scream in frustration. After all that she had gone through, just these last few days, and her own sister-in-law could think that she was in constant rapture with the Spirit of God. But Dinah said nothing. That is what they think of me, these women who call me Prophetess. That is what I am to them, filled with light, as alive and powerful as the wind. Then let it be. Let them believe it, I'll not tell them no. I'll claim nothing for myself but what is true, yet if they choose to paint me in brighter colors than life, that is the gift of God to me. It gives me the power to teach them and be believed, and because of that I can help them to be glad in their suffering.

Sally opened the door to leave, and there stood Emma, across the hall, a statue of cold hatred with her eyes fixed on Dinah as if she had already been watching her through the door.

"Good day, Sister Emma," Sally said. Emma did not answer. Sally looked back at Dinah as if to say, Would you like me to stay with you?

"Good-bye, Sally. Give my love to Charlie and to Harriette."

As soon as Sally was gone, Emma walked briskly into the room and closed the door loudly behind her.

"Mrs. Handy," Emma said. "I had no intention of speaking to you while you were in my house. But while you are here, I must insist that you refrain from teaching impressionable young girls to give their husbands up to sanctified adultery."

Almost in answer to Emma's words, the pain where Dinah's womb had been erupted again, and she winced in spite of herself.

"Oh, does the truth hurt you?" Emma asked, not realizing Dinah's pain was physical.

"The Prophet of God," Dinah said softly, "is not an adulterer."

Emma's voice was loud enough to be heard throughout the house. "Don't tell me what the Prophet is and what he isn't! Where were you in the years when he had to leave me and the children living on the charity of people who did not want us in their home? Where were you when his babies died? Where were you when he was in jail under sentence of death and I tried to keep the Church alive with the so-called Brethren resisting every step of the way? Where were you when the mob came into our home and dragged him from my bed and took him out to try to make a steer of him?"

"It would have been no worse than what you did to me."

It wasn't even true, Dinah knew it; Emma had never meant her to fall, and it was Bennett who took her womanhood from her. But Emma had engaged the battle, and this time Dinah would cut as deep, and with any weapon she could use.

"I didn't do that to you." Emma's voice was uncertain, for she felt responsible and was ashamed—that was part of her rage at Dinah, that she felt responsible for Dinah's pain. "I was angry, I didn't even know the stairs were there—"

"You have your wish for me, Emma," Dinah said. "Joseph will never come to my home to see his sons and daughters. You are the unchallenged mother of all his children, though you must remember that we are not his only wives."

"You are not his *wife*."

"Once you were the strength of the Church when he was in jail. But now, Emma, the true Church is the men and women who have entered into the Principle, and you are not the strength of *that* Church. When Joseph wants his wife to help him in his work, he will not look to you. He could have. He wanted to. But you refused him. So now take care of your children, Emma Smith. Have your house, pretend your husband has no other wife, hold your Relief Society meetings and do your good works. But as long as you refuse to accept the Principle, you are not his helpmeet, and I am."

The pain in her belly silenced her. Only then did she hear her words. This is not what I meant to say to Emma, Dinah thought. I meant to plead with her. I meant to love her and to try to make things right.

Emma stood near the closed door, looking at Dinah with red-rimmed eyes.

"I'm sorry," Dinah whispered.

"Perhaps," Emma answered, with a soft and bitter voice, "perhaps you ought to wonder if God has judged that you aren't fit to raise a child."

I am no match for Emma, Dinah realized, when there are no rules. For that was the fear behind her other fears, that God intended all along that she should never have a child of her own.

I will not stay here, Dinah decided. I cannot stay here with this woman who wants to destroy me even though I loved her. I cannot stay because I know that I did her an injury which was the source of all my own pain now.

She rolled over and let her legs slide off the bed, slipped down into a kneeling position.

"What are you doing?" Emma asked.

Dinah tried to stand. Using all the strength of her arms she tried to throw herself into a standing position, but all she succeeded in doing was rising a little and turning as she fell again. The sudden lurch sent pain like childbirth into her loins. If I cannot walk, I'll crawl, but I won't stay here another moment. She began moving toward the door. But she could not even crawl, for when she tried to bring her leg forward, the pain in her abdomen was more than she could bear. She fell forward, and her forehead struck the wooden floor.

"Are you out of your mind, Dinah? Get back in bed."

If she could not use her legs, her arms would do. She pulled herself forward, sliding along the floor.

"You'll hurt yourself."

I have already been hurt, Dinah answered silently. She heaved herself another few inches toward the door. It was the last exertion her body would endure. She felt something give way inside, felt blood begin to flow, and she retched with the pain though she had eaten nothing.

Emma flung open the door. "Help me!" she cried. "Come help me!"

Since everyone in the house had been listening to the argument upstairs, they heard and obeyed at once. It was the Lawrence girls and Emily Partridge who helped Emma lift Dinah into the bed. They saw Dinah's blood on her nightgown and slick on the floor, they saw Emma's stern, tight-set face, and they remembered that they, too, were Joseph's wives, and believed that Emma hated them the same. They did not know that Emma did not fear them at all, and so did not hate them for being Joseph's wives. They could not see Emma's deep remorse at Dinah's sufferings. And because she sent them out to fetch a doctor, they did not see her lean and kiss Dinah's unfeeling lips, did not hear her whisper, "You're the woman I wanted to be for him. How could he help but love you more than me?" They did not see her embrace Dinah and cry for a few minutes. Dinah, unconscious, did not see it either.

It would have changed the future if Dinah had known how Emma felt.

But then, it would not have been Emma if she had been able to show her feelings when Dinah could see them.

Dinah awoke with Joseph sitting beside her bed. She was disoriented. The room was wrong. "Where am I?" Dinah asked.

"In Vilate's house," Joseph answered. "I had you moved in spite of the doctors' advice. I had a feeling that being in my house might hinder your recovery."

Dinah remembered what she had said to Emma. "I was cruel to her, Joseph."

"That was days ago," he said. "Emma told me all that was said, by both of you. She asked for my forgiveness."

"So do I."

"Foolish, both of you. Who am I to forgive you? It's the two of you who are bleeding, and then you come to me, when I'm uninjured, and ask me to forgive you both for loving me. Never mind. I was a fool to dream that the two of you could ever share a home even in the best of times. This isn't the best of times."

Dinah reached out for his hand. "Joseph," she said, "am I going to die?"

"They told me yesterday that if you ever woke up again, you'd probably live."

"I'm awake," she said.

"I asked the Lord for a favor. Now and then he grants me one. But I suspect he was acting for the good of the Church."

Dinah closed her eyes. "I haven't been very good for the Church, either."

Joseph touched her cheek. "When the word spread through the city that Sister Dinah was dying, do you know what happened? There were already hundreds looking on like sentinels when you were carried to the carriage and brought here. They've been coming in a constant stream, hundreds of women. They come into the house and tell each other stories about how you helped them. There've been enough tears shed downstairs to put the Mississippi into flood. They hold prayer circles and vigils and testimony meetings all over the city. Your funeral would have been a marvel."

"Will they be terribly disappointed that I'm going to live?"

"They'll get along."

"Joseph," she asked, "will you still—come to me, even though I'll never have your child?"

"Do you think I càme to you only for that?" He bent and kissed her. "Besides, we have children. Val and Honor, they're ours, remember."

She shook her head. "No they're not, Joseph. I dream of them all the time, I was dreaming of them just now before I awoke. I saw Val as a little copy of his father, and Honor as pretty as Matthew's sister Mary. I'm too late already. Even if I had them now, they'd never be mine."

"Dreams can lie."

"I have no children," Dinah said.

Joseph held her hand, and she could see prophecy come into his eyes. "You'll have ten thousand children," Joseph said. "All the children of the Kingdom of God will honor you, and your own works will praise you." Then he kissed her again. "And your husband will love you forever, worlds without end."

He left her, and she thought of the hundreds of women who had heard her speak, who had prayed with her, the thousands who had read her poetry or believed the rumors of her prophecies spoken in tongues. These are my children. God did not want me to close myself within a single home and bear ten children and raise perhaps half of them to adulthood. *I* wanted that, but God had other plans for me. I must open myself into every home, and bear ten thousand daughters of the Spirit before my life is through. And she lay in her bed and wept in relief until the weakness of her body overtook her and she fell still.

Joy and torment, peace and pain, they were faces of the coin, they were hours of the day. The only life worth living, Dinah told herself, is the life with equal balance of fulfillment and regret. Only the cattle in the field have utter peace. Only the gnats with lives measured in days die unencumbered with regret.

The next day she asked for pen and ink, and began to rime her way through all these thoughts. Sonnet, couplets, anything small and neat—they were such comfort, for when she had cut idea or passion down to fit such little forms they were small enough she felt no terror of them anymore. They became comprehensible, they had meaning, they were sometimes even beautiful, and they began appearing almost every day in the *Times and Seasons*, so that even before she could get up from her bed, she had resumed her ministry.

⇘ 42 ⇙

Charlie, Sally, and Harriette
Nauvoo, 1842

HARRIETTE! THE GARGOYLE that had always loomed over them, her face set in stone so that it could never smile, living like an unattached shadow in the interstices of the family's life—Charlie suspected for a moment that Sally was insisting he marry Harriette so that he would suffer for the Principle as much as she. But of course she wanted no such thing. *Sally* thought of Harriette as a beloved older sister. How could Sally know that Charlie was afraid of her?

I'm not afraid, he told himself. I just don't like her. But if Sally could consent to the Principle, how could Charlie refuse Harriette? So he said yes, with far more confidence than he felt, and then spent the next hours wondering why God had consigned him to this deplorable fate. Perhaps I'll be lucky, and the Lord will let my life be mercifully short.

But Sally had said that Harriette would say yes. Sally said that Harriette already loved him. He began to remember the

595

face of the sphinx as she watched him. He had always thought
she disapproved of him—after all, she was his senior by nearly
two years, and she had been the chaperone at times when
Charlie was afire with adolescent lust. Now he realized that
her sternness might have been concealment of affection that
she dared not show.

Her secret love for him made her suddenly fascinating. Now
he remembered that Hariette had interpreted the poems Charlie
sent to Sally from Washington—Herrick's Julia poems, with
talk of "liquefaction of her clothes" and "sweet vibration each
way free"—how that must have stung Harriette to be so privy
to her sister's conjugal affairs, all the time wanting the man
that Sally could not fully understand. No wonder she brooded
over the wedding, not like a vulture, as Charlie had thought at
the time, but like a tragic widow hovering at the grave of a
love she could never have. She must have grieved that night,
must have been mourning during all our joy, and yet she never
gave a sign of it. And now, because Charlie and Sally were
obedient to the Lord, Harriette would now have what had long
seemed so impossible to her.

This new image of Harriette did not make her more desirable
to Charlie, but it made the idea of marrying her more tolerable;
to be able to view himself as charitable and noble appealed to
Charlie, and his role within the romantic tale he spun was so
admirable he almost liked it.

Facing Harriette, though, that image faded. For he *was*
afraid of her. Sally sat in a corner of the room as Charlie
proposed. It was excruciating to speak so frankly of marriage
with his wife looking on. What flustered him most, though,
was a feeling that for Harriette's sake he should say at least
something about love. Even in the midst of his most romantic
version of this tale he had not been able to fool himself into
thinking that he *loved* her. And yet surely a woman deserved
to hear of love from the man who would be, after all, her first
husband.

"Charlie," Harriette said, in her distant, aloof way, "it's
sweet of you to try, but I don't expect you to say that you love
me. You only just learned about the Principle—it would smack
of adulterous desires if you had actually been feeling more
affection to me than would be appropriate for a sister-in-law.
You are only proposing marriage to me out of obedience to

the Lord. I expect no more than that."

Charlie's first impulse was to protest, but she had seen
through him, and so he didn't bother. If she was willing to be
honest about it, so was he. "Then it's settled," he said with
relief.

"Far from it," she said. "I will not marry you, Charlie, if
you intend to congratulate yourself on your charitableness for
all our lives together. Some things must be clearly understood.
I do not expect you to love me as you love Sally, but I expect
you to do your duty to me. A wife is a wife. There is no reason
to believe that I will be any less fertile than my sister—I have
a right to an equal crop of children, as your wife, and the only
way to an equal harvest is to sow an equal amount of seed."

Charlie tried to swallow with a dry throat. This was the
Harriette who had terrified him all along, not the heartbroken,
romantic wallflower he had conjured up.

"When our children are born," she said, "I am aware that
in order to satisfy the world they might have to be raised without
the name of Kirkham. Nevertheless, I want them to have no
doubt that you are their father, and not the slightest suspicion
that you might love Sally's children more. Do I have your oath
on that?"

"I've never known a child of my own. I don't know how
I'll treat a child."

"I want your solemn oath before God, Charlie."

It angered him a little. "Do you think I'm so unrighteous
that I'd neglect my children? Have you ever known me to fail
in my duty?"

"Wives have few enough rights in marriage under the law—
but there's no law that will protect a plural wife or her children.
To a judge our children would be bastards, and I would be a
paramour with no recourse. I know you're honorable, or I'd
never bother to ask you for an oath—what is an oath to a
dishonorable man?"

So Charlie swore in the name of Christ that as far as a mortal
man could manage it, he'd not stint her or their children in any
of the natural rights of a family.

When he had finished swearing, she nodded gravely. "I
have already promised Sally that I will be her true sister, not
an older sister as I was when we were young—neither of us
will try to rule the other. And when I make the vows that I

will make to you, I will mean them, Charlie. You may be sure of that."

"Thank you," he said. He wondered if the words sounded as stupid to her as they did to him. Then he realized—if she and Sally had already made promises to each other, then Sally must already have broached the subject.

"I didn't want you to propose," Sally said from her chair in the corner, "if she wasn't going to say yes."

"Thank you," Charlie said again.

"Harriette and I have worked out housing arrangements," Sally said. "Dinah will be in Vilate's house for weeks, and then with your parents for some time after that, till she has her full strength. Harriette will live in Dinah's house to take care of it for her. We understand that it is possible for a discreet man to meet his wife there unobserved."

"That sounds like a good idea," Charlie said. It would be a relief not to have to sleep with either wife in this little house, where no room's activities could be kept secret from someone listening in another.

"We thought of having you alternate weeks," Sally said, "but we decided it would be safer if you kept an irregular schedule at first."

Charlie almost asked what it was they were scheduling. He figured it out for himself in time.

"But I think it shouldn't be hard for you to build the addition to the house that you've been talking about, only a little larger than we had thought. You should be able to get it finished by the time Dinah needs her house back. It will seem perfectly natural even to the most suspicious minds if you and I move into the new wing, and let my spinster sister live in the old part of the house." To Charlie's surprise, at the words *spinster sister*, both Sally and Harriette smiled, and by the time Sally had finished her speech, they were both laughing aloud.

How can they laugh? Charlie thought. It worried him that Sally was sounding every bit as sure of herself as Harriette. They had planned everything so neatly. He began to wonder if marrying sisters was such a good idea. They knew each other better than he knew either of them, and when they agreed on something they would always outnumber him. He felt a momentary temptation to reject their plans, even though he couldn't think of anything to object to, just because he needed to make sure they knew he would not be put upon. But that would be childish—he couldn't imagine himself saying, with a straight face, It's my house and so I'll make the rules. That was the way that he and Robert had been. There were many ways for a man to be with a wife. Surely there were as many paths open when a man had to deal with more than one at a time.

"I'm beginning to think I may need a book of advice on this," Charlie said. They were still laughing from before, and laughed again at this.

"I don't know of one," Sally said.

"Perhaps something translated from the Arabic," Harriette suggested. And this time when they broke up laughing, Charlie could not help but join them. They laughed and laughed together until the tears streamed down their cheeks. Then Charlie went and found Heber Kimball, who came to Charlie's house at four o'clock in the afternoon and performed the marriage in the bedroom, so that no chance visitor would catch them in the ceremony.

Before administering the oaths, Heber made a little speech. "This is a hell of a place for a wedding," he said. "Last time you got married, Charlie, the whole city came, I hear. But let me tell you—all the guests, all the drinking and dancing and singing, all the friends congratulating you—that's what the world does to make up for the fact that those public weddings are till death do them part. It's a marriage as the world knows how, and no better. When I seal you together, Charlie and Harriette, it's not a marriage that ends with death. Do you hear me? Celestial marriage is just that—for this life *and* the next life. When you take these oaths, you're sealing yourselves up for eternity." Then he had them hold hands, and he said the oaths, and each of them said yes at the right time, and it was done.

But it was not over. Sally caught Heber by the arm the moment he let go of Harriette. "Why should *they* be married for eternity, when Charlie and I are only married till death!"

Heber was flustered. "Joseph isn't sealing first wives yet— he wants us to wait until the Temple's built."

"That'll be years," Sally said. "Why should I wait? What if I die in childbirth before the Temple's finished?"

"Well, I'm sealed to Vilate, aren't I? And the Prophet did it himself, so it must be all right. I suppose you want me to do it now?"

"Yes," Sally said.

"Women are like that, Charlie. You haven't been at this marrying business as long as I have, but they keep on telling you what to do as if they thought they had a right to an opinion. Get what they want, too, mostly."

So Charlie took wedding vows for the third time in his life. He wondered fleetingly how many more times he'd take such vows before he was through. *I wonder how I'm going to live through the next few years. Truth is, I only have to worry about a few months—by then if I'm not dead I'll probably be used to it.*

There was no lingering after the wedding. Charlie was still keeping the Word of Wisdom, so there were no toasts. Heber just made small talk with them for a few minutes, then took Harriette by the arm. "I hope you'll allow me to take you to your new house in my carriage," he said. "Actually, it isn't my carriage. But then, it isn't your house."

Harriette smiled at him. To Charlie's surprise, her smile was merry, her eyes full of mirth. Here Charlie was feeling nervous as a goose on Christmas Eve, and Harriette was having the time of her life. It didn't seem fair, somehow. Why should she be so glad to marry a man who isn't glad to marry *her?* Heber reached back and closed the door behind them, and in a few moments the carriage drove off.

"Well," Sally said at last.

"Yes," Charlie answered.

"You didn't even kiss her, Charlie," Sally said.

Charlie wasn't sure if she was reproaching him or being grateful. Didn't matter. Sally would be spending tonight alone, and so he took her in his arms and held her a long, long time, until she stopped crying. Then she made Charlie offer a prayer for the three of them. He didn't know what to say. "This wasn't our idea, Father, it was yours," he said. "We aren't asking you to make it pleasant. We're just asking you to give us the strength to bear the burden. And if you can find a way to make us happy, too, we wouldn't mind." Then he felt inspired to give Sally a blessing, putting his hands on her head and saying some unplanned words that surely came from the Spirit. It wasn't prophecy or a miracle or anything like that, but it was a sign that the Lord approved of what they were doing. Charlie was in sore need of such a sign, and took it gratefully. Then he, too, left the house, to begin a roundabout journey that would get him to Harriette after dark.

"Be careful, Charlie," Sally told him at the door. "You might lose your way in the dark."

"No chance of that," Charlie said. "My luck's been running the other way lately." He kissed her again and left.

It was night, and he stood at the door of Dinah's house. Brother Joseph has stood here before, he realized as he studied the grain of the wood on the door in the moonlight, the Prophet has been here before me, and on the same errand. The difference is that God has spoken to the Prophet face to face, and I got this commandment second hand. He did not let himself think of the fact that Brother Joseph also had Dinah waiting on the other side of the door. She was Charlie's sister, but that didn't keep him from knowing she was one of the most beautiful women in Nauvoo. Not even his utmost charity could convince him that Harriette was in that group.

He knocked, and almost at once heard the scuff of slippers on the rag rug floor. The scuffing stopped near the door, but the latch did not rise. In the pause he remembered his own timidity on that night with Sally, when he had been so frightened he could hardly unbutton his waistcoat. And remembering that night, he also remembered the Bible that had been there on the bed, and the passage that the ribbon had marked. The Song of Solomon; Harriette's favorite passage in all of scripture; surely it was for tonight that Harriette had marked the book, though she could not have known that this night would ever come. She had marked the verses, and Charlie knew what would most gladden her to hear.

"Open to me, my sister, my love, my dove, my undefiled," he said through the door. "For my head is filled with dew, and my locks with the drops of the night."

The latch rose, and the door opened, and Charlie came in to her. He learned that the severe dresses had concealed a supple, vulnerable body, that the sternness had been a mask for a yielding heart. In the darkness Charlie was enlightened, for he had not imagined that two women could love so differently; in Harriette's arms he was not the man that Sally had so often held. He knew within five minutes that he had never understood Harriette at all before, that she was not at all what she had always seemed; and within an hour he began to wonder if he had really known himself. For here he lay with the warmth of a woman's skin at his cheek, tired and tingling with new-finished love, and as he had in his most romantic dreams imagined, he whispered to her,

> *Sabrina fair,*
>> *Listen where thou art sitting*
> *Under the glassy, cool, translucent wave,*
>> *In twisted braids of lilies knitting*
> *The loose train of thy amber-dropping hair;*
>> *Listen for dear honour's sake,*
>> *Goddess of the silver lake,*
>> *Listen and save.*

And then, her voice not a whisper but a tone so soft that he felt it more than heard it, felt it at the thousand separate points where her body touched him,

> *Thus I set my printless feet*
> *O'er the cowslip's velvet head,*
>> *That bends not as I tread.*
> *Gentle swain, at thy request*
>> *I am here!*

Then she laughed silently. He felt the movement, and asked why.

"What would Milton say, that old Puritan," she answered, "if he could see the use we put his verses to!"

Charlie laughed, too, and was far happier all that night than he would ever have dared to think possible.

The addition to the house was framed and roofed, brooding over the old house, almost enclosing it.

"Looks like that big new house just had herself a little old baby," Caleb the carpenter said to Sally.

"I just wonder if anyone will be able to tell the old house is still *there*, once the walls are done." She had been watching him splitting clapboards, and now he stood with the heavy froe in his hands, dripping sweat like a rainstorm, panting a little. The finished clapboards had grown from a mere sheaf into a haystack in one afternoon.

"Oh, there's a lot of the old house sticking out the back, Sister Kirkham."

Sally laughed a little. "It looks silly. Like a wart."

"I heard your husband mention he planned to face the old house in new clapboard, once the addition's done."

"Yes," Sally said. "You'll be working for us here for a while yet, won't you?"

"Not me," Caleb said. "I'll be dead."

"What!"

"I figure my life will probably end around six-thirty this very day. I've sweated more water this afternoon than I've drunk in my whole life. I've done more clapboards today than all the carpenters in Chicago do in a week."

"Then take a rest, Brother Caleb!"

In answer he set the froe against the end of a board and began pounding with the mallet, pushing and twisting on the handle, so that the wood shrieked and slowly, delicately split at exactly clapboard thickness. "There's sort of a law among house-builders, Sister Kirkham. Never rest while the owner's watching."

"Have I been watching long?"

"Only all day, Sister Kirkham. If you hadn't gone inside for a few minutes half an hour ago, my bladder would've bust. Begging your pardon."

"But I understand that resting is part of the job. You can rest when I'm here."

"I've been doing this for thirty years, Sister Kirkham. It'd drive me crazy to set down with the owner watching. I just can't do it."

Sally smiled and patted his sopping wet shoulder. "I'll stay away. Except for now and then."

"Oh, we don't mind you looking on now and then. After all, you can't help but be interested in how it's getting along—"

"I'm eager, Brother Caleb. I want this house finished tomorrow."

"Well, in that case you want Brother Joseph, he's the one who does the miracles here."

Sally meant to leave immediately, as soon as Caleb finished this board. But with a cracking sound the wood took a sudden eccentric split, ruining the last two feet. Caleb started to say something, then caught himself. "Dammit, Sister Kirkham, I can't even cuss proper with you looking on!"

She went inside quickly then, closed the door behind her, and sat and looked at the table. Must get dinner ready right away. Must do a washing. We're nearly out of butter and I haven't gone to Sister Calliver's to pick up our eggs. Sally knew all the work she hadn't done, and yet all she could think of was the addition to the house. All she wanted was for it to be finished, so that Charlie would no longer have to take unnecessary selling trips just to be able to spend a night at the little cabin on Temple Hill on the way out and on the way back. So that Charlie's life would not take place where she could not be a part of it. So that she could have her sister back again. Sally sat on the chair and let herself imagine the way it would be—Harriette there all day while Charlie worked, so that it could be the way it was before that Day, the two sisters talking always, doing everything together, having no secrets from each other.

There was a knock at the door. Sally looked at the mantle clock. She had been sitting there for half an hour. Doing nothing. What am I becoming? she asked herself as she went to the door. What kind of wife spends a whole day in which she does no work at all?

It was Harriette at the door. "The house is so beautiful already," Harriette said. "I was at Sister Calliver's, and she said you hadn't been by yet for the eggs. Where should I put them?"

Sally blushed. "I was going to get them."

"Here?" Harriette was setting the basket on the table in the kitchen. Sally followed her in.

"Yes, of course."

"I thought you wouldn't mind if I got them for you. The building must be disrupting everything. Well, if you're fine, I'll just go see Dinah. She wanted me to come by this afternoon to talk about a—"

"Go ahead and go, you don't have to tell me your errand, I don't care." The words surprised Sally even as she said them. But she couldn't think of anything to say in apology.

It was as if Harriette had just been waiting for Sally to say some such thing, for almost without a pause her tone changed completely. She didn't even bother to finish her sentence. "So you don't care? Well, *I* care. I used to think my sister and I were better friends than any other women I knew, but I was *wrong*, and it may not bother you, but it bothers *me*."

"Don't talk as if it were *my* fault. You're always in and out of here in such a hurry you haven't said ten words to me in a row since—"

"Since! Yes, *since!* Why do you feel like you need to *punish* me—"

"Punish *you!* I've been walking around like a dead woman, no one to talk to for three weeks, the poor workmen actually had to yell at me to get me inside this house, and *you* have an errand, *you* have to visit Dinah, *you* never even sit down here and *talk* to me!"

Harriette walked to a chair, sat down hard, and said, "Here I am."

"Not like that!"

Harriette turned sideways in the chair. "Now?"

And in spite of herself Sally had to laugh. "I think we're fighting."

"It makes me feel like a little girl again," said Harriette. "It's been years."

"Why don't you talk to me anymore?"

"Why haven't you even invited me to dinner?"

"You know you're always welcome."

"And how would I know that?"

"Because I'm telling you, now. Oh, Harriette, I've missed you."

Harriette seemed surprised. "Have you?"

"That's the worst thing. Dinah told me wives were supposed to become sisters—but we've become strangers, Harriette. I was afraid of losing my husband. I never thought I'd lose *you.*"

Harriette looked off toward the corner of the room.

"Harriette, aren't you listening to me?"

Harriette nodded. "Oh, yes. I've thought the same things myself. But I also thought—maybe it would be better that way. Not to talk at all. Not to see each other."

"Why! It's been so lonely these last weeks!"

"When we used to talk, Sally, you spoke freely about Charlie. Can you speak as freely about your quarrels or your hopes or even your love for him when you're telling it to his wife?"

"I don't know."

"Almost everyone who's living the Principle is keeping separate houses for the wives, Sally. I'm so afraid our plan is a mistake."

"I don't know if we can talk about everything, Harriette,

but surely we can talk about *some* things."

"I'm not talking about talking." Harriette lifted her chin in the proud way she did whenever she was feeling frightened. Almost no one but Sally knew that it was a sign of fear. "I'm talking about living here together. Taking our meals together. I don't know if I can live in the same house with you."

"Do you think I'll be so terrible?"

"You'll be an angel, that's not what worries me."

"I'm not even as jealous as I thought I'd be, Harriette. I lie awake sometimes, but not because the two of you—just because I need him in the house with me. If I knew he was in the house, even if he were with you—"

"Sally, I remember when we were very small. You were three and I was six. We were in the street—Mother was taking us to market with her—and three other women stopped and looked at you, and chucked you under the chin and all the other things that ladies do to babies—"

"I used to hate it—"

"And they said, 'Oh, she's so beautiful.' And you said, 'Yes, I'm the most beautifullest girl in the world.'"

"Did I really say that?"

"You were only three. That's what Mother said, 'She's only three, and she hears that all the time.' Only I stood there, I remember standing there and thinking—I've never heard that in all my life. No one has ever said, Oh, Harriette, you're so beautiful."

Sally was perplexed. All these years, and Harriette had never shown the slightest sign of jealousy. The difference in their looks had never been a barrier between them. "Why should that hurt you now, Harriette?"

"Oh no, you misunderstand me. I've never hated you for that, I've always been glad for you. No one's taken more pleasure from your beauty than I have, Sally. I don't even envy you now, because I think that Charlie loves me anyway. I really think he does."

"He won't stop loving you if you live here with us, Harriette. If he were going to compare us, he already would."

"What do I care if *he* compares. Don't you see, Sally? There is my little cabin, in Dinah's little cabin, there in the light of the fire, when we talk about the most difficult doctrines and say poetry to each other and—love each other, Sally—I can pretend, just for a few hours, that *I* am the most beautifullest girl in the whole world. I have to laugh at myself even talking about it. But I can tell you anything, can't I, and you never think I'm a fool for it, do you? When I live with you, Sally, and have that silly little dream broken every day, I won't be miserable, I won't suffer, I won't mope around the house and grieve. I know it's foolish even now. I just don't want to lose it, that's all. I have to move in with you soon enough. I just want to keep my foolishness a little longer. Those old women just annoyed you with their cooing and petting. You don't know how precious a thing it is."

Harriette was not a weeper, but Sally knew when she needed comforting, and so they sat on chairs beside each other, held each other's hands and talked and talked, and then prepared dinner together, all without deciding that they would. And when Charlie came home there were three places set at the table, and two wives to serve him.

At first Sally almost laughed at Charlie, he was so embarrassed. He hardly said anything at all, just let the sisters talk. It was the way it had always been between them, with one exception. Sally had never seen Harriette so bright and happy in front of anyone but Sally and their mother before. And as the meal went on, Sally began to feel uncomfortable herself. As Charlie joined in the conversation it became almost irritating, for he and Harriette were so natural with each other. They had never *been* that way before. He even had a pet name for her—he called her Sabrina, and she called him My Gentle Swain, and then they stifled their laughter and acted embarrassed, as if it were a secret they had to keep. Gradually Sally began to understand that it could not be the same old Harriette and the same old Charlie, all living with her in the same house. Charlie and Harriette had changed each other. Only three weeks and they were new people, and Sally, who hadn't changed, Sally was the stranger in her own house.

"What's wrong?" Charlie asked.

"Nothing." Sally realized that they had finished eating, and her plate was still almost full. "Oh. I think I'm not very hungry, that's all."

"You aren't very talkative, either."

Don't you dare to criticize me. "Nothing to say, I suppose."

"The house is going up remarkably fast. Old Brother Caleb

tells me I should hire you out to buildings that are going up behind schedule—you'll have them right on time within a day or two."

He meant it in good humor, Sally knew that, but it still annoyed her. "I'm terribly sorry if I've been bothering the workmen. From now on I'll only use the back door, so they won't have to see me at all."

"I didn't mean to give offense, Sally."

Harriette spoke. "Never mind, Charlie." She smiled gently at Sally. "I knew it would be this way. I tried to tell you, Sally. I've changed, and it's not what you wanted it to be. I'm glad we had dinner tonight, because now you'll know that you don't really want me over here after all—"

Yes, Sally thought, that's right, it was a mistake, just my own foolishness in not understanding at all the way it would be. Go back to your cabin, and I'll go back to moping around the house like a martyr, like a Christian in the lions' den, waiting for the lions and getting so damned impatient when they never come.

"No," Charlie said.

"Charlie, Harriette's right—"

"And I said no. It's better *this* way."

"But it isn't, Charlie! Harriette will come visit me when you're gone, that'll be all right, won't it, Harriette?"

"Excellent idea!" Charlie said, with far too much enthusiasm. "And I'll wear a bell so that you can hear me coming and never be together when I'm here. If I ever forget my bell, I can call out, 'Unclean, unclean,' so that one of you can jump out the window and run away, in fear that you might actually have to see that I love you both. We wouldn't want *that*, would we, because *we* know that no man can really love two women at the same time. It isn't natural. Of course, *you* both love dozens, hundreds of people. You can both love each other, and me, and Dinah, and your families, but God help us all if I should dare to love two people in the same room at the same time."

"Don't be angry, Charlie," Sally said.

"I can if I want."

"I won't complain," Sally said. "I'll do better."

"So will I," Harriette said. "I was so happy to be together like this, that's all, but I'll be more careful in the future—"

"No!" Charlie shouted. "You haven't been listening to me! I don't want you being careful! Out there, out in the street, there we can be delicate and pretend to be strangers and watch every word we say. But here in my home, here with my"— he lowered his voice—"with my wives, I will say what Charlie Kirkham really feels like saying, I'll feel what I feel like feeling, and so will you. We will *not* tell lies to each other, we will tell the bloody truth and get used to it. And then, by heaven, we will be happy."

Sally was abashed. The one thing she had not expected was that Charlie would take charge. This was between her and Harriette. No one had ever interfered between her and Harriette before.

"You're right," said Harriette.

"Come help me with the dishes, Harriette," Sally said.

"We will both help you with the dishes," Charlie said.

"You're terrible at dishes, Charlie," Sally said.

"Don't complain," said Harriette. "When he breaks enough, you get a new set."

The evening lasted until late, and though it was still awkward, Sally got better at pretending not to be annoyed. It still bothered her when Charlie and Harriette had a joke between them that Sally didn't understand. It was always a reference to some poem or other, and it made her feel stupid not to know what they meant. Sally liked poetry, but she couldn't hold it in her head the way they did—she could hear a poem once, then forget the title so quickly that later in the day Charlie would mention it and she'd not know what he was talking about. He had never criticized her for it, and still occasionally read to her, but now Sally realized how much he had needed someone to share his love of poetry. And it was the other wife, not her.

What do I have to offer him? What does he really get from me? I'm not clever, I just work in the house and try to look pretty for him when he comes home. He could replace me with a painting. I should get his father to paint me and then I could go away. What he gets from me in bed he gets as well from her. And I'm far too dull and stupid to satisfy him in conversation. Hearing the way they talk together, about doctrine, about literature, about the government of the city, it's a miracle he ever stayed awake this past year, forced to converse with me alone for hours on end.

Stop it, she told herself. Smile. Take part in the conversation.

"How can people say such things about Brother Taylor?" she asked.

Charlie looked embarrassed. "Tyler, Sally. I was talking about the President of the United States."

"The names sound so alike," Sally said, laughing lightly. Silently she retorted, I've only been in America for twenty months, and *I* didn't have four months in Washington, so don't you dare to despise me for my ignorance! Then she had to watch in misery as they changed the subject to one they knew she could handle: gossip about whose business was doing well and whose wasn't in Nauvoo. It went on forever. I can never compete with her, Sally realized. Beauty is only good to attract a man—it's the mind of a woman that will keep him, especially a man like Charlie, who lives in his mind and not in his body.

Yet that night, when Harriette was gone and Charlie lay in bed with her, it was only to the body that Sally had recourse. It was the final indignity when Charlie gently kissed her and said, "Sally, I'm tired tonight—all I want to do is sleep."

She tried to keep her crying silent, but the bed shook as her shoulders trembled, and Charlie said, "Sally, what is it, tell me what's wrong. If it means so much to you tonight, of course I will—"

"It doesn't. I'm sorry. Go to sleep."

"I can't sleep when you're crying and I think it's probably my fault."

"It isn't."

"You were crying louder and louder to make sure I'd hear you. Now I've heard you, tell me what you want to say."

Angry, she rolled over abruptly to face him. "If it had been Harriette tonight, would you have been too tired?"

"Is that it! Well, my darling, if you really want to know, after the first night Harriette and I have had intimate relations four times, and another five nights we have merely lain in bed and talked or read. You're ahead, seven to four. I see now why you were so eager tonight—you wanted to double her score."

"I don't want to know about it!"

"Then why did you bring it up?"

"You made me tell you!"

"I wondered when it would come to this. What a liar you were tonight, pretending it was *her* you missed, that you weren't the least bit jealous that she was my wife. I could laugh."

"Why don't you read to *me* at night?"

Charlie got up and lit a candle. "All right. You want reading, you'll get reading. But first get out of bed and wrap your hair the way that Harriette does. And make sure you have five new poems memorized each night, because I'll expect you to recite to me from memory—"

"I can't do that! I'm not Harriette!"

"Then why in the name of heaven do you want me to treat you like Harriette!"

"I don't! I don't want you to treat me at all! Why are you even here with me tonight? You know you'd rather be with her!" She was so angry she wanted to break something, tear something. All she could find was the pillow. She plumped it savagely, then threw herself down on it. Unfortunately, she was higher in the bed than she had thought, and she banged her head against the headboard. The pain was sudden and stayed with her, throbbing. She moaned and held her head and rolled away from him. To her fury, he was laughing.

"It isn't funny!"

"I'm sorry," he said. He climbed back onto the bed and tried to comfort her.

She pushed him away. "I hate you," she said.

"Good," he said, removing her nightgown. "Then this'll make you suffer all the more."

Afterward they talked for a few minutes before sleeping, the way they always did. "That didn't solve anything, you know," Sally said.

"So? It was your idea anyway," Charlie said, yawning. "I always wanted to grow up to be a monk."

She didn't answer. Just lay there, realizing that perhaps something had been solved today, after all. The three weeks of hiding from each other had ended. Sally could get on with life. There were many things to hate about living the Principle. But at least now Sally knew what they were. That was an improvement, to know what the problems were, instead of waiting in dread for them to happen.

"Your worrying is keeping me awake," Charlie murmured.

"I'm not even moving."

"I know." He poked at the taut muscles of her thigh. "You're rigid as a wall."

She was. Consciously she forced herself to relax her arms and legs, relax the tightness across her stomach; she nestled against his back and rested her arm on him. I can't be rigid, she decided. There's no way to survive this if I cannot bend.

They were still putting new clapboards on the exterior walls of the old house when Harriette moved in. But Dinah was better now and needed her house again, and so Harriette put her few clothes into a box and waited for her husband—no, her brother-in-law Charlie—to come with his new shay and bring her home.

Harriette did not want to leave this miserable little hut. It was not entirely her fear of living in the same house with Sally; even though they would maintain their own sections privately, there was bound to be even more tension than before. Yet that was merely a cross she had to bear—the price she had to pay for the husband God had given her at last. Charlie was worth ten times the cost, she knew. Yet she was also reluctant to leave Dinah's cabin because she had liked the way of life there. Dinah complained of having her husband come to her so ir-regularly, complained of the uncertainty of such solitude. But Harriette reveled in it. She had no previous marriage to compare it to. It was like the lovers of ancient poetry—Troilus coming secretly to Criseyde, with a prophet as their Pandarus; Uther coming in the darkness, disguised, to get Prince Arthur on Ygraine. Harriette had wanted to conceive her first child here. Perhaps, she thought with a moment of hope, perhaps she already had.

The shay approached up Mulholland, which had just been graded; it was a cheerful sight in the morning sunlight, the dust rising behind the little two-wheeler, the single horse tossing its head. Charlie had brought Dinah, of course, and she waved a greeting with such vigor that Harriette was glad in spite of herself. Dinah had a way of deciding what the prevailing mood would be, and no one could resist her decision for long.

Charlie helped Dinah from the shay, and Harriette took her by the arm and waist to lead her into the house. "I'm not so weak anymore," Dinah insisted, but Harriette noticed that she leaned a little and walked with uncertain steps. "You've kept the flowers growing," Dinah said with pleasure. "Oh, I've missed this wretched little place!"

Harriette brought her inside, and Dinah walked around and touched everything. "It's so funny to think," she said, "that all these things that have so many memories for me, have completely different memories for you."

"Not so different, perhaps."

Charlie spoke from the door. "Is this box all you have, Harriette?"

"Yes, Charlie."

"Take your time with it, Charlie," Dinah said to him as he picked it up.

He was gone. "Welcome home," Harriette said.

"It's a lovely place. I wonder who the first bride was to welcome her husband here."

"Some goddess, I think."

"Proserpine?" Dinah asked.

"Proserpine was married to Death."

"Pandora then. The one who was married to Cupid, and he forbade her to see his face, but she brought a lantern and surprised him, and so she lost him."

"Psyche."

"Oh," Dinah said. "I thought it started with a *P*."

"It does."

"I had a factory education. She wasn't a goddess though, was she."

"Just a mortal that a god had chosen to love."

Dinah took Harriette by the hands. "And now I'm evicting you."

"It was time for the idyll to end, I think."

"I wrote a poem for you. No, that's a lie. I wrote it for Emma, but I think you'll understand it, and it's certain I can never show it to her. I can never publish it, either. So I expect you're the only audience it will ever have. Do you want it?"

"Of course."

Dinah opened the bag she had carried with her, and took from it a sheet of paper. She folded it carefully, then lit a candle and sealed the paper with the dripping wax. "Don't open it," Dinah said, "until one night when you're sleeping alone, and you think that surely God must have a better plan for us than this."

Harriette took the paper, then kissed Dinah on the cheek.

"You're older, Dinah," Harriette said.

"Having your womb mutilated has a way of aging you."
Dinah was smiling when she said it.

"I didn't mean that you *look* older." In fact, though, she
did. "I meant—I don't know. You're only a year older than I
am. But you carry yourself as if you knew more than me. More
than anyone. Tell me, Dinah, do you know everything?"

"Oh, yes," Dinah said. "That's why I'm the Prophetess."

Harriette had never heard Dinah call herself that name,
though everyone in Nauvoo knew who was meant whenever
someone said it.

"A woman who can't have children has to have something
to do to keep herself busy."

Harriette studied her face. Dinah meant her bitter words to
be taken jokingly. But her face was too wan from long illness
for the joke to come off properly. "So you'll be mother to us
all?"

"Oh, I don't think so. Just an aunt, I think. A funny maiden
aunt."

"Not a maiden."

"To the world. I thank Father every night that there are
some like you, who know me for the silly girl I am and don't
get fooled by my fine speeches and my blessings and my poetry."

"Sorry. I *am* fooled. I want you to give me a blessing."

Dinah smiled and reached out her hands, held Harriette's
head between the palms of her hands, and with no hesitation
at all said, quietly, "Harriette my sister, you are one of the
greatest of the daughters of God. He has given you a husband
who will love his family more than the world. The Lord will
give you more children than any of your husband's other wives.
You will see all of your children live to adulthood. And you
will never be a widow in your life. You will know all the days
of your life that you are the most blessed of women, and you
will be happy. That is what you deserve at the hands of the
Lord. I speak in the name of Jesus Christ. Amen."

Harriette felt weak, for Dinah's hands and Dinah's words
had filled her with such power that it seemed as though her
heart hadn't the strength to continue on its own. "Dinah," she
said. "Is it true?"

"You know it is. Of course, Brother Taylor would be very

angry. He keeps complaining to Joseph about the way the sisters are usurping the authority of the priesthood by giving blessings and making prophecies."

"What does Joseph say?"

"That if the Brethren were living up to their priesthood responsibilities, the Lord wouldn't have to rely on women so much to do his work."

They laughed, then kissed and embraced each other, and finally Harriette took leave of her. Dinah herself was balm for a fearful heart; but on the way home, sitting beside Charlie in the shay—careful not to touch him or look at him lest someone see and understand their true connection—she thought over and over again about the words of the blessing. It was too perfect. She could not believe it. No woman lived to see all her children survive to adulthood. No woman was happy all the days of her life. Yet Dinah had said it, and so it must come true.

The lecture hall was crowded. Springfield, Illinois—John Bennett thought with satisfaction of all the legislators who would fill a dull evening by hearing Dr. Bennett lecture on the strange and terrible practices of the Mormons. Oh, they'd get their money's worth tonight. And when it was time to vote on extending the Nauvoo Charter, they'd think twice about leaving so much power in the hands of Joseph Smith. No man does to me as you did, Prophet Joe, and goes unpunished.

The theater manager introduced him glowingly with all the titles Bennett had given him to read. Noted scholar, surgeon, founder and fellow of the University of Columbus—or had he told him Louisville?—no matter—and above all former mayor of Nauvoo and Assistant President of the Mormon Church. "Who is in a better position to expose Mormonism than one who has been deep in that pernicious conspiracy, but saw the light and left it just in time?"

That was his cue. He gave his cravat one last tug and stepped onto the stage. He knew he looked immaculate, the perfect gentleman in this town where anyone with a clean suit was taken for a dandy. He began his lecture by describing how he had suspected Joseph Smith of nefarious purposes from the start. "I was unable to believe that such a monster as he was reputed to be could possibly have influenced so many of my hapless fellow-Americans to follow him. I determined that I must study what he was and discover what he planned, and to do so the only means that seemed sure of success was to join his church and try to gain this man's confidence. It is a sign of how much God communicates with him that never once did God give him the tiniest hint that I was anything but the most sincere of dupes to his nonsensical religious claims. He believed me, they all believed me, and there were times when belief was so contagious that I almost believed myself."

On and on, the now familiar words. The city of Nauvoo is filled with puppets, and Joe Smith and his henchmen, the apostles, pull the strings. You can't hold office in Nauvoo without Joe Smith's approval, and we all know how to get his approval. Joe Smith drives in a fine carriage while people are dying of hunger and disease. Joe Smith waves a hand and a man can lose his job. Bennett hardly had to think of what he was saying anymore. He just watched and listened to the crowd, tuned his voice to fit their mood. And this crowd was hot, outraged. The poor bastards took democracy seriously. Half the people in the hall had probably paid or received a bribe in running the state of Illinois, but still he could get them angry at the only un-bribable man that Bennett knew.

By the time he got to spiritual wifery, the audience was ready to believe anything. Especially something titillating. Especially when it showed the so-called Saints to be lustful hypocrites. All bastards like to believe that the righteous are only pretending. So he told them of Women leaving their husbands to join harems to satisfy the lust of Joseph Smith or Hyrum Smith or the other lecherous leaders of the so-called church. Young ladies taken into locked rooms and there shouted at and harangued and lied to and threatened until they finally consented to become Joe Smith's spiritual wives and let him have his way with them. And when Smith finished with them, he rented them out as whores to the apostles.

"There are those who say that I am afraid to name names. Well, my friends, I had thought to spare the tender feelings of members of the fair sex, but in the interest of your right to know the truth, I must tell you what I myself know, the tragic tale of Dinah Kirkham. A poor English girl, destitute, friendless, her family stricken with poverty. But pretty? She was pretty, and Joe Smith gets first picks in Nauvoo. He inducted her into the secrets of eternal intercourse and heavenly harem-ism. But where, you ask, was her family? Had she no brothers to protect her? She had one, yes. A tall, strong young man. But he was so obedient to the Prophet that this young English gentleman was bought off. Joe Smith arranged a loan for him and he built himself a factory, so he could get rich and play the duke, lording it over the mere Americans around him. Joe Smith sent him off to Washington, where he went to parties and balls while Joe Smith got his sister in the family way with a child that for delicacy we will refer to as being of questionable legitimacy. Now tell me, gentlemen, if it's natural for a *man* to behave that way when his sister's virtue is attacked? Would you have done as he did? Or would you look to find where last you put your musket, your powder and ball, and would you answer Joe Smith as such men should be answered! When a spoonful of lead served hard and fast in the center of his black, black heart!"

He had them. They rose to their feet and shouted threats and oaths that were a joy to hear. If Joseph walked into this hall, this minute, he'd not leave the place alive. Keep this hatred, people. You are all cattle, you are all swine, but keep this hatred and give me my vengeance. I gave Joe Smith his charter, I gave Joe Smith his city, I gave Joe Smith his political influence and even saved his life, and he begrudged me my pleasure even while he was rutting with half the women of Nauvoo. *He* had Dinah Kirkham, that bastard, and wouldn't even let me have a few girls in my examining room. Well, Joe Smith, think of the faces of this mob in your sleep, if you can sleep. I'll have them at your throat one day, and you will die knowing that John Bennett's friends fare better than John Bennett's enemies.

But there was nothing for the mob to do tonight, so he wound down his lecture with hints of orgies in the half-built temple and occult sacrifices in the Masonic Lodge. He spoke of a woman who had tried to kill herself rather than endure the obscene rituals of Mormon baptism for the dead, and he hinted that abortion was treated as a holy sacrament. And just when the poor bastards were getting hot to hear the detailed descrip-tions of these obscenities, Bennett coyly stopped. "It would be an offense to public decency," he said, "to continue my sci-entific discussion in a hall with ladies present. So I invite all gentlemen who have a scientific interest in the practices of this strange religious sect to come back tomorrow night to hear my second lecture, in which I will acquaint you with the details of the debauches practiced by the Mormons."

Several people called out "smut merchant" and "pornographer," but Bennett didn't mind. He only smiled and pointed toward the person who had called the loudest and said, "There are always those who prefer to remain blind to the truth because the truth is ugly, and they would rather not see it. But Mormonism is a cancer growing in the very bowels of our society, and we must examine it, find its limits, discover the extent of its poisonous influence, and then cut it out to save the rest of the body."

He left the stage sure of a full house tomorrow. He could make more money in three weeks doing these lectures than he had made in a year in Nauvoo. That's one thing he owed to Joe Smith—the best damn source of income he'd ever had.

Joseph came for Dinah just after dark, his carriage newly washed and Porter Rockwell wearing an unusually clean suit.

"You shouldn't bring the carriage right to the door," Dinah rebuked him as he led her from her house.

"I can't very well ask you to hike a mile, can I?"

"I could do it. I'm much stronger."

"Tonight, you and I are going to your brother's house as husband and wife, not as thieves afraid of getting caught." To prove his point, he kissed her out in the open before lifting her into the carriage. When he was inside, he pointedly opened the carriage curtains so that anyone with sharp eyes could see who was riding with the Prophet.

"Joseph," she said, "this isn't wise."

"Tonight somewhere in Illinois Dr. John C. Bennett is telling every curious bastard with a dollar for a ticket all about how I seduced poor Dinah Handy and made her part of my harem. Let the devil make it look as ugly as he likes, I'm proud to have you in my harem, ma'am, and I am not going to hide you tonight."

She laughed and rested her hand on his thigh, but she also kept her face out of the moonlight that streamed in the window. She would not enjoy this evening if Joseph were made to suffer because of it. .

They were the last to arrive at Charlie's new house. Joseph boldly led her through the front doors, and loudly introduced her as Dinah Smith before the door was fully closed, but to her relief he didn't carry it to extremes—he made no effort to open the curtains so that passersby could see just who was the Prophet's consort tonight.

Hyrum was full of wit tonight, and Heber was jovial, and even Brigham managed to be decent company, and all the women were the sisterhood that Dinah wanted them to be. Especially Charlie and his wives. Who would have thought it; my brother Charlie, of all people, the first to make the Principle work as it ought. For Harriette had never been so beautiful, and Sally never so serene as when Charlie held their hands and offered the prayer over the food. And I, too, Dinah thought, I have never been so happy as tonight. For in this house, with these people, I am Joseph's wife. His true wife when he is with the truest Saints. I could not ask for more.

Charlie had relaxed from the Word of Wisdom enough to serve wine with the dinner tonight, and when the forks were still and the toasts began, Dinah carefully rose to her feet and proposed one. "To the day when all wives live in such harmony as Sally and Harriette, and to the day when we will not have to close the curtains on such a gathering as this! Come quickly!"

"Quickly," some murmured, and "Amen," and they drank, and then Joseph arose and kissed her hand and lifted his glass and said, "Brothers and sisters, to my wife." No one blamed her that she put her hands to her face and wept for joy.

Then Joseph gathered them all into a circle and said a prayer to dedicate the house.

When the guests had gone, Charlie, Sally, and Harriette cleaned up together, and when the work was done, Charlie kissed Sally good-night at the door of her room, and then brought Harriette up to bed. To Harriette's relief, Sally still seemed glad the next morning. Harriette began to think it might work out well after all.

And it did work out. She and Sally never quarreled. Any loneliness one might feel on the nights that Charlie was with the other could be borne well, for they both knew he would be theirs the next night. Even the private jokes, the little habits that grew up between Charlie and each of his wives, became a part of the life of the house, no more noticed, in the main, than the pattern on the china or the shadows of the furniture on the wall.

Why, then, Harriette asked herself one night, why do I still have times like this when I want to scream and run from this house and hide somewhere in the woods for a year or two? She tried to think what had gone wrong today. Only little things. Harriette hadn't put enough starch in Charlie's collars. Sally didn't fuss about it, just said, "Oh, by the way, Charlie usually takes more starch." And Harriette smiled and nodded and why not? What was wrong with that? Sally had been married to him longer, she knew what he preferred. But Harriette could not help suspecting that Charlie had no preference and never noticed if his collars were starched at all, that it was Sally who wanted his shirts that way.

Even if that's so, she insisted to herself, so what? Sally never imposes her will on me. We decide the housekeeping assignments together. She never makes me feel that she's following after me to check up on my work. We do practically everything alike in the house anyway—we've done housework together for twenty years. We even cook the same dishes, and agree on how much salt there ought to be in the soup.

But Harriette's uneasiness remained. Charlie had a way of saying, "Remember when we bought the chiffonier?" though he and Sally had bought it long before Harriette joined the family; "I told you the Pierces were coming over tonight," when in fact he had told only Sally. And tonight—yes, that was why she felt so out of sorts—tonight they had been sitting together in the parlor. Charlie was reading the *Times and Seasons,* seeing how his advertisements looked and making fun of the typographical errors, while Sally repaired a damaged shirt and Harriette hemmed an apron. After a while Harriette realized that Charlie had forgotten she was there. When he looked up from the paper or spoke without looking up, his comments were all directed to Sally, and he was content when only Sally answered. Harriette was sure it was her imagination. But when she did make a comment, Charlie looked at her with just a little startlement. It wasn't so much that he would even notice it himself, but it was real.

This was what bothered Harriette tonight: Charlie and Sally had a web of habit that had grown up between them for many,

many months. They had a past together that Harriette could never be part of. It was childish of her even to care, she knew. Yet she was envious nonetheless; envious even of the tragic memory of little Alexandra, for that pain, which Charlie and Sally had in common, bound them in a whole that excluded Harriette. Even the pain because Charlie had not ever seen the child—even that was part of Harriette's irrational jealousy. If anyone knew what she felt, they'd laugh at her. She even laughed at herself, and then went on feeling just the same.

It will pass, she told herself. As we have more and more experiences together, those parts that I'm not part of will be smaller and smaller in proportion. Be patient.

Still she lay awake, alone in her bed, a book of poetry open before her filled with words that said nothing. What is poetry to Charlie? A decoration in his life, while Sally is his heart. Not that I ever want to displace her. Someday my thread will be as thoroughly woven into the fabric as hers is.

The book tipped forward as she dozed for a moment, and when she startled and lifted it again, a folded paper, sealed with a few drops of wax, slipped from the leaves and lay upon the sheet. It was the poem Dinah had written for Emma and given to her. Harriette opened it and read again.

> *I look in the mirror.*
> *The glass is my friend.*
> *I count all the wrinkles.*
> *They never end.*
> *He touches my forehead.*
> *He kisses my cheek,*
> *And I know he is thinking of her.*
>
> *We walk by the temple.*
> *We rest by a tree.*
> *He looks to be thinking,*
> *But not of me.*
> *He stood here before,*
> *And the memory's good,*
> *And I know he is thinking of her.*
>
> *I see how he watches*
> *Her step and her smile.*
> *He laughs and he listens,*

> *And in a while*
> *He gives her his hand—*
> *But that hand is mine!*
> *It is not. It was given to her,*
> *That terrible stranger,*
> *My beautiful sister,*
> *His wife.*

It was unlike anything that Dinah had ever written before. Gone were the long involved sentences, the rhyming lines that never lacked a mate. Gone, too, was the neat certainty of most of her poems. In this one she seemed unsure of what she had to say. It could be spoken by first or second wife alike, in equal pain. And yet it was a love poem. And not a love poem for the husband.

That was the meaning of the poem, and the meaning of the pain that Harriette felt. It was the love between the wives that made the Principle both terrible and glorious. It was the daily forgivenesses, the quiet bearing of a burden that accumulated every little pain, and above all the knowledge that her sister shared a burden at least as heavy as her own. Most women marry, Harriette realized, but never the same man at the same time. Sally and I know each other's lives more perfectly than any other women can hope to know each other. We are each other's school for charity. If we live through this and love each other at the end, no one can say we don't deserve to be called saints.

➤➤➤ BOOK EIGHT ⬅⬅⬅

*In which Providence finally
lets the lamb
find out why he was fattened
and protected all these years.*

❧ First Word ❧

Polygamy is the great smokescreen of Mormonism. For a hundred years whenever people spoke or wrote of Mormonism, it was that peculiar institution that drew their attention. A generation of readers of pulp fiction grew up with a picture of Mormons as dour-faced patriarchs who sent out handsome young missionaries to seduce or kidnap young girls and bring them back to their harems. Those who did not think Mormon polygamy was a moral outrage found it to be a bizarre curiosity.

I, however, never thought of polygamy that way. Even though the Church had forsaken the practice years before I was born, I was aware almost from infancy that my grandparents had grown up in plural families—my one grandmother even told me stories of the day her father brought home Aunt Velora, the second wife. So the Principle did not seem strange to me, and I knew from the start that most of the titillating tales of polygamy were nonsense. With rare exceptions, the men and women who practiced the Principle were quite Victorian in their moral attitude. Polygamy was not promiscuity—all the children of all the wives were loved and cared for by their fathers, and adultery was regarded by the Church as a sin next to murder in seriousness. Women were never physically forced into polygamy, and while some no doubt were pressured into marriages they did not want, I suspect that there were no fewer non-Mormon girls pressured into equally detestable monogamous marriages. And some of my female ancestors, like Dinah Kirkham, were ardent advocates of the Principle. I know of no serious student of Mormon history who has found evidence to justify any other conclusion than this: Whatever other faults they might have had, Mormon men and women were almost never hypocritical about polygamy. It was not an excuse for promiscuity and exploitation. They entered the Principle as a sacrament and lived it as a serious family responsibility.

Yet a puzzle remained for me. Why did the first Mormons, reared in the puritanical tradition of New England, ever accept the Principle in the first place? Even Joseph Smith himself wrestled with the doctrine for a decade before he began to impose it on the Church, and it is almost impossible to find a record of a man or woman who was glad to learn of the commandment. Many, perhaps most, of the people who were taught the doctrine rejected it outright, and often they were so shaken by it that they apostatized and began to fight against the Church. Joseph Smith's assassination can in large part be blamed on the practice of polygamy. Almost no one liked the doctrine, yet Joseph Smith died for it, hundreds of Saints went to jail for it, the Church was nearly destroyed for its sake. Even today, Mormons who, like me, grew up knowing the truth about polygamy still shudder at the thought of ever being required to live that law ourselves.

I have often wondered if, on an institutional level, polygamy did the Mormon Church harm or good. The death and suffering during the exodus from Nauvoo, added to the community pain caused by the deaths of

Joseph and Hyrum, weigh heavily on the negative side. By the end of open polygamy in 1890, fifty years of struggle between the Church and the federal government left the Church broken and defeated, the Saints exhausted, the economy of Utah Territory in a shambles. The price for the peculiar doctrine was high.

But the benefits to the Church as an institution were high, too. Polygamy intensified the Saints' dedication to the Church. Once men and women entered plural marriages, they were utterly committed to Mormonism. There could be no turning back without deserting helpless, beloved children, without renouncing wives or husband. A polygamous Mormon was forced to turn inward to the Church, for the outside world viewed him or her with pity at best, revulsion at worst. The long series of battles with the federal government taught generations of Saints to have a higher loyalty to their Church than to their government, a loyalty that continues even today. Mormons still treasure the myth of persecution: abuse a Mormon because of his beliefs, and he is almost grateful for the chance to bravely resist you, for it proves that he is worthy of the sacrifices of his ancestors. Polygamy named us as a people, and though polygamy is gratefully behind us now, we still live on the strength of its legacy.

That analytical view is possible only from a distance. Dinah and Charlie took a much more personal view. And that nearsighted, subjective, personal version of events may well be the only one that has any truth or importance to it. For all my words about the function of polygamy, the fact is that Charlie and Sally and Harriette, Joseph and Dinah, Heber and Vilate and hundreds of other Saints lived with it, paid its terrible price, and emerged from that peculiar institution stronger than ever. To my mind, at least, their response to the crisis of their faith ennobled them. And yet I suspect that my own response to the doctrine would have been like those who either left the Church in fury or pretended that it was just an aberration and hoped that it would go away. It is Emma whose acts I most sympathize with. I am not made of the same stuff as my ancestors. There's a limit on how much I'm willing to sacrifice for my faith.

The years from 1842 to 1844 were crowded with events, according to the documents, but to me they seem like endless maneuvers to delay the inevitable end. The battle lines were drawn, the armies assembled, and for two years the armies perched on opposite hills and shouted at each other, fired warning shots, set pickets, sent forays, laid ambuscades, and yet dared not commit themselves irrevocably to battle. In the end, while all these little maneuvers fascinate me, they are footnotes to the story I am telling. Joseph Smith struggled to hold the Church together as polygamy threatened to tear it apart; he fought to win political power for the Church, even to the point of running for President of the United States, sending out troops of missionaries to campaign for him; in the end, watching the government turn into a weapon against him, watching the strength of the Church bleeding away as Mormon after Mormon defected to the anti-Mormon camp, he knew that it was impossible for the Church to fulfil his dream within the borders of the United States, and before he died he had already set the plans in motion for the westward migration that finally happened under the leadership of Brigham Young.

What finally brought matters to a head was the Nauvoo *Expositor*. The enemies of the Church published the newspaper right in Joseph's city. Its first and only issue was filled with specific allegations concerning polygamy in Nauvoo. The *Expositor* forced Joseph Smith to commit himself. The Mormons who still had no idea that Joseph Smith himself was the source of the doctrine of polygamy demanded that any polygamists be prosecuted. As Mayor, Joseph Smith would have had to lead the prosecutions himself, and all the facts that would have come out in a trial would have destroyed the Church. Even a trial for libel was impossible for the same reason—too many of the allegations were true, or true enough that the world would never appreciate the fine distinction between the Principle and John Bennett's version of events. The alternative was to deny everything, declare the *Expositor* a public nuisance, and stop its publication. That was the course that Joseph chose, and as a result, instead of the outside world seeing Mormons as a persecuted minority struggling for religious freedom against a mob, the world saw the Mormons as an arrogant theocracy, trampling on the Constitution by denying freedom of the press. After all the months of maneuvering, Joseph Smith found himself surrounded, and there was no way out.

—*O. Kirkham, Salt Lake City, 1981*

❧ 43 ❧

Charlie Banks Kirkham
Nauvoo, 1844

CHARLIE ALWAYS FELT A LITTLE silly wearing his sword as an officer in the Nauvoo Legion. He hadn't the faintest idea what to do with it, and never unsheathed it for fear of hurting someone. He only held his rank because prominent citizens were expected to do their civic duty in the militia; but in the frequent military parades in recent months Charlie's company became known as the best in the Nauvoo Legion. Charlie was dependable, so his soldiers had actually practiced marching in regular lines; Charlie had money, so his soldiers were all well-equipped. Naturally, Brother Joseph and the Nauvoo City Council decided to assign their destruction order to him. He was not pleased that his little company of soldiers was called into action for such a messy business as wrecking the paper. Not that he minded seeing the Nauvoo *Expositor* put out of business. After reading some of the terrible things that were said about him and his wives, Charlie wouldn't have minded if the publishers were hanged. What he minded was having some responsibility for performing the act himself, for he had learned enough about American public feeling during his months in Washington to know that when the soldiers began to hammer at the door with their muskets, they were opening the door for the destruction of Nauvoo.

Still, Charlie was not one to hang back from his duty. He was one of the first militiamen to pass through the door into the printing office. Two of his soldiers had their muskets pointing at the terrified typesetter.

"I'm just a typesetter," he said. "I don't write the stuff, I just set it up."

"Don't point your guns at him," Charlie said. "They might go off."

"It's OK. They only got powder and wad."

"I don't want you catching him on fire, either."

The young soldiers reluctantly lifted the muzzles toward the ceiling—all but one, who pointed the gun downward, whereupon the gunpowder dribbled out on the floor. "Next time," Charlie said, "remember the wadding."

The marshall had several men going at the press with crowbars. Charlie watched the machinery come apart and remembered Don Carlos in the cellar before he died, pumping his heart out on just such an apparatus. It made him sad to see how frail the press really was.

"Come on, Charlie," the marshall said. "The quicker begun, the quicker done."

A philosopher, Charlie thought. "Come on, men, carry all the paper out into the street. We want a bonfire big enough to see in Iowa." The men soon had a human chain going, passing the bundles of paper from arm to arm out of the shop.

His men were having trouble getting the type. The typesetter was clinging to the case, his mouth set in such a determined expression that Charlie was afraid violence might be necessary. Still, it was always better to try reason first.

"Friend," Charlie said to him. "We're just doing a little scientific experiment here. We're trying to find out if little pieces of metal with backward letters on them are worth dying for. What do *you* think?"

After another moment's hesitation, the fellow decided he

had things yet to do with his life. He had been pulling with such force that the three men trying to get it from him nearly fell over when he let go. Then they wrestled the type case outside and dumped it into the street. Charlie watched from the window. The flames from the burning paper were yellow, anu he could hear the roar of the fire above all the shouting.

One of his soldiers, a boy not much younger than Charlie, sidled up to him at the window. "Were you really gonna to kill him?"

Charlie shook his head. "But I'm flattered that he believed I might."

The boy thought for a moment. "Would've been a hell of a lot more exciting if you did."

No doubt. And then they would have had a murder trial on their hands. As it was, Charlie wondered if he'd be sent to jail for this. True, he was only obeying orders, but that wouldn't save him. His name had long been prominent in anti-Mormon diatribes—putting him on trial would be worth the show even if he was acquitted. Still, the enemy was hunting buck, not rabbit. It was Joseph who was in the greatest danger. Even as Charlie sent his men marching back and forth to grind the metal type into the street, he was planning what might be done to get out of the trouble this was going to cause. And by the time the show was over, with all the furniture and fittings and materials broken and lying in the street, Charlie knew what he had to do.

It was a week before he had a chance to talk to Brother Joseph. By then it was plain to everyone that things were getting out of hand. Thousands of militiamen were drilling in nearby cities, boasting loudly of how they planned to invade Nauvoo whether Governor Ford officially called them out or not.

"I have a dozen horses stabled for you across the river in Iowa, with guards day and night," Charlie told the Prophet. "There are a dozen boats up and down the river ready to take you across. I've also outfitted four wagons on the Iowa side with everything you'll need to set up a forward camp in the Indian Territory, where the Church can come to join you."

Joseph looked at the lists and maps Charlie had given him. "Charlie, don't your factories keep you busy anymore? What do I want with this?"

"You've said before that you mean to lead us west. If you're going to be alive to do it, you'll have to be a few hundred miles away from what passes for civilization around here."

Joseph looked over at Hyrum, who shrugged and said, "I'm glad somebody around here is thinking."

"I've ridden out storms before." Joseph pushed the papers away from him across the table. "They've even arrested me."

"This time is different," Charlie said. "This time it looks like you violated the Constitution."

"I didn't violate the Constitution!"

"I didn't say you did. I said it looks like it, and it does."

"The Constitution doesn't protect libel."

"Then you should have prosecuted them for libel." Charlie smiled, to let Joseph know he was playing the devil's advocate.

"That's just what they wanted me to do, so they could call every apostate and traitor as a witness against me. I'd win the case and they'd convince the whole world that we practice Bennett's brand of spiritual wifery."

"Then you should have ignored them."

"That would've been like admitting they were telling the truth. I had no choice but to do what I did."

"Oh, I know that," Charlie said. "That's why I've got a dozen horses and four wagons full of supplies. I've also got men ready at a moment's notice to ride with you, day or night. It's all paid for out of my pocket, and it's going to be ready whether you like it or not. I just wanted you to know where they were."

"I'll never use them, Charlie. Do you think I'll run west and leave the Saints here surrounded by armies the way they were in Missouri? You weren't here, Charlie, but I won't do that again—I won't sit off helpless in the distance, hearing reports of little children being murdered and women being raped while I can't do a damn thing to stop it. They'll never dare arrest me when I'm in Nauvoo, surrounded by the Legion."

When Joseph had his mind made up, it was like talking to a wall. Charlie looked to Hyrum for some cue; Hyrum only smiled and shrugged. Charlie took that as encouragement and went on. "Brother Joseph, up to now you've had public sympathy with you, and your enemies knew it. But now you've done something un-American."

"What do you think they did to our newspaper in Missouri!"

"I didn't say it was fair. I just said that as far as public opinion is concerned, they're free now to do whatever they dare."

Joseph stood up and looked down on Charlie with fire in his eyes. "Who the hell are you to tell me I don't understand. You aren't even American!"

"I've lived for months in Washington."

"You're only a boy!"

"I'm twenty-one. When you were twenty-one you translated the Book of Mormon."

Joseph made as if to answer. Then, slowly, he sat down. "I was a boy then too."

"Charlie," Hyrum said, "he knows you're right."

"I know nothing of the kind," Joseph retorted.

"He knows you're right, but he wants so bad for all this just to go away that he's pretending that it will."

"Hyrum, sometimes." Joseph glared at his brother.

"The horses are there," Charlie said. "If I have enough warning, I'll be on the other side of the river when you get there, to make sure it goes smoothly. If anybody follows you, we'll hold them off as long as we can."

"I told you. I won't be going."

Charlie got up from his chair and walked to the door. "I think I'll have a carriage waiting over there, too, in case somebody's injured and can't ride."

"The boy's deaf," Joseph said to Hyrum.

"Thanks, Brother Charlie," Hyrum called.

"Good-night," Charlie answered.

It was daybreak, and Charlie woke up stiff from sleeping on a dirt floor. He got up at once and went to the door of the cabin. Joseph should have been here by now. It was a dangerous crossing. Charlie could not help but fear that the boat might have capsized.

He walked down to the shore. The water was higher today than it had been yesterday, when Charlie himself crossed. Several whole trees were rushing by out on the water, signs of heavy rainstorms upriver.

"Look at him!" someone shouted. "Just standing around, couldn't even fix breakfast!"

It was Hyrum, emerging from the brush downstream. To Charlie's relief, Joseph appeared next, followed by Porter

Rockwell, with fat little Willard Richards puffing along behind.

"I thought you were drowned."

"Damn near were," said Rockwell. "I thought we were dead a million times."

"I'll help you saddle up the horses," Charlie offered.

"No," Joseph said. "We aren't in that big a hurry. Do you have any paper and ink here?"

"In the supply wagons somewhere. They're on about a mile inland."

Willard Richards produced a scrap of paper from his pocket. "Will this do?"

"Pen and ink?"

Charlie had those. Joseph scrawled out a message to Emma. "I want her out of Nauvoo," he said as he handed the message to Rockwell. "Hyrum's family too. Not a Smith left in the city. Tell them to send all Hyrum's and my personal belongings downriver on the *Maid of Iowa*, then up the Ohio to Pittsburgh. Or somewhere. Maybe they don't have to go that far to be safe. I don't want a mob getting their hands on my son and holding him as a hostage against my coming back. If there isn't a single Smith left in Nauvoo, the Saints will be safe."

Rockwell looked at the note in his hand. "Back across the river?"

"It's daylight now. Bring somebody back with you to help you bail."

They waited for hours in the cabin as the day got hotter and hotter. Joseph kept telling stories and joking until Charlie wanted to shout at him that it was no time for joking, with the world coming down on them. But he held his tongue. Instead he escaped the relentless good cheer by repeatedly going outside to scan the river to see if anyone was crossing. No one did until Rockwell and another man came across at midmorning.

It was Reynolds Cahoon, and he brought a letter from Emma. Joseph read it in silence, then turned away, handing it to Hyrum as he walked off alone toward the horses. Charlie read the letter over Hyrum's shoulder. She was pleading with Joseph to come back and submit to arrest. The governor had promised protection for him if he did. Otherwise, there'd be no controlling the mobs. Nauvoo would be sacked, the Saints driven out or killed.

Charlie looked at Cahoon. "You can tell the Saints that if they don't want Brother Joseph alive, they aren't worth his dying for."

Cahoon glanced at Charlie, then glanced away as if he were unworthy of notice. It was Joseph who had to be persuaded, Cahoon knew. He wouldn't waste time arguing with anyone else.

"Brother Joseph," he called, and followed the Prophet.

Joseph was leaning on the cabin wall, stroking the muzzle of one of the horses tethered there. "Charlie," he said, "you didn't tell me your horses were a bunch of old nags. I've given better horses than this to the knacker."

"I'm not a very good judge of horses," said Charlie.

"So I see."

"Brother Joseph," Cahoon said. "You've never seen the people as scared as they are now, with word going around that you've left the city."

"They only want *me*, Reynolds. If I'm out of reach their threats won't come to anything."

"And then what, Joseph? What do the Saints do then? Leave Nauvoo, leave another temple unfinished, give up our homes again? The governor gives his personal guarantee that you'll be protected."

"Last time I trusted a governor, I nearly ended up in Missouri hanging on the end of a rope."

"That was Governor Carlin. This is Governor Ford."

"The kind of man likely to get elected governor of any state isn't worth the money he was bought with." Joseph looked Cahoon in the eye. "If I give myself up, Cahoon, the Saints will never see me again."

"Sister Emma doesn't think so," Cahoon said. "Sister Emma thinks it's your responsibility to act for the good of the Church."

"That's what I'm doing."

"Sister Emma told me that you always said if the Church would stick to you, you'd stick to the Church, and now trouble comes you're the first to run!"

Joseph reached out and took Cahoon by the lapels. "Emma didn't say that."

"No," Cahoon admitted. "She only told me people were saying that. She says that the people are losing heart. Some folks say that if you can't even stick around when you've got the governor on your side, you're no good to the Church alive *or* dead."

"They're just scared," Charlie said. "They won't feel that way in a few days."

"There are mobs out there!" Cahoon shouted. "I don't want no immigrant telling me how we're going to feel in a couple of days! I made that march across Missouri, and I sure as hell ain't gonna do it again, not if the Prophet's sitting fat and sassy out in Iowa somewhere making flapjacks so we can have a nice hot breakfast when we get there!"

Charlie was about to answer when Joseph silenced him with a hand on his shoulder. "If my life is of no value to my friends, it isn't worth much to me, either," Joseph said. He turned to Hyrum and Port. "What should I do?"

Port rested his hands on the pistols at his belt. "You're the oldest, I figure you know best. But however you make your bed, I'm lying in it with you."

Joseph chuckled. "But I'm not the oldest. You are, Hyrum. What should we do?"

"Let's go back."

"No," Charlie said.

"You got no vote," Cahoon said.

"You're the President and I'm the Patriarch," Hyrum said. "We ought to act for the Church's sake whatever happens."

"We'll be butchered," said Joseph. He wasn't arguing, just stating a fact.

"The Lord's hand is in this, Joseph. Live or die, it'll be how the Lord wants it to be."

Joseph started toward the river. Rockwell stopped him. "That skiff ain't worth a damn. There's some men fetching a better boat from upriver. Be here in an hour or so."

Joseph looked around as if uncertain where he was. "Charlie," he said. "Ride to the wagons and get some paper. I need to write some letters. Might as well use your handwriting."

Charlie was no horseman, and the horse was none too sure-footed herself. Charlie kept kicking her and then wishing he hadn't as she lurched and stumbled along the uneven path. He was petrified the whole time, sure that he would end up with a broken leg somewhere, and all for some paper. No one would write any epic poems about his self-sacrifice in undergoing agony so Joseph could write some letters. More likely a nursery rhyme.

> *Charlie K*
> *Was killed today*
> *While going for the paper.*

He kept trying to think of a rhyme for paper. Taper. Caper. Epic poem or not, the paper was what Joseph had sent him for; and by God Joseph would have it as fast as Charlie could possibly get it.

When he got back to the cabin, Joseph wasn't there. Hyrum saw Charlie's expression and put him at ease at once. "He hasn't gone, Charlie. He's off in the woods praying."

Rockwell, Richards, and Cahoon were waiting, too. "You let him go alone?" Charlie asked.

Rockwell snorted. "If I had my way he wouldn't go to the privy alone, but nobody tells Joseph what to do."

"I think," Hyrum said, "that if Joseph had his choice how to die, he'd rather be found praying than any other thing."

Charlie set the paper on the stones of the cold hearth. The room was underfurnished. He had meant to take care of that, but there hadn't been time. Now it wouldn't matter.

He felt Hyrum's hand on his shoulder. "Thanks for bringing the paper, Charlie."

"I wish it had been an army of angels."

"I guess the Lord got out of the military business after the Old Testament." Hyrum drew him to the door, led him outside. "Charlie," he said, "I wish you hadn't seen Emma's letter."

"I wish I hadn't, either."

"I'm afraid you don't understand why she wrote it."

"She doesn't give a damn about his life."

"That's why I wanted to talk to you, Charlie. Emma's always been a bluntspoken woman. She says what's on her mind."

"She's bringing him back to die."

"She doesn't believe that. Besides, Charlie, we've played this whole scene through before. In Missouri Joseph was in the hands of the mob, under sentence of death, while the Saints were being driven from their homes through the snow. It was a terrible time—but one sure thing was that the Lord protected Joseph. Didn't protect a lot of others, but the Lord kept Joseph alive. Cooped up in that little jail with his people suffering so, it used to drive Joseph half out of his mind. Once he said to me, 'At least they could have the decency to kill me instead of torturing me like this.' Emma knows her husband. Whether the Lord protects him or not, if the Saints were in trouble and Joseph wasn't with them, he'd hate himself."

"It hurt him that they don't care for his life."

"Yes. The timid Saints hurt him a little. But Emma didn't hurt him. He knows Emma."

Joseph's voice came from around the corner of the building, not ten feet off. "Hyrum, is there anybody you haven't got all figured out?"

Joseph came around the building. Hyrum grinned at him like a silly boy. "I thought you were going into the woods."

"Too many bugs. They're in league with the devil. It's hard to pray when you're swatting flies. Got the paper, Charlie?"

So Charlie scribed for the Prophet one last time, rode across the river with him, and said good-bye to him at the Nauvoo wharf. Joseph insisted they arrive there where enough people would see him that there'd be no more talk of him running away. Charlie offered to stay with him, even to surrender with him.

"No, Charlie. You're the man I needed if I were going to do the sensible thing. Now you just go home to your family. They're all the duty you've got now. You just take care of *them*." Then the Prophet kissed him and sent him on his way. It was the last time Charlie saw him alive.

❧ 44 ❧

Dinah Kirkham Smith
Nauvoo, 1844

DINAH HEARD ABOUT EMMA'S letter to Joseph before Reynolds Cahoon got to the boat—the one thing in Nauvoo that functioned better in time of panic was the gossip mill. Dinah knew at once that he'd return and give himself up. She wasted no time condemning Emma. She did not even bother to try to find Joseph and persuade him not to surrender. All through Charlie's quiet preparations for Joseph's flight west, Dinah had known what Emma knew—Joseph would never go through with it. The Church was Joseph's life, and he could not separate himself from it. The difference was that Emma had the courage to tell Joseph so.

I was never worthy of him, Dinah realized then. Even now, I hate the fact that he is going. Even now, if he were here, I would plead with him to be weak, to deny his whole life, to stay alive so I could have him another week, another year, for all my life.

Joseph came to her that evening, came when it was still light in the sky. He did not bother hiding. He stood openly at her door, with several men at his carriage looking on, and he did not even bother to go inside the cabin before taking her in his arms and kissing her. Then he turned and faced the men to make sure that they had seen.

"We've been publicly denying the Principle so long," Joseph said to her, "that some folks might want to claim I never practiced it at all. I don't want it to be your word against theirs." *After I'm dead.* Those were the words he didn't say, but Dinah heard them.

He came inside then, and just held her, standing in the middle of the floor, just stroked her hair, her cheek. "You may just be the most beautiful woman I ever married."

"You say that to all your wives."

"If I tried to say good-bye to all my wives, Dinah, it'd be three days before the Governor got his hands on me."

"Are there so many?"

"The Lord gave me a lot of wives. Just didn't give me much time. There's quite a lot who have a ceremony to remember. Precious few who have anything else. I guess I didn't set a very good example."

"I wish you wouldn't go."

"I will, though. Like a lamb to the slaughter. But it's funny—I was terrified all the time getting across the river to try to escape. Scared half to death. And now, when I know I'm going to die, I'm as calm as a summer's morning." He kissed her lightly. "You tell people. After I'm dead, you tell them that I wasn't afraid to die. My conscience is clean toward God or anybody. When they kill me they'll be killing an innocent man in cold blood. You write that." He grinned. "Feel free to improve it a little if you like. Heroes need grand speeches. That's one thing I always wanted, to be the hero of my own story. Got my wish."

He walked toward the door.

"Joseph!" she cried.

"Did I forget something?" he asked.

"I want to confess something."

"It's my own sins I'm worrying about right now, Dinah."

"It's a lie I told, and I want you to know the truth." *Before you die.*

"I already know more truth than a man can know and stay alive in this world."

"When I married you, I told you I only did it out of obedience to the Lord."

"I know. I told you the same thing."

"It wasn't true. I dreamed of you in England, I wanted you when I saw you wrestling in the mud, and if God hadn't given me consent to love you I would have loved you anyway, sin or not. I'm sorry that I lied."

He touched her cheek. "I'm sorry," he whispered, "but I told the truth."

She had determined not to cry, but now she changed her mind. "If you die, Joseph, I'm the one you died for, I and all your plural wives."

He kissed her again. "I never asked the Lord to take *this* cup from me." Then he smiled. "But don't take too much glory on yourself, Dinah. I won't die for you. I won't even die for the Church, or for God. If I die, it's because I saw the world true and told people the truth about what I saw. And if it takes my blood to convince them that I meant it, I hope I spill ten gallons of it."

She wiped her eyes on her apron. "You haven't got ten gallons."

"They'll be disappointed. They all want so bad to have a little of it on their hands." He opened the door.

"Can't you stay a little longer?"

He shook his head. "If I've got one night left in Nauvoo, I'm going to spend it with my children. I want them to remember their father. They're young enough they might forget. But you——I don't think you're about to forget me."

As he walked outside, she felt the ground trembling under her, heard her own name in her mind and could not think of what it meant. "What will I do without you?"

"You know what to do." She followed him out the door, stood beside him. "You just make sure that what I built, stays." He was looking westward, but she knew he wasn't talking about the Temple or the city.

He embraced her again, quickly, and then ran toward the carriage. Ran like a boy bounding across a field, as if he were chasing a butterfly, Dinah thought. As if he were excited to find out what the next part of his life was going to be.

He stopped in the middle of swinging up into the carriage. He was holding to the carriage roof with one arm, waving the other. She waved back. Then he pointed at her. "You!" he shouted. "I'll be waiting for you!"

"You'd better be!"

Then the carriage started moving, and he ducked inside, and the door closed, and that was the last time Dinah saw him alive.

❧ 45 ❧

Joseph Smith
Carthage, Illinois, 1844

THE DOOR OPENED AND the jailer came in. Joseph had his mouth full or he would have greeted him. Joseph was getting along rather well with this jailer. It helped that Governor Ford had helped him get settled and parted with him on friendly terms—the jailer no doubt was influenced by that. As a result, Joseph and Hyrum, the two prisoners, were kept in the relative freedom of the debtors' room, upstairs in the jailhouse, instead of being locked in a cell. They could have almost any visitors they wanted. Joseph didn't abuse that privilege, or he might have had an army there. He was not lacking for would-be bodyguards, but he did not want to endanger anyone's life but his own. He had finally managed to send everyone away except Willard Richards and John Taylor, who were not easy to get rid of. The truth was that Joseph was glad of their company.

Joseph wasn't sure, though, how far the jailer's liberality would extend. Prisoners were not usually supposed to have weapons. Willard Richards's cane was harmless enough, but Brother Markham had left a huge hickory stick that he called a "rascal beater," and Cyrus Wheelock had smuggled in a six-shooter, which now rested in the bottom of Hyrum's pocket.

"Supper any good?" the jailer asked.

"Stone cold," Hyrum said.

"Always is." The jailer looked around a minute. Joseph watched him, wondering if the man was simply doing his duty or if he meant to betray them. Joseph saw the bulge of the pistol in Hyrum's coat pocket and wondered if Hyrum would be able to shoot the man if he turned out to be an assassin.

"You know," the jailer said, "you'll probably be a lot safer in the cell."

"No doubt," Joseph answered. He looked at the little barred window on the heavy cell door and thought how convenient it would be for a murderer to stand there and fill the cell with bullets. "We'll go in after supper."

"Damnedest prisoners I ever knew," the jailer said. "I don't often have 'em sitting with their friends."

Willard Richards looked up from his plate of potatoes. "You mean I'm not a prisoner?"

"You know you're not," Hyrum said.

"It's the most insulting thing I ever heard of," Willard said. "Why aren't I important enough to arrest?"

"Don't worry," John Taylor said. "If somebody breaks in here to kill Joseph, they probably won't check to make sure they only kill legally arrested men."

The jailer was annoyed. "Nobody's getting in here, boys, so don't you fret. This jail's the most solid one in the state, or so the Governor said."

"No doubt the Governor has been in all of them to see," Willard answered.

"You just go into the cell after supper," the jailer said. "Your friends can wait right here. And if you start worrying, you just remember that the Carthage Greys are standing guard outside this jail. Ain't nobody can get to you without getting by them first."

"Now I'm worried," Joseph said.

"Our Carthage boys are true blue." The jailer went back down the stairs, leaving the door open behind him.

Joseph got up and closed the door. "Eat slow," he said. "I

don't want to be locked into that little place."

"Will they try anything tonight?" Willard asked.

"I don't know." People always expected a prophet to know things like that. It was no good explaining to them that the Lord didn't work that way. "But I'll sleep a whole lot easier if I know that you and John aren't in here."

John Taylor wiped his mouth on his napkin. "I won't sleep at all if I'm not."

"If something happened to Hyrum and me, they'll need you in Nauvoo. The other apostles won't be back for weeks yet."

"If the Lord needs us to be in Nauvoo, he'll see to it we get there."

It wasn't worth arguing. John had his stubborn face on, and when John Taylor was stubborn he didn't bend very easily. Joseph already felt control of things slipping out of his hands. For so many years now he had felt the whole Church, all the Saints as if they were an extension of himself. An injury to one part was always his own injury; he felt the pain more than anyone. Now, though, he felt himself going numb, going paralyzed. He was separating from the greatest part of himself. The most important part. All he had left was his own body, and he felt lost. It hadn't been like that in the Liberty jail. There he had been in agony for the suffering of the Saints. Now he couldn't even be sure that they existed, not the way it had always been before. He knew what it meant. The Lord was getting things ready for his death. It meant that when he died, the Church wouldn't die with him. He should be glad of it. He was, in a way. But that single, vulnerable man he had become—that man was afraid to die. He wondered if he would disgrace himself.

Willard tried to tell a story, but after a while John told him to be quiet. "I want to hear any sounds there might be outside." And so they sat in silence, not even looking at each other as the afternoon sunlight dazzled in the room, went gold, went red, and then began to grey out toward night.

There was a scuffing noise outside, down in the square. Joseph opened his eyes. John Taylor was sitting bolt upright, and Willard Richards was standing by the door. From below they heard a young voice complaining. "But we outnumber them!"

An older voice faded in and out: ". . . mouth shut, boy . . ."

Another voice: ". . . blanks, better check . . ."

Hyrum languidly got to his feet. "Sounds like they didn't let everybody in on the plan."

Willard rushed to the window. Huge and heavy as he was, Joseph marveled at how quickly he could move, and how quietly. Willard peered out, then came back, his face sick with fear. "They're all around the jail. Faces painted up, looks like."

"Uniforms?" John Taylor asked.

"Of course not," Hyrum said. "They're pretending to be Indians." He took the pistol out of his pocket and looked at it. "I hate to use these things. I don't even like to see them used."

They heard a noise in the room below, then the sound of someone coming up the stairs. Outside someone shouted unconvincingly, "Surrender!" and a few shots were fired. Trying to make it look like the Carthage Greys put up a fight, Joseph thought with amusement. All it does is prove in the eyes of God that they knew that what they were doing was wrong. Hypocrites confess by their own effort to conceal. Joseph found himself mentally composing a sermon on the subject as John Taylor snatched up Markham's rascal beater and Willard Richards took his cane. The door opened a little, and Willard Richards threw himself against it, all three hundred pounds of him. There was a shout of surprise or pain outside the door. Joseph stood up. He ought to be standing up for this.

The men on the stairs began to shout. Terrible oaths and threats. I ought to be contemplating the glory of God. At least having a vision. That's what prophets are supposed to do when they're about to die. The door pushed back open slowly despite Willard's weight against it. Hyrum took his position opposite the door and aimed his pistol. The barrels of two or three muskets poked into the room and discharged, even as John hammered them down with his rascal beater. Hyrum cocked the pistol. There was more shouting, and suddenly the door swung open wider. Hyrum thought of firing. Joseph could see it in his face. But he never pulled the trigger. Half a dozen shots came from the doorway all at once, and Hyrum's clothing blossomed with wounds. Willard screamed something and jammed the door shut, almost catching John as he stabbed outward with his stick. Joseph saw all that even as he ran to Hyrum.

"I'm a dead man," Hyrum said. One of the bullets had struck

beside his nose, and the blood was smeared all over his face. Joseph eased Hyrum to the ground. It wasn't supposed to be this way. Something had gone wrong. Joseph was supposed to die, not Hyrum. Hyrum was supposed to succeed him at the head of the Church. Wasn't that what Joseph had planned? He took the pistol out of Hyrum's hand. The handle was sweaty. It was still cocked. Hyrum never did them any harm at all, Joseph thought, not even to defend himself. Didn't they know who their enemy was? I am their enemy. And he strode to the door, which was being forced open again, and discharged the pistol six times.

Joseph ran back from the door. He had seen flesh and clothing burst with the impact of the bullets, and it frightened him. That isn't what I lived for. I never killed anybody before. And in spite of himself he hoped that they weren't hurt too badly. He even wanted to apologize, the way he always did when he hurt somebody wrestling. Hyrum lay dead on the floor. Joseph looked at him for a moment, and wanted to apologize to him, too. But then he couldn't think what it was he should have done differently. Couldn't think of a thing in his life that he should have changed.

Behind him the shouting was worse. He turned. The men were inside the room now; John Taylor was near the window. When had he gone to the window? The bullets struck him, too, and he fell inside the room, writhing in pain on the floor. Joseph couldn't feel his pain, though. Not even now. Willard Richards was screaming at him from behind the door, where he was pinned when the mob had at last pushed it open. Only safe place in the room, Joseph thought. The biggest man here, and he's the only one who found a hiding place.

Why was everyone standing there, waiting? Why had everything stopped? Were they leaving it up to him again? Was everything going to stay as it was until he moved and changed it? Even now, did they have to depend on him to take charge of his own death? All right, then. He threw the empty pistol to the ground and ran to the window. You want Joseph Smith? Here I am. Not hiding from you in a room. You don't have to come in and get me. I'll come out to you.

He had one foot on the sill when a bullet struck him in the other leg, knocking it out from under him. Don't be so impatient, I'm coming. He lay on the sill, straddling it, one arm and leg outside. He felt the bullets pierce him on both sides, as if some were trying to push him out, the others push him in. Out, he decided, and felt himself slide from the sill toward the open space outside. The pain struck him then, and he felt his mouth open as he cried out, "Oh Lord my God!" He wasn't quite sure himself whether he was giving the Masonic cry of distress or a complaint. The ground came as the most powerful blow he had ever been struck, and he felt himself bounce into the air a little. He tried to raise himself up. Stand up. Arise. Then he realized that his cry had been neither distress nor complaint. It was a greeting.

❧ 46 ❧

Requiem
Nauvoo, Illinois, 1844

DINAH SAT ALONE AT her writing table. It was well after midnight, but she did not think of sleep. Her journal lay before her. She flipped through a hundred leaves covered with her smooth handwriting and wrote "June 29th" at the top of the first blank page.

Funeral today. I did not want to see his body. I was not interested in Br. Ph.'s sermon. Only E. and M. were allowed to mourn. I sent word for certain widows to come to Ch.'s house. There we bore testimony to each other that his words were true, his works were good, and that all that God gave him in this life would be his forever and ever. When we meet him again, we will all stand forth in full light of day. For this reason we rejoiced instead of grieving. We resolved to be sisters always. Did they think their bullets could tear apart what God joined?

They called me the Prophetess tonight, she remembered. Even the other wives, who should have known I was just a woman in the same hidden agony as they. But she was not unhappy that they did not know her. Dinah, as she really was, was no wiser than any other woman—she could not have comforted these women, for she had no comfort even for herself. Yet the Sister Dinah they called the Prophetess had power to heal broken hearts and make the darkest of futures bright, for they believed in her, which would make her promises come true. So she would be Joseph's helpmate, and speak for him out of the grave.

She set to work. She knew what was needed. No bloody anthems calling for revenge. Only elegy, lament, and above all vows that the martyr did not die in vain. Before the Saints can lose heart, I will tell them that they will not lose heart; before they begin to abandon Zion, I will tell them that they are too faithful ever to give up. I will tell them they are willing to die as Joseph did, and they will read it and believe it and so it will be true.

She wrote seventeen poems that night, and recorded them all in her journal when they were finished. All would be published in the *Times and Seasons* during the next week, under six different names. Some of them were among the worst poems she ever wrote. But three of them were among her best, and two of these, set to music, would become beloved hymns of the Church.

She finished at first light, but still she did not sleep. Instead, after copying the poems into her journal, she carried them to the *Times and Seasons* office. The staff was already there, preparing that day's edition. The editor didn't even read them, just took the top six from the stack. "Which of these do you want under your own name?"

She chose one.

He handed the other five to the typesetter. "Make up names for these," he said. Then he carefully printed Dinah's name under the one that she had chosen. Mrs. Handy, he wrote. But he knew better. "God bless you, Sister Smith," he said, and held her hand a moment before letting her go back out into the morning.

The sun came up as she walked home, the light blinding her so she could hardly see her own house for all the brightness.

It was the glory of the resurrection and he stood by her door, clothed in glory. Have you come for me? she asked him silently. He did not answer. When she reached the door, he was gone, and the sun no longer dazzled her eyes. He would not come for her yet. Not for days, not for weeks, not for years. Time without him would be long. The hours with him were so few that she could remember them all; standing there at her door she remembered every moment of him in a single instant, held the sight of him all at once in her eyes, the sound of his voice frightened and loving and angry all at once, and all at once against her body, his hands, his lips. He touched her, not in the past, but in the present and forever.

Then, as suddenly as it had come, that clear sense of him was gone. She could not hide, then, from what she had lost. She stumbled into the house, curled herself upon the bed and wept for the first time, and the last time, until sleep took her.

⇒⇒⇒ BOOK NINE ⇐⇐⇐

*In which Providence sets up shop
in a new location
with different management.*

❧ First Word ❧

The men who planned Joseph Smith's death no doubt expected that with the Prophet gone the Mormons would all give up and go home. They believed their own image of the Mormons as puppets under his satanic control; with the strings cut, there would be nothing to keep the Mormons together. They didn't realize what Joseph Smith had found out all too often: if the Saints were sheep, they were the most stubborn, self-willed, cantankerous herd a shepherd ever had to deal with. Any Saint who got to Nauvoo had already passed through such a gauntlet of pressure and abuse from unconverted family and friends, had already sacrificed so much money and time and effort, that he or she was not about to give in just because the world had martyred another prophet. Indeed, that was all the more reason to continue God's work: Joseph had sealed his testimony with his blood.

Besides, precious few of them had any home left to go back to.

Joseph and Hyrum were dead at the jail. John Taylor hovered near death from his wounds, but gradually recovered. Willard Richards escaped with only a nick in his ear. He was pinned behind the door for just a few seconds, but that was long enough to save him from the fusillade. The citizens of Carthage, fearing vengeance from the Mormons—after all, they had heard so much about how monstrous the Mormon people were—fled their city, and frightened people in all the nearby towns huddled, waiting for the Mormon counterstroke. It never came. There were those among the Saints who wanted to give the blow, but John Taylor sent word from the prison that the Saints were to fire not a single weapon in vengeance. Taylor, whose blood had been mingled with that of the martyrs, was obeyed. Western Illinois did not suffer the bloodbath that had been so feared. And the non-Mormons settled back to watch the Church dissolve.

Brigham Young heard the news of Joseph's death in Boston, where he was on a mission to promote Joseph's candidacy for President of the United States. He wept, for no man loved Joseph more than Brigham did. Then he packed up and headed for Nauvoo. The campaign was over, and the Lord would want him with the Saints.

Sidney Rigdon, Joseph's First Counselor in the presidency of the Church, heard the news in Pittsburgh. He had gone to that unlikely place after a long series of quarrels with Joseph, after which the Prophet had stripped him of almost all his authority; but now that Joseph was dead, Sidney felt the burden of the Church descend upon him.

Even John C. Bennett had sudden stirrings of long-dormant faith. He wrote to offer his services as President of the Church—hadn't Joseph once made him second in the kingdom? Wisely, however, Bennett did not actually enter the city of Nauvoo, and thus extended his life by many years.

Within the weeks following the martyrdom, a battle for the succession quickly developed. Three main parties emerged, each with a strong legalistic claim. Joseph had several times promised that his son, Joseph Smith III, would succeed him, a fact well known to many of the Saints. However, it had long been Church practice that in the absence of the President, the First Counselor presided—in this case, Sidney Rigdon. The third claim was the most tenuous: in an 1835 revelation, Joseph Smith had declared that the Twelve Apostles, acting as a quorum, were equal in authority to the presidency of the Church, and presided over the Church in their absence. Sidney Rigdon argued that because he was a member of the presidency, the presidency was not absent; Brigham Young, as president of the Quorum of the Twelve Apostles, held that the Presidency of the Church was dissolved when Joseph died and did not exist, and the Twelve now presided. It gets very, very intricate.

And the truth is that while the three parties were arguing legal points, the Saints would make their decision on completely different grounds. No one could seriously deny that Joseph wanted his son to succeed him—but the boy was still a child, and the Saints were not interested in being governed by Joseph's obnoxious brother William, or by the boy's mother, Emma. It was not until many years later, when Joseph III was grown, that he was set up as head of an alternative church.

The choice between Sidney and Brigham was harder. Sidney was a master orator, and he had been one of the leaders of the Church almost from the start. He had had a falling out with Joseph, his health was weak and his leadership uncertain, but the Saints still had great affection for him. Brigham Young, on the other hand, was known to be a strong and effective leader. Of all the highest men in the Church, only Brigham Young and Heber Kimball had never failed in their perfect loyalty to the Prophet. There were more than a few who disliked Brigham Young, but none who thought him incapable or suspected him of not wanting to carry forward Joseph's work.

In the confusion following the martyrdom, Dinah's decision was quick, and her reasons clear. Sidney Rigdon had rejected the Principle. Emma would certainly get rid of it as quickly as she could, if her son became titular head of the Church. Only Brigham Young was committed to preserving it, and therefore, for those who had accepted the difficult commandment, there could be only one choice. To support anyone else for the leadership of the Church would be to deny the very Principle for which, to a large degree, had cost Joseph his life.

So Dinah resolved to do all she could to help Brigham Young get control of the Church. There was a dangerous period after Sidney Rigdon arrived and before Brigham got there, during which Sidney did his best to get himself in an unassailable position. Dinah worked among the plural wives, and the plural wives pressured their husbands—delay, delay until Brigham comes. Most of the Saints still had no idea the Principle was really being lived, but the highest leaders of the Church knew the law and were, by and large, living it. Dinah's influence no doubt helped, for Sidney was held back until Brigham Young arrived, and after that Brigham was at least a match for Sidney, ploy for ploy.

The climax of the struggle came at a great outdoor meeting of the Saints. It looked like such a meeting would play into Sidney's hands—he was the orator, and Brigham was not. But Sidney was not well; Brigham stage-managed the event to advantage; and, in the end, God was on Brigham's side.

Or so the story goes. In the mythology of Mormonism, while Brigham Young was speaking to the Saints, the people saw him change before their eyes. Instead of Brigham, it was Joseph Smith talking to them; then the vision faded, and it was Brigham Young again. The Lord's intent had been made plain. The mantle of the Prophet had fallen upon Brigham Young. He was the chosen leader, and the Saints voted overwhelmingly to follow him. Sidney Rigdon faded into obscurity, as far as the Mormon Church was concerned, and Brigham Young became one of the great figures of American history—or American legend, at least.

The problem with this story is that no one seems to have seen this vision at the time. All the accounts of the miracle were written down as remembrances, years later. The contemporary journals say nothing about it. One would think a mass vision of that sort would at least get mentioned; there would at least be some record of people talking about it. And yet the story does not seem to be a fabrication, either. The people who wrote about it in later years were honest men and women, and few of them had any reason to lie.

It was in Dinah's journal that I found a possible answer for such a contradiction:

Meeting today in the grove. Spent all morning and all dinner hour talking to people. Told them to choose as Joseph would have them. What is good for the ch[urch]? What will help the k[ingdo]m survive? Must have repeated 100 times what Heber told me yesterday—when Brigham speaks, it is Joseph you are hearing. I can not tell whether my work had any influence. It is surely God's will and the Spirit must do more than my words. Never the less, vote unanimous for B[righam] Y[oun]g. The Pr[inciple] will endure.

To me this is at least an adequate explanation of the myth. No one is lying. Many of the Saints listened to Brigham Young with the idea already planted that when he spoke, it was Joseph Smith talking to them. They were not confused—they knew it was a figure of speech. Yet as they talked about the experience to others, they used the ready-made language that Dinah and Heber had given them. The figure of speech became cliché; the cliché began to be taken as literal truth; and as memories grew faded, the figure of speech took the place of memory and the one certain thing that witnesses could say was that, whatever else was said and done that day, when they watched Brigham Young, it was Joseph Smith they saw.

I made a mistake when I found this in Dinah's journal. All excited, as we amateur historians invariably are, I mentioned the discovery to a few dozen people working there in the Church Archives. The next day, Dinah's journal was unavailable for my use. It was being "microfilmed." Neither the book nor the microfilm ever appeared.

At first I was angry. How dare they suppress truth, I thought. But in the months since then I have come to understand that there are different kinds of truth.

To me, the truth is What Actually Happened. Yet it is impossible to know anything approaching the whole truth about past events. Even the people living them could not possibly understand. That truth is always out of reach.

To the guardians of the myth who pulled Dinah's journal from public access, the only truth that matters is the survival and continuation of the Church. For the Saints to have the kind of trust in their leaders that binds and has always bound them together into one of the most unified communities in the world, they must believe that their leaders are chosen by God. The kind of political struggle that went on after Joseph Smith's death seems to call that into question. Even the legalistic view of the Twelve as successor to the President is not enough to balance that. The direct intervention of God is the only view of that time that promotes the faith of today. And to those whose responsibility is the preservation and growth of Mormonism, the myth of the Mantle of the Prophet is far truer than the version I believe in.

I'm not even sure I believe in my version, anyway. History is never anything more than an imaginative reconstruction of the past. Some of it is better than the rest. But how do you decide which is good history, and which bad? I'm pretty sure I know what Dinah Kirkham's answer would have been. If she had heard me babbling a theory that undermined the mythic view of the succession of Brigham Young, and if she thought my theory might be believed because of her diary, she would have walked to thé shelves herself and burned the offending book, even though it was the only tool I had to reconstruct her life in these pages. For she never regarded the facts of her life as being important at all. Only the Church mattered. Only the future was true. I think perhaps I love my ancient aunt too much now—I would like her to approve of what I've done.

—*O. Kirkham, Salt Lake City, 1981*

≫ 47 ≪

Exodus
Nauvoo, 1846

JOHN KIRKHAM WAS THE first of his family to leave Nauvoo. The decision was forced on him early. As it became more and more obvious that the Saints would be forced to leave the city, there began to be less and less money to spend on luxuries like portraits. By the end of 1844, John had no income at all. And as the winter went on, he realized that there would be no income for him as a painter for years to come—if he remained with the Church. Out west it was desert country. Out west everyone would have to scrabble for survival. There'd be a need, not for eyes that saw truth and beauty, but for eyes that saw usefulness and fertility.

In the spring of 1845 he packed.

"Where are you going?" Anna asked him.

"I've lived on Charlie's charity long enough," John said. "I've had two requests for portraits from Chicago. I'm going there. I'll send for you when I'm making enough money to support us both."

She did not believe that he would ever send for her. He could see it in the distant expression on her face. To her it was just another abandonment, and this time she was determined not to care. "Do what you like," she said.

She let him kiss her good-bye.

"You don't believe me," John said, "but this time I *will* succeed. And I *will* send for you."

"But will I come?" she asked softly.

He looked at her face, the way it was getting lined and loose with age, though she was only forty-six years old. All the best years gone, John realized, hers as well as mine. But still, that doesn't mean there can't be good years. I've learned some lessons. I'm not a child now, at last I'm not a child, and I *can* be a good husband for you. Not here, not with the Church. Maybe in Chicago. If not there, New York or Boston or Washington. I *can*.

"I hope you will," he said.

He looked out the window of the coach as it rolled through Nauvoo on the way east. He had no regrets about leaving the place. Joseph had forgiven him for his adultery, but it had stood as a barrier between him and everyone else since then. Or maybe it wasn't the knowledge that he had gone awhoring. Maybe it was just the fact that he was a painter, that his whole life was just making pretty pictures to hang on walls. These practical people just couldn't understand a grown man spending all his time doing something so useless.

Between the buildings he caught glimpses of the Temple; the walls were now up, and the roof was going on. These people *should* have understood him, for they were much more like him than they knew. The mobs were gathering outside the city again; they meant to drive the Mormons into the river if they could not get them out any other way; that Temple would have to be abandoned, and soon, unless the Saints figured out a way to carry ten thousand tons of limestone with them into the west. Yet there they were, working harder than ever to get it finished. Joseph's Temple would be built, it would be dedicated, or they would die trying. And they wondered why John Kirkham had to paint. Maybe there was some difference between them, but if there was, John couldn't figure it out. Soon enough he stopped trying. The Temple was out of sight, and the city at the foot of the lake would soon become his home.

People didn't care so much about God there. John would get along.

Almost as soon as Joseph and Hyrum were buried, Charlie had begun dismantling his factory. Because he acted so quickly, he got good prices for his soap- and candle-making equipment. Within a few months, when everyone in Nauvoo was trying to sell their goods to raise money for the westward trek, people lost everything they owned for a few hundred dollars cash. Charlie had memorized Adam Smith as a child; he could not easily be taken by surprise.

The wheelwright business he kept, and expanded into a full-fledged wagon-making shop. There was good business in Nauvoo for a wagonmaker.

When Father left Nauvoo, Charlie took his mother in. Soon Dinah also moved in, and both their little homes were sold for what cash they could bring. Dinah, Sally, Harriette, and Anna began working constantly on sewing canvas wagon covers. The whole family became a thriving business. Someone looking on might well have thought that Charlie was the consummate profiteer, making a fortune from his people's distress.

Whoever thought that would have been wrong. Charlie was selling the wagons for barely enough to feed his workmen and his family. He sold wagons on credit to Saints that he knew would never have the money to pay. He watched his account books go deeper and deeper into the red, and cared not at all for the impending ruin, as long as he had cash to buy lumber to make the wagons. The Saints would need his wagons, and so his wagons would be there.

If he had learned one thing from Joseph's death, it was this: that even a good man who loves his wives and children can die. When the news came from Carthage, Charlie did not even weep. Just spent the day playing with his three one-year-old sons. Early in 1843, Sally had borne him twins, and within a week Harriette had given him another son. Sally's boys were named Joseph Smith Kirkham and Hyrum Smith Kirkham. Harriette's son was Nephi Clinton Kirkham. They all walked at nine months, and by the time of the martyrdom they were beginning to talk. The day the news came, Charlie played as if to put a lifetime's worth of it into one afternoon. They ran around and around in the yard, weaving in and out among the stacks of lumber and of finished wheels. He tossed them up into the air and caught them; let them grab on his coat and pull him down into the dirt and wrestle with him; let them teach him all their fingerplays. Harriette and Sally, weeping in grief at the death of the brothers in Carthage, were far more comforted by Charlie's frenetic playing than they would have been if he had tried to find words to comfort them.

The change in him was not a fleeting thing. He kept his sons with him as much as possible. They toddled around with him through the shop; he did his books almost always with at least one child on his knee, and never scolded unless they spilled the ink. People got used to seeing him on errands in the town, his shay aswarm with boys climbing in and out while he was inside doing business.

He also changed toward Sally and Harriette. He was more affectionate. He was with them more often. He listened much more seriously to their problems; he sought out their advice for his own. It was as if he no longer felt the need to rule in his home; now he merely wanted to live in it, and live happily, and let them show him how.

In the spring of 1845, he introduced his family to a thirty-four-year-old woman named Maria Jones. She was a widow; her husband and children had been murdered in the persecutions in Missouri. She was frightened; it was happening again. Within days it was clear to Sally and Harriette what Charlie had in mind, and they gave consent. He married her, though she was so much older than the rest of the family; she took her place with a needle, stitching canvas, and the family upheld her as the fear in the city grew. She changed the family almost unobtrusively; with her there it was impossible for anyone in the household to regard their problems as real suffering. And her growing hope in a time when the rest of the city was despairing helped the Kirkhams to run against the grain. They managed to be glad.

By the fall of 1845 the financial situation was getting desperate. No one was giving credit to anyone in Nauvoo. Charlie had to pay cash for any lumber that he got, and now most of the lumbermen were trying to get him to take green wood. Charlie knew that wagons built with wood that hadn't been properly aged would soon be worthless—he refused the wood. His stockpile diminished. He called together his wives, his sister, his mother and told them the problem.

"What do you want us to do?" Harriette asked.

"We have one stockpile of good lumber that we haven't touched yet," Charlie said. "But it's as much yours as mine."

"Whatever it takes to make good wagons," Sally said, "we'll do."

So the family moved into the cramped space above the factory, and Charlie's workmen carefully dismantled Charlie's house. He still made wheels and axle-trees out of the little good new lumber he could get, but the wagons that rolled away from his factory had boxes floored with floorboards from his house, and the white clapboard sides of his wagonboxes became at first a joke and then a mark of pride among the Saints.

When at last the mobs delivered their ultimatum in the dead of winter in the first months of 1846, Charlie's family left behind the ruins of a house and an empty factory for his creditors to fight over. Their four wagons were filled with supplies enough to support the families of five of Charlie's workmen; eventually the supplies were stretched to save the lives of twenty other families. Charlie drove the first of his wagons out onto the Mississippi ice himself. His sons, now almost three years old, shouted with excitement and jumped up and down in the wagonbox behind him. It was the best day of their lives so far. And their father was not far from sharing their opinion.

Brigham Young was standing on the western shore to greet the wagons. He waved to Charlie as he neared the roadway up the bank, and cried out, "Blessed is the man who has a quiver full!" Charlie waved back, his sons cheered, and Charlie's workmen brought the rest of his wagons up the road behind him.

John's letter arrived the day that Anna was to leave. She held it in her hands, not even rereading it, just stood there in the middle of the empty factory until Dinah came back into the house to fetch her.

"Mother," she said, "they say the ice could break up this afternoon. If we're going to cross at all this week, we have to cross now."

"Someone dropped the letters by," Anna said. She held out her husband's letter. Dinah read it.

"I never thought he'd do it," Dinah said.

Anna smiled. "Neither did I." That was the one thing she had counted on—that when John left her this time, he had left for good. There was no room in her plans for this.

"What are you going to do?"

Anna took the letter back and looked at it, hoping to find somehow the answer written in the brief paragraph.

> I have ten commissions already, and enough money to rent a decent house. I am ready for you now. If you need help with fares to come, write and I can easily borrow enough for that.

That was all. It seemed not to occur to him that she would not come. He was proud of himself; he signed the letter "your husband John," and Anna could see in the words "I am ready for you now" a declaration of—of what? Adulthood?

But he had been gone nearly a year, and in that time Anna had become a part of Charlie's household. She was not like Dinah, following a separate path even while fitting in with Charlie's wives and children. Anna felt sometimes like another child in the home; she did her work, but never had to make any decisions, and was free to give affection and receive it without any responsibilities at all. She did not regard it as a loss. She regarded it as the first happy year of her life, at least that she could remember. She had been a parent for so long; it was good to leave that duty to her children. Charlie and Dinah were so strong that Anna didn't need to be.

What was John offering that made it inconceivable to go to him? She was not afraid of struggle or hard times—there would be no lack of those in the journey west. But that struggle would be somehow outside her. She would do her assigned duty, and someone else would make sure that it turned out all right. That was it. After doing her best, someone else would make sure that her best was good enough. It was too late for John and her; she had gone to that well once too often, and she was dry. She thought of him and yes, she still loved him. But she no longer wanted to live with him. She wanted, now, to be carried along in someone else's current, to drink from someone else's fountain.

She carefully folded the letter. She opened her bag, which was sitting on the well-swept floor. They had left the factory clean. Pride insisted on that. From the bag she took the wooden box where she kept all the forbidden treasures that were behind her now. She set John's letter inside.

"What's in that box, Mother?" Dinah asked.

"Letters."

"But I thought I saw Robert's handwriting."

"Oh, yes. He's written to me several times."

"You never told me."

"Should I have?" Anna wondered if she had done wrong.

Dinah shook her head. "I suppose not. How is he?"

"He stood for Parliament."

"And?"

"He lost. He makes speeches. He's very, very rich. He has seven children, and Mary is well and happy. John's son Corey ran away from home. Robert didn't seem surprised."

Anna waited. If Dinah asked, then she would tell her.

Dinah asked. "And Val and Honor?"

Anna reached into the box, shuffled through the letters. Near the bottom she found the letter she was looking for. It was in Matthew's handwriting. She held it out to Dinah.

Dinah looked at it as if she were afraid to touch it. "What does it say?"

"He will let you attend any Church you want. He wants you to come home to your children. Val wrote a little letter at the end. His father must have told him what to say. Don't read it."

Still Dinah did not take the letter. "How long ago did it arrive?"

"Six months or so after the Prophet was killed."

"Why didn't you give it to me?"

"Because you were happy." Again Anna studied her daughter's face. Did I do wrong? Your life is chosen, it is lying before you—do you want to go backward on the path now? "When John came home," Anna asked, "was it good for you?"

Dinah took the letter from her, opened it and read. When she got to Val's childish scrawl tears slipped down her cheeks. Anna noticed how, once a tear had taken a certain route, all the tears afterward went the same way. Curious.

"Should I go to John, do you think?" Anna asked.

Dinah folded up her letter, handed it to her mother. "No, Mother."

"And I don't think the celestial wife of Joseph Smith can

go to Matthew Handy, and rear his children, and be a quiet wife in a Manchester home."

"No, Mother." Dinah took the box, closed it, dropped it back into Anna's bag. Anna felt her daughter's arm around her trembling as they walked out of the factory together.

Dinah stopped at the gate in the picket fence in front of where the house had used to be. Anna also looked back at the foundation stones, still crisply arranged in their neat rows, marking off too small an area to have ever been that lovely, lovely place.

"No regrets?" Dinah asked.

For a fleeting moment Anna heard her voice as if she were a little girl. It shouldn't have stirred such memory. Dinah had never asked Anna for advice when she was young; why should it seem familiar now? Yet it *was* her little girl beside her, and Anna was her wise mother, if only for a moment. She must answer her daughter truthfully. "I treasure my regrets," Anna said. "I worked so hard to earn them. They're all that makes my memories worth keeping."

They looked at the bare ground, the empty factory, the neat piles of scrap wood for only a few moments more. Then they went to Charlie's shay, got in, and Dinah drove south, into the emptying town.

Dinah drove briskly along, despite the ruts in the ice-crusted snow that made the shay bounce murderously. After the day Dan drove her to Warsaw, Dinah had made sure she learned how to handle the vehicle herself. There was no business in the cold winter streets, though it was a business day. All the traffic was riverward, or up and down the hill to the Temple. It was dedicated now. They had decided to call it finished even though a good deal of furnishing and fitting was not done; God would accept as much as the mobs had let them do. Now they were doing the ordinances day and night. Dinah had helped with the endowments at first. She had even thought to stay in the city until the last of the Saints left, months from now, to help with the sacred work. But yesterday Brigham Young had accosted her after a temple session and berated her for thinking she could get out of her responsibilities.

"People are cold and hungry and sick in the camps on the other side," Brigham said. "What are you doing here where it's cozy, when you're the only woman I know who can keep their hope alive?"

In Brigham's backhanded way it was praise; it was a calling; she came back to Anna last night and announced that they were going to join Charlie at the Sugar Creek camp the next day. Mother made no argument. These days she never did. Until half an hour before, Dinah had thought her weak because of it. Now, having read what she had read, having seen the choice that Mother made, Dinah knew better. Anna had not chosen the problems in her life, but she had chosen what she would do with them, and she was not about to reverse her course now. Neither will I, thought Dinah. In the harbor at Liverpool I made my choice; I can't unmake it now.

"Why are we going south?" Mother asked.

Dinah realized for the first time that she was driving the wrong direction. The river crossing was west of their home. She shouldn't have driven south at all. Now she was near Water Street, miles out of their way.

"I think I wanted to drive by the Temple again," Dinah said. But that answer would not do. They were already well past the Temple. Then she knew. Three blocks to the west was Emma's home. She was going to see Emma.

She turned the horse, and the shay moved briskly along. Once in winter the road near Emma's house would have been a sea of mud or a treacherous slick of ice from all the traffic coming and going. Now there had been only a half-dozen visitors since the last snowfall day before yesterday. The Church was going on, and Emma was staying behind. Why have I come here? Dinah asked herself. She stopped the shay, handed the reins to her mother, and got down.

"I don't know how to handle this," Anna said.

"If the horse starts going, pull sharply and say whoa." Dinah walked toward the porch. She tried to step where other visitors had stepped, but her stride was not long enough, and she kept breaking through the crust until her boots were icy cold halfway up her calf. At last she got to the porch, still wondering why she had come.

What do I have to say to Emma? They had hardly spoken since that one quarrel in Emma's house. They had worked together in the Relief Society almost as soon as Dinah had recovered from her fall; Emma had invited Dinah to serve as secretary of the organization, and they had been courteous to each other, for Joseph's sake. For the sake of the sisters of the Church. But since the Prophet's death they had hardly seen each other. There was no conflict. They simply had no reason to be together. There was no work that brought Dinah to Emma's door; Emma had no need that would make her call for Dinah to come. Until this moment Dinah had never wasted much thought on the matter—she was too busy preparing for the exodus. Now she realized it with a sense of loss. If things had worked out better, she and Emma would have been sisters forever. Now Dinah stood on Emma's porch and was afraid to knock. They had become such strangers that Dinah did not know what to expect from her, or even what to expect from herself.

Ashamed of her own uncertainty, Dinah turned to go. She heard the door open behind her. "Dinah," Emma said.

Dinah turned, slipping a little on the ice and catching herself. "Emma," she said.

"I saw you from the window. You didn't knock."

"I thought—"

"Will you come in?"

"My mother's waiting in the shay."

"Just for a few minutes."

So Dinah waved to her mother and went inside. Emma's house surprised her. It looked oddly clean, uncluttered, prim. Suddenly Dinah realized that this is how Emma always wanted her home to be, except that Joseph's work made it impossible. Everything was in its place. Everything was under her control. It was small, but it was, triumphantly, her own.

"I see you like my home," Emma said.

"It will be a while before I have a home again."

"Brigham wants me out of this one, too. It seems it belonged to the Church, not Joseph."

Dinah winced with embarrassment. Brigham undid much of his own good work with his insensitivity to what was proper and decent. "I'm sorry," she said.

"Oh, I've given up being sorry about things," Emma said. "I refuse to poison my life with hatred."

Dinah could hear the pain of regret, the poison of hatred behind the words. It was not hypocrisy, though. Emma was merely stating her intention as if she had already accomplished it, that's all. And Dinah had no doubt that Emma would some-day succeed in forgiving Brigham Young for having supplanted her son in the leadership of the Church; that she would someday forgive herself for having wasted her last years with Joseph in a futile struggle over polygamy. But Dinah suspected that Emma would never forgive Brigham for trying to evict her from her house; nor would Emma forgive herself for having written to Joseph, bringing him back across the river to his death.

"It's the small things that are unbearable, I think," Dinah said. "The large ones are too hard to hold."

"Yes," Emma said. "Can I give you something to drink?"

"No, thank you. Emma, I don't know why I came. I was heading for the river. This is far from the quickest way there."

"You're leaving today? I thought you were in charge of washings and anointings at the Temple."

"Brigham—Brigham wants me to go."

That was all the difference between them now. What Brigham wanted, Dinah would do.

"Dinah," Emma said, "do you ever miss him?"

It was a brave thing for Emma to ask. It deserved a truthful answer. "I miss him less now than when he was still here. I used to wait in my cabin, wondering if he would come and see me. I used to save up things to say to him." Now, Dinah thought, now I say everything to him as I think of it. I catch myself talking to him all the time, under my breath, my lips moving. People think I'm losing my mind, talking to myself. I'm just telling Joseph everything. I even joke with him. He laughs, I know he's listening to me; I'm sure of it except when I think about it. That's the way I get by without going mad with missing him. I go a little bit crazy, that's all.

Emma smiled wanly. "It wasn't so much different for us, then. Even when he was here, he wasn't here. I had to take what was left over between meetings. Sometimes I was even jealous of my children. They had more time with him than I had." Emma laughed bitterly. "I might have done things dif-ferently, if I had known how little time there was. It might have gone so differently."

"No," Dinah said. "Not if you were still you, and Joseph still Joseph."

Emma looked off toward a side window. Dinah thought she saw a glint of light from her eyes. "I think that was the problem.

Joseph needed a better wife than me."

Dinah knew now why she had come. She got up from her chair, walked behind Emma, put her hands on the woman's shoulders, gently touched her, comfortingly. "Emma, in all his life, the one thing Joseph did that he knew he had done exactly right was marrying you."

Emma made a small sound in her throat.

"Joseph loved you more than anyone but the Lord. You bore him all the children that he knew. No one ever moved you from your place in his heart."

Emma was weeping. Dinah tasted the words she had said in her own mouth. What was so sweet to Emma was pure bitterness to her; if the words had not come to her lips from the Lord, Dinah would never have said them, for she didn't want them to be true. Yet they *were* true, and Dinah did not shrink from it. The Lord had brought her to Emma's house to say it. Now it was said, and Dinah could go.

She stopped at the door, for Emma was speaking to her. "I don't believe," she said with a tremulous voice, "I don't believe that Joseph ever had another wife." The words cut deeply into Dinah; it was the last thing she would have thought that Emma might say, especially after the comfort Dinah had given her. "I was his only wife!" Emma insisted. "He was a true prophet and I was his only wife!"

Dinah walked out and closed the door behind her. She was shaking with rage; it was hard for her to walk. How could Emma dare to say that to her? But by the time she reached the shay, she knew: Emma would not have dared to say anything else. A lie she could live with. What she could not live with was a memory of Dinah as her husband's wife and, at the same time, as her true friend. Emma had chosen to remember Dinah as her friend. So be it, Dinah thought. We all have to find our own way through the world.

She drove north to the road across the ice into Iowa. The ice was groaning, and the men there almost didn't let her across. They only let her go because the shay was so light. Dinah and Anna reached the other side safely, and rode directly to the camp at Sugar Creek. It was the place where Saints who were ill-supplied and unprepared waited until they could move on. The only virtue of Sugar Creek was that it was out of the reach of the mob. It was still well within the reach of fear, of misery, of hunger, sickness, and death. Dinah could see at once why

Brigham had wanted her there. And as if to prove to any doubters that the move was irrevocable, that afternoon the ice broke up and the river was uncrossable by any means for many days.

There were twenty burials that week in Sugar Creek—twenty that Dinah knew about. The ground was too cold for proper graves; the Saints cut the earth as deep as they could, then covered the bodies with stones to keep out the animals. The hardest thing was burying the babies. Those were the ones that Dinah allowed herself to weep for. The others had all freely chosen their lives. Their deaths were offered up as sacrifices to God. But the babies chose nothing, and now would never choose, and Dinah wept for them.

But it did not break her heart. Nothing broke Dinah's heart. She went through the camp at Sugar Creek, smiling, saying prayers, giving blessings, midwifing births, and especially taking note of who was starving but too proud to ask for help. Brigham had asked her to report such cases directly to him. "I want to make sure that people like that survive," he said. "Otherwise we'll end up with a Church full of complainers and a cemetery full of Saints, and frankly I'd rather see it just the opposite."

After the morning's visits through the camp, Dinah knew of two families that had eaten nothing since two days before. The supply wagon Charlie had left behind for her was nearly empty now; she had to go to Brigham for immediate help, instead of staving off the most urgent need herself.

Anna was in the tent, coughing violently.

"I have to go see Brother Brigham," Dinah said.

Her mother only coughed. She had had a chronic cough since Dinah could remember—people who lived long in Manchester usually did. But the cough was getting worse. The hard winter in a makeshift camp, on low ground where there was almost always morning fog—it made everyone who was sick at all get sicker. Dinah worried about Mother sometimes, when she had time to worry. "Are you all right?" Dinah asked.

"Just the cough I got in Manchester. Coal smoke." Anna coughed again.

"If anyone comes, tell them I'll be back before dark, unless they've moved unusually far today."

Anna nodded, and Dinah left.

The shay made good time over the wintry road. In a way it was frustrating that the advance company of the Saints had made so little progress in the last three days that Dinah, in Charlie's one-horse vehicle, could overtake them in only a few hours of urgent driving. But the horses pulled the wagons very slowly, and tired quickly. They were discovering that although oxen pulled slower than horses, they held up better and by day's end were invariably stronger than any horse. Bit by bit the Saints were learning what nomad nations had learned long ago: endurance is speed.

Brigham sent his wagons ahead and sat on horseback to converse with her. She was surprised—it should have taken only a moment to write the names and get her estimate of what was needed. And in fact they finished with that in the first few minutes. That was not what Brigham meant to talk to her about.

"Several of the Brethren and I have been concerned," he said, "about Joseph's and Hyrum's widows. The plural ones, that no one knows about except us who live the Principle. No one thinks of them as widows, don't you see. There was some opinion that as celestial wives for eternity, they couldn't re-marry, seeing as how if they had two husbands it would make a hell of a mess to sort out in heaven—which wife belongs to which man, that kind of thing. But it occurred to us that if we have the authority to seal a man and woman together in eternity, we certainly have the authority to seal them together in plural marriages for this life only, till death do them part. Even though none of us are exactly prosperous at the moment, we've decided that to give these women proper protection, and to raise up a progeny for Joseph and Hyrum, we're willing to marry their widows during this mortal life. The reason I'm telling you is to see what you think."

"Are you asking my opinion on a matter of doctrine, Brother Brigham?"

"I never have before, and I don't aim to start now. What I'm asking is, do you think these women will accept?"

"Is this the will of the Lord, Brother Brigham?"

"I'm not the prophet that Joseph was, Sister Dinah, but I know good sense when I hear it, and good sense is always the will of the Lord."

"Try to sound a little more definite, and I think that after due consideration almost all of the widows will accept."

"What about you?" Brigham asked.

"I'll encourage them to accept. I think it's sensible myself."

"That isn't what I was asking."

I know what you were asking, Brigham, and I'm saying no. "Brother Brigham, you called me away from the Temple to serve the Saints at Sugar Creek, not to be taken care of by a husband. Am I doing what the Lord wants me to do?"

"Yes."

"Then don't trouble me with distractions. Send me what supplies you can. Loaves and fishes especially, if you can spare any." She clucked, and the horse started forward. She caught only a glimpse of Brigham's face. He was angry. Well, let him be angry. Let him stew over it for a week. I buried a husband a year and a half ago, and fourteen babies just this week, and I'm trying to feed five hundred people with provisions enough for two hundred, while they're dying of as many diseases as they can think of. It's a poor time to propose marriage. Brigham never has had much of a sense of proper timing.

Still, she might have been more polite about the way that she turned him down. It *was* a proposal of marriage from a proud man, after all. She was in a bad mood. She planned how to apologize to him. And then just after dark, when she got back to her tent, she forgot all about Brigham Young. For there were two sisters in the tent, preparing her mother's body for burial. Even though Dinah had long since stopped depending on her mother, still it had never occurred to her that her mother could ever break, that anything would be too much for her. Anna Kirkham had lived through terrible suffering and came out stronger than ever, always stronger than ever. Who would have thought hunger and cold weather in Sugar Creek would take her?

Yet Dinah did not cry. Now of all times she had to serve the people who watched her, looked to her for strength. She led the singing of the hymn at the brief services for those who had died that day, and her voice did not break. She made her full round of visits through the camp, and was still awake when the supply wagon came, so she could see to it the food was distributed according to real need, and not just to those who asked the loudest. It was well after midnight in the bitter cold, with the camp still and no one but a few sentinels about, when Dinah sat alone beside the fire and gave a few tears to her mother, and remembered her as she was the day they put their belongings in the cart and moved to the vile cottage by the River Irk. The way she argued with the carter, the way she cleaned up the filth downstairs and insisted on living as civilized people despite their poverty. She remembered her mother standing on the stairs with a drunken man trying to come up. Dinah and Robert had crept out, terrified, but they knew from their mother what they ought to do. Never surrender. Kill or die if you had to, but never, never give up. She remembered the man crying out as he fell backward down the stairs, his whimpers as he ran away. So much for you, death. So much for you, despair. And Dinah smiled, and her grief was purged enough to bear.

Then she went back into the tent, searched in her mother's bag, found the box of letters, and emptied it into the flames. Almost at once she snatched one letter out, blew on it until it no longer burned, and then tore off the childish scrawl at the bottom. That part she put back into the box; the rest of the letter joined the others in the fire. All the might-have-beens did not so much as turn the fire blue. Just a minute's brighter flare, and they were ash.

Dinah did not lie awake afterward. She did not even think about the empty bed beside her, where her mother had slept the night before; where her mother had died today. She had to get what sleep she could, for her work would begin at dawn tomorrow, and she could not afford to be weak in the morning.

❧ 48 ❧

Dinah Kirkham
Winter Quarters, Iowa, 1846

DINAH COULD NOT HELP but look ahead. Not that she didn't have enough to keep her busy in the present—all the way across Iowa she had nursed the sick, dressed the dead for burial, encouraged those whose courage failed—but she knew that things would change here in Winter Quarters. Things were already changing. Now in its second spring, Winter Quarters was becoming a city. A tent city, but much more permanent than the way the Saints had lived out of wagons during the weeks of travel across Iowa. The last of the Saints were out of Nauvoo now. And, miraculously, the living who arrived outnumbered the graves left along the road from Sugar Creek to here. Now the companies of fifty families were becoming stable; people were ordering their lives in new patterns. It was good, Dinah knew that; but she also knew she was a woman alone, and the patterns were growing up without her.

The idea of being alone did not terrify her. She liked it in many ways. Her work was demanding and she had no distractions. More, there was no conceivable way that any other man could take Joseph Smith's place. The problem was that she could see the end of her work ahead. All the widows of Joseph Smith that she knew about had found other husbands. Not celestial husbands, of course, for they would all belong to Joseph forever. Their husbands took them as plural wives for this mortal life only, to care for them and raise up children to be part of Joseph's eternal progeny. And Dinah saw that the women who had taken Brother Brigham were already taking ascendancy in the Church. The wife always shared in the station of her husband—that was a law for the whole world. In the Church, it held as much for plural wives, too. It had been the same in Nauvoo, she saw now. She had sustained Joseph, yes, but Joseph had sustained her as well.

She was not ambitious. She examined her own heart and was sure that she was not thinking of marriage only because she wanted to make sure she was at the center of power. In her life she had never thrust herself forward, had been content to minister quietly to those who needed her. Prominence had been a gift of God to her; perhaps also a curse, but still not something she had fought for or even dreamed of. Her only reason for wanting to ensure for herself a position of influence was that without it, she would not be able to keep her promise to Joseph. She had already done her best to make sure the Church was led by a man who would continue the Principle, the only man who was strong enough to hold the Saints together. But that was done now. What else would she live for? How else would she be Joseph's true wife, if not by being a leader among women, helping to strengthen the Saints and so strengthen the Church from the heart outward? She had no orphaned children to rear, as Hyrum's widow Mary had. She had only a motherless Church, which had been given to her to nurse, to raise up in place of her own lost children. If she did not have that anymore, she did not know what her life would then be for.

She had not been wrong to reject Brigham Young at Sugar Creek—the man had no sense of proper timing. Now was the right time to accept his proposal, if she was to live the only life she could conceive for herself. It had been almost a year since his proposal, of course, and he might not want her anymore. That, however, was in the hands of God—if God wanted her in the role she chose, Brigham would accept. If not, then she would try to find another path for whatever years she had ahead of her.

There was only one drawback. Much as she respected Brigham Young, she did not like him much. He hadn't the gentle heart that Heber Kimball had; he seemed much more full of himself, much more certain that if he and God ever disagreed, it was God who would have to go back and think it through again. Keeping her position of preeminence among Mormon women might not be worth it, if being married to Brigham Young was the price she had to pay.

As if Providence were determined to make her choice more difficult, Heber proposed to her before she could get an appointment to talk to Brigham Young. It was the first day of April, and she was walking along the bluff overlooking the miserable mudwash they called the Missouri River, trying to discover if this was what passed for spring in this flat country. To Dinah, spring had always been a certain sort of bird, trees greening up, blossoms surrounding her. Here it was the grass getting some green around the roots, the rodents getting feisty on the prairie, and rain instead of snow when anything came out of the sky at all. Across the river she could see the wooden markers of the cemetery. It was the closest thing to a forest this place could claim. And she knew there were three bodies for every grave that was marked.

So she wasn't in a cheerful mood when Heber rode up on a horse that danced in the most annoying way.

"You shouldn't walk out here alone!" he called. "There *are* Indians, you know."

"Can't you get your horse to hold still?" she retorted.

"It's happy. It's spring."

"Is that what they call it?"

Heber dismounted and walked beside her, leading the horse. For a few minutes he said nothing at all. She wondered if somehow he had learned to respect other people's silence. Soon enough she discovered that he was trying to figure out the delicate way to say something difficult.

"Sister Dinah, you ought to marry me, you know." Apparently he had given up and said it in the way that came naturally.

"Because you're such a fine strapping young buck?"

"That was Vilate's reason, but you come too late now. No, you ought to marry me because you know you're going to have to marry somebody, and I'm the only man I know who isn't scared to death of you."

She chose to ignore the last comment. "Why do I have to marry somebody?"

"Who's going to have time for a widow when we're breaking virgin ground? You going to go around with a bucket and plead for donations? Or do you plan to do your own plowing?"

"I might." Of course that was absurd. She was just being defiant and knew it. "I can live with my brother Charlie."

"A brother's a brother. A husband's something else."

"I never thought of it that way."

"Your brother's first duty is to his wives. You'd be in the way and you know it."

"I've had a shortage of other offers."

"Like I said. They're afraid of you. Well, you don't think it's because you aren't pretty, do you! Dammit, woman, you're still the prettiest girl in the camp, and there are some pretty women here."

"Brother Heber, I thought you had enough wives by now to keep you cooled off, even in the springtime."

"I'm just saying I wouldn't be marrying you out of charity. I can tell you this, too. I've loved you dearly ever since I baptized you, and Vilate—to tell you the truth, she brought it up herself. Said it was a damned shame that of all the widows left behind by the martyrdom, you were the only one who was still alone. She said she thought the family that had you would be the luckiest in the Church."

"Vilate thinks more highly of me than I deserve."

"That's what I told her, but she insisted."

Dinah laughed in spite of herself.

"What I proposed was marriage."

"There'd be no purpose in it, Heber. I'm barren as a brick."

"I already knew that. Furthermore and besides, you knew I knew it. So don't go trying to make up reasons just to get rid of me."

"I'm sorry, Heber."

"Is it someone else? Not that I'm jealous, mind you. Just curious."

"Yes, it is."

"And Brigham told me he had no intention—"

"Not Brigham. Joseph."

Heber stopped abruptly, and his horse ran into him. It nearly knocked him down. "Sister Dinah, you can't tell me you mean to stay single just because——"

"Heber, I just mean to tell you that I'll marry the man I think that Joseph would want me to marry. I made some promises to him, and I have to marry a man who'll give me the means to keep them. If I married again for love, or even for good company, I'd have said yes fifteen minutes ago and we could have saved ourselves a lot of breath."

He stood there nodding, looking thoughtful. Looking a little sad, too. "You know," he finally said, "I'm just giving you my opinion, but it's the honest truth. I think it's a shame that after all you've been through, after all you've given up or lost or gone without in your life, I think it's a damned shame that you still have to bend your life to fit other people instead of going straight ahead with what makes you happy."

It touched her that he cared for her so much; she leaned up and kissed his cheek. "Heber, you're the best man alive."

"Nothing I say is going to convince you, is it?"

"Heber, my life is going just right for the kind of person I am. It really is."

"You're happy?"

That was an unfair question. Right at the moment, no. Right at the moment she was still grieving for Joseph, still lonely for her mother, still empty in the place where her love of her own children ought to be. But happiness wasn't a momentary question. Dinah thought back to the path of her life, all its turns, and wondered which of them, even the most painful, she would choose to undo, if it meant losing all that came after. The only one she even paused over was the day that Joseph died—but that was the one thing that wasn't her own choice, not at all within her power to change. If happiness isn't looking back and being content with the road you already traveled, she told herself, I don't know what it is.

"Yes, Heber. I'm happy."

He studied her face a moment more. Then he smiled. "If you're lying, you're too good at it for me to catch." He walked around to the other side of the horse and scrambled on. Then he reached down a hand to Dinah. "Climb on up and come back to town," he said.

"Does anyone know you came out here to propose to me?"

"A couple of people."

"Then I have no intention of riding into camp behind you on a horse. Tongues would wag, Brother Heber."

"Tongues always wag!"

"I'll walk, thank you kindly, sir."

He kicked the horse's flanks and rode ahead a little way. Then he stopped and shouted back at her. "Madam, if you was my mule I'd shoot you!" She laughed at him, and he laughed back, and they stayed friends. That was what she loved most about Heber. He stayed friends.

Brigham was very busy. He put her off for three days, what with having to get ready, at last, for the first company of pioneers to leave the banks of the Missouri and head west in earnest for the Great Salt Lake Valley. It wasn't until April fourth that she got a time with him—her birthday, she remembered with sudden pleasure. I'm twenty-seven, going on ninety.

When she got into his tent, there was William Clayton, ready to take notes as with any other meeting.

"You won't be needed, Brother William," Dinah said.

William looked startled. "I stay for all the meetings."

"Not this one," she answered.

William looked at Brigham, who gave him no answer, not even a gesture. William waited a moment more, then packed up his writing kit and walked out. "I'll be just outside if you want me," he said.

"He sounds," said Brigham, "as if he thought I was entering a lion's den."

"While *I* really have. The Lion of the Lord, of course," she said, with just enough archness that he laughed.

"Let me guess what you came for. If you're asking for a place in the first company of pioneers, forget it. You're needed here, and if I had my way, which I seldom do, we wouldn't have any women in the first company at all."

"I haven't the slightest desire to be in the first company."

"What then? You said it was a matter of urgency. So important that it had to take up an hour of my few precious days before we go."

"I'm here to accept your proposal of marriage. I want the ceremony to be performed before you go."

Brigham raised an eyebrow. "Are you confusing me with someone else?"

"At Sugar Creek, in Iowa."

"That wasn't a proposal!"

"I know. It was the most cowardly display of hinting around I've ever seen. But I've decided to forgive that and marry you anyway. Unless you're going back on your offer."

"You as much as told me to drop dead!"

"I would never say such a thing to the Lord's anointed."

He roared, deliberately, though he must have known it wouldn't frighten her. "By damn, woman, I have sixteen or so wives already, more or less, and I don't need more!"

"I haven't come to plead with you," she said quietly. "You made me an offer, you never withdrew it, and now I'm accepting it. Come now, take your medicine like a man. Marrying me is not like marrying a rattlesnake, you know."

"The dissimilarities are only superficial."

"You consider yourself a good judge of men, I think. How good a judge of women are you?"

"Now, don't put it on that basis, Sister Dinah. You know that I know there's no finer woman in this Church for the sorts of things you're good at."

"And I'm good at nearly everything that matters." He was getting there.

"When I proposed to you at Sugar Creek I did it with trepidation. I'm a man who likes domestic peace. Let me war with the nations, but have a quiet home."

"I rarely speak. I never raise my voice."

"When you turned me down I breathed the biggest sigh of relief you ever heard! I was facing southwest and damn near blew down every tree in the state of Missouri."

"Are you sticking by your word or not, sir?"

"I think out west I'll build a separate house, just for you. Which I'll lock from the outside, as a public service."

"Then you'll marry me?"

"Yes."

"Before you leave next week?"

"Why such a long engagement?"

Because I want to stay here in Winter Quarters as one of the President's wives. She did not say it. It was easier to deal with Brigham if he did not know what you wanted. "I'm afraid with so much else on your mind you might just forget to send for me."

"Tomorrow, then, if you want."

"Today. Before I leave this tent."

"All right, today! Call William in here, I'll have him—"

"Just a moment."

He stopped. "Having second thoughts?"

"I just have a couple of conditions for you."

"You have conditions for *me?"*

"First, that I be free to teach school or hold Church positions."

"Of course."

Patience. I'm building up to the big one. "Second, that I be allowed to publish and speak as I have always done, with no husbandly interference."

"I'm still the President. If I see false doctrine, I'll stamp it out."

"You will never see false doctrine from me. And the third condition—"

"Out of how many?" He tapped on the writing table.

"Three. You heard, I am sure, about my accident some years ago, and the service I received at the hands of Dr. Bennett. As far as I am concerned, the only reason for a woman who is eternally married to Joseph Smith to allow another husband into her bed is to raise up children for *him.* That is impossible for me. Also, I am not starved for the pleasures of the marriage bed; I've quite had my fill for a lifetime. In short, sir, this is a platonic marriage."

His eyes narrowed. "Marriage is marriage."

She couldn't help being flattered—he had been looking forward to bedding her. "You don't need me. I'm eternally married to another man. Intimacy for its own sake would be tantamount to adultery."

"That's not doctrine."

"Nevertheless, if you come near me with tender thoughts of conjugal bliss, I warn you, I'll cut it off."

"Sister Dinah, if I ever came near you it would shrivel up and fall off of its own accord!" He got up and stormed out of the tent. For a moment she thought she had pushed him too far, that he would not marry her after all. Yet she dared not be any more submissive to him, or she'd never have the freedom to do the work she had to do. Brigham was too strong a man, if once he thought he owned you. She would just have to do the best she could without being married to the President of the Church.

Then the tent door opened again, and Brigham came back with William Clayton and two other elders in tow. The marriage would take place after all. She wondered if she was relieved or disappointed. "Brethren, you are to witness an act of supreme courage. I am marrying this woman under the Principle of Celestial Marriage. However, the marriage will be for our mortal years only, since, to my blessed relief, she will be the responsibility of poor Brother Joseph in the next life. William, make it quick, I have a busy day."

Clayton fairly raced through the words—but all the words were there, and the marriage would stand. When it was over, Brigham turned to her, took her squarely by the shoulders, and kissed her passionately in full view of the other men. If he had grinned at her when he finally ended the kiss, she would have hit him, witnesses or no. But he wasn't so much as smiling. In fact, he looked furious, and he shook a finger in her face. "And don't you forget it!" he said.

He turned to the bewildered witnesses. "I have already taken as much time as I can spare on this matter. Please sign your names in the book as witnesses to this marriage."

While one signed the book that Clayton offered him, the other looked from Dinah to Brigham and said, "I'm not altogether sure I *witnessed* a marriage."

"Brother Scoville, you have more sense than I gave you credit for. You will surely rise in the kingdom. Now sign the book."

He signed, and so did Dinah and Clayton and Brigham himself. Then Brigham ushered her to the door. "I regret that I won't have a chance to see you before I go," he said. "But don't think that I won't expect a reckoning from you when I get back. I'm leaving Brother Parley in charge of this camp till I return. But I assure you that I'll be a lot easier in my mind knowing you're carrying on the work that you've been doing all these years. I am the head of this Church right now, Sister Dinah, but you are its heart. And if being married to me will help you accomplish your work, I'm glad to make the sacrifice."

So in spite of the bluster he knew what she was doing and saw the value of it. That was the first moment that it occurred to her that she might actually enjoy being married to Brigham Young. That it might not be nothing but a sacrifice. And she hoped that it might not be a pure sacrifice for him, either. After all, now and then God allows his servants a little joy on the side—why not in this?

He held out his hand to shake hers. She took it and kissed his palm. "I'll miss you, Brother Brigham," she said.

"Oh, will you?"

"Who'll roar to wake up the roosters in the morning when you're gone?"

He was still laughing when he closed the door, and she smiled too, all the way back to her tent. There was a child there waiting for her. Could Sister Dinah come? My sister's baby's coming early. Could Sister Dinah give a blessing and help with the delivery?

Sister Dinah could. The baby lived. Cried a lot, but it lived.

⇥⇥⇥ BOOK TEN ⇤⇤⇤

*In which Providence at last
frees the servants from their work.*

❧ First Word ❧

So many pages now I have written and you have read,
and yet I have barely touched the surface of the information that I have. Twenty-three notebooks are filled
with facts about Dinah and Charlie Kirkham; there are
nearly a hundred books on my shelves that I could use.
For this is exactly the point where the real documentation
begins. Till now I have pieced their story together from
hints, from scraps of information, from their own journals, from my own unreliable sense of what makes people
do the things they do. Now when they arrive in Utah the
data suddenly comes in floods. Dinah Kirkham gave
more than three thousand speeches in her life—I have
every one of them that was written down. I have the
minutes of five hundred meetings. I have the pertinent
quotations from a thousand newspaper reports and journal entries. There are essays and analyses of her life. As

for Charlie, though he was far less public, there are the journals of his children, their reminiscences, his own records of his mission to England, his financial maneuvering to save the Church from bankruptcy in 1888, an endless pile of contracts and deeds and notes and leases.

And yet I look at the page in front of me and I know that I am through. The book is finished. For there are no surprises left. Through the rest of their lives Dinah and Charlie faced an endless series of problems, but they resolved them exactly as you would expect. All the experiences that changed and shaped them are accomplished; from now on they merely continued to be themselves, and either forced the world to change a little to accommodate them, or ignored the world and let it slide on by, unnoticed and unnoticing. It mattered to them, mattered very much. But it did not change them. Their character was set; the rest, to me at least, is just endless application.

In Utah, once she got there, Dinah became preeminent among Mormon women, and something of a legend in the Church. For years Brigham Young refused to reorganize the Relief Society, perhaps afraid of setting up an organization that might compete with the priesthood. If that was his fear, it was partly justified. For when Dinah at last was allowed to reestablish the Relief Society, it at once became the Church's most effective organization. It has become a joke among the Saints: if you want anything to get done right and on time, assign it to the Relief Society. Never, though, did Dinah say or do anything to set her organization against Brigham's leadership. She argued with him, true, sometimes even in print. But she always acted for the good of the Church, and the good of the Church, to her at least, always included keeping one man at the head. Whenever it came to a choice between getting her own way and keeping Brigham's authority intact, Dinah invariably gave in. It was not weakness on her part, I think. It was strength. It was keeping her promise to Joseph. The Relief Society was not all she did, either. She was an active campaigner for temperance and women suffrage; she wrote ardent polemics and gave passionate speeches in favor of the right of Mormon women to live in polygamy if they wanted to; and above all, she remained the Prophetess, giving blessings, speaking in tongues, comforting and encouraging the Saints from Canada to Mexico.

As for Charlie, he settled into happy anonymity. He made money, but never much more than he needed to maintain his family. He married six wives and fathered twenty-nine children, and loved them all devotedly. He served a few missions for the Church, and while the general run of the Church membership never knew his name ("Oh, yes, Aunt Dinah's brother") a few of the Church leaders regularly came to him for advice on running the business of the Church. Even for advice on their own business affairs, and in fact he made more money for the Brethren than he ever made for himself. Some more dedicated businessmen couldn't understand why Charlie Kirkham was so respected—he wasn't rich and seemed to have no ambition at all. He was simply happy. Not that his life went smoothly. His fourth wife, Verda Pratt, simply could not bear the strain of plural marriage, and after several years of terrible conflict that worried Charlie endlessly and made a shambles of domestic life, she divorced him, left the Church, and took their only child, Raymond, off to San Francisco. Charlie always grieved for that one wife and that one child who were lost. He also grieved for the five children who died before him, and for Harriette, the only one of his wives who was not widowed when he died in 1896. But such griefs were no contradiction to his happiness. The Church has largely forgotten him except for one hymn that he wrote which is still often sung; to me, however, Charlie epitomizes the early Saints at their best.

I am doing what I vowed to myself I would not do when I undertook this book: I am praising instead of telling the tale. I've lived with them too long. So I'll stop my eulogy and tell you instead of the last two changes in Dinah's life. Not changes in herself, but changes in the role she had to play. They are little chapters, because they are little stories, and then I will be through.

                              —*O. Kirkham, Salt Lake City, 1981*

❧ 49 ❧

Dinah Kirkham Young
Provo, Utah, 1877

IT WAS THE LAST night away from home—tomorrow they would make the last fifty miles from Provo to Salt Lake City. Brigham would return to his official residence and Dinah to her quite unofficial one, the house that served her as home and general headquarters of the Relief Society. Brigham had taken her along to Utah's Dixie for the dedication of the St. George Temple, the first one finished in Utah. She had helped teach the sisters working there how to do their part in the ordinances. Even after the dedication, however, the work had gone on; their progress northward through Utah was like a state procession, and Dinah gave more speeches than Brigham did. She was tired. It would be good to get home.

The others rushed inside the house to get out of the dusty wind. It was Dinah's nephew Joseph's house—he was stake president and mayor in Provo, and Dinah wasn't anxious to go in, because the talk would all be Church work and in all honesty she was sick of hearing about quorums and meetings and tithing and buildings and co-ops. Besides, she loved the coming of a thunderstorm. She stood in the yard, letting the hot wind fling dust and sand against her as the clouds rolled in from the southwest. It was so dry here; she could feel how the valley waited in agony for the storm to come. It would bring life in the water that stood and soaked deep; it would bring death in the rain that cut along the surface sharp as harvest knives. She had often stood this way before, feeling the electric air in the lulls of the wind and, as always, she remembered: This is how I waited for Joseph to come to me. In love and dread, I waited for him; and this is how Joseph waited for God.

"Aunt Dinah!" It was Charlie's boy Joseph, who fancied himself a grown man now at the ridiculously childish age of thirty-four. He was far too young for his responsibilities. A man that age was still trying to figure out how to be a father.

"Aunt Dinah!" So many people called her that, and even though Charlie did his best to fill the territory with her nieces and nephews, most of those who knew her as Aunt Dinah were no more kin to her than to Chief Walker. She didn't like such overfamiliarity. It wasn't respectful of her office. But it wasn't worth quarreling about.

"Aunt Dinah." Joseph took her by the arm. "President Young is asking where you are."

"He knows where I am."

"You shouldn't be outside. There's going to be lightning."

"God has my consent to strike me down if he likes. I've been through worse."

"Were you praying out there? I didn't mean to interrupt if you were."

"No. I just move my lips when I think." They went inside.

The house was already quieting down for the night. Everyone knew that Brigham liked to retire early when he was traveling. Now he was sitting on the davenport, waiting for Joseph's wife to declare that his room was ready. His was always ready first; everyone knew that Dinah didn't mind waiting for her room until after Brigham was tucked away in his.

"Sit with me, Aunt Dinah," Brigham said when he saw that she had come inside. "Sit and speak to me of anything except religion. I already know everything about religion."

She smiled and sat by him. "You look tired," she said.

"Heavy lies the mantle of authority upon these weary shoulders. What time is it?"

"You're the one with the watch," Dinah answered.

"I'm too tired to lift it out of my pocket."

Dinah sighed and pulled it out for him. He liked to be babied. "The big hand's on seven, the little hand's pretty vague but seems to indicate somewhere between eight and nine."

"Watch how you tease me, Aunt Dinah."

"Don't *you* call me that."

"Will if I want. Maybe I'll confine you to five minutes next time I call on you to speak."

"I'd be grateful."

"It would break your heart."

Joseph walked in just then, looking flustered and embarrassed. "One of my children has some miserable disease, Dorcas tells me. We'd send the other children to sleep with a neighbor tonight but they're already asleep. My wife and I are already going to sleep in the parlor—would you mind terribly if we put you both in the same room tonight?"

Ah, the agony the poor boy was suffering. Dinah couldn't resist making it just a little worse. "Out of the question. Brigham snores as if it were his duty to rouse the dead for resurrection morning."

"I sleep the sleep of angels," he protested.

"You don't mind, then?" Joseph asked. The boy had some wit—he knew when he was being taken.

"Lay our bodies down anywhere," Dinah said.

They supped lightly. Brigham hardly ate at all, since he kept up a constant stream of anecdotes about the trip. Dinah watched him in silence. She had judged him right a thousand years ago, when she decided he was the only man to lead the Church after Joseph. He had fought off drought, the U.S. Army, apostasy, the temptation of the gold rush, and a plague of federal officials sent to Utah to enforce the antipolygamy laws, and somehow he was still alive, and so was the Church. Indeed, because of his work it looked as though the Church would live for a long time. But the sagging flesh of his face, the age spots on his hands, the sunken appearance of his eyes all testified that the Church would definitely outlive Brigham Young. Though he might surprise us all, Dinah thought, and live forever.

It occurred to her that, after all these years, she loved him. Not just as a Saint should love the prophet. Not even as the president of the Relief Society should love the President of the Church. She loved him, to her surprise, as a husband. Why haven't I noticed it before? She really ought to mention it to him before one of them died.

The supper ended. They walked upstairs—slowly, because stairs weren't easy for either of them. They closed the bedroom door behind them. And discovered that, despite their age, they were shy. The double bed was a challenge. In all their years of marriage they had never shared a bed. Brigham hadn't even tried—he hardly lacked for company. And Dinah, for her part, had never yearned for him. Until tonight. Until she stood near the door of the room and thought, Is it too late to become Brigham's wife? Joseph would not begrudge her a wife's privilege now. She was old enough not to care that it would be inconsistent of her to suggest it. An old woman had a right to be different from the young one she once was.

He noticed her eyeing the bed. "Never fear," he said. "I shall sleep before my body hits the bed."

"At least make sure you're well-aimed, then. I'm not up to lifting you."

"Turn your back, Dinah, and I'll turn mine, lest we offend by revealing our carnal secrets to each other."

Carefully they undressed with eyes averted. Chastely clad in nightgowns, they climbed into bed at the same time. "Can it bear the burden?" Brigham murmured. The bed groaned. "Have faith, little bed." Then, settled in comfortably, Brigham leaned over to the nightstand and blew out his candle.

Dinah, of course, did not blow out hers. Instead she pulled out her third book of the journey, a humorous thing called *Roughing It*. She had been told the author had some unkind things to say about Mormons. She always made it a point to read unkind mentions by popular writers.

"Don't tell me you're going to read!" Brigham said.

"I always do," she answered in surprise.

"Every night?"

"I can't sleep unless I read first. It's when I do my best studying."

"I have more respect for the cost of candlewax."

She smiled benignly, then opened the book and turned to

the passage she had left off with. In a few moments she heard Brigham begin to snore—far more loudly than nature could possibly allow.

"Deceit is beneath you," she said.

"It isn't deceit, it's retaliation. Can't sleep with a light on."

"And I can't sleep without reading. Your discomfort will end with a little patience. But if you get *your* way I'll be awake staring at the ceiling all night."

"I'm President of the Church."

"I'm a lady. Try to learn some manners."

"What's the book?"

She turned so he could see the cover. Of course, the candlelight made it a silhouette to him, perfectly black. "Tell me the title," he growled.

"*Roughing It*. By Mark Twain. He has a bit about meeting *you*. Do you remember him?"

"Mark Twain? No. Or was he—he couldn't have been that Missouri fellow?"

"He's from Missouri."

"Cocky little runt, if I remember him. Very full of himself. Seemed to think everything was quite amusing. I thought him an ass. What did he think of me?"

"He didn't like you half so well. No, I won't read it to you, you'd only get angry and torment me with your torrent of self-defense. What I intend to read you is his hideous lies about Mormon women."

"Did any of our women speak to him?"

"The Principle seemed to fascinate him. I quote: 'With the gushing self-sufficiency of youth, I was feverish to plunge in headlong and achieve a great reform here—until I saw the Mormon women. Then I was touched. My heart was wiser than my head. It warmed toward these poor, ungainly and pathetically "homely" creatures, and as I turned to hide the generous moisture in my eyes, I said, "No—the man that marries one of them has done an act of Christian charity which entitles him to the kindly applause of mankind, not their harsh censure—and the man that marries sixty of them has done a deed of open-handed generosity so sublime that the nation should stand uncovered in his presence and worship in silence."'"

She closed the book with an emphatic thump. The bed was shaking. She looked over at Brigham to see his eyes squinted closed as he shook in silent paroxysms of laughter. "It wasn't *that* funny," she said.

He only laughed harder, tears squeezing out of his eyes.

"You might think to defend the women of the Church. Or the Principle. He *is* laughing at sacred things."

"Let him laugh. I'd far rather have the world's scorn than the world's pious outrage. No one ever killed for scorn."

"I'm disappointed in you. Shall I spread the word that Brother Brigham thinks us all an ungainly lot?"

He turned on his side, facing her, and smiled. "Not all. I saw to it that he didn't ever see our real beauties."

"Hid the pretty ones away, did you?"

"Kept them all for myself. And farthest away, where none could see, I hid the sacred virgin of Manchester, who was captured away by Heber Kimball and kept untouched in the harem of the grand sultan of Salt Lake City, that vile and reprehensible Brigham Young."

"I'm hardly a virgin."

"Madam," he said, "after thirty years of abstinence, you became an honorary virgin. In another five years you become one in fact."

Since he brought up the subject, perhaps—

"I never aspired to renew my virginity," she said.

"You never aspired not to, either."

"Perhaps we're old enough to be above such things as adolescent lust."

"I have always thought that lust, like wine, matures with age."

"You're not supposed to know anything about wine," she said.

He reached and touched her arm. Instead of recoiling, which he plainly expected her to do, she leaned into his arm, bent to him and kissed him.

"Are you sure you want to go through with this?" he asked her. "I thought you never changed your mind about anything."

"Don't tell anyone," she said.

But twenty minutes later, they had to admit defeat. Brigham was dejected. "It's never happened to me before," he said.

"My fault," she said. "I'm just too old."

"Dinah, I am an expert in what happens to women of middle age when their corsets come off. You are the only one of all my wives who wears a corset for modesty rather than buttress-ing."

She chuckled.

"I wasn't being clever," he said. "We're being punished." He lay on his side and traced patterns on her skin.

"For what sin?"

"For abstinence where God never meant his children to abstain."

"So it's my fault after all?"

"You were such a beautiful girl, Dinah. But formidable. I should have braved the fortress long ago, when I still had vigor for it."

And they began to reminisce about times that had been painful to live, but were good to remember. All the time they talked, he touched her, and she caressed him in return, and after a while he smiled and said, "Miracle of miracles," and they finished what they set out to do after all.

Afterward she lay in his arms, his breath against her cheek. "If I had known you would be so lovely at fifty-eight, madam," he whispered, "I would have picked the lock of your door twenty years ago."

"And if you had come to try it, perhaps I would have let you in."

"I've loved Joseph and admired him and sometimes almost worshiped him, but this is the first time that I've envied him. You'll be his in the next life."

"You've had me as a wife longer in this one."

He kissed her lovingly. "You don't know what a crushing blow it would have been, if my failure had been more than temporary. I've been compared to Moses in other ways, but I had always hoped to earn his epitaph."

"Epitaph?"

"Deuteronomy 34:7. 'And Moses was an hundred and twenty years old when he died: his eye was not dim, nor his natural force abated.'"

"I'll see to it that it's engraved on your headstone. If they doubt it, I'll swear to it. And if I die before you, I'll leave a deposition."

"You won't die before me."

"My mother died younger than I am now."

"You're tougher than she was."

"I don't think so."

"If you plan to die before me, Dinah, you'll have to hurry."

She stroked his cheek but did not argue with him. It was true. And he needed no comfort. If any man had little cause to fear death, it was Brigham Young.

There's a voice in me, Dinah. It says Hurry hurry hurry. Hurry and get the Temple dedicated. Hurry and get the quorums reorganized. Hurry and set the order of the Twelve so John Taylor will succeed you. Hurry and set things right with your most cantankerous wife. All done now. All finished, or nearly so. And when it's done, do you know what will happen?"

Of course I do.

"He'll come for me."

"The Lord?"

"The Lord's too busy. No, the man God put at my head years ago, who has guided me ever since. Joseph. I've felt as though he is still watching over the Church, saying, No, Brigham. Careful, Brigham. What are you so timid about, Brigham? And now he'll come and say, Well, you're finally ready. Come on into the Kingdom, I've got work for you that's been piling up for years."

He smiled, but his eyes were filled with tears, as if to say, Hasten the day. He said nothing more, just lay there until he slept.

Dinah blew out her candle. But she did not sleep for a while. Just lay awake, wondering if Brigham was right. If Joseph comes for him, might he not also come for me? What will I say to him then? And as so many times before, her lips moved in silent rehearsal for that conversation, until at last she slept.

Brigham died four months later, calling out Joseph's name. Dinah was not there; she was in a meeting of the Relief Society presidency. She did not grieve; she merely thought congratulatory thoughts, and envied him a little.

The day before the funeral she submitted a letter of resignation to John Taylor, who as President of the Twelve had already taken over the leadership of the Church. The day after the funeral, the letter came back with a curt note in Taylor's own hand:

Sister Young, I am returning this letter because it is not appropriate. Upon the death of the President of the

Church, all officers who are not ordained priesthood authorities are automatically released from their positions. Therefore the office of president of the Relief Society is vacant, and with thanks for your competent service for these many years I inform you that the place will be filled by another sister.

She took it well. It was his right. It was time for someone else, and she didn't mind giving up the office. She did resent the ungenerous word *competent*, but even at that she refused to harbor ill feeling. She even understood. The Saints weren't used to anyone but Brigham at the helm; the last thing he needed was to have a woman who was called the Prophetess diluting his authority.

The only reason she reconciled herself to this change so easily, however, was because of what it surely meant. My work is finished; the Lord has released me from my duties. Now I'll have a pleasant few months in which to write some poems, read some books, plant a garden, visit Charlie and his children and grandchildren, even sleep more than five hours a night. Soon enough the Lord would take her.

After she had been out of office for a few years, people began coming to her door. Some of them were old acquaintances, wanting to know what she was doing these days. But most of them were strangers, or people she had met but once at a conference somewhere. Aunt Dinah, you changed my life. Aunt Dinah, I have a problem and I need advice. Aunt Dinah, can you give me a blessing? It was a good thing, she knew, and she enjoyed the visits, but surely this was not what God kept her alive for.

Then, in 1890, John Taylor's successor, Wilford Woodruff, gave up the struggle with the government and issued the Manifesto, renouncing the practice of the plural marriage in the Church. Then the visitors came to Dinah's door pleading for her to help them understand how God could change a law that had been so vital for so many years; or asking her to denounce the Manifesto as proof that Wilford Woodruff did not have the authority to speak for God. To all of them she said the same thing: A prophet taught us the Principle; a prophet has told us to stop practicing it. If he does not have the authority to end the practice of plural marriage, then no prophet had the authority to begin it. You cannot pick and choose among the prophet's words and take only the ones you like. Now go home and obey the Lord. They went home. Most of them obeyed the Lord. She watched the Principle fade from the Church, despite a few dying gasps, and thought: I saw it born, I saw it die, and I helped the Saints endure both passages. That must be why the Lord persists in leaving me alive. Now my work is done, and I can go.

But the Lord delayed. The Lord postponed her death. The years passed, and still she was alive. She began to wonder whether God had any sense of timing at all.

⇘ 50 ⇙

Dinah K. Young
Salt Lake City, 1896

As she walked from the carriage to Charlie's house, Dinah heard the booming of fireworks celebrating the end of Utah's direct rule by the federal government. Utah was a state, and at last the Saints would be able to govern themselves. She tried not to think of what had been given up to achieve peace with the government. The Lord moves in mysterious ways.

Children were shouting far down the street. No, not down the street. They were playing in the back yard of Charlie's house. They did not know that their grandfather—or was he their great-grandfather?—was dying inside the house. But that was right. Children should not be interrupted by death, not the death of an old man.

But he isn't an old man, she thought. He's younger than I am, and he has no business dying now. There should be some order in these things. He still has a young wife, who is pregnant with their first child. Surely God would have taken account of that and taken Dinah in his place.

She did not knock at the door—Sally always chided her if she acted so formally. Inside, there were men and women of many ages, and many children, too, sitting or standing or walking, conversing quietly or weeping or just silent, staring into space.

"Aunt Dinah," someone murmured in greeting, and then others noticed her and came to shake her hand or embrace her. Many of them were almost strangers to her. She had to ask their names. You're the one who lives in Mexico. You came all the way from Ephraim. Oh, yes, Hannah's girl, you married Peter Black's boy. Slowly she made her way to the stairs, then excused herself and began to climb. Charlie had sent for her. He wanted to talk to her before he died.

The wives were gathered in Charlie's room. Sally, Maria, Hannah. Where was Harriette? Oh, yes. Harriette died years ago. I must remember not to ask for her—it annoys the children, they think I'm losing my mind. They don't realize that when you live at the edge of death you can't possibly keep straight which of the people you know have already stepped over, and which are still lingering like cowards on the brink. At this age it doesn't make much difference, does it?

Sally, Maria, Hannah. Who was missing that should be there? The young one, of course. Gwen. She must be in the house. If she isn't here in this room it's because we're going to talk about her.

"Did you come to talk to me or admire my wives?" Charlie's voice was so soft that for a moment Dinah didn't realize he had spoken.

"You sent for me," she said.

"There weren't enough people here," he answered. She laughed. Was he smiling? Was that all the laughter he could manage now?

"Well, then, let's get on with it. What is it you want to tell me about Gwen?"

They looked startled. Dinah loved doing that. She used her brains, and they all assumed she was getting revelations.

"Her baby's not due for three more months," Hannah said. "We don't know what to do with her."

"I'm not rich," Charlie said.

"We all have children with plenty of money," Maria said. "And we're all old women. Except Gwen."

"It was stupid to marry her in the first place," Sally said. Everyone knew that she wasn't angry. She had merely become outspoken in her old age.

"No it wasn't," Charlie said quietly.

"Seventeen years old then. And doesn't have a baby till six years later. You should have listened to me, Charlie. I don't know whose timing is worse, yours or hers."

"Don't scold," Charlie said. "I wouldn't have married her if I hadn't thought I was going to live forever."

"You'll get tired," Maria told him. "Let us tell it."

"I'll be quiet," Sally said. "Then he won't get angry."

Dinah listened to their explanations, but she did not need to be told. Gwen was still young, still pretty. Charlie had no fortune to support her, only a little money when all debts were settled and the house was sold. It wasn't fair to leave her still in her youth, with a baby; she needed someone to look after her, help with the child, let her have some freedom so she might find another husband.

Charlie had married her in the last few weeks before the Manifesto. It had been common practice then for young women to marry into grand old polygamous families. Now Mormons no longer entered into polygamy. She was already a relic, and too young to live the rest of her life that way. It would be hard for her to find a young husband when she was sealed to another man. Now that a man couldn't marry several wives, young Mormons wanted to make sure their one wife was sealed to them for eternity. Otherwise she and all their children would, by the law of the Church, belong to the first husband forever.

"With all that against her," Hannah said, "she doesn't need to be tied down with a child, too."

"I should think," Dinah said, "that the child would be a comfort to her."

The wives looked at each other. Charlie shook his head. "She's a good woman, Dinah, but I don't think she wants to be a widowed mother."

Now Dinah understood why they were being so careful to explain it all to her. A decision had already been reached; they did not want advice. They didn't want someone to help Gwen out for a while. They wanted someone to take the child.

"Do I look to be the right age to take on such a responsibility?"

"My granddaughter Sally Ann lives close to you," Sally said. "She says that she'll look in on you now and then."

"Then let her take the baby."

Hannah looked at Dinah helplessly. "Dinah, Gwen says she'll only give the baby up if she gives it to you."

"Then she should keep it! I'm a doddering old woman and I'll probably be dead before Christmas."

Charlie raised a hand, beckoned to her. "Dinah," he said. "How many times have I ever told you what to do, in all our lives?"

"Never that I can remember."

"I was saving up for now."

"If you tell me that I should do it for my own good—"

"Gwen adores you, Dinah."

"I've only talked to her a few times."

"Her mother always told her as she was growing up that when Gwen was an infant, dying of a disease that made her so weak she couldn't even cry, Aunt Dinah Kirkham prayed for her, and she was healed."

"Am I to be punished for that now?" But Dinah did not feel as flippant as she sounded. She felt a circle closing around her. She felt a change coming in her life. She was not looking for any change but death.

"Gwen wants to keep the baby and sacrifice her future to rearing it. You see, she loves me. And loves the idea of a baby. She doesn't know yet that the child will grow up and leave, and there she'll be in her forties with nothing, with no one. I want her to give up my baby so she can have a life of her own. She's given enough to me these six years of marriage. To all of us."

"She's a good girl," Hannah said.

"Dinah," said Charlie. "It's killing me faster to talk so much."

"Charlie, I gave up the idea of children fifty years ago. I'm too old."

"Dinah, listen. I've been worrying about you. I kept trying to understand why God was keeping you alive so long after your life's work was over. I was praying about it. And that's when I thought of this. It's not just for Gwen. You've been Aunt Dinah to three generations of the Church. Now here it is: the Lord wants you to have a child. You will be giving a gift to Gwen and to the child and to me. Will you be like Sarah, and laugh at the Lord behind the door?"

Dinah thought of a scrap of paper that she kept in a small wooden box on her bureau at home. She hadn't read the words for years. She only looked at the childish scrawl now and then with a vague yearning that she refused to name. She named it now: Gone. Lost opportunity. The part of life that she had given up for the gospel's sake. God had given her three years of marriage to Joseph Smith, thirty years of service to the Church, and twenty years of wasted time since then. She had kept busy enough, writing reminiscences of Joseph and Brigham and Heber, writing poetry, and talking to the endless stream of pilgrims who found her door and said, You came to my mother; you blessed my brother; you spoke once and changed my life; I wouldn't be so happy today if it hadn't been for you. It was pleasant, but it was wasted time. And under it all had been this small feeling: Gone. The little boy calling out to her on the boat. The little girl crying for her mother. And now a mother wants to give her child to me.

"Do you really think the Lord wants me to do it?"

"You're the Prophetess," Charlie said. "I can't speak for the Lord. But I tell you that *I* want you to do it. I'll go a lot easier knowing Gwen is free and my child has a good mother."

"For a man who's dying you talk a lot." What would Joseph tell me to do?

"Say yes and leave me alone to be with my wives."

Joseph would say, When the Lord opens a door, a wise man walks through it. "Yes," Dinah said. Then she bent to Charlie and kissed him. "You're a good brother, Charlie. I'll miss you."

"I'll say hello to all your friends for you," he said.

She left him with his family then, and went looking for Gwen. She was not far off; she was only waiting for Dinah to leave before she went back in to be with her husband. Dinah was not halfway down the hall before she emerged from an open door.

"Aunt Dinah?" she said.

Dinah looked at her. She was well along into the pregnancy, plumping at the waist and bosom, but still thin at the face, still frail and hopeful-looking. "Why did you marry him?" Dinah asked, because old people can ask anything they like.

"Because I loved him. I never knew my father. Charlie was the closest thing I had to a father. I grew up next door."

"Yes, I knew that." Charlie had told her once—it was Charlie, wasn't it?—that Gwen had proposed to *him*. Marry me, before the church gives up the Principle. "I told him that I'd take your child, if you wanted to give it to me."

Gwen started to cry, suddenly, without restraint. In surprise Dinah held her, let her sob into her shoulder. Was she crying because she would have to give up her baby? Or in gladness that Dinah would take it?

"Thank you," Gwen said.

Gladness, then. I only wonder—will *I* be glad? And the child—will the child be glad of this?

Charlie died that night, reciting poetry up to the last moment. His last words were a poem by Herrick. Sally declared that he did it because he knew she never liked that poem.

Four months later, Gwen gave birth to a daughter and named the child LaDell. Dinah reared her from infancy. She was a bright and beautiful child, but to Dinah's surprise she learned things that Dinah never meant to teach. She learned to be stubborn; she learned to think of herself as the equal of any person or any problem. When LaDell became a woman, she went to college in New York and became a skeptic and had a love affair that went sour. Every day Dinah prayed for her and worried about her and wrote letters to her—and one day Dinah realized: For years I did all this for other people's children. This child grieves me, but she is my own, and that makes even the grief into a kind of gladness.

❧ Last Word ❧

Robert Kirkham was one of the richest men in England by the age of forty. He served in Parliament for many years, and it was thought by some that if he had not died before Gladstone he might have been Prime Minister.

John Kirkham did quite well as a painter in Chicago, and eventually had exhibitions in Boston and New York. He was planning a London exhibition when he died in Philadelphia at the age of seventy. His reputation did not long survive him.

Emma Smith eventually married a man named Lewis C. Bidamon, and was very happy. Her son, Joseph III, became president of the Reorganized Church of Jesus Christ of Latter Day Saints, and Emma claimed until she died that her husband never taught or practiced polygamy.

Heber Kimball, always Brigham's closest friend, served as President Young's First Counselor from 1847 until he died in 1868 at the age of sixty-seven, a year after the death of his first wife, Vilate.

Sally Clinton Kirkham survived her husband by only two years.

According to the Charles Banks Kirkham Family Organization, there are now more than seven thousand living descendants of Charles Kirkham, more than four thousand of whom still bear the Kirkham name.

Matthew Handy was still an executive in Robert Kirkham's railroad organization when he died of pneumonia in 1881.

Valiant Handy became a newspaper publisher in Manchester. He died in a railway accident at the age of fifty.

Honor Handy married a barrister named Hartman and lived in London until her death in 1926. She learned in 1919 that her mother was still alive, but too late to communicate with Dinah before she died.

LaDell Kirkham Richards now lives in Salt Lake City, where she is retired from medical practice. Her husband is professor emeritus at the University of Utah. She is still active in local politics, and has written a children's book.

Dinah Kirkham visited LaDell in New York City in 1919; during their time together they were reconciled, and Dinah was writing an affectionate letter to her surrogate daughter when she died on the train home, about two hours outside of Ogden, Utah. At first the Mormon Church tried to keep notices of her death small—her first obituary in the *Deseret News* ran only eight lines. Presumably the authorities were not anxious in 1919 to remind everyone of Dinah Kirkham, who had been such a prominent figure during the polygamy era. But the non-Mormon Salt Lake *Tribune* ran a full-page article on her, and after that the *Deseret News* ran four pages of reminiscences of "Aunt Dinah." Though her last official service was forty-three years before, she had not been forgotten. Her funeral was attended by an estimated thirty thousand mourners. According to some observers, most of those who came were far too young ever to have known her. She was one hundred years old when she died.

🕊 Acknowledgments 🕊

This book would have been impossible without the help of Jared B. Ames, who tracked down the endless details of nineteenth-century life; Steve Knight, who provided insights about the practice of plural marriage; the helpful employees at the LDS Church Archives; the Charles Banks Kirkham Family Organization; an agent and an editor who share the annoying belief that perfection can be improved on; and my wife, who read everything as it came from the typewriter, made me rewrite most of it twice, and in the meantime kept the children alive and taught them that once they had a father, and someday would have a father again.

And special thanks to LaDell Richards, who was my only living bridge to the past. Without her hours spent answering questions and telling memories, I could not have come so close to knowing Dinah Kirkham.